# THE WITCH'S MONSTERS

## COMPLETE COLLECTION

SARAH PIPER

**The Witch's Monsters: Complete Collection**

**Blood & Midnight**
**Blood & Malice**
**Blood & Madness**
**Blood & Magick**

Copyright © 2021, 2022 by Sarah Piper
SarahPiperBooks.com

**Excerpt from Wicked Conjuring**
Copyright © 2023 by Sarah Piper

Published by Two Gnomes Media

Cover design by Malice & Mayhem

All rights reserved. With the exception of brief quotations used for promotional or review purposes, no part of this book may be recorded, reproduced, stored in a retrieval system, or transmitted in any form or by any means without the express permission of the author.

This book is a work of fiction. Names, characters, places, businesses, organizations, brands, media, and incidents are either products of the author's imagination or are used fictitiously. Any resemblance to actual events, locations, or persons, living or dead, is entirely coincidental.

v1

E-book ISBN: 978-1-948455-99-2
Paperback ISBN: 978-1-948455-98-5
Audiobook ISBN: 978-1-963657-09-8

# BOOK SERIES BY SARAH PIPER

<u>Reverse Harem Romance Series</u>

Claimed by Gargoyles

The Witch's Monsters

Tarot Academy

The Witch's Rebels

---

<u>M/F Romance Series</u>

The Witches of Wayward Bay

Vampire Royals of New York

# DEDICATION

*To the woman who missed someone so much,
it hollowed out her fucking insides.*

*To the woman who saved up her tears for the shower,
where no one could hear her cry.*

*To the woman who fell to her knees
over a song, a scent, a photograph.*

*To the woman who stood alone at the witching hour,
forehead pressed to the window,
wondering how the fuck it'd even happened.*

*To the woman who didn't know
if she could drag herself up off the floor
to face another day.*

*I see you, you fucking goddess.
I've always seen you
You were never alone.*

*Just because you fell apart
doesn't mean you're broken.*

*So, scream if you have to.*
*Cry.*
*Shatter.*
*Fucking feel it.*

*You're still the baddest bitch.*

*This story is for you.*

# BLOOD AND MIDNIGHT

BOOK ONE

# PROLOGUE

## HALEY

There's an old adage about the difference between falling in love with a hero and falling in love with a villain. Go for the latter, it says, because a hero would ultimately sacrifice you to save the world, but a villain? He'd burn down the world just to save *you*.

Sounds pretty epic, right? And let's be honest—who doesn't love a bad boy?

The thing about villains, though… Ultimately, they're just the heroes of their own stories. Still fighting for a cause. Still trying to prove something to the world.

Trust me, I've fallen for both. And those assholes? They broke my heart every damn time.

So now I've got a new saying:

*Screw* the heroes and villains.

I want the *monsters*.

Dark. Vicious. Depraved. The men who slide into your heart like a surgical blade, so sharp you don't even feel it until you're on your knees, trembling and soaked in blood.

A monster won't try to woo you with roses and chocolates, with sweet promises whispered across satin pillowcases. He'll kick down a fucking door to get to you, though. Snap a man's neck just for leering. One threat against you, and he'll tear out the guy's throat with his teeth, then kiss you with a mouth full of blood, no apologies.

A monster's got nothing to prove and nothing left to lose.

And in bed?

*Damn.*

He'll *own* you, pushing until he finds the very edge of your limits, then smashing right through them. And oh, how you'll *beg* him for it—beg him to break you, again and again and again. To absolutely ruin you for anything less than a life of obsession and fire.

And while the hero slays his dragons and the villain burns down the world for the woman he loves, the monster will simply hand you the matches and gasoline, step aside, and smile as you burn it down yourself.

Because all along, the monster always knew you could.

He just had to make sure you knew it, too.

# 1

## HALEY

*T*he blood on my boots was still wet when I stepped inside.

My weapons needed a good cleaning too, but the novitiate asked me to leave the daggers and stakes at the entrance, and I obliged.

The Temple of the Dark Moon, she reminded me, was a holy place.

*Right.*

Appropriately chastised, I nodded and followed the swish of her long black robes across the threshold, my eyes widening as the interior came into view.

The temple had probably been beautiful once, but now it lay in ruins. Half the ceiling had caved in, and broken pillars of onyx and moonstone flanked the inner sanctuary, several of them reduced to rubble. Deep, angry gouges scored the masonry as if some feral god-beast had been locked up inside.

Everything smelled like rot and death.

*What the hell happened here?*

Hoping whatever it was had already been dealt with, I lowered my eyes and quickened the pace.

"Yours?" the novitiate asked from beneath her dark hood, and I knew she meant the blood I'd tracked across the chipped marble floor. I wondered if she'd be the one mopping it up later or if that would be my job now—one of the many menial tasks the Goddess surely had in store for me.

"No." I scraped the toe of my boot along the floor and left another

"

smear, which was about all the acknowledgment the previous owner of the blood deserved. "Listen, I'm sorry about the mess, but I was summoned here kind of last-minute and I didn't really have time to... I mean... Should I bathe before I meet her?" I dragged the back of my hand across my forehead, skin gritty with dirt and sweat and probably more blood. "Maybe do a purifying juice cleanse or... something?"

With a serene smile, the novitiate lowered her hood and said, "The Goddess Melantha does not require purity of body. Only purity of intent."

She looked younger than I expected—only a teenager—and she wasn't a witch. Just a regular human girl. I wondered what she'd done to end up a servant in the realm of the Dark Goddess, a place you couldn't even access without being summoned by the deity herself, then portaled in by her magick. Ruined or not, this temple was more than just a holy place—it existed in a liminal space all its own, nothing but stars and darkness as far as the eye could see.

Didn't the girl have parents? Friends? *Someone* missing her on the other side?

A sharp pain lanced my heart, but I breathed through it. I had no idea how long the girl had been here, but this was merely day one for me, and I had a long road ahead. I needed to stay grounded. Committed.

"How will she know my intentions are pure?" I asked. "Is there a test?"

"Fear not, Daughter of Darkwinter. I'm certain Her Holiness will be quite impressed with your offering."

Ignoring the Darkwinter bit, I forced a smile and scratched the back of my neck, sneaking a covert whiff of my armpit.

*Let's hope her Holiness is impressed with Eau de Urban Warfare, because that's about all I'm offering at the moment...*

"Come. She's expecting you." Still wearing a look of pure serenity, she continued on through a doorway at the back of the temple sanctuary, gesturing for me to follow.

The antechamber was small and intimate, much less imposing than the main temple. The warm glow of hundreds of candles flickered across plain mud walls and a low ceiling, the ground nothing but bare earth. My boots sank into it with every step, and as the scents of candle wax and dirt washed over me, I let out a sigh of relief.

This room, at least, had remained untouched by whatever monster had gone batshit crazy in the sanctuary.

My eyes adjusted to the candlelight, my gaze drifting to the stone altar in the center of the room—a large slab covered in fresh flowers and bowls of fruit, ringed by votive candles in red glass orbs.

Offerings, I assumed. For the…

*Oh, shit.*

I gasped as I finally spotted the boy, no more than ten or eleven, lying in repose on the altar. His skin was milk white, the robe they'd dressed him in much too large, as if it was borrowed in haste from someone much older.

Someone much closer to death than this child should've been.

"How did he pass?" I whispered.

"He didn't." The novitiate frowned. "Melantha's son is very much alive."

"Her *son*?" I couldn't hide my shock. The Dark Goddess was tens of thousands of years old—probably older. Lots of witches prayed to her, worshipped her, wrote volumes about her history and magick. I'd never once heard of a child. "How long has he been like this?"

"Six months." She sighed, running her fingers through the sweep of dark hair across his forehead. "He was cursed by a dark fae warlord called Keradoc. A vicious monster who punishes children for the sins of their parents."

An icy shiver ran down my spine. Dark fae were powerful, but Melantha was a dark *goddess. The* dark goddess. How could a fae warlord have gotten anywhere *near* her child? And what sin could she have committed to provoke such terrible retribution?

"He's alive," the novitiate continued, "but his soul is trapped in moonglass." She retrieved a small wooden chest from the offerings at his side, opening it to reveal a glass-like sphere as delicate as a soap bubble. At her gentle touch, it glowed with a bright, pearlescent sheen. "It's made from pure moonlight, cast with dark fae magick that's been banned for thousands of years."

"Because it's a prison," I said, disgust churning inside. It wasn't the first time I'd encountered moonglass. According to legend, the very first fae created it by deceiving the moon into lending the fae her light, then forging the magickal globes to trap the souls of their enemies. Eventually, they'd release those souls into the most hostile fae realms, sentencing them to an eternity of torment. "How did this happen?"

She met my eyes, but her serene smile was gone, replaced now with a look of grim determination. "What matters, Daughter of Darkwinter, is that you alone can free him."

"Me? But… how?"

"Breaking the curse requires the blood of the one who cast it."

"Keradoc. Of course." I blew out a breath, the tightness in my muscles loosening as the pieces clicked into place. I was a blood witch—a damned good one at that. Melantha needed me to do some sort of spell to help the child. "So, when do we start?"

"You will travel to his realm as soon as possible," she replied. "Once you've extracted the blood, you'll return to the Temple of the Dark Moon to perform the spell with Melantha, breaking the curse and—"

"Wait. Did you just..." I blinked at her, my mind racing to keep up. "You don't have his blood? Then how can I do the spell?"

"As I said, once you return to the Temple—"

"Her Holiness expects me to hunt this guy down? Some psychotic warlord from a realm I've never been to?"

She arched an eyebrow, as if in warning. "Her Holiness granted you untold strength and power in your time of need, for which you so eagerly pledged your service."

Tension simmered in the air as she glared at me, making my skin hot and itchy.

"I know. It's just..." I took a breath, trying to regroup. Who *was* this girl, anyway? Where were the other novitiates? Melantha's soldiers? "Forgive me, but when Her Holiness summoned me, I was under the impression I'd be meeting with her elite guard."

"Elite? Hardly." A bitter laugh rang out through the small chamber. "No honor among them. No fortitude. I'm sorry, but the Guard of the Dark Moon is no more."

A prickle of unease tingled at the back of my mind. What the hell did "no more" mean?

Fired? Furloughed? Executed?

Crushed to death by falling pillars?

None of this made any sense.

I paced before the altar, my sudden movement snuffing out a few of the votives. "The guards are gone, so now it's on *me* to assassinate some creepy warlord?"

"Not assassinate, no. If Keradoc dies before we perform the spell, the blood will be useless." She grabbed a taper candle and touched it to one of the votives, reigniting the flame. "You must retrieve the blood without harming him—without so much as *alerting* him—or all will be for naught."

"Are you serious? You just said he's a warlord!"

"And you're a formidable blood witch, are you not? One with access to spells and magick you're only just beginning to tap into."

"I'm good at what I do, sure. But dark fae warlords? I'm not... Look, you seem... knowledgeable. Clearly, you're fond of the boy." I smiled, fighting to keep the desperation from my voice. "Maybe you should go instead? I'll stay here and keep an eye on things until you get back." I took the taper from her hand and lit the remaining votives. "See? Already getting the hang of it."

She pinched one of the flames between her thumb and forefinger, the frustration in her eyes finally boiling over. "One candle remains unlit to honor the darkness that exists in all of us, without which we can never know the light."

"Right." I raised my hands in surrender. "I should've known that, but I didn't. That's what I'm trying to tell you. I'm not the witch for the job. I'll do anything else she asks of me, but—"

"*This* is the quest the Goddess has set out for you," she snapped. The girl was unraveling, her eyes blazing, her voice nearly trembling. "Are you reneging on your sacred vow?"

"No, of course not. I just think we should look at all the options. I'm sure if we put our heads together, we can—"

"How *dare* you question the will of the Goddess!" she bellowed, the force of it making the ground rumble. Her eyes turned a fiery red, two hot embers smoldering in a shadow-dark face. Flames crackled suddenly at her feet, the inferno rising higher and higher until she was completely engulfed.

The mud walls cracked and bubbled around us, and I watched in mute horror as her robes burned away to reveal a body as black as the night sky, pale white serpents slithering around her thighs and torso. Her limbs elongated before my eyes, twisting like those of an ancient tree, hands and feet curling into monstrous talons. Two massive black wings burst from her back and smashed through the walls of the antechamber, each feather dripping with blood.

The altar remained untouched, the boy undisturbed.

I stumbled backward, my heart slamming against my ribs.

The novitiate.

All along, it was her. Melantha.

And this was her true form. Dark and magnificent. Hideous and terrifying.

I dropped to my knees, half-tripping, half awed, and bowed my head. "Forgive me, Your Holiness. I was wrong to question you."

Sharp claws pierced the underside of my chin, forcing me to look up and meet her fearsome gaze. I blinked through the pain, ignoring the warm blood trickling down my neck.

"Daughter of Darkwinter," she said, her voice echoing across the night like a death knell. "If you value the lives of the sisters you fought so bravely to protect in Blackmoon Bay, you *will* achieve this task. By blood and by blade, as you have promised."

*By blood and by blade.*

The words of my spell echoed as clearly as they had the night I'd first spoken them.

> *Blood of hell, blood of night*
> *I call on the darkness to show us the light*
> *May evil and malice and violence intended*
> *Return to its hosts uprooted, upended*
> *Dark Goddess I bend, Dark Goddess I bow*
> *Hear my petition, and thusly I vow*
> *My service is yours, by blood and by blade*
> *Until my last breath shall deem it unmade.*

That night, my allies and I—my sisters among them—had been trapped in a prison compound hidden in the Olympic National Forest. We'd managed to free the prisoners—dozens of witches and other supernaturals captured by human hunters and the corrupt fae they were working for—but soon our enemies surrounded us, outgunning us four to one. They were hybrids—nearly unstoppable beasts with the combined powers of vampires, shifters, and genetically altered super-monsters we couldn't even identify.

Even with our own formidable team of supernatural heavy-hitters, there was no way we could've survived their relentless attack.

In a last, desperate move, I petitioned Melantha for the strength and magick to turn the tides. She answered my call at once, and thanks to her, we earned our victory—first retaking the compound, then finishing the job last night at the Battle of Blackmoon Bay.

The battle for our lives and our home. For everything we held dear.

I glanced down at my boots, the last of the blood soaking into the dirt, along with any hope I had of avoiding this disastrous mission.

If I refused her, everything I was able to accomplish through the spell would be undone. The city of Blackmoon Bay would fall. My sisters—the family I'd only just discovered—would die. And everything we'd fought so hard to save would just...

It would end.

A surge of renewed strength shot through my limbs, my blood simmering with magick. *My* magick.

"My service is yours," I said now, repeating the vow I'd made that night. "By blood and by blade. Until my last breath shall deem it unmade."

"Rise, Daughter of Darkwinter."

I got to my feet and met her gaze once more, hoping like hell we were done with the Big Goddess Energy show. I'd seen enough of her scary magnificence to fill my nightmares for the next decade, thanks.

Her dark wings fluttered in the breeze, and the same rot and ruin I'd smelled in the sanctuary assaulted my senses. I tried not to recoil.

"Are you prepared to accept this task?" she asked. "To see it through by any means necessary?"

"I am," I said firmly. I was in it to win it now, no going back. With what I hoped was a confident smile, I asked, "What must I do?"

Melantha extended her arms. One claw held my weapons. The other clutched a glass vial about the size of a tube of lipstick.

After re-securing my stakes and blades, I took the vial and peered inside. Magick swirled beneath the glass, red smoke shot through with threads of black and gold. It was oddly mesmerizing.

"Keradoc dwells in the dark fae realm of Midnight," she said. "This portal spell will take you there, but you won't survive it alone. There's a man in your home realm—also fae—one rumored to have escaped Midnight alive. You must ask for his assistance."

My heart stalled. All the confidence I'd conjured up evaporated in an instant.

The ground spun out from beneath my feet, and I fell back to my knees, my lungs struggling to suck in air.

Deep inside, beneath all the magick and fire, behind all the parts of myself I'd sharpened into weapons and hardened into shields, a tiny box lay hidden, bolted with iron chains and encased in cement. That box held my darkest, most private pain. All the ghosts that had the power to eat through my very soul.

I'd sealed them away years ago, vowing to never open that box again, no matter how often it called to me. And though it still rattled inside on occasion, for the most part, I'd kept it on strict lockdown.

Until now.

*The dark fae realm of Midnight... One rumored to have escaped... Ask for his assistance...*

Her words were the bolt-cutters on those iron chains, unleashing all the pain I'd so diligently buried. It seeped into my heart, burning it like hot acid, taunting me from across the long years as if no time had passed at all.

Midnight. The most treacherous realm in the universe, controlled by the darkest of the dark fae. A place where the sun never rose and so much blood had been spilled upon its war-torn lands, the lakes and rivers ran red. Melantha was right—there was no way I'd survive it alone.

And the fae who had?

There was no way I'd survive *him*, either.

Not again.

"I will return you to the mortal plane," the Goddess continued, as if I wasn't falling apart before her eyes. "To the city of—"

"New Orleans," I whispered, and she nodded, sealing my fate.

A tear slipped down my cheek.

New Orleans. The one place I swore I'd never, ever go. A place that terrified me even more than Midnight.

No, not because of the ghosts that haunted the city's many cemeteries and historic landmarks.

Because of the ghosts that haunted my heart. The ones she'd just set loose.

"And this… this *fae*," I said, still unable to speak his name out loud, even after all these years. "If he refuses to help me?"

Her black lips twisted into a cruel grin, her wings spreading to their full, terrifying span. The ground rumbled beneath her feet, but instead of flames, skulls rose from the dirt, a dead army blooming at her command.

Behind me, a portal opened, ready to ferry me to New Orleans.

To him.

"Convince him, Darkwinter," Melantha hissed. "Or the ones you claim to love will suffer the consequences of your failure."

I nodded and took a deep breath.

Fought off an onslaught of memories—strong hands sliding into my hair. Eyes the color of molten silver. Promises whispered, promises broken. The salty taste of tears and the dull ache of wounds that never fully healed.

I took a step backward, then another.

Closed my eyes.

And tumbled, ass over teakettle, into my own private hell.

# 2

## HALEY

*T*wo years.

That's how long I'd spent convincing myself this place didn't exist. Convincing myself that Elian's return from captivity in Midnight and the subsequent launching of a whole new life in New Orleans—one that *didn't* include me—was just a rumor.

Now, standing before the entrance to his exclusive French Quarter club, I could no longer deny the truth.

*Saints and Sinners*, the sign read. To humans, it was just another abandoned cathedral with blown-out windows and crumbling spires, complete with a hulking gargoyle perched above the main archway.

But for those of us who could see past the illusion of the fae glamour, a set of glowing silver doors awaited—an invitation I still couldn't bring myself to answer.

There were no bouncers or velvet ropes, no demands for the secret password. Just the ancient gargoyle and the doors and a small plaque reminding me this was hallowed ground, so could I please check my weapons at the armory inside the narthex?

I practically snorted.

*Fat fucking chance.*

This was no Temple of the Dark Moon. Just because Elian's den of supernatural sin was housed in an old church, that didn't make it hallowed ground any more than it made him a priest.

No one showed up in a place like this looking for redemption, anyway.

They showed up looking for an escape.

Or in my case—to beg.

*Damn it.* The thought of even *facing* that prick again—let alone asking him for help—tied me up in knots. But what choice did I have? My sisters' lives depended on me seeing this all the way through, and Elian truly was my best shot at surviving the horrors of Midnight.

Probably my *only* shot.

So, decked out in a new lace dress the color of the stars and thigh-high leather boots I'd picked out just to make him suffer, strapped from hip to ankle with weapons that would finish the job if the outfit failed, I pushed open the doors and stepped inside.

And immediately fell under its spell.

Everything about the place was designed to hypnotize, from the rich, blood-red walls to the restored stained-glass windows that pulsed with magick. Suspended in gilded cages from the ceiling, painted fae couples performed dances so erotic, I was already wishing for a cold shower. Semi-private candlelit alcoves lined both sides of the former cathedral, and the pews had been removed from the nave, the flooring replaced with black marble that glittered with tiny silver points.

It looked as if the club's many revelers were dancing across the night sky.

I was relieved not to spot Elian among them. Despite the fever-inducing performances of the fae dancers, five years' worth of resentment and abandonment issues still simmered inside, and one look into his entrancing silver eyes would set it all ablaze.

Not a fire I wanted to face while sober.

Chin raised, shoulders squared, I beelined for the bar and slid onto an empty barstool at the end, trying to spot any potential threats. Hunters were always my first concern, but we'd taken a pretty big bite out of their organization during the Battle at Blackmoon Bay. Those who remained loyal to their fucked-up cause would likely be licking their wounds for a good long while.

Here at Saints and Sinners, vampires and fae made up the majority of the clientele, all of them rich, well-dressed, and predatory. The fae were even more refined than the bloodsuckers, their otherworldly beauty as mesmerizing as it was dangerous.

The bartender, though... He didn't fit the profile. Demon. Rough around the edges. A head of messy, jet-black hair and a mouth so sultry it was almost a crime to look at. He wore a white dress shirt and dark slacks but no tie, his sleeves rolled up to reveal muscular forearms mapped with scars.

My own scars practically tingled in response.

As he finished up with one of his vampire customers, I studied him. Another sexy scar ran the full length of his face, slicing through his eyebrow and ending in the dark stubble along his jaw. A black patch covered the injured eye.

When he finally made his way over to me, he nodded and set a coaster on the bar, but didn't smile or say hello. Just waited, arms crossed over his broad chest, one blue eye glowering at me like he was daring me to ask about the missing one.

What I *really* wanted to ask was what time he got off work and how soon he'd like to get started on becoming my next ex-boyfriend, but...

"Drinking or leaving, new girl?" he asked, smooth and cold as ice. "You're holding up the line."

I took a deep breath, trying to re-focus on the mission.

*Midnight.*

*Begging.*

*Elian.*

"Drinking. Definitely drinking. I'll have... I don't know." I offered a flirty smile. "Whatever you think I'll like."

He leaned in close, his demonic scent enveloping me. It reminded me of the smoke that lingered in your hair when you spent too much time by the fire, a hint of lemon simmering beneath it, and holy *hell* did I want to jump across the bar and—

"I need a bit more to go on," he said, then shot me an icy grin to match his voice. "If it's not too much trouble for you."

"Fine. Let's do something with a kick, but nothing boring or predictable. That rules out whisky, vodka, and tequila. I'm not a huge fan of bubbles either, and I don't like anything too milky. Sweet's good, but not *too* sweet, and a little fruit is fine, but nothing *super* fruity, unless it's—"

"Sorry I asked." Without waiting for me to finish, he wiped his hands on the towel draped over his shoulder, selected a martini glass from the rack overhead, and turned toward the multi-colored bottles lined up behind him.

Before I could offer any more helpful pointers, a wave of vertigo hit, alerting me to the presence of a vampire. One getting way too close and personal.

"Did it hurt?" A husky voice breathed in my ear.

I turned to meet his gaze, resting bitch face locked and loaded. "Excuse me?"

"When you fell from Heaven?" He spread his arms and grinned as if I might find the whole package so charming I'd leap into his embrace, wrap my thighs around him, and ride him all the way home.

"Not as much as it did when they cut off my horns and tail," I said. "Anyway, I'm all set here, so… Have a good night."

"Can I at least buy you a drink, beautiful?"

"No, thank you. I'm not interested."

His face fell, then twisted into a scowl. "You don't have to be such a bitch."

"Actually, I do. Because otherwise bloodsuckers like you assume a smile or a kind word is a full-on invitation to Pussytown, and I promise you, friend. *That's* an exclusive ticket."

"Check the guest list again." He reached over and touched my hair, bringing a lock to his lips before dropping his hand to my thigh and giving it a possessive squeeze. "Pretty sure I'm on it."

*Pretty sure you're going to regret touching me, but ooh-kay…*

"Well, since you're so persistent," I cooed, "maybe I *should* check." With a faux-seductive smile, I slid my fingers into the top of my boot, seeking that cold, comforting piece of wood I never left home without.

One minute, the hawthorn stake was minding its own business in the boot holster. The next, it was jammed into the back of the fucker's hand.

Such was the beauty of my sharp and pointy friend.

He jerked back with a howl, the hawthorn poison already paralyzing his fingers. I yanked the stake free, spun it in my palm, and shoved it against his crotch, stopping just short of inflicting a more serious injury.

"Touch me again, bloodsucker," I hissed, "and your hand won't be the only thing going limp."

"Go… go fuck yourself, bitch."

"I'd return the sentiment, but I'm pretty sure that hand won't be up for the job any time soon." I laughed. "Get it? Hand? Job?"

He bared his fangs, then stumbled away like a wounded, dejected bird.

"First drink is on me," the bartender said. "That was the best thing I've seen in months."

I reached forward and yanked the towel off his shoulder, then wiped the blood from my stake. "Thanks for the assist, demon."

"You had it handled. Be grateful I don't toss your ass out for smuggling in that stake."

"This teeny tiny little thing?" I finished cleaning it off, then slipped it back into the holster. "It's not like it was going to kill him."

Wooden stakes could poison the fuckers—hawthorn was especially good at interfering with their healing abilities, and a well-placed stake to the chest would knock them out for hours—but still, that was just a temporary fix. Killing vampires required decapitation or burning, and I wasn't about to ruin my new outfit with all *that* mess.

"In any case, best not to draw too much attention." The bartender set down the martini glass, now brimming with pale amber liquid. A single mint leaf floated on top.

"What is it?"

The barest hint of a smile quirked his lips. "It's called a Fallen Angel."

It was the smile that saved him. *Asshole.*

Hiding my return grin behind the rim of the glass, I took a sip, then another.

*Damn,* that Fallen Angel concoction was good—good enough to savor over a long conversation laced with innuendo. A conversation that on any other night might've led to a kiss and maybe even an orgasm or two.

But tonight?

I tipped back the glass and chugged it all down. Then, before I could talk myself out of it, I said, "I'm looking for Elian."

# 3

## HALEY

*I* blew out a breath, seriously impressed with my ability to say the bastard's name without crying and/or breaking something. Progress!

The sexy bartender, however, was *not* impressed. Quite the opposite, actually.

"Elian," he said flatly, folding his arms over his chest again, and I swear the temperature dropped ten degrees.

It didn't feel like jealousy. Aside from a little teasing, he wasn't exactly putting out any "let's take this back to my place" vibes. So why did he clam up when I asked about Elian?

"Is he in tonight?" I pressed.

The guy sized me up with his singularly intense blue eye, which apparently found me lacking. When his gaze finally made its way back to mine, he scowled as if I'd just threatened *his* dick with the stake. "Who the *fuck* wants to know?"

"Pro-tip, buddy. Usually, when a person straight-up tells you they're looking for someone? Dead giveaway right there."

Glaring. He had it down to a science. The eye, the ticking jaw muscle, the flex of those pin-me-down forearms.

I tried to glare right back at him, but when it came to squaring off with intimidating, hot-as-hell demons, I was out of practice. "You *do* realize the size of your tip is inversely proportional to your bullshit, right?"

"What do you want with… *Elian?*" His lip curled when he said the name—a reaction I understood all too well.

"I need to speak with him. It's private and it's important. So if you could just fix me another drink for the road and point me in the right direction, I'll gladly—"

"Are you a dancer?"

*A dancer?* Was this demon for real?

I reached for my stake again. It wouldn't take much. I could probably put it through his good eye before another insult had time to fall out of that sexy mouth.

The thought calmed me almost as much as the booze.

"I'm more of a stabby, pokey kinda girl," I said. "With a little magick thrown in for fun."

"Well, we're all set on security detail and spell casters, so unless you can work that stabby, pokey bit into a cage dance, we're not hiring."

"You think I'm here about a job?"

"Not sure I care enough to give it much more thought, honestly." He grinned, but I could tell he didn't mean it. Something about all this had gotten under his skin. Something about Elian.

I opened my mouth to push him on it, but before I could utter another word, he flicked his hand to shoo me away, already turning to the next customer.

"Enjoy your evening, *angel*," he said over his shoulder.

Enjoy my *evening*?

It'd taken me two years and the threats of a scary-ass goddess to work up the nerve to set foot in this city, a killer outfit to walk through those silver doors, and a good dose of booze just to say Elian's name without a string of curses attached.

And this demon thought I was *done*?

I was on a hot streak—no way was I bowing out now.

I waited until he finished up with his other customers, then tapped my empty glass. "Still needing that second drink, friend."

He watched me for a beat, then muttered something inaudible before clearing away the empty glass and reaching for another. "Shall I start a tab, then?"

"I'm not staying long enough for that." I opened up the black hole otherwise known as my purse, emptying its contents onto the bar as I searched for my money.

Cell phone, lipstick, lip gloss, a vial of shifter blood.

Hand sanitizer, emergency tampons, emergency black tourmaline, breath mints.

Three vampire fangs, black eyeliner, a stun potion leftover from the Blackmoon Bay fight, Melantha's portal spell, a hair tie, and…

*Aha!* Sweet, shiny credit card of questionable remaining balance. After today's shopping spree in the Big Easy, I wasn't too sure how much farther it would get me, but hey. Hope sprang eternal.

"Let's give this one a whirl." I held out the card, but the demon didn't take it.

His gaze was on the glass vial from the goddess, utterly transfixed. The blood-red smoke roiled inside, its black and gold threads shimmering.

He glanced up at me again, and I braced for another argument. A brush-off. Anything but what flashed through that stone-cold eye.

Recognition.

The demon *knew* that particular magick. Which meant…

*Holy shit.* Had he been to Midnight too? Was that how he knew Elian?

He reached across the bar and covered the vial with his hand, his voice turning dark. "Put it out of sight. Now."

I did as he asked, too stunned to do anything else.

"Wait here," he said in that same deadly tone. "Do *not* leave this bar."

"Okay, but what about my—" *Damn.* He was already gone. "Drink," I said with a sigh. I was just about to hop behind the bar and make something myself when the vertigo hit me again, this wave so strong it nearly knocked me off my barstool.

I fisted my stake and palmed the stun potion, slowly turning to face the newcomers—three of them this time.

My wounded bird was flanked by two of his friends, each one more despicable than the last. Whatever supernatural genetics made most vampires hot as fuck and impossible to resist? Clearly skipped this lot.

A quick scan of my surroundings and my heart sunk. No sign of the demon, and the other patrons in the vicinity were too wrapped up in their own flirtations and petty skirmishes to pay any attention to mine.

*Shit.*

"Sorry, boys," I said as the vampires crowded in close. "You really *aren't* on the guest list."

"It's not pussy we're after tonight, witch," my original stalker said, ever the romantic. His hand hung limp at his side, the skin black and blistering. "We're here for—"

I shoved the stake into his chest, taking him down for the count, then hurled the stun potion at the second vamp's feet. It exploded in a bright yellow starburst, freezing him on contact, but the third one wasn't close enough to the blast to feel its effects. I tried to reach for one of my daggers, but he was too fast, too strong, and too smart.

He was on me in a heartbeat, hauling me out of the stool and locking me in a vise grip, my back against his chest.

"Got any more tricks, witch?" he growled in my ear.

I struggled against his hold, but it was no use. My arms were pinned at my sides, my feet no longer touching the ground, and I had maybe a minute before the stun potion wore off on the other vamp. "Let me go and I'll show you all *sorts* of magick."

"I don't think so, pretty girl." With a sick groan of pleasure, he clamped down hard on my neck, fangs piercing the skin. Before I could even cry out, he'd drained enough blood to make my world spin.

I fought to remain conscious, to reach the dagger in my boot, to do something other than let this asshole finish me off. The temporarily stunned vamp was already on his feet again, stumbling toward me with rage in his eyes, fangs bared, mouth practically foaming for a taste…

Someone slammed into us from behind, breaking me out of my captor's relentless hold and knocking me to the ground as another man—the bartender, I realized—staked my two attackers in quick succession.

*Guess I'm not the only one good with the stabby, pokey bit…*

I caught his gaze and managed a quick smile of thanks, then turned my attention to the guy who'd knocked me down.

The *fae* who'd knocked me down. Half-vampire too, I realized, dressed in a three-piece black Nehru suit that perfectly hugged his leanly muscled frame.

My mind spun.

*How was this possible?*

He was partially on top of me from the fall, one hand cradling the back of my head, lips muttering my name like a prayer. His long hair brushed across my face, a fall of silver waves and intricate braids I itched to run my fingers through.

Only the strongest magick could erase time, and there was no magick more powerful than scent for yanking you right back into the past. It washed over me like a dark curse—the particular mix of bergamot and rain that could only belong to him.

Butterflies danced through my insides, my heartbeat quickening.

When I finally found the courage to meet his eyes, my breath hitched, and not just because his weight was half-crushing my lungs.

Five years ago, he walked out of my life without so much as a good-bye… and crushed my fucking heart.

"Elian," I whispered.

Accidentally.

*Shit.*

His molten silver gaze swept down to my lips, then back to my eyes. A cocky grin curved his mouth, tugging slightly higher on the left.

It did things to me, that crooked grin. Always had. Bad things. Stupid things. And before I knew it, I was grinning right back at him.

Elian brushed his thumb across my lower lip, eyes sparkling, his touch making me shiver. "Still dreaming of me, little sparrow?"

"I am," I admitted.

Then, just to prove it, I did something I'd been *dreaming* about every day for the last five years.

I punched that sexy, silver-eyed fae-hole right in the mouth.

# 4

## ELIAN

Mouth full of blood, aching jaw, and a throbbing hard-on I couldn't do a damn thing to fix?

Not exactly the made-for-tv reunion I would've scripted, but it could've been worse.

After what I'd put Haley Barnes through, I was lucky my cock was still attached to my body.

"Ouch!" she hissed, jerking away from my touch. "Careful."

"Damn it, Haley." I tipped her head to the side and got back to work. "Hold still."

Normally, I liked a woman squirming on my desk, but the bullshit with those vampires made my blood boil. Inspecting the gaping holes in Haley's neck, it was all I could do not to smash something. Vampire skulls would've been my first choice, but Jax was already dealing with those fuckers.

Now, alone in my office with the woman I'd ghosted five years ago for the first time since my big disappearing act, I was seriously regretting sending away the demon.

"How much longer?" she asked.

"Almost there." With the gentlest touch I could manage, I finished cleaning out the bite wound, then pressed a gauze pad to her neck, taping it around the edges. She wouldn't let me near the knuckles she'd split clocking me in the face, though—pretty sure she wanted to keep that particular injury as a souvenir.

Couldn't exactly blame her.

I ran my finger along the tape to secure it, and she shivered, then swatted my hand away and yanked her hair forward, covering up the evidence.

"Sorry," I said, completely out of my depth.

"For what, exactly?"

I gestured vaguely. It was a lot to encompass.

*Fuck.*

Half a decade of radio silence, no explanation, a broken heart she damn sure didn't deserve, and *that* was all I could say to her? Sorry for... whatever?

Jax was right. I was seriously fucked in the head.

Arms wrapped tight around her chest, one leg crossed over the other, booted foot bouncing, Haley shook her head and let out a bitter laugh, probably reconsidering the whole letting-me-keep-my-cock thing.

Five years. Five fucking years of fantasizing about the woman, and now I was ready to bash my own brains in as punishment for all the weak-ass memories it'd served up. They were *nothing* compared to the real thing, and she'd only gotten more stunning with time.

I sighed, the sound of it laced with regret. "Haley, I didn't—"

"Save it. I'm not here for the overdue explanation." She glared at me with the gorgeous green eyes that still haunted my dreams, but they were different now. Harder. Edged with a deep, dark anger trying real damn hard to mask the pain.

*Then why are you here, sparrow?* I wanted to ask. *Come to turn my life upside down? Congratulations, woman. Mission fucking accomplished.*

But I said nothing. Just nodded and waited her out. She'd get to it when she was damn good and ready, just like she always had.

Jax didn't know the story either. All he'd said before the vamp attack was that a green-eyed witch had shown up at the bar asking for me by a name I'd left behind years ago, and she was packing weapons, an attitude, and a portal spell to Midnight.

I knew right away it had to be her. Knew right away she had to be in some deep shit, too.

"Where's the hot demon?" she asked, hopping to her feet.

I tried to pretend the question didn't send a bolt of jealousy straight through my gut. "Cemetery out back."

"Smoke break?"

"The only thing smoking will be the vampires who touched you, but

I'm afraid you'll have to wait until sunrise if you want to see *that* show live and uncut."

Her eyes widened a fraction, the faintest flicker of a smile touching her lips, but she turned her back on me before I could really enjoy it.

*That's right, little sparrow. Don't say I never did anything nice for you.*

She paced my office, checking out all the shit I'd collected in here, none of it particularly meaningful. Aside from the private bar set up behind my desk, it was mostly just dusty tomes and relics left from the original church. Still, she examined each shelf with interest, as if an old bible or wine-stained chalice might give her a clue about why I'd done what I'd done.

She'd known me as fae, but I was half-vampire now, my senses picking up more than she probably realized. The rapid-fire beat of her heart. The familiar strawberries-and-cream sweetness wafting from her skin, mingling with the intoxicating scent of her blood and—even more impossible to ignore—the scent of her arousal.

The woman might've hated my guts, but old habits died hard.

And if I didn't stop staring at her ass in that tight lace dress, I was going to die hard, too.

*Damn it, Haley. You should've stayed far the fuck away from me...*

I sat in my leather chair and steepled my hands on the desk, my gaze everywhere but on her. A blur of dark hair here, a flash of those boots there, a quick glimpse of black lace stockings... Bits and pieces. It was all I dared to take from her now, and even *that* felt selfish.

Fate had given me a choice five years ago, and I'd picked wrong. Now, there *was* no choice. Only consequences.

So, as badly as I wanted to give her the answers she was seeking from those musty shelves—as much as I *owed* her those answers—I couldn't do it. Couldn't risk her life just to ease my guilty conscience.

It was time to put those walls back up. Time to freeze her ass out, once and for all.

She'd hate me forever, sure. But I'd rather she hate me on her feet than love me from the bottom of a fucking grave, and right now, those were the only possible outcomes.

"So this is your life now, huh?" She finally turned to face me again, doing a damn good job of keeping her shit together, despite the raging heartbeat. "Serving up fae strippers and designer drugs to the supernatural elite? Impressive, Elian. Truly."

"Serving up *fantasies*," I corrected, still not meeting her gaze. "And try not to judge me too harshly. It's a lucrative endeavor."

"I'm sure it is."

I propped my hands behind my head and grinned, focusing on a spot just past her shoulder. "Stick around. Maybe you'll see something you like."

"Aside from your bartender?"

I let that one go. She deserved to take a few more jabs at me.

"And this… this vampire business." Her gaze roved over me, nearly setting me on fire. "All part of your fantasy schtick? Give the highborn fae girls a taste of the dark side? Bet they *love* that."

"Certainly doesn't hurt," I said, grin still firmly in place. "But it's no schtick. I was turned a few years back."

"By force?"

"Necessity."

In my case, there hadn't been a difference, but I wasn't about to get into all that. Pretty sure Haley hadn't come all the way to Louisiana just to hear my Midnight sob story.

"Don't feel *too* sorry for me, though," I added. "Thanks to my fae blood, I ended up with most of the perks and hardly any of the weaknesses. Super speed and strength, healing, mental influence, and no aversion to sunlight."

She flashed a cruel grin. "You're saying I could chop off your head and you'd survive?"

"That's… untested."

"Can I try?"

"No."

"Let me know if you change your mind."

Ignoring the offer, I said, "Really, the only downside is the minor inconvenience of my complete dependency on human blood, but that's… manageable."

Silence drifted between us once more, and she blew out a breath and glanced up at the ceiling. I didn't need to look at her to know she was holding back tears.

"God. What *happened* to you, Elian?"

"He goes by Saint now," Jax said suddenly. He'd just stepped into the office, his white shirt stained with vampire blood, but otherwise no worse for the wear.

"*Saint*?" Haley laughed again, and damn if the sound of it didn't stir a deep longing inside me. "And let me guess," she said to Jax. "You're Sinner. A little on the nose, no?"

"We're all sinners, angel," the demon said, no trace of irony. "Even you."

*Asshole.* Thirty seconds in the same room together, and I already hated the way those two were eye-fucking each other.

"*Jax,*" I said, a little harsher than necessary. "You take care of our guests?"

"Tied up, staked, and awaiting the sunrise barbecue."

"Excellent."

Burning by sunlight was the most painful way to take out a full-blooded vampire, and the fact that we were making them wait for their demise, conscious but paralyzed, made it all the sweeter. As a general rule, I tried not to make a habit of murdering my clientele, but sometimes exceptions had to be made.

"Jax, huh?" Haley flashed the demon a genuine smile I wanted to steal for myself. "Okay. Much better than Sinner. Do you—"

"And what business brings you to New Orleans, Ms. Barnes?" I asked coolly, rummaging through some papers on my desk as if I had better shit to do—*anything* to do but sit here and watch the former love of my life fawn over the fucking demon I wanted to murder on the best of days.

The look she shot me made my balls shrivel, but the faster we got down to it, the faster we could both move on.

Again.

"I was hoping we could talk privately," she said.

"Whatever you need to say, you can say it in front of Jax."

Mostly because I was too chicken shit to be alone with her again.

"Fine," Haley said. "Let's just rip off the Band-Aid then, shall we? I need to get to the realm of Midnight and then back to the Temple of the Dark Moon. Alive. And I need to do it soon, or everyone I love is going to die." Then, with a bright, heart-stopping smile, "So, what are you guys doing later? Fancy a road trip? My snack game is *killer.*"

# 5

## ELIAN

*Fuck.* I'd really hoped Jax had been wrong about that portal spell.

"Why Midnight?" I asked.

Haley sighed, her megawatt smile dimming. "For reasons I have *no* interest in sharing, I'm in debt to the Goddess Melantha. She needs a blood witch to sneak into the realm and retrieve the blood of some warlord... Kayden? Karaden?"

"Keradoc?" I asked, and she pointed at me with finger guns and winked.

Normally, I might've found the gesture adorable. But now?

My heart dropped into my stomach.

How the hell had Haley Barnes gotten mixed up with Melantha and fucking Keradoc of Midnight?

"*Saint,*" Jax warned, as if he knew exactly where my mind was heading. "Don't even think about—"

I lifted a hand and cut him off. Ignoring his glare—along with every alarm blaring inside my head—I said, "Define *retrieve*, Haley."

"Retrieve," she replied. "As in steal. And I need your help getting in and out. I wouldn't mind a few pointers about this warlord douchebag either, but that's just frosting on the cake as far as I'm concerned. Escort me, and I'll handle the rest."

"Steal. You want to steal the blood of the warlord of Midnight, and you're asking for *my* help?" I laughed, forcing myself to shore up those walls around my heart. "Ask me again, sparrow. Put a little more oomph into it this time."

"Seriously?"

"*Very* seriously. In fact, for something like this… Yeah. You should probably beg." I stood up and leaned back against the bar, my gaze raking down her body, then back up. "Feel free to get on your knees—probably won't convince me, but who knows? Maybe I'll be inspired by your performance. Wouldn't be the first time."

Hurt flickered in her eyes, but I couldn't let it get to me. Couldn't give in. Couldn't deal with *any* of this shit—not now.

In a soft voice that cut deeper than the dagger strapped to her thigh, she said, "Were you always such a prick?"

*Only since I walked away from the best thing in my immortal life to chase after a ghost…*

"Was a time when you liked pricks," I said.

"Well now I like men, so you can sit *your* prick-ass down."

I shook my head. *The nerve of this woman…* "Is someone paying you to fuck with me, Haley, or have you just lost your damn mind?"

"The fact that I'm even here should be a pretty good indicator of my current mental state." She shoved her hands into her hair, stopping just short of tearing it out. "Let me break it down for you, okay? Basically, I'm supposed to portal on over to some deadly dark-fae realm where the sun never shines and the good guys never last, hijack the blood of a psychotic warlord without killing him, and zip back home like fucking Dorothy with the ruby slippers. Only I don't have ruby slippers, Elian. I have you. The asshole bloodsucking fae who *somehow*—even though he's a spineless amoeba who needs to crawl back into his petri dish and *ripen* for a few more decades—holds the distinguished honor of being the only guy to ever escape Midnight alive. So I'm sorry if my sudden arrival is confusing or annoying or inconvenient for you and Mr. Tall, Dark, and Demon over here, but seriously? How fucked am *I*?"

"On a scale of one to ten," Jax said, still glowering at me, "you're fucked by a magnitude of a thousand, give or take."

He was right. Didn't matter that there were actually *three* of us who'd escaped Midnight alive; Haley was well and truly fucked. Whatever she'd gotten into with Melantha was so far beyond fixable, the best I could do for her was hand over a pile of drugs, say goodbye, and put her in a permanent coma.

"Aren't you going to call him a prick, too?" I asked.

"Jax? He's just being honest. *You're* being a prick."

"Honesty doesn't preclude prickishness. In fact—"

"You know what? I didn't come here to reminisce about my penchant for pricks, thanks." She crossed the office and stood before my desk again, staring me down. "Are you going to help me or not?"

*Shit.*

My cock throbbed at the proximity of her. The fall of dark brown hair over her breasts. The lace top of her dress, dipping just low enough to make my mouth water...

Fucking witch was putting me under her spell without even trying.

"I'm not an inter-realm Uber, Haley," I said. "So unless there's a fantasy I can conjure up for you, no. I can't help."

"You know what my fantasy is, *Saint*? A man who keeps his promises. A man who doesn't pledge his immortal love one night, then vanish into the mist the next." She leaned across my desk, black manicured fingertips pressed against the glossy mahogany, the scent of her red-hot blood rushing over me in a seductive wave. "You *owe* me this, asshole. So man up, help me get it done, and I'll be out of your life again before you can say 'how much for the fae lap dance.'"

Darkness swirled in her eyes. It'd always been there—the quiet rage, the simmering fury she hid so well with jokes and smiles. But still... the Haley I'd walked out on all those years ago was softer. Hopeful, despite what she'd been through. This one was hard-edged and gunning for a fight, ready to blow up her whole life over some debt to a goddess she had no business fucking with in the first place.

It broke my heart to see her like this.

Turned me on like nothing had in years, but damn.

What was her life like now? In all the time that'd passed since our last kiss, what mountains of shit had fate thrown at her?

Or were all those hard edges because of me? Because of what *I'd* thrown at her?

*Fuck me.* In that moment, all I wanted to do was take her into my arms, push her down on my desk, and claim her until she knew *exactly* how sorry I was. How much I'd truly missed her.

But I wasn't that man anymore.

Haley was right—I *was* a prick. Worse.

And I needed to *stay* worse. For both our sakes.

"You're welcome to hang out for another drink," I said. "Maybe that fae lap dance you mentioned. On the house, of course."

Disappointment chased the darkness from her eyes.

Never before had I so badly wanted to kick my own ass.

"Tempting offer," she said, her tone dripping with sarcasm. "Unfortunately, I think I left my kneepads back at the Temple of the Dark Moon." She stood up to her full height and headed for the exit, those sexy boots thudding across the floor, her hot little ass swishing. "I'll be sure to give Melantha your regards. Thanks again for reminding me *exactly* why I never came looking for you here. Enjoy your fantasy life, Saint. Sweet dreams."

She grabbed the door handle, and my world ground to a screeching halt.

*Fuck.* Five years on, and she was still as stubborn and fiery as the night she'd pushed me off a pier in Blackmoon Bay for spilling coffee on her shoes. It was the first time I'd ever seen her, standing out behind Luna's Café, her long hair blowing into her mouth, eyes flashing in the dark. I'd sworn it was an accident, but we both knew I was full of shit. I just wanted a reason to talk to her, and I panicked and pulled a dick move with the coffee.

So, into the water I went.

Then she felt bad about it and jumped in after me.

She splashed me.

I dunked her.

We'd started the night nearly drowning each other in the Salish Sea. Ended it with me drowning in the taste of her as I made her come on my tongue, again and again and again. She was wild. Insatiable. So passionate her touch set my skin on fire.

Of all the exotic drugs we served at Saints and Sinners, the fae magick, the cocktails that would've been illegal in a human bar, Haley Barnes was still my favorite fucking addiction, and I'd never stopped fantasizing about her.

Now she was here. In New Orleans. In the club I'd built for the sole purpose of giving people the very escape I could never truly find for myself.

One good tug on that door, and she'd be out of my life again—probably for the last time.

*Let her walk, asshole. Just let her go...*

It was the smart thing to do, sure. Cut it off, forget she'd ever set foot in my city. Forget how damn good and right she felt in my arms when I'd knocked her away from that bloodsucker tonight. Forget the way my insides twisted up when she'd looked into my eyes and whispered my real name.

*Elian...*

Yeah, letting her go was definitely the right call.

But no one had ever accused me of being a fucking hero, and they weren't about to start now.

"Wait," I said.

One word. Barely a whisper.

But Haley heard me. She always knew exactly what I was thinking anyway, whether I said it out loud or not.

She sighed, then turned to face me, her face etched with so much sadness it made me want to choke the life out of something with my bare hands.

"I'm not here to fuck with you, Elian," she said softly, a tear sliding down her cheek. "I'm in a jam, and I don't know where else to go. I wouldn't ask if it wasn't life-or-death."

I closed my eyes and sighed. Her pain was too close, too raw. It took everything in me not to go to her, gather her close, and promise I'd find a way to fix this without her ever having to set foot in that hellhole.

But that was a fantasy even *I* couldn't produce.

"We'll figure something out," I said instead. "Tomorrow. We'll make a plan to get you where you need to go."

Even with my eyes closed, I felt the red-hot burn of Jax's scornful gaze as deeply as I felt the hope rising in hers. But for all my protests, the demon *had* to know how this would play out.

Hell, I'd known it from the moment he stormed into my office ranting about the witch at the bar holding a one-way ticket to hell.

After two years as free men, barely outrunning the ghosts forever nipping at our heels, it'd finally come to this.

We were going back to Midnight.

And this time, we probably *wouldn't* escape alive.

But Haley would. I'd make damn sure of that.

# 6

## JAX

*I*t was an hour before sunrise when the last inebriated vampire stumbled out of the club and I finally tracked down Elian again.

*Damn it.* Saint, not Elian. The witch was getting in my head—definitely not a good sign.

He was holding court on one of the velvet couches in the former choir loft that overlooked the club, the VIP lounge he'd designated for our more exclusive clientele.

Two lilac-haired fae women writhed in his lap, one kissing his neck, the other moaning softly as Saint dropped little black pills onto her tongue. Two demon cocktail servers lounged beside them, thoroughly engaged with each other.

Saint's mouth shone red with blood from a fresh feed, though I had no idea who'd offered up the vein this time. Fae blood was the most exquisite in terms of taste, but it didn't sustain him. He needed regular infusions of human blood for that, and the supply was always an issue. We usually imported it for our vampire customers from a network of blood banks down in Mexico, but the human authorities were starting to crack down on our smugglers, squeezing the supply and pushing up our costs.

Live-feeding was the best alternative, but Saint didn't allow humans in the club, and outside he kept a low profile, avoiding humans whenever possible. All of us did—most humans didn't know the supernatural world existed, and we preferred to keep it that way. Exposure was bad for business and bad for our health.

I folded my arms across my chest and leaned against the massive pipes, all that remained of the cathedral's original organ. Images of the woman—Haley—flickered through my mind.

After promising to meet Saint at his home in the Garden District the following afternoon, she'd said her goodbyes and headed back to her hotel, and he'd spent the rest of the evening making arrangements with our top advisors to keep the business running during his... unforeseen absence.

Direct quote.

Operational and profitable at all times—that was the deal. All part of the fucked-up agreement we'd made with the crooked Midnight fae who'd helped us escape. And in the two years we'd been smuggling drugs out of Midnight, we'd done everything in our power to keep things running smoothly, to keep bringing in the green for everyone involved, and—most importantly—to keep the entire hustle off Keradoc's radar.

For all Saint's bullshit, Haley was a complication I hadn't seen coming.

What was her deal, anyway? Clearly, she and Saint had been in a relationship, but I couldn't make sense of it. The woman was a little on the crazy side, sure. But she was smart. Confident. A fighter. Drop-dead beautiful.

What the hell had a witch like that *ever* seen in a grade-A fuckup like Saint?

He whispered something into the pill-popping fae's ear, no doubt weaving some vampire-influenced fantasy she'd paid for, then finally met my gaze across the dim space. "Something I can do for you, Mr. Tall, Dark, and Demon?"

"No," I ground out, and we both knew I wasn't talking about whether he could do something for me.

"No?" he asked.

"*Hell* no. Would it help if I added a fuck? Fuck no. As a matter of fact, fucking hell no. Saint, you're a crazy fuck, but this... this is next-level insanity, even for you."

His silver eyes burned into me, even as his hand roamed down to the fae's ass. He gave her a quick swat, then all four of his guests rose from the couch and exited the loft.

"You've got history with her," I said once we were alone.

"Ancient, over, and not up for discussion." He retrieved an envelope from his inside jacket pocket and tossed it to me.

I opened it up. Thumbed the thick stack of money inside. "Fuck is this?"

He rose from the couch and headed for the bar, pouring himself a bourbon. "Insane or not, Jax, I don't have a choice."

"Because you owe her?"

He didn't respond.

"Haley's calling in your debt," I said, "so you're calling in mine? That's how this works?"

"I'm paying you. It's not the same thing."

"And you know I can't take the money, which makes it *exactly* the same thing." I shoved the envelope against his chest. "Newsflash, asshole. I'm not interested in playing escort to some witch who used to suck your—"

He grabbed my wrist. Leaned in close. "Careful, hellspawn."

His pupils were so dilated they almost swallowed the silver in his eyes. The sickly sweet scent of Devil's Dream clung to his breath. I didn't need to see his tongue to know it would be covered in the drug's signature black whorls.

Apparently, the fae woman wasn't the only one popping the pills of Midnight.

*Fuck.*

Back in The Black, they called it. Dancing with the Devil, visiting an old friend, tripping down memory lane. There were as many terms for the addiction as there were for the drug itself—Devil's Dream, D2, Dizzy Devil, Sweet Dream, The Black, Dark Delight. It obliterated your inhibitions, erased your conscious awareness, and put you in a state of pure euphoria, leaving you wide open to the twin powers of imagination and suggestion. Combine that with vampire influence whispered in a willing ear, and you had the perfect recipe for crafting the ultimate fantasy… assuming you could pay the price.

Saint had always struggled with the stuff—in Midnight and New Orleans both. After nearly burning down the club in a drug-induced haze six months ago, he'd managed to stay clean, but an hour with his ex had sent him running right back into the Devil's arms.

I broke out of his grip and poured myself a bourbon. Saint didn't need me to enumerate all the ways in which he was slowly killing himself. I suspected he'd been hoping for that exact outcome ever since we escaped that shithole realm.

I used to resent him for it. Hell, maybe I still did.

He didn't sell Midnight's exotic drugs here in the States because he wanted to—he did it because he had to, same as I did. Taking them, though? That *was* a choice.

And when it came down to choices—no matter how many he'd been given—Saint had never managed to make the right ones.

"We're not talking about an overnight trip to the coast," I said. "There are people in Midnight—fucking *mercenaries*—still out for your blood."

He met my gaze again, his eyes glassy. The fact that he was still on his feet at all spoke volumes about the tolerance he'd built up over the years. Even after taking enough Devil's Dream to turn his eyes black, he was still nowhere near the unconscious delirium it promised.

"*Our* blood," he said. "Isn't that what you mean? You. Me. Hudson. Blood before roses, right?"

*Blood before roses.*

The old vow echoed, the blood oath the three of us had sworn to one another in the Hollow—the neighborhood where we'd first crossed paths inside Midnight's walled city of Amaranth. Where we'd first figured out how to turn the realm's infamous corpsevine plant into the pills that would ultimately buy our freedom... And promptly enslave us.

It felt like a lifetime ago.

Saint grinned, black eyes haunted by the ghosts of everything we'd done. Everything we were *still* doing. Memories, guilt, leverage... What did it matter? All of it bound us like the iron chains we'd left back in the Hollow.

A bitter taste filled my mouth. A lot had happened since the days of blood oaths and brotherhood.

"Fuck you." I shoved him away and turned my back, unable to look into those drugged-out eyes for another moment. "The realm is at war. Always has been, always will be. Even if I *did* want to help your witch, what makes you think we could survive another go? That we could even reach Amaranth City before some rebel faction wasted us?" I shook my head and laughed. "Maybe you should get in touch with Keradoc yourself. Negotiate a peace treaty—you'd have a better chance at *that* than making it through the realm alive."

Now it was Saint's turn to laugh. "And what would peace do to our supply chain?" He poured himself another drink, then resumed lounging on the couch. "It's a balancing act, Jax. We don't want the realm blowing itself to bits, but we still need them at war. A peaceful, law-abiding realm is no good for us."

"Tricky thing, this war profiteering."

"The Empire doesn't run itself, brother." He held up his glass in cheers, then sipped.

It was an old argument between us—one I'd never win because the bastard was right. And however repugnant it was, the Empire—the code name he'd given our operation—was what kept us alive.

Then *and* now.

"Haley needs my help," he said. "Sure. But this isn't about her at all. She brought us an opportunity. A golden fucking opportunity we'd be fools to squander."

"An opportunity for death? Great. Sign me up."

"Not ours, Jax." He stared into the amber liquid in his glass, dark eyes glinting with a malice I hadn't seen since our last days in Midnight. "*His.*"

# 7

## JAX

"Keradoc?" I asked. "Are you high? Wait—don't answer that."

"Then don't ask."

"Saint, there's no way. No fucking way. Besides, Haley said she needs to get the blood without killing him."

"Everyone needs *something*, Jax. Sometimes I can meet those needs, sometimes I can't."

"And most of the time, you just plain *won't*." I sipped my bourbon, half-wishing it was as good as Devil's Dream at obliterating my thoughts. "Why would you risk your life for a doomed assassination attempt on Keradoc?"

"For fuck's sake. He's the warlord responsible for the genocide of tens of thousands of people. Do I really need a reason?"

"He's the warlord you smuggled weapons for in the Hollow. Your drug enterprise is probably still funding half his campaigns."

"*Our* drug enterprise. And as for the things I did and why I did them… Let's not confuse survival with loyalty, shall we?"

"Saint—"

"I've got unfinished business with the warlord of Midnight," he snapped. "Leave it."

Saint had unfinished business? I nearly snorted.

We *all* had unfinished business. Midnight wasn't exactly the kind of place that let you tie up loose ends, say your goodbyes, and fuck off to the next chapter in your happy little life.

As far as I knew, Saint, Hudson, and I were the only bastards who'd ever left at all, and the things we had to do to escape… I fought back a shiver. It wasn't just the drug smuggling. Leaving that place might've saved our lives, but it broke something inside each of us I was pretty sure we'd never be able to put back together again.

Hudson still didn't speak, not that he ever did in Midnight. But now, he disappeared into himself for days at a time, not eating, not sleeping. I kept waiting for the night he'd hop on his motorcycle, head out on the interstate, and disappear forever.

Since we got back, I hadn't been able to sleep more than an hour a night either, the nightmares too fucking close. Too real. And don't even get me started on the headaches.

And Saint… No matter how many pills he swallowed, no matter how much blood he drank, no matter how much fae pussy he chased, that poor fuck was as twisted up now as I'd ever seen him in Midnight.

Yes, the three of us had called ourselves blood brothers once. Bonded for life.

But life in Midnight turned out to be a lot shorter than we expected, and now we were here, facing an entirely different reality.

Most of the time, I still wasn't sure we'd made the right call leaving that fucking place.

"Besides," Saint said now, "taking Keradoc off the board could be a lucrative move for the entire operation."

"How do you figure?"

"Within the instability lies the opportunity." He scratched his jaw, considering. "A power vacuum would leave room to maneuver some of our people into influential political positions. Positions we could leverage to get more resources. More products—I'm talking stuff beyond D2. Midnight is a veritable blank check, Jax. One *we* could write and cash."

"Sure." I huffed out a laugh. "Less a juicy cut for the middlemen."

Aside from Keradoc and his extended family, an elite group of dark fae sorcerers and witches were all that remained of the pureblood Midnight fae. As purebloods, they could travel freely between Midnight and our realm, no portal spells or dark bargains necessary. They were easily bought, completely amoral, and notoriously honorable in that honor-among-thieves sort of way—perfect combination for drug smugglers.

*Those* were our so-called people. The ones who'd aided and abetted our escape. They'd been helping us move product and payment between realms ever since, and so far, it'd worked out.

But the only reason we had to move product at all was to keep those dark fae happy. As long as the drugs and money kept flowing, they'd ensure no one ever looked too hard for the three monsters who'd supposedly slipped through Midnight's cracks.

Payoffs made the world go round—it was as true in Midnight as it was here in NOLA.

"Or," I said, "we could try to buy our way out of this shit and find a legitimate way to live out the rest of our miserable immortalities."

"Go legit? A one-eyed demon, a mute shifter, and a strung-out vampire-fae mutt who can't get through a day without a stiff drink or a handful of little black pills?" Saint laughed. "Sorry, but I think our straight-and-narrow days are over."

"They don't have to be."

"Face it, brother. We're falling from grace like meteorites hurtling to earth. Might as well enjoy the spoils on the way down." Saint leaned his head back against the couch and sighed. He was motionless for so long, I wondered if the Devil's Dream had finally taken hold. But after a few long moments of silence, he sat up again and said, "I need you with me on this, Jax."

"Yes, you do."

"If you won't take the money, what the fuck do you want?"

"I *can't* take the money," I said. The asshole fucking knew it, too. He'd saved my life getting me out of that shithole, and I still owed him for it. Only reason I still worked for him—otherwise I'd be halfway around the world by now, as far away from *Saint Elian* as I could get.

Demons were notorious for making deals, and when it came to the desperate and depraved, we held all the bargaining power. But on the rare occasion a demon found himself on the receiving end of a favor? Fuck. Carrying debts of any sort—financial, emotional, physical, even just implied—chipped away at our power. The longer it took us to crawl out from under it, the weaker our ties to our physical bodies became, until one day we found ourselves smoked to oblivion, no chance of re-spawning.

I'd lost enough of my natural-born demon mojo in Midnight. I couldn't afford to lose any more just because Saint wanted to ease his conscience with a payoff.

"How about a little honesty instead?" I offered.

"Ha! That's a new one." Saint tipped his glass toward me and grinned. "I'll do my best. No promises."

I crouched down before him. Placed a hand on his knee and looked into his glassy black eyes. "Tell me this is just about Keradoc."

"I want him dead," he said firmly, and because he was half-tanked and his guard was down, he didn't have the mental fortitude to uphold the facade. To keep me out of his head.

Yes, he wanted the warlord on ice. But that wasn't the real reason he was so hell-bent on going back to Midnight. Not even close.

I got to my feet, trying to keep my annoyance in check.

Mostly, I fucking hated the burden of being a fear demon. But at times like this, I appreciated the insight it gave me. No, I couldn't read minds, but I could sense what people were most afraid of, and that was damn near the same thing.

Nothing revealed truth like fear. Dig deep enough, and I could turn that fear against a person, making them believe their darkest terror was playing out before their very eyes, much in the same way Saint could use his vampire influence.

Depending on how hard I pushed, that kind of manipulation could shatter a person's mind.

I didn't need to manipulate Saint, though. The drugs had eradicated his mental vigilance. Now, he telegraphed his fears like a child trembling over the monsters in the closet.

It all came back to the witch.

Saint really *had* loved her. *Still* loved her. And the thought of her coming to harm in Midnight fucking gutted him.

I headed to the bar. Abandoned my glass and went straight for the bottle.

"I do this for you, we're done," I said, taking a swig. "My debts are cleared. Understand? The minute we get back—*if* we get back—I'm leaving New Orleans. Leaving the Empire. Leaving this fucking country. Leaving *you*. And I never want to see you again, Saint."

He nodded as if he'd been expecting as much, though a hint of sadness flickered in his black eyes. "Promise to send me a postcard from your glamorous new life, and I won't stand in your way."

Ignoring his pathetic attempt at humor, I said, "So what's our move?"

"We need to coordinate this from the inside."

"Agreed."

"I'll send word to Gem, let her know the boys are heading back to the Hollow."

I allowed a thin smile. Of all the pureblood Midnighters, Gem was one of the good ones, just as her name implied. "You think we'll actually make it into Amaranth City?"

"With her help, we've got a shot. We'll need supplies, though—more than we can bring through Haley's portal. A place to crash. Midnight currency. Intel on Keradoc's whereabouts, and no, before you even say it, I *won't* be telling anyone about my plans—or Haley's, for that matter. That information's on a strictly need-to-know basis, and right now? You, Hudson, and I are the only ones who need to know."

"Hudson?" I groaned and scrubbed a hand over my jaw. "Don't even *think* about dragging him into this shit. Haven't you done enough damage? He's barely—"

My words fell away as the man in question landed in the loft, tucking his wings behind him.

For a massive gargoyle shifter who towered close to eight feet tall in his winged warrior form—a mix between man and winged beast, with bulging human musculature, talon-like claws, and smooth, slate-gray skin —he moved with the grace of a ballerina. Even in his human form—blond, bearded, and covered in tattoos that made him look more like a motorcycle club president than a mythical beast—he was silent and stealthy.

"Good to see you in living color again, Hudson," I said, and I meant it. By day, the sunlight turned him to stone. But after sunset, he was free to roam in his winged or human form. Lately, though, he'd been spending most of his time stoned by choice, perched on the cathedral eves or hiding out in the gardens behind Saint's place.

He nodded hello but didn't say a word, as usual.

"Hudson's the only one who can get everyone across Beggar's Moat," Saint said matter-of-factly, and from the incurious look on the gargoyle's face, it was clear he'd been listening in and was fully up to speed. "Unless you're ready to grow a pair of wings along with the balls you're still working on."

Hudson folded his arms across his massive chest and grinned, his fangs catching the light. Man or beast, it was the closest he ever got to laughing.

With a contempt I didn't bother to veil, I glanced down at the black smoke now curling off Saint's fingertips—side effect of the Devil's Dream. "Keep dancing with the Devil, Saint, and we'll see who needs new balls."

"Don't tell me you're losing your nerve." Saint lifted his hand to his mouth and blew, making the smoke dance. His grin stretched wide. "A fear demon, scared of a little trip to the dark side?"

"You know better than that."

Midnight was a brutal place, every square inch fraught with the kind of horrors that could reach into your chest and carve out your heart—the kind of horrors that would send most men to an early grave just to escape the memories of what they'd seen. What they'd endured.

But no, the prospect of going back there didn't scare me. I was largely incapable of fear, rational or otherwise—all part of the forced indoctrination of my particular demonic breed.

Didn't mean I was completely immune to it, though. And right now, one thing had me by the fucking throat.

Haley Barnes.

After two years of walking through life like a lukewarm corpse, Saint was coming back to life.

And he could say whatever the fuck he wanted about assassinating Keradoc, but I'd seen his truth, and it wasn't the prospect of spilling the warlord's blood that'd suddenly set his cock on fire.

It was a gorgeous, green-eyed witch who'd shown up at the club with a devious smile, a portal to Midnight, and a heart full of fury for the man who'd broken her.

I'd seen *her* truth, too. Yes, she had eyes that lit up the room and a smile that could bring a man to his knees. But that pitch-black flame inside her burned so hot, it was a miracle she hadn't incinerated herself.

She wasn't just an angel.

She was an angel of darkness.

And we were about to see just how far she was willing to fall.

"What do you say, brothers?" Saint asked. "Up for a rendezvous in the old stomping grounds?"

Hudson scratched a claw behind one of his horns and nodded.

I took another hit of bourbon first, but yes, I nodded, too.

And Saint...

Well. That asshole just laughed, as if he'd known all along his brothers wouldn't let him walk into the fires alone.

"Excellent. We'll finalize the plans with Haley at my place over lunch. In the meantime, the sun's almost up." He popped another pill into his mouth, grabbed a fresh bottle of bourbon from the bar, and headed for the exit. "If anyone needs me, I'll be in the cemetery furiously jerking off to the smell of flambéed vampire."

# 8

## HALEY

*I* wanted to hate it.

The lawn was overgrown, the paint chipping, and the humidity so thick my hair needed its own zip code.

But the sight of Elian's butter-yellow mansion made my heart ache with longing.

He'd stolen it. The future we'd always planned. The dream we'd created together.

A new life in a city drenched with magick that made our skin tingle. An old home in the Garden District—an original we could restore from the ground up. Businesses in the Quarter—a club for him, a witchy café and bookstore for me. Music and revelry floating on the air at night, the song of crickets drifting through the windows, the soundtrack of a beautiful life.

Had this house always been his—some weird double life he'd never confessed to? All the lovely pictures he'd painted in my mind… Was it all just to torment me?

Or had he bought this place after his return from Midnight, trying to torment *himself*?

*Yeah, and speaking of tormenting yourself…*

That's exactly what I was doing with all this pointless speculation. I'd spent *years* missing him. Now I was going to miss some pie-in-the-sky daydream about a future that'd never stood a chance? Screw that. I had a *real* life to miss—with people who actually cared about me. Sisters and friends. A coven of witches waiting for me back in the Bay.

Elian was nothing more than an escort service now—a means to an end. The sooner we wrapped up this mission, the sooner I could get back home.

No one answered the door when I rang the bell, and peering through the thick, dusty windows didn't reveal any signs of life either. So, after a quick walk to a corner café for a coffee refill, I stashed my bag on the porch and headed into the backyard to wait.

The place was something out of a fairytale. Southern live oaks and flowering dogwood trees circled a small pond, curtains of Spanish moss dripping from every limb. Bright pink azaleas bloomed at their feet, and a wooden footbridge arched across the pond like a pathway to a secret world.

A stone gargoyle sat at the water's edge, catching my attention. It was an odd placement for a garden statue, and he reminded me of the one who'd perched on the cathedral at Saints and Sinners.

I never knew Elian had a thing for them.

As I approached the pond, a sense of calm washed over me. Removing the dagger holstered beneath my sundress, I took a seat in the grass beside the gargoyle, hoping he didn't mind the intrusion.

We hung out in companionable silence for a few minutes, but as soon as I finished my chicory coffee, I was overcome with the inexplicable urge to talk to the guy.

Yes, the gargoyle.

Further evidence of Elian's deleterious effects on my mental state, but for now, I was rolling with it.

"Tough talk, Gargs," I said. "Am I a *complete* idiot, or just three-quarters' worth? Don't get me wrong—it's not like I came here expecting him to grovel. But is it crazy to trust him with this? He really wrecked me, you know? And not in the good way."

I laughed and swatted away a mosquito, but before I could speak again, a wave of emotion rose in my throat. Memories bombarded me from all sides—memories I'd taken out and examined so many times before, all the edges should've been worn smooth by now.

No such luck. These babies were as sharp and painful today as they'd been the morning after he'd left.

*Motherfucker.* How was it possible I had any more tears left for the man?

I closed my eyes, letting a few of them slip down my cheeks. Prying open the door to the past was a dangerous habit—one I thought I'd kicked. Yet there I was again, cracking it open and peering inside. An inch at first.

Then a foot. A little wider, and…

Boom. I was right back in Blackmoon Bay, shoving a cocky, silver-eyed fae off the edge of a pier.

"I was in a dark place when fate put Elian in my path," I told my silent friend. "Even after I invited him back to my place that night, I thought we were just heading for a one-night stand. A little horizontal adventure to take my mind off the shitshow of my life."

It *was* a shitshow, too. I was barely nineteen. The grandmother who'd raised me after my adoptive parents died in a car crash had suddenly dropped dead of a heart attack. No warning, no goodbyes. I was lost without my Nona—a complete disaster. I got mixed up in dark magick— lots of forbidden shit. Bailed on college, sold Nona's house, and wandered the country until I finally ended up in Blackmoon Bay.

Turned out I'd been born there, though I hadn't known it at the time. Somehow, the city had called me home.

I was looking for something, though. A purpose. A reason to get out of bed each day.

Instead, I found *him*.

"I know this sounds cliché," I said, "but with Elian? It really was love at first sight."

A week after our so-called one-night stand, I was moving into his apartment. A month later, we were already talking about New Orleans. About forever.

Sometimes, you just knew.

And sometimes, your intuition needed to be drop-kicked into the nearest dumpster and set on fire, but hey. Hindsight, right?

"I was with him for three years," I continued. "Three of the most intense, mind-blowing, soul-shattering years of my life. God, even our fights were hot." I gathered the hair at the nape of my neck and fanned my face, trying to convince myself the sweat trickling down my back was from the Louisiana heat and *not* the vivid memories of Elian's tongue on my nipple, his hair tickling my stomach, one hand wrapped around my throat and squeezing—oh, *fuck*… just right.

We were good together in every way. No secrets—or so I'd thought. No shame.

"But one night I just got this really bad feeling," I said. "He'd been acting strange all day, and even after he'd spent two hours in bed giving me the most intense orgasms of my life, whispering over and over how much he loved me, something still felt off. I woke up in the middle of the night feeling like someone had ripped something out of my chest. I glanced at the clock on the nightstand—three-thirty-three AM. And before I even rolled over to check on him, before I trailed a hand across the sheets to touch his shoulder, a deep sadness washed over me and I just... I *knew* he was gone. Not in the bathroom, not out for a nightcap, but *gone*."

Memories of that night tore through my heart, and I unsheathed my dagger, the familiar feel of the smooth bone handle steadying me.

"I got up and searched the place," I said. "The only things missing were a backpack, his wallet, and some clothes. He didn't even take his keys or phone. He left almost all of his possessions behind, yet I still knew he wasn't coming back. It was as if our very connection had suddenly shattered—everything we'd meant to each other, everything we'd promised." I turned the blade, catching the sunlight and reflecting it onto my face. "Losing someone you love is hard enough, but the not knowing? It makes everything so much more unbearable. You think you can handle shit, but the brain *hates* a mystery. Things need to be solved. Cases closed. If you don't have the answers? Your oh-so-helpful brain fills in all the blanks for you. And let me tell you something, Gargs—brains are mean little assholes. Be grateful you don't have one."

The breeze whispered across my shoulders, and I ran my fingers along the flat of the blade, the metal warm from the sun.

Elian *left* me that night—I wasn't stupid. He'd packed a bag. Fucked me like he knew it'd be our last time. But I still spent months searching for him. Scouring every fae and vampire club in the vicinity, asking every connection, friend, and supernatural neighbor we'd ever encountered if they'd heard from him.

After six months of bashing my head against nothing but dead ends, I was starting to think maybe I'd imagined him. Dreamed up my fae soulmate as some kind of manifestation of all the people I'd lost in my life. All the people who—by choice or the cruel winds of fate—had left me.

The months dragged on. Everyone else seemed to forget he'd ever existed, but me? I was still waking up every single night at three-thirty-three and crawling the walls in the dark, my heart pounding so hard I swore it would kill me, mind spinning with the same pointless *why, why, whys?*

"You know what I finally figured out?" I glanced over at my new friend, silent and stately as ever. "Sometimes, things just end. They're messy and complicated and it sucks, but life doesn't owe you answers and a neat little bow to tie things off. Sometimes, all you get is a smashed heart and a choice: make friends with the pain and move forward, or curl up on the kitchen floor, fall back into the past, and fucking *drown* there. I didn't want to drown, Gargs. I wanted to fight."

I told him about my so-called rise from the depths of that dead sea—leaving Elian's apartment, joining Bay Coven, practicing my blood magick, trying to build an actual life for myself that didn't involve looking at old pictures and waiting for them to talk to me. I made new friends, found things to smile about. I even met a new guy—a wolf shifter. I thought I could love him, too. Not right away, not in the same reckless, passionate tumble I'd experienced with Elian. But in a mature and stable way—one that would last. It's what I thought I'd wanted, and for a long time, things were good. Not amazing, not butterflies-with-every-searing-hot-touch, but good.

Then, just as I was finally getting my footing again, it happened.

A mutual witch friend who'd moved down south had heard about a club in New Orleans. Saints and Sinners, it was called. An abandoned cathedral bought and resurrected a few months earlier by a silver-eyed fae with a crooked grin and a clever tongue.

A man who'd allegedly done the impossible:

Escaped the deadly realm of Midnight after years of exile.

His name was Elian.

"I wept to know he was alive," I said. "Wept to imagine what he must've endured in captivity. Wept to think he might soon return to the Bay, or call or write me, and what would I even say to him? I was in a different place in my life at that point. Stronger. Older. Content with my wolf shifter. But I still cared for Elian. I wanted him to know he'd always have a friend in me. One who wanted him to be safe and happy, no matter how badly things had gone between us. But Elian... He never reached out, and I was too scared to make the first move. I figured he had his reasons—reasons he didn't want to share, or couldn't share, and I tried to accept that. But I couldn't.

"My witch friend had visited the club a few times since then—told me about the wild parties, the fae women, Elian at the center of it all like some giant supernova. I wanted to be happy for him, but all I could think about was the fact that in all her visits, for all that he'd rolled out the red carpet for her, he'd never *once* asked about me. It was like I'd stopped existing for him the same way *he'd* stopped existing for everyone else years earlier."

I ran my thumb along the blade of my dagger, accidentally nicking myself. Blood welled on my skin, and I stared at the little red beads. They glinted like rubies in the sunlight.

I pressed my thumb to the blade again, just enough to make it sting.

"I started waking up every night at three-thirty-three again," I said. "Started having nightmares about him being trapped in Midnight. The questions I'd *sworn* I put to rest were back with a vengeance, scampering around my mind all day and night like rats. I'd do my best to keep it together at home, then lose it in the shower, hoping my boyfriend didn't hear me. I didn't have the courage to tell him about Elian—about how often I still thought of him. Missed him. It was tearing me up inside—I could barely function anymore. Eventually, I got fired from my job. I blew up my relationship, pushed away most of my friends. I sank right back into my old, desperate patterns, and it was only the barest shred of pride that kept me from hitching a ride down to New Orleans and making a scene so explosive, it would put Elian's craziest parties to shame."

Another breeze cut through the humidity, carrying the scents of jasmine and the still waters of the pond. I shivered, despite the heat.

The worst night of my life was slowly clawing its way back to the surface, strangling me in its icy grip.

I hadn't thought about it in a long time—not even when I'd finally seen Elian last night—but suddenly, it was all around me again. The darkness. The cold.

"My friend called me one night," I said softly. "Said she was at the club, and Elian was heading down to meet her, and did I want to give him a message? Feeling brave, I told her to say hello for me, and to call or text later if he wanted to say hello back."

I shook my head and groaned, the old shame rising inside. "You never think you're gonna be that girl, Gargs. The one who holds her phone and literally stares at the screen for three hours, waiting on the ping that never comes. And it didn't, of course. It was never going to. So, as the sun started to rise on yet *another* day without a word from the man who still owned my heart, I decided I was finally done. Just done. I chucked my phone in the toilet, stripped out of my clothes, and turned on the bathwater."

A deep, shuddering breath rattled through my lungs. I'd never told this story to anyone. Not to my sisters, not to my coven mates, not even to my journals.

Now, I was telling it to a statue beneath the gentle sway of Spanish moss, feeling safe and calm in a way I hadn't since my high school years in Nona's kitchen, doing homework at the kitchen table while she baked her world-famous lasagna.

"The next thing I was consciously aware of," I said, "I was naked in a scalding hot bath with a bottle of pills in one hand and a kitchen knife in the other, trying to decide which would kill me faster. Pills were unreliable, I figured, so I went with the knife. A vertical slit from wrist to elbow, as deep as I could stand."

I shivered and traced the tip of my dagger along the scar, a pink and silver ridge about the length of my pinky. The skin was numb there. It didn't want to remember that night, either.

"There was a lot of blood," I said. "More than I was expecting. And seeing it, that bright red mess... Something snapped inside, like someone just yanked off the veil and shined a flashlight in my face. Maybe it was Nona, or my dead parents, or the sisters I hadn't even met yet. Maybe it was fate itself, reminding me I still had important shit to do. But in that moment, I heard a voice in my head, clear as a bell. *Stop hoping*, it said. *Just stop.* At first, I thought it was encouraging me to give up, but it wasn't. It was saving me."

My friend's reports of Elian's party life in New Orleans had reignited hope inside me, and every day that passed, I was *hoping* I'd see him again. *Hoping* he'd finally explain. *Hoping*, above all else, he'd finally fucking acknowledge that what we'd shared had meant something to him, even if we had to let it go.

All that hope? I was poisoning myself with it.

"So I stopped hoping," I continued, "and instead tried to think of one simple thing—one *real* thing—I could appreciate. First thing that popped into my head? Nona's lasagna. I'd just made a batch the night before, and suddenly, I *had* to survive, if only to taste one last bite. So I made myself a deal: Get out of the bathtub, stitch up the arm, and warm up the damn lasagna. If I still wanted to opt out after all that, I could get right back in the tub. But you know what, Gargs? Once I had that first hot, gooey bite, I wanted another one. So I made a new deal: Stay alive long enough to eat one whole piece. One piece became the rest of the pan, which got me through another week. Then I found something else to appreciate. On it went, a few hours or days at a time, all these little moments of appreciation and bargaining until I finally realized I didn't want to get back in that bathtub. I was ready to fight again."

It felt like a thousand years ago, that fight. I thought it would've ended by now, but it didn't.

I was *still* fighting. Every single day.

Seeing Elian last night, as beautiful and alive as I'd ever known him, still rocking that stupid smirk and those eyes that could melt my soul...

I could very easily let him break me again. Slip right back into the darkest hours of my life. Slice the vein. Slide under the water. Goodbye.

But I'd survived that darkness. And in the years that followed, I survived other darknesses as well—the brutalities of the hunters. The deaths of friends and loved ones. The war in Blackmoon Bay.

Now, I had to survive Midnight.

And survival, I was starting to realize, wasn't an endpoint you reached. It was a process you endured—an endless cycle of trying and sometimes failing, but ultimately getting up again to fight another day.

Maybe I'd never be completely free of those ghosts. Maybe looking into Elian's eyes or saying his name would always cut me open. Maybe I'd start waking up at the witching hour again, my heart bleeding, the pain so deep it would drive me to my knees.

Didn't mean it had to control me, though. Didn't mean I had to give up fighting.

The love I had for him, the love I lost, the darkness... All of it had shaped me into the woman and witch I was now—a witch who'd called upon the dark goddess and wielded that incredible magick to save her family. A witch who'd found the strength to face the man who'd nearly broken her, just so she could repay her debts and save them again.

So, pain? Darkness?

Yeah. Maybe surviving meant learning how to appreciate those things, too.

Sitting in the sun-dappled grass with the gargoyle, I carved a pentacle into the soft ground at the edge of the pond with my dagger, then wrapped my hand around my blade and jerked it hard, cutting a deep slice.

It wasn't mutilation, though. It was magick. A blood spell for strength and courage. A thank-you to myself for not giving up. For learning, day by day, to spin the pain of experience into the gold of wisdom.

I made a fist, squeezing the blood onto the pentacle.

*I will not give up. I will not stop fighting. I will not drown.*

It felt like a promise. A sacred oath between my heart, my soul, and fate itself.

The blood glowed bright, then sank into the ground with a quiet hiss.

The softest breeze carried away my silent vow.

And in its wake, a dozen black roses bloomed in the mud.

**9**

## HUDSON

$S$ aint was my boy and all, but damn. My boy was a fucking liar.

He'd told me about the witch last night—about this Midnight run we'd all signed up for, come hell or high water. But now that the woman was pouring her heart out—not to mention her blood—I realized he'd glossed over a few key details.

Like the one about how he'd jacked up her life. Broke her heart so bad she'd made a date with Death and damn near sealed the deal.

*Fucking Saint.*

I'd never learned why or how he'd ended up in Midnight. Same with Jax. Just wasn't the kinda group therapy bullshit you shared in a place that had you running for your life more often than kicking back with friends over a few beers. Out there, no one had a past. No one had a future. All you ever got was the moment. Sometimes, not even that.

But now? I wanted to know all of it. Every gritty detail.

What the hell was so bad about his old life that it'd driven him to bail on a woman like Haley? A woman who'd clearly loved his dumb ass?

*Still* loved him, if the heartache in her voice was a sign—and in all my centuries of taking accidental confessions just like this one? Yeah. It usually was.

I wasn't able to *feel* anything in my stone form—no human touch, no sense of my own body, no rain, not even the fly-by bird shit that hit me on the regular—but I could sure as hell see and hear everything, and my brain worked just fine too.

Saint had really done a number on her.

Babygirl was a fighter, though—had to give her credit. Pulling herself out of that dark hole? Showing up here asking for his help? That took a serious set of lady balls, and hers were made of steel.

Even with them crocodile tears slipping down her cheeks, she still looked like a warrior.

She reached out and fingered one of her roses.

"Fuck," she whispered, her mouth rounding into a soft little o. "What the fuck is *wrong* with me?"

Wasn't often I shared a smile these days, but hell. If I was in my human form, I definitely woulda had one for her.

I'd been alive for damn near a thousand years, and I'd seen enough crazy shit to make even the most depraved, twisted sonofabitch gouge out his own eyes.

But this?

This was something else.

She and the others might not realize it yet, but I saw the truth in them black roses. Behind Haley's bright green eyes, a spooky-ass little monster girl lurked in the shadows. She was a fighter, yeah. A survivor, just like she'd said.

But she was a hell of a lot more than that, and she was only just *beginning* to taste her full power.

"So listen, Gargs." She glanced up at me and smiled, warmer than the sun on my stone heart. "Didn't mean to get so heavy on you on our first date. But you'll keep my secrets, won't you? You're a vault. Yes, I realize I'm confiding in a statue, and yes, I realize I'm probably having a breakdown—one more secret for you to keep. Oh! Along with my horticultural disaster. Wow. Haley Barnes, everyone. The crazy just keeps on coming!"

She reached for a big ol' clump of Spanish moss that'd fallen in the grass and hastily covered up her roses.

Too bad. Beauty like that deserved to be seen.

Satisfied with the mossy camo, she sheathed her blade, strapped the holster back around her thigh, grabbed her coffee cup, and got to her feet.

Her dress was the color of apples. A quick breeze blew it up around her waist, giving me a shot of white lace panties and the leather holster. Haley just giggled, though.

"Hey hey," she teased. "Confession *and* a show—lucky you!"

If I wasn't already stoned, the sight of her woulda made me *rock* fucking hard. How the fuck was I gonna keep my shit together around her after sunset, when I was back to being a man?

No wonder Saint was tripping over his own balls just to help her. Pretty sure Jax had fallen under her spell too, though he'd be the last to admit it. That demon always liked to play it cool.

So yeah, *this* adventure was off to a good start.

Smoothing out the dress, Haley beamed up at me and said, "Thanks again for climbing aboard my crazy train. I think it's safe to say we've reached our final destination—I'll try to keep the breakdowns to a minimum. Let's just hope Saint's house is stocked with as much booze as his club."

Then, she leaned in real close—close enough I could see the golden threads in her green eyes—and ran a hand along the edge of my wing.

*Aw, hell.*

If I could've spoken, I would've told her *I* was the one losing my damn mind.

Because right then? The touch of her hand? The magnetic pull of those eyes?

Everything just fucking changed in a blink.

Everything.

Fuck.

*Fuck.*

No. No fuckin' way. I had to have imagined that. Right?

*Touch me again, babygirl. Just need to be sure...*

The softest breeze ruffled her hair.

"Did you just...?" She cocked her head and narrowed her eyes. "I could've *sworn* I saw your wing twitch."

*If that's true, shit just got a whole lot more complicated...*

Haley shook her head and laughed. "I'm totally blaming the heat on that one. It's gotta be at least two hundred degrees out here, and your girl is *wilting*. How do any of you survive this place? Guess I dodged a bullet, huh? Okay, I need to get inside that house before I melt. Assuming I make it through the day without getting arrested for murdering a fae and a demon, I'll stop by and visit again later. Maybe find some hedge trimmers for those creepy roses."

She reached for me once more, this time placing her hand flat against my chest, her palm still wet with blood.

A bolt of electricity shot right through me, jolting my heart and sizzling across nerves I didn't even know existed.

She felt it too—I could see it in her face. Her eyes widened, and she sucked in a sharp breath.

Thing is... In my stone form? I shouldn't have been able to feel it. Shouldn't have been able to hear the sudden jackhammering of my heartbeat.

It shouldn't have started beating at all. Not until the sun dropped and I shifted into one of my other forms.

But there was no denying it. Inside the stone shell, I was fucking alive.

She kept on staring at me with them wide eyes, her hand trembling against my chest, and I *knew*. Sure as I knew every chip in my stone gargoyle form, every notch and tear in my wings, every scar and line of ink tattooed on my human chest.

I hadn't experienced anything like it in nine centuries. Nine fucking centuries, and I'd damn near forgotten how it felt. Forgotten I was even capable of it. Forgotten it was a real thing and not just some story I'd picked up along the way and turned into a false memory.

But suddenly, at the press of her hand and the touch of her blood on my stone, there it was.

The bond.

If I could've roared right then, I would've.

Unlike Jax and Saint, I was born in Midnight. Bred in captivity to serve as a guardian to the original Midnight royals—the most honorable gig our kind could've hoped for in that hellhole.

Fucked up as it was, the place was home—only one I'd ever known.

Until two years ago when I was betrayed by my own kind, and Saint smuggled me out to save my ass from being pulverized. Not even Jax knew the whole story, but we weren't about to leave him behind. Saint made the arrangements for all of us.

Blood before roses—the three of us were tight like that.

So last night, when my boy said he needed help with this mission? I was all in, no question. Ain't never turned my back on him, not once. On top of that, throw in a chance to go back and hunt down the motherfuckers that'd taken everything from me? Done and done.

But now? Shit just got real in a whole different kinda way.

The bond only meant one thing.

Haley was fated for me.

My charge.

My twin heart.

My mate.

No, I wasn't talking about love and marriage and all that happy horse-shit. Fate had a fucked-up sense of humor, and it didn't always work out the way you thought it oughta. More often than not, a gargoyle and his fated mate *despised* each other.

Didn't make a damn bit of difference to the bond, though.

Whether she ended up hating me or loving me, whether she wanted to be my friend or something else entirely—good or bad—fate had just sent me a message.

I was chosen as her guardian. She was chosen as mine to protect.

Non-negotiable.

Starting right now.

"Haley!" Saint suddenly called out, heading across the lawn. He was carrying a few bags of restaurant food—I recognized the smell of Cajun Jeb's.

Haley gave me one more smile. Felt like a gift. Then she lowered her hand and turned to face him, taking that electric zing with her.

"Sorry to keep you," he said, charming as ever in a fitted suit the color of sand, white shirt open at the top. "I was out picking up lunch—took a little longer than I'd hoped."

"Totally on brand, Elian. But... bright side?" She plucked one of the bags from his arms and peeked inside. "This time, you only left me hanging for an hour instead of five years. And you brought food. Hallelujah praise the goddess, maybe you *can* be trained!"

On the inside, I was laughing my rock-hard ass off.

*Good girl.*

"Haley... What happened to your...?" He reached for her wounded hand, but stopped just short of touching her.

She flexed her fingers and shrugged. "Just a little blood spell. It'll heal up in a few minutes."

"But... on its own? How?"

"Blood magick. It's is a hell of a drug." She flashed Saint a killer smile he didn't deserve, keeping her other hand—the one with that fat scar along her wrist—tucked under the food bag.

Something told me he hadn't seen it last night, either. Might not have been so smug if he had.

Saint glared at me now, a warning flashing in them nickel-plated eyes like I needed to know something, and fast.

What the fuck he was trying to warn *me* about, I had no idea. Didn't care, honestly.

Homeboy shoulda been warning himself. 'Cause here's what I *already* knew: He'd hurt her in the past. Bad.

And as soon as the sun set and I was back to being a hot-blooded man again?

*Fuck* Cajun Jeb's jambalaya. That fae-fucking sonofabitch was gonna taste my fist.

# 10

## HALEY

*I* followed Elian into the house, as grateful for the air conditioning as I was for the food.

*Phew.* New Orleans needed a level-ten boob sweat warning stamped right there on the welcome sign.

The interior was even more picture-perfect than the outside, completely remodeled but still retaining its original charm. Lush draperies hung over floor-to-ceiling windows, and crown molding wrapped around the tops of the high walls, everything done in an elegant palate of creams, sages, and black. Nothing was out of place—I'd be surprised if Saint had even spent much time here.

I took a moment to look around, bracing for the same gut-punch that'd socked me outside. It didn't come, though. My spell seemed to be working, keeping me grounded. Keeping me sane.

*Just a beautiful old house,* I reminded myself. *Just a means to an end.*

The kitchen was a massive affair of exposed brick walls, granite countertops, and stainless steel appliances, ending in an eating nook with French doors that led out to a sunny patio.

At the center of the nook, Jax was seated at the table reading the newspaper—like, a *paper* newspaper, not a tablet—which was about the quaintest thing I'd ever seen. He'd ditched last night's white button-down for a faded black Dead Weather T-shirt that clung to his muscled chest, his hair damp from a recent shower.

He looked and smelled good enough to lick—a situation that was *not* helping me recover from the heatstroke.

Maybe NOLA needed a warning sign for him, too.

"Hey there, sinner," I said with a smile. "Fancy meeting you here."

He glanced up from the newspaper and flashed a grin—there and gone again—and I practically swooned.

*Pay no attention to the diamond-hard nipples your lush mouth has suddenly inspired...*

"Angel," he said neutrally, returning his attention to the newspaper. "I trust you didn't have any problems checking out of the hotel?"

"Funny enough, someone had already paid my bill." I turned and glared at Elian, who was busy retrieving plates and silverware for our feast. "Any guesses who?"

"Don't read into it," he said. "The owner's a demon. He owed me a favor."

"Don't we all," Jax grumbled.

"What are you doing here, anyway?" I asked Jax. "Come to see me off?" I set the bag on the table and started pulling out the takeout containers. Southern, spicy goodness wafted up, making my stomach grumble. "I think I love you."

"After one night?" Jax ruffled his newspaper. "Didn't realize I made such an impression."

I rolled my eyes. "Yeah, I was talking to the jambalaya."

"She does that," Elian said. "Talks to her food."

Jax looked up at me and lifted his brows, like, *Are you going to let him get away with that shit?*

No, I was not.

"I think we need some ground rules here, Elian," I said. "Rule number one—don't do that."

"Don't do what?"

"Point out all my cute little quirks and foibles like you've got the inside scoop on all things Haley Barnes. It was a long time ago."

"But that's... that's a thing you still do," he protested. "You literally just did it."

I grabbed the biggest container and popped off the lid, then took a seat right next to the demon. "Do you mind if I make out with you a little, just to piss him off?"

Jax leaned over, his breath stirring my hair. "Just so I'm clear... Still talking to the jambalaya?"

"Obviously." Ignoring the shiver of pleasure that rolled across my shoulders at the demon's proximity, I snatched a spoon from Elian's hand and dug in, skipping the courtesy of dishing it into a bowl. Elian had made me wait in the hot sun for an hour without so much as a note taped to the door. Manners were no longer high on my list.

By the time I glanced up from my jambalaya snog-fest, the room had fallen silent, and both guys were watching me as if they'd never seen someone have an orgasmic culinary experience before.

"Want some?" I asked, though it came out more like "wan thub" on account of the red-hot deliciousness filling my mouth. I scooped up another spoonful and lifted it toward Jax, but the demon didn't bite. Just glared at me in that unnervingly hot way of his.

"Jax is *here*," Elian finally said, "because he's coming with us."

"As is Hudson," Jax said. "Our other… associate."

*Coming with us? Other associate?*

"I'm not following," I said to Elian. "Why would you drag more people into this?"

Elian and Jax exchanged a loaded glance. They seemed to be having an argument without words.

Apparently, Elian lost.

Through a tight jaw, he sighed and said, "I wasn't the only one to escape Midnight, Haley. Jax and Hudson were with me. We survived the streets together, and when the time came to leave, we made it out together."

"So now you're going *back* together? I don't think so, Musketeers." I shoved the spoon into my mouth, but the spicy food wasn't enough to rival the hot guilt bubbling inside me. "Elian, I can't do this without you. We both know that. But I can't ask your friends to—"

"We're not friends," Jax said, at the same time Elian said, "It's already done."

I turned to Jax, my eyes misting. "Don't be crazy. You don't even know me. Why would you agree to this?"

"I have my reasons." He grabbed the spoon from my hand and dipped it into the container, then lifted it to my lips. With another smirk, he said, "Eat, angel. Or you'll be fighting Hudson for the scraps."

I did as he asked, my eyes locked on his mouth, my skin heating up in a way that had nothing to do with the spices *or* my guilt.

Elian grumbled under his breath, but that was another thing I wasn't about to let him get away with.

Keeping my gaze locked on Jax, I grinned and said, "Elian, that's a *great* idea—thanks for offering. I'd love something to drink. Lemonade? Preferably spiked? And something for the demon as well. I think he's a little... thirsty."

Jax laughed. "Oh, I think I'm keeping this one, Saint."

*Good.*

Because I was pretty sure I'd be keeping him, too.

# 11

## HALEY

*A*fter I'd demolished most of the food and sucked down just enough boozy lemonade to fortify all those emotional buttons Elian liked to push, we cleared the table and got to work.

For all his many, *many* flaws—and I do mean *many*—Elian was at least taking this seriously. In the time since I'd dropped the Midnight-or-bust bomb last night, he'd already sketched out a map for me, and now he spread it out on the table and gave me the grand tour.

It was a vast realm, rippling with jagged mountains and drowning in nearly bottomless lakes, some made of blood, others made of fire. Aside from a few small outposts established by the soldiers of the many ongoing wars, there was only one urban center—Amaranth City—built in the north along the shores of the Sea of Tranquility. The Razorback Mountains protected its western border; a range called Dead Claw protected the east.

The remainder of the realm stretched out to the south, each section of the map more treacherous than the last—tar pits, ice cliffs, meadows filled with poisonous flowers and razor-sharp grass. At the southernmost edge was Boiling Glass Sands, a desert so hot the ancient sands had long ago turned to glass. Elian said the Midnight fae had relinquished the region to the dragon lords millennia ago, but no one knew for certain whether the fire-breathers still existed; anyone who got close to the glass simply... melted.

Three-thousand-degree heat would do that to a body.

Blackbone Forest lay about thirty miles south of the city. According to

Elian, it was mostly just bare trees and scorched earth, very little flora or fauna, largely ignored by the many factions fighting for control and the many beasts that would otherwise devour our bones.

That's where we'd be portaling in. According to Elian, anything closer to Amaranth had a higher probability of being watched, or—considering how often war erupted there—was too much of an unknown quantity. We couldn't risk portaling into the middle of a battle.

As for the city itself? Amaranth was warded against portals.

"And all these rebel factions," I said. "They actually *want* these lands? Talk about shady real estate dealings."

"Wars have been waged over less," Jax said. "By monsters and men alike."

I studied the map intensely, trying to picture myself trekking across such an inhospitable place.

*Guess I won't be needing any more cute dresses now…*

"Your primary objective in Midnight," Elian said, "is to locate Keradoc, get close enough to work your magick, and steal his blood, all without him detecting our presence."

"Oh, is that all? Easy peasy." I dropped my head into my hands and groaned. Seeing the map just made the situation all the more real.

The Goddess had to be *nuts* to think I could pull this off. *I* had to be nuts.

Maybe that's what she'd been counting on.

*Bring me your demented, your unstable, your overly-eager-to-prove-their-worth-after-suffering-years-of-crushingly-low-self-esteem…*

*Damn*, I really wanted another drink. But I was pretty sure a hangover would be about as useless as the cute wardrobe for getting me through Midnight.

"Hey. I know it's overwhelming," Elian said, coming around to my side of the table. "Looking at it all at once, sure. It feels damn near impossible."

"Not just near, Elian. *Actual* impossible."

He crouched down beside me and put a hand on my knee. Not sexual, not dominating, just… encouraging.

The gesture made my eyes glaze with emotion. It was like a glimpse of the Elian I used to know. A glimpse into the past.

"The best way to tackle something like this is by breaking it down into several smaller missions," he said. "The first mission? Packing up, which we'll do tonight when Hudson gets here with the supplies. The next mission is getting through the portal to Blackbone Forest. After that, we get a new mission. See how this works?"

"Lasagna," I whispered, the knots in my stomach loosening. It was just like I'd gotten through the dark days after the bathtub incident. First, warm up the lasagna. Then take one bite. Then a piece. Then the whole pan.

"Is that one of her things too?" Jax asked Elian. "Calling out random foods?"

"I'm... not sure. Maybe she's hungry again?"

"How is that possible? She ate all the jambalaya and most of the cornbread."

"Not to mention the dirty rice," Elian said.

I laughed as the two of them studied me like some kind of zoo exhibit. "I'm good. I promise. Let's get back to these near-but-not-quite-impossible missions, yes?"

Elian got to his feet again, pacing in front of the table as Jax and I returned our attention to the map.

"Other than the soldiers," Elian said, "the majority of the population lives here in Amaranth." He leaned over and circled it on the map. "You want to get to Keradoc? We'll need to get inside the city first."

"Isn't he out fighting battles and slaughtering innocent villagers?" I asked. "I mean, warlord, right? One job."

"There are no innocents in Midnight," Jax said.

"And Keradoc's not a soldier," Elian said. "He's a politician who *plays* at being a soldier, waging his wars from behind a desk safely locked away in a fortified tower. The only time his weapons see any action is when he's bored and orders his minions to bring him something to decapitate or set on fire."

"You're saying he's got a thing for vampires," I said, and Jax laughed. I was truly starting to like the guy.

Ignoring us both, Elian said, "We won't be able to figure out Keradoc's current location until we're in the city. There, even the walls have ears. So, our first order of business in Midnight is getting from the portal..." He made an X over Blackbone. "...to the city. The southeastern quadrant is the weakest point, so that's our objective." He made another X near the city, then circled it.

"Is there a checkpoint or something?" I asked. "Watchmen? Or do we just... show up?"

He drew a curved line with several Xs running along the bottom of the city, all the way from the Razorback Mountains to Dead Claw.

"Vanderham's Wall," he explained. "And the watchtowers. The wall itself," he said, drawing another curve just beneath the first, "is protected by a trench that spans thirty feet across, thirty feet deep."

"Beggar's Moat," Jax said. "Just about the *last* fucking place you want to be."

"A moat?" I asked. "Seriously? As in, alligators?"

Jax ran a finger across the moat. "Worse. Way worse."

"It'll take about two days to reach the wall," Elian said. "There are primarily two ways in." He drew a line from the center of the wall out across the moat. "The drawbridge, which is lowered from the gatehouse twice per night, allowing Keradoc's soldiers to come and go, along with any other assholes unlucky enough to be in his service. Mostly military and their outfits—medics, cooks, and the like. Suppliers and traders come and go as well, maybe a few hunters looking for their next trophy from Dead Claw, although most of those fools never make it back."

"So the rest of the people inside the city are prisoners?" I asked.

"Aside from Keradoc and the other pureblood Midnighters, *everyone* in the realm is a prisoner. The ones who make it through the wilds and into the city are more protected, but they're not free, Haley."

"So why does Keradoc let them stay?"

"Every emperor needs his peasants," he said. "The working class keeps the city running, which keeps the ruling class in power. The rich get fat and happy off the sweat of their labor, then toss them a few bones once in a while to lull them into complacency. If they start to grumble about inequality, the ruling class simply starts another war, finds them another scapegoat, makes them fear and loathe and turn on each other to divert their attention from the true injustices baked right into the system."

"On and on the machine grinds," Jax said. "Until it grinds us all to dust."

I blew out a breath. For all its reputation as a vile, terrifying kingdom of bloodthirsty exiles, Midnight didn't sound all that different from the rest of the world here at home.

"Anyway," Elian continued, "one of us alone could easily sneak in with one of the supply caravans. But with a group, our best bet is option two—going *over* the wall."

"Over it?" I asked.

"That's Hudson's area of expertise," he said. "We don't need to worry about the details right now."

I shot him a dubious look, wondering just what sort of "associate" this Hudson guy was. Did he build catapults? Was he a dragon? How the hell was he going to get us over that wall?

Leaving it for now, I said, "Once we're in, that's it? We figure out where Keradoc's secret warlord hidey-hole is and storm the castle? Make it home in time for Mardi Gras?"

"Not exactly." Elian capped the pen and tossed it on the table. "Once we're inside Amaranth City, we'll need to reassess the situation on the ground day by day. Tracking down Keradoc won't be easy—he's not one to leave the city's protective boundaries, but that doesn't mean he's easy to find. We're talking setting up tails, stakeouts, bribing everyone from house servants to guards."

"And let's not forget, *brother*," Jax said with a sneer. "Not everyone in Amaranth will be rolling out the red carpet for their three favorite fugitives."

Elian sighed. "No, they won't be."

"Why?" I asked. "What did you guys do?"

When he looked at me, all the confidence drained from his eyes, leaving only sadness and regret behind. In a soft, broken voice, he said simply, "We got out, Haley. And they didn't."

Again I wondered what his life had been like in Midnight. What he'd even done to get exiled in the first place. As I understood it, unless you were a pureblood, there were only two ways into Midnight—portal magick from a dark goddess or witch, or committing a crime against the high fae so vile, they had no choice but to banish you from all the decent places of the world.

Which of those two tickets had Elian punched? Or Jax, for that matter? What about Hudson?

I came to New Orleans begging Elian for help—partly because the Goddess ordered me to and partly because I didn't have any other options for getting into Midnight. Elian was my shot. My one shot.

But underneath all that logic, there was another part of me that'd truly wanted to see him. That wanted to believe, however naïve and ridiculous, he'd still have my back.

Now, more than ever, I needed that to be true.

But I was also staring down the prospect of a long-term stay on planet hell—months, from the sound of it—facing more dangers than I could possibly imagine, and my only escorts were a man I hadn't yet laid eyes on, a battle-scarred, one-eyed demon who'd *clearly* seen some shit, and the vampire-fae who'd already betrayed me once.

What if they led me into a trap?

What if things got heavy and they turned on me to save their own asses?

What if Elian bailed on me again?

I sighed. Legit concerns, maybe. But ultimately, none of them mattered. I needed to get to Midnight, and I couldn't do it alone. That ship, however rickety, had sailed.

Absently, I rubbed my thumb along the scar on my wrist.

*Come on. You've survived worse. You're surviving right now—present tense. Whatever it takes. You've got this. You've fucking got this...*

"Hey." Jax got to his feet and glanced out the window. Headlights cut a path through the trees. I hadn't even realized it'd gotten so late. "Looks like Hudson's back."

I got to my feet too, nerves tingling down my spine.

This was it. The third guy. My final escort to Midnight.

And quite possibly to my doom.

# 12

## HALEY

*A* huge beast of a man pushed through the kitchen door, arms laden with bags from a local hunting and sporting goods store.

Presumably the promised supplies—I spotted a couple of tent boxes and some sleeping bags, along with some outdoor gear. I didn't see any ingredients for S'mores, though, which didn't bode well for our Blackbone camping excursion.

I tried not to show my disappointment.

*Sacrifices, girl. We're all making them.*

The guy dropped the bags unceremoniously on the floor, then stood up to his full height, casting a shadow that went on forever. His eyes met mine across the distance, and my stomach dropped into free-fall.

"Hudson," Jax said. "Haley. I believe you two have already met."

"Um." I scanned the guy from head to toe and back again, which took a long time because dude was *massive*. Six-and-a-half feet of solid muscle, white V-neck tee stretched across a torso that looked like it was sculpted from marble, every inch of visible skin on his arms and neck covered in tattoos. Sun-streaked, messy blond hair fell to his shoulders, setting off eyes the color of milk chocolate. He had a beard too, slightly darker than his hair and just this side of scruffy, practically *begging* for someone to run her fingers through it.

Not that I was volunteering.

Out loud.

*Anyway...*

"Pretty sure I'd remember if I'd met *you*," I said, heading over to shake his hand.

The moment our palms connected, an electric zap shot up my arm, straight to my heart.

I let out a gasp, and Hudson's lips twitched. Not quite a smile, but close.

There was something oddly familiar about him. About that little spark.

"Are you going to tell her," Jax said to Elian, "or should I? Preferably before he proposes?"

"Oh, for fuck's..." Elian sighed. "Haley, you spent the afternoon mooning over him in the garden. Hudson's the gargoyle. That's how we're getting over the wall—gargoyles fly."

"Like the one out by the pond?" I asked, still dazed by his hulking presence. "And the one at Saints and Sinners?"

"*Same* one," Elian said, gesturing at Hudson like he was Vanna freaking White showing the good people what they'd won. "Garden statue, cathedral ornament, man about town."

A hot rush raced up my entire body, toes to eyeballs. "Wow. So that whole time I was out there spilling my guts, you were just... And I... Right. This is *super* fucking awkward."

He squeezed my hand and winked, both gestures so quick and easy I almost missed them.

He still hadn't spoken a word, but somehow, I understood him.

*Don't worry,* he seemed to be telling me. *Your secrets are safe with me.*

I relaxed and finally released his hand, but that little spark lingered in my heart.

Jax grabbed a beer from the fridge and tossed it to Hudson, who caught it with one hand and popped the top in a move so smooth I felt like I was in a beer commercial.

*Good with his hands, check and check...*

"Are you from New Orleans originally?" I asked, and he shook his head.

"He's not much of a talker," Jax said, and I wondered if that applied in all situations or just social ones.

Like, did he talk in bed? In a dirty way? *Could* he? If I strategically positioned myself beneath him without clothes on and asked nicely?

*I wonder how that scruffy beard would feel between my thighs...*

God, what was wrong with me? First, I was lusting after the demon. Now the gargoyle, too?

This was all Elian's fault. Why the hell did he have such hot friends?

I glared at him as if he might answer my unspoken question.

He glared right back, firm and commanding and *not* fucking around.

My thighs clenched.

*Shit.* How the hell did he still have that effect on me?

No matter. Elian was a high-speed, hot mess express, and even though I maybe, possibly, very probably still had feelings for him—stupid ones, obviously—that didn't mean I had to act on them. I had *zero* interest in climbing aboard that train-wreck-in-waiting.

*Restraint.* That was my word of the year.

For Elian, I mean.

Jax and Hudson? I'd have to figure out different words for them.

"Well," I said with a bright smile, "he's covered in tattoos and his very presence seems to be irritating the fuck out of Elian, so obviously Hudson's one of the good guys."

Hudson raised his beer and smiled. A tiny one, barely peeking out from behind the facial hair, but the sparkle in his eyes said it all.

I trusted him immediately.

"So you three were… friends?" I asked. "In Midnight?"

"*Were*," Jax said, at the same time Elian said, "more like brothers."

I glanced at Hudson, who nodded but still hadn't said a word. So far, he had my vote for the sanest guy of the bunch, but for all I knew, that would change the minute he opened his mouth.

I was starting to get the sense they *weren't* friends—not exactly. Especially Elian and Jax. But clearly, something still bonded them, even years after they'd escaped Midnight. There was a deep loyalty there, a ride-or-die current running just beneath all the sniping and heated tension.

That, at least, was comforting.

"Hey," Elian said softly, and I jumped. He was close now—so close his breath tickled my neck. I hadn't even heard him approach. "You know we're going to see this through, right?"

I turned to face him. Searched those silver eyes. Searched my own heart.

Once, Elian had been that guy. The one who could make a promise like that without hesitation. A promise that could carry me through anything.

But now?

I swallowed hard, my throat suddenly tight. "How do I know I can trust you?" I whispered. "All of you? I still don't even understand why Jax and Hudson agreed to this."

"Well, Jax is a demon," Elian said, "and demons don't like being in debt. He's essentially doing this for me. Ergo, if he fucks you, he fucks me, and then—"

"Not literally, of course," Jax added, coming to stand beside Elian.

"—*and then* he ends up back in my debt," Elian continued. "So, for the sake of self-preservation, Jax can absolutely be trusted. And Hudson? He's a gargoyle. You couldn't ask for a better guardian. Strong, loyal to a fault, mean as hell in a fight, and he's *always* got my back, which means now he's got yours, too."

The gargoyle crowded in next to Jax and put his giant hand on my shoulder, giving it a squeeze.

I still couldn't explain it, but something about him made me feel instantly safe. Protected, just like I'd felt in the garden.

Maybe it was all part of his gargoyle vibe. Before tonight, I'd never actually encountered one.

I put my hand on top of his. Squeezed him right back.

Sometimes you spent every day with a person for years, yet you really never knew them.

Other times you spent five minutes with someone and it was like you'd known them a lifetime.

That's how I felt about Hudson. Like I'd just been reunited with my oldest friend.

To Elian, I said, "I notice you didn't rattle off *your* qualifications for a position in our circle of trust."

This got a smile from both the demon and the gargoyle. Even Elian himself grinned, crooked and sexy as ever.

*Damn it, thighs. Enough with the clenching. You're going to chafe.*

"I'm an excellent map-maker," he said, counting off on his fingers. "I'm fast, have superior senses, and can carry a pack more than ten times my body weight." Then, his voice turning as serious as his eyes, "I won't let you down, Haley. Not this time."

I let out a long, slow exhale and looked over each of them in turn.

Hudson, the strong and silent gargoyle protector.

Jax, the demon fighter who called me angel and gave me the best kind of shivers.

Elian, the vampire-fae who'd once taken my heart and still hadn't returned all the pieces, suddenly back from the dead.

My escorts. My monsters.

Every one of them had a dark past. Every one of them had probably done things—terrible, horrifying things I couldn't even imagine. Things that ate them up inside, no matter how tough they played it on the outside.

We weren't so different, my monsters and I.

But right now, standing in that New Orleans kitchen as we prepared for the most dangerous mission of our lives, our pasts didn't matter. All that mattered was the promise Elian had just made me.

A promise I was making to them as well.

I looked into Elian's eyes once more and I smiled.

"Yes," I said. "We're going to see this through."

Jax nodded.

Hudson nodded.

Elian held my gaze for another beat, then he nodded too. "Excellent. We leave before first light."

I forced a laugh. "No rest for the wicked, huh?"

"No, sparrow." His silver eyes turned fierce. "No rest for *any* of us until we get you back here in one piece."

# 13

## ELIAN

$\mathcal{M}$y sweet little sparrow hadn't earned her nickname touring the karaoke bars of Blackmoon Bay—as much as I would've *loved* to see that.

No, her singing was more of an involuntary reflex. A *post-orgasm* reflex that'd driven me fucking wild since the first time I'd discovered it, not long after she moved into my place in Blackmoon Bay.

Here in New Orleans, Haley had just wrapped up an hour-long shower in my guest bathroom—the last indoor plumbing she'd get to enjoy for months.

And now, the sparrow was singing again.

*Fuck.*

I knew a bad idea when one blindsided me—hell, I was the *king* of bad ideas—but this was a wreck I couldn't fucking divert.

My hand was already on the doorknob. Logic? Reason? Those assholes were long gone. All I had left was the Devil's Dream dissolving on my tongue and the moron sitting on my shoulder, laughing his balls off.

*It's your fucking house,* he goaded. *Do whatever you want.*

I didn't bother knocking. Just turned that knob, pushed open the door, and waltzed right in.

"Shit, Elian!" she shrieked, clutching the towel she'd just finished securing around her body. Her hair hung in a dark wet curtain, dripping over her shoulders. "I'm half-naked in here! What is *wrong* with you?"

I cursed myself for my terrible timing. Thirty seconds earlier, and the view would've been a lot better.

"I heard you singing," I said.

"Was I singing a song called 'Elian, please barge in here uninvited and annoy me in that oh-so-special way only you can do?' No? Of *course* not, because I'm still working out the lyrics for that one and it's not ready for prime time. Now, if you don't mind..." She fisted the front of my shirt and tried to push me out, but I wasn't budging.

I grinned at her, and her eyes softened just a fraction.

I stepped closer. Gazed down into her heart-shaped face. "I know I'm not supposed to keep pointing out all your little Haley-isms, but—"

"But you think I'll find your refusal to honor my wishes endearing? Because—*bzzt!*—thank you for playing! Please try again."

"*But*," I continued, stepping closer until I had her backed up against the sink, no escape. "I remember *exactly* what it means when you sing in the shower, little sparrow. And I just had to know... What inspired tonight's musical selection?"

Her cheeks flamed, but she didn't look away. Didn't flinch. Didn't go for the dagger she'd left beside the sink. Just glared up at me with those fierce green eyes, water beading across her shoulders, a few drops rolling down the hollow above her collarbone.

It took everything in me not to lower my mouth to her throat and lick.

Suck.

*Bite*.

"If you remember what it means," she hissed, "then you should also remember your services *aren't* required. I've already taken care of things, thanks."

"A little self-love in the shower? Definitely not enough to satiate *your* appetite." I put my hands on the edge of the sink, caging her between my arms. Heat radiated from her freshly showered skin. She smelled, as always, like strawberries and cream. "I remember that too, sparrow."

"New rule—you do *not* get to call me that anymore. Furthermore, you can't just... Holy shit, Elian. What the hell happened to your face?" She reached up and grabbed my jaw, jerking my head to the side. "Looks like someone picked you up by your feet and used your head as a croquet mallet."

"It'll be back to normal soon enough," I said. Then, tossing out the words she'd thrown at me earlier, "Vampire healing. Hell of a drug."

"What are you healing *from*?"

"Hudson. He and I had a few... words."

Well, that wasn't entirely true. *I* had words. He had mean glares and a hard-as-rock fist, which gave me even *more* words as I connected the dots on his sudden flare-up of psychotic over-protectionism.

It was a little crazy, even for Hudson. Didn't take me too long to figure out what was going on.

He'd bonded with her.

Fucking gargoyle. Nine hundred years without a bonded mate, and fate decided to offer up Haley? *My* Haley?

My blood still boiled just to think of it.

"Elian," she demanded. "What the hell did you do to him?"

"*Me*?" I laughed. "Thanks for the sympathy. *I'm* the one with the nearly dislocated jaw."

"I'd bet my favorite stake you had it coming. Hudson's a total sweetheart—he wouldn't hit you for no reason."

"You've known him all of an hour."

"Oh? Is there an official amount of time for when you can say you've known someone? A few years, maybe? Or is it that you're supposed to live with them, fall in love, and plan a whole future together first? Because that plan didn't work out so hot for me, so I'm thinking maybe time and proximity aren't always factors in how well you know a man."

I closed my eyes. Bit back a curse. Gave her a little space.

"I deserved that," I said.

"Maybe, but..." She bit her lip and lowered her eyes. "I'm sorry. I can't keep blowing up at you about the past. You're helping me now, and that's enough."

I moved in again. Tucked my finger under her chin until she met my gaze once more. "There's a lot you're not saying. Don't think I'm blind to it."

She nodded. "But I told myself I wouldn't ask you."

"Ask what?"

The breath left her lungs in a rush, stirring the steamy air between us. "What you did to get exiled to Midnight. You... you must've had your reasons for leaving that night, but... Anyway, it doesn't matter now. No going back."

Yeah, I had my reasons. At the time, I thought they were good ones. Honorable, even.

If I could go back and change things...

No.

As fucked up as it sounded—as much as the woman's very presence was tearing me up inside—I still couldn't say I'd do things differently with a second chance. Going to Midnight… It was something I had to do back then, just like I had to do it now.

Hurting Haley, though… That was the one thing I *would* undo.

"Haley, you have to know I—"

She held up her hand, cutting me off. "I told you, I'm not interested in rehashing the past. I don't need to know how you got to Midnight. But there is something I *do* need to know. Something we didn't cover earlier."

"Anything," I breathed.

"How the hell did you guys get *out*?"

"Midnight's… Well, it's not much different from any other place. A few bribes here, an exchange there, an agreement or two…"

"I guess everyone has a price," she said.

"Absolutely. The question is… Are you willing to pay it? Can you bear that cost for the rest of your life?"

She held my gaze for a long time, searching my face as if the answers she swore she didn't want were written there.

If she noticed my blown pupils, she didn't mention it.

Instead, she said sadly, "What did it cost you?"

"More than you can imagine."

Tears tracked down her cheeks, and I reached for her, cupping her face and swiping them away with my thumbs. She didn't pull back.

"I never stopped thinking about you, little sparrow." I held her face in my hands and drew closer, whispering against her lips. "Not once."

It was a confession I never would've bared if I'd been off the Black, but the inhibitions were down and the words were out and—like everything else in my fucked-up existence—I couldn't take them back.

"Elian…" She lowered her eyes again.

"Tell me you didn't think about me too," I said softly. "Tell me you banished me from your mind the night I walked out on you. Tell me you weren't thinking of me in the shower tonight, and I swear to you, Haley, I'll walk out of here right fucking now and never bring it up again."

She shook her head, a broken laugh escaping. "I can't."

*Damn it.* I was playing with *serious* fire, but having her this close again, her tears on my skin, her breath in the air, I couldn't let her go.

*Just another minute,* I promised myself. *Two tops.*

I wasn't so stoned I couldn't tell the difference between reality and my own twisted bullshit. I still knew I wasn't allowed to kiss her, to touch her any more intimately than I already had, but the Dream gave me just enough of a push to keep me walking along that razor-sharp edge.

*Ask her,* the moron on my shoulder said. *You know you want to.*

"Do you remember the first time I caught you singing in the shower?" I whispered.

She nodded, the blush rising in her cheeks. "I wanted you. Needed you, actually, but you were fast asleep and I didn't want to wake you."

"But you woke me, anyway. The sweetest, most off-key melody I'd ever heard stirred me from my dreams. I headed into the bathroom and found you leaning back against the tiles in the shower, your hand between your legs, your skin flushed. Even through the steam on the glass, I knew you'd just made yourself come."

"I was thinking of you. The way you kissed me. All the things you…" She swallowed hard, the blood racing through her veins, calling out to me just as her songs still did. "…the things you did to me earlier that night."

"You opened your eyes and caught me grinning at you," I whispered, afraid anything louder would shatter the moment. "I was so hard for you, I thought I might explode." My own words painted the fantasy, mixing with the Dream in my system to bring it to life as if it were unfolding right here, right before my eyes. I was hard for her again, my balls aching. "You weren't shy about it, though. You smiled right back at me, you wicked girl. And when I stepped into the shower, you *begged* me to touch you."

A teasing smile touched her lips, her eyes glassy, as if she was tripping right along with me. "You refused."

"I wanted you to make yourself come again. I wanted to watch. And you know something, sparrow?" I leaned in close, lowering my mouth to just a hair's breadth from hers. "You *wanted* me to watch, didn't you? Wanted to tease me and drive me wild."

Her breath caught. She nodded, unable to deny it.

"Do you know how many times I've played that movie in my mind?" I asked, tracing a fingertip along her jaw, following the path of another rivulet of water down her throat. "How many nights I've stood in the shower, still hard for you, remembering the sight of your fingers sliding over your wet skin? The taste of your kiss on my lips? Your breathy moans as you brought yourself right back to the edge?"

"Elian, I… I…" She closed her eyes and shook her head. Muttered a curse.

When she glanced up at me again, the haze had cleared, her eyes flashing with anger.

"Stop," she commanded. She leaned back against the sink, her hands instinctively going to her dagger, as if the damn thing were a security blanket. "Just stop."

I raised my hands and stepped back, shrugging as if it didn't matter to me one way or the other. As if it didn't feel like she'd just punched a hole through my chest and yanked out my heart.

"I'm not one of your clients, asshole," she snapped. "So stop incepting me with your hypnotic fae illusions and creepy vampire... *whatever* it is you're doing."

I didn't have the heart to tell her the only power I was using was words. The story of our shared memories unearthed from the deep and brought back into the light.

What Haley and I had shared? It didn't need a vampire's influence or a fae's trickery. It was powerful and magickal in its own right. And even though I'd fucking destroyed it, it still tethered us. Across the years. Across the realms. I could still feel her under my skin. In my soul.

Yeah, I was an asshole to barge in on her tonight. An asshole to push things as far as I had.

But I couldn't leave it like this.

If she knew what this was doing to me right now...

*No.* Vulnerability was the surest way to get yourself killed.

I plastered my smile back in place, as cocky as she'd ever known it.

"Too bad you feel that way," I said. "Might be your last chance to, ah... *sing* for me before we ship off to hell."

"Pretty sure I'm already there."

"If that's true, then why is your blood racing?" I held my palm in front of her chest, close enough to feel the heat of her skin, but not touching. "I can hear it, little sparrow. Zipping through your veins like it's trying to escape."

"Hmm. Are you sure it's *my* blood you're hearing?" Haley laughed. Then, with a cocky grin of her own, she slammed her hand against my chest.

Blood leaked from a fresh gash on her palm, soaking into my shirt.

The magick hit me at once, a hot flush that burst from my chest and skittered across my skin like fire. Stars blinked before my eyes, and the edges of the room darkened. The ground spun out from beneath my feet.

I caught myself on the edge of the sink just before I fell.

"It worked!" She clapped her hands and bounced on her toes, so fucking cute I couldn't even be pissed at her for whatever mojo she'd just unleashed.

"What... did you do?" I panted, still dizzy. Weak. Not a good look for a vampire-fae, I'll tell you that much.

"Oh, is there something you *don't* remember about me? That I'm a blood witch, maybe?" She laughed, the sound of it echoing off the tile walls.

"But this is..." I clutched my chest, the breath slowly returning to my lungs. "This is different."

"Yeah, that particular spell is a *new* Haley Barnes trick." She waggled her fingers in front of my eyes, showing off a silver ring with a polished dark-red stone. "Bought it from a blood priestess last night in Tremé. She said the bloodstone was spelled to enhance my natural gifts and allow me to temporarily manipulate blood flow in an assailant. Don't you just *love* when a product works as advertised?"

I nodded, still trying to blink the stars from my eyes, though at that point I couldn't be sure they were from the magick and not from the whirlwind of Haley Barnes.

"But now that you've had the pleasure of nearly losing consciousness at my command," she added, her smile bright, "you can add it to the list of things to remember about me. Write it down. That way, the next time you barge into my shower uninvited, you'll know what to expect."

With that, she pressed her hand to my chest again and shoved me and my still-raging hard-on right out of the bathroom.

"Save your fucking fantasies for someone who wants them," she snapped, "because I sure as hell don't."

The door slammed in my face.

My breathing returned to normal.

I leaned my forehead against the wood and sighed.

*Fuck.*

Haley didn't want my fantasies? Yeah, they weren't for her. They were never for her.

They were for me.

Because like I'd told her, the price I'd paid to leave Midnight was higher than she could've imagined. And now, a fantasy was the closest I could ever come to making my little sparrow sing for me again.

# 14

KERADOC

$\mathcal{L}$ ieutenant General Oona of Midnight stood before me at the council of war, her sky-blue hair pulled tight, her face grim. "We've lost Hanging Lake, sir. The Road of Silence has been overrun."

The other generals and commanders seated around my table grumbled, but I kept my face impassive.

Named for the mutilated corpses the raven gryphons hung from the surrounding trees, Hanging Lake was actually a swamp, a fetid pit of despair that stretched on for miles along the southwestern borders of Midnight. The swamp's value was purely strategic; it surrounded both sides of the Road of Silence that led into Razorback range, keeping all but the most intrepid travelers and traders from wandering too close to Amaranth City.

Most could neither outrun nor outwit the vicious raven gryphons, and the slaughtered remains of those who'd tried had long served as a deterrent to any upstarts.

So how the hell had we lost control?

"Darkwinter?" I asked, though I already knew the answer. The Darkwinter fae were the toughest of the rebel factions—the only faction we truly needed to fear, assuming the others didn't unite under a common banner. They'd been steadily gaining ground for months, portaling in all across the realm, each new platoon stronger and more fearsome than its predecessor.

"Yes, sir." Oona held my gaze, her spine straight as an arrow. "Reports from the northern front have also confirmed additional Darkwinter vessels moving in across the Sea of Tranquility."

So the enemy fae had found dark witches powerful enough to portal in not just their men, but their ships as well?

Again, I fought to hide my displeasure.

Despite its moniker, the northernmost sea was anything but tranquil. Roaring as high as a mile above sea level, its waves were notoriously savage, pulverizing most ships within seconds. What the water could not destroy, the sub-zero air temperatures and brutal hurricane-force winds usually did, not to mention the array of fiendish sea creatures circling the depths, always in search of a feast.

Long before Amaranth City was built, the Sea of Tranquility protected Midnight's northern border from invaders, fae and demonic alike. It was so untraversable, our own people had never even built warships. We scarcely knew the true depths of that perpetually storm-tossed sea or the terrifying creatures that inhabited its watery kingdom.

"How are they even navigating it?" one of the commanders asked.

"Our troops claim their ships are unassailable," Oona said. "They cut through the waves like hot knives through butter, allegedly impervious to both the cold and the threats of Tranquility's native monsters."

"We *must* mount an attack," he replied.

I shook my head. "Our gargoyle squadrons simply aren't capable of an aerial assault in the extreme cold."

"Unchallenged, they will surely reach this city," he said. "This castle."

"Yes, and we must defend both at all costs." I turned my attention back to Oona. "I want more men moved to the outposts along the shoreline. Find out what they need in terms of additional weaponry, and see to it they get it. Assume a prolonged siege."

"And if the arriving Darkwinter troops are as fortified as their ships?" another general asked.

"We will face them nevertheless."

"The Fog of a Thousand Knives, sir," Oona said. "The shoreline outposts are closed until it lifts—two to three more weeks, at least."

A chill crept into the room.

The Fog of a Thousand Knives descended upon the shoreline twice annually, lasting anywhere from four to six weeks. No one knew what caused it exactly, or how long it'd been haunting the north. No one who'd been caught in the mist had ever survived to tell the tale; anyone trapped in its white claws was immediately liquified. By the time the Fog receded, the beach would be stained with the blood of its victims.

My composure finally unraveled. "Do any of my commanding officers have a damned bit of *good* news to report? Have we managed to reclaim any territory from Darkwinter? Made any new gains in the east?"

Silence.

All eyes were downcast, save for Oona's.

There was a reason she was my most trusted advisor—one that had nothing to do with blood ties.

"See to it our additional troops are prepared to move north as soon as the Fog allows," I commanded. "In the meantime, send reserves to the Road of Silence. I want a full assessment of the situation, as well as ongoing reports on Darkwinter's movements. Every time one of those bastards so much as shits in the Haunted Wood, I want to know about it."

"Yes sir," came the chorus of replies.

"We'll reconvene in three nights' time," I said. "Dismissed."

As one, the council rose from the table and saluted, fists pressed together over their hearts.

I gestured for Oona to remain.

"What of our prisoner?" I asked when we were finally alone. Other than two very handsomely paid dungeon guards, Oona was the only one I trusted with knowledge of his existence.

But even she didn't know his true identity.

"Weaker by the night, sir."

I nodded, twisting the ring on my finger. Through the magick that bound me to him, I could feel his body failing, his soul aching for release. But if that happened before my armies reclaimed full control of the realm…

*No.* I wouldn't even allow for the possibility. Mine was a plan *years* in the making. Executing it had required exceptional vision, strategy, precision, and commitment.

I'd come too far to surrender now.

"See to it that his health is stabilized," I said. "Ask the guards to relocate him if you must."

"Relocate him?"

"The dampness and mold are likely impacting his lungs. Move him to the second level and increase his food and water rations as well. I want him alive and healthy, but not strong. Not clear-headed. Understand?"

"Yes, sir."

"What news of the Hollow?" I asked. "Have the peasants decided to revolt yet?" At this, I allowed a small smile, which Oona returned.

"Not yet, sir, though we're seeing increased signs. Dwindling access to food and water is causing unrest. Petty squabbles are turning more violent. Drugs and weapons seizures are on the rise from sources we've not sanctioned for the trade." She sighed. "If I may speak plainly, sir?"

"Please."

"It's been three years since the last Feast of Midnight. Perhaps it's time to host another? Give the people something to celebrate?"

I closed my eyes and sighed.

The Feast of Midnight.

In days of old, the ruler of Midnight began the tradition, hosting what would then become an annual gathering. For reasons that had always evaded me, he invited the filthy rabble of Amaranth City off the streets and into his home for a night-long celebration of food and sex and wine, offerings for our continued victories over the forces—natural and other-wise—constantly seeking to destroy us. The ruler, along with wealthy guests who'd paid for the privilege, would attend a more exclusive version of the event on the upper levels of the castle.

Feast of the Beast, as it was colloquially known, though I was never certain whether the beast referred to the host, the copious amounts of exotic meat he served, or the base impulses of the masses.

I'd always found it barbaric, but the people loved it. The ruler's feigned generosity gave them hope, and the briefest taste of luxury easily put them back into the barely conscious slumber from which the ruling class so readily profited.

The idea turned my very blood to ice, especially since it was now *my* home that would be opened to every street rat and urchin in Amaranth City, *my* feigned generosity put on full display.

But Oona's thinking was sound. The people needed something to cele-brate. Something to pacify them.

"Very well," I said. "We shall give them their meat and ale. Let them cling to their ridiculous traditions."

"A wise choice, sir," Oona said. "I'll appoint advisors to see to the arrangements and keep you apprised of the plans."

"Thank you." I rose from the table and gazed out the tower window.

Situated in the center of the city on a rise that offered a three-hundred-sixty-degree view, the Castle of Midnight had been in the family for millennia, an architectural marvel as well as a fortress. In the long dark of Midnight's many wars, the Castle had never fallen.

Now, gazing south across Amaranth City and beyond Vanderham's Wall, I wondered how long that would remain true.

As if in response to an unasked question, red lightning flickered on the southern horizon, sending an unexpected jolt of fear skittering along my spine. It settled in the pit of my stomach with a dull fizz, like sparkling wine gone suddenly flat.

"Sir?" Oona asked. "Are you unwell?"

I stared out at the dark sky. Nothing moved but the clouds scudding over the two visible moons. No more lightning. Not even a flicker of starlight. The third moon wouldn't rise for hours.

"Father?" she pressed, finally dropping the pretense of military rank as she placed a hand on my arm.

The touch drew my attention, and I glanced into her eyes, violet like her father's.

In that moment, she was no longer a lieutenant general. Just a concerned daughter. Daughter of the monster who ruled this land with fists and swords and manipulation, no atoning for the blood he'd spilled along the way.

The concern in her voice softened my hard heart, but I wouldn't allow her to glimpse it. Oona wasn't accustomed to gentleness. She'd grown up the target of threats and abuse that had only grown worse with time, with the pressure of our many endless wars.

Showing vulnerability now would only confuse things. For both of us.

"Your concern is misplaced," I said firmly.

"But I thought—"

"See to our prisoner, Oona. And let the cooks know I'll be taking dinner alone in my chambers tonight."

"Shall I join you there? We could review the maps, maybe look at alternate routes around—"

"What part of *alone* was unclear to you?"

She didn't flinch. She was too good a soldier for that.

But I'd seen the flicker of sadness in her eyes, and it cut me in a way I preferred not to dwell upon.

"Of course," she said. "Goodnight, Father. Sir." She bowed her head, then stood up straight and saluted.

"Dismissed," I replied, and then she was gone.

Guilt simmered, but Oona was strong, just as her mother had been.

I glanced out across the wall once more and sighed.

I only hoped her strength would be enough to save her.

# 15

## HALEY

*There's beauty in darkness. Remember that when we get where we're going.*
*—H*

I stared at the note, scrawled hastily on the back of a receipt for wool hiking socks and MREs, tucked under a vase of fresh flowers that someone had left in the guest room while I'd showered.

Not just any flowers, either.

Black roses. *My* black roses.

I couldn't help the smile that spread on my face or the warmth that followed.

The biggest, baddest guy of the bunch, and when it came down to it, Hudson was just a big ol' squishy teddy bear in the body of a stone giant.

Maybe I should've been mortified to discover I'd bared my soul to *him* in the garden and not an inanimate statue, but I wasn't. That covert wink had said it all. He really was a vault—safe and secure. Reliable. Strong.

Besides, I'd taken him on a deep dive into my ocean of crazy, and even after he'd shifted into a man with functioning legs, he hadn't gone running for the hills.

He was a rock.

And honestly? Between the old flames Elian was stoking back to life and the new ones Jax was igniting, a rock was just what I needed.

Not that Hudson didn't have the power to stoke flames.

Just that not everything with every hot guy had to be about sex.

Even though I hadn't really... ahem... *sung* for anyone other than myself in a long time. And I was a thirsty bitch who would've loved to share my vocal gifts with a partner. Hell, at that point, I was ready to put on a full-blown concert, complete with T-shirt cannons and pyrotechnics and a Madonna-style cone bra, if that's what it took.

Alas...

Duty called.

I folded up the note and tucked it inside the pack I found on the bed. There were some clothes laid out as well—cargo pants, sports bra, a fitted moisture-wicking shirt, hiking boots, all in my size. They'd thought of everything.

I dressed quickly, finishing up just as someone knocked on the door.

"Come on in," I said, knowing it wouldn't be Elian. He wouldn't have bothered with the knock.

It was Jax, the scent of campfire and lemon trailing in with him as he stepped inside and closed the door.

"Looks good on you," he said. "Not that you can trust the opinion of a one-eyed demon, but..."

"Thanks," I said with a smile. "I'm used to a different sort of look."

"Short dresses?"

"Sometimes, yes. My other favorite is leather and metal. All depends on whether I'm hunting down bloodsuckers—"

"Or trying to drive your ex crazy?"

I laughed. "Yeah, well. Pretty sure my crazy-driving days are over. I'm Rocky Mountain Barbie now."

"Pretty sure you've still got some crazy in you." Jax's smile faded. "You about ready?"

"Does it matter if I'm not?" I sat down on the bed, fingering the strap of my new pack. "Wait—let me rephrase: no, hell no, not even close."

"Haley..." Jax ran a hand through his black hair and sighed, then came to sit beside me. "What Saint said about trusting us... Look, I won't pretend to know what the two of you went through before he showed up in Midnight, and I sure as hell don't know what's waiting for us when we get back. But he was right about one thing. We *will* have your back."

"I know. I'll have yours, too."

"Is that so?" he teased.

"Of course! What the hell kind of a witch do you take me for?"

"No idea, but something tells me you're kind of a badass."

I propped a hand on my hip and glared. "*Kind* of?"

"Okay, okay. Full-on badass." Jax smiled, then grabbed my hand, shocking the hell out of me.

His touch was strong and reassuring, and in the wake of its warmth, I rested my head on his shoulder and closed my eyes.

"You think I'm crazy, don't you?" I whispered.

Jax's breath stirred my hair. "I think… I think you're doing what you believe is best to save the people you love."

"Nice save, demon." I laughed. "Who knew hellspawn could be so diplomatic? Maybe you should consider running for office."

Jax wasn't laughing, though. He pulled back and gazed into my eyes, a sadness rising in his that made my heart squeeze up. "Saving the people you love is never crazy, Haley. Just be sure you don't lose yourself in the process."

I nodded and promised I wouldn't, but could I even keep a promise like that?

How could I make sure I didn't lose myself when I'd never even found myself in the first place?

"Take a few more minutes and do what you need to do," Jax said, giving my hand one last squeeze before letting go. "But we need to get going. We don't know how long the portal transition will take, and if we don't get enough of a jump on sunrise, we'll have to wait until Hudson can shift back again tomorrow night."

"How does all that work, exactly?" I asked. "With his shifting?"

"Daylight always turns him into stone. Any other time, he can shift at will among three forms—human, stone, or his winged warrior form, which is sort of crossed between the two, but more massive and with wings."

"Stone by daylight. Okay, I need to set a watch or something—that seems like an important thing to keep track of."

"Won't be an issue in Midnight. The sun doesn't rise there—just three moons."

"Seriously? I was hoping that was just hyperbole."

"Nothing you've heard about that place is hyperbole." He put his hand on my shoulder, his gaze stern. "Remember that, angel. Because the minute you forget, it'll get us all killed."

Loaded up with our gear, the four of us stood on the damp earth on the far edge of the pond, gazing into the thicket of live oaks in the shadows just beyond.

"Will it hurt?" I asked, one hand clutching the portal spell, the other nestled tightly in Hudson's grip.

"No," Elian said. "Just hold on to us, and don't let go. As long as you focus on keeping the portal open, and the three of us keep visualizing Blackbone Forest, the magick should guide us straight there."

"From your lips to the Goddess' ears." I took a deep breath, inhaling the fragrant scent of night-blooming jasmine, realizing it could very well be the last time I ever smelled it.

I closed my eyes and whispered a prayer for my sisters, sending them all my love.

Then, with nothing left to say, I opened my eyes, tossed the vial to the ground, and stomped on it.

The portal shimmered to life before us, swirling with reds and golds and black, just like it had inside the glass. Hudson's grip tightened, nearly crushing my fingers. Jax moved closer, lacing his fingers through my other hand. Elian hooked his fingers through the back of my waistband.

And together, my monsters and I stepped into the light of the portal.

Into the darkness of another realm.

And into a volley of flaming arrows sailing right toward us.

# 16

## HALEY

own! Now!" Elian shoved me hard from behind, and we all dropped to the ground as the arrows whizzed overhead, leaving trails of smoke behind them. All around us, fires burned unchecked.

Ash and fire choked the air, making my eyes water. Through the haze about fifty feet out, I counted a dozen soldiers moving through the bare trees, their arrows knocked for another volley, bows aimed toward the sky.

"Fae. They're not after us," Elian said, and we all looked up at once. Two dark, winged figures cut through the glow of a blood-red sky, letting loose an earsplitting cry that sent shivers down my spine.

"Raven gryphons." Jax cursed as the beasts flew closer. "What the fuck are they doing this far east?"

"Hold!" came the command from the fae troops. "Hold! On my mark!"

I watched in a state of shock and wonder as two monstrous black birds the size of large SUVs swooped down to the treetops. They had the heads and wings of ravens, the limbs and tails of lions, and talons that looked like they could tear through concrete.

"Fire!" shouted the commander.

The troops unleashed another volley, their arrows whistling. The gryphons soared higher, avoiding a direct hit.

"Holy shit, they're fast," Elian said.

They screeched into the night, circling once before swooping back down, heading right for the fae.

The commander shouted again. "Fire at will! Fire at will!"

This time, some of the arrows actually hit the wings, but they had little effect on the huge gryphons, the fires fizzling out almost immediately. The winged beasts crashed through the dead trees and snatched up three fae, rending them apart in a shower of blood and gore that sent the others scampering off toward us.

"Get up!" Jax hissed, helping Elian to his feet. "We need to move before we're spotted by the gryphons *or* the fae."

Before I could say another word, Hudson hauled me up by my pack and set me back on my feet, his hand clamping around mine again.

Heads ducked, the four of us took off in the opposite direction of the advancing line. I chanced a quick glance behind us; the gryphons were busy turning the soldiers into their own personal buffet.

All around us, the bare, pitch-black trees of Blackbone Forest rose like skeleton fingers reaching up toward the stars. The sky glowed orange-red with the fire that raged behind us, chewing through the underbrush with a sound like a runaway train.

I choked back a cough, forcing my lungs to keep breathing despite the acrid air. My heart pounded, ears ringing with the roar of the fire and that awful screeching, all of it now mixing with the terrified cries of fae soldiers as the gryphons continued their relentless attacks.

It felt like we'd been running for hours when Jax finally stopped us at the top of a rise, bending over to catch his breath. Hands on his knees, he glanced up at me and said, "You okay?"

"Midnight makes one hell of a first impression," I said, finally letting loose that cough. The air was marginally cleaner up here, but the sky still held that ethereal orange glow. In the distance, I could just make out the silhouettes of the two gryphons, their forms growing smaller and smaller until they finally vanished.

I was pretty sure none of the fae had survived.

"The Midnight welcoming committee could use some new blood," I said. "Because that *completely* sucked. Didn't you say this forest would be deserted?"

"It should've been," Elian said.

Certain we were alone, we took a moment to check over our packs and each other for any signs of loss—gear, blood, or otherwise. All signs indicated we'd survived the literal trial-by-fire. After a quick water break, we started moving again, heading deeper into Blackbone.

Jax stayed by my side, with Hudson taking point and Elian bringing up the rear. We walked in silence for a few minutes, our gear clinking, boots hitting the scorched earth with soft thuds.

Then Elian said, "You were right about the gryphons, Jax. They shouldn't be roaming this far east. Their domain is the Hanging Lake."

Jax nodded, turning to glance at Elian over his shoulder. "Things have changed since we left."

"War will do that to a place," Elian said. "I wonder what other surprises we'll find. I don't—"

"Guys!" I gasped as a new shadow moved over us. "We've got company!"

A third gryphon glided overhead, passing us before it circled back for another look.

*Fuck.* My gut told me we had mere seconds before he spotted us.

Jax grabbed my arm, but I shook free and dropped into a crouch, unsheathing my dagger and drawing a pentagram in the dirt. A quick slice of my palm and a tight fist, and my blood spilled onto the symbol.

The gryphon let out his war cry and dove, and I called out my spell.

> *Beast of darkness, beast of night*
> *My blood is your weakness, my blood is our light*

I slammed my palm against the dirt. The pentagram glowed as bright as the fae arrows, then exploded in a flash of red light, rising like a wall before us just seconds before the gryphon crashed through the trees.

The beast hit the wall head-on. Magick sizzled across his feathers, lighting him up as if he'd been electrocuted, unleashing a cry of pure agony.

I jumped to my feet. "Move! It won't hold him for long!"

We darted down the other side of the rise and into a new section of Blackbone. The bare trees offered no cover, and minutes later, the gryphon was back in the air and hot on our trail, the smell of scorched feathers so strong it made me gag.

Even at a run, I saw his dark shadow slithering along the ground. Felt the air current shift above me as he dove.

My heart jumped into my throat.

"Haley!" Elian shouted from somewhere behind me. "Get down!"

I dropped and covered my head, and in a blur of vampire speed and grace, Elian catapulted over me, his sword held high.

The gryphon cried out, a great flapping of wings sending a hot current rushing over me.

Blood rained down, splattering my hair, my pack.

I didn't even have time to process what'd happened before Hudson barreled into me, tucking me against his chest and rolling us away mere seconds before the mutilated gryphon dropped from the sky, plowing into the ground where I'd just been crouching.

Still caged in Hudson's arms, I thrashed frantically, scanning the scene.

"Elian!" I called out. "Elian!"

"Here," came the reply. "All hail the victorious gryphon-slayer."

He emerged over the top of the dead beast like a champion dragon-slayer of old, pack dangling off one shoulder, his sword at his side. Blood ran down his face and covered his clothes. He looked like a demon straight out of hell.

But the vampire-fae merely tossed his pack to the ground and laughed, white teeth flashing in the dim. "You should see your face right now, sparrow. Priceless."

"For fuck's sake, Saint," Jax said, staring at the gryphon and its killer in disbelief. "How the hell...?"

Hudson finally released me, and I jumped to my feet, charging right for the cocky fae.

"Seriously?" I glared at him, hands on my hips. "I totally weakened him for you."

"Yes, and that was quite an impressive bit of hocus-pocus, witch."

"I know, right?" I flipped the bloody hair over my shoulder and preened, more relieved to see that stupid fae than I cared to admit.

Elian kicked at the creature beneath his feet. "You know, these assholes wouldn't be half bad if I could figure out how to compel them. Maybe strap on a saddle."

"Hard pass," I said. "But you go right ahead. In the meantime, I need to change this bloody shirt before I puke. Any idea where the ladies' room is?"

Elian laughed, but before he could shoot out his next retort, his face paled, his eyes going wide.

A dark shadow swept over him.

I sucked in a breath and blinked, and just like that, another gryphon swooped in. Before he could even raise his sword, the beast plucked Elian from the dead gryphon like an owl plucking a mouse from the field.

His sword fell to the ground.

And the gryphon soared into the smoke-filled sky.

<h1 style="text-align:center">17</h1>

HALEY

"Go!" Jax shouted at Hudson. "I've got Haley. Go help Elian!"

Hudson met my gaze for an instant, my eyes wide with fear, his own pained, then took off at a sprint, his human form already beginning to morph. His muscles stretched and elongated, bones shifting, his body gaining in height and mass as the warrior form took shape. Hands and feet became talons not unlike those of the gryphons, and as his clothing fell away, his skin turned a deep slate gray. By the time the massive leathery wings burst from between his shoulder blades, Hudson was already airborne.

I watched him soar higher and higher, following the path of the gryphon until both of them vanished into the darkness. I spun around in circles, head tipped, searching in all directions for any more assailants.

"I think we're in the clear," Jax finally said. "They don't usually hunt in packs. That they were here at all is a fucking mystery."

"But Elian's… That thing took him and…" I swayed on my feet, images of the dismembered fae soldiers flooding my mind.

Jax caught me and held me upright, his mouth close to my ear. "Pull it together," he whispered. "Elian's stronger than he looks, and Hudson's already on his way. We've fought these things before—they just took us off guard tonight. It won't happen again."

"But—

"They'll be back before you know it. Trust me—we know how to survive Midnight. That's why you came to Elian for help, right? So stop freaking out before you lose your shit and make a mistake that gets us killed."

I nodded, blowing out a shaky breath.

Jax was right. They were practically locals. *I* was the newbie here. And this was only day one. Hour one. *Disaster* one of what was probably many more to come.

If I lost it now, the mission would be over before it'd ever really begun.

Digging another water bottle from my pack, I did my best to rinse the gryphon's blood from my hair, then swapped my shirt for a clean one.

"Hungry?" Jax asked, searching through his pack. "I'm guessing that blood spell took some of the wind out of your sails."

I nodded, offering a grateful smile. "If I ever say no to food, *that's* when you need to start worrying."

"Fresh out of jambalaya, but I've got an oat-and-honey granola bar and some beef jerky, if you're interested."

That got an even bigger smile. "Throw in a Fallen Angel, and you've got yourself a deal, demon."

"Don't tempt me."

"Is that even possible?" I teased, happy for the distraction it provided. Without it, I'd start thinking about Elian and Hudson and that freakshow fucking bird. "Aren't demons supposed to be the tempters in this operation?"

"Free advice?" Jax tossed me the food, then readjusted his eye patch, his mouth pulling into a surly scowl. "Don't *ever* give a demon reason to tempt you."

I tried not to shiver at the dark warning in his voice.

I gobbled up the jerky, then the granola bar. Feeling a little more grounded, I left Jax to brood alone and headed over to check out the gryphon carcass. The thing was even more terrifying up close. The beak alone was as long as I was tall, lined with two rows of black, razor-sharp teeth.

A fresh wave of fear barreled into me, and I turned back toward the demon. "Why aren't they back yet? What's taking so—"

"Um, Haley? Less talking and more..." He grabbed my shoulders, then stepped us a few feet to the left.

A heartbeat later, another dead gryphon crashed to the ground with a thud.

Two figures emerged from the trees behind it.

Hudson was back in his human form, naked and glistening with sweat, his powerful muscles rippling beneath his skin, and yes, friends and neighbors, the answer to the question on *everyone's* minds…

Those tattoos really *did* go all the way down.

He caught me staring. Winked.

Cheeks flaming, I managed to drag my gaze away from him long enough to check on Elian, who was still wearing that same smug, victorious grin he'd had after taking out the other gryphon.

"Two for two," he said breathlessly, stumbling toward us. "If anyone's keeping score."

"You're okay," I breathed. I scanned him from head to toe, not entirely sure I could trust my eyes. "I thought you were a goner, you dick."

"All good, sparrow. Just… just a little…" He blinked, then fell forward, collapsing into my arms.

"Jax! What's wrong with him?"

"Fuck. He needs to feed," Jax said. "Come on, let's get him on the ground."

As Hudson dressed and checked our perimeter, Jax helped me get Elian situated against a tree. We cleaned the blood from his face, then fished out a couple of blood bags from the stash, helping him feed. But even after downing two in a row, he still looked pale and listless.

"It's not going to be enough," Jax said. "I was afraid of that."

"We've got plenty more."

Jax shook his head. "He burned through too much energy fighting the gryphons. They've got their own sort of dark magick, and it takes a bite out of you just as sure as those claws and teeth. Cold blood isn't going to cut it. He needs to feed from the source."

"Source?" Alarm spiked in my chest. "Are there even any humans in Midnight?"

"In the city, yes."

"Jax. That's a two-day hike. He'll never make it."

"You got a plan B? I'm all ears."

"No, but…" I bit my lip, not sure if this was a good idea or a fucking disaster-in-the-making, but at that point, I was pretty sure things couldn't get much worse. I pushed up my sleeve and made a fist, bringing my veins to the surface. "How about a plan B-positive?"

Jax glared at me, his blue eye boring right through me. "*No.*"

"Why the hell not?"

"Once he starts, he might not be able to stop. If he takes too much, you'll—"

"He won't. You'll keep a close watch. If it looks like he's about to O.D. on the good shit, just cut him off."

"Have you ever tried to cut off a starving bloodsucker mid-feed?"

"Have you ever tried to tell a Scorpio-sun, Aries-moon blood witch that she can't do something?"

Silence.

I glanced at Elian. His eyes were closed, his head lolling to the side. I tucked one of his silver braids behind his ear, my hand trembling for more reasons than I wanted to think about.

In a quiet voice, I said, "I told you before we left New Orleans, Jax. I've got your backs, same as you've got mine. So either help me or stand aside, because I'm not letting him die here tonight."

Jax sighed, but finally agreed. Kneeling beside us, he gave me a quick nod, then gripped Elian's shoulder. "Careful, Saint."

I took a deep breath. Pressed my wrist to Elian's cold lips.

He tried to swat me away, to turn his head, but he was too weak to fight me.

"Bite me, bloodsucker," I said, cupping his chin to hold him steady. "Or you're going to give me some weird complex about how my blood is undesirable and I'll end up in therapy and I don't have health insurance so I'll have to—"

Fangs pierced my skin, a sharp pain shooting up my arm. But before I could even cry out, the pain receded, chased by a pleasure so intense, I almost came.

"*Damn*," I whispered, and Elian's gaze locked on mine, new life flooding into his eyes, their silvery depths swirling with desire as he licked and sucked.

Tasted.

Devoured.

Left me weak and panting and—

"Slow down, Saint," Jax said, but Elian ignored him, sucking harder, his eyes fierce and fiery, my skin burning under the instant press of his mouth.

"That's enough."

I was vaguely aware of the demon's command, but I didn't dare pull away. Didn't dare deny Elian the blood he needed. Didn't dare deny myself the exquisite pleasure of—

"I said that's *enough*."

I hadn't even felt Jax reach for it, but before I knew it, he had my stake out of its thigh holster, the pointy end pressed to Elian's throat.

Elian shot him a vicious glare, but—with a final swirl of his tongue against my skin—he released me.

Blood shone on his mouth, his lips pulling into that crooked grin I loved as much as resented.

"Haley, you good?" Jax asked, sliding my stake back into place.

Blinking, I tore my gaze away from Elian's ruby-red mouth and glanced down at my wrist. The wound throbbed, every beat of my heart sending a matching pulse of desire through my core.

But unlike the asshole vamps who'd bitten me at Saints and Sinners, Elian had infused the bite with his healing magick. The bright red punctures immediately began to close, leaving nothing behind but a smear of blood and a deep, endless ache between my thighs.

"I'm fine," I told Jax. Then, forcing a bright smile, I looked at Elian once more and said, "And you? All better, gryphon-slayer?"

He held my gaze for a long moment, flickers of desire still flashing in his eyes. He reached for my hand, gave it a quick squeeze. "Rest assured, sparrow," he whispered. "Your blood is *highly* desirable—no therapy needed."

---

We packed up in silence, hiking another couple of miles through Blackbone before deciding to stop for the night.

Well, for whatever constituted "the night" in a place with three moons and no sun.

The guys insisted on setting up camp, so while they hammered tent stakes into the ground with mallets and generally played out their macho outdoorsman fantasies, I found a quiet spot nearby and took a seat.

Other than the occasional smack of a mallet or the snapping of branches for firewood, the forest was oddly silent. We'd moved far past the main area of the fires; all that remained was the vague scent of woodsmoke. It reminded me of Jax.

All around me, the finger-bone trees reached out, black and barren, strangely beautiful. There were no crickets or night birds, no rustling of leaves, no skittering of nocturnal creatures.

Yet the place held its own beauty. When I placed my palms against the dirt, I felt the hum of its magick running just beneath the surface, wild and untamed. Dark. Enchanting.

I took a deep breath and tried to figure out that strange, foreign feeling settling over me.

*Peace.*

Despite the beating we'd taken on arrival, something about Midnight had called to my soul in a way not even Blackmoon Bay ever had. Now, in these quiet moments, I could almost hear my soul whispering right back.

*This is where I'm supposed to be…*

But that was impossible. Crazy. Midnight was the worst place that'd ever existed.

Wasn't it?

"Good news and bad news," a smooth voice said from behind, and I turned to see Jax approaching, a mug of something hot in his outstretched hands. "Good news, we got the fire going, and I thought maybe you could use a—"

"Yes." I didn't even care what it was—I was so happy for a mug of hot liquid, it could've been straight out of Elian's blood bags and I would've dogged it. I took a sip, pleased to learn it was actually mint tea. "Tea is excellent news. So what's the bad?"

He crouched down beside me and frowned. "We lost two of the tents in the chaos, so there's only one left."

I laughed. "Bad news for you guys. That tent's *all* mine."

"But—"

"Hey, you're the one who was all, 'trust me—we know how to survive Midnight.' Since you're so intimately familiar with the place, you should have no problem sleeping out in the elements."

"You're not willing to share? Not even with one of us?"

"Yes. Hudson."

Jax laughed. "He doesn't sleep. He'll be keeping watch."

"Then he'll be watching me sleep in the luxury of my own private tent." I beamed at him and took another sip of tea. "This brew is excellent, by the way. Did you make it yourself?"

Jax shook his head, but there was no malice in his eye. "I thought it might help you sleep. In your own private tent. While the rest of us freeze our assess off outside. Why the fuck did I ever agree to help Saint with this shit?"

"Aww, you'd better stop saying such sweet things, sinner. Otherwise, I'll start getting the wrong idea."

"And what idea might *that* be?" he grumbled.

"That you *like* me."

He held my gaze for a beat. Two.

"Finish your tea," he said with a smirk, "and get your ass in that tent before Elian beats you to it and I have to stake his ass for being rude."

"Yes, sir." I took another sip, then turned to him and said, "Thanks, Jax."

He let out a huff. "For being so damn sweet?"

"Among other things."

And I meant it, too.

Especially an hour later, when I was safely tucked inside my tent and zipped up in my sleeping bag, far from prying eyes and superior vampire senses.

Because for the first time in five years, when I quietly slid my fingers between my thighs, the name I whispered into the darkness wasn't the name of the accursed silver-eyed fae, but a grumpy, blue-eyed demon whose smoldering gaze made me feel like I had a delicious new secret, all for me.

# 18

## ELIAN

$\mathcal{I}$ had every intention of sneaking out of camp without making a fucking nuisance of myself.

But as soon as I passed Haley's tent, the soft, off-key melody of a badly butchered Led Zeppelin song floated to my ears, and I fucking tripped over my own stupid feet.

"Fuck," I muttered, barely catching myself before I face-planted into the still-smoldering fire pit.

*Gods be damned, Haley Barnes. Forget the dangers of Midnight. You and your insatiable appetites are going to kill me before any of them get another shot.*

The tent unzipped with a whoosh.

And there she was, blinking up at me with a wide, dreamy gaze, her cheeks stained with some new blush.

I knew *exactly* how that color had gotten there, too.

"Fuck," I muttered again, because when it came to Haley, there just weren't enough of them to cover it.

"Elian?" Her voice was soft and low in the quiet dark. "I thought you guys crashed already. What are you doing?"

*Resisting the urge to climb into the tent, tear off your clothes with my teeth, and fuck you with my mouth until you're singing loud enough to wake the dead of Midnight...*

"Just wondering if you're taking requests, little sparrow." I smirked and tapped my lips. "Radiohead, perhaps?"

Her sweet blush darkened, making my cock twitch. The taste of her intoxicating blood still lingered in my mouth—reason number one why I had to get the hell out of Blackbone Forest—and soon.

"Oh my God!" she whisper-shouted. "Were you *spying* on me?"

"There's a rumor Thom Yorke is fae—that's how he's able to hit those otherworldly notes."

"Elian!" She huffed out an exasperated breath, but she couldn't hide the smile curving her lips.

I tried not to gloat. The naughty little witch *liked* that I'd caught her.

*The more things change, the more they stay the same...*

Her green eyes flashed with mischief, then narrowed, finally noticing my pack. "Going somewhere?"

"Amaranth City."

"Alone? Now? In the middle of the... well, whatever the hell time it is?"

"I can move faster on my own."

"But... Why? We'd planned on a two-day hike. We haven't even talked about our next mission yet."

"Jax was right—the cold blood bags aren't cutting it. It's not just the gryphon attack—it's this place. It's more draining than I remembered." I hauled my pack higher on my shoulder and glanced around. The trees were still and silent. Fucking eerie, this place. I was pretty sure I'd never get used to it. "The longer I go without access to a live blood source, the more danger I'm putting everyone in."

"Right. I'll be sure to expedite your Martyr of the Year nomination." She rolled her eyes and pushed up her sleeve, revealing her creamy skin and the blue veins pulsing beneath. "You need a top-off? I'm good to go —promise."

My mouth watered at the sight of it, at the soft pulse throbbing in her veins. It echoed in my eardrums, damn near hypnotizing me.

*Bite her,* the asshole on my shoulder said. *She's offering the vein—fucking take what's yours...*

I closed my eyes. Bit back a curse.

I wanted nothing more than to drop to my knees and do just that. Fucking take it. Feed on her in all the ways I still fantasized about. Ways that would leave us *both* breathless and ruined.

But that was a sure path to disaster.

"Thanks," I said, meeting her eyes once more. "But it won't be enough. We can't risk it, Haley. I need to go."

*Or I'm going to drain you dry...*

Yeah, the scent of her blood was pushing me to an edge I did *not* want to cross, and I needed another food source. But it wasn't the only reason I had to get away.

Being this close to her again after so many years… It was screwing with my head. The way she looked at me was just…

*Fuck.*

Long before I'd ended up in Midnight the first time around, I'd spent decades surviving through lies and trickery. Then I met her and my world turned inside out. She'd seen me right from the start—right through all the masks, the bullshit.

After, when I got out of here and landed in New Orleans, I'd promised myself I'd make it real easy. No close ties. No intimate relationships. I'd built our Empire on fake smiles and the promise of escape, and people loved me for it. Fae, vampires, demons, witches—they all wanted in on the party. All wanted to be friends with the Saint of New Orleans, the fae who could take away their pain and absolve them of their sins.

It was all bullshit, nothing real, but it was easy. I knew what they wanted. They knew what they were getting. Add in a few smiles and comp VIP tickets, and I'd never want for company.

But people like Haley Barnes would always need more than I could give now. Not because they demanded it, but because they fucking deserved it, and to offer them anything less was un-fucking-acceptable.

Now, when she looked at me with those big green eyes, I tried to imagine what she saw.

And I fucking *despised* it.

So yeah, maybe that made me a coward. But I couldn't afford to be distracted—not out in the open like this, where my complete inability to get my shit together and function like a real man would put everyone at risk.

Especially her.

I crouched down in front of her. Pulled the sleeve back down over her wrist. Took her hand, just for a minute. "I'll see you in the Hollow in two days. By then, I'll have everything set up for us. We'll be safer in the city—all of us."

She pulled her hand away, tucking it deeper inside her sleeve. "What's the Hollow?"

"Our old… neighborhood, for lack of a better word. We've got someone on the inside—she knows we're coming. She's just waiting for me to make contact."

I heard the skip in her heartbeat at the word "she," but she didn't ask for details.

"Okay," she finally said, though her eyes had lost some of their sparkle. "And Hudson and Jax—"

"They know I'm leaving. They'll get you there safely." I got to my feet, readjusted the pack.

Haley stood up, too. "Will you do me one favor, if possible?"

*As long as you don't ask me to kiss you…*

"Anything, sparrow."

"The blood source… Will you ask first?"

"Ask *what*?"

She glared at me like I was the realm's biggest idiot. Which, admittedly… Yeah. I was definitely in the running.

"Permission," she said. "Consent is sexy, Elian."

"I'm a vampire now. Pretty sure 'sexy consent' doesn't apply to feeding."

"Yes it fucking does, and I'm asking you—against all odds—to at least *try* not to be a murderous asshole, if at all possible."

"And if it isn't possible? If I can't find the *one* human in all of Amaranth City who might be happy to offer up the vein? Would you rather I starve?"

"Of course not. If push comes to shove… Fine. Bite whoever you need to bite. But *only* if it's a break-glass-now kind of emergency."

I laughed. "Good to see you're still adhering to that rock-solid moral compass, Haley. Downright inspiring. In fact, maybe I'll write a song about it. And speaking of songs…" I nodded at her tent. "Don't let me keep you. Seemed like you were having a pretty good night, all things considered."

She glared at me a minute, then narrowed her eyes and said, "You sure you know what you're doing, *Saint*?"

*Considering I'm about to walk away from you again? No, not in the slightest.*

"Guess we'll find out, won't we?" I winked at her.

She pressed her lips together and sighed, clearly holding back.

"Haley, listen to me. I know I haven't always… I didn't…" I struggled to find the damn words. Words I actually meant, even if they weren't all the ones she deserved. "You said you needed my help getting you into and out of the most dangerous realm in the known universe, and you've got it. So everything else you feel about me, everything I did in the past, everything you *think* you know… I need you to put all that shit aside. Right now, the past no longer exists. Blackmoon Bay, New Orleans, the lives we had before—dead. There's only this shithole and the things we all need to do to get through it, and one of those things is you trusting me." I gripped the straps of my pack with both hands, because if I didn't, I'd grab her instead. "The guys will take care of you. Stick with one of them at all times. You hear me?"

She let out another sigh, but eventually nodded. "Yeah, I hear you."

"Good. Okay. Right. So, anyway… Yeah. I'll… I'll see you soon."

No response.

I turned on my heel. Heard the change in her heartbeat—the telltale spike.

"Elian, wait."

I blew out a breath. Turned around, even though I was terrified of what I might find in her eyes next. Terrified she might give me a reason to stay.

But Haley merely smiled at me. A small one, but real. Real enough, it almost had me tripping over my damn feet again.

"Be safe out there," she said. Then, with a new twinkle in her eye, "And for the record? Thom Yorke is *definitely* fae."

# 19

## JAX

The three of us left camp a couple of hours after Elian when we figured out none of us could sleep, anyway.

The hike kicked off slow and groggy, but things started looking up when we found a freshwater lake. We took turns washing up, doing our best to ignore a group of imps on the shore taking turns flaying one another's skin off and feeding it to some creature they'd trapped.

Fucking Midnight. Sometimes, it was even worse than hell.

Considering Haley had never set foot in this fucked-up nightmare world, though, she was holding up pretty well. *Better* than well; after the bath, she perked right up, her cheeks pink, her eyes bright as we continued on through the endless night.

About a mile beyond the lake, Hudson took off to scout ahead. Haley and I climbed another rise, and a small meadow opened up on the other side, silvery-blue in the moonlight, streaked with black vines and tiny white flowers—a plant I'd recognize anywhere.

"Corpsevine," I said, gazing out across the expanse. A small wooded area edged the back side. "Fuck."

"What's wrong?"

"Corpsevine is the raw material used to make Devil's Dream—a potent hallucinogen. Most of the fields are already marked off. This one looks untouched—it probably hasn't been noticed or cataloged. Which means—"

"As soon as people find it, they're going to be fighting over it."

"Exactly."

"What's the deal with the drug? Do people smoke the flowers or something?"

"No, they're dried and processed into pill form. It's sold in Amaranth City and… Well, New Orleans, primarily."

She blinked up at me, the pieces clicking into place behind her eyes. "So, *that's* why Saints and Sinners is so popular."

"One of the reasons, yes." I turned away from her, looking out again across the vine-laced meadow. "We're smugglers, Haley. We've got people here in Midnight handling production and portaling, and we sell it back in our realm. Everyone gets a cut."

"Is that how you three met? Dealing in Amaranth City?"

There was no judgment in her tone, just an earnest curiosity, which I appreciated. Last thing I wanted to do was justify our survival methods to a tourist who hadn't even seen the *real* shitshow of Midnight yet.

"It's… kind of a long story."

"Look around you, sinner. All we've got is time."

I let out a long breath. She was right, and something told me if I didn't spill it, she'd pester me for the rest of the hike.

"Those of us exiled to Midnight are the worst of the worst," I began. "Most of us are portaled into the realm far away from the city, dropped into battles more often than not. Military duty isn't exactly a volunteer thing here."

She shivered next to me, and I resisted the urge to pull her close.

"Anyway," I continued, "if you make it as far as Amaranth City, you stand a better chance at surviving. But surviving behind the wall requires a different set of skills."

"Skills you obviously have," she said. "Okay. So you, Hudson, and Elian made it to Amaranth after your arrival."

"Well, Hudson… He was born here. And don't ask me any more than that—it's not my story to tell, and I don't even know most of the details. But yes, Saint and I made it to the city. Different timelines—I'd been here a while by the time he showed up—but eventually, our paths crossed. Not long after that, we met Hudson. We all hit it off. Didn't take us too long to put our heads together and figure out we had some… complementary talents."

She flashed a wicked grin, her eyes sparkling with new mischief. "Oh, I *bet.*"

The look in her eyes sent a shock of heat straight to my cock.

*Bad idea, asshole. Bad, bad idea…*

Dismissing the sudden onslaught of images featuring Haley on her knees and me telling her to suck harder, I said, "Saint was a smuggler and a con who could just about charm a corpse out of the ground. And Hudson—"

"Let me guess. Muscle?"

"Exactly. Also a good scout. Flying is dangerous in Midnight—you risk being shot down by a solider's flaming arrows or attacked by a raven gryphon—but gargoyles are fast, strong, and extremely agile flyers. That worked out in our favor, especially when we had to meet up with people we didn't know very well."

"Okay, so Elian was the mouth, surprising no one. Hudson was the eyes and the muscle. That makes you…" She glanced up at me and narrowed her eyes, assessing. "The brains?"

"I have certain… abilities," I hedged. "Manipulation techniques that allow me to read things about people—things they don't always want to broadcast."

"Such as…?"

*Don't even ask, angel.*

Glaring at her, I ignored the question and started down the rise, leading us to the edge of the field.

"Okay," she said, seemingly content to move on. "You guys hooked up behind the wall and decided to parlay your talents into a drug-smuggling operation?"

"No, we didn't start out dealing in Dream—that came later. At first, it was just… well, whatever people needed. Saint had a way of finding things for people, or finding other people who could get the first people what they needed. Through that, he developed a reputation as the guy who could get anyone anything—weapons, booze, sex, spells, poisons and hexes, information—and he built this whole network of associates who came to trust and rely on him."

"When does the mystical fae crack come into play?"

"Drugs were already rampant in the city, same as anywhere else—people want their medicine. Something to take away the pain, you know?"

She nodded.

"But Saint… He was always one step ahead of the game. By the time some new designer drug hit the streets, he was already looking for the next big thing. Eventually, we found it. One of the trading caravans came through Amaranth selling corpsevine flower as a cure-all. Total bullshit, but we started experimenting with it. And we figured out if you dried the flowers under the full triple moon—it only happens once every two months or so—you could activate the hallucinogenic properties with dark fae magick. From there, you could process it into pills."

"Wow. Not only do you sell it, but you *invented* the crack? It's like I'm standing in the presence of drug-dealer royalty."

"I wouldn't go that far. But yes, we discovered it."

"Devil's Dream," she said. "Interesting name."

"D2, Black, Dark Delight. There are a lot of names for it, but the end result is the same: it takes you right out of your mind and into another place entirely. Swallow enough, and eventually, you'll no longer be able to tell fantasy from reality."

With a soft sigh, she dropped her pack and crouched down for a closer look. "This is the stuff you guys import back home?"

"No. This is the raw material—completely inert." I crouched down next to her and plucked a flower from the vine, then handed it over. "We can't do anything with it on the earthly realm. It has to be processed here first— the moonlight and the fae magick are what make it possible."

"Why do they call it corpsevine?"

"It grows mostly on old battlefields where many dead have fallen. Their blood and bones nourish the soil. It's said the potency of Devil's Dream lies in its connection to death—that it brings you as close to the other side as you can get without actually stepping over."

"And people put this into their bodies? Willingly?"

I nodded. "The euphoria is like nothing you've ever felt, Haley."

She looked at me, her brow furrowed, but there was still no judgment there. "You've done it?"

"At this point, you'd be hard-pressed to find anyone in Midnight who hasn't."

"And Elian?" She turned back to the field and ran her hands just above the flowers, not quite touching them. "It explains a lot. I've seen him popping pills. Seen the fog in his eyes."

I didn't respond. His was another sad story that wasn't mine to tell.

"It's not dangerous to touch this stuff, right?" she asked. "The flowers won't fuck me up or anything? Because hey, no judgments, but the only hallucinations I'm into are the ones induced by early onset food coma after I go all in on a plate of nachos."

I couldn't help but laugh, grateful for a break in the heaviness. "You're fine, angel. The plants themselves are harmless."

"In that case." With another of her sexy-as-sin mischievous grins, she got to her feet and bolted out into the middle of the field.

I stood up and watched her, that bright smile beaming at me across the expanse.

*Holy fuck,* she was beautiful. Crazy, just as I'd suspected. But she was definitely getting under my skin, and I wasn't sure I could keep her at arm's length much longer.

Wasn't sure I even *wanted* to keep her at arm's length, which was… problematic, to say the least.

"Get your demon ass out here, sinner. You're missing the best part." She got down and stretched out on her back, arms and legs splayed like a child making a snow angel.

Unable to resist, I dropped my pack and trotted out there.

The first moon shone down on her, catching the highlights in her dark hair, casting her in an otherworldly glow, and for a second I swore she looked like she was born here.

"Less staring," she said, "more getting down here with me. You've *got* to see this view."

Rolling my eyes, I dropped down into a crouch beside her and looked up.

She grabbed my arm, tugged me until I fell on my back.

I opened my mouth, all set to give her some smart-ass comment about tricking me into getting horizontal for her, but the view stole the words right out of my mouth.

Gazing up at the sky, I lost all sense of time and place. Way out here, far from the torchlights of Amaranth City, even farther from New Orleans, the red-and-gold stars of Midnight were infinite.

It was better than Devil's Dream. Better than any drink I could whip up at Saints and Sinners. It was fucking majestic.

"Kind of amazing, isn't it?" she said softly. "Before we left New Orleans, Hudson told me—well, *wrote* me—there's beauty in darkness. This is exactly what he meant, Jax."

I barely had the words to respond. "I… I've never… seen it. Not like this."

"Really? How long did you live here?"

I let out a deep sigh. "Eighteen years, four months, and six days before Saint pulled me out."

A soft gasp slipped out from between her lips, but she didn't say anything. After a beat, I felt the soft touch of her hand against mine as she linked our pinky fingers.

Something jabbed me then, right in the heart.

We stayed like that, side-by-side on our backs on the field of the dead, and I'd never felt so alive. My body burned with the need to do something, to touch her, but...

*Fucking Saint.*

I closed my eyes. Forced those ridiculous notions right out of my head.

But then, out of nowhere, Haley said, "Jax? I kind of want to kiss you."

# 20

## JAX

nother unplanned, uninvited smile stretched across my lips. I turned on my hip to face her, shocked to find she was already facing me, her eyes glittering, her body surrounded by the ethereal white flowers.

"You're not talking to the jambalaya again, are you?" I teased.

"Not this time. And granola bars and MREs don't inspire the same level of affection."

"I see," I said, hoping like hell she couldn't hear my heart slamming against my ribs. "Is this a what-happens-in-Midnight-stays-in-Midnight thing?"

"It could be."

Sure, it *could* be. Just a little fun, right? No harm, no foul. A lot of women believed they could have that with me.

On some level, I got it. The scars, the mystery of the missing eye, the whole bad-boy-who-goes-good-for-you fantasy. And if Saint was any indication, I fit the profile; Haley had a thing for walking disasters.

But while I'd promised him I'd take care of her—and something about the woman brought out my protective instincts like nothing else ever had—that didn't change who I was at the core.

A demon. A killer. A monster.

Being in this place only served to remind me of that.

I didn't know what Haley saw when she looked at me the way she was looking at me now, but it wasn't the truth.

"As tempting as your offer sounds..." I shook my head and flipped onto my back, swallowing my disappointment. "You don't want me to kiss you, angel. Trust me on that."

"I didn't say anything about *you* kissing *me*. I said *I* wanted to kiss *you*."

"*You* want your doom."

"Maybe I do," she whispered, shifting closer and sweeping her fingers through my hair.

Her touch was electric, and it made me shiver.

*Fuck.*

I was already fucking hard.

"Jax," she whispered, her soft breath tickling my cheek, just below the eye patch.

And that was it.

I rolled on top of her, propping myself up to keep from crushing her completely. Her body was warm and soft in a hundred different ways—a hundred ways I hadn't felt in so long, I barely remembered how good it could be.

*What are you doing to me, angel?*

"What's *this* new game?" she teased, wriggling beneath me. "You've got me at a disadvantage here, but I think I'm okay with it."

"No more games," I said. Then, staring at her lush mouth, I whispered, "Tell me what you *really* want from me, angel. You sure it's just the kiss of doom?"

"You think you can give me what I want, demon?" she teased, her nipples hardening beneath me.

"Oh, I *know* I can give it to you. But be warned—you might not like it once you've got it."

She slid her hands behind my neck. Then, in a hot whisper against my mouth, "Why don't you let *me* be the judge of that?"

*Fuck me. I'm done.*

My resistance shattered, along with my instinct to protect her from my demon side, and any remaining shreds of loyalty I had for Saint.

I crashed into her lush mouth, stealing the offered kiss before she could change her mind.

The taste of her... It shot through me like a spark, igniting a fire inside that threatened to consume us both.

But after just a few seconds of pure bliss, she was already pushing against my chest, struggling to break free.

I pulled back. Tried to hide my frustration.

"Giving up already, angel?" I teased, though I knew *right* where this was heading. I'd known it from the moment she'd said she wanted it.

One taste, and she'd be running for her life, just like everyone else.

"Oh my God," she gasped, her eyes wide. "You're... you're a *fear* demon."

"Finally figured that out, did you?"

She touched her fingertips to her mouth, a shiver racking her body. "It's... so cold... I feel like... like I'm drowning and... Jax?" Panic filled her eyes. "What's happening to me?"

"That's the fear," I said. "The closer I get to someone, the greater the effect. Intimate contact? Sorry, angel. You just got the highest dose possible, outside of me intentionally forcing it on you."

"Were you... were you born like this or...?"

"Breathe, Haley. You need to breathe. You're freaking out on me here."

"Move." She shoved against my chest. "Move!"

I rolled off, and she got to her feet. Took off running without another word, crashing through the field and into the wooded area just beyond.

A wicked grin slashed across my mouth, matching the wicked fire in my balls.

*Sorry, angel. You've just signed your death warrant.*

# 21

## ELIAN

About a mile out from Amaranth City, atop the towering White Cliffs of Oshen, I looked out across a largely unobstructed view of the moat crossing and gatehouse at Vanderham's Wall.

Flat on my belly, I crawled to the edge of the cliff and peered through my binoculars, trying to suss out the situation.

Clusterfuck.

The drawbridge was down, but the crossing was jammed up by a caravan that trailed back about a quarter-mile. By the light of their magick torches, I counted about a dozen shepherd wagons pulled by twice as many Mares of Night—massive, horselike beasts that looked more demonic than equine, with all-white hair and bright red eyes that glowed in the dim. Midnighters had figured out how to tame them with iron and magick centuries ago, but the wild ones were so feral they made the raven gryphons look like winged kittens.

All of them were waiting for entry into Amaranth City.

Had to be a trading party. I had no idea where they'd come from, but it was a miracle so many had survived the trek without a military escort.

It was the first bit of good news I'd gotten since I left Haley back at camp. Traders—even ones strong enough to cross the realm—weren't warriors. They were merchants.

In other words, con artists—my favorite fucking kind of asshole.

Con artists always thought they had the upper hand, which made them easy to kill; they were always so busy trying to separate you from your wallet, it rarely occurred to them you were planning to separate their heads from their bodies.

I tucked away the binoculars and made my way down the steep rise, doing my best to conserve my dwindling energy. The mile-wide swath of land that stretched from the bottom of the cliffs to the edge of Beggar's Moat was bleak and barren, nothing but obsidian sand and the bones of those deemed too fetid for even *these* cursed grounds to swallow.

There were no shadows cast but those from the wagons. No places to hide.

I'd have to rely on my vampire speed and, if someone spotted me before I wanted them to, my influence.

I checked my pack. I'd sucked down all my extra blood bags hours earlier, but I couldn't afford to screw up now. I needed one last burst of energy and speed—along with a little trickery—to get to the caravan.

At the bottom of the cliffs, I dropped the pack and dug out a change of clothing—an Amaranth guard uniform I'd stolen before we'd left last time. I had no idea if they were still using the same ones, but the travelers might not notice, anyway. Just had to look close enough to the part, turn on the charm, and hope they weren't as clever as they believed.

After I walked as far as I dared across the black sands, I blurred to the very last wagon, pressing myself against the back and taking a minute to catch my breath. Pinpricks of light danced before my eyes. I needed to fucking eat, and soon.

The entire caravan fucking stank. Rotten food, dead animals, personal waste, road reek. Somewhere near the rear was likely a cart carrying the few of their dead they'd managed to recover from whatever shit had befallen them on the trek, but that was always a wasted effort. Soon as they got to the bridge, the guards would force them to dump the corpses into the moat.

Amaranth City had enough of its *own* dead to contend with, *fuckyou-verymuch*.

I wondered how many travelers from their original party were left. Seemed kind of quiet—just the soft nickers of the mares and a few grumblings from the people who'd left their mounts and ducked inside the wagons to wait out the traffic jam.

From what I could pick up, it sounded like Keradoc had ordered extra patrols, though no one seemed to know why. I heard snatches of everything from "Darkwinter fae enemies" to "arrival of a weapon that would turn the tides of the war" to "Keradoc's balls were hanging a little too far the left tonight, so he decided to take it out on his city watch and give them all extra work to do."

Whatever the reason, it sounded like I'd be here for a while.

Most of the wagons were fitted with three doors—one in the back and two smaller doors on the sides to allow for shift changes on and off the mares without having to stop. It was also fun to flip off the guy behind you and piss out the back, but that wasn't what I'd come to do tonight.

Certain no one had seen me, I stashed my pack under the wagon, then slipped in through the back door.

Two men—a human who looked about as old as the grains of sand outside the door and a fae whose face had recently been chewed on by something bigger than him—glanced up from a card game in progress, immediately reaching for the daggers on their hips.

"You're no guard of Amaranth," the fae said, taking in my red-and-black uniform. "They wear blue."

"Good to know," I said. "Would you mind standing up?"

He got to his feet and unsheathed the dagger. "What the fuck do you—"

I grabbed his head and snapped his neck, then turned the quivering old human into a juice box—not about to look *that* gift horse in the mouth.

The blood rejuvenated me at once, bringing with it a flash of guilt I quickly dismissed.

Wasn't exactly consensual, but... I was pretty sure it would meet Haley's qualifications for a break-the-glass emergency.

Working quickly, I stripped the fae and swapped my uniform for his traveling clothes—not much more than a pair of dusty cargo pants and a dark gray hooded cloak. I stashed the bodies in one of the hollow storage benches that lined the walls, just in case someone decided to poke their head in the door looking for these two.

I found a rucksack too, and when I left the wagon I'd forever think of as my dining car, I retrieved my pack and shoved it inside.

I looked like one of them now. Smelled like them, too. Made my eyes burn.

I hoped like hell the place Gem found for us had running water.

Keeping my head low, I walked up the line, passing the corpse cart and another wagon that seemed to be filled with medical supplies, for all the good it did them. A few travelers were hanging out outside, trying to get a peek at whatever was holding up the line ahead. I grunted my greetings and kept on moving, not bothering to offer condolences for the bastard whose clothes I'd stolen.

By the time they all made it over the bridge and realized they'd left the last wagon in the dust, they'd be tucked away in one of Amaranth's many taverns, and some terror or another—one much bigger than a vampire-fae—would have already destroyed the wagon and claimed the two corpses inside it as a meal.

I kept walking, searching for my jackpot—a.k.a. the booze cart.

Every caravan had one—traders, hunters, and military alike.

A traveling bar and distillery was a source of comfort on a long journey. A place to gather after a long night's ride. A sanctuary to drink to the fallen they'd lost along the way.

More importantly? It was a fucking bomb on wheels.

I found it about four wagons from the bridge entrance and slipped unseen underneath it. Waited. Each time another wagon moved onto the bridge and the line crept along, I crept right along with it.

And then, it was finally time. We were at the bridge, about to start the crossing, no chance for another traveler to pop in for a drink.

Just before the wheels started turning again, I slipped out from under the wagon and let myself in through the side door.

The occupant, a low-level crossroads demon, was busy rearranging liquor bottles, his back to me.

"Sorry, friend," he said, not even turning around. Apparently, my foul stench marked me as one of their own, no visual confirmation needed. "We ain't open. You'll have to wait till we get across the—"

I punched a hole through his back and tore out his spine just as his horseman whistled to the mares. The wagon bumped onto the drawbridge, its wheels somehow managing to find every crack and divot in the old wood.

I waited until we reached the center of the bridge, then opened the side door and pitched his remains into the moat.

The guards never cared about shit like that, and most of the other travelers were too worried about their own business to notice. People were always falling off the wagon, so to speak, or getting thrown off, or—for those looking for the *worst* way to go—jumping.

It was an unexpected treat for the ghouls that dwelled there. I didn't have to watch to know what was happening; the second the demon hit bottom, they converged, rending skin and muscle from bone, consuming it until there wasn't so much as a drop of fucking blood left.

Then they dropped to their knees and wept, a sound so haunting it always made me want to retch, cry, and punch something at the same fucking time.

They looked like rotting skeletons, the ghouls, draped in nothing more than a vaguely transparent layer of tattered skin suggesting the person they once were.

Such was the fate of the soldiers of Midnight. *Keradoc's* soldiers. Outside the city walls, all who died in battle were left to rot. What the beasts of Midnight didn't pick clean eventually decomposed in the fields. After that, the poor bastards would rise again in Beggar's Moat, cursed to forever guard the city that'd turned its back on them.

Demon attendant properly disposed of, I pulled out the liquor bottles and dumped them, dousing the interior of the wagon, no surface left dry.

Minutes later, we reached the end of the bridge and pulled to a stop at the gatehouse for the inspection, which was little more than a payoff.

One I wouldn't be making tonight.

The guard didn't knock. Just opened the side door and stepped in, probably already salivating for the cash—and the liquor—he'd been counting on.

*What do you know—the uniforms really are blue now.*

He caught my eye. Nodded, real friendly, like they always were when it came time to get their palms greased.

"Nice night for a barbecue," I said. Then I flicked my Zippo to life, tossed it at the guard's feet, and slipped out the other side in a vampire blur so fast, even the most reliable witness would've had trouble convincing a jury he'd seen anything other than a smudge in the night.

I was a safe distance away when the fucking thing exploded, undoubtedly sending the rest of the guards into a tizzy, no time to pay heed to any possible rumors of a stowaway.

Hey, I liked covering all the bases.

Pulling my hood up, I tucked in with the rest of the rabble in the street, my stink unnoticeable in the river of filth and shit that was Amaranth City.

One last glance over my shoulder, and I smiled.

I'd fucking made it.

That old guilt soup started boiling in my gut again, but this time, I didn't ignore it. I welcomed it.

Used to be shit like this was easy. Pleasurable, even. But those days had died the night I left Midnight, vowing never to return.

Now that I had?

I didn't want it to be easy anymore. Killing someone—human, fae, demon, guard, innocent, guilty as sin—it *shouldn't* be easy. Ever.

But one thought of the witch with the off-key songs and the power to make me dizzy with a murmured spell and her little magick ring, and I knew I'd keep right on killing—anyone, anywhere, anytime I deemed it necessary to keep her safe—no matter how much it ate me up inside.

Making sure I hadn't been followed, I cut down a familiar alley, slipping into the shadows once again.

But something moved behind me.

And before I could turn around, the short sword was at my throat, a stake pressed between my shoulder blades.

## 22

### ELIAN

*Y*ou've got some nerve showing up here, bloodsucker," a female voice hissed, low and gravelly.

Demon, maybe?

I wasn't sure. Too many other smells and sounds in this putrid asshole of a city to get a good read.

"You know how to use that sword, assassin? Or is this some kind of fucked-up gang initiation that's only going to get you killed?"

"Bit of both, perhaps?" My assailant laughed and lowered her weapons, then stepped in front of me and pushed back her hood. Chin-length purple hair curled around a smile as bright as the blaze I'd left behind. "By the moons and stars, it's good to see you again, Saint."

I wrapped her up in my arms, crushing her against my chest. "For fuck's sake, Gem. I was about to *waste* your beautiful ass. I thought you were a demon."

"And I thought you'd at least give an old friend the courtesy of showering before manhandling her, but you know what they say—nothing in Midnight is ever what it should be."

"You'd think I'd remember that by now." I released her, stepping back to take a good look. Other than Jax and Hudson, Gem had been one of the only people I'd ever trusted in Midnight. Hell, one of the few I'd ever trusted *anywhere*. "How the hell did you find me so quickly?"

"Really?" With a laugh, she glanced over her shoulder, where a fiery orange light glowed in the distance, flickering against the roughly hewn black stone buildings that surrounded it. "Where there's smoke—and an explosion, and murder, and a lot of baffled city watchmen bumbling around with their dicks in their hands—there's fire. And in this case, by fire, I mean you."

"What can I say? I love to make an entrance."

"Speaking of entrances, where are the rest of my boys? Don't tell me they sent your scrappy ass back here alone."

"They're still a day behind. Had to leave them to make the trek with Haley," I said, my heart kicking me in the ribs at the reminder. I knew they'd take care of her, but damn. Leaving her behind—again? I *really* needed to stop making that a thing. "I need blood, Gem. Human. Live."

"Don't worry, bloodsucker," she said with a grin. "You know I've got you covered."

Haley's words echoed.

Again.

*Consent is sexy, Elian…*

I sighed. Fucking woman was going to get me killed.

"Hate to ask," I said, "but… Willing?"

Gem lifted a brow. "Don't tell me you've gone soft on me, Saint."

"Never. Just… trying to mitigate rumors about a vicious new vampire on the scene. People start nosing around, asking too many questions… That could be bad news for us. I'm trying to keep a low profile this time."

She glanced back at the inferno still raging near the gatehouse. "Low profile, sure. Looks good on you, Saint. Really." With another laugh, she looped her arm through mine and sighed dramatically. "Oh, all right, I'll free the guy I've got tied up in the apartment and find someone a little more… agreeable. If you insist."

"I knew I could count on you, Gem. Always."

"Saint, I…" She hesitated, something darkening her eyes, but before I could ask her where her mind had wandered off to, she was back with a conspiratorial grin. "Tell me about this mission of yours. I want all the details."

"That, I'm afraid, will cost you." I put my arm around her. "A few drinks, perhaps?"

"You mentioned something about a witch in your message. That's Haley, I presume?"

"Yes," I said. "She's a blood witch. She has business in the city."

"She must be the reason you're not tearing off my clothes. Not that I'm jealous or anything. Just need to make sure I'm not losing my sparkle."

I laughed. For all our years of flirting, Gem and I never actually hooked up.

"Pretty sure you could never lose your sparkle," I said.

"Good answer. Now come on—I've got you all set up. A place not far from your old digs. You ready to be back?"

Back. In Amaranth City.

In the place where at least a third of the population wanted me dead, another third would definitely sell me out to the first group if the price was right, and the last third would be more than happy to stand on the sidelines with some beer and popcorn to watch the slaughter.

I took a deep breath and nodded.

"Ready as ever, Gem. Lead the way."

## 23

### HALEY

It was no conscious decision on my part—I simply ran. Ran like my life depended on it, my heart close to bursting, my lips still icy from the demon's kiss.

The moment we'd come together, I felt it, like a fist punching right through my chest and yanking all my worst fears to the surface. They'd flashed before my eyes—losing my sisters. Getting trapped in Midnight. Watching Elian die. Flashbacks to the prison compound the hunters had trapped me in. Shit from my childhood—from before I was adopted—I wanted to leave in a fucking graveyard.

The more distance I put between us, the better I felt. When the chill finally subsided, I stopped to catch my breath in the woods, hands on my knees, eyes shut tight. I hadn't gone far—I could still see glimpses of the silvery-white field through the trees.

No Jax, though. Maybe he'd decided to give me some space.

I wasn't sure exactly how it worked—how much of it Jax could control —but kissing him seemed to unleash it all. Logically, I wasn't scared of *him* —not really. I'd simply reacted to the images of my own fears shoved in my face. But in that moment, it'd all felt so real.

I opened my eyes and stood up. My hands were still trembling.

*Fucking demon.*

A twig snapped, and I glanced up to see Jax slowly approaching, our packs slung over his shoulder. His face was unreadable.

"I tried to warn you," he said, stepping closer.

I crossed my arms over my chest and took a step back, still fighting off a shiver. "You could've been a little more specific."

"Would you have even believed me? Would it have stopped you?"

Heat pooled between my thighs—another reaction. Purely instinctual. Purely... *fuck.*

Horror-movie slideshow notwithstanding, that kiss had been...

I blew out a breath, forcing away the memories of his hot mouth. The smoky taste. The fire that had raged inside me when he'd finally given in and...

*No.*

I couldn't go back there. Not in my mind. Not in my reality.

Didn't matter how sexy he was or how damn fine he'd tasted. Kissing demons in the dark was far too fucking dangerous.

"I didn't need to see that stuff," I said. "I can't... I can't be worrying about all my old demons, no pun intended, when I'm trying to focus on this crazy-ass mission in the most crazy-ass place in the universe. This isn't about me, Jax. I've got sisters. Three of them. I didn't even know they existed until recently, and if I don't see this through—if I don't get this dude's blood and get back to the Temple of the Dark Moon—Melantha will kill them."

He dropped the packs and closed the space between us, reaching out to cup my face. Sympathy flashed in his eye, but it quickly turned to something else—something wicked and predatory.

"I know," he said darkly.

"You know?"

"I'm a fear demon, Haley. Everything you saw just now? I saw it too. I can sense your fears. All of them—fears about the future, fears you experienced last year, right down to the fear of drowning you've had since you were a child."

I pulled away from his touch and shook my head.

"Your whole life," he said, "you've been afraid of your birth mother. She murdered your father—her own husband. She tried to drown you. She tried to steal your magick—your legacy."

Ouch. Right to the fucking bone, that one. It felt as if he'd shoved a knife into my gut.

"Stop," I whispered.

Still, he kept coming. Another step, too fucking close. Another reminder. Another twist of the knife.

"You suffer from an almost debilitating fear of abandonment," he continued, "firstly from your mother, but also because your adoptive parents and grandmother died, leaving you behind. Saint bailing on your relationship only further served to—"

"I said *stop!*" I unsheathed my dagger. "Get out of my fucking head!"

"Haley, I'm telling you," he warned. "If you don't deal with this shit, you're—"

"Fuck off and deal with *this*." I sliced my palm and slammed it into his chest, the spell already on my lips. He stumbled backward, then fell on his ass, and I pounced.

Straddling him, I gazed down into his face, his eye wide, his breath short and ragged.

"You feel that, Jax? The lightheadedness? The muscle weakness? Your heart's beginning to slow. If I don't call off the spell, you'll pass out. Maybe even die. Scared yet? You fucking should be. Fear demons aren't the only ones who can unleash terrors."

"Haley," he whispered, reaching for my face with a shaky hand.

But he wasn't scared—I could see it in his eye. Just sad and a little pale.

And, as much as it pained me to admit…

Hard.

For me.

*Fucking asshole.*

I could've pushed it further. Could've rerouted the blood to leave his dick as limp as an overcooked lasagna noodle.

But now, with that rock-hard bulge pressing urgently against my core, all I wanted to do was…

*No.*

Jax was a fear demon. If merely kissing him for ten seconds had sent me fleeing for my life, what would a dose of that red-hot demon dick do to me?

I was in so far over my head, I might as well be drowning all over again, just like my birthmother had intended.

I sighed. My spell was already fading. It wasn't intended for long-term use, anyway—just a quickie to help you escape a jam, like if you were about to get jumped or groped.

But the thing about escaping was you had to actually, you know, *go*. Away. You couldn't just sit on top of your would-be assailant, subtly grinding against him, dreaming about that sweet, sweet Demon D.

After a beat, Jax sucked in a breath, the color finally returning to his cheeks.

I slammed the dagger back into its sheath.

Before I could move to let him up, Jax wrapped his hand around the back of my neck and pulled me down close, a new spark alighting in his eye. "You shouldn't have done that."

Another shiver snaked down my spine, but it wasn't his touch that was cold. He was as warm as any other man. But his touch? It brought out the cold from deep inside me—and that's where the *real* terror lived.

Where his power lived.

Jax squeezed my neck. Arched his hips, ever so slightly, making me feel it. Feel him.

Time stopped. The world stopped. Right now, there was nothing outside the trees that mattered.

"Jax," I whispered, but it was too late.

He flipped us so he was on top, his weight pressing me into the soft ground, hands clamped down over my wrists, his body warm and solid and delicious and...

Oh, hell, I was fucked.

"What... what are you doing?"

"You were right, angel. I couldn't give you what you wanted. So now I'll have to give you what you need."

He claimed me in another kiss—bruising, fucking incredible. The fear rose again, but this time it had no face. No images. Only a feeling of ice-cold dread and dagger-sharp edges slicing right through me, a contrast to his hot mouth and fiery touch.

Resisting the urge to run again, I slid my hands up inside the back of his T-shirt, clawing at his shoulders as he continued to own me with his mouth.

He finally broke our kiss. "Think you can hurt me again, angel?" he growled in my ear. "Do your worst."

"I hope you feel this all fucking night." I raked my nails hard down his back.

He hissed in my ear, then licked his way down to my neck, biting me so hard he drew blood. I cried out, but the pain quickly turned to pleasure as the warm trickle slid over my skin.

Like a man unhinged, he grunted and tore open my shirt, kissing and biting his way down my chest, my stomach, his mouth searing every inch of exposed skin. When he got to my pants and underwear, he didn't even bother taking them all the way off. Just yanked them down to my knees, then buried his sexy demon face right between my thighs.

I moaned and fisted his hair, which only encouraged him to go harder, tongue lapping my clit as he shoved two fingers inside me and fucked me fast and furious.

I gasped and writhed, his mouth and fingers driving me closer and closer to the edge, harder, faster, so intense I couldn't even catch my breath before…

"Right there. I'm… yes! Jax!"

A starburst of blinding, white-hot ecstasy exploded inside me, waves of pleasure rolling through my body as the demon sucked my clit and curled his fingers, hitting the perfect spot, making good on his promise to give me *exactly* what I needed.

"Jax," I whispered again, the night sky tilting sideways, and he got to his knees and glared at me, his mouth glistening with the evidence of what he'd done.

I hadn't even finished shuddering through the last aftershock when he flipped me onto my stomach, grabbed my hips, and hauled my ass up in the air.

He was behind me now, one hand on my backside, the other unzipping his pants.

His cock teased against my still-dripping pussy.

"Okay?" he growled.

One question.

One answer.

"Fuck yes," I breathed, and he slammed into me from behind, letting loose a deep, possessive growl that made me weak.

He fucked me hard and deep, fingers digging into my hips as he claimed me, owned me, marked me.

I arched my back and he fisted my hair, pulling it hard and forcing me up onto my knees as he continued to rock against my ass. I reached behind with both hands and clawed at his sides, and he returned the attack with a bite on my shoulder, then pushed me back onto my hands and knees, taking his fill any way he wanted it.

We were animals in the dirt, scratching and biting, fighting, fucking, and I'd never felt anything so raw. So primal. So perfect.

The heat was rising inside me again, building, winding me tight as he sped up his thrusts. He slammed into me one last time, growling as he shuddered against me, coming in a hot torrent that sent me right into another spiral. I choked out his name, and he pulled out and brought his bare hand down on my ass with a crack that echoed through the trees, and I came so hard I had tears in my eyes.

## 24

# HALEY

*Y*ou're singing," Jax said as we continued walking north through the woods.

"Humming, technically. Is that a problem?" I laughed. "After all the noise we made earlier, I didn't think a little music would suddenly give away our position."

"It's not a problem. It's… cute."

Heat crept into my cheeks, and I knew I should've left it at that.

But I just couldn't help myself.

"It's… a thing I do," I confessed. "After."

"After…? You mean… oh. Oh! Well, *damn.*" He arched an eyebrow, mischief flashing in his eye. "Is that why Saint calls you—"

"Yes. Can we move on?"

He stopped and grabbed my hand, pulling me close. With a hot kiss behind my ear, he whispered, "No. I want to make you sing again."

"Too late," I teased. "You ruined the mood with all the talking."

"Let me make it up to you." He kissed his way down my neck, reaching for the zipper on the shirt I'd changed into after he'd ruined the last one. I was just about to give in, just about to let him drag me to the ground for another go, when a rustling in the trees ahead stopped us cold.

"Jax?" I whispered. "Did you—"

He clamped a hand hard over my mouth and dragged me to the ground, but not for anything fun.

"Stay here," he whispered, hot and low in my ear. "Don't make a sound. I'll be right back."

I nodded, watching with my heart in my throat as he took off in the direction of the sound. Seconds later, a young fae soldier emerged onto the path about twenty feet in front of me, stopping to scan the area.

*Shit.*

I slid the dagger from my holster. I had maybe five seconds before she spotted me.

A noise behind her caught her attention, but it was too late.

Jax was already on her. He grabbed her head, and I held my breath for the telltale pop of a snapped neck.

It never came.

The fae's arms went limp at her sides, and she dropped soundlessly to her knees, Jax crouching down behind her, still holding her head.

Even from this distance, I could tell she was beautiful. Ethereal.

Staying low, I crept a little closer.

*What the fuck is he doing?*

Suddenly, all the color drained from her face, her eyes wide with fear. I'd never seen anyone look so flat-out terrified. I wanted to run to her. To shove that demon away and save the poor creature from whatever torment he was undoubtedly inflicting.

But movement in the trees a dozen feet behind them caught my eye.

Another soldier. Female, just like the first.

She lifted her bow. Knocked an arrow. Aimed it right at Jax's head.

I didn't think. Just whipped my dagger at her, straight and true. It zinged through the air, blade over handle, and hit the mark—the soft hollow just above her collarbone.

She let out a strangled gasp, then dropped to her knees.

Jax turned around just in time to see her faceplant.

Without a second thought, he pulled a dagger from his boot and sliced his fae's throat.

"Jax!" I bolted up from the ground and ran to him, but pulled up short when I saw the fiery rage burning in his eye.

"I told you to stay *put*," he growled. "What the *fuck* were you thinking?"

*Excuse me?*

I folded my arms across my chest and took a step backward, glaring right back at him. "I'm sorry. Was that demon-speak for 'thanks for saving my ass?' Because yeah, you're welcome."

"Fuck, Haley. You killed her. You fucking killed her."

"Um…" I gestured at the dead fae at his feet. "Hello?"

"I didn't want to kill them. Leaving a trail of bodies—Midnight soldiers—is a sure way to get tracked."

"Then what the hell were you doing to her? Before you sliced and diced her, the poor thing looked like she was about thirty seconds from dying of fright."

He sighed. Glared. Waited for me to catch up, which…

*Holy. Fuck.*

"You fear-mojo'd her."

"My intention, had you let me take care of things, was to scare her so badly she'd take off, forgetting she'd ever seen us."

"And her little friend back there? Did you think she'd just wait in line for her turn?"

Jax said nothing.

"You didn't even know she was there, did you?" I asked.

Silence.

"Okay, so why did you end up killing her after all that?" I asked. "Why not let her go?"

"Because the trauma of seeing her partner assassinated might've been enough to shock her out of the fear-haze and alert the rest of her squad to our presence."

I walked around the dead fae slowly, still trying to process what I'd seen.

She really *had* looked like she was about to die of fright.

"What did you show her?" I whispered, almost afraid of the answer. "What was her worst fear? How does it even work? When we were together, I didn't… I didn't feel anything *close* to that. I mean… She was *terrified*, Jax."

He gripped my jaw and leaned in close, his grin turning cruel. "You just got front-row seats to the kind of terror a direct hit from a fear demon can unleash, and that's not even the worst I've got. Still think you can outrun your demons, angel? Or are you ready to wise up and stay the fuck away from me?"

"Fuck off." I jerked away from his touch and stalked off to go retrieve my dagger.

He grabbed my arm, hauling me back. "Leave it."

"But it's—"

"I said leave it. We need to move. Now." He held my gaze for another beat, shaking his head as if he couldn't have been more disgusted. "Before you do something *else* to give away our position."

# 25

## HUDSON

*S*tone City wasn't a city, but that's what they called it—a mountainous region dotted with caves named for the wild gargoyles who called it home. It was all part of the Dead Claw range that stretched far to the north.

It was also where my people lived. Where I'd been born.

While Jax and Haley'd had their little… *ahem*… private moment in the woods, I'd headed east for a quick flyover of the homeland. Quick, because anything out in the open like that could get you noticed *real* quick. But still, I needed to see it.

Between our current route and Stone City, I spotted a few skirmishes on the ground. I recognized the Darkwinter insignia on some of the uniforms—looked like they were making a push toward Dead Claw, probably hoping to find a way into Amaranth through the mountains, but they'd have to face the gargoyles, too. Wouldn't be an easy victory.

Keradoc's soldiers were holding them off for now, but from what I could tell, the ground was soaked with just as much Midnighter blood as Darkwinter.

Whole thing was fucked.

Once I reached Stone City, wasn't long before I started getting that feeling like I was being watched and had to double back. But I got a glimpse, which was a start. The place was still there, still just as over-crowded as I remembered. Lots of old memories, but no obvious signs of the fuckers that'd sold me out two years ago.

Not a problem. I'd track them down soon enough.

Once Haley got what she needed from Keradoc and we put her on the express train back the fuck to New Orleans? Yeah, I had some personal business to take care of here. An old score to settle. I suspected it was the same for Saint and Jax, but like I said, Midnight wasn't a group-therapy kind of place. Whatever those guys were up to, they were keeping it to themselves for now, same as me.

It would all come out eventually, though. Always did. And the longer we stayed in this place, the more we were gonna need each other again, just like old times—*that* was a fact.

But right now, the main thing that bound us was Haley. Her mission had become ours. Keeping her safe and helping her see it through was our only priority.

I'd just gotten back when I spotted her and Jax tumbling out of the woods, looking like they'd done a hell of a lot more than roll around half-naked in the dirt.

First came the demon, storming away from her like she'd just dipped his balls in kerosene and was packing a flamethrower.

Haley stalked out next—no flamethrower, but man, did she look pissed.

Still in my warrior form, I glided down and landed in front of her. Gave her a good once-over, just to make sure she wasn't bleeding or broken.

Then I just stared at her, waiting for her to spill it.

"I'm fine," she insisted, even though she wasn't.

I could wait her out, though. One thing I'd learned about Haley in our short time together? Babygirl couldn't keep it locked up for too long. Not with me. Not when something was eating her up inside.

"Okay, so I'm assuming you saw all that?" she finally said.

I shrugged and rocked my hand in a so-so gesture.

"Just... don't tell Elian, okay? I mean, not that you're... talking. But... you know. Don't leave him any notes or give him any winks or gestures."

I cocked an eyebrow. Tried not to smirk.

"It's none of his business what I do, where I do it, or who I do it with. Plus, he's just gonna go psycho on Jax, and for no reason, because there's *nothing* going on between us. And even if there *was*, why should Elian care? He's the one who ended things with me. No, I take that back. He didn't end things. He just walked away, leaving *me* to tie up all the loose ends and I... You know what, Hudson? I love talking to you, but I think it's a little early in our relationship for the post-woods, walk-of-shame, justifying-my-bad-life-choices convo."

She tried like hell to hold on to that anger, but we both knew it wasn't meant for me, and eventually, she gave up. Just lowered her eyes and shook her head, her cheeks blushing.

"Sorry, Gargs. I know you're just trying to look out for me."

I reached out. Tugged a few sticks from her hair and smoothed it out so she didn't look like such a hot, freshly fucked mess—as much as I appreciated the look.

It was a small thing, that touch. Barely anything, really. But damn, my fingers were on fire.

Frustration simmered in my blood. Just this once, I wanted the damn bond to be more. To actually mean what all the fairytales said. Mates, in every sense of the word. True partners. Lovers. Friends. The whole kit-n-caboodle, right down to the cheesy framed photos and matching monogrammed bath towels.

No idea if regular couples did that kinda shit, but if so, I was fucking in.

She pursed her lips. Shot me a look that I wanted to memorize for the rest of my immortal life, that perfect mix of sass and sweetness.

"You okay?" she asked. "You look a little… pensive. More than usual, I mean."

I forced a smile. Nodded. Turned away from her before I did something even more stupid—more dangerous—than touching her damn hair.

"Hey, will you do me a favor?" she asked. When I turned back to face her, she held out her hand and said, "Will you stay on the ground with me? Just for a little while?"

I probably shoulda left her, right then. Gestured to the sky, my duty, and taken off, keeping an eye on the path ahead, staying far above it all.

But one look into those green eyes, and my stone heart was as good as melted goo.

I took her hand, so tiny in mine, doing my best to ignore the fire shooting up my veins as we walked on in peaceful silence. Every few minutes, a light breeze would blow her hair, and the silky strands would tickle my arm, and Jax got so far ahead of us I lost sight of him completely.

We caught up with him not long after in a clearing at the base of a sheer rock face, a freshwater stream cutting through the middle. It was a good place to stop, so we set up camp and made a fire. Haley wasn't hungry for dinner—just wanted to crash.

I waited until she was tucked safely into her tent. Waited until Jax gave me the look—the *what the hell did I do?* look.

Then, with no more warning than a low growl, I slammed the fucker against the rock, hand around his neck, his feet dangling a good foot off the ground.

"Ease off," he said, more annoyed than frightened. "This shit between me and Haley has nothing to do with you."

I lifted my eyebrows. Pounded a fist into my chest, then into his, indicating our tattoos. The oath.

"You think I'd let a woman—a witch—come before my oath?" he shot back. "Saint may be a rotten fuck, Hudson, but I will *always* honor my oath. You should fucking know that by now."

I *did* know that, and his loyalty to our bond wasn't what I'd meant at all, the dumb fuck.

I pointed at the tent, then back to my chest, then his.

Haley was one of us—that's what I'd meant. She didn't need no tattoo or blood oath to prove it. It just *was*.

Eventually, the asshole got my meaning. I saw it rise in his eye like the moon, and I let him drop, shooting him one last warning glare, just to drive the point home.

"I won't hurt her," he said, his voice soft with a hint of regret. "Not again. You have my word."

I nodded, which was about all I could give him just then.

"Are you taking first watch?" he asked, rubbing his neck. He was lucky I hadn't broken it.

I shook my head and pointed at him.

Tonight, I was putting *him* on perimeter watch.

Me? I'd be keeping watch over that tent and the witch inside it, making damn sure she didn't end up with any more hurt in her eyes than the sonofabitch had already put there.

# 26

## HALEY

After a night with little sleep followed by hours of hiking in uncomfortable silence, Jax and I finally made it to the top of the White Cliffs of Oshen.

Hudson landed behind us moments later, and together, we peered out across the black expanse that led to the City of Amaranth and its imposing wall.

"Wow," I said, the sight nearly stealing my breath. "Looks like *some-one's* architect has Mordor on his inspiration board."

Jax let out the faintest laugh. I smiled in response, but didn't show it to him. He'd been a total jackass to me, so no, he wasn't getting any of my personal sunshine tonight.

*Or any of my screaming orgasms either…*

Ignoring the pulse of heat between my thighs, I turned to ask Hudson about the plan for getting over the wall.

But before I even opened my mouth, the rain started.

And it… burned?

"Um, guys? Is this normal?" I held out my hand, catching a few glowing drops. They sizzled into my palm like sparks.

"Shit! Starshowers!" Jax grabbed me and pulled me close just as Hudson stretched his massive wings over us, shielding us from the rain.

"Are they really falling stars?" I asked as the red-and-gold sparks hissed into the grass around us.

"Just a name," he said. A few of the sparks were starting to catch, igniting a series of little fires in front of us. "We can't stay here. We need to move."

"But what about the plan? How are we—"

"No time for a plan, Haley. Let's go."

"But—"

"Hudson has to take us over the wall. It's the only way. *That's* the plan, okay? So do me a favor and just... Just hold still and don't freak out."

The showers picked up in intensity, and a gust of wind sent a spray of sparks flying into my chest, a hundred points of heat biting into my skin. I patted myself down, tamping out the embers.

It was raining fire. It was fucking raining fire.

Flames surged up from the grass behind us, and without another second to waste, Hudson lifted me and Jax off the ground, tucked us in close, and took off at a run, leaping from the cliff and soaring out into the falling-star night.

I couldn't scream. Couldn't even catch my breath. All I could do was cling to Hudson's massive arm and do my best to ignore the vertigo, the bite of the starshowers nipping at my legs, and—if I was being totally honest—the thrill charging through my bloodstream at the sheer fucking wonder of it all.

Midnight was deadly and dark and terrifying, sure.

But it was also fucking amazing.

We swooped down across the abyss, skimming along the black sands before taking a sharp turn upward at Beggar's Moat, where I caught a brief glimpse of the creatures dwelling in its shadowy trench, lit up by the starshowers.

Skeletons. Shambling, shivering skeletons.

I bit back a gasp. Definitely worse than alligators.

We zoomed up Vanderham's Wall, sparks pinging off Hudson's leathery wings as he cut through the air. When we reached the top, two guards spotted us, shouting and pointing but making no move to leave the relative safety of their tower—especially not for a lone gargoyle and a couple of carry-on bags with no visible weapons.

We sailed up and over, then dropped down to street level on the other side, Hudson landing with a graceful thump.

Thankfully, the starshowers fizzled out fast. People who'd clearly just run for cover spilled out onto the streets again, dousing small fires with buckets of water that seemed to be kept on hand for just that purpose.

Jax led us through a maze of alleys to a no-name pub in the Hollow neighborhood—the rally point, he'd said. Elian would supposedly find us there.

While he went inside to check things out, Hudson and I ducked under a tin overhang, and I took a minute to catch my breath and take in my surroundings.

The city was black and craggy, as if the surrounding mountains had started crumbling and the inhabitants decided to carve out homes rather than clear away the rocks. Newer buildings had been erected too, and now the city was a mix of crumbling rock-hewn structures, sleek black skyscrapers, and a mass of single-story shacks with tin roofs, all of it thrown together with no rhyme or reason. From our spot beneath the overhang, I could just make out the rise in the city center, the castle looming at the very top.

And the people. So many people. Every supernatural race, every age, every social status—whatever that even meant in a place like Midnight.

I couldn't stop staring.

The air smelled like roasted nuts and raw meat and garbage and fire and so many different things I could scarcely separate them all. There were no cars in the streets, no modern transportation, but I spotted a few wagons drawn by demonic-looking horses, along with some rickety old bicycles and a few rickshaws for rent. It seemed that most of the city's residents got by on foot.

Everywhere I looked, magick and firelight flickered in the windows, bright eyes in a face of shadow and rock. The same light burned in the streetlamps that lined the alleys.

My own magick surged, tingling along my arms and legs, making my heart race.

Amaranth City was filthy and cramped and louder than a concert, but it was easily the most breathtaking place I'd ever seen.

And when a familiar face finally stepped out from the pub and into the flickering torchlight of the streetlamp above me, Amaranth City started to feel, inexplicably, like home.

"Elian," I breathed, my knees nearly buckling with relief.

"Glad you finally made it, sparrow. Welcome to the Hollow."

His eyes were glassy, his smile too wide.

My heart sank.

I glanced over at Jax, who'd just exited the pub behind Elian. His jaw was tight. He gave me a quick shake of his head.

*Fucking Devil's Dream.*

I had no idea whether Elian had brought a stash with him or scored one the minute he got to Amaranth City, but obviously, he'd found a way to get his fix.

Was this why he'd left camp? Not for blood, but for pills?

I blew out a deep sigh, trying not to let my disappointment—or my worry—fester.

I *hated* Elian for what he'd done to me all those years ago.

But more than that, I hated him for what he'd done to himself. For what he'd done—was *still* doing—to the man I once loved.

"So, what happens now?" I asked, if only to take my mind off everything else.

Elian flashed his cocky, crooked smirk. *That*, at least, hadn't changed. "Now, little sparrow, we go home."

---

The third-floor apartment was located inside a modern, plain black building about a block from the pub. It was a no-frills kind of place, but it was a lot more spacious than I'd expected. It looked like dozens of other apartments I'd seen in Blackmoon Bay, with plain wood flooring and white walls, minimal decor, and appliances just a little smaller than average. The entrance was off the kitchen, which opened into a common area with two fold-out couches and a small bathroom off to the side. Down a hallway at the back of the apartment, I spotted a large bedroom with its own private bathroom.

"What she lacks in elegance she makes up for in hot water, indoor plumbing, and electricity," Elian said, showing me around. "Gem managed to scrounge up some shampoo and conditioner for you—luxury items in these parts."

"Hot water?" I gasped. "*Conditioner?*" All my exhaustion drained away in an instant at the prospect of a real shower.

Jax let out a low whistle. "You must know people in high places, Saint."

"Once a deal-maker, always a deal-maker." Elian held Jax's gaze for a beat, a million unsaid words passing between them.

I had no idea how he'd managed to score such a place either, but right then, I didn't care.

"Work it out, boys." I claimed the bedroom as mine, dropped my pack on the bed, and headed right for that hot shower.

As much as I wanted to luxuriate in all my sudsy glory for the next three to five days, I also knew we had work to do. I wrapped it up quickly, then changed into a fresh set of clothes from my pack.

By the time I got back to the common area, Jax and Elian were already heading out the door.

"Where are you going?" I asked, twisting my wet hair into a bun.

"Back to the pub to meet up with Gem," Elian said. "She might have some intel on Keradoc."

"Great! I'm coming with you."

"No, you're not."

"You got me into Midnight, Elian. And Jax and Hudson got me to Amaranth City. But if I'm going to pull off a blood heist, I'll need as much information about Keradoc as I can get. Every little piece of gossip or news could end up being important later, and the more ears we have to the ground, the better our chances of picking up on something useful. So, yes. I *am* coming with you. And you're going to shut up and take it like a man, or I'm going to tell your friends about the *adorable* nickname we had for your—"

"Wow, would you look at the time?" He huffed out a nervous laugh and offered me his arm. "We'd better get going if we want to find a good table!"

I smirked at him and squeezed his arm, more than happy to gloat.

*Haley Barnes, you've still got the touch.*

## 27

ELIAN

As an immortal fae, I'd lived a lot of fucking lives. A childhood I barely remembered in the royal fae court of Autumnshire, back before we lost my brother Evander. Our family's banishment to the material realm. The darkness that eventually landed me in Blackmoon Bay, where I finally met Haley, my light. The all-too-brief years we'd shared that were still—of all the lives I'd lived before and since—my fucking favorite.

After the Bay came my first tour of Midnight.

Then New Orleans, Saints and Sinners, the empire that Jax, Hudson, and I built.

And now, I was back in Midnight once more, all of my lives converging and colliding like someone had tossed them into a blender and hit puree.

Felt like they'd tossed me right in there, too.

We sat huddled around a sticky table inside the dark, dank pub, the whole place reeking of bodies and spilled ale. It was a long way from the cool refinement of Saints and Sinners, but something about the nameless pub in the Hollow would always feel like home.

Still, I couldn't risk being recognized. Right now, Gem was the only resident of Midnight I trusted, and until I could determine otherwise, I'd be operating under the assumption that everyone else was an enemy out for blood.

I sank a little in my chair. Drew my hood low, throwing my face into shadow.

"It's so nice to finally meet you, Haley Barnes," Gem said, beaming at her. "Saint's told me almost nothing about you, a fact which speaks even louder than words."

Haley laughed, but I didn't get the joke.

"Save it, Gem," I warned. "I'm not paying you for your comedy."

"Well, you should be. I'm pretty hilarious." She laughed again and tipped back her ale, but I knew the woman. Part of it was an act—blending in, playing the easy-going party girl. Her eyes were sharp though, darting around every dark corner, cataloging every new patron that walked in and every old one that stumbled out.

Gem was one of the Midnight elite, a pureblood fae witch who could travel freely between this realm and our home realm. She could also travel freely between Keradoc's ruling class and the class of miscreants and reprobates that made up the majority of this city, which came in handy for picking up intel from both camps.

In the time I'd known her, she'd gained a reputation as a tough and loyal friend who looked out for the real people of Amaranth and did what she could to keep Keradoc's nose out of our fucking asses, which was the only reason Jax, Hudson, and I were able to get our empire off the ground and keep it running in NOLA.

She took her cut, of course, just like everyone else, but that was fair. She earned it.

And now she'd be earning a little more.

Since I'd left Midnight, she'd stepped in to fill the void, serving as the woman who could get anyone anything, anytime—for the right price.

The most valuable of her offerings?

Secrets.

"What's the word, Gem?" I asked. "I'm hearing whispers that Keradoc's losing his touch. Can't keep his territories."

She glanced around the pub, then nodded, leaning in close. "Darkwinter's got him *real* twitchy these days."

"Darkwinter?" Haley's eyes widened, her neck turning blotchy.

"Are you familiar with the bloodline?" Gem asked her.

Adrenaline spiked in Haley's blood, mingling with a hint of fear. I could smell them both, souring her.

*What the hell's got her so worked up about Darkwinter?*

"Somewhat familiar," she replied cautiously. "My allies and I recently fought some of them in Blackmoon Bay. They'd been working with human hunters to hybridize supernaturals and create large-scale magickal weapons."

"Fuck, Haley." My gut clenched, guilt surging anew, reminding me just how much of Haley's life I'd missed.

Did this fight have anything to do with her debt to Melantha? With the reason she was here now?

"It's all good." Haley shrugged, forcing a smile. "We nailed the bastards and shut down the entire operation, but... Yeah. Darkwinter left a bad taste."

"Well, we've got ourselves an infestation here," Gem continued. "They've been spilling over our borders like bog roaches, mowing down Keradoc's troops faster than he can keep up. I just heard they took the Hanging Lake and the Road of Silence."

"Seriously?" Jax asked. "How'd they manage that?"

"No idea. They're allegedly moving in from the sea, too. Got some kind of crazy powerful ships."

"You think they're poised to take over?" I asked. "Turn this place into a Darkwinter satellite realm?"

"If I were Keradoc?" She nodded and lifted her glass. "That's what'd be keeping *me* up at night."

We shot the shit a little longer about the perils of Darkwinter, the festering lands of Midnight that were quickly falling under their control.

But Haley had gone completely silent after her comment about the fight in the Bay, her heart still fluttering like a trapped bird.

I leaned in close. "You okay? You don't look so hot."

"What?" She turned to me and plastered on a smile. "No. I mean, yes, I'm fine. I'm just... You know, I think I'll head back to the apartment. I should probably... practice some of my spells." She rose from her chair and nodded at Gem. "Nice to meet you, Gem. Thanks again for finding us the apartment."

"Anytime, hon. You need help getting back?"

"I'll take her," Jax said.

I didn't want to make a big deal about her leaving, but what the hell? After the fight she'd put up about coming with us, now she was ready to call it a night?

Something was definitely going on with her, and I was pretty sure it had to do with Darkwinter and the shit she'd gone through back in the Bay.

Shit I should've been able to help her with, but couldn't, because I'd fucking bailed on her to come to this hellhole and...

I blew out a breath. "I need another drink. You good?"

"I could use one too," Gem said. "But let me get it. You stay here, Mr. Low Profile."

By the time she fought her way through the crowd at the bar, Jax had returned.

We settled back into the Darkwinter convo again, but then out of nowhere, she said, "So, Jax. You gonna look up Oona while you're here?"

My heart almost seized in my fucking chest.

"Gem," I hissed. "Oona… She died."

Last thing we fucking needed was Jax tripping down memory lane. I needed him focused on Haley, not on the past.

Gem's face paled. "Died? But—"

"I saw it happen," I said. "Killed by her own father's guards. Fucking sick."

I felt Jax's eye burning right through me.

*Fuck.*

"I… I'm so sorry," Gem said, sounding genuinely astonished. "I had no idea."

"You know, I've been meaning to ask you about that night again, Saint," Jax said cooly. "Now that we're back at the scene of the crime, so to speak."

He flashed a grin that cut right to the bone.

Before he could spit out his question, I clamped a hand over his shoulder and said, "We've been over this, Jax. Oona's dead. Keradoc ordered the hit. How many more times do you need to hear it?"

"As many as it takes until I'm convinced you're not lying to me."

"Trust me, brother. You do *not* want to go chasing after ghosts. Not in this city."

"Maybe I fucking do." Jax pushed back his chair and got to his feet. "Good to see you again, Gem."

"Fuck you going?" I asked him.

He didn't answer. Just glared at me with the all-seeing eye, then took off.

"There's something you're not telling him about Oona," Gem said once he was gone. "Spill it."

With a grin, I picked up my mug and dumped some ale onto the floor, knowing damn well that's not what she'd meant by "spill it."

"For Oona of Midnight," I said anyway. "May she rest in peace."

Gem scoffed at me, but when it was clear I had nothing more to say on the matter, she let it go.

"All right, Saint. I've held out long enough. Time for you to tell me what you're *really* doing in Midnight, and why the hell you're asking me so many questions about Keradoc."

I finished my drink. Set down the mug. Looked hard into her eyes. "We need to get close to him, Gem. Tell me how to fucking do it."

A slow smile stretched across her face, lighting her up like the moons in the pitch-black sky. "Oh, I've got just the thing for you, Saint. And I've been waiting for a chance to see you and the boys in tuxes for a *long* time."

## 28

## HUDSON

*a*fter a shower, I headed into the common area wearing nothing but sweatpants, thinking I'd have the place to myself for a bit.

But Haley was sitting on the floor, surrounded by potted plants and a few vials of blood and a bunch of them sharp knives she loved so much. The space was filled with candles, and a pentacle glowed on the bare wooden planks in front of her.

"Practicing," she explained when she caught me watching her. "Sorry if it's a little… extra. Then again, it's not like I ever claimed to be anything else, so… Working as designed?" She shrugged and wrinkled her nose, and I grinned, real big this time. She brought it outta me like no one else could.

"So, bare chest and gray sweatpants, huh?" She took in the sight of me, her eyes roving down to my bare feet and back up again. "*Now* who's casting dark magick?"

*Anyone casting spells around here, babygirl, it's you.*

Ignoring her sinful little smirk, I grabbed two beers from the fridge, handed one to her, then took my favorite spot on the couch.

"You want some company up there?" she asked, already getting to her feet.

I shot her a look, like, *Do you really need to ask?* Then patted the spot next to me.

She curled up beside me, tucking her legs up, but I grabbed her feet and pulled her legs across my lap. I liked having her close. Liked being able to keep in contact—made me feel better about all the things outside these walls trying to hurt her, like maybe I could actually keep her safe from some of them.

"I was out with those guys earlier," she said, sipping her beer. "Trying to get some intel on Keradoc from Elian's… friend. Gem?"

I nodded. Gem and I went way back, even before Saint was in the picture. I knew they'd gotten close during his time here, so if Saint thought we could trust her on this mission? Then I backed him. After all, she'd helped us get out of this place when my ass was on the line. I'd always be grateful for that.

"She seems smart," Haley said. "Really knows her way around the streets, you know? I respect that."

She gazed down into her beer bottle. Ran her thumb up and down the neck.

I tugged on a lock of her hair. Smirked at her when she finally looked up.

"*What?* I'm not jealous. I'm just… cautious. New people… It's hard to trust, you know? Especially with something so important to me."

Yeah, I couldn't argue with her there. Trusting the wrong people had nearly cost me my life.

We sat in silence for a while, listening to the sounds of the city outside —fighting, mostly. Glass shattering. Thunder in the distance, though it was muted compared to the rest.

When I looked over at her again, I found her staring at the tattoos on my chest, mesmerized.

I curled my arm and flexed, and the sweetest blush crept into her cheeks.

"Sorry," she said. "I'm just… You're covered. And they're fucking incredible." She reached for my shoulder, fingers hovering just over the tattoo that took up most of my upper arm—two daggers crossing beneath an eye. "May I? I've always been fascinated by tattoos. Well, that and scars. I kind of see them as two sides of the same coin. Scars are the stories of the things that happened *to* us, things that were chosen *for* us. But tattoos are the stories we choose for ourselves. Both can be beautiful. A record of our lived experiences, you know?"

I leaned into her, and she brushed her fingers over my skin, making me shiver.

Her touch was… fucking indescribable.

The gray sweatpants suddenly seemed like a real bad choice.

But Haley wasn't paying attention to the situation in my lap. She was tracing the lines of my tattoos—my stories. The daggers and the eye. The raven gryphon feather. The triple crescent moons. The fleur-de-lis I'd gotten when we'd first ended up in New Orleans. The weeping skull with its mouth full of roses.

*Blood before roses,* it said beneath.

"I've only got a couple of tattoos," she said, and held out her wrist.

I ran my thumb along the writing tattooed there, bisecting the long, vertical scar. I'd noticed it that first day in Saint's garden, but hadn't been close enough to read it until now.

"This too shall pass," she said, soft and slow, like maybe she needed to hear it again.

Haley sighed.

I swiped a thumb across her cheek, erasing the tear that'd slipped out.

"I got it after… the bathtub incident," she said softly. "I wanted the reminder that pain like that doesn't last forever. But over time, I started taking it as a reminder that peace and joy don't last forever, either. Maybe that sounds morbid, but I find it comforting. It makes me appreciate everything a whole hell of a lot more than I used to because I know nothing is guaranteed. Not love, not health, not money, not friendship. But that doesn't make those things any less valuable, you know? In some ways, it feels even *more* valuable because it's fleeting, and…" She rolled her eyes and grinned. "Okay, I'm doing it again. Babbling your ears off."

I smiled at her and shook my head, letting her know I didn't mind. Matter fact, I could've listened to her babbling my ears off for another few centuries at least. Maybe even longer.

"Hudson, can I ask you something?"

I set my beer on the end table. Tucked a lock of hair behind her ear.

"How is it that we're in the most dangerous place in the universe," she said, "yet I've never felt so safe anywhere than I do right here? With you?"

I flexed my biceps for her again, and she laughed.

But just as quickly as the laugh had sprung up, it died, and a whole mess of tears spilled from her eyes.

I drew her close, wrapped her up in a hug.

A tremor rolled through her body, and I tightened my hold, wishing I could take away her pain. That I could go back in time, hunt down all them motherfuckers who'd ever put a crack or dent in her heart, and tear the flesh right off their bones.

But I knew Saint would be on that list.

And hell, maybe she'd be on his list too.

Sometimes things just got to a point with people where blame no longer served a purpose. Everyone was suffering the same damn misery.

Haley blew out a shaky sigh and pulled back, smiling at me once again. "Not only do I feel completely safe with you, but you're also the guy who gets me to reveal my deepest secrets and ball my eyes out, all without saying a word. Oprah could learn a thing or two from you, Gargs."

She tried another smile, but once again, it dropped right off her face.

This time when the tears started, she blinked them away, refusing to let another one fall.

She musta seen the worry on my face.

"I'm okay," she insisted, trying for another smile. "It's all good."

I touched her wrist tattoo again, and she nodded.

"Exactly. It'll pass, right? Always does. No point in falling apart over it."

I shook my head and frowned.

"Okay, it's... not all good? It's terrible and awful and we should probably just throw ourselves into Beggar's Moat and save fate the trouble?"

I shot her a stern glare and pressed my finger to her lips, and she nodded and quieted down, like she knew I needed a minute to gather my thoughts.

Just then, I felt like I needed an hour. A lifetime, and I still wouldn't have known how to do this.

I cupped her face, my big hands nearly swallowing her up. My heart thudded in my chest, blood rushing to my ears, the whole room going a little fuzzy.

Back in New Orleans, Haley had come to me—trusted me with her secrets—before she'd even known I was a real man. But that day in Saint's garden out back, something told me she sensed I was listening anyway.

Now, I knew she was listening to *me*.

Most people, when they encountered someone who didn't talk much... Well, most of them just started ignoring you after a while. Like, if you couldn't entertain them with your jokes and stories, if you couldn't ask them questions about their oh-so-fascinating lives, if you couldn't brag about how much money you had in the bank or what kind of car you drove, you weren't worth their time.

Haley was different, though. She listened to me in different ways—in all the subtle ways most people didn't bother with—like maintaining eye contact and noticing body language and being okay to just hang out in the silence together.

She always seemed to know what I needed.

Just like I always seemed to know what she needed.

She was mine to protect. If she needed *anything*—a hug, a loan, a kidney, a place to hide a fucking body—I was all over it.

Right then, with her still half-trembling in my arms, I knew the thing she needed most was for someone to tell her everything was gonna be okay, and mean it. To remind her that she didn't have to face the harsh world alone.

And suddenly, after more years than I could remember, I no longer wanted to just write it down on the back of a receipt. I wanted to taste the fucking words in my mouth. And I wanted to give those words to her—in my own voice.

I swallowed hard. Pressed one of her hands to my heart, still holding her face.

Another tear slipped down her cheek.

I took a deep breath.

And I opened my mouth.

"It's okay, babygirl," I said. "I got you."

The words rumbled through my chest, deep and gravelly, the sound of my old voice a shock to my ears. If I didn't know any better, I would've sworn there was another man in the room.

But it was just me and Haley, all alone in the candlelight, her eyes going so wide I saw the flames dancing in them.

This time when she smiled, it stuck.

"Hudson," she whispered, "thank you."

And I knew it wasn't just for the message, but for the words. For sharing them with her like some precious gift.

I kissed her forehead and pulled her back into my arms, and she snuggled in close like the whole fucking world could go to shit and it wouldn't matter, not a damn bit, so long as I kept my promise.

"I got you," I said again, only a whisper this time, because like she'd said—sometimes a fleeting thing was all the sweeter. "So fall apart if you need to, 'cause I *swear* I ain't letting you go."

**29**

## HALEY

$\mathcal{I}$ woke up in my bed a few hours later, half-smothered by a sleeping, tattooed giant in gray sweatpants.

It took a few minutes to extricate myself. My big teddy bear looked so sweet and peaceful, snoring lightly and taking up most of my bed, I didn't want to wake him. Something told me it was the first time he'd slept in a long time.

I closed the door softly, then crept into the kitchen, unable to help the smile that spread on my face.

Until I found Elian standing at the counter, arms crossed over his chest, glowering at me like he'd just discovered I'd eaten his leftovers and had been waiting hours to ambush me.

"Sleep well?" he practically grumbled. His jaw ticked, and his pupils were large and glassy.

Technically, there was no morning in Midnight, but it still felt too early for a little wake-'n-bake with the Devil.

I blew out a breath. I no longer had a say in Elian's choices—if I ever really did.

He kept on glaring at me, though, which was getting annoying.

Forcing myself not to roll my eyes, I said, "If you're not careful, Elian, you'll infect this whole city with your joyful attitude, and the next thing you know, they'll be painting rainbows and unicorns on the wall and breaking out in musical numbers in the streets. Is Jax back yet?"

"Why?" he snapped. "Worried he'll find out who you spent the night with, *angel*?"

"Okay, first of all? Don't call me that. Secondly, it's none of your business who I spent the night with. The only thing I want to hear out of your mouth next is confirmation that Gem stocked this place with coffee, or I can't make any more guarantees about your personal safety."

Elian turned his back on me to mess with something on the counter. When he faced me again, he held out a steaming mug of black coffee that called to my very soul. I hadn't even noticed the coffeepot behind him.

I took the mug with a nod of thanks and a genuine smile. Elian almost smiled back.

After a few sips, I leaned back against the counter next to him and said, "After we left you guys last night, Jax told me he was going up to the city center to dig up some more dirt on Keradoc. I figured he'd be back by now."

"Haven't seen him," he said. He shifted to stand right in front of me—all the better to glare down at me with those judgy silver eyes. "Haley? Honestly. What are you doing with Hudson?"

I took a few gulps of fortifying coffee, then grinned. "Oh, that's easy! If you head on over to Wikipedia and look up the entry for… What was it called again?" I tapped my lips. "Oh, right! Even More Shit That's None of Elian's Fucking Business. Can you spell all that, or should I write it down for you? I don't want you to miss out—it's a good entry. It'll save you from wasting your breath asking me shit like this."

He stepped close to me, crowding me against the countertop, his bergamot-and-rain scent making my heart rate kick up even more than the fresh jolt of caffeine.

Another second of *that* stupidly sexy nonsense and I couldn't even hold his gaze anymore—just dropped mine into my mug, grateful I had something else to focus on.

"It's the worst of the worst who end up in Midnight," Elian said, his voice low.

"Jax told me Hudson was born here."

"Doesn't mean he isn't just as bad as the rest of us. Or worse."

I laughed. "Oh, yes. Hudson's a real monster, all right."

"Haley—"

"As hard as it is to believe, some guys really *are* genuinely kind and sweet."

"And some are just good at putting on a show."

I patted his chest. "And thanks to all of *yours*, I've developed a keen bullshit detector. So, as much as I appreciate your opinion about my bedroom companions—which is not at all—I don't need a babysitter."

"I'm just telling you to be careful. I know you guys are getting close, and that's fine. Just don't piss him off. He's not—"

"If he's so big and bad, why is he even here?" I finally glanced up at him again. "I thought you trusted him. You said he'd always have my back."

"Yeah, within the parameters of this mission—protecting you and getting you in and out of Midnight. How was I supposed to know you two would get cozy?"

"You're being ridiculous."

"Really? Do you ever wonder why a thousand-something-year-old gargoyle looks like he could be the frontman of a motorcycle club?"

"His lifestyle choices have nothing to do with—"

"It's not a lifestyle choice, Haley. It's basic mythology. When a human dies by a gargoyle's hands—either by outright murder or by the neglect of his duty—the gargoyle incorporates part of that human's soul into his own, kind of like an atonement. He carries it with him for the rest of his eternal life. Hudson's whole big, burly teddy bear thing you love so much? That's not entirely *his*."

"You're saying he's just… acting out some other guy's life? A guy he *killed*?"

"No, he's not acting. His thoughts are his own, his values, the man he is at his core. But certain aspects of his personality, the way he looks and dresses, the way his words form into thoughts, the way he'd talk if he could... It's hard to explain, but a lot of what you're seeing and reacting to is essentially a piece of someone else."

"A piece of… someone he killed?"

"Not *someone*. *All* the ones. Including some you haven't seen yet. And *that's* what worries me, Haley. The ones you haven't seen. Because some of those aspects are downright—"

"Again. You're being ridiculous."

"I'm just telling you your sweet little cuddle-buddy isn't all he's cracked up to be, and all I ask is that you be a little smarter about that."

I shook my head. Nothing Elian had said would change the way I felt about Hudson. If this soul-incorporating thing was part of gargoyle mythology, then it was all just part of what made Hudson who he was—a friend I'd come to care about. One I trusted with my life.

One who was probably as tired of Elian's bullshit as I was.

"What are you doing?" I asked.

"Trying to protect you from—"

"No. You're not acting like a concerned friend. You're acting like a jealous ex. All this stuff about Hudson? You know damn well he'd never hurt me, no matter what kind of soul-mashup he's got inside. You're just pissed because you think I slept with him."

He huffed. "Didn't you?"

"Literally, yes. As in, I curled up against his chest, with all my clothes on, and fell asleep. And it was the best night's rest I've had since we got here, so please prepare yourself, because it might just happen again, and I wouldn't want you to get all hyper-protective and vamp out on me over—"

"For fuck's sake." He finally broke away from me, giving me some much-needed air, but it was only so he could reach into his pocket for another little black pill.

It was the first I'd seen one up close, tiny and unassuming, and I watched with fascination as he pressed it to his tongue, magick swirling briefly in his mouth before he snapped it shut and swallowed.

When he looked at me again, the tension had left his jaw, his eyes turning even darker and more glazed than before.

He was killing himself. Fucking killing himself, one little pill at a time.

Anger flared inside, but I tamped it down.

In so many ways, I understood him. That urge. That sliding scale between desperately wanting to live, desperately wanting to die, and the dead center of not really caring one way or the other.

When I'd met Elian, we were both closer to the center. But now, it felt like he was sliding toward that black edge where he might just decide— one night when no one was watching—to hurry things along.

Elian didn't know just how close he'd driven me to that very same, very dark edge—and he didn't need to.

But I wasn't about to let him fall over it now.

"Do you want to die?" I asked.

He offered a lazy, crooked grin. "Do you want me to die?"

"Why do you do it?"

"All part of the fantasy, sparrow. You should try it—might help take the edge off if you escaped your reality once in a while. Might make you a little less uptight."

"You think I don't know how to escape reality?" A bitter laugh hissed through my lips. "It's ironic that you ended up in the fantasy-dealing business, Elian. That people actually *pay* you for this shit. Me? I never needed a pill or fae illusions or the thrall of a vampire. I spent so much time making up fantasies about *you*, half the time I couldn't even remember what was real."

"Yeah?" Guilt flickered in his eyes. His smile faded. He stepped closer. "What kind of fantasies?"

"All different kinds. Sometimes the one where I woke up and found you in bed, just like always, and realized my life without you was only a bad dream. Other times it was the fantasy where you came home to me, telling me you'd finally remembered our life together after being in a coma for five years. There was the one where I'd be in a restaurant with some other guy, and you'd walk through the door and see me there, and you'd fall to your knees and beg me to forgive you and take you back." Emotion rose in my chest as all those old, useless dreams came rushing back. "Then there was the most painful one. The one I distracted myself with for hours on end, forgetting to eat, to shower, to sleep."

Elian swallowed hard. Reached up and tucked a lock of hair behind my ear, his glassy-eyed gaze turning soft. Sad. "Which fantasy was that, sparrow?"

"The one where you'd never even left me at all."

A tear slid down my cheek, and Elian followed it with his fingertip, lingering on the corner of my mouth.

"Three-thirty-three in the morning," I whispered. "It's the loneliest time in the world, Elian. When the rest of the city is asleep and you're wandering your own house like a fucking ghost. Do you have any idea how many three-thirty-threes I suffered through? Staring out the window onto the dark streets of Blackmoon Bay, trying to walk backward through time in search of the *one* thing I could've done differently, the *one* thing I could've said to make you stay?"

He cupped my face with both hands, his breath warm on my lips, sickly sweet from the drugs.

"I'm sorry," he whispered. "I never meant… I'm so sorry."

"Those were my fantasies," I said. "They gave me hope. And let me tell you something. Hope? It's a drug worse than your Devil's Dream. A drug that causes delusions so powerful, you re-route your whole life around them until all you have left are the bullshit stories you tell yourself just to get through another day." I closed my eyes and leaned into his touch, stealing a little of its warmth. "Those fantasies were killing me. So, I came up with a new one."

"Tell me," he whispered.

I opened my eyes. The guilt etched into his face was nearly over-powering.

I didn't want to carry it for him. Not a single ounce.

"The one where you *died*," I said. "Every other fantasy got locked in a box, because they were too painful to deal with. And now I'm standing here watching you pop your little pills and you're looking at me like that and we both know *damn* well I'm still in love with you—I always will be. But all I can think is… All I can think is that I wish it were true. I wish you really *had* died. Because grieving for a corpse is a hell of a lot easier than grieving for a man who's standing right in front of you, disappearing a little more each night." More tears fell, and I swiped at them hard. "So that's all I've got left for you, Elian. All the blood. All the broken pieces. The fucking mess. Take a good look, because this is the *last* time I'm shedding a tear for you."

He stared at me in silence, but didn't take too long to recover. He moved in close once again, pushing me against the counter, sucking all the air out of the room.

"You wished me dead, sparrow?" he breathed, looming over me. "Well guess what? I *was* dead. I died the night I walked out on you." He fisted my hair, his hips pinning me in place, the heat of his body radiating through his clothes and straight into my skin. "You want me on my knees? You want me to bleed for you? Fine. Here it is. I was a dead man. A fucking ghost. Then out of nowhere, you walked into my bar with your vampire stakes and your green eyes and that hot little lace dress, and for the first time in five fucking years, my heart started beating again. Damn near thought I was having a heart attack. You tell me you still love me? Fuck, Haley. I'd give *you* the last fucking breath from my lungs if it came down to it. But I can't. No matter how badly I want to, I just can't. So you go on pretending I'm dead if it helps you get through the night, but don't for a *second* think you're the only one staring out that window at three-thirty-three, wondering what the fuck you could've done to change things."

He didn't let me go. Didn't back up. Just kept standing there with his hands in my hair and his body so close I could feel his heart banging against his chest, could see my own reflection in the depths of those bottomless black pupils.

His gaze swept down to my lips, and he lowered his mouth to mine, the barest brush of a kiss…

A noise on the stairwell, and a second later, the kitchen door swung open.

Jax.

Elian closed his eyes. Slipped away from me.

And I went right on back to wishing he was already dead.

# 30

## JAX

he tension in the kitchen was as thick as the Fog of a Thousand Knives, and one look at Haley and Saint told me it was probably just as deadly, too.

They broke apart immediately, but neither one of them said a word. Just kept stealing glances at each other when they thought the other wasn't watching.

Something churned in my gut like battery acid, but I wasn't about to name it. Not now.

"Everything okay?" Haley asked, putting on a bright smile. I would've loved to bask in it, but it wasn't her real smile. Didn't even light up her eyes, which I could see now were rimmed in red.

*Fucking Saint.*

What the hell had he done to her this time?

I glared at him, but one look into those eyes told me he was so far into the Black, he probably couldn't even hold a conversation.

Ignoring him, I headed to the small kitchen table and set down my bag, retrieving the box from inside and handing it to Haley.

This time, I got a glimpse of the real smile, which made some of that battery acid evaporate.

"What's this?" she asked.

"This," I said, "is demon-speak for thanks for saving my ass. Something I should've said a while ago. But don't get your hopes up, angel. It's not an engagement ring."

She cracked up. "Glad you clarified that. For a minute there, I saw a box the size of a swordfish and got excited. For a ring, I mean. Not actual swordfish. Which, come to think of it, I haven't had in—"

"Haley?"

"Yeah?"

"Open the box."

She let out a little squeal, then popped the lid.

As soon as she saw the dagger inside, she gasped, removing it and wrapping her hand around the bone handle, turning it to inspect the blade. "This is gorgeous, Jax. *Way* better than a ring."

I laughed. "Yeah, well. I know it sucked when we had to leave yours behind. Soon as I saw this one, I wanted you to have it."

"It's perfect. Look at the detailing on the blade! And the weight… It's like it was made for me."

"There's a sheath in the bag, too. Should fit on your current holster, but if not, we can get you something else."

"Thank you. I love it!"

My chest puffed up. Couldn't be helped. "Yeah?"

"Seriously? Best present ever. Hands down."

Her eyes were all sparkly again, her cheeks pink, all evidence of the earlier tears gone.

The fact that I'd even noticed as much? Probably a warning sign, but I didn't care.

Haley was right that first night at camp. I *did* like her.

I watched her now, the smile curving her lips, the light in her eyes, and a feeling of rightness settled over me.

I'd come back to Midnight not just because Saint had dragged me into another of his epic fucking messes, but because I thought it would give me a chance to finally find some fucking answers. Answers about the night Oona died—about Saint's version of events that'd never quite added up.

But all night, as I'd walked the alleys of the city that'd claimed the woman I'd once loved, all I could think about was the woman I'd left at the apartment back in the Hollows.

My angel of darkness.

Oona's death had damn near destroyed me, and after years of chasing the ghosts of all those unanswered questions, after years of nurturing a festering rage at the unjustness of it all, Haley Barnes had taken me completely off guard.

She'd snuck up on me. Her laugh, her fire, the taste of her kiss, the feel of her fevered touches in the corpsevine field, the sound of her moans as I'd made her come for me…

I didn't know what the fuck it all meant, if anything. But right then, staring at her in our kitchen in the Hollow, I knew I wanted more.

More than just a mission.

More than just a roll in the corpsevine.

More than I'd ever admit to anyone—even her.

*Especially* her.

"Thank you so much, Jax," she said now, stretching up on her toes and kissing my cheek.

I sighed and ran my hand down her back, my thumb grazing the soft skin that peeked out beneath the hem of her T-shirt.

Saint, who'd gone so still and silent I'd forgotten he was even in the room, groaned. "While you were out on your little shopping spree, Jax, *I* actually managed to find some useful intelligence."

Still holding Haley in my arms, I glared at him, shocked he could even use the word 'intelligence' in a sentence, given how stoned he was.

"So, if you don't *mind*," he continued, rolling his eyes, "I'm much more interested in discussing Keradoc than watching you fondle my ex."

"So don't watch," Haley said, flashing me a devious little grin that had my cock twitching.

*Damn it.* All I wanted to do was drag her ass into that bedroom and make up for the two days we'd wasted avoiding each other.

But if Saint had found good intel on Keradoc, we needed to hear it.

"Out with it," I said.

"The Feast of Midnight," he said with a flourish. "Also known as the Feast of the Beast. Also known as our best shot at getting up close and personal with the warlord we so know and love."

"Also known as a thing that hasn't happened in years," I said. "They don't do the feasts anymore."

"Ah, but they do!" Saint beamed. "Resurrected from the dead for one night only, and it's happening in less than two weeks."

"What's the Feast of Midnight?" Haley asked.

"Some bullshit party the ruler of Midnight throws to convince the people he gives a shit about them," I said. "It's the only time his castle is open to the public."

"Concurrently," Saint added, "he hosts a soiree for the upper-crust. Very exclusive, invite-only, lots of ass-kissing and deal-making. Those rich bastards are the only ones who'll get anywhere near Keradoc. They don't even host the parties on the same floors."

"So, what are you thinking?" I asked, my interest definitely piqued. "Can we bypass security? Have Hudson get us in from the top, maybe?"

"Not a chance. The place will be crawling with soldiers. The main floor is one thing—they'll be admitting every criminal and murderer from the Hollow to the Sea. But the exclusive party? Fourth-floor ballroom. And *no* one's getting up there without an invite."

I nodded, seeing right where this was headed. "You've already talked to Gem about this."

"She's already working on my list."

"What's on the list?" Haley asked.

"Two tuxes, three forged tickets to the soiree of the century, weapons to be strategically placed ahead of time by the most disloyal castle staff money can buy, a formal gown with easy access to said weapons and the ability to conceal a contraption that can extract someone's blood without that person's awareness. Oh, and the contraption itself—we obviously need that. Let's see... Floor plans for the castle, a list of additional guards and servants open to bribes, no less than three escape routes... Yeah, I think that about covers it. Oh! I forgot to ask her about shoes." He pulled a notebook out of his back pocket and scribbled it down, along with a few other notes.

"Pretty sure you're missing a tux and a ticket," Haley said.

"Hudson doesn't need one. He'll keep watch from the roof. If hell breaks loose, he'll swoop in and... well, break it looser. And whisk us out of there in a flash of those glorious wings and talons." Saint spread his hands like a magician revealing his final trick.

"You make it sound so easy," Haley said.

"The logistics are always easy. It's the execution that fucks people." He flashed the crooked grin that'd closed more deals and sealed more fates than there were stars in the Midnight sky, then returned his attention to his notebook, frantically scribbling once again. "Fortunately for us, I'm an *expert* at not getting fucked."

Haley and I exchanged a glance, both biting back a laugh.

Then, leaving Saint to his maniacal plotting, Haley grabbed her new dagger, and we snuck off to the bedroom to execute a few plans of our own.

# 31

## HALEY

$\mathcal{N}$o sooner had Jax peeled me out of my T-shirt and closed his hot mouth around my nipple did my bedroom door crack open, ushering in a sliver of light and a vampire-fae who seemed determined to piss me off.

We'd been sniping at each other for a week straight, ever since we'd started planning for the Feast of Midnight heist. First, it was an argument about the best way to infiltrate the party and get close to Keradoc, and wasn't there a way I could just steal his blood without actually touching him? From a safe distance across the room, perhaps? Then Elian decided I wasn't spending enough time practicing my blood spells. The asshole had even picked a fight about whether the gown Gem had procured for me would draw too much attention and blow our cover.

*Yes, friends and colleagues, a little side-boob-and-shoulder combo is all it takes to raise the alarms of Midnight. I sure hope the embroidered potato sack I ordered as backup will arrive in time!*

Idiot.

So forgive me, Father, for feeling less than hospitable while my jerky ex-boyfriend crashed my private party with my demon lover, but…

What the fuck did he want to fight about now?

"Haley, look," Elian said, his voice low and serious. "We need to talk. There's something you need to know."

Jax and I froze in the bed. Apparently, Elian hadn't noticed I was otherwise occupied, which shouldn't have surprised me. Elian was a selfish prick who rarely noticed anything unless it had to do with him, and those pills had put a serious damper on his vampire senses.

"A little busy right now," I finally said.

"Busy? But you're... oh. *Fuck*," he muttered, finally figuring it out. "I should've known."

"You should've *knocked*," I said. "What do you want?"

"I told you, I need to talk to you."

"*Busy*," I said again. I rolled onto my hip to face him. Jax drew closer from behind, lips hot on my bare shoulder, hand sliding invitingly around my hip and down between my thighs, teasing me through my panties. Only a thin sheet covered us—all that kept our intruder from getting a full show.

"You expect me to wait?" Elian asked, annoyance darkening his tone.

"She's worth it," Jax said, taunting him. "But you'll have to take a number—assuming she'll have you at all."

Elian let out a hollow laugh. "Didn't peg you as the share-and-share-alike type, brother."

Jax's fingers tightened possessively on my hip, but he shrugged and said, "Her bed, her rules."

"I need to talk to Haley."

"She's a little busy at the moment. Maybe try back in an hour?"

"I'll wait."

"You sure about that?" Jax kissed the back of my neck, his fingers skating lower, just behind the top edge of the lace.

I tried not to shiver.

Elian folded his arms across his chest and leaned back against the door. That asshole fae wasn't going anywhere. Not until he got his way, which I wasn't about to give him.

So, dropping all pretense of modesty, I slid out of Jax's hold, hopped out of bed, and waltzed right over to him.

Staring him down in nothing but my black lace G-banger, I folded my arms under my bare breasts and said, "What was it you needed to talk to me about, Elian? The weather? Tomorrow's breakfast options? My shoe selection for the party? Or are you here to warn me about my poor choices in men?"

Elian swallowed hard, his gaze locked on mine, cold and impassive. There was no hiding the hitch in his breath, though. The flare of his nostrils as he took in the scent of my bare skin.

There was no hiding the resulting throb of desire between my thighs, either, but like I said—we were well past the pretense of modesty.

"I told you I'd *wait*," he ground out. "So go ahead and get back to… whatever it is you're doing."

"Whatever it is I'm doing? Really? Is it unclear what I'm doing? Did you need a diagram or something?"

A buck-naked Jax joined me by the door, stepping up behind me and placing his hands on my hips, his hard cock nudging me. Kissing the sensitive spot behind my ear, he said softly, "A live demo could also be arranged."

I glared at Elian, my heart pounding as his rain-and-bergamot scent collided with Jax's smoke-and-lemons. I felt like I was caught between a storm and a fire. I didn't know which would kill me first.

Elian glared right back at me, his eyes flashing in the darkness, pupils nearly blown from the Dream, his breath quickening. A low growl rumbled in his chest, the warning of an apex predator.

He wasn't going to back down.

I closed my eyes. Tried to calm the frantic beat of my heart. Tried to talk myself into kicking Elian out, bolting the door, and climbing right back into bed with Jax as if we'd never been interrupted in the first place.

But deep down, where all my darkest truths lived, another secret rose to the surface:

I didn't *want* Elian to back down. I wanted him to watch. I wanted him to burn for me the same way I still burned for him.

Jax nipped my earlobe, then dragged his hot mouth down my neck and across my shoulder, one hand sliding up to cup my breast, the other gliding down over the front of my panties.

I leaned my head back as he tugged my nipple, my eyes opening just a fraction, my body relaxing into the pleasure of his touch. Through a heavy, half-lidded haze, I watched Elian's vicious gaze rove down my body, heat rising in its wake.

A quiet moan escaped my lips, and Jax slid his hand lower between my thighs, cupping me and rubbing the lace. It scraped against my clit, making me gasp.

"You're so wet, angel," he breathed, increasing the pressure. "Do you like it when he watches me touch you?"

"I'm… I don't know. It's… I'm just…"

*Oh, God…*

My entire body tingled, my skin hot, nerves buzzing with anticipation. But…

Was I even *allowed* to like this? Elian was my ex—one I still had intense, complicated feelings for. Jax was his friend—sort of. One I was also developing feelings for, and they didn't exactly get along. What Jax and I did behind closed doors was one thing, but this? Letting Jax drive me wild while Elian stood by and watched? Knowingly tormenting the man I'd once promised my heart?

It *had* to be wrong.

Didn't it?

"He's a vampire," Jax whispered, teasing my nipple to a hard point, his fingers moving harder and faster over the panties. "He already knows your answer. He can hear your heartbeat. Feel the rush of blood through your veins." He bit my neck, then kissed a searing hot path back up to my ear. In a low, hot murmur, he said, "The scent of your sweet pussy is making him drunker than all the little black pills in the realm."

"Jax," I breathed, though I couldn't tell whether my soft sigh was a warning to stop… or a plea to keep going.

He released my breast and grabbed my hair, fisting it so tight it made my eyes water.

*Fuck, yes…*

"Look at him, angel. Look at what you're doing to him." His mouth was still close to my ear, breath hot on my skin. "Now, I'm going to fuck you. Right here. And unless you say otherwise, he's going to stand there and watch while I make you come all over your demon's cock. Isn't that right, Saint Elian?"

I almost came right there. His dirty mouth, his hot breath, the sudden heat rising in Elian's eyes…

Holy fuck, I'd never been so turned on in my life.

I met Elian's gaze again, the fire in his eyes a reflection of the same fire burning in me, white-hot and all-consuming. Destructive. Chaotic.

Unstoppable.

Elian didn't say a word. Just clenched his fists at his sides, his jaw so tight he was nearly trembling.

He could've left, I reminded myself. Could've turned around, opened that door, and walked right out.

But he didn't.

"Yes," I finally whispered, answering for both of us.

Jax tore my panties off so fast, the lace burned my hips. He brought them to his face and inhaled, then stuffed them into Elian's pants pocket.

Still, the vampire-fae didn't move.

Gripping my thighs, Jax lifted me right off the ground, wrapping my legs around his hips from behind. I tipped forward, catching myself on Elian's shoulders as Jax slid into me with a hard thrust.

"Jax!" I cried out with a gasp, the new angle of my body giving him even deeper access. He rocked his hips, hitting me just… just right.

Elian grabbed my wrists, my hands still clamped on his shoulders, his back firm against the door. I waited for him to shrug me off, to let me fall, to do *something* other than drill into me with those penetrating silver eyes, but he didn't move. Didn't speak. Barely even breathed.

"Elian," I whispered, my eyes blurring with tears. The pain and longing in my heart intensified, mixing with the tremors of pleasure coursing through my body at Jax's every touch.

More than anything, I wanted Elian to kiss me. To claim me right along with Jax, even if it was just for tonight. Even if it was destined to become nothing more than another memory haunting my dreams, slicing me up like a razor blade every time I touched it.

I whispered his name once more, and a new fire blazed in his eyes. He released one of my wrists and trailed his fingers up my arm, goosebumps rising in his path.

Then he wrapped his hand around my throat, squeezing just tight enough to make it hurt.

Just tight enough to let me know he remembered *exactly* how I liked it.

*Oh, fuck…*

A fresh bolt of desire rocketed between my thighs, and Jax slowed his movements behind me, the subtle tease of his cock making me ache. He tugged on my hair again, his other hand firm around my hip, fingers digging into my flesh.

My thighs clenched tighter, and I crossed my ankles behind him, drawing him in deeper. I strained to get closer to Elian, but between Jax pulling my hair and Elian's tight grip around my throat, the kiss I so desperately wanted remained just out of reach.

This was… this was fucking crazy. I was pinned between them, the demon whose every touch made me feel like I needed to go to church and beg for absolution and the vampire-fae whose smoldering gaze still had the power to make me weak.

I hadn't seen that look in five years—not like this, close and raw. For all the shit he'd put me through, for all the nights I'd spent curled up on the kitchen floor, for all the hours I'd spent cursing his very name…

God, I'd fucking *missed* him. I *still* missed him—maybe even more now, having him so close but never close enough.

I was his captive—heart, body, and soul.

Why hadn't he turned around and walked out of here? Did he want me as badly as I still wanted him? Was this all just a game to him?

And was Jax truly okay with this? No, the demon and I weren't in a relationship. Hadn't really talked about anything other than enjoying each other's company in Midnight. But most guys weren't into sharing, no matter how much they might've joked about it, no matter how casual the hookups.

Was it crazy to think he didn't care that I so obviously wanted Elian? Wanted them both?

I was confused and angry and completely overwhelmed, but *damn*, I'd never felt anything so intense—so hot—in my life.

I didn't want it to end.

"Elian," I whispered, my breath shallow beneath the press of his fingers. Tiny pinpricks of light danced across my vision. "Jax. You... you're so... Both of you..."

"We're so *what*, angel?" Jax whispered.

"Yes, little sparrow," Elian finally managed, his breath ghosting over my lips. Heat pulsed from his fingers, radiating through my skin. "Do tell."

Jax thrust in deeper once more. I closed my eyes and melted into him, a bead of sweat trickling down my spine, his name on my lips like a curse.

When I finally opened my eyes and met Elian's gaze again, he smirked. Crooked. Cocky.

Jealous.

"Demon got your tongue?" he asked, his smirk turning cruel. "Maybe we should let your insatiable little cunt do the talking instead."

Elian might've thought his words would cut deep, but all they did was turn me on.

Keeping a hand wrapped around my throat, he released my wrist and slid his other hand down my abdomen, palm flat against my skin, fingers whispering closer...

"Please," I whispered. Begged. "Touch me, Elian."

His fingers trembled against my skin as if it burned him, but he didn't pull away.

"Touch me," I begged again.

"*Damn it*, Haley," Elian ground out. "Don't—"

"Don't what?" I whispered. "Admit that I want you? *Both* of you? It doesn't have to mean anything more than—"

"It will *always* mean more," he hissed.

Anger flashed in his eyes, his private war waging endlessly behind them. He clenched his jaw, grip tightening on my throat as Jax railed me from behind, every thrust making me hot and dizzy.

A roar exploded from Elian's chest. Fangs descended, and in a flash he brought his mouth to the spot between my neck and shoulder, his lips and breath caressing my skin, a soft contrast to his rage.

It *wasn't* a caress, though. It was a warning.

I felt the graze of his fangs, the sharp points scraping across my flesh, his hand still trembling against my abdomen, fingers inching closer but not close enough, my breath ragged, my body wound tight as my monsters pushed me down deeper into that dark well of pleasure.

If this was how I was going to die, well…

*Fucking bring it.*

Jax slid a hand around my hip, fingers dipping low between my thighs where Elian had refused to venture, teasing and stroking, pushing me closer and closer to the edge of white-hot bliss as I awaited the exquisite pain of Elian's bite.

"You're close, angel," Jax murmured. "I can feel it."

A shudder wracked my body, heat building in my core as he circled my clit, his pace quickening, his cock hitting me deeper, harder, my thighs tightening around him, the wave of intense pleasure rising, cresting, and then… *oh, God…*

Elian released my throat, and the air rushed back into my lungs just as the wave broke, crashing over me with a force that nearly blinded me.

Jax slammed into me with a desperate growl, shuddering against my backside as he came hot and hard, my pussy clenching around him, my body drowning in ecstasy.

I cried out for my demon, and Elian grabbed my face and sealed his lips around mine, inhaling my moans of pleasure like a drug as I rode out the intense orgasm, the wet heat of his mouth radiating across my tongue, the bastard fae stealing the very breath he'd only just allowed me to claim.

I ached for his real kiss, the slide of his tongue, the slice of his fangs, but I knew he wouldn't give it to me. Not like this. He was too proud, too wounded, too fucked up to go back on whatever promises he'd made himself all those years ago—whatever he'd done to cut me loose and burn the cords that'd once so tightly bound us.

He nipped my lip as he pulled back, finally drawing blood.

It wasn't enough, though. With Elian, it would never be enough. Not unless he decided to let me back into his heart.

A warm, wet trickle ran down my chin.

"If you were singing for *me*, beautiful sparrow," Elian breathed, his eyes blazing once more, "I wouldn't allow an audience."

His tongue darted out to trace the path of the blood from my chin to my lower lip, but that's as far as he went.

All too soon, he turned away, severing the last of our momentary connection.

Jax pulled out and gently set me back on my feet, wrapping his arms around my middle. His release slid down my thighs.

I leaned back into his embrace, anchoring myself.

Elian sighed. Held my gaze for a thousand years, a thousand mysteries burning in his.

Only one thing was clear.

Between the three of us, everything had just changed.

No one spoke.

And when Elian finally turned and stalked out that door without so much as a backward glance, it felt like I'd lost him all over again.

# 32

## JAX

"Tell me something, angel," I said. "Why him?"

We were standing in the shower after that crazy shit with Saint, my hands gliding up and down Haley's soaped-up curves as she slathered conditioner through her hair.

She twisted it into a loose knot on top of her head, then stepped close, sliding her hands up over my shoulders. Her nipples hardened against my chest, and when I palmed her perfect backside, she grinned.

She looked sad, though, and I didn't know whose ass I wanted to beat harder—Saint's, for breaking her heart all those years ago, or mine, for asking about it now.

It was none of my business. But before I could tell her to forget it, she sighed and said, "it may be hard to believe now, but the Elian I knew back then was kind and sweet and funny. I mean, yeah, he's always walked on the dark side. But he was... I don't know. Different before. Not so jaded and selfish."

Selfish wasn't a word I'd use to describe Saint, but I wasn't sure what to call him, either. In the time I'd known him, he'd shown a strong sense of self-preservation, coupled with a razor-sharp ingenuity that was just this side of dangerous. That combination often spelled disaster for anyone crazy enough to get caught up in his bullshit, but it could just as easily save someone's life as wreck it.

I'd been on both sides of it. Still was.

Like most of the dark, damaged, and depraved of Midnight, Saint was a complicated fuck.

"Sometimes he'd just sit in the dark with me," Haley said, "breathing with me, letting me listen to his heartbeat. It always brought me back from the edge."

Her eyes flooded with tears, and my heart squeezed.

"The edge of what, angel?"

Despite the hot shower, a shiver rolled through her body, and she drew closer to me. "Have you ever felt completely broken? Like you weren't even a whole person, but a collection of jagged pieces, some of them missing, some of them smashed beyond repair?"

I didn't know what the fuck to say to that, so I tightened my hold on her.

"There have been times in my life…" she said. "I mean, it's never totally gone, but it's not as bad now as… Anyway, back then, a lot of times I'd slip into these dark moods where I was convinced I was just this broken, unfixable thing. But Elian… He never made me feel that way. Never treated me like I was a burden just for having feelings or expressing shitty thoughts. Never told me to look at the bright side or be more positive or any of that bullshit people throw at you under the guise of helping when all they're really doing is trying to make themselves more comfortable with your pain. He didn't try to glue me back together—and it wasn't because he agreed I couldn't be fixed. He just never believed I needed fixing at all. 'Falling apart doesn't mean you're broken,' he used to tell me." She sighed. "Sometimes that was all I needed. That one little reminder, and I knew it would be okay, even when it hurt."

"Why the *fuck* did he leave?" I hadn't meant to say it out loud, but loud it was.

"I don't know, Jax." She blew out a breath, hot mist across my chest, then pulled back. When she looked up into my eyes again, I thought she might say something else about it, but then she just shook her head and lowered her gaze. It landed on the tattoo over my heart—a skull weeping blood, mouth full of roses.

"Hudson has the same one," she said softly, reaching up to trace the outline.

I could hear the question in her words, and I nodded. "Saint too."

"From your time together here in Midnight?"

"We took an oath," I said. "After one of Keradoc's victory parades."

"Victory parades? But he hasn't even won the war."

"And if he ever does, and the fighting actually stops and the monsters of Midnight unite in peace, the whole place will crumble. Midnight runs on corruption, greed, and violence. It doesn't work otherwise." I closed my eye and dipped my face into the spray of water, eye patch and all. I never took it off around her, and I never would. Haley didn't need any more nightmares.

"After the battles," I continued, "his soldiers would bring the wounded back to the city and parade them through the streets until they either bled to death or passed out and got crushed in the procession. Not just his enemies, which would've been horrifying enough, but his own fighters too. Anyone who got themselves injured was weak, he'd reasoned, and needed to be culled from the herd."

"Holy fuck."

"The worst part was seeing the family and friends of the wounded. They'd throw themselves in front of the procession, begging for the soldiers to free their people, but most of the time they got crushed, too."

My gut twisted at the thought. Saint didn't think Keradoc was doing the parades anymore, but every time I stepped out into the street now, I looked over my shoulder, half expecting to see the half-dead armies marching through a river of blood.

"This one night," I continued, "the parade got out of hand. The injured weren't dying fast enough, so the Midnight soldiers starting killing them —just picking them off. Knives, arrows, immolation. People—not the ones unlucky enough to have someone marching in that mess, but the others— watched the procession from their windows and balconies. They cheered for the violence, egging on the attackers. They dropped roses down on the bloody streets, chanting for Keradoc. The bastard himself never bothered attending, though. He'd tell his generals he didn't think it was prudent for a leader to sully himself by publicly supporting such barbaric traditions, even though they'd all been carried out on his orders."

"And the soldiers called this a *victory*?"

"All they had to do was murder their own men, and they were champions." I pressed the heel of my hand to my good eye, wishing I could stamp out the memories. "Later on, the three of us headed outside. The streets were littered with roses and blood and death. So we stood, right out in the middle of the city, and made our oath. Sliced our palms, clasped hands, and swore that no matter *what* happened to us in Midnight, we'd never turn on each other like that. We'd protect each other. Before glory, victory, or love, the three of us would come first. Even before honor. Didn't matter that we weren't born as brothers, or that we weren't even the same species. That night, we became blood."

"Blood before roses," she whispered, and I nodded.

"That old saying, 'blood is thicker than water?' Most people assume it's talking about your blood family—parents, siblings, whatever—and telling you they're the most important people in your life. No matter what abuses or atrocities they commit, it doesn't matter, because they're your blood."

Haley nodded, her eyes darkening. "I've always hated that saying. Family—a bond like that—should be *chosen*. Sometimes you choose your blood relatives, but that's not always a given."

"No, it isn't. Which is why some people believe the saying is actually a bastardization of the original, which is, 'the blood of the battle is thicker than the water of the womb.' The people who fight side-by-side, the people who spill blood for you... That bond is stronger than a connection forged by the chance pairing of two people creating biological offspring. I always took it that way, anyway. So when I say Hudson and Saint were my blood... I *chose* them that night, Haley."

She took my hand. Ran her finger along my palm, right across the spot where I'd sliced it open for the oath.

"And now?" she asked. "Are you still choosing them?"

"Now it's... complicated. You know, sometimes things happen and you just... I don't know, Haley. Bonds break."

"*Elian* breaks them, you mean."

"No, it's... It wasn't all his fault. Not this time. We all played our parts. We're *still* playing them. But Saint... He certainly doesn't make it easy to keep choosing him."

She reached up and traced the arch of my eyebrow. "He makes you sad."

"Not just him," I said, forcing a smile. "Saint may be a grade-A dickhead, but he can't take credit for *every* fucked-up thing that's ever befallen me. Believe it or not, angel, I haven't always been such a charming gentleman."

That got a smile, but it wasn't enough to chase the new worry from her eyes.

"Sometimes when you look at me," she said, "I feel like... like you're seeing someone else. A ghost."

"Sometimes I feel like I might be."

She blinked up at me, water dripping from her long lashes, waiting for an explanation I wasn't sure I wanted to give her. Wasn't sure I even could.

But then my lips were moving, bringing the past into the present, words tumbling out before I could stop myself.

"Oona," I whispered, as if she really was a ghost. "She was a dark fae—

one of the pureblood Midnighters. Keradoc's daughter, actually, though I didn't learn that until after. When his people found out we'd been together, they killed her. Saint thought they were trying to send me a message."

"Oh my God," she gasped.

"He was there—said he tried to help her, but it was too late. Too much blood. Oona died in his arms, and there wasn't a damn thing to be done. It all happened so fast, and I... The guards were after us. We had to run, and..." I squeezed my eye shut, just barely keeping the worst of the memories at bay. "An hour later, we were in New Orleans, Midnight firmly in the rearview."

"Jax, I'm so... Fuck. I don't even know what to say."

"It was a million years ago, Haley. It's done."

"But you—"

"Look, we don't need to do this," I said, already kicking myself for opening up a damn vein. "Really."

"Jax, look at me. Please."

Biting back a curse, I opened my eye. Looked down at her soft, creamy skin. The rivulets of water running over her dark nipples.

*Fuck*, this was not how I saw this night going. I was standing in the shower with the hot, naked, insatiable witch who'd given me the most intense fucking orgasms of my life, and we were wasting time talking about dead soldiers and blood oaths and murdered exes?

"Jax—"

"I told you, it was a long time ago. I shouldn't have mentioned her."

"Did you love her?" she whispered, her face so earnest, so sweet, it threatened to carve me right open all over again.

"I *don't* love, Haley. Period."

"Because you were hurt?"

"Because I know where loving someone leads."

"To... being in love?" She tried to laugh, but it fizzled out quickly.

Inside, I felt the old devils clawing at my heart. Burning it. Slicing me open only to heal me and do it all over again.

"Do you know the first thing you learn when they turn you into a fear demon?" I leaned in close. Gripped her jaw and forced her to meet my gaze. Then, in a dark whisper that left her trembling, "Behind every fear, every horror, every blood-soaked nightmare that leaves its victims screaming into the darkness lies but a single root, and no, it's not cancer or spiders or the monsters lurking under the bed. It's something *much* more dangerous."

# 33

## JAX

*Y*ou asked me once if I was born like this," I whispered, my mouth so close to hers I could taste her every ragged breath. "No, I wasn't born a demon, my sweet angel. I was human once—centuries ago—dragged to hell for my irredeemable sins and forged into the monster standing before you now."

"I… I'm sorry. I didn't know."

"From my first day in those fiery pits, they beat me. Tortured me. Stripped me bare of everything I ever knew and loved as a man. Then, certain I was sufficiently weak and malleable, they rebuilt me to their exact specifications, force-feeding me every single fear imaginable—dying alone, suffering, getting devoured by snakes, waking up during surgery, drowning, burning alive, losing loved ones, facing war, falling from a great height, getting diagnosed with incurable diseases, and yes, even facing those monsters under the bed. I lived through every single nightmare as though it was real—as though it was mine. And then, I did it again. Again and again, every day for a hundred years in a place where an hour feels like a lifetime. And do you know why they subjected me to such tortures?"

"No," she whispered, eyes wide, her body still trembling in my hands, warm and wet.

"Because a fear demon needs to learn how to look into someone's soul and recognize his worst terrors without succumbing to them, all so we can turn them into weapons against him." I released her jaw and slid my hand down to her breast, the other gripping her hip. Drawing slow circles around her nipple, I said, "So when I tell you I don't love? No, it's not because I was hurt. It's because I've lived through every man's worst nightmares, and I can tell you with utter certainty the only *true* fear—the seed that blooms into all the others—is love."

She searched my face. Gripped my hand to stop my incessant circling. "You're wrong."

"I wish I was, angel. But I'm not."

"But… love? That's ridiculous. What about fear of abandonment?"

"You mean fear of being abandoned by the people you love?"

"Fear of death?"

"Fear of losing your loved ones, losing time with them, or leaving them behind to face life without you, because they love you and you know it will devastate them?"

"Loneliness?"

"Longing for someone to love and to love you back—partner, family member, community, friend, or otherwise?"

"Pain?"

"Haley, it's still about love. Ultimately, suffering is—at its heart—a separation from or betrayal by the love we're promised, explicitly or otherwise. When pain is inflicted by someone who's supposed to care for us, it feels like a deep betrayal. If it's our bodies, then *we're* the betrayer, or maybe it's our gods—after all, aren't they supposed to love us? If a stranger hurts us, it's a violation of a sacred social contract—an implicit agreement to look out for one another, to love thy neighbor. When someone breaks that contract? We feel it on a soul level."

"Then what about the monsters under the bed? Surely that's just—"

"A perceived loss of safety and security, which is another form of love, and the failure of a loved one who should've protected us."

Her brow furrowed, and I could tell she was searching her mind for the loophole, but there wasn't one. Not for this.

"People are made to love," I said. "Humans and supernaturals alike. Anything that prevents or breaks that bond? Give it all the trappings you want, but that's still the *ultimate* fear."

"Humans and supernaturals are made to love?" She gave me the saddest fucking look in the world. "But not you?"

I shook my head.

"Jax, come on. It *has* to be more complicated than that."

"Does it?"

"Look, I don't know the first thing about being a demon, so I'm not trying to, like, witchsplain you or anything. But—"

"Tell me your worst fear," I said. "Dig deep."

"I don't have to dig—it's easy. Screwing up this quest and losing my sisters to the Dark Goddess. If I don't get Keradoc's blood, she'll... And I'll... Oh, shit." Haley blew out a breath, then rolled her eyes. "Okay, point made. I love my sisters. Ergo, love is the root of my fear of losing them. Let the gloating commence."

"No gloating necessary. However, I will make *one* small point of clarification..." I slipped a finger under her chin, tilting her face toward me once more. Her hair slipped loose from the knot, falling down her back and unleashing the scent of coconuts. "I know what *truly* frightens you, angel, and it isn't the thought of losing your sisters to Melantha."

"It... isn't?"

I brought my hand back to her breast, palming it, then squeezing, making her moan. Her eyelids fluttered closed as she leaned into my touch.

"You've been hiding it," I said softly, her nipple hardening at my touch, "ever since we set foot in this realm."

She shook her head, but didn't deny it outright. Didn't back away from me.

"You've been doing a damn good job keeping it under wraps from everyone else," I said, "but you can't hide it from me. One look into your eyes, and I see *everything* that haunts you."

I slid my hand down past her abdomen, slowly parting her thighs and dipping between them.

She clutched my arms and sighed. When she spoke again, her voice was breathy and faint. "Don't, Jax. Please don't."

"Don't what? Touch you?" I pressed my palm to her clit, gliding over her hot flesh, teasing her entrance. "Don't kiss you?" I brought my mouth to her ear, licking the edge, making her shudder. "Don't make you shatter for me?" At that, I slid two fingers inside, pumping her slow and deep.

A soft whimper escaped her lips.

In a dark whisper, I breathed, "Or are you telling me to look into those gorgeous green eyes and pretend I don't see the darkness lurking behind them?"

"Jax..." She tightened her grip on my arms, her mouth parted, cheeks darkening as I fucked her faster and deeper with my fingers.

"I'm telling you, angel. Inside you is an abyss so black it could turn even the most fearsome monsters into smoke if you let it. But way down at the bottom of the well, a little voice is shouting at you to lock up all that darkness and throw away the key."

"I… can't. I'm… oh, fuck. You're—"

"Yes, angel, I know *exactly* what I am. And I know what you are, too." I palmed her clit again, pulsing my fingers inside her wet heat. "That little voice telling you to run and hide? To pretend you don't feel the things you feel about me, about Saint, about this fucking place? To put on a smile and go back to being the sweet little sunshine girl that never admits how dark things truly get for her?"

"That's not… No. I'm…" With another soft moan, Haley rocked her hips, taking me in deeper, riding me, even as she tried to deny herself the pleasure. The truth.

"You're not afraid of Melantha's wrath," I said. "You're afraid if your sisters knew the truth about you—if they saw the same darkness *I* see in your eyes—they'd abandon you." I slid my fingers in deeper, faster, her body already starting to quiver around me. "And you're afraid they'd be right to, because deep down you're a bad girl, and bad girls don't deserve love."

"Don't… don't say that," she panted, squeezing her eyes shut even tighter, as if that alone could make it all go away. "Please don't say that."

"I'm only saying it to tell you it's a fucking *lie*. That voice inside you? It wants to keep you small and afraid because it thinks that's the best way to keep you safe. But that's a lie too—nothing can keep you safe from that kind of darkness, and every day you believe that lie and allow yourself to shrink is another day some part of you fucking *dies*."

Another whimper. Fingernails digging into my arms. She was about to come, but I wouldn't let her. Not yet.

I jerked my fingers out, spun her around, and pushed her face-first against the tiles, pinning her with a hand between her shoulder blades.

"Jax," she breathed. "I need… I'm so close… I just need…"

"Tell me," I growled. "What does my angel need?"

"Hard… Make it… hurt. Everything inside me is just… I need it to hurt. I need to fucking *scream*."

"You will, angel. Because no matter what you believe, I'm not afraid of what's inside you. I'm fucking *drowning* in it." I fisted my cock. Slid it between her curves, teasing her even as my balls ached to unload. "When you show someone who you really are? When you trust someone enough to give them even a glimpse? That's living, not shrinking. That's courage. And anyone who turns their back on you after that never deserved your love in the first place."

I slammed into her pussy, making her cry out in a fierce roar that ricocheted off the tiles, echoing through my very bones.

I grabbed her hands. Pinned them to the tiles above her head.

Fucked her harder, deeper. She pushed back to meet every thrust, her whole body jerking, already so close to the edge she was barely holding on.

"I made you come once already tonight," I said. "But that was for Saint. Now I need you to come for *me*."

I clamped a hand hard over her mouth, not wanting to share this with anyone. Her body was mine. Her pain. Her pleasure. Her screams.

One more deep, hard thrust, and that was it. She fucking shattered, frantic and desperate, biting my hand hard enough to draw blood as her pussy clenched around me and she rode out the intense wave, trembling and bucking until she had nothing left.

I gave her a minute to come back to her body, then slid out from between her thighs, spun her around to face me, and pushed her onto her knees beneath the water spray. I fisted her hair, still thick and slippery with conditioner, every lock like spun silk in my hand.

"Okay?" I asked, running a thumb along her lower lip.

In response, she took my thumb into her mouth and sucked. Hard.

Then she started humming a new tune, all for me.

I almost came right there.

Still humming, she moved her lips from my thumb to my cock, her tongue darting out to tease the tip as she fisted me. Water slid down her face like rain, and she blinked up at me with those devious green eyes.

I stared down into them, watching the darkness swirl.

My cock pulsed in her hand, and she grinned, wicked and powerful. Fucking beautiful.

She needed this as badly as I did. Craved it. The roughness. The realness of it all.

In a place where blood rained from the sky and ghouls begged for bones outside the city walls, sometimes it was easy to forget that even immortal beings could still ache and bleed and die.

Not tonight. Right now, right here, we both remembered.

She parted her lips and took me in deep, her sweet music vibrating across my flesh, my hands buried in her hair as I fucked her hot little mouth until she gagged.

"Right there, angel," I growled. "Right fucking there."

She looked up at me then, another flash of pure wickedness, then sucked me in deep and raked her nails down my abs, blood mixing with the water, and I hit the back of her throat and came so fucking hard I thought I might actually disappear.

I waited until she sucked down the last drop, then pulled out and slumped back against the tiles, my whole body spent and shaking.

Haley was still on her knees. And when I looked down at her again, she smiled.

A little bit devious. A little bit sweet. All angel.

And suddenly I remembered the day of our arrival when we fought off the raven gryphons. I remembered the blood in her hair. Remembered the fae nearly ambushing us in the woods after the first time we'd been together.

Remembered the image of Saint's worst fear in full technicolor detail—Keradoc, his violet eyes alight with pleasure as he swung a sword and chopped off her head.

And right there, out of fucking nowhere, I felt it.

A flicker in my heart that had absolutely *no* business showing up again. *Fear.*

Without another word, I stepped out of the shower and toweled off. I left her there on her knees, still panting, her eyes dark and dreamy as the water slid down her sexy-as-hell curves.

She flashed me a smile, her cheeks dark with a blush that threatened to make me hard all over again. "Feel free to invade my shower anytime, sinner. My door is always open for you."

I forced a smile. "Good to know. Anyone else on that list?"

She rolled her eyes and got to her feet, then turned her back on me, granting me a view of her fine, perfect ass before yanking the shower curtain closed and cutting me off.

I debated sticking around, waiting for her in bed for another round.

But then the sword flashed in my mind, and my heart stuttered again.

No, I couldn't stay. What I *really* needed to do was hunt down a bottle of something strong enough to chase away that flicker, right along with the rest of the damn ghosts trapped in my head.

I grabbed my clothes off the floor. Headed out into the hall, pulling her door shut behind me.

Saint was *right* fucking there, standing across from me in the dark, leaning back against the wall with his arms folded over his chest.

He'd probably been there the whole time, the sick fae fuck. Probably still hard from what I'd done to his woman earlier. From what he'd witnessed and heard just now, undoubtedly imagining his own cock in her mouth every time I slammed into her with a grunt.

Not like she hadn't given him the opportunity.

"Enjoy the show, asshole?" I asked.

He glared at me in the darkness, his silver eyes flashing. It took him a minute to find the words, which was unusual for Saint.

But then, finally, he leaned in close and said, "You hurt her, demon, and I'll take the other eye, too."

A sharp ache tore through my skull, the memory of a hot blade in my flesh. *His* blade.

"I'll let you in on a little secret, Saint." I grinned, lowering my voice to a whisper. "That little witch *loves* when I make it hurt."

He punched me so hard in the face my head snapped back, but I just kept smiling, even as my head throbbed so badly it felt like my skull was caving in. Even as the blood gushed hot and salty from my nose.

I dragged my hand through the mess. Smeared it across his mouth and clutched his face, making sure he tasted it.

The tattoo on my chest blazed.

"Blood before roses, Saint," I said. "*Choke* on it."

# 34

## ELIAN

*L*ong after I'd washed the demon stink from my mouth, I could still taste Haley on my tongue—her breath, her blood, the intoxicating scent of her desire.

*It wasn't desire for* you, *asshole. It's Jax she wants now.*

My fist crashed into the bathroom mirror, spiderwebbing it.

I stared into a dozen jagged shards of glass. And a dozen broken versions of the same man stared right back.

I never should've come to Midnight.

I wasn't talking about this time—no way would I have let Haley face this hell on her own.

I was talking about the last time. The *first* time.

If I'd ignored my instincts then, would she still be with me now? Would we be happy and warm and safe in Blackmoon Bay? Or maybe living the life we'd so often talked about in New Orleans, her with her bookstore and café, me with my club?

How many more nights, weeks, *years* would I spend playing this game?

I'd almost told her the truth tonight. The story she so desperately wanted to know but didn't have the heart to ask. She had a right to it. It was her story as much as mine.

But seeing her in bed with Jax…

I clenched my fists. My hand fucking throbbed, slower to heal than it should've been.

*Good.*

I slipped a pill from the bottle and pressed it to my tongue. Held my breath, waited for the familiar tingle to set in.

It didn't.

I popped another one. Stuck out my tongue and watched the Dream's black whorls dance across it.

It took a few minutes, but eventually, I felt something. The whorls grew blacker, and the dark fae magick buzzed in my mouth, sliding down my throat and slowly working its way into my bloodstream.

Shutting my eyes tight, I yanked her panties from my pocket. Pressed them to my mouth. Inhaled. Tried like hell to ignore the agony tearing through my heart, but of course I couldn't.

I'd never quite mastered that fucking trick.

Tears brimmed behind my eyelids, then spilled, my entire chest cavity about go supernova.

Sometimes it felt as if leaving her had hollowed me out inside. Carved the beating heart right from my body.

And other times, like tonight, I knew that heart still existed, because every time it fucking beat, a bright burst of pain reverberated throughout my entire being.

How the fuck was I even breathing?

*"Touch me, Elian. Please..."*

Her desperate whispers floated through my mind, unleashing a thousand memories just like it. A thousand other breathy moans, a thousand other nights when she belonged only to me. When I still had a right to touch her at all. To call her mine.

*"Haley,"* I ground out. Her name felt like razor blades in my mouth, but I couldn't stop. "Haley," I whispered. "Haley."

I unzipped my pants and fisted my cock with the panties, stroking once, twice. I moved slowly at first, dragging the lace across my sensitive skin, imagining the scrape of her fingernails. Her teeth.

I was rock hard in an instant, my cock throbbing for her. Aching.

I tightened my grip and stroked again. Again. A little harder this time. Harder still. Faster, faster, the sweet memory of her moans crashing through my head, her fists tight on my shoulders, the taste of her breath in my mouth, the scent of her drenched pussy overwhelming me as the demon fucked her so hard she shattered...

*"Fuck..."* I shuddered into that black lace, coming in a fast, red-hot rush that left me trembling, my head falling against the broken mirror, breath fogging the glass.

Jerking off into her panties after I'd watched another man fuck her into oblivion was beyond pathetic.

But it was all I had.

There was a time when I enjoyed fantasizing about my little sparrow, even when it hurt.

Now, it did more than hurt. It carved the Haley-shaped hole in my chest deeper, bigger.

It fucking gutted me.

I tossed the spent panties in the trash and showered off the rest of my release, but until they made a soap to get rid of guilt and self-loathing, I was stuck with that shit. It burned through me like fire.

But for now, I needed to lock it all down.

The Feast of the Beast was in three days. We'd planned to attend together, but that was no longer an option. I needed to do some recon on the castle, see if I could identify all the possible points of failure ahead of time—before the only people in the world I gave a fuck about risked their lives walking into a death trap.

And I still had to figure out how the fuck I was going to kill Keradoc. For all our arguing about plans and timing and wardrobe choices, the assassination was a detail I still hadn't been able to wrap my head around. It would have to wait until after Haley got the blood she needed but before anyone figured out who we were, and that wouldn't give me much time to maneuver if things went sideways.

I needed to think. And I couldn't fucking do it with Jax banging my woman into a wall every night, the sounds of her pleasure floating on the air like all the ghosts I was still trying to outrun.

Gem's place was the only safe haven now. No fucking demons. No exes. No ghosts. Besides, she'd been on a need-to-know basis since our arrival in Midnight, and the time was finally here. She needed to know.

Showered and dressed, I scrawled out a hasty note, telling Jax I had some things to wrap up and would meet them inside the castle in three days.

Then I drew my hood low over my eyes, shouldered my pack, and headed out into the perpetually dark streets of the Hollow, half hoping someone would leap out of the shadows and stake me before I reached my destination.

## 35

HALEY

*I*t's okay, babygirl. I got you.

Though Hudson hadn't uttered another word since the night I'd fallen apart in his arms, those were the words that gave me strength now, as Jax and I stepped through the polished obsidian doors of Keradoc's castle.

Our gargoyle was covering the exterior in his winged warrior form, keeping watch from the stone turrets. Jax would have my back on the inside in case anything went south.

But Elian?

None of us had seen him since that intense night in my bedroom.

Jax told me he'd left a note—that he was working closely with Gem to ensure everything was set up for us tonight, leaving nothing to chance. That I shouldn't fret. That Elian would show up, no matter what had happened—or *hadn't* happened—between us.

But a fissure of worry had opened up in my chest all the same.

"Haley." Jax tightened his grip on my elbow and leaned in close, brushing a kiss to my temple. "He'll be here, angel."

I nodded and smiled because I wanted to believe him. Also, because he was wearing a fitted tux that made him even more drool-worthy than usual, even though he'd outright refused to let me bedazzle his eye patch.

But as we made our way into the castle's main parlor, a deep dread settled into my stomach. Not necessarily about Elian, though his absence

184

certainly didn't help; I hated how we'd left things that night—how he'd turned his back and walked out.

Still. Personal issues aside, tonight was the most important night of my life. Of my sisters' lives, though they had no idea any of this was even happening. I tried to imagine them at home now, practicing their magick and keeping one another company. Getting together for dinner or drinks or just to chat.

Living their lives—lives I would do everything in my power to protect.

Even if it killed me.

The parlor was a mass of sweaty, filthy bodies—fae, demon, vampire, human, witch—all of them crushed together, elbows and punches flying as they jockeyed for a closer spot at the buffet tables and open bars. They were dancing, too; whoops of laughter and catcalls rang out above a cacophony of discordant music—some kind of dark techno that thumped through my bones. The whole thing reminded me of a frat party, completely off the rails, and if someone busted out a beer pong table or announced a wet T-shirt contest, it wouldn't have surprised me in the slightest.

But once we got through the public party and over to the sleek winding staircase that would take us up to the exclusive level, everything changed.

Getting through security took a good twenty minutes. Two different soldiers frisked us, then wanded us with some kind of magickal device that supposedly identified hidden spells and potions. Our tickets were scrutinized so closely, I started to fear we'd already blown our cover—that at any minute, the guards would haul us down to the dungeons.

But eventually, they cleared us, and we made our way up the winding staircase to the fourth-floor ballroom, my heartbeat steadying a little more with every step as I borrowed some strength from my fearless, superhot demon.

As if he could sense my thoughts, Jax slid his arm around my shoulders and drew me a little closer, whispering into my hair for the hundredth time in an hour, "You're fucking *stunning*, Haley Barnes."

Heat rose in my cheeks. I was pretty sure I'd never get tired of hearing it.

The truth was, I *did* look pretty damn fine tonight. The dress Gem had picked out for me was black, of course—a strapless silk gown with a long sleeve on one side. The fitted bodice was hand-embroidered with tiny red roses that trailed down along the skirt, which flared out to my ankles in a series of layered petals—easy access to my thigh holsters, assuming I could reunite with them soon.

All part of the plan.

I'd left my hair down, curled in loose waves that Jax couldn't stop touching.

*Jax…*

I'd meant it when I told Elian I was still in love with him. I probably always would be. But I couldn't deny the feelings simmering for my demon, either. Even Hudson had found a place in my heart—a place that was quickly expanding to allow for the possibility that he could be more than a friend, too.

Something about these men—these monsters—belonged to me. And I belonged to them. Whatever happened in Midnight, whichever paths we walked when all was said and done, they'd never leave my heart.

The ballroom was as massive and ostentatious as I expected, like something straight out of a Regency romance novel. There were a few hundred people gathered there, some dancing, some drinking—a more refined version of the party exploding downstairs.

We didn't spot Keradoc, though.

"Remember," Jax said. "Long black hair. Violet eyes. He'll be the best-dressed fae here. And he's *extremely* compelling, so you're gonna need to watch yourself at all times."

I grinned. "I don't know if you know this about me? But I'm pretty good at fending off unwanted advances from creepy supernatural men."

Jax cupped my face and brought his lips to my ear. In a dark whisper, he said, "And that sounds like a fun game for us to play later, angel."

Laughing, I slipped away from him and headed into the bathroom located beside a tapestry of a fiery lake—the place Gem was supposed to leave my package.

Lifting the top of the toilet tank, I choked back a sob of pure relief. There, taped inside, was the promised leather pouch.

Gem had come through for us. She'd fucking come through.

I removed the pouch and retrieved my weapons—my favorite hawthorn stake that'd somehow managed to survive the long trek from New Orleans to Midnight. The dagger Jax had given me. My thigh holsters. And there, last but certainly not least, a tiny glass vial no larger than my pinky finger, fitted with a needle so short and thin I could only see it when I held it beneath the torchlight.

It was attached to a leather bracelet that fit snugly against my wrist, just inside my sleeve.

When I was ready to do the blood extraction, a quick flex would release the needle.

A magickal numbing agent would ensure Keradoc didn't feel a thing.

Then, assuming his blood responded to the call of my magick, I'd be able to guide it straight into the vial without it losing any of its potency.

The Goddess didn't require much—even a few drops of his blood would be enough to break the moonglass spell—but I wasn't taking any chances.

Locked and loaded, I searched my face in the bathroom mirror, trying to find the woman that Jax had seen the other night in the shower when he'd whispered all my secrets.

*Inside you is an abyss so black, it could turn even the most fearsome monsters into smoke...*

*You're afraid if your sisters saw the same darkness I see in your eyes, they'd abandon you...*

*Nothing can keep you safe from that kind of darkness, and every day you believe that lie is another day some part of you fucking dies...*

*I'm not afraid of what's inside you. I'm fucking drowning in it...*

Jax was right. I *was* dark.

And I was magick.

And here in Midnight, in the place I should've feared more than any other, I'd never felt more at home.

---

As soon as I emerged from the bathroom, a pair of strong arms encircled me, dragging me into a nearby closet full of musty old cloaks and a long-forgotten suit of armor.

The scent of campfire and lemons was a dead giveaway, even before his fingers started sneaking past the petals of my dress.

"Jax!" I breathed. "What the hell are you *doing?*"

His reply came low and raspy in my ear, making me shiver. "You thought you could parade around looking like this and expect me to keep my hands off you tonight?"

"I figured the whole risking-our-lives, one-man-short, dangerous-blood-heist-in-a-castle-full-of-armed-soldiers thing would put your dick on ice—at least for a *few* hours."

"Not happening, angel," he murmured, his kisses growing as urgent as his touch. "I'll *die* if I don't taste you."

He finally found his way between my thighs, fingers gliding over my exposed clit.

"Jax, I… Oh, *fuck*," I breathed, clutching his arm. "Why are you so good at… at being the *worst*?"

"Because you *love* the worst. The more important question is… Why the fuck aren't you wearing panties?"

"You kept ruining mine, so I solved the problem by removing the temptation."

"You've merely created a *new* problem, angel."

He slid two fingers inside me, a slow, delicious thrust that left me trembling, but just when it started to feel *really* fucking amazing, he pulled out, then reached for the stake strapped to my thigh, freeing it. Beneath the silky fabric, he ran the tip up along my thigh to my hipbone, then slid it across to the other one before dipping lower. Lower.

Lower still.

He grazed my clit, then dropped to his knees and pushed open the panels of silk, baring me.

I was powerless to do anything but sigh as he worked his sinful brand of magick, one touch, one kiss at a time.

With the very stake I'd used to paralyze the bloodsuckers who'd attacked me at Saints and Sinners the first night I'd met him, the demon traced delicate patterns on my skin, then followed with his tongue, each stroke burning like a magick rune.

"Do you trust me?" he whispered.

"Are you serious? Fuck no!"

"Good girl."

"Jax, wait. I don't think we should be… I'm… Oh, well that's just… *so* not fair."

He licked my clit, then sucked it between his teeth, giving it a teasing nibble before pulling back and drawing another soft circle with the stake.

"I'm going to make you come," he said. "But there's a catch."

"I don't… care…" I panted, fisting his hair. "Whatever it is. Just… don't stop."

"You can't sing for me tonight, angel. You can't make a sound or we'll be discovered, and our whole plan will be shot to hell."

"Maybe you should've thought of that before you dragged me into the closet and—"

He tapped my clit with a light slap, then descended, his mouth and breath and tongue licking and teasing, pushing me closer, then pulling back to draw more maddening strokes with the stake until I was so wound up I worried I might actually explode, nothing left but a pile of black silk petals to mark my passing.

"Jax," I breathed, and he slid his tongue across my clit once more, then thrust his fingers inside, fucking me right into oblivion as I held my breath and shuddered against his face, not making a sound.

When I finally stopped shaking, he slid the stake back into the holster and got to his feet.

Then, cupping my face and lowering his mouth to mine, he whispered, "Every time you feel that stake rub against your thighs, I want you to think of my mouth. I want you to remember how hard I made you come on my tongue. And I want you to know I'll be waiting for you to return to me, so I can do it all over again later."

His eye blazed, but no, these weren't just the dirty words of a hot demon looking to get laid later.

The look in that eye was fierce. Protective.

And if I didn't know better...

*Don't be ridiculous, girl. Jax is incapable of love. Fear demon, remember? You're seeing stars because you want to, and that's a dangerous game you can't afford to play right now.*

"I knew it," I said with a wink. "You totally like me."

He grinned and swatted my ass, and then he was off, ready for us to go our separate ways and carry out the plan.

I waited a full minute before making my exit. And when I did, a new kind of magick sang through my veins. I felt strong and powerful, confident.

*I can do this. I can totally fucking do this.*

I slipped into the ballroom. Grabbed a flute of champagne from a passing butler. Cataloged all the exits. Located Jax across the room. Scoped out the magickal chandeliers, the gorgeous crown molding. The Midnight elite in all their finery.

And then, suddenly, there he was.

Our mark.

Keradoc.

Flanked by two heavily armed fae guards, he began a long, slow walk from the back of the ballroom to the center, the crowd parting for him as he passed. A small plattorm had been set up for him, and when he reached it and stepped up to the podium, the entire ballroom erupted in applause.

I was too far back to clearly make out his features, but even at that distance, I could still feel his magnetic charm. He hadn't even said a word yet, and already I felt myself leaning closer, eager to hear it.

He waited forever before finally lifting his hands and settling the crowd, then—after a brief welcome—launched into a doozy of a patriotic speech that could've given every evil dictator back home a run for their money.

To hear him tell it, Midnight was and would always be theirs. He rambled on about a major show of force, the arrival of a new weapon the enemy would never be able to defeat... I mean, honestly. Had this guy even looked out a window lately? Did he not see his entire realm burning at the hands of the Darkwinter fae?

As he *finally* wrapped up the monologue that sent the crowd into a full-on rapture, I made my way to the other side of the ballroom, still scanning for signs of Elian. I spotted Gem, but just as I was about to head over and grill her on Elian's whereabouts, the air shifted behind me, and a dark wave of magick whispered across my skin.

"Normally, I execute party-crashers," came a smooth voice, low and dangerous in my ear. "But I might be willing to make an exception for you."

Tensing for a fight, I slid my hand to my side, fingers brushing the hilt of the dagger holstered just beneath the silk petals.

Then, I turned around to face the man who'd made the mistake of threatening me, coming face-to-face with the most entrancing violet eyes I'd ever seen.

# 36

## HALEY

$\mathcal{I}$t was hard not to stare.

The warlord of Midnight was damned intimidating.

Unlike Elian, who'd incorporated enough modern touches into his personal style to help him blend in back home, this guy was pure, O.G. fae.

His long black hair shimmered with strands of silver, woven in a mix of intricate braids and loose locks. His fingernails were as black as his hair, each one filed to a sharp point. Even his clothing was black—embossed silks tailored perfectly to his lean body and an open, collarless jacket made of some kind of leather, the edges trimmed with delicate silver and violet swirls that danced in the light.

It brought out his eyes, which now had me pinned in place, completely mesmerized.

Also, if more guys wanted to start wearing black eyeliner back home? I'd fully support that endeavor.

"Would you grant me the honor of a dance?" He held out his arm and smiled once more, a warning hidden in the depths of that violet gaze.

I couldn't help but test his boundaries, just a little.

Folding my arms across my chest, I gave him a once-over. Then, in my most sultry voice, I said, "Do I have a choice?"

"No. Not unless you want me to reconsider my exception."

"Right. The one where you *don't* toss me to the ghouls?"

"That would be the one, yes. Though I feel compelled to tell you that tossing you to the ghouls is just one of the myriad ways in which I might decide to… deal with you. A dance would be much more pleasant. For you, at least."

He flashed a devastating grin, and I flashed one right back, and the next thing I knew, I was allowing him to sweep me out onto the dance floor.

His scent was overpowering up close, like wild roses encased in ice, mixed with a hint of deep, dark earthiness I could only describe as… forbidden. For all the power locked away in his lean muscles, he held my hand with a delicate touch, his other hand warm and gentle on the small of my back, holding me just a little closer than what might be considered proper for polite company.

Across the ballroom, I caught sight of Jax, who watched me with a mix of concern, lust, and jealousy. I wasn't sure which of those feelings dominated, but my demon was definitely spring-loaded and ready to pounce, should the need arise.

But I didn't feel threatened by Keradoc. Not even with all his subtle taunts about executions and the current of dark power crackling just beneath the surface of his touch. In fact, now that I was in his arms, breathing in his heady scent and gazing into those captivating violet eyes, I felt an inexplicable connection to him. Even my magick responded to his presence, a soft hum buzzing through my veins, warm and electric.

Keradoc twirled me, then captured me in his embrace again, pulling me even closer.

"I didn't realize you'd be so beautiful," he murmured in my ear. "So… enchanting."

Fighting off a shiver of pleasure, I said, "Didn't realize? What do you mean?"

"I… I simply meant…" He faltered, then smiled once again, dazzling as ever. "When I saw you earlier this evening. I'm embarrassed to confess… I was watching you speak with another. A demon, if I'm not mistaken? With an injury to his eye?"

"Oh, *that* guy?" I forced a laugh. "Some rando looking for a little company. I never even caught his name."

He lifted his brows, amusement glinting in his eyes. "You didn't?"

"Not everyone is worth learning something about, your… your Highness? Grace? I'm sorry. I don't know what to call you."

"Keradoc will do just fine. Midnight is not a monarchy, Haley."

My name was like melted chocolate on his lips, the smoothness in his voice making me swoon. He spun me out again, then drew me back, fingers tracing slow, almost imperceptible circles on my bare back.

There was something almost… familiar about him, though I was sure we'd never met. I'd never even laid eyes on the man until he gave that speech.

Now, as one song bled into the next and Keradoc continued to waltz and twirl me across the ballroom, I felt myself falling under his spell.

Whether it was his natural charm or just another trick of the dark fae, I couldn't say.

But one thing was certain: I needed to pull my head out of the clouds, refocus on the mission, and get this thing over with before I lost my opportunity.

Listening to the cadence of the song, I waited until I knew he was going to dip me, then I slipped my hand along my thigh, making a tiny slice with the perfectly positioned dagger just before he brought me upright.

Blood welled in the cut, just enough to coat my bloodstone ring. Under the guise of wanting to hold him closer, I rested my head on his shoulder and muttered my spell, so softly not even a vampire would've been able to hear it.

> *Blood of the realm, blood of the night*
> *Follow the magick, follow the light*
> *Midnight fae, I summon thee*
> *With these words, so shall it be*

By the time I glanced into those violet eyes again, my hand was already sliding into his hair. With a slight flick of my wrist, the needle pierced his skin.

Keradoc didn't flinch, and I tried not to sigh in relief.

Then, bringing his lips to my ear again, he said, "Tell me something, Haley. How does someone as beautiful and… refined… as yourself end up in a place as treacherous as Midnight?"

I forced a laugh as his blood continued to fill the vial, warm and tingling against my wrist, the magick inside me heating in its presence.

"Oh, you know how it is. One minute you're doing a little unsanctioned magick, dabbling a bit too deeply in the dark arts, messing with the wrong people… And all of a sudden you're being hurtled through a portal to a prison realm full of creeps and monsters and—I mean, not that it's *all* creeps and monsters, of course. It's actually quite lovely once you get used to it."

He laughed, rich and buttery, and the soft snick against my wrist told me the contraption had done its job.

Adrenaline flooded my insides, making my heart gallop in my chest.

The song was winding down, but it seemed Keradoc wasn't ready to let me go just yet. I tried to gently extract myself from his hold, but he only tightened the embrace.

"One more song, if I may? I'm sorry, but it's not often I have the pleasure of dancing with such a lovely companion."

Seeing no way out of it, I smiled. "Last song, buddy. I've got my eye on some appetizers at the buffet table I don't want to miss out on."

"As you wish." He dipped me low, then drew me up again, his footsteps quickening to keep pace with the new song, faster and livelier than the others. With each new dip and turn, he danced us further away from the crowds, deeper into the shadows at the edges of the ballroom, my stomach full of butterflies as the room spun into a blur of colors and his scent washed over me and his strong, firm embrace held me close and then, like a bucket of ice water straight to the face, I realized…

I'd never told him my name.

He'd called me Haley, all smooth and melted-chocolatey, but I was sure of it—I'd never actually shared it.

*So how the fuck does he know who I am?*

"Keradoc, how did—"

Before the words were out, he spun me away once more, then released me.

Straight into the arms of one of his guards.

"Take her to the throne room and wait for me there," Keradoc ordered, then reached out to touch my face, a cold finger trailing down my cheek. "Thank you for the dance and the enlightening conversation, Haley. We'll pick up where we left off very soon."

*Wait… was that silver flickering in his eyes?*

It was my last conscious thought before the guard blew a handful of sparkly gold dust into my face and threw a bag over my head, and it was lights out, Haley Barnes.

# 37

## HALEY

*I* came back to consciousness slowly, my head heavy, my vision blurry. The ringing in my ears made me so dizzy I wanted to puke.

Where the fuck was I? How long had I been here? Did Gem or the guys even know I'd been taken?

Sucking in a deep breath, I tried to get a feel for my surroundings.

I was on my knees, wrists and ankles bound with rope, hands tied behind my back. Someone had stripped off my weapons.

The vial was gone too.

*Fuck.*

Fear surged in my chest, but I tamped it down. I couldn't afford to freak out. Not yet.

I took another deep breath. Did a quick scan of my body. Other than a spinning head and a little chaffing from the rope, it didn't feel like they'd roughed me up too badly. I wasn't bleeding. Still had my clothes on, aside from the underwear I hadn't bothered with. I could still feel the buzz of magick in my veins. And…

*Yes.* The ring. They'd ignored the bloodstone ring.

Another bolt shot through my chest. Not fear this time, but adrenaline. My vision started to clear.

Dais. I was on my knees in front of a black dais in a massive throne room, all black—the walls, the polished marble floor, the velvet drapes hanging over the windows. Magick torches lined the walls, and at the top of the platform, a shadowed figure sat on an imposing throne made of skulls, bones, and polished obsidian.

Keradoc.

*Fancy yourself a king now, do you?*

Violet eyes blazed through the darkness, glaring down at me.

"Enter," he called out gruffly, and a heavy door clanged open a few dozen feet behind me, chains rattling.

Footsteps echoed across the floor, along with the clink of swords slapping against armor and the sound of something being dragged.

I swallowed hard. Refused to look. Because if Keradoc's guards had taken any of my men…

The stench of wet fur and blood plowed into me. Seconds later, two beasts were deposited unceremoniously at my side.

Certain they weren't mine, I darted a quick glance.

Shifters, though it was hard to tell what type. Wolves, most likely. The poor beasts were caught mid-shift, with the heads and torsos of men, the arms and legs of… something else. Both were emaciated, with bruised faces and ribs poking through open wounds on their skin.

Tears glazed my eyes. Poor fucking creatures. I didn't care what they'd done to end up in Midnight. They didn't deserve what'd happened to them. Didn't deserve whatever punishment Keradoc was about to dish out now.

I twisted my wrists, trying not to draw too much attention. If I could just get the rope to cut deep enough to spill some of my blood, I might be able to conjure a spell…

"Anything to say for yourselves, filth?" Keradoc asked, finally tearing his gaze away from me to look at the other prisoners. The gruffness had faded, replaced with the smooth, hypnotic tone he'd used on me in the ballroom. Its liquid warmth washed over me in a soothing wave.

The logical part of me insisted it was fae magick. That he was trying to entrance me.

It didn't feel like fae trickery, though. No more than it had in the ballroom.

*Yes, and look how well* that *worked out for you, dumbass.*

Next to me, one of the shifters spit on the dais. The other said nothing.

Keradoc rose from the throne, taking his sweet time, his steps silent and graceful as he descended the platform. One of the guards stepped forward and handed him a gleaming sword that looked as if it'd just been forged.

Either that, or it'd never seen battle.

Keradoc approached the shifter farthest from me, who lifted his chin defiantly. Touching the tip of the sword to the prisoner's throat, Keradoc said, "You have been charged with treason, sedition, and conspiracy against the realm. How do you plead?"

The shifter lifted his chin higher. Opened his mouth to speak.

But Keradoc had already raised the blade.

It happened so fast, I didn't even have time to duck.

I heard the zing of the metal cutting through the air, felt the bite of a sharp point grazing my neck.

A lock of my hair fell soundlessly to the floor, and beside me, two heads dropped. Their bodies slumped forward, blood spilling like wine tipped from a glass.

It pooled beside me, inching closer, finally soaking through my dress.

The acrid tang of it tickled the back of my throat. Magick rushed up my spine, but that was just an instinctive response to the presence of so much blood. I couldn't actually cast a spell unless I used my *own* blood.

"Is there a problem, witch?" Keradoc asked. "Seems you've got something to say."

"You didn't even wait for their plea," I blurted out. "You just beheaded two shifters—residents of your own realm—and you didn't even hear their plea."

"Treason carries the punishment of death," he said, his voice eerily calm. "They're lucky I made it a quick one."

"Oh? Was that for my benefit? Trying to frighten the fragile, helpless witch into confessing her secrets by showing her what a big, scary fairy you are?"

Behind me, one of the guards cleared his throat, but said nothing.

"I never pegged you as fragile or helpless, little thief," Keradoc said. "Only presumptuous." He walked around me in a slow circle, examining me as if I were a prized steer at an auction, then finally stopped to stand behind me. I could feel him looming, the air heavy with his cloying scent, but I wouldn't give him the satisfaction of tipping my head up to look at him.

"How the fuck do you even know those shifters were guilty?" I snapped, past the point of caring whether I pissed him off. He was either going to behead me or keep screwing with me, and if he chose the former? Fine. I'd make *damn* sure I was still cursing him out when my head rolled. "Who appointed *you* judge, jury, and executioner? Last I heard, you were just a self-appointed, washed-up warlord moving pieces around a chessboard with one hand and jerking off with the other. And who made that throne, anyway? Are those even real bones? Because I'm pretty sure I saw a DIY kit just like it on Amazon."

A shadow shifted over me, the scent of roses receding.

A chill crept across my shoulders, making me shiver.

And once again, Keradoc of Midnight swung his sword.

I gasped, but the pain never came.

The ropes fell away from my wrists and ankles. I was pretty sure he'd slashed a few stitches on my dress too. But...

Holy *fuck*. Had I not been so busy trying not to pee myself, I might've taken a moment to be impressed with his swordsmanship.

Turning back to his guards, Keradoc said, "Leave us."

They did as he asked. When the door finally slammed shut, he sighed and tossed the sword to the floor, like he couldn't even stand to hold it. The metallic clang echoed across the cavernous room, making my teeth clench.

"On your feet, witch."

I stood up slowly and rubbed my wrists, trying to figure out my next move. Try to go for the sword? It was mere feet away from me, but... No. He'd almost certainly beat me to it. Hell, he'd probably set the whole thing up as a test, just to see how far I'd push him.

I got the distinct feeling the guy was bored and looking for a challenge.

Why keep me alive otherwise?

So the sword was a no-go. I had no weapons, no jewelry but the ring, and my fingernails weren't long or sharp enough to cut my skin and draw blood. If I acted quickly, though, a hard bite to the fleshy part of my hand could do the trick...

I feigned a cough, lifting my hand to my mouth, and—

Keradoc grabbed my wrists and hauled me against his chest—another dance, but this one was much rougher than the last. Much more intense.

And Keradoc, the fucking creep, was hard as hell.

An answering pulse of desire throbbed in my core.

That *had* to be a fae trick. Keradoc was a fucking murderous asshole. A sociopath. We were standing in a pool of shifter blood, for fuck's sake, all because he'd felt like playing with his big sword.

"Tell me something, witch," he said. His cold-roses scent washed over me again, mixing with that forbidden earthiness that'd called to me earlier, all of it conspiring with his smooth voice and warm body to shatter my resolve.

None of this made sense. Why the fuck did he sound—did he *feel*—so familiar?

"If treason is punishable by death," he murmured, his gaze sweeping my face, "what is the appropriate sentence for a thief who attempts to steal the blood of the… what was it now? Ah, yes. The self-appointed, washed-up warlord of Midnight?"

He released me and retrieved a vial from his pocket, holding it before my eyes. *My* vial. His blood swirled inside, flickering with magick.

He dropped it. Stomped on it.

*Fuck. Me.*

I swallowed the tightness in my throat, refusing to shed so much as a single tear. This was far from over. There *had* to be another way. As long as I was still breathing, there was another way, and I'd fucking find it.

"How about a duel?" I asked, biding my time. "Fight to the death. Witch versus warlord, no holds barred."

His eyes flashed with mischief. "Do you honestly think you'd stand a chance?"

"Give me a sword and let's find out."

He bent down and scooped up the discarded sword, turning it over in his hands as if he were actually considering it. Torchlight flickered along the blood-stained blade. "As entertaining as a deathmatch sounds… No, little thief. I'm not sure that would be prudent. You seem quite… determined."

"Don't tell me the big, scary fairy is afraid of a little witch."

"Something tells me I *should* be." He lowered the sword to his side, and a smile finally cracked the stone-hard face. Not the smooth, charming grin of a fae spell-weaver entrancing his prey, but the smile of a real man. A fae who was as much human on the inside as I was.

And in that moment, his entire face changed.

Literally.

The sharp angles smoothed out just a bit, the nose widening. And those violet eyes, so cold and deadly, turned… silver.

I sucked in a sharp breath.

It was all just a fae glamour, and in that brief instant, I saw right through it to the real man beneath.

*Ellan.*

A wave of relief swept me up and propelled me right back into him like a boat tossed against the rocks. I threw my arms around his neck, tears hot on my cheeks.

"I was so worried about you," I breathed, burying my face in the crook of his neck. "You have no idea."

Then I pulled back, looked once more into those familiar silver eyes, and slapped him across the face.

"*That* was for scaring the hell out of me," I snapped, then whacked him again. "And for making me worry about you for three fucking days." I lifted my hand once more, this time making a fist. "And *this*—"

He grabbed my wrist, those silver eyes boring straight into my soul. They were clear tonight, no trace of Devil's Dream. No trace of anything but white-hot fury.

His vise grip tightened, crushing the bones of my wrist.

"I thought you were dead, dickhead!" I shouted, the agony in my wrist intensifying. "And all night you're just… what? Fucking with me? Where's Keradoc? Is this even his castle? Or was this all just another one of your bullshit schemes?"

His brow furrowed, a look of genuine confusion settling into his features. His eyes flickered between silver and violet.

I had a million more questions, and they all rushed through my mind at once. *Where the hell have you been? Why didn't you get in touch with us? What kind of glamour is this? Why did you kill those shifters? Why did you act like you didn't recognize me when we danced?*

But none of that mattered. Something else was welling up inside me too, chasing away all the questions—the new as well as the old.

I no longer cared where he'd been.

No longer cared why he'd left me all those years ago.

No longer cared why he'd gotten exiled to this terrible realm in the first place.

Suddenly, I just wanted to kiss him. I *needed* to kiss him.

"I hate you," I whispered.

Then crashed into his mouth.

He resisted for a second, then dropped the pretense, releasing my wrist and kissing me back.

The sword clattered to the ground, and he lifted me up, claiming me with his brutal mouth as my legs wrapped tight around his hips. Without breaking for air, he turned and lowered me to the dais, kneeling between my thighs, pushing me down against the steps as he devoured me, his hands winding into my hair, his breath hot, tongue sweeping into my mouth, cock grinding against my center, every touch sending spasms of pleasure straight to my core.

And in that moment, here's what I knew:

The kiss was epic. The kind they wrote songs about. The kind that would, if things progressed, have *me* singing.

It turned me inside out and left me reeling.

It made the stars scatter behind my eyes.

It filled me with a fire unmatched by any I'd imagined from such an explosive reunion with the man I'd loved for most of my life.

But here's what else I knew:

The man kissing me senseless right now? It *wasn't* Elian.

Not even a glamoured version of Elian.

Didn't matter that we hadn't kissed in years. Didn't matter that so much had changed between us, we were practically strangers.

Some things you just knew. You just fucking *knew*.

I shoved hard against his chest, and the imposter pulled back, just as breathless as I was.

Hands still in my hair, rock-hard cock straining against his silken finery, he stared down at me with heavy-lidded eyes, violet once again. "It seems our realms have rather different interpretations of dueling. Admittedly, I like your version better."

"You… You're not…" I sucked in a sharp breath and pressed my fingers to my tingling lips, mind reeling. "Who the *hell* are you?"

A slow, devouring grin slid across his mouth, his face flickering back to the version I'd seen earlier. Menace flashed in his eyes.

"Kiss me like that again, Daughter of Darkwinter," he whispered, "and I'll be whoever you need me to be."

*Daughter of Darkwinter?*

No. There was no way he knew about that. Not even Elian knew about that. Only my sisters, who I hadn't spoken with since I left Blackmoon Bay and had no idea I was even here, and…

*Oh, fuck.*

The goddess Melantha.

"The question remains," Keradoc said. "Are *you* going to be what *I* need?"

At that, he smiled and lowered his mouth to mine once more, then pursed his lips and blew out a sweet, gentle breath, so soft it tickled my lips. Golden smoke swirled up before my eyes, and all at once, the room spun.

For the second time in an hour, my world turned black.

## 38

## ELIAN

"Where the fuck have you *been*?" Jax fisted my lapels and hauled me close, his fury barely contained. "Tell me you've got Haley. Tell me you didn't fucking blow this and risk her fucking life, you piece of shit, or I swear I will throw you over the wall and feed your useless ass to the fucking ghouls."

*Fuck.*

Adrenaline spiked. I tried to swallow down my fear, school my features, but it was no use. Jax could sense it a mile away.

No, it wasn't his bullshit threats that had me tied up in knots.

It was fucking Haley.

Despite Jax's accusations, I'd been here the whole fucking time. Gem and I had been keeping watch all night, taking turns checking on Haley while we cased out the best opportunity for me to get my shot at Keradoc. I knew Haley had gotten her weapons. Knew she'd fucked Jax in that damn closet, too.

And I knew my girl had sealed the deal, accomplishing what she'd set out to do—get that Midnight bastard's blood.

But now, Jax and I were alone in a little-used parlor adjacent to the ballroom, and Haley was nowhere to be found.

"Last I saw her," I said, "she was dancing with Keradoc. She already got the blood, Jax. I saw it happen—figured she'd make her way back to you so you could take her home."

"I can't fucking find her!" he roared. "I saw her with him, too. Twirling around the ballroom like a fucking ballerina. The next thing I knew, she was gone."

Gone?

No. It wasn't happening. It wasn't *fucking* happening.

"Get Hudson," I ordered. "If someone grabbed her, they can't have gotten far. We need to do a full sweep outside. Make sure no one—"

"Saint!" Gem burst into the room in a blur of red dress and purple hair, her cheeks streaked with mascara-stained tears. "Thank the devil. I've been looking everywhere for you guys. They've taken Haley!"

"Where?" Jax asked. "Who? Gem, what the *fuck* did you see?"

Fresh tears glazed her eyes. "This is all my fault. I should've left her more weapons. I should've stayed by her side. But they were dancing right out in the open! I never thought he'd—"

"Gem." I put my hands on her shoulders, trying to calm her the fuck down. "Breathe. You need to fucking breathe and tell us exactly what you saw."

"I don't know… I mean, one minute she was dancing with Keradoc, and then he just… handed her off. I almost didn't see it, it happened so fast. But then I caught a flash of their uniforms."

"Whose uniforms?" Jax asked.

"His guards. They were waiting in the wings, Saint. Fucking guards, like he'd positioned them right there the whole time. So either he knew what Haley was planning, or he wanted her for… for something else. Either way, they nabbed her."

"Fuck." It took everything I had not to smash my fist through the fucking wall, but that wouldn't help anyone, least of all Haley. "Any ideas where they would've taken her? Holding cell? Private chambers?"

"Throne room," Gem said. "That's where he… I mean, if she's… if she's still alive, that's where she'll be."

"She's still alive," I insisted, refusing to allow for the possibility of anything else.

"Keradoc took her just so he could force her to bend the knee and kiss the ring?" Jax let out a bitter laugh. "I don't think so. What the hell is going on, Gem?"

"No, he…" Gem swallowed hard. When she spoke again, her voice was a brittle whisper. "Some prisoners he kills right away. But others, he… He toys with them first. Torments them. And then, once he's bored of his sick little games…" She closed her eyes and shook her head, tears falling.

"What happens then?" I whispered, my heart lodged so far into my throat, I nearly choked on it.

She opened her eyes, nothing but two pits of hopelessness. "He chops off their heads and adds the skulls to his throne."

I'd never fallen into a meat grinder before, or been set on fire, or had my skin flayed off and my ass dropped into a salt bath.

But in that moment? I was pretty sure any of those options would've felt better than the agony ripping through me.

"If we've got any chance of saving her," Gem said, rubbing the tears from her eyes and straightening her spine, "we need to move. Now."

"We can't just go storming in there," I said. "The castle is crawling with soldiers. We won't get anywhere *near* that room. If they even *suspect* we're on to them—"

"There's a back way," she said. "But if we don't go now… Look, it's not just her life at stake. If Haley breaks and tells them she wasn't working alone, they'll lock this place down faster than the ghouls in the moat can eat a corpse."

Jax nodded. Straightened his jacket. Cracked his neck. When he met my gaze again, his blue eye blazed, his whole body trembling with a rage I hadn't seen since I carved out his other eye.

He looked like a fucking omen of death.

"Lead the way," he ground out.

We followed Gem back down to the main level, fighting our way through the throng of drunk and filthy masses and out the main entrance. More revelers spilled out onto the grounds, which slowed us down, but made it easier not to draw attention. After what felt like a fucking lifetime, she finally got us to a servants' entrance at the rear of the castle, unguarded but for a cook on a smoke break.

He pointed at us as we approached, then exploded in a hearty laugh.

Devil's Dream colored his tongue and clouded his eyes, the poor fucking idiot.

Jax grabbed his head and grinned. "Goodnight, asshole."

He snapped the guy's neck and dragged him inside, stashing the corpse in a meat locker, and on we went, following Gem through a maze of servant passages until we finally ended up one level above the ballroom. Music and revelry hummed below our feet.

"It's here," she finally said, stopping at a set of wooden double doors, plain and unguarded. "It leads into a small sanctuary behind the dais. We open these doors, we'll have maybe ten seconds before anyone spots us. I'll get Haley. You two take down the soldiers and Keradoc."

"Let's fucking do it," Jax said, and I nodded, fangs descending, adrenaline coursing through my blood. My mouth was already watering for a taste of Midnight blood.

Keradoc's, if I got lucky and he didn't.

Gem drew her short sword and pushed open the doors.

We followed her in, and in the span of a single breath, a few things became readily fucking apparent.

This wasn't some sanctuary behind the dais. Just an ordinary fucking room currently occupied by a firing squad of a dozen Midnight guards with crossbows, all pointed at me and Jax.

Gem had fucking betrayed us.

Half the crossbows were loaded with hawthorn stakes for me, the other with good old-fashioned bolts for Jax.

I didn't need a closeup to know they'd be carved with devil's trap sigils —a demon's worst nightmare. As soon as one of those fuckers nailed him, he'd drop, completely immobilized.

Gem lowered her sword and stepped behind us, pushing us forward. "On your knees, tough guys."

Outnumbered and outgunned, we did as she asked. My heart fucking liquified.

"I trusted you," I breathed. "I thought you were one of us."

"I'm sorry," she said coldly. Flat. Nothing like the Gem I knew. The Gem I thought I'd always known. "But it's like I always say, *Elian*... Nothing in Midnight is ever what it should be."

She crossed over to join the firing squad. Then, her gaze locked firmly on mine, she stepped behind them and said, "Fire at will."

# 39

## HALEY

*S*eriously? This is your A-game, Keradoc? Fairy-dust roofies and some light bondage?" I struggled against the ropes binding me to his throne, but it was no use. Unlike the last rope, this stuff had been spelled.

I had no idea how long I'd been unconscious this time, but judging from the numb ass, it'd been a while.

Where were Jax and Hudson? Gem? Elian? Did they still not realize I was missing?

Or had they been captured, too?

Had Elian even shown up tonight?

"Let me go," I gritted out, "and I promise I won't throw your corpse to the ghouls after I kill you."

Standing in front of his precious skull throne, Keradoc glared down at me, unimpressed. "I don't know the guise under which you were sent here, Daughter of Darkwinter, but your purpose is neither to kill me nor to steal my blood. You're here to help me win this war."

"Don't call me that. I'm not Darkwinter."

He set his hands on the arms of the throne and leaned in close, his scent nearly suffocating me. "I can *smell* it on your blood, witch. The darkness in you."

I fought back a shiver. "How can you smell *anything* with all that cheap cologne you're drowning in?"

"Taunt me all you wish. Melantha assured me your ancestry can be traced and verified."

*Melantha.*

So it was true, then. The bitch betrayed me.

Fury boiled up inside.

But... Why had she gone to all the trouble of sending me on this doomed blood-heist mission if her intent was to turn me over to Keradoc? It made no sense.

Still, my gut told me he wasn't lying. Not about this.

"Melantha?" I sneered. "The same one who ordered me to steal your blood for a spell to free her son? Yes, she's certainly a reliable narrator. Good call trusting her."

"Her son?" He let out a dark chuckle. "It seems Melantha was hedging her bets. I regret to inform you she has no children—only tricks."

"Says the master illusionist himself. Nice glamour, by the way. Might want to touch it up a bit—it's starting to show your age. And those eyes... Are they violet? Silver? Who can tell?"

He hesitated, just for a moment. Just long enough to let me know my arrow had hit the mark.

*So it was a glamour. And he didn't realize it was faltering.*

"Why did she want your blood?" I asked, taking advantage of his momentary distraction. I needed to get him talking. Ranting. Ranting villains always increased your chances of mounting a successful escape.

"She's trying to blackmail me into reversing her permanent banishment from Midnight. With my blood in her possession, she could've crafted all sorts of curses to harm or manipulate me." He sighed, as if the topic bored him. "You're a blood witch, Haley. You know how this works."

"But it sounds like you guys already made a deal, no? She gift-wraps me in a nice little bow and delivers me to Midnight, and you let her back in. Right?"

"That was the agreement, but I never had any intentions of honoring it. I suppose that's why she made a backup plan."

"She wanted a win-win," I said, the pieces finally clicking into place.

Melantha must've figured it would go one of two ways—either I'd get the blood and make it back to the Temple, granting her the powers she needed to blackmail him, or I'd fail and Keradoc would get to keep his so called present, granting her that shiny new passport to Midnight as a thanks.

"Well, fuck her," I said. "She's officially on my shit-list. Hey! Here's a thought." I flashed my most award-winning smile. "Maybe we should team up and kick her ass? The enemy's enemy is my friend?"

"Oh, but we *are* teaming up." A cruel smirk twisted his otherwise handsome face, and a chill skittered down my spine. "To make a weapon."

His earlier words echoed, the speech he'd given the crowd. Something about... a weapon the enemy could never defeat?

And if he needed Darkwinter blood to make it...

"It's me," I whispered, more to myself than to him. "I'm the weapon."

"Did you not wonder why it was so easy for you to traverse this treacherous realm?" Keradoc asked. "To breach my wall without the guards raising the alarm? To slip into my castle with a forged invitation?"

His words crashed over me in a dark wave. I'd thought we'd just gotten lucky with our escape from the raven gryphons and the relatively unimpeded trek to the wall. With the starshowers that'd distracted the guards. With securing Gem's help.

But no—luck had nothing to do with it. Keradoc had been expecting me all along, and he'd rolled out Midnight's version of the red carpet, luring me right into his trap.

He must've seen the realization dawning on my face, because when he spoke again, his tone dripped with smug satisfaction. "You will use your blood magick to summon your Darkwinter ancestors. Our necromancers will take care of the rest."

I closed my eyes, trying to recall everything I knew about my Darkwinter heritage. I'd only just found out about it recently—it all came out during the attacks on Blackmoon Bay, and since then, I'd been doing my best to ignore it. We fought against Darkwinter in the Bay too, just like Keradoc was doing in Midnight. They were evil assholes. I didn't want to believe I'd come from them—who would?

But now, I could no longer deny the truth.

My sisters and I were descendants of one of the very first witches and... wait for it... her Darkwinter lovers.

Yes, lovers. Plural. Apparently, it runs in the family.

My sister Gray had said something about a spell with the ancestors. If I remembered it right, there was a way you could summon them and resurrect them into new vessels. *Living* vessels.

Is that what Keradoc intended?

To resurrect Darkwinter ancestors into the bodies of Midnight soldiers?

Holy shit. The existing Darkwinter soldiers—Keradoc's invaders—would have no choice but to surrender. Not unless they wanted to dishonor their entire bloodline and slaughter their own family members.

Sort of.

I opened my eyes again, my head spinning. This was insane. All of it. *They* were insane. Melantha, Keradoc, the Darkwinter fae... Why didn't they just fuck off to their own private island and kill each other there? Leave everyone else out of it?

"You *will* help me, Haley," Keradoc said.

I lifted my chin, just like the wolf shifters had done earlier. "And if I refuse? You can take my blood, but you can't force me to do a summoning spell. The magick won't work if my heart isn't in it."

He retrieved a dagger from inside his jacket—my dagger. Fresh blood had only just begun to dry on the blade.

I shuddered to think whose it might be.

Keradoc grinned, then dragged his tongue along the blade, his eyes wicked and cold.

How could I *ever* have mistaken Keradoc for Elian?

Yet... he wasn't the real Keradoc either, was he? Just someone wearing the *illusion* of Keradoc.

How many layers deep did the glamour magick go?

And who the hell *was* the guy behind all the masks?

"If you refuse to aid me in defeating my enemies," he said, "your friends will suffer the same fate as the wolf shifters you so ardently defended earlier."

Alarm shot through my chest.

"What friends?" I forced a laugh. "If I had friends, don't you think they would've rescued me by now? I came alone at the behest of Melantha. If you don't like how this little blind date of ours is turning out, take it up with *that* bitch."

"Tsk tsk," he said. "Lying, on top of all the crimes you've already committed? Unwise."

Before I could say anything else, he snapped his fingers, and the door at the rear of the room creaked open.

Four guards entered, once again dragging prisoners.

Only this time, they weren't treasonous wolf shifters.

They were my men.

My monsters.

My fucking heart.

Hudson wasn't with them—the only glimmer of hope.

But Jax and Elian were. It was the first I'd seen my vampire-fae in days.

The guards dropped them on their knees at the bottom of the dais, barely conscious, both bleeding from multiple wounds—hawthorn stakes for Elian, metal bolts for Jax, likely cursed to trap demons. It was the only thing that would've rendered him so weak.

They both looked up at me, agony twisting their faces when they saw me tied to the throne.

I couldn't help the pained gasp that escaped, the tears that leaked from my eyes.

I could hardly breathe.

Blood soaked their shirts. Their faces had been severely beaten, eyes swollen and blackened, teeth missing. Jax's eye patch was gone, revealing a crater of old scar tissue and fresh gashes.

Thanks to the hawthorn poisoning his system, Elian wouldn't be able to heal. I couldn't even imagine his suffering.

And yet, when he finally turned away from me to look at our captor, it seemed as if he was suddenly gazing upon the face of a god.

Elian's breath caught, and for a moment, he stopped breathing altogether. Tears streamed down his face, but the pain in his eyes was gone, replaced with relief. With joy.

I glanced at Keradoc.

The glamour was fading again, and now he looked more like Elian than he ever had earlier. Same silver eyes. Same face.

Still on his knees in a rapidly spreading pool of his own blood, the real Elian smiled, his lips curving into that sexy, crooked grin I loved so much.

And when he finally spoke through that broken, bloodied smile, he whispered a name I'd only ever heard him say in the throes of his most fearsome nightmares, thrashing so hard he'd torn off the sheets, bolting upright in a cold sweat and clinging to me in the darkness as if the devil himself was on his way to personally drag him to hell.

*"Evander?"*

# BLOOD AND MALICE

BOOK TWO

# 1

## HUDSON

*A* dark little whisper nagged inside, making my wings twitch. *Something sure as shit ain't right.*

From my perch on the highest turret on the eastern side of Keradoc's castle, I scanned the scene, looking for signs of trouble.

Seemed like the whole of Amaranth City had turned out for the Feast of the Beast, and the few who *hadn't* shown up were most likely out casing houses and apartments, helping themselves to the revelers' unattended loot.

Course, the thieves would most likely be tracked down and murdered within a day, but that was all part of the game. Real entertainment was scarce in Midnight; everyone had to make their own fun.

Bass thumped from the ground floor, the music even louder than the shouts and whoops of the drunken assholes in attendance, all the noise making the stones beneath my feet vibrate. The place was so packed, half the guests had already been pushed out onto the grounds. Everywhere I looked, people were either fighting or fucking—sometimes both. All around the castle, the ground was muddy with spilled booze and puke and blood. I wondered whose sorry ass would be tasked with tomorrow's cleanup.

Grateful for the relatively fresher air up on the turrets, I took a deep breath and dropped into a glide, circling the perimeter. I spotted three of Keradoc's gargoyle guards making the rounds, but they looked to be about as drunk as the rest of the riffraff and were easily dodged.

Clearly, the warlord needed better security. Not that I was gonna drop *that* little comment in the suggestion box.

Shitty security or not, I wasn't about to let my guard down. Haley was counting on me. All of them were. And that voice inside me wasn't getting any quieter.

Took me a while, but after my fourth loop around the property, I finally spotted them—Saint and Jax following Gem through the melee outside. They weren't looking up at me, though. Too focused on their destination.

*The hell they going?*

I followed from above as they elbowed their way through the mass of sweaty bodies and headed for a back entrance—kitchens, most likely. Some servant or cook was standing outside the door, but Jax took him out.

*Shit.*

That whisper inside me grew to a shout. No way would Jax kill some random fae on a whim—not even one of Keradoc's random fae. Way too risky, especially with Haley involved.

I was about to drop down and follow them into whatever shitstorm they were gearing up for, but a new threat buzzed through my blood— sharp and sudden and utterly unmistakable.

*Haley.* She was in trouble, and fucking scared. Thanks to the bond, her fear was so palpable, it may as well have been my own.

Leaving Jax and Saint to fight their own battles, I zoomed back up toward the fourth level, following the insistent pull of my connection to Haley. The pain. It felt like a fishing line reeling me in, a sharp hook right through the gut.

In seconds, I knew *exactly* where she was.

Throne room. I was intimately familiar with it. Centuries ago, before my life went to shit here and I was relegated to working private security gigs for Midnight's drug and weapons dealers, I was head guardian to one of the Midnight noble families. They spent a lot of time hobnobbing at the castle, kissing the ass of a different ruler while Keradoc was still clawing his way to power. Keradoc was no different though—all them fae fuckers liked to keep my kind close. Gargoyles were better than fae at taking bullets and arrows.

But Haley certainly wasn't there as an ass-kissing noble tonight. Or even as a spy.

She was a prisoner.

I saw her the second the windows came into view, bound to the throne on the dais.

The pain in my gut turned to raw fucking rage.

*Hell no, asshole. Wrong fucking night, wrong fucking witch.*

I tucked my wings close and arrowed straight for the windows, ready to smash through the glass, grab that purple-eyed fae fucker, and rip the spine from his body. But just before impact, a hot streak sizzled up my spine, tearing through me with an agony that left me gasping for air. My back twisted against the pain as my muscles seized up, sending me into a fucking tailspin.

I crashed to the ground behind the castle like a warplane shot out of the sky, sending up a wave of mud and debris.

My thick hide saved my bones from shattering, but it still fucking hurt like the devil. I had just enough strength to roll onto my back and wipe the muck from my eyes. I wasn't far from where I'd seen Gem take Jax and Saint. The door they'd ducked into was mere feet away.

But it may as well have been a hundred miles for all the time I had to get there.

Before I even fully caught my breath, my attackers were already swooping down for the kill shot. Dark shapes closed in fast from overhead—fifteen seconds until impact.

Wings. Claws. Horns and fangs.

Fucking gargoyles.

Not the drunk mercs I'd seen earlier, but street fighters. No sense of honor or loyalty among them—and yeah, I was speaking from experience.

Garrison, Draven, and—worst of the lot—Mad Marco, who made up for his lack in stature with balls-out craziness. Three of the six Stone City homegrown assholes who'd slaughtered people I cared about, destroyed my old life in Midnight, and left me for dead.

Twice.

Haley's fear spiked again, sending another zing straight to my gut. Pretty sure the other guys were in deep shit, too. I needed to get to them—and fast.

I closed my eyes. Gave myself one more heartbeat to get my lungs working and get my ass out of the dirt.

Rage was the best fuel there was, and between Haley's fear and my old enemies attacking me, I was *furious*. I stoked those flames hard, let them propel me out of the mud and onto my feet. I was still in warrior form, nothing broken far as I could tell, but I wasn't about to give anything away.

Keeping my wings limp and my shoulders hunched, I struck a weak pose as all three of 'em landed and closed ranks around me, claws out and snarls twisting their gruesome faces.

Unlike last time they'd gotten the drop on me, they'd come alone tonight—no dark witch to do their bidding. But whatever they'd hit me with in the sky wasn't gargoyle-made. It was magick. And there was a hundred percent chance they were packin' more, because pricks like them never fought their own battles.

"Look what the cat dragged back from the human realm, boys." Marco started in right away, predictable as fuck. His eyes were wide and crazy, his familiar gap-toothed grin splitting his face—the rare gargoyle who looked the same amount of ugly whether he was a statue or a human. Now, in his warrior form, he shook out his tattered wings and shifted from one foot to the other, twitchy as hell. "Guess your vacation on the other side didn't work out so well."

"Welcome home, motherfucker." This, from Garrison, the biggest and dumbest of the lot. Talked a good game but sucked in a fight.

I pretended to cower in silence, keeping my head low. The closer they got, the less energy I'd have to expend taking them down, and no, that wouldn't hamper my enjoyment of it in the least.

"What's wrong, Hudson?" Marco taunted, tilting his head and peering up at me with those crazy eyes. "After all these centuries, you're still not talking? Not even to your oldest friends?"

Talking? Totally unnecessary, much as he liked to flap his lips. Midnight-bred gargoyles were connected—long as no one was actively shielding, we could tap into one another's minds to communicate. I'd been shielding against every last one of them fuckers since I set foot back in this realm, but now it was time to send out a broadcast.

*That you, Marco? Hard to recognize you when you're not cowering behind a witch. Shit, boy. You're a lot shorter than I remember.*

"And you're a lot more *alive* than I remember," he sneered. "Guess we'll have to do something about that." He slammed a fist into my gut. I was ready for it though—saw it coming a mile off. I doubled over, feigning pain, and the other two rock-heads pounced on cue.

*Yeah. Not happening, fuckholes.*

I reared up to my full height and smashed my fists into their faces, sending them both sailing backward through the air. They hit the ground with twin thuds, and I spun around, landing a solid kick to Marco's chest. He stumbled back but didn't go down.

With a fierce growl, he came at me again, slashing his talons across my chest. I dodged the worst of it and ducked low, then plowed into him headlong, taking his ass down.

Set to the soundtrack of the still-thumping party music, we wrestled on the ground, trading punches and slashes—a blow to the jaw here, a gash along the ribs there. I was bigger and stronger, but that little fucker was fast and wily. One cheap knee-shot to the balls, and he sent me rolling off him, giving him just enough time to scramble back to his feet.

Ignoring the throbbing pain in my groin, I sucked in a breath and rose to face him once more. Garrison and Draven were back in the mix now, all three of the beasts circling me like wild dogs, panting and growling, salivating for a bite. Blood and sweat dripped into my eyes, but I didn't dare blink. Didn't dare give them fuckers a chance to take me out.

Three on one? They probably could've, had they been smarter.

Yet no one made another move.

Whole thing was fucking futile, anyway. Gargoyles in warrior form were nearly impossible to kill—aside from a soft bit of flesh at the throat that could be pierced with a sword or an arrow, we had thick, ultra-protective hides, massive muscles, and we could escape most ground skirmishes by taking flight. Best chance at killing us was to take us by surprise in our human form or get us to turn to stone, then smash us like bad pottery.

But here, tonight?

Without a sunlight spell to turn my ass to stone—or a few sharp weapons and better aim—these fuckers didn't have much of a shot, and they damn well knew it.

Which meant…

*Fuck.*

They weren't here to take me down. They were just a distraction.

I could still sense Haley, though the signal was getting weaker. I hoped that didn't mean *she* was getting weaker.

"What's wrong?" Marco asked, wiping the blood from his mouth as he leered up at me. "Lose another one of your charges? Guess some things never change."

"Too bad, really," Draven piped in. He licked his lips and grunted. "Such a pretty little witch. I would've loved to have a go at that."

The tremble began in my hands, quickly shooting up my arms and across my back. My muscles tensed for another fight, talons curling, everything inside me eager for a bloodbath.

*You're fucking dust,* I sent out. *All of you.*

Marco nodded, finally shutting his trap and letting his thoughts come to me instead. *Someday, maybe. But not tonight.*

He raised his arms and pointed something at my chest. A gun, I realized. Manmade. Useless against me.

I spread my arms and smiled, welcoming the nip of those useless little bullets. *Looks like someone's got a new toy. Compensating, maybe?*

*You tell me, cocksucker.* Marco fired off a whole mess of rounds, the bullets biting into my hide like annoying mosquitos. I plucked one of them from my chest and tossed it at him.

He hit me with one last shot in the gut.

When he was done jerking off his new gun, he stood there watching me expectantly, smoke curling from the end of the barrel.

*Yeah,* definitely *compensating.* I laughed, inside and out, and stalked toward him, my talons itching for a chance to spill more of his blood. All of it. *Got anything bigger, or is that the best you —*

All at once, my body froze up on me, and a new grin lit up that motherfucker's face.

A dozen tiny explosions tore through my insides, chewing through bone and muscle, unleashing a flood of pure, white-hot agony.

These were no ordinary bullets. None that I'd ever had the fucked-up pleasure of being shot with, anyway—not in the realms of monsters *or* men—which was saying a lot.

*Fuck. Me.*

I stumbled to my knees as my muscles stiffened. Everything inside me was turning to stone, but not because I'd shifted. Felt like I'd chugged a few hundred gallons of cement.

"Ultraviolet bullets," Marco boasted out loud, admiring his gun. "They ignite on contact—little balls of sunshine packed into a human death machine. Say what you will about dark witches, Hudson, but they really are ingenious bitches when they need to be."

Before I could even ask what constituted a witch's need for ingenuity, he lifted the gun again. Stepped close.

Then he spat in my face like a fucking coward. Jammed the barrel into the spot between my eyes and...

*Bang.*

My world disappeared.

# 2

## KERADOC

*vander.*

The name slipped from the fugitive's lips and right through my defenses, prodding at something that felt like a memory. Images flashed in my mind—a fae child laughing, his silver eyes alight with mischief as he bent his head close to share a secret. A father playfully wrestling with his boys in the soft grass. The scent of sweet cakes cooling on a sill…

Another time, another place. Certainly not mine.

Blinking away the odd images, I stepped down from the dais, leaving the Darkwinter witch bound to the throne behind me.

Still on his knees, the vampire-fae fugitive my guards had captured gazed up at me strangely, his silver eyes so like my real eyes. Similar too were the set of his jaw and the sharpness of his cheekbones, and the grin that tipped higher on one side than the other. It was as if we'd been cast from the very same mold.

But for the glamour I'd been wearing for the last eighteen months, I could've been gazing into a mirror.

"It's really you," he whispered as I approached. Blood leaked from a half-dozen wounds in his chest, hawthorn stakes jutting out at odd angles, sapping his strength. His pain must've been unbearable, yet his eyes held only wonder. Happiness.

*Evander…*

"No one gave you permission to speak, slave." One of my guards kicked the prisoner in the back, sending him sprawling. He caught himself on his hands with a grunt but made no effort to get back to his knees. A coughing fit seized him, wringing the blood from his lungs out onto the polished floor. The guards had dragged away the remains of the executed shifters but had yet to clean up their mess. Now, it mingled with the blood of my new prisoners in a dark, wet stain. The scent of copper and fear hung heavy in the air.

"Keradoc!" the witch cried out, as fiery as ever. I didn't need to turn around to know she was still struggling against her bonds. "Help him! *Help* him!"

At her desperate cries, the second fugitive—a one-eyed demon shot full of metal bolts—winced, as if the fear in her voice hurt him even more than the devil's trap sigils sucking away his life force.

Even more than watching his mate suffer brutally on the floor beside him.

The vampire-fae lifted his head once more. His arms trembled. Blood leaked from his nose and mouth, but he was still staring at me with awe.

"Do you not remember?" he whispered. "Do you not know your..." His words trailed off into another wet cough that seemed to stretch on for an eternity, but through it all, one word rang out clear, whispered over and over again like a prayer.

*Evander. Evander. Evander.*

The echo of it unleashed another flicker of images—two fae boys swimming in a cool emerald-green lake, diving for make-believe buried treasure. A mother calling them back to the shore for lunch, the sand pink and glittery beneath her bare toes. The rustle of the breeze through treetops dripping with silver leaves.

An odd warmth spread through my chest, quickly chased by a sucking emptiness so cold it left me gasping.

I cleared my throat and dismissed the visions, reclaiming my focus. This was obviously another of Melantha's games—some wicked spell meant to disarm me and distract me from her machinations with the Darkwinter witch.

No matter. When this war was finally over, I'd make the dark goddess pay. By the time I finished with her, the banishment she was enduring now would look like a pleasant vacation.

"Keradoc," the witch called out again, cutting straight through my thoughts like a blade through flesh.

I turned to her, drawn by the anger in her voice. The righteousness.

The contrast of the raw bones and sharp, polished obsidian of my throne against her soft skin and artfully painted face was so striking, it nearly stole my breath. Death and beauty, darkness and light. Both suited her equally.

A smile touched my lips. For all Melantha's tricks, the blood witch Haley Barnes was *not* a disappointment. Not only was she beautiful, she was sharp-tongued, passionate, clever, and just this side of mad.

Precisely how I needed her.

No witch in her *right* mind would attempt the ancestral ritual required to channel her Darkwinter kin—Midnight's most formidable enemies. Haley herself would certainly refuse at first, but I had no doubts she'd come around soon enough.

Now that I'd captured her companions, persuading her to cooperate would be much easier.

"*Do* something," she implored, and the fire sparking in her green eyes ignited a more recent memory—one I could absolutely claim as my own.

*Her lips crashing into mine as she wrapped her legs around me, stealing a kiss that left us both breathless. The feel of her silky hair in my hands as I laid her on the dais and gave her what she seemed to so desperately want...*

The taste of her still lingered on my tongue, threatening to make me hard again.

But no. It wasn't me she'd wanted. The witch had seen through my glamour, however briefly, and mistaken me for another.

Her vampire-fae, I realized now. The Midnight fugitive who seemed to be wearing my real face.

More dark magick. More trickery.

My blood simmered as Melantha's betrayal burned through me anew. Was there no spell she wouldn't conjure, no illusion she wouldn't cast in her endless attempts at vengeance?

I clenched my fists and closed my eyes, forcing myself to remain steady. In control. Unraveling in front of my guards and prisoners would put everything at risk, and I'd worked too hard, too tirelessly for that.

"Evander..." the fugitive said once more, his voice a gurgling whisper as he continued to drown in his own blood. New images flashed through my mind—fae children chasing each other through a thick forest. A festival in the heart of the oaken woods, boughs glittering with lights, couples dancing merrily as red and gold leaves fluttered on the breeze like birds...

Behind my eyes, a dull ache throbbed to the beat of an old song lingering on the edge of memory...

"Please, Keradoc." The witch's voice cut through the din, chasing away the music and the visions both. When I opened my eyes again, I found her gazing back at me, her face pained.

I climbed back up the dais and approached the throne. "What was that, little thief?"

The demon responded before she could find her words. "Touch her and you'll—"

One of my guards shot him with another bolt, silencing him.

"I'll… I'll do anything you ask of me," the witch stammered. "Just stop hurting them. Please… please don't kill them." Tears brimmed in her eyes, dousing the last of her fire. She was suddenly exhausted and weak.

Pathetic.

Anger stirred inside me. This woman, this formidable witch had traveled to Midnight and risked her life in an attempt to steal my blood. My blood! Even after I'd exposed her lies and taken her prisoner, she'd continued to taunt me, to fight me, to burn with indignation.

Yet now, at the sight of her wounded companions, she crumpled like a flower crushed beneath a soldier's boot?

Had I been wrong about her mettle? Her power?

"Help them," she begged again, not meeting my eyes.

I gripped the arms of the throne and bent low, leaning so close to her the berries-and-cream scent of her skin filled my senses. Ignoring the stirrings of my cock, I said softly, "My apologies, little thief. I can't quite hear you above the pathetic moans of my prisoners. Did you have a request? "

"Yes." She finally glanced up and met my eyes. That old fire blazed anew, and at my answering grin, she flashed one of her own. Sly. Triumphant. *Wicked.* "Get fucked, asshole. You're going *down.*"

**3**

HALEY

Thanks to Keradoc's obsession with sharp objects—obsidian and bones, in this case—I finally sawed through the fae-spelled ropes and sliced a deep gouge in my palm, coating my ring in fresh blood.

Now, I took more than a little pleasure in watching that smug grin fall off the warlord's face.

"Get fucked, asshole. You're going *down*." I slammed a blood-soaked palm against his chest. Power scorched the air as a blast of magick exploded at my touch, sending him crashing down the dais.

With another quick spell, I called up a magickal barrier around the guys. The guards rushed forward, but it was too late. I leaped from the throne and bolted down the dais, sealing myself inside the barrier with Elian and Jax before Keradoc could bark out an order to attack.

A wall of bright-red magick surged and crackled around us, enclosing us in a temporary safe haven impervious to weapons and fists.

Finally righting himself, Keradoc commanded the guards to break through, but they were no match for the magickal shield.

"Nice work, angel." Jax managed a thin smile, but he was fading fast. Blood soaked into his shirt around the bolts and leaked from a deep gash on his forehead, sliding into the cavern of his missing eye.

He couldn't even lift a hand to my shoulder without wincing.

"Sit tight," I told him. "We'll figure this out. Just... just give me a minute."

I reached out to touch the barrier. It brightened in response, but just

223

like that night in Blackbone Forest with the raven gryphon, I had no idea how long it would hold.

Didn't matter, though. Five minutes or an hour, eventually it would fizzle out, and we'd have to fight our way out of this room.

I needed to get my men back on their feet.

I dropped down in front of Elian, gently helping him to his knees. He was the priority—he'd lost more blood than Jax, and that much hawthorn crammed into his body posed a major risk of permanent damage. If I could get the stakes out quickly, his natural healing would hopefully kick in. Then we could use his vampire blood to heal Jax.

Forcing a smile, I said, "No offense, Elian, but this is the *worst* rescue attempt ever. It's like you've never even seen a superhero movie."

"Sparrow." He cupped my face with a bloody hand, too weak to even smile back.

I hadn't seen him since that night in the bedroom with Jax when he'd refused to kiss me, and suddenly there he was, his blood on my face, regret heavy in his voice, the scent of death sharp on the air...

All of it threatened to break me.

"I'll fix this," I said firmly, trying to convince us both. "Hold still."

A brutal cough rattled through his chest, wet and wheezing. When he looked at me again, his eyes were glassy, his brow wrinkled in pain and confusion. He blinked slowly, then looked up at our captors.

"Evander," he whispered, but then shook his head, his brow knitting in confusion as if he no longer recognized the name.

I had no idea who Evander was, or why Elian was so oddly fixated on Keradoc, but it would have to wait.

"Elian," I said, "listen to me. We need to remove these stakes, and—"

"No," he panted, shifting his attention back to me. A new urgency flashed through his eyes, clearing away the haze. "You must... get out. Run, sparrow. You... go."

All around us the magick flickered, the guards hitting the wall with fae magick and weapons both, Keradoc pacing like an animal trying to sniff out the weak spot.

"Haley." Jax coughed, blood splattering his lips. "It was Gem. She... she betrayed... You need to leave."

"Gem?" I gasped. "Shit. Shit! Okay. Guys? I need you both to stay focused. Jax, we can heal you with Elian's blood. He just needs a minute to regain his strength. I need to get these stakes out, so shut up and let me concentrate."

Elian pushed my hands away, dark blood leaking from his mouth in a seemingly endless stream. "Go. Find… find Hudson and—" Another wet cough strangled his words.

Next to us, Jax sucked in a sharp breath and closed his eye, a shiver rattling his body.

He could sense it, I realized. My fear.

It surged up inside me, but quickly fizzled in the wake of another emotion.

Raw, unchecked rage.

*Fuck. This.*

I *refused* to be scared. There was no reason for it. Both of them were going to be just fine. Hudson was fine. All of us were absolutely fucking *fine*. We just needed to get on our feet—first mission. That was our lasagna. Stop the fucking bleeding and get these guys back on their feet.

"Here's the deal, Elian," I snapped. "I'm really mad at you, asshole. Like, *really* mad. For a lot of things, not the least of which—" I gripped his shoulder and unceremoniously yanked out one of the stakes. "—is your vanishing act this week. We don't hear from you for days, and suddenly you show up shot full of hawthorn and dragged in by armed guards like a stuck pig?" I ripped out another stake, enjoying his grunts of agony. "What kind of vampire *does* that? God, I should put you out of your misery right now. One less cocky, obstinate, irredeemable bloodsucking fuckstick in the world." Another stake removed, another clattering to the ground as Keradoc and his guards continued their assault on my barrier. "But you know what, Elian? *That* would be giving you an easy out, and you haven't earned it. So if you fucking die on me here? Yeah. We're gonna have a *serious* problem—way more serious than a few branches of hawthorn impaling your chest." I freed the last stake, then met his eyes once more. Not taking any chances, I sliced open my wrist with the stake, sucked the wound to get the blood flowing, then jammed it against his mouth. "Now feed, before I shove every last one of these stakes back in and finish the job Keradoc's guards started."

He tried to turn away, but the temptation of my fresh blood on his lips was too much to resist, as I knew it would be. He grabbed my wrist with a trembling hand and licked the wound, then sucked, his eyes locked on mine in a fierce battle of wills. We both knew he had no choice but to feed, but he wasn't about to do it happily.

Too bad. I needed him alive more than I needed him happy.

Ignoring the surge of pleasure in my veins, I let him take his fill, waiting until the first pangs of dizziness hit me before I finally tore my wrist from his mouth.

The color had returned to his face, the haze clearing from his eyes. The gaping wounds in his chest started closing. Slowly, but still. Progress.

Blood ran down my arm. I lowered it to my side and curled my fingers, letting it pool in the cup of my hand until it coated my ring. Then, pressing my hand to the floor, I whispered another spell. The magickal shield brightened in response, but the incessant barrage of dark fae magick was taking its toll.

We didn't have much time.

"We need to help Jax," I said to Elian.

Wiping the blood from his mouth, he nodded and crawled over to the demon, who was turning paler by the second. Elian bit into his wrist and held it to Jax's mouth, urging him to drink as I carefully removed the bolts.

Even with the healing magick of vampire blood coursing through his system, Jax's wounds would still take time to heal. But devil's traps could drain a demon's life force at the soul level, and their removal had an immediate effect. All at once, the color returned to his skin, and after another minute, he finally turned away from Elian's vein, offering a curt nod of thanks.

"Better?" I asked.

"Nothing I won't survive." Jax wrapped an arm around his midsection, stifling another bloody cough as he scrambled to his feet.

I helped Elian up, and the three of us let out a collective sigh.

"Gem betrayed us," Elian said, leaning on me hard. A slight tremor still rattled his muscles, reverberating into my shoulder. "We planned for everything—*everything* but that."

Anger rolled off him in hot waves, infecting me and Jax both.

"We'll deal with her later," Jax said. "We need to find a way out."

"There are too many of them." I blew out a breath. "Once this barrier drops, they'll attack us."

"If Keradoc wanted us dead," Jax said, "we'd already be in the moat."

"Agreed," I said, "but there's a lot of gray area between keeping someone alive and keeping them alive and *unharmed*. I'm really not in the mood to get my ass kicked."

"You might not have a choice tonight, angel." He nodded at the show of force. The guards who weren't working on dismantling the barrier had their weapons drawn, every last one of them waiting for their shot— waiting for Keradoc to order them to take it.

Keradoc glared at me through the barrier, his eyes blazing, his rage so palpable I could practically taste it. Even through the magick, his sweet rose scent stung the back of my nose.

Memories collided suddenly in my mind, making me shiver. The dance, the sound of my name on his lips, the ferocity of our kiss, all of it spinning around my head like he'd spun me around that ballroom…

My magick flickered.

"Sparrow." Elian leaned close, his body still trembling and weak. "You… you need to go."

On my other side, Jax nodded. "We'll hold them off. You break for it."

"Shut up," I snapped. "Both of you. We go out together, or we go down together. Non-negotiable."

They tried to argue, but it was pointless. I'd no sooner leave them behind than they'd leave me. The problem was neither of them was strong enough to walk out of here without a lot of help—not when we'd still have to fight our way past the guards and whatever else awaited us outside this room, not to mention the party still raging down on the main level.

*Shit, shit, shit!*

Where was Hudson? What the hell had Gem done? Where had she gone? Was she still in the castle, waiting in the shadows for another opportunity to stab us in the back?

I glanced around frantically for another escape, my magick waning. Everywhere I looked, I saw another guard. Another obstacle. Another dead end.

I wanted to roar. After all that blood and magick, after finally getting the guys on their feet, we were no better off than when Keradoc's guards had dumped them on the floor. Elian didn't have the strength for a vampire blur, Jax didn't have the energy to work his fear mojo, and my magick was completely tapped out.

The barrier surrounding us faded to a dull pink.

We had minutes. Maybe seconds.

The guys closed ranks around me.

And then, with nothing more than a soft hiss, the magick fizzled out, leaving us completely exposed.

# 4

## HALEY

old your fire." Keradoc lifted a hand to the guards behind us, but his eyes were locked on mine, his gaze triumphant.

I felt Jax and Elian tense beside me, both of them spring-loaded for an attack.

"Don't," I whispered. "We're severely outnumbered."

"Never stopped us before," Jax said.

"Certain death?" Elian laughed. "I like the odds here, brother."

"Guys," I warned, but it was too late.

For two supernaturals who acted like they wanted to murder each other on the best of days, they sure didn't have any trouble teaming up to ignore me.

As one, they sprang into action and lunged for Keradoc, and I watched with fresh horror as two bolts zinged through the air, nailing them both in the back.

Once again, my men fell to their knees.

Unruffled, Keradoc stepped swiftly past them, brushing off his shoulder. He was still dressed in his party finery—black silks and leather swirled with delicate silver and violet embellishments—and if not for the sheen of sweat on his brow and the tiny flecks of blood dotting his cheek, he would've looked like the perfect gentleman and host.

He still hadn't dropped his gaze from mine, and as he approached, I felt powerless to do anything but watch… and wait.

Gone was the faltering glamour I'd seen earlier, leaving only Keradoc in its place—sharp jaw, penetrating violet eyes, sensual mouth.

Everything about him appeared kingly and entitled, his movements slow and deliberate, and in that moment, I wanted nothing more than to see the fae's dark head on a pike.

Yet the longer he stared at me, the farther my thoughts strayed, sweeping me up again in the memory of that sensual mouth claiming mine, his hands in my hair, his cock grinding against me on the dais…

I closed my eyes and took a step back, trying to shake myself loose from the grip of those images. From the feelings they unleashed inside me, hot and prickly and terrifying.

Intriguing.

When I opened my eyes again, the bastard was still watching me, a new glimmer shining in his violet eyes.

He arched a delicate eyebrow, as if he'd been reading my thoughts.

Through the burn of my cheeks, I lifted my chin, refusing to be cowed.

The situation was grim, sure, but not impossible. Like Jax had said—if Keradoc wanted us dead, we'd be swimming with the ghouls by now. He'd already admitted he needed me for the ancestor spell, which meant I had some leverage to play with. And since the guys were still in possession of their heads, even after attempting another attack against him, maybe they had some leverage, too.

It was a thin hope based on even thinner logic, but with Jax and Elian immobilized, Hudson MIA, and no other friends in sight, that hope was all I had to cling to.

He finally stopped before me, so close I could see all the shades of color in his irises. Not just violet, I realized now, but violet flecked with gold, ringed in deep indigo, the colors seeming to shift before me in an endless dance. He lowered his gaze to my mouth, and I sucked in a sharp breath, heat snaking down my spine.

*Kiss me like that again, Daughter of Darkwinter, and I'll be whoever you need me to be…*

"A heroic attempt, Miss Barnes," Keradoc said, and it took me a beat to realize he was talking about the blood magick, not my kiss. "Truly. But as I'm sure your companions can attest to—assuming their brief sojourn to the earthly realm didn't wipe the lesson from memory—Midnight has no need of heroes." Still glaring at me, he snapped his fingers, and several of the guards stepped forward. "Put the two fugitives in a cell. I'll deal with them later."

Jax and Elian groaned in protest, but groaning was about all they had the strength for. The guards grabbed them roughly. Elian coughed up more blood.

"If you still expect me to do your bidding, warlord," I said firmly, choking back my panic, "I expect you to leave my men unharmed."

"Your so-called men are nothing but lowly fugitives. They gave up the right to fair treatment the night they plotted with the dark goddess to betray me, defy their sentences, and escape my realm."

I narrowed my eyes. The dark goddess? *Melantha* had helped them escape?

No wonder she knew about them—knew to send me to New Orleans to ask for Elian's help.

My mind reeled with new questions, but there was no time to ask them. The guards were already hauling Elian and Jax out, leaving a trail of blood in their wake.

"Give the order," I said, "or all of this will have been for nothing. I don't care what you and Melantha hold over my head. I won't help you if you hurt them, Keradoc. That's a promise."

The muscle in Keradoc's jaw ticked in annoyance, but after making me suffer through another long, admonishing glare, he finally nodded.

"Remove the bolts and dress their wounds," he told the guards. "Keep the demon and the fae together, isolated from the other prisoners."

"And give them food and water," I added. "*Fresh* food and *clean* water."

Another glare. Another sigh. And finally, a half-nod. "Water," he said. "For now."

It was more than I expected, so I kept my mouth shut.

"And the witch?" one of the guards asked.

"Leave her." Keradoc's teeth flashed in the torchlight, and he leaned closer once more, reaching for a lock of my hair. In a soft, soothing voice that sent chills racing across my shoulders, he whispered, "It's time I had a conversation with my little thief about consequences."

# 5

## HALEY

$\mathcal{I}$ was alone again with the warlord of Midnight, my insides trembling as he continued to stare at me, cold and unflinching. It felt like he was looking right through me, peeling back every layer, dismantling every wall I'd spent so many years erecting.

I studied him as well, still trying to understand what I'd seen behind his glamour. He was the warlord of Midnight—at least, that was the role he was playing. So why did he need to hide behind a mask?

More disturbing than that, though, was the strange connection I felt to him. Not just because of the intense kiss we'd shared, or because I'd used my magick to influence the flow of his blood, or even because I'd *sworn* I'd seen Elian's silver eyes flickering behind Keradoc's violet ones.

No… Something *else* bound me to this fae—a dark magick that hummed between us like an electrical current, barely perceptible but lingering nevertheless. My body responded to his presence even now, drawn to him in ways a captive should never be.

And in those violet eyes, I saw it too—the same curiosity about me as I felt about him. The same wonder.

The same desire.

After what seemed like an eternity, he finally turned his back and headed for the exit.

The breath rushed from my lungs in an audible sigh.

"Come," he demanded, the sharp, icy tone echoing with his footsteps across the floor.

I was still vibrating from the adrenaline coursing through my system, weakened from the magick I'd conjured, terrified for Jax and Elian, completely confused about my reactions to the man, and also—for the record—starving. Unless he was promising me dinner, I had no intentions of following that asshole *anywhere* alone.

When he realized I hadn't moved, he stopped before the exit, barely turning his head to spare me a glance. "Is there a problem, Miss Barnes?"

"I was waiting for you to say 'please,' but apparently, you're about as big a fan of manners as you are of free choice, so it looks like I'm pretty much screwed."

"Categorically untrue." He approached me again, his eyes glinting with some new trickery. "I'm a huge proponent of choice. In this moment, you've got two: follow me out of this room on your own two feet, or I shall render you unconscious and drag you out by the hair. Take your pick, witch, and make haste. I've got business to attend to."

"Wow. So the big, scary fairy gets off on making idle threats to women. *Very* impressive, Keradoc. You totally deserve a cookie." I rolled my eyes and stalked past him, knocking into his shoulder.

In a move so fluid it was no more than a blur in my peripheral vision, he spun and gripped my upper arms, hauling me backward against his chest. His fingers dug so hard into my flesh I knew he'd leave a bruise.

In a low, dangerous voice, he whispered, "Would you prefer I show rather than tell? Even in a realm so brutal as ours, I'm *not* known for my mercy."

"Really? And here I thought you were a big ol' softy, what with you beheading a pair of shifters, sending your guards to ambush my men with crossbows, tossing them into the dungeon half-dead and bleeding, not to mention drugging me with your fae roofies." I jerked free of his grip and turned to face him, rubbing my throbbing arms. "Twice, I might add. And I don't care how many guards you have at your beck and call. You manhandle me like that again, the next time I work my magick, I'll blast it straight up your arrogant fae ass."

A slow grin stretched across his mouth, a menacing slash of red in a face too pretty to be so dark. "You think me cruel, little thief?"

"Among other things, yes."

"Cruelty is a tactic that wins wars."

"Cruelty is a tactic relied upon by men with small dicks who lack the confidence to communicate and the courage to fight fair."

"I see. So in your neat-and-tidy little worldview, the meek shall inherit the earth—or in this case, Midnight?" He scoffed. "Only two kinds of people believe that, Miss Barnes. The extremely privileged and the extremely naïve, neither of whom have any right to criticize the things the rest of us must do to survive."

*Survive.* The word pricked at my insides, igniting a flurry of fresh outrage.

"You aren't a survivor, Keradoc," I practically spat. "You're the reason people like me are forced to survive. You stand there reeking of wealth and power, smiling for your guests, opening your home to the masses as if you're some benevolent god from above when in reality you're nothing but a murderer, a kidnapper, a torturer, and a warmonger with legions of minions falling over themselves for a chance to do your bidding. The only battles your sword has ever seen are the ones dropped at your feet for your entertainment, and you know *nothing* about my life—nothing but the few things you believe will serve your interests. So the next time you want to lecture me about privilege and naïveté, you pompous dick, do your fucking homework."

This time, I didn't turn away or try to stalk past him. I stared him down, fury simmering between us, waiting for him to make another move —to tie me up again, to blow his gold fairy dust into my face, to gut me with the dagger he'd stolen from me.

But Keradoc only glared at me, the indignation in his eyes warring with his unchecked curiosity and, if I didn't know any better, arousal.

Saying nothing, he finally turned and marched toward the door. This time, he didn't stop to see if I was following, and for the briefest instant, I considered bolting in the other direction, taking my chances with another doorway, a window, anything but whatever Keradoc had in store for me.

But Gem had already betrayed us. The guys had been ambushed. Keradoc knew the game right from the start, and he'd likely planned for every contingency.

If there was truly another escape, he wouldn't have turned his back on me.

I closed my eyes. Drew a deep breath.

*Survive,* I told myself, the word never far from my thoughts. *No matter what.*

It was my next piece of lasagna—make it through the night alive. Not just for myself, but for Jax and Elian. For Hudson, wherever he was. For my sisters. I had no idea if Melantha knew I'd failed in my quest to retrieve Keradoc's blood, but right now, I had to hope she didn't. Had to hope that my sisters were okay.

And as much as it burned me to admit it, that fae asshole was my best shot at coming up with a plan to keep them safe. Melantha was as much Keradoc's enemy as she was mine. That right there was some common ground.

Something I could potentially exploit as readily as he was planning to exploit my Darkwinter connection.

*Survive.* The word echoed once more.

I nodded. Shored up my walls. Promised myself I'd do just that.

And right now, surviving meant putting one foot in front of the other and following my captor into the dark abyss that awaited me.

# 6

## HALEY

With smooth, graceful steps, Keradoc led me down the long corridor outside the throne room and up a narrow, winding staircase that climbed so high I grew dizzier with every step. There was no railing and no light to guide the way, only the glint of silver on his clothing a few steps ahead and the cold, damp stone surrounding us—sometimes smooth and polished, other times as rough and unrefined as the walls of a cave.

Again I thought about slicing my palm, trying to tap back into my magick. But I was running on empty, in desperate need of food and sleep, and worried about the guys. Fear and exhaustion? Perfect formula for sloppy mistakes. Keradoc would be expecting another attack, and we'd already encountered a dozen more guards, some pacing the halls, others scuttling down the stairs like roaches, their armor and weapons brushing my chest as I stepped aside to let them pass.

Best I just bide my time. Gather my strength. Observe, assess, and make a plan.

My thighs and calves burned with every step, but finally, after what felt like hours, we reached the top of the staircase. It was all I could do not to drop to my hands and knees and kiss the ground.

The landing opened up right in the center of a massive gallery that stretched out about fifty feet in both directions, with towering stained-glass windows at each end like some kind of gothic cathedral. The walls were the same rough-hewn black stone as the staircase, only now they glowed a soft orange from dozens of magickal chandeliers hanging from the ceiling, the endless black rock broken only by a series of ornately carved oak doors. I had no idea what lay beyond them, but the whole place was, like so much of Midnight, strangely beautiful and intriguing.

"The entire castle was once a mountain," Keradoc said, his voice softening with a hint of wonder that took me by surprise. "Legend has it the trolls carved it into a castle with their bare hands."

"Trolls? They're a thing here?"

"No one knows for certain. None have been sighted for a good five hundred years or so." This time, the smile he shared was playful rather than cruel, and damn if it didn't send a little spark to my heart. "Fear not, Miss Barnes. Should any trolls breach the walls and attempt to reclaim their home, I shall personally slaughter them and present their heads to you on silver platters."

I shrugged as if his teasing *hadn't* thrown me completely off guard. "If you're looking for the perfect gift, K-Doc, I'm more of a chocolates-and-weapons kinda girl. Actually, if you wouldn't mind returning that dagger you stole from me and sending me on my merry little way, we'll call it even. Hell, I'll even send you a thank-you card when I get back home."

He shook his head, his eyes dancing in the light. He looked younger somehow, as if a little teasing had the power to erase years of brutal existence.

Maybe it did.

"Fair offer," he said with a wink, "but I think I'll pass, clever little thief."

"Worth a shot, though, right?"

"I suppose so." Still smiling, he gestured for me to follow him once more, and together we continued down the left branch to the very end of the hallway. He paused before a set of carved double doors, each side boasting one half of a massive tree lush with star-shaped leaves.

The craftsmanship was exquisite—a delicate, beautiful work of art that seemed out of place in this hall of rough stone.

"Wow," I breathed, unable to stop myself from reaching out. At the slightest brush of my fingertips against the polished wood, the leaves glimmered with silver light. "That's incredible!"

"The doors were crafted by the fae, of course. Trolls aren't known for their artistry." Keradoc grabbed the polished door handles, then turned to me once more, his face so close I could see the silver light of the leaves reflected in his dark pupils. "The entire floor comprises the living quarters for myself and my guests—primarily fae nobles and their families, or the occasional military commander. More often than not, it's just me and my..." He trailed off, the barest breath of sadness lingering.

*You and your what?* I wanted to ask. *Partner? Concubines? Imaginary friends?*

I closed my eyes and blew out a breath, trying to shore up my walls again. Every minute passed in Keradoc's presence only confused me further, shaking my confidence and sending my nerves into hyperdrive. Who *was* this man? This enigmatic fae? In the span of a couple of hours, he'd gone from legendary warlord to smooth-as-silk conversationalist to ballroom charmer to illusionist to kidnapper, and now he was showing me around the castle like a proud homeowner welcoming an old friend?

"As much as I appreciate the historic-homes-of-Midnight tour," I said, opening my eyes to meet his intense gaze again, "why did you bring me up here, Keradoc? Where are my men? Is this all just... just a game of show-and-tell to you? What am I *doing* here?"

My questions erased the last of the mirth between us, and his gaze turned as cold as the walls, his jaw tightening, his spine straightening as if he just remembered he was supposed to be detached and demanding, not friendly or playful. With a great sigh, he pushed open the massive doors and stepped aside, gesturing for me to enter ahead of him.

Another command.

I did as he asked, immediately drawn in by the sight before me. It was a massive suite, featuring a large common room with a fireplace, several couches, and an eating area set along the back with a dining table fit for a dozen people. A row of tall, glass-front doors opened onto a balcony offering a stunning view of the city and the mountains to the east—the Dead Claw range, if I remembered right. There were two large bathrooms accessible from inside the suite as well as from the main hall, both with massive black onyx tubs I was already dying to sink into. At equal intervals around the common room, I counted six alcoves carved right into the stone, each one large enough for a four-poster bed, an armoire, and a small desk. More magickal chandeliers hung from the ceiling in every room, flickering in time with the fire.

Like everything else in the castle, the suite was a mix of medieval royal opulence and primitive, rough-hewn architecture that made me feel like we'd tunneled into some ancient dwarven city beneath the mountains.

"Stunning," I whispered, though I hadn't meant to say it out loud.

"I'm pleased you think so," Keradoc said from behind me, his sudden nearness startling. I'd been so lost in the splendor of it all, I hadn't sensed his approach. "This is your home now, Miss Barnes. Take your pick of the bedrooms and make yourself comfortable. I'll have some clothing sent up for you later."

Though I sensed it was coming, his words hit the bottom of my stomach like cold rocks. It didn't matter how beautiful his castle was or what comforts he was promising. All the opulence in the world couldn't disguise what this place truly was.

"This is no home," I hissed, whirling around to face him. "It's a prison."

"You're not my prisoner."

"No?" I pressed a hand to my chest, feigning a relieved laugh. "Wow, so glad we cleared *that* up. Awkward! Anyway, if you'll kindly show me to the dungeons to collect my friends, we'll be on our way. Great party, though. We'll have to do it again a year from never."

"I cannot allow you to leave the castle unguarded. But that's merely a safety precaution. And just for tonight, I'd like you to remain in your suite —there are too many unsavory guests afoot, most of whom have the manners of wild boars. But once I'm rid of them, you'll be free to wander the castle as you wish. I'll show you the kitchens tomorrow, the gardens... well, what passes for gardens in Midnight. You'll have free rein."

"Gardens?" I mocked. "Why didn't you say so? You're right—totally not a prison. Do I have to sign up for my time in the yard? When do I meet my cellmate? I sure hope we have the same taste in music!"

"Throw a tantrum if you must, but I think you'll find me quite accommodating, provided you hold up your end of the bargain."

"We're bargaining now, are we? I don't recall any negotiations. You're getting your weapon. What am I getting?"

"You and your companions are still breathing, are you not? That will continue to be the case for as long as you continue to cooperate."

"Yeah? And how long do you expect me to stay here, *cooperating*?" I made air quotes around the word.

"As long as it takes you to craft the ritual, call upon your Darkwinter ancestors, and secure our victory."

A bitter laugh slipped from my lips. "Let's get something straight, Keradoc. War is *your* game. *Your* victory. I'm just a pawn, so stop pretending there's anything mutual about it."

He opened his mouth to respond, but a sharp rap on the door cut him off.

"Enter," he said gruffly.

A fae woman with hair the color of pale sapphires and eyes the same shade of violet as Keradoc's stepped through the doorway, escorted by two fae guards. All three wore the same dark-gray military uniform, but significantly more patches and pins decorated hers.

The guy on her right was a new face, but I recognized the one on her left as the fucker who'd kicked Elian in the back in the throne room. He glared at me now, his face contorted with unchecked hostility.

A chill skittered down my spine.

"Forgive the interruption, sir," the high-ranking fae woman said. "I come with urgent news from the north."

"What is it, Oona?" Keradoc's voice was tight and exasperated, but that's not what caught my attention.

It was the name. Oona.

Just like the fae woman Jax had loved. The one who'd supposedly died on her father's orders.

On *Keradoc's* orders.

# 7

## HALEY

*I* turned away from the fae guards and stared into the fireplace, schooling my reaction.

Oona. It *had* to be the same woman. Even if Oona was a common name among the fae, what were the chances that two of them had been in Keradoc's close orbit? With violet eyes, besides?

No way. She was definitely his daughter.

So she wasn't dead, then. Which meant Elian had lied to Jax. Why?

And what would Jax do when he found out?

A mix of emotions churned through my gut—worry and sympathy for Jax, rage at Elian's capacity for treachery, and there, simmering beneath it all, a big helping of red-hot jealousy.

I shoved it all aside though, forcing myself to take in whatever information I could.

"Two warships bearing the standard of Darkwinter have been spotted near the harbor," she reported. "None have disembarked—presumably on account of the Fog—but it's only a matter of time. The Fog is already beginning to thin."

*Fog?* Was she serious?

"Your enemies are afraid of a little fog," I blurted out, turning to face Keradoc, "and you think you need *my* help?"

"The Fog of a Thousand Knives, Miss Barnes," he said. "So named for its ability to slice anyone it touches into ribbons so microscopic, whole bodies become liquified in seconds."

Bile rose in my throat at the thought.

Keradoc must've seen the revulsion and fear on my face. His eyes softened, and he joined me by the fireplace, his voice low and soothing when he said, "Amaranth City is the safest place in the realm, and the castle is the safest place in the city. Neither the fog nor the enemy will reach us here."

He touched my shoulder, his skin warm, his eyes gentle. For a moment, it felt like we were the only people in the room.

I wanted that momentary comfort… and I hated him for it.

For all of it—the cruelty, the imprisonment, the beheadings, the way he'd allowed his guards to treat Jax and Elian. But mostly, I hated the kindness in his eyes, the softness in his touch. It was all a lie, another fae manipulation designed to weaken my defenses.

"And which enemy are you referring to this time?" I asked. "From what I hear, you've got a whole list of monsters waiting in line for a chance to chop off your head and mount it on the wall like a trophy."

All the kindness in his eyes drained away, leaving only the ice-cold warlord behind.

Good. I'd much rather face the ugly truth than a beautiful lie.

"Children playing war games do not concern me, Daughter of Darkwinter," he said, his voice loud enough for everyone to hear now. "Your esteemed ancestors, however, *do* concern me."

Turning back to Oona, he said, "What else?"

"Dead Claw, sir. There's another Darkwinter party on the eastern front moving north toward Stone City."

The muscle in Keradoc's jaw ticked. "Alert the squadron at the Stone City outpost they've got Darkwinter inbound, if they're not already aware. I want those bastards stopped before they get anywhere near the wall."

"Consider it done, sir."

With a curt nod, he dismissed them, then joined me once more at the fireplace.

None of this made sense. If she was Keradoc's daughter, why did she speak to him so formally? Was that just a military thing? And if he and his guards had ever truly threatened her relationship with Jax, why did she seem to respect the man so much? The way she looked at him went beyond a daughter's love for a father or even a general's respect for her commanding officer. It bordered on admiration.

I had a million questions, but for now, I held my tongue, waiting for Keradoc to make the next move.

"Do we understand each other yet, Daughter of Darkwinter? Or do you need additional persuading? I would be more than happy to have your friends moved to… less hospitable accommodations than they're currently enjoying, and that's saying something."

Thoughts of Jax and Elian shivering their assess off in some rank dungeon zapped the last of my strength. The craziness of the evening caught up with me in a rush, tears stinging my eyes, my limbs trembling with exhaustion. Suddenly, all I wanted to do was curl into a ball and pass out in front of the fire.

"I'll do as you ask, Keradoc," I said wearily. "Because you're holding us hostage and I've got no good choices here. But I'm telling you—I don't know the spell to summon my ancestors, I've got literally *zero* connection to them, and I can't perform a summoning ritual of that magnitude and complexity under pressure. Even if I was on board with this plan—which, make a note of this for posterity, I'm absolutely *not*—it's not something we can force."

"Force? No. But plan and prepare for? Together? That's something we can certainly do." He stepped close again, his sweet scent drenching the air around me. "I'm not the enemy, Miss Barnes. Remember that."

His smile was sad, his eyes softening as he captured me in another entrancing gaze, and like a fool I let my mind fall back into memories of that kiss.

"Haley," he whispered, his hand reaching for mine, our fingers brushing.

"You know nothing of it," I hissed. But of course it was bullshit.

My gaze dropped to his mouth, my stomach fizzy as he leaned in close, his warm breath tickling my lips as he…

Clamped a cold iron cuff over my wrist.

"What… what is this?" Shaking free of the trance, I clawed at the iron uselessly. "What have you done?"

Magick bit into my skin. Dark magick. *His* magick, crawling up one arm and down the other, spreading through my veins like ice. My teeth began to chatter, my skin erupting in goosebumps.

"Relax, Darkwinter," he said, shaking out his fingers. They looked red, as if they'd just been burned.

The cuff, I realized. Iron was poisonous to fae.

"It won't harm you," he said. "It's merely a dampener cuff. It will ensure your magick can't be used in an attack or in any other way that might undermine or harm me during your stay."

I cursed myself for being so stupid. So weak. Why had I let my guard down around him? Why had I thought, even for a second, that he was capable of even a shred of compassion?

"And you expect me to perform a complicated blood ritual while neutered?" I snapped, still trying to pry off the cuff. "I'm not sure you've thought this all the way through, genius."

"You're not neutered, just muted. You'll still be able to practice summoning spells and other small magicks, provided they're not intended for use against me or my guards or staff. Then, when the time is right to call upon your ancestors, the cuff will be removed and you'll have access to your full power."

"Yeah? And what makes you so sure I'll behave myself on *that* night if you don't trust me to do it now?"

"I have every confidence you and I will have reached an understanding by then. Perhaps even a level of trust."

"Right now, I trust you to be a complete asshole, and I don't see that changing any time soon."

"Nevertheless, this is your reality now. I suggest you make peace with it, and channel all that fire into crafting an effective ritual. Now, I must return to the party and ensure the remaining guests are ushered away without incident. If there's anything I can do to make your stay more palatable, well..." The grin returned, only now it was the grin of a dark wolf, his eyes shimmering like raw amethyst in the firelight. "My chambers are right down the hall. Should any *needs* arise..." His eyes trailed down my body, then back up, blazing a hot path. "Don't hesitate to knock on my door."

"I'd rather knock your head into the wall."

"You could certainly try." He gave me a small, mocking bow. "I remain, as ever, at your service."

And with that, Keradoc of Midnight was gone, leaving me furious, bone-tired, and—worst of all—dangerously, impossibly, *ridiculously* aroused.

"Fae magick," I said, desperate to convince myself that's all it was. "Hell of a drug."

# 8

## ELIAN

Are we dead yet, brother? Wasn't expecting the afterlife to smell so rank."

Yeah. Jax hadn't said a word, and I was talking to the fucking shadows again. Shadows and rats and the ghosts of ten thousand men who'd taken their last broken breaths in this dungeon long before we showed up.

How long had it even been since they'd staked us, beaten us, thrown us down here?

Hours? Days? An eternity?

There was only one way into the dungeon—the steel door they'd dragged us through—and no one had come or gone since.

The whole place reeked of death.

Jax and I were shoved into one of a handful of barred cells, all of them empty but for a lone prisoner in the cell directly across from ours. Now, a pained gasp emanated from his side of the dungeon, but I had no idea who or what lurked behind those bars. It was so dark, I couldn't make out much of anything beyond our immediate area—beyond the wet stone and waste and the moldy rags that were probably once prisoners, their bones picked clean by rats. It hurt to breathe. Hell, I wasn't even sure I remembered how. Everything attached to me was bleeding and raw, inside and out, and my whole body trembled with a gaping, soul-sucking need for *one* thing. One fucking little black pill to make it all go away.

But that old Devil wasn't dancing with me tonight. Only those ever-shifting shadows and my rancid thoughts and the demon I still called my brother, slumped against the damp stone wall right next to me, the sound of his ragged heartbeat and the acrid scent of his warm, hellspawn blood the only evidence he was still here with me.

Hell, maybe he *wasn't* here. Maybe we'd died in that throne room together on our knees, and this was our purgatory. Or maybe we'd never even escaped Midnight at all. Maybe the last two years in New Orleans had all been a fucking dream and we'd been trapped in the dungeons the whole time, wasting away breath by breath. Memory by memory.

"Jax," I whispered for what felt like the hundredth time. "Jax."

No response but the squeaking of another rodent gnawing at what I now realized was a festering corpse in the far corner. A red-haired fae from another realm, naked and long since forgotten.

My mind spun, still trying to piece together how everything had gone to shit at the Feast of the Beast.

The pain of Gem's betrayal cut through me anew. How could she have set us up like that? How had I not seen it coming?

And Keradoc... What game of illusions was he playing? For those few hazy moments, kneeling in a pool of my own blood before the dais, I'd looked upon his face and seen...

No. Impossible. Just more ghosts and wishful thinking and the byproducts of a mind long ago poisoned by drugs and fantasies.

"But I could've *sworn* it was him," I said anyway, as if I still needed someone to convince me otherwise. "Silver eyes. Those silver fucking eyes. I saw them, Jax. Clear as the first moon. But then they vanished. *He* vanished. Fucking illusion magick, or... I don't know. Another one of Melantha's games or the Dream finally scrambling up whatever's left of my brain."

Next to me, Jax coughed, the sound of it rattling through his chest. I'd taken out the second round of bolts and fed him more of my blood, but healing was slow going for both of us. The guards weren't exactly gentle when they tossed us into the cell, and the water Keradoc was supposed to send us still hadn't materialized.

"I lost him again," I said, my mind swirling in and out of consciousness, traveling through time and memory. "All of them. They were never the same after that. It should've been me, Jax. Not him. He was the good one. It should've been me."

Jax coughed again, the scent of a fresh spray of blood tingeing the air.

My stomach churned with hunger for it, but even if I'd wanted to drain him dry, the demon blood wouldn't sustain me, and there were no humans down here. Not tonight.

"Did you ever have one?" I asked, my speech starting to slur. "A family? Were you someone's son? A father? A brother?"

At that, the demon finally spoke, every word gritted out through teeth clenched in pain. "What the *fuck* are you on about, Saint? A brother? More blood and roses bullshit?"

"My family… my fae family. A long time ago."

"You had a family? Good for you. They know what a fuckup you are?"

"Yeah, I think they might."

"And Haley? What about her? What about *her*, you fuck? You left us days ago without a word, nothing more than some bullshit note, and I defended you. I looked into her sad, worried face and actually defended you. Where the fuck were you?"

"With Gem. Figuring out the plan, just like I said."

"Trading secrets with the enemy. Playing right into her fucking trap."

"If I'd known she was planning to stab us in the back, I would've—"

Jax coughed again, cutting me off.

Just as well. When it came down to it, I had no explanation. No excuses. I was the one who'd trusted her, who'd spent so much time with her—then and now. I should've seen it coming. Yeah, Gem was an old friend—one who'd proven her loyalty long ago. But still. There *had* to have been signs. Signs I fucking missed, and *that* was on me.

"I'd say I was sorry," I said, "but I don't think you're the one who needs to hear it."

"You sure about that, asshole?"

"Haley—"

"*Don't*," Jax warned. With a surge of renewed energy, he shot out a hand and clamped it around my throat. "Say her name again, bloodsucker, and I'll tear off your fucking head."

"I damn near destroyed her, Jax," I rasped. "Again. So many fucking times, and she didn't deserve it. *Doesn't* deserve it. All my bullshit and the secrets and the lies and… *Fuck.*" I was rambling again, memories and regrets crashing through my mind faster than I could parse them. Beneath the demon's crushing grip, fresh fear tightened my throat, churning through me like gasoline waiting for the match. "She was taken. She was taken because she trusted me—once again—to take care of her. And once again, I failed. I failed the woman I was supposed to love and protect and fucking cherish for the rest of my pathetic immortal life. And where did that immortality get me? I'm shot full of holes that won't heal right because my blood is tainted, and I'm locked up in this shithole, trapped in this dank-ass prison in the worst place in the fucking universe with no company but a dying demon who'd just as soon see my ashes in an urn, and all I've got to show for it is—"

"Saint, you're on my *last* fucking nerve right now and believe me, after what we just went through? I don't have any nerves left to spare." Jax jerked his hand away, and I sucked in a breath. "So either make a *fucking* point, or shut up and let me think, because one of us has to figure out how to get out of this mess—to find Hudson and get Haley back and get her *far* the fuck away from Keradoc—and clearly you're not the man for the job. In fact, you're not the man for *any* job, because you can't even go five minutes without killing someone or blowing something up or creating a major catastrophe the rest of us have to clean up and you know what, asshole? Yeah, I *would* like to see your ashes in an urn. Because I'm exhausted. You fucking *exhaust* me, *Saint* Elian. So right now, I need you to do me and Hudson and the woman you claim to love and the dead guy rotting behind us and every last bog roach in this dungeon a favor and stop. Fucking. Talking."

Stop fucking talking? Stop fucking talking.

Yeah, I could do that. I could definitely do that. I *wanted* to do that—one right thing in a lifetime of utter wrongs, but suddenly the walls were closing in and the air was evaporating and my heart wanted to pound right out of my chest and I couldn't fucking breathe…

"Jax," I gasped. "Wait. I'm not… I'm not well. It's the… the… the…" I lifted a hand, the tremor so severe it was all just a bloody blur at the edges of my vision. "I'm losing it. I'm losing… and I can't… I…"

He looked over at me then, his eye widening at the sight, a glint in the darkness. I tried to imagine what it looked like to him—me, strung out and shaking, begging, losing my shit while the rats continued to gnaw and the roaches continued to scamper and death breathed on the back of my neck…

"You're in withdrawal." He closed his eye and bit off a curse. "Perfect. Anything else you'd like to fuck up for us this evening?"

"I… I… I don't have any more pills on me. I didn't want to take anything before the Feast and I didn't bring any because I wanted a clear head and I thought we'd be back at the apartment and on our way out of this fucking realm and now I'm—"

"Now you're fucked."

I nodded, but he already knew the deal. He'd seen it enough times before.

"Did I say you were on my last nerve?" he snapped. "That was a lie. I've got none left for you, *brother*."

"But do you have… do you… the pills, Jax? Do—"

"Fuck you," he ground out, then reached into his pocket. He retrieved a small silver pillbox, tipped one of those little black beauties into his hand.

He'd always carried them, just in case. *Always.* I nearly wept.

"More," I said. I didn't even have the strength to reach for the pills myself. All I could do was beg. "More, Jax. One isn't enough. I… I need…"

He glowered at me like he really was debating ripping off my head, which… yeah. I definitely deserved it. But he shook out another pill anyway, and grabbed my jaw in a murderous grip and dropped two pills on my tongue.

I closed my mouth. Turned away from him. Moaned in relief as the drugs started to dissolve.

After a long pause, Jax sighed and said, "You need to kick this shit, Saint. If not for yourself, then for her. Do it for her."

His voice was soft—kind, even—yet it felt as if he'd just lit me on fire.

I clenched my fists in my lap, trying to keep the fury at bay. "Just because you're sharing her bed now doesn't mean you get to tell me what to do for my—"

"Your *what*, Saint?" he hissed, all the kindness evaporating. "Your long-lost love? A woman you abandoned without cause? A woman whose heart you keep on shredding every time you look at her? She's still in love with you, asshole, and all you're doing is rubbing her face in it like it's all some fucking game to you. She would've given you the world, and you turned your back on her for *this* place. How the fuck do you even live with yourself?"

If I had any strength left in me, I would've torn out his throat for that.

"You have no fucking *idea* what I did to get here," I said. "Why I did it. Why I left her and what it does to *my* fucking heart every time I look at *her*. You wanna talk about the past? You wanna compare notes? You were in Midnight long before I ever showed up, so you tell yourself whatever lies you need to about what kind of man you are, but don't you *dare* pretend you're not going to destroy her life."

He snorted out a harsh laugh, but didn't respond, and for a long while we both just sat there stewing in our own rage and misery, his heart banging around behind his busted ribs, the Dream taking its sweet time working through my bloodstream.

When Jax finally spoke again, his voice was so empty and broken I couldn't even be sure I hadn't imagined it.

"Fuck you, Elian," came the whisper, and when I forced myself to look at him, his cheeks were wet with tears. "Fuck you and everything you are and everything you did and everything we *both* fucking lost along the way."

The stale air shifted beside me, and he groaned as he pushed himself to his feet, one arm clutched around his midsection.

"Going somewhere?" I asked.

"We've got a witch to save, you dick." He kicked my thigh. "And by the way, since I'm pretty sure you and I are both going to die tonight, I might as well tell you I'm halfway in love with her. So fuck you for that, too."

The admission tore a fresh hole in my heart, but I'd known it was coming. I could see it in his eye that night he fucked her in front of me, and again when he'd come out of the room later and found me in the hallway. It wasn't just vengeance, wasn't just some twisted shit to pour salt in my wounds.

He'd already fallen under her spell. And I was pretty sure the feeling was mutual.

It killed me to even think about it, but deep down, I had to accept it. I just wanted her to be okay. To be happy, if that was even still possible. And if Jax was it for her, I'd accept it. Support it, even.

Not that I was about to admit it.

I dragged my ass to my feet, still leaning back against the wet stone for support. The Dream had settled me a bit, smoothing out some of the tremors, but it hadn't yet dropped me into the numb haze I knew was coming. It was like the calm before the storm—a brief moment of clarity and okay-ness before it sucked me in deep.

"Yeah, well, you're an asshole, Jax," I said. "You've always been an asshole. And as much as I'd love to murder you for falling in love with a woman you should've had the decency to stay far away from, I can't, because I still need your help getting her out of this hellhole and eviscerating the purple-eyed freak who took her."

"Same page, dickhead. Same page."

The words felt like a promise. An alliance, and I let them bolster me.

"The plan is still the plan," I said firmly. "Assassinate the warlord. As far as getting his blood for Haley? That's a lost cause at this point."

"Agreed."

"Once she's out of danger—"

"We're taking down Gem and the guards."

I nodded. "So you got my back on this, demon? Come what may?"

This time, he didn't hesitate.

"Blood before roses, you sick fae fuck." He smacked the back of my head, then gripped my hair, holding tight as he glared at me, and I could see from the ferocity in his eye how much he meant it this time.

How much he'd *always* meant it, despite all the shit we'd put each other through. Shit I still couldn't even bring myself to confess.

A knot of emotion tightened my throat, but I swallowed it down. Buried it.

"Whatever happens tonight, brother," I said, "we're getting her out."

"We're getting us *all* out."

I shook my head, adamant. "Haley comes first. That was *always* the deal, and nothing's changed on that front."

He let out a heavy sigh, but then he nodded, and once again I trusted it. Whether he wanted to admit it or not, the demon was *more* than halfway in love with her. He'd do whatever was in his power to keep her safe, just like Hudson would.

"Any ideas where our gargoyle might be?" I asked, fresh worry chewing through my gut. Hudson was fierce and I knew he could look out for himself, but it wasn't like him to no-show when we were in deep shit. Something was definitely wrong.

"He's not here," Jax said. "If he was, he would've been the first one storming that throne room the second trouble hit."

"Let's hope he's in a better place than we are."

"Hope isn't a viable strategy, Saint. Chances are, we're looking at another rescue mission. That's if he's still—"

"He is. And we'll find him." I blew out a shaky breath, knowing our chances were slim to none on all fronts, but we had to fucking try. "Once we figure out how to bust out of here, I want you to head up—"

A new commotion from outside the main door cut me off—sounded like the guards returning. Arguing.

Suddenly, the door heaved open, bathing the dungeon in torchlight that had Jax and me wincing.

"…are they doing in *here*?" A sharp voice was saying. Female. Official-sounding. "Who authorized this?"

"Keradoc ordered the fugitives to be placed in custody," came the reply —a gravelly voice belonging to one of the guards who'd tossed us in here.

"No prisoners are to be housed on this level while prisoner 6712 is in holding," the woman said.

"But we were told to isolate them and—"

"Wait here and stay out of my way," she commanded. "I will deal with this myself, since you're obviously too incompetent to follow even the most basic orders."

Whoever this woman was, it seemed she outranked the lowly guard. I caught the outline of his hunched form as he nodded and stepped back, and then the door slammed shut once more, bathing the room in darkness and locking the woman inside with us.

Jax and I exchanged a glance. This was our shot.

The prisoner in the other cell tried to speak—6712, I presumed—but his words were weak and watery, and the woman ignored him. She headed right for us, her face shadowed, her every footstep echoing through my skull as I gathered my strength and prepared to—

*Wait… No. It can't be. Is that…?*

I narrowed my eyes, desperate to make out her features in the utter darkness, but I couldn't.

Not until it was too late.

She reached the bars of our cell. Peered inside.

"Holy shit," she breathed. "Saint? Is that you? And… Jax?"

Her violet eyes widened, and in them I saw the shattering of the fragile peace Jax and I had just managed to stitch together.

I saw the shattering of our bond, once and for all.

The demon peeled himself off the wall and took a wobbly step toward her. Wrapped his fingers around the bars. Gasped.

Then, in a pained voice that punched a fist straight through my chest, he spoke the name of the woman he once loved. The woman I'd sworn to him—on our very oath—was dead.

*"Oona?"*

# 9

## ELIAN

"Oona," I echoed, not sure what else to say. Her name hung in the stale air like another corpse.

I still couldn't believe she was here. Now, of all nights, in all places.

I'd never trusted her back then—not until my final hours in Midnight the last time around. Before that, she'd been spending a lot of time with Jax, and I knew there was something fucked about her—just knew it. But he'd refused to see it.

So I followed her. Spied.

Took a few weeks, but I finally nailed her. Turned out she wasn't just some hot little blue-haired fae who liked to hang out at the pub in the Hollow and play Midnight card games with my demon brother.

She was military. Keradoc's Lieutenant General. And worse, his fucking daughter.

I wanted to kill her. Almost did, too, but she talked me out of it. Convinced me she really did love Jax, but couldn't escape her duty to the realm. To her father, despite his legendary cruelty.

Now, Jax continued to stare at her, his every cell already vibrating with the rage I knew was gathering inside him. I could practically hear it—the rush of blood, the thrum of his heart, the tightening of his muscles.

For his sake—and because I'd believed her—I let her live that night. Buried her secret deep inside, right along with everyone else's. And in exchange, she owed me. Perpetually. That was our arrangement, and it worked out well for both of us. She got to keep Jax and the illusion she was just another fae making her way on the mean streets of Amaranth City. I got intel on Keradoc and his officials whenever I needed it, and access to resources that would've otherwise been far out of my league.

Then, two years ago, Hudson's past came back to bite him in the ass, stirring up the kind of trouble that earned most people a one-way trip to the bottom of Beggar's Moat. The gargoyle never would've told me about it directly—rather than risk us getting involved and getting hurt, that sonofabitch warrior was ready to let himself be captured, tortured, and executed by Keradoc's men.

Lieutenant General Oona of Midnight got wind of the mission before it all went down, though. Knew Jax and I were close with Hudson. So she tracked me down, told me the story. Knew as well as I did the only way to keep Hudson's head attached to his body was to smuggle him out of Midnight and hide him in the earthly realm.

Getting out of Midnight was an impossible feat. No one had ever done it before. But with the right connections, help from the inside, and a good bit of forbidden magick cooked up by one terrifying dark goddess who'd been slumming it in Midnight recently, maybe we could beat the odds.

And, Oona reasoned, if I was going to smuggle out Hudson, I'd be taking Jax with me—those were her terms. Terms I happened to agree with. But we both knew Jax would never willingly leave her behind, and she'd never turn her back on her duty, so she couldn't go with us.

The only way then, she reasoned, was for Jax to believe she was dead.

A few nights later, when the plan finally came together, I knew we'd only have one shot to get out—one fucking shot. Me, Hudson, Jax. All or nothing. So, in my efforts to convince Jax he had no reason to stay, I'd painted the most grim, disturbing, hopeless picture my mind could craft, using my vampire influence and fae magick and everything I possessed to make him believe it.

It was quite a fucking performance.

Oona was Keradoc's daughter, I told him, pushing my influence deeper into his mind until the belief took root. Her father found out about their relationship—a daughter of Midnight fucking a lowly demon exile—and ordered his own men to kill her. I told him I'd witnessed it. Told him about the blood—so much blood. Told him about her strangled gasps as she supposedly died in my arms. Told him about my wasted efforts to save her, and how those same guards were after *him*, and he needed to leave Midnight with me and Hudson right fucking then or we were all going to be food for the ghouls.

I did not, however, tell him about Oona's demands of me. About how desperately she'd wanted Jax to have a better life, far away from the dark corners of the Hollow and her father's cruel regime. About why Hudson needed our protection in the first place.

"Why?"

It was only a whisper, but it dragged me right back to the present. Jax was still staring at Oona, and he didn't even turn to face me when he spoke, his voice soft with that quiet fury.

I'd never seen him so beside himself. Not even after I'd told him his woman had died, carved out his eye with a hot blade, and pushed him through the portal out of Midnight.

I opened my mouth to respond, but before I could figure out what the fuck to say, Oona was already talking.

"It was my idea, Jax. I begged him to manipulate you into believing I was dead so you'd leave Midnight with him."

"*Oona.*" I shook my head, imploring her to shut the fuck up. Jax was going to hate me enough after all this—why saddle him with the burden of hating her as well?

"No," he said, as if he couldn't believe it. "No."

"It's true," she said. "It was the only way. I'm sorry."

He finally turned to face me then, his skin pale, his remaining eyelid twitching like he was T-minus thirty seconds from detonating.

"Why?" he said again, taking one step, then another, until we were nose to nose at the back of the cell.

Oona unlocked the bars and stepped inside our cell, but didn't come between us.

"I had an opportunity to leave Midnight," I said, forcing a steely calm into my voice I damn well didn't feel. "I wasn't about to leave you here."

"Why, Saint?" he demanded once more. "Why? Because you fucked up your life with Haley and you couldn't stand the fact that I found even a *shred* of happiness with a woman here? Or was it because you needed a demon lapdog to peddle your drugs and work behind your bar in New Orleans? Someone you could keep beholden to you for a fucking eternity, all because you let him believe you'd saved his fucking life?" He let out a bitter laugh, then slammed me against the wall, his fist wrapped tight around my throat. "You never saved me, Saint. All you did was drag me out of one prison and into another. I would've rather *died* that night."

Pain bolted through my heart. That's what he fucking thought? What he wanted?

That old devil dropped onto my shoulder again, taunting me.

*Who gives a fuck what that asshole thinks? Should've left his ass here to die if that's what he wanted. Hell, there's still time.*

"It was the only way to get you out, Jax." Oona placed a hand on his shoulder. "You wouldn't have left me otherwise."

"Damn right about that," he said, still glaring at me. "Because I—"

*Loved you,* he wanted to say, but didn't. I could just about taste the words on his breath, not that he'd ever said them out loud before. Fear demons weren't supposed to love, but I knew how he'd felt about Oona.

Knew how he felt about Haley now.

"It was the only way," she said again. "I wanted—"

"Stop." He finally released me. Turned to face her.

The dungeon fell silent once again. Even the rats had stopped squeaking, and prisoner 6712 seemed to be holding his breath.

Or maybe he finally died.

Oona tried to reach for Jax's face, but he jerked back from her touch.

"Say something," she whispered. "Please, Jax."

"Where is the witch?" he demanded.

Oona sighed, blinking rapidly as if she were still trying to put all the pieces together. "The Darkwinter witch? You know her?"

"Where," Jax said again, low and dangerous, "has your father taken her?"

Whatever she was about to say next, she swallowed it. Closed her violet eyes. Let out another deep sigh. When she looked up at him again, the confusion had cleared away, leaving only the grim determination of a soldier following orders.

"The Darkwinter blood witch is under guard on the top floor—he's put her in the guest suites. But you won't get far, Jax. He's got men positioned outside the entrances and on the balconies."

"Excellent," he said. "The more people I get to kill tonight, the merrier." He yanked a stake from the holster at her hip, whirled on his heel, and shoved it straight into my chest.

"What the fuck?" I sputtered, stumbling backward against the wall. I slid down into a boneless heap, the last of my strength abandoning me.

Oona spared one last look for Jax, then crouched down to help me. With a swift jerk, she ripped out the stake and pressed her hand to the wound, slowing the blood until my body started to heal itself—as best as it could, anyway.

The whole thing was over in less than fifteen seconds, but those precious seconds were all the time Jax needed to make his move.

The bars slammed shut behind him, and he twirled a keyring on his finger—one he'd obviously taken from her. He also held one of her daggers.

Oona got to her feet again, leaving me on the ground. "Where the hell are you going?"

"I'm going to track down Haley, find a way out of this nightmare, and murder as many Midnight soldiers as I can along the way."

"What about us?" I asked.

"*You* can fucking rot." He glared at me, then turned that crazy blue eye on Oona. "Both of you."

He unlocked and opened the steel door. The guard Oona had argued with was still standing there. He had just enough time to reach for his weapon, but he wasn't quick enough on the draw. Jax slit his throat, then dumped the body inside, slamming the door on all of us as he slipped away.

Oona slumped down beside me on the damp ground. "Why didn't you tell him the truth?"

"You just said it, Oona. He wouldn't have left Midnight if he'd known you were still alive."

"No, I mean the truth about why you had to leave. About Hudson."

I closed my eyes and shook my head.

"It isn't my story to tell," I said, which was the truth, sure. But only half of it.

The rest of it I kept to myself—the part about how most of the time, it was easier to keep giving someone a reason to be disappointed in you than it was to carry the burden of his gratitude, or worse—the expectation that you could be counted on to do the right thing again.

That night, Oona and I had set out to save Hudson's life, and we'd succeeded. Whether Jax knew all the details was irrelevant.

She seemed to understand it—or at least understand that I had nothing more to say on that particular matter. With another deep sigh, she rested her head on my shoulder and pulled her knees up to her chest.

"Please tell me he at least had a better life," she said, the hope in her voice almost too much to bear. "Even just for those few short years you were out. Tell me what we did that night was worth it, Saint."

I said nothing. The Devil's Dream was finally kicking in, cocooning me in its familiar numb haze.

"Saint?" she prodded, lifting her head, and I sighed and finally looked into those teary violet eyes, and I knew—I *knew* she still loved him, knew she'd do it all over again if she thought for one *minute* it would give him a better life. Yes, even if it could only be better for a few short years.

I knew it because I'd do the same thing for Haley if I could. The same thing for Jax, even if he kept right on hating me for it.

Oona nudged me with her elbow, but still, I said nothing. Not a damn thing.

Partly because I was finally too stoned to string together any more coherent words.

But mostly because I was locked in the dungeons of my worst enemy, blood leaking from more holes in my body than I could count, my soul as close to Death's door as it had ever been, and I couldn't bring myself to tell one more fucking lie tonight.

# 10

## JAX

Keradoc's castle was as cold and black as the man's heart, a maze of damp stone passageways that twisted in all directions like tangled vines. Left, right, up, down, a confusing network no doubt meant to frustrate any would-be intruders and allow the lord of the manor to cower beneath his desk from a safe distance.

No matter.

I needed it tonight. The harsh, frustrating brutality of it all. Gave me something to focus on other than Saint's betrayal.

*Oona's* betrayal. Her rise from the fucking dead and her reappearance in my life at a time that was rapidly becoming its lowest point.

I wasn't sure which of them I despised more. Tough call, but I'd meant what I said in the dungeons. After what the two of them cooked up together? They could both fucking rot.

*Liar…*

Dismissing that little voice whispering at the base of my skull, I pushed on. Right now, my priority—my only priority—was finding Haley.

Trusting Saint was a mistake I'd never make again—especially not when it came to her. When Saint finally found his way out of the dungeons, if he still wanted to assassinate Keradoc? Fine by me—I wouldn't stand in his way. But that motherfucker was on his own.

And so was his blue-haired co-conspirator.

*Fucking Oona.*

I couldn't believe she was alive. That Saint had so thoroughly lied to me that night. That Oona herself had been complicit in the act.

*Fuck.* Their treachery tore a fresh wound in my heart all over again, more painful than the still-bleeding holes from the devil's trap bolts. But as much as seeing her tonight gutted me, it also proved something. I wasn't in love with her. Not any more—and hell, maybe I never was. Not really. When I looked back on what we'd shared, the glimmer of my feelings for her felt like a pale, flickering candle compared to the inferno burning inside me for Haley.

*Haley. Hold on, angel. I will find you.*

I repeated the words in my mind, the mantra keeping me on track.

I didn't want to risk backtracking the same way the guards had dragged us in, but after a few more twists and turns through the damp lower levels, I managed to find a back stairwell. Judging from the musty odor and the thick layers of slime covering the steps, it hadn't seen much use—probably just the occasional servant or spy.

Back on the ground floor, I melted into the still-raging party crowd, my gaze finally zeroing in on a servant. Exiting the kitchens with a tray full of bubbly balanced on his fingertips, he was clearly heading up to the executive level; the rabble on the main floor didn't get their drinks delivered on silver platters.

I ducked into a shadowy alcove. Waited for him to get close enough to grab.

His neck snapped with an audible pop. Amid the chaos of the party, no one heard the champagne glasses shattering.

Two minutes and another dead servant of Midnight later, I was dressed in a tux just this side of snug, the black cummerbund fashioned into a sleek new eye patch, his silver tray in hand. After a quick trip to the kitchens to replace the drinks I'd spilled, I was on my way back upstairs.

With a brief nod, I acknowledged the guards monitoring access to the upper levels, sending out a faint pulse of generalized fear and uneasiness —just enough to keep them worried about their own bullshit instead of scrutinizing my half-assed disguise.

*That's right, assholes. Nothing to see here. Just another poor chump serving drinks to the overlords of Midnight…*

It took me another hour of dodging Keradoc's guards, searching the nooks and crannies, and climbing more twisting, turning tunnels and staircases before I finally found my way to the castle's topmost level—a massive gallery lined with dozens of oak doors that led off into what I assumed were suites and bedrooms, maybe a study or parlor or whatever the fuck kind of rooms the dark warlord of Midnight required.

The two guards positioned outside the doors at the very end were a dead giveaway, though—that's where Keradoc had stashed Haley. It had to be.

Still hidden out of sight on the landing, I tried to cobble together a plan. I had no idea how many guards were on the other side of the doors, but if I didn't take down the first two, it wouldn't matter. The doors were a good fifty feet from the landing. I couldn't just run over there, dagger drawn for a little slice-and-dice. They'd shoot me full of bolts faster than I could say *boo*.

Time to go old-school, then.

For all the humanity the devils of hell ripped from my soul to turn me into a demon, the fact that they'd left me with a conscience was a fucking mystery. Guilt chewed at the edges of it now, but I ignored it. Took a deep breath and closed my eye. Blocked out all sense of right and wrong as I cast my awareness out into the darkness, searching for the one thing that could help me now.

And there it was. A whisper of fear slithering in the depths of memory. One of the guards had been betrayed as a young man. Tortured, brutalized, nearly murdered for his foolish, misplaced trust.

I focused on that ugly memory, tugging it to the surface of his consciousness until I felt the shift in his energy and knew he was looking upon his fellow guard with a suspicion that bordered on paranoia.

They didn't even argue. One minute, they were standing side by side in front of the doors, hands resting casually on their weapons. The next, one guard stabbed the other in the neck, his body dropping with a soft thud as he choked on his own blood.

Still caught in the grip of his worst memories, the murderous guard darted down the hall, heading right for me. The closer he got, the easier it was for me to push into his mind, to mine the wounds of his past until he was nothing but a sweating, whimpering mess.

He barely noticed me as he blurred past at a run, then crashed through the stained-glass window at the opposite end, leaping to his death.

Thick rivulets of blood coated the remaining shards of glass. The sight was enough to unleash a flood of guilt if I let it, but I didn't. *Couldn't.* Getting Haley out of here was my only concern, and if I had to sacrifice a thousand Midnight soldiers to get to her, I'd do it in a heartbeat.

I headed for the end of the hallway, where the first guard's body lay in a lifeless heap against the doors.

Haley was just inside—I could sense her fear, tempered only by a fierce determination.

"I'm here, angel," I whispered. But just before I reached the double doors, they swung inward, and Haley stepped out.

The dead guard fell backward, landing at her feet. She startled and gasped, but I grabbed her and clamped a hand over her mouth, pulling her away from the body. Pulling her close.

"Don't scream, angel," I whispered into her ear. "It's me. Just me."

She sighed and relaxed into my arms, and I took a moment just to hold her. To inhale the sweet scent of her, willing it to chase away the blood and rot that stained my soul. The warmth of her, the softness, the aliveness... Hell, for a minute I almost forgot we were in this terrible place at all.

She was still dressed in her gown from the Feast of Midnight, though it was torn and filthy now, ruined with blood. Saint's blood. Mine. Hers as well, leftover from her earlier spells.

I understood that's how her magick worked, but the idea that she'd spilled even a single drop of her own blood for fucking Keradoc sent me into a fresh rage. It trembled through me in a wave, my arms tightening around her.

She finally wriggled free and looked up at me, her eyes flooding with relief.

"Jax," she whispered. "Thank the gods and the devil both, I knew you'd come. Where's—"

"Did he hurt you?" I blurted out, taking her face in my hands. "Did that monster put a hand on you?"

She sighed and bit her lip. Lowered her eyes. For a second that felt like an eternity, no words followed.

And for that split second of not knowing... *Fuck*. The very idea that he'd touched her made me wish I'd slaughtered more than just a few guards and servants tonight. It made me want to burn down the entire castle and everyone in it.

"Keradoc didn't... he didn't touch me," she finally said. "Not like that. He just..." Haley shook her head, her brow furrowed as if she couldn't find the words.

"You're not convincing me, angel."

Haley sighed again and lifted her hand, showing me a wrist cuff she hadn't been wearing earlier. Iron. I knew immediately what it was for.

"We'll get it removed," I said, hoping that was the worst of it. "Right now, we just need to get the fuck out of here. Okay?"

"Jax, when they first brought you to the throne room… You saw him, right?"

"Haley, we don't have time. We—"

"Just tell me what you saw when you looked at him. Please, Jax. It's important."

I blew out a breath. "Keradoc?"

She nodded.

"Black hair. Purple eyes. Soon to be a corpse, if I've got any say in the matter. Does that answer your question? Because—"

"Something was off, though." Her eyes clouded, the wrinkle between them deepening. "I could've sworn he was wearing a glamour. And it looked like—"

"Haley, I will *gladly* analyze everything from his glamour to his hairstyle to his fashion choices to the twinkle in his fucking eyes, in whatever level of excruciating detail you wish, but not until I know you're safe and we're both far, far away from this fucking cage. Now take your pick of weapons from the dead guy, and let's go."

I finally got through to her. Her eyes cleared, and she nodded once before kneeling down to search the guard. Would've been great if she could've taken his uniform, but it was covered in blood. We'd have to figure out another disguise for her on the way.

She took his belt and holsters, along with a stake and two daggers. "Damn. As much as I'd love to play around with that crossbow, it's too bulky to run with."

"Devastatingly sexy *and* tactical?" I couldn't help but grin. "I knew there was a reason I liked you."

"There are lots of reasons you like me. Now get us the hell out of here, sinner."

# 11

## JAX

ollow me, angel." I grabbed her hand and we headed for the gallery stairwell, keeping our eyes peeled for an ambush. I had no idea whether anyone outside had seen the jumper fall out the window, but eventually someone would find his body, along with his partner's at the end of the hall. Oona had said there were more guards posted on the balconies too—I didn't know how many, or whether they'd seen Haley leave her suite, but I wasn't sticking around to find out.

"Did Elian get out already?" she asked as we began our descent. "Do we have a rallying point? Do you know if he found Hudson? Shit, everything happened so fast before. And Gem! Where the hell is *she*?"

I said nothing, but she must've felt the uncomfortable shift in my mood, because hers changed as well. She slipped free of my grip and stopped on the stairwell.

"Jax." Her voice held a hint of panic. "Is Elian… Is he okay?"

"Far as I know."

"But where is he?"

My gut soured, and I muttered, "Rotting in the dungeons, which is a better place than he deserves."

"Wait… *What? What* happened? How did you manage to escape without him?"

"Oh, I don't know. Probably had something to do with me locking him in a cell and stealing these?" I retrieved the keys I'd stolen from Oona and dangled them in front of her.

"You locked him in a cell and *left* him there? What is *wrong* with you?"

"The list is long and sordid, and I'll enumerate it for you later, point by point. But first—"

"What about all that blood before roses stuff? We can't just abandon him, Jax!"

Oh, she was dead wrong about that. I could very easily leave Saint Elian to the rats and roaches of Midnight. After what I'd discovered tonight, there was nothing left tethering me to that bastard. No debts, no loyalties, and certainly no brotherhood. He'd pissed all over that bond the night he'd told me the woman I loved had been executed.

Blood before roses? Right. Those days were dead to me now. *He* was dead to me.

But Haley wasn't having it, of course. Snatching the keys from my hand, she said firmly, "Take me to the dungeons or tell me how to get there myself. I'm not leaving him."

*Fuck.* I should've seen it coming. Should've had some story cooked up in advance—we got separated, I lost him, he's long gone. Better yet, I should've told her he was dead, just like he'd told me Oona was dead.

Why the hell wasn't I a better liar?

I slumped back against the wall and closed my eye. Didn't matter what stories I invented. Haley could always see right through everyone's bullshit, anyway. Mine. Saint's. Hudson didn't shovel as much of it as the rest of us, but if he did, she'd be the first to call him on it.

I waited a beat. Said nothing. My eye socket burned and itched behind the cummerbund, as if it were Saint's ghost come to fuck with me.

Seconds passed. Minutes. The rock walls seemed to be growing moldy around us, closing in tight.

"Jax." Haley broke the silence first, her voice considerably softer now. I couldn't decide whether that made me feel better or worse. "What is this about? I know you guys have issues, but this feels… different."

I shook my head, not even sure where to begin. "He lied to me about… about something he *damn* well shouldn't have."

"Oona," she whispered, and my eye shot open to meet her gaze. Her eyes shone bright with sympathy, and she reached up to touch my face. "I saw her, Jax. After Keradoc brought me to the suite, she showed up with a report on Darkwinter's ships. You saw her too, I'm guessing."

"She found us in the dungeons. She was as surprised to see me as I was to see her, believe me." Fresh anger simmered to a boil inside, and it took some monumental restraint for me not to slam my fist into the rock wall. "He told me she was murdered, Haley. Swore it on our oath. It's the only reason I agreed to leave Midnight. He knew I would've stayed behind otherwise."

"He must've had his reasons for lying."

"Sure." My laugh rang hollow in the cramped space of the stairwell. "Just like he had his reasons for abandoning you and breaking your heart?"

I regretted the words as soon as they escaped my mouth, but Haley didn't flinch.

"I'm not saying they're *good* reasons," she said. "Only that Elian isn't... I don't know. He hurts people, Jax. Fucks us over in ways we probably don't even know about half the time. But he's not cruel."

"Does it make a difference? Someone stabs you with a blade, you're still bleeding—maybe even dying—whether they meant it or just tripped and fell in the dark."

Haley shook her head. "I have to believe he had his reasons for the lies, the abandonment... even if we don't know or understand them. And no, I'm not making excuses for him—what he did to you was a dick move. A *seriously* dick move that I'm ready to strangle him for on your behalf. But is that really enough to just... just leave him for dead?"

"You know what, angel? Yes. It *is* enough. You know why? Because I'm fucking sick of it. Saint's got reasons for everything—as many reasons as he's got pills, and I've been putting up with both for far too long." I turned my back and continued down the stairwell, hoping like hell she'd just shut up and follow me. We hadn't even reached the executive level yet, and I still needed to figure out how to disguise her from the party guests, dodge the guards, avoid another encounter with Keradoc...

But there was no angel behind me. Only darkness.

I climbed the few steps back up to her and reached for her hand. She didn't resist, but didn't move from her spot against the wall.

"I left him in the cell with Uona," I explained. "She's the lieutenant general. She'll get him out. The two of them will hatch some scheme, make their escape, and *very* likely find some other poor sucker to swindle along the way, but I'll tell you something, Haley. It's not going to be me. And it's not going to be you, either. So you know what? *Fuck* Saint. Let's go."

"We're *not* leaving him here, Jax."

"Sorry, angel." I shook my head. "I'm done. Done choosing Saint when all he does—all he's *ever* done—is choose himself. Every fucking time, every opportunity to do the right thing, he picks wrong. If the situations were reversed, he'd throw us both to the ghouls without a second thought."

"I wish that were true. It would make everything a lot easier, including telling Elian to fuck off for good." A sad smile curved her lips, a tear slipping down her cheek. "But you don't believe it any more than I do, so stop trying to convince yourself."

"I'm not the one who needs convincing. I'm..." I took a deep breath, tried to put Saint out of my mind. This wasn't about him. Not anymore. "Listen to me, angel. Everything else aside? I made a promise that I'd get you out of here tonight, no matter what. *You're* the priority here—for me and Saint both."

"Unfortunately, I made a promise, too. Before we left New Orleans, I told you I'd have your backs in this place—all of you. I gave my word, and that means something to me, Jax. Even without a matching secret-society skull tattoo. So if you have that much contempt for Elian—if you're truly ready to turn your back on everything he ever meant to you, I won't blame you. But I won't join you, either." She turned her face and kissed my palm, then pushed past me on the stairs. "Tell me how to get to the dungeons, or I'll have to find my own way there."

"Wait," I said, blowing out a heavy sigh. "Wait."

I put a hand on her bare shoulder, and she stopped, her muscles tense, her hair tickling my skin.

"I'll take you to him," I said softly. "We'll get him out. But only if I can beat his ass later, and you promise not to interfere."

Without turning around, she put her hand on top of mine and squeezed. Then, in a soft, melodic voice that lifted my spirits right out of the darkest depths, she said, "Jax? If you're beating that boy's ass later, not only will I not interfere, but I'll be the one cheering for you in the front row with a bag of white cheddar popcorn and a peach margarita, and *that* is a promise."

# 12

## HUDSON

*I* wasn't one of them twisted fuckers who got off on pain, but when I finally regained consciousness? God *damn*, was I ever wishing for it.

Pain woulda meant I was still alive. Pain woulda meant my muscles and nerves still worked, and if they still worked, maybe I still had a chance at saving my girl.

But right now, there was only darkness and silence and a cold, empty ache where my heart should've been. My entire body was locked in my stone form, but it wasn't by choice. I couldn't shift into my warrior or human form, couldn't sense all the things I should've been able to sense as a gargoyle—where the fuck I was, for starters.

It meant one of two things.

I was either dead…

Or Marco's sunshine bullets were working some seriously dark mojo, keeping me locked up and helpless, just like the spell the fucker had used on me back in the day.

Either way, I had to keep fighting. Far as I was concerned? Marco was just another obstacle to overcome. Hell, not even Death himself could keep me from getting back to Haley, no matter how long it took.

So I did the only thing I could do. The only thing—in that moment of pure helplessness—that felt right.

I reached out to her. Called on our bond—something solid and real in this completely fucked-up realm of illusions and betrayals.

267

Took a while. Hours, maybe. No sounds, no sights, not even a whisper of a hint as to where those motherfuckers had locked me up. But then, out of fucking nowhere, I felt it.

A surge of pure panic. Haley's panic—same kinda thing I felt before, but way more urgent now. Desperate. *Fuck.* I had no idea how much time had passed since I'd seen her on the dais, but she was still in trouble.

Alive, fighting back, but in trouble.

And I was here. Not dead, I was pretty sure now. Just trapped. Ambushed by the same enemies who'd murdered my...

*Fuck me.* Tonight had all been a setup, just like before.

And now it was Haley's head on the chopping block.

The realization unleashed something dark inside me—something wild and primal and just desperate enough to make me absolutely lose it.

Rage? That shit was my *own* form of dark magick, an old companion I kept chained up in the basement of the worst parts of my soul until I needed to set that motherfucker free.

Like right. Fucking. Now.

I pictured her. My mate. My woman. Thought of the warlord's hands on her, spilling so much as a single drop of her blood.

That old companion exploded out of his chains and burst through my chest like a bomb, colliding with Haley's magick, all of it amplified by our bond and my fierce need to protect her.

For the second time that night, I swore I'd died.

But no. I wasn't dead.

I was fucking free.

I was human again, naked, stashed in some cold, dark cave I didn't recognize. I quickly shifted into my warrior form. Stronger that way. Faster.

Way better for busting heads.

Marco and his fuck-faced little pals put a lot of trust in that magickal little gun of his. They'd only left two guards at the cave entrance—probably figured I wasn't going anywhere on my own, so why waste resources?

These assholes weren't even gargoyles, but vampires—I could tell from the smell of 'em. Standing around with their dicks in the wind like they didn't have a care in the world.

Why would they? Their prisoner was supposedly locked in a permanent stone coma.

My lips curled into a twisted grin. They weren't expecting me to find the motivation, but they'd obviously never met Haley fucking Barnes.

*Good lookin' out, babygirl.*

The bloodsuckers didn't even scent me coming.

I made sure they heard me, though. Right at that last second. Stretched out my wings as far as they would reach in that cave and let loose a roar that burned my throat raw.

They spun around in a blur. And I smiled, more than happy to show them the face of their impending demise.

Fangs descended, but I wasn't in the mood for a tussle. I was in the mood to grab 'em both around the throat and repeatedly bash their skulls together until there was nothing left but the bloody stumps of their necks.

So that's what I fucking did.

Beautiful sight, that. Work of art, really.

I pitched the mutilated corpses back into the cave, then took off at a sprint, leaping out into the cool Midnight air as my wings fully unfurled behind me.

I was on the western side of the realm—some cave system in the Razorback range. The flicker of campfires dotted the mountainside, and I was pretty damn sure I could find Marco and the boys if I looked hard enough. Pretty damn sure I could catch them by surprise and tear off their fucking wings—a fate far worse than death for a gargoyle.

I could practically smell the foul blood spilling from their backs. Hear their pathetic cries. It made my cock hard just to imagine it…

But vengeance would have to wait.

Haley was still in trouble—I could feel it now, stronger than ever.

So I took all that rage—centuries and centuries of it—and chained it back up in the basement.

Then I banked north toward Amaranth City.

Toward the woman who'd saved my life in more ways than one, more than ready to repay the favor.

*Hold on, babygirl. Your Gargs is on his way…*

# 13

## JAX

et back," I whispered urgently, pulling Haley into the shadows of another corridor, shielding her from the guards' view.

*Don't look,* I muttered silently as they marched down the passageway perpendicular to ours. *Keep right on walking. Do not look this way...*

Haley gripped my hand and nodded toward the other end of our corridor, but that was a no-go. It opened back up into the main parlor, where Keradoc's servants had been trying to corral the lingering party guests. The crowd had thinned substantially; our chances of being spotted were much greater now.

I shook my head. All we could do was wait for the guards to pass.

Only it wasn't just a few guards, we quickly realized. They were transporting prisoners—three dozen or so, as far as I could count, made up of every race imaginable. Demons with glowing red eyes. Vampires, their mouths bloodied from a fresh feed. Wasted humans already well on their way to the afterlife. Shifters and gargoyles in chains, Hudson thankfully not among them. And fae, battle-worn and weary, their innate magick dim.

All of them wore armbands with the same black-and-gold insignia.

"Darkwinter," Haley whispered, and I nodded. Her heart beat so hard I could see the pulse of it in her neck, throbbing with every thunk of the guards' boots. "They're all wearing it. Even the non-fae."

It made no sense. Darkwinter fae were an exclusive bunch. Why the hell had they allowed the others to wear their colors? Their symbols?

"Where are they taking them?" she whispered.

I couldn't answer her. Not until I'd made damn sure Saint and Oona weren't among them.

*Fuck.*

Call it instinct, call it some twisted, misplaced sense of history. Call it fucking crazy, because I shouldn't have given a shit what happened to either of them.

But I did.

A red-hot bolt of guilt seared my gut, but then the last of the guards passed through without incident, and I smothered it.

Certain we were in the clear again, I blew out a breath and we slipped back into the passageway, continuing on in the opposite direction of the prisoners. If memory served, there was an exit at the end that led into the Sanctuary—a walled garden that hid a secret underground entrance to the dungeons. The prison guards used it to sneak away during their shifts to score drugs and sex with the castle servants.

Saint, Hudson, and I had brokered many a Devil's Dream deal inside that garden.

I just hoped the entrance to the dungeons was still intact, and that any wandering guards and servants would be more interested in the party tonight than a clandestine roll in the garden.

"They're new captives," I explained, finally able to answer her question. "Keradoc and his men will probably interrogate them."

"And then what?"

"If they're following the typical Midnight protocol…" I scratched behind my eye patch and shrugged. "They'll likely beat the hell out of them, lock them up in close quarters, starve them for a few days, and then —when they're good and feral, rotting from the inside out, they'll load them into wagons and dump them over the wall."

"Into Beggar's Moat?" she asked with a horrified gasp.

"Ghouls gotta eat too," I said plainly. "Same as everyone else."

"But how do ghouls even eat?" she asked, her eyes shining with an innocent, naked curiosity that would've had me grinning if not for the morbid topic—and the fact that if we didn't find a way out of there, we'd be sharing the same fate.

Still, I answered her questions as best I could, if only to pass the time on our endless creep along the cold, black passageway. "It's a gruesome, terrifying thing to witness, and I pray you never have to see it, which gives you an idea of how bad it is because demons don't, as a general rule, pray."

She smiled, a ray of light in the darkness.

"When a body is dumped into the moat," I continued, "dead or alive, the ghouls are drawn to it at once. They swarm, fighting over the meat in their endless quest to consume. They know nothing else, Haley—just the frenzy of the feed. Then, when the last bit of flesh has been picked from the bones, and the marrow sucked dry, and every last drop of blood licked from the dirt, the ghouls fall to their knees and weep."

"They're begging," she said softly. "That's why they call it Beggar's Moat."

I nodded, a heavy sadness settling over me.

Midnight was a terrible place. I'd spent nearly two decades here and never had any false illusions about that.

But somehow, painting these pictures for her… It made me see it in a whole new way. Not just as a terrible place, some cruel fate heaped upon even crueler monsters and men. But as… as a home. As a place like any other.

Stripped of its violent history and all the men who'd written it in blood, *every* place had the potential to be something different, something better… if only someone wanted to make it so. Decided it. Instead, Midnight's fae founders had turned a realm of magick and wonder and otherworldly beauty into a vicious torture chamber that left no soul untarnished, no heart unbroken.

I laced my fingers through Haley's and squeezed, quickening our pace.

"Is that where *all* the prisoners end up, or just the Darkwinter captives?" she asked.

"It's everyone, Haley. Everyone with the misfortune of getting caught committing whatever bullshit infraction Keradoc decides is a punishable offense. Could be you murdered someone, could be you smell a little funny that day, could be you're just breathing too much air in his presence. If you're unlucky enough to end up in the dungeons, you either die in a cell or you die in a fall over the wall. Either way, you're ghoul fodder."

She didn't speak for a long moment, but I knew what she was thinking. I could practically hear the wheels turning in her head.

"Saint and Oona excluded," I said, as if suddenly, after all the ill will I'd wished on them both, I needed to hear it myself. "Oona's a high-ranking Midnight officer and Saint's—well, he's a snake charmer who can talk his way out of anything. As much as I want to set his ass on fire most days, I wouldn't have left them if I thought they couldn't escape."

"That doesn't mean they *did* escape."

I stopped and turned to face her, tipping her chin up until she met my gaze. "I *promise* you, angel. Saint is fine. I'm pretty sure this is a wasted trip—he and Oona are likely long gone by now."

She smiled, but it didn't quite touch her eyes. A hint of accusation still lingered behind them.

*Fucking Saint. I really hope you're okay, you asshole...*

And I did hope it, too. Not just for his sake, but for mine. Call me a selfish prick, but I didn't want to see that look in Haley's eyes *ever* again.

"Guess we'll know soon enough," she said, pointing ahead. "Look."

I followed her gaze to a welcome sight—the proverbial light at the end of the tunnel.

There, through a small doorway and a gate rotted with age and decay, two moons shone down on a tangle of vines, trees, and flowering bushes.

And—thank the devil—the garden was empty, just as I'd suspected.

"That's it," I said. "Come on."

With renewed hope, we headed out through the gate, stopping at the center of the Sanctuary before a towering fountain of two sculpted fae warriors, one carved of onyx and the other moonstone, their swords clashing in perpetual battle. Blood spilled from wounds at their necks, collecting in a pool at their feet, where it churned and bubbled in an endless dance.

"Is that... Holy shit, Jax. Is that real blood?" Haley stepped closer, but I stopped her with a firm hand on her shoulder.

"It's the blood of the realm. No one actually knows where the blood comes from, but it never evaporates, never freezes, never stops running. It's forbidden to touch or drink it—hence the vampire skulls." I nodded at skulls piled around the base, their fangs still gleaming.

Those fuckers always thought they could outwit whatever gods, goddesses, or entities haunted the realm of Midnight, but they never did. The moment the blood touched their lips, they died.

A shiver rolled through her body, and she rubbed her arms, chasing away the chill. "Where's this secret entrance? And please don't say we're wading through vampire skulls to get there. I'm really not dressed for an excavation tonight."

"No skulls, angel. Just a few plants and a little dirt." Still gripping her shoulder, I guided her toward the far wall covered in shadow and creeper vines. From here, it looked like a solid wall, but that was just the fae glamour.

"Ouch! Damn it!" Haley suddenly yelped. "What the *hell*?" She glanced down at her feet, stomping at some invisible assailant in the tall, leafy grass. "If that was a fucking snake, I'm out. Elian's on his own."

"Not a snake," I said, my heart leaping as I finally caught sight of the vines shifting on the ground. Panic gripped my throat, damn near cutting off my air. "Haley, listen to me. We're going down, and it's gonna hurt. You need to fight hard. Kick, punch, claw, whatever you need to do. Take a deep breath right fucking now and hold it or—"

"Wait, what?" Her fear spiked, sending my own into overdrive as the deadly chokeweed vines slithered around our ankles and up our legs.

"Hold your breath!" I shouted, but I knew the command didn't make sense, and there was no time to explain. The chokeweed swept our feet out from under us, dropping us flat on our faces as their sharp, golden thorns burst from the vines, tiny black blooms unfurling beside them.

We had seconds before those blooms released their toxic gas.

"Jax!" she cried out, swatting uselessly at the vines as they ripped into her skin. "What do I do? I can't get to my daggers!"

She was panicking, confused by the sudden threat. I knew she'd fight hard no matter what, but there was only one way to fight chokeweed, and it wasn't with daggers or blood magick.

*Fuck.*

No time.

"Close your eyes!" I ordered. "I need you to trust me and close your fucking eyes right now!"

She finally did as I asked, no more questions, which made what I was about to do a hundred times worse.

*I'm so sorry, angel.*

Cupping her face, I called on one of her oldest memories—her oldest fears. I'd seen it the first time we kissed in that corpsevine field—her own mother trying to drown her—and now I drew it to the surface like I was drawing poison into a syringe.

I released that vile memory into her conscious awareness, amplifying it, making her believe it was happening right now.

In an instant she sucked in a breath and held it, then thrashed wildly, kicking for all she was worth. Her sharp, jerky movements knocked the blooms off the vines, neutralizing them.

*Good girl.*

I did the same, the thorns tearing through our clothes and skin, but unlike the poison, gashes were survivable.

After a few minutes of us thrashing around on the ground, the vines finally receded, but they'd come back soon enough. They always did.

I got to my feet and hauled Haley up.

"What… what the fuck happened?" she panted and coughed. Blood slicked her arms and legs, and her eyes were wide with fright, like she still couldn't be sure she was out of the water.

"Chokeweed. Its thorns tear, the vines constrict, and the flowers release deadly gas. Only way to fight it is by aggressively shaking it loose, hard and fast. There wasn't time to explain. I had to improvise. I needed you to believe you were drowning. It was the closest thing I could think of and… Fuck, Haley. I'm sorry. I never would've put you through that if I thought there was another way."

I reached for her, but she flinched away at my touch.

"It's all right, angel," I said softly, guilt burning inside. If there was a medal for the number of times you could hurt a person in the span of an hour, I was pretty sure I'd win it. "You're safe now."

"Am I?" She glanced up at me, the terror still lingering. Then she closed her eyes. Took in another breath, blew it out slowly. When she looked at me again, those eyes were guarded. "Just… Look, I understand why you did it, but that was… Shit, Jax. You dug deep on that one. I need a little space."

"Haley, we can't—"

"Please. Just… I need a minute."

"You don't have one."

The chokeweed was already sprouting up again, creeping toward us like the fucking ghouls of Beggar's Moat in search of a warm body.

"We gotta move. Now." Without waiting for her response, I grabbed her arm and dragged her toward the glamoured entrance in the garden wall, but it was too late. The chokeweed covered the entire Sanctuary, new vines awakening with our every footstep.

"Fuck!" I lifted her off the ground and away from the vines, but no matter how hard I stomped them down, they just kept coming back. They covered the entrance, covered the wall, covered the fountain, slithering toward us like snakes. I might have been able to outrun them alone, but not with Haley in tow.

"What do we do?" she breathed. "What the fuck do we do? My magick isn't working!" She tried to call up a spell with her spilled blood, but that fucking cuff was muting her, and it fizzled out at the first flicker of light.

Still holding her in my arms, I smashed down more vines and tried to head back the way we'd come, thorns ripping at my legs, the telltale bright green gas drifting upward. We weren't going to make it. Not to the glamoured entrance, not to the old gate we'd come through. The vines were too thick, too strong.

"We hold our breaths," I said again. "That's what. And then we—*wait*. Haley, look!"

A dark shadow passed overhead, then circled back, swooping lower.

A shadow in the shape of a massive gargoyle.

I laughed, relief surging through my limbs when I recognized our long-lost brother. "Looks like we fly, angel. We fucking fly."

# 14

## HUDSON

*H*er fear was sharp and sudden, and it churned through me like acid, so painful it had me clutching at my chest and struggling for breath.

An icy chill gripped my whole body, shaking me like a rag doll. I was a hundred feet off the ground, yet I felt like I was drowning.

I pushed myself harder, faster, soaring right for Vanderham's Wall. There were no starshowers keeping the guards hidden in the towers tonight, and they were more than happy to use me for target practice.

Fortunately, they weren't as fast or determined as a gargoyle on a mission to protect his charge, and once I was over the wall and on the ground, it wasn't long before I lost them in the dank allies of Amaranth City.

Fast as I could on foot, I made my way to that fucking castle, the bond an urgent, incessant tug. When a fresh bolt of terror rattled through my bones, I leaped up into the air once more, keeping an eye out for Marco and his crew. My hope was they were off drunk or stoned somewhere, comfortable in the assumption I was locked up in that cave.

Cocky motherfuckers always made the best enemies.

High above the castle, I circled the grounds, my gaze roving over the last of the inebriated Midnighters stumbling home after gorging themselves in every way possible at the Feast. The taste of Haley's fear grew sharper, sharper still, until finally…

There.

I spotted them in the walled Sanctuary, Jax holding her close as he smashed his foot down on…

Aw, hell.

Chokeweed.

*Motherfucker.*

Stuff would cut you to shreds and poison you at the same time, just to make sure it got the job done.

I tucked my wings in close and dove down, pushing myself faster and faster until I had them both in range. Jax glanced up just in time to see me coming and lifted Haley up high. I snatched her out of his arms, then reached for him, but he shook his head.

"I'm going back for Saint!" he shouted, thrashing free of the vines around his legs. "Get her out of here and stay out of sight—I'll find you in the Hollow. Gem can't be trusted!"

It was the last thing he said before he took off, fighting his way back through the chokeweed to that spot in the wall the guards used sometimes to sneak in and out of the dungeons.

I assumed that's where Saint had gotten held up.

Haley struggled for a minute, desperately reaching for Jax, but my girl wasn't stupid. No way could she fight through those vines—best to just let the demon do what he needed to do. The demon would be fine—we'd all tangled with the stuff more times than I cared to remember.

Just another one of Midnight's many fucking charms.

Eventually, Haley let him go, stopped squirming around, and held on for the ride.

I tucked her in close and zoomed straight up, getting us up to a good cruising altitude before leveling out again.

Two of the three moons hung high over the horizon, and I'd hoped to take a moment to catch my breath, check on my girl, and enjoy the view. But one glance ahead shot *that* plan to shit.

Dark shapes scudded across the moons, and a flurry of dark wings nearly blotted out all the light.

Gargoyles. Not the assholes from before, but Keradoc's official team picks—bunch of bloodless mercenaries and sell-swords who didn't give a fuck whose heads they had to sever to make a buck.

"Incoming!" Haley shouted, and I banked a hard right, rolling to avoid a barrage of arrows on fire with purple magick. One caught the tip of my wing, tearing a hole right through it, but I ignored the pain and rolled again, narrowly missing another hit.

Fucking hell. Wasn't bad enough they'd sold out their own kind. They had to bring dark witches in to fight their battles, just like Marco. The whole lot of 'em seemed to forget what it meant to be a gargoyle. A protector.

Tightening my grip on Haley, I flew in a sharp zig-zag pattern as they fired another volley, the magick singeing my hide with another near-miss. I dropped down low, trying to lose them among the crowded, mismatched buildings of Amaranth, but the fuckers were relentless.

I circled back over the castle again, then headed north, wishing like hell I could fly us all the way out to sea. I glanced back over my shoulder. Counted. Six, as far as I could tell, armed and magicked to the teeth, ready to take us down.

"Hudson, the Fog!" Haley shouted, and I banked just before we hit the wall of deadly mist.

*Fuck.* I hadn't even seen it creep up. Shouldn't have even been there at all—that shit had never come so close to the city center before.

If she hadn't spotted it, we'd both be soup by now.

My gut churned with new worry. I had to get her the fuck out of there, and fast.

"Hold on, babygirl," I grumbled, then did a hard one-eighty, heading right back toward our attackers. I waited until they let loose another volley, then dropped into a free fall before zipping right back up again, trying to shake them loose.

I was heading for the wall. If I could get past the guards again, I could take her into the mountains. Or the woods. Or anywhere that wasn't the fucking city that seemed determined to kill us both tonight.

But good news apparently traveled fast, and as soon as we got near the wall, I spotted another squadron waiting on the ramparts, several of 'em perched and ready to take flight, the rest with their dark witch-enhanced bows drawn.

I made a sharp turn to double back, scanning ahead for another route. The way back to the castle appeared clear, but the new gargoyles were hot on our trail.

Seconds later, the original fuckers cut in from the east.

They were herding us back toward the castle, and there wasn't a damn thing I could do about it.

I tried to shake them off, to zig-zag again, to fly higher, but there was truly no escape—Fog of a Thousand Knives to the north, tower guards to the south, gargoyle mercs fucking everywhere.

Before I could even decide my next play, a burst of heat exploded across my wings. In a flash of purple light, a net of pure magick tangled around us, immobilizing me in midair.

We dropped like a hot rock, crashing down onto one of the castle's many balconies. It was all I could do to protect Haley from the fall, cradling her close as I took the brunt of the impact on my side. Pain ripped through my hip and shoulder, but adrenaline quickly chased it away as a dozen winged warriors landed soundlessly around us.

Two fae witches stood among them, just as I'd suspected.

And there, at the center of it all, was the warlord himself, his hair slightly windblown, cheeks flushed, as though he'd been standing out there the entire time awaiting our impending arrival.

Our capture.

"Are you fucking kidding me?" Haley shouted at the prick. She tried to stand up but I kept a tight grip, not wanting her to go anywhere near that bastard. Not as long as I could help it.

He leered down at us, his lip curled in disgust.

Never before had I so badly wanted to debone someone.

He didn't even bother acknowledging her. Just took one look, then turned on his heel and snapped his fingers, lord of the fucking manor. The witches stepped forward at once.

"Bring them to the war room with the other fugitives," he commanded. "And this time, when I tell you to secure them, I mean it."

# 15

## HALEY

*I*n a cavernous room on one of the castle's upper levels, Keradoc stood at the head of a conference table with his arms crossed over his chest, glaring down at us and looking supremely pleased with himself.

Gone were the formal silks from the party, replaced with an intimidating military ensemble that could only be described as Fuck Around and Find Out—The Dark Fae Collection.

All black, of course, and perfectly tailored to suit his lean frame, with a mix of soft leathers and hard, polished metals I was pretty sure didn't even exist on the earthly realm. Various pins and badges decorated his uniform, and nearly every inch of him was strapped with weaponry of the sharp and pointy nature.

A particularly stunning dagger hung from a holster at his hip, the jewels encrusted on the hilt almost an invitation to grab it, jerk it free, and shove the blade right into his chest.

Somehow I resisted the urge, glaring at him with the daggers in my eyes instead.

He glared right back, fury simmering in that violet-eyed gaze.

Everything about him was spotless and precise—but for one thing.

His boots. They were covered in blood splatter. It was the same story with the rest of the guards who stood at attention behind him—more than a dozen fae, not counting another dozen on the opposite wall, and several who'd been left outside to man the exit.

Where the witches and gargoyles had gone, I hadn't a clue. Seemed Keradoc had a whole host of supernaturals at his beck and call; all he needed to do was snap those elegant fingers and issue a command, and they'd come running, guns—and magick—blazing.

I recalled the prisoners from earlier. The Darkwinter fae and their company.

Jax was right—Keradoc and his men had likely interrogated them. And in the end, when he'd wrung out every last bit of useful intel, he—

I swallowed hard, lowering my gaze once more to his blood-stained boots.

"Now that we've all gotten a live demonstration of what happens when you try to escape," the warlord said, "I trust we won't be repeating the mistake. Is that a fair assessment? Or am I being too presumptuous? Admittedly, I wasn't expecting you to push things so far on your first night as my… guests."

One eyebrow raised in a perfect arch, he looked at each of us in turn.

Jax, still bloodied from the chokeweed encounter, his jaw clenched tight, rage radiating off him in waves.

Elian, pale and bruised and—if his blown pupils were any indication—tripping on the Black.

Hudson, still in warrior form, his wings bound to his back with iron bands that wrapped around his torso.

They were all draped in heavy chains spelled with fae magick so dark I could practically taste it, like burnt toast and ozone.

Keradoc hadn't bothered restraining me. Even if my magick wasn't muted by his cuff, he knew damn well I wouldn't make a move against him now—not while the guys were immobilized and Keradoc's backup team had tripled in size.

It was an intimidating show of force, but I'd seen his cruel side in the throne room. Seen what he'd done to those shifters for their so-called treason. The fact that the guys were still alive and relatively unharmed—even after our attempted escape? That told me *exactly* what I needed to know.

Keradoc needed them, just like he needed me.

The question was… what the hell did he need them *for*?

"Takes a real man to hold off on making threats until his enemies are all chained up," I said. "They teach you that at the Academy for Warlords and Supervillains?"

Keradoc bristled but didn't take the bait. Instead, he lifted a hand and glanced down at his black fingernails, sighing as if I were nothing but a petulant child. "Miss Barnes, do you have any idea what it costs me to keep prisoners alive in this castle?"

"Do *you*? I wasn't aware you kept them alive long enough to work out the financials."

A dark laugh slithered out from between his lips. "Fair point. In truth, I'd much rather toss you all over the wall with the dead as a reward for my ghouls. Alas, my priorities require a different approach." His smile fell. "I need you alive. *All* of you."

*Just as I thought.*

"What the hell do you want with us?" Elian asked, his words slurring. Jax still hadn't spoken, but the intensity of his gaze told me exactly what he was up to. Trying to find the chink in Keradoc's armor. Trying to mine his fears.

A shiver wracked my body as images of the Sanctuary flashed through my mind. The chokeweed. Jax's warm hands cradling my face, his touch calming me, like he alone had the power to save me.

Then, the water rushing over my head. The darkness. The cold.

I blinked away the memories. The old as well as the more recent. I was alive. That's what mattered. And so was my demon.

I wondered if a man like Keradoc even *had* fears. Jax believed the root of all fear was love, and he'd made a pretty compelling case for it. But if that were true, then he was out of luck tonight.

Keradoc was fucking fearless. Had to be. No love had ever touched that cold, dead heart. Not even his so-called daughter's. Of that, I was certain.

Unbidden, his earlier words came back to haunt me.

*Kiss me like that again, Daughter of Darkwinter, and I'll be whoever you need me to be…*

I sucked in a breath as the memory of that kiss, that passion swept over me, flushing my cheeks.

As if he could read my thoughts, Keradoc lifted that brow again, curious rather than authoritarian this time, his eyes glittering with something I couldn't quite pinpoint.

Intrigue?

I lowered my gaze back to his boots. The ones he'd probably used to stomp on heads. Because that's who Keradoc was—a cruel, murderous man-child who snapped his fingers and swung a sword whenever something didn't go his way. I refused to give that kiss—or him—another thought.

What mattered now was that the guys and I were together. Stronger because of it. We just had to figure out how to stay that way long enough to formulate a solid escape plan. Preferably one that didn't involve killer weeds or gargoyle archers or magickal nets or infuriating captors with deep, penetrating, violet eyes…

"As I've already explained to Miss Barnes," Keradoc continued, "I need her to craft and perform a ritual to summon her Darkwinter ancestors. The details are not important, but their resurrection will ensure our victory. The—"

"Darkwinter?" Elian gaped at me, some of the fuzziness clearing from his eyes. "Since when do you have Darkwinter ancestors? You're a witch, not a fae."

*Shit.* I'd nearly forgotten how far behind Elian was on the life and times of Haley Barnes.

"It's a long story," I said, "but let me give you the highlights reel of everything you've missed in Blackmoon Bay. Let's see… I've got three sisters. When we were little, our evil bitch of a mother murdered our father and tried to drown us because she thought we were trying to steal her magickal legacy, which all stemmed from this crazy prophecy about the Silversbane witches—four witches who would one day rise up to unite our kind against hunters and other oppressors and bring the sisterhood of witchcraft back into the light."

"Silversbane?" Elian asked, astonished. "You're talking about the Silversbane prophecy? You… you're one of the four?"

I spread my hands and flashed a cheesy grin. "In the flesh. Descendent of one of the very first witches and—oh, you're going to love this part— her Darkwinter fae loverboys. Of course, this was before Darkwinter turned into the vile scum they are today, so I can't exactly blame a girl for going out and getting herself some of that hot, hot Darkwinter D, if you know what I'm saying."

I was pretty sure no one in that room knew what I was saying, but I smiled anyway. I had the Silversbane family tree to thank for my own insatiable appetites—a thing for which I'd always be grateful.

"Haley, that's… You've got sisters?" Elian asked softly.

Suddenly, he was looking at me as if I were the only other person in the room, his eyes shining with something I did *not* want to see there. Something I *refused* to see, because seeing it brought me too close to the past. Too close to that old love, that connection, that closeness that had always come after we'd shared our most intimate hopes. Our stories.

He'd always known how important family was to me. And if he'd still been with me in the Bay, he would've been the first person I'd told after I'd discovered I had sisters. Real sisters.

"Sisters," I repeated, speaking over the tightness in my throat. "We were all born in Blackmoon Bay, too. But after the attempted murder of four innocent girls, my granny—blood relative granny, not the Nona I've mentioned in the past—got with her coven and did some dark memory mojo to convince my mother we were all dead, then temporarily bound our powers, messed with our memories too, separated us, and shipped us off to be raised by new families, totally unaware of one another's existence. Granny happens to be the King of Hell's side piece, so obviously I didn't trust her story at first, but it turns out it was all true—it all came out during an epic battle in the Bay against the very Darkwinter fae dicks that are attacking Midnight. Seems they've got quite a hard-on for invading territories that don't belong to them. Anyway... yeah, you're looking at a super-special Darkwinter-fae-Silversbane-witch hybrid that our man K-Doc here believes can help him win his war against my own people. Aren't you sorry you ghosted me?" I laughed, then turned back to Keradoc, leaving Elian in shocked silence. Blinking up at the warlord with a faux-innocent gaze, I said, "Anyway, what were you saying? About why you needed the guys? As far as I know, none of *them* have Darkwinter ancestors."

Keradoc stared at me for a long beat, as if he was trying to figure out whether to laugh, run for cover, or just grab his trusty old sword and take my head off, nipping all that crazy in the bud.

In the end, he only sighed. Again.

It was a thing with him, I was quickly learning. The epic sighs.

"No, Miss Barnes. They do *not* have Darkwinter ancestors." Keradoc retrieved a small glass bottle from his breast pocket and set it on the table in front of Elian. Dozens of tiny black pills glittered inside. "*They* will be putting their talents to use on a weapon of a different sort."

# 16

## HALEY

"Devil's Dream?" I grabbed the bottle for a closer look. Elian's eyelid twitched.

"Unless my intelligence agents have deceived me," Keradoc said, his attention shifting between Elian, Jax, and Hudson, "you three are the men responsible for the current epidemic raging through Amaranth City."

"That's quite an accusation," Elian drawled. "Got any proof?"

"I'm well aware of your exploits in Midnight and back in your home realm." Keradoc rested his black-tipped fingers on the table, leaning close to Elian. "I'm well aware of how you escaped Midnight. I'm well aware of who assisted you, and I'm well aware of what those individuals received —*continue* to receive—as payment for services rendered. I've known all of it from the start, and I've allowed your operations to persist regardless of your status as fugitives and criminals, so kindly spare me the tedium of your denials."

Wisely, Elian said nothing. Jax said nothing. And—spoiler alert— Hudson remained silent as well.

"What I require now," Keradoc continued, "is for you to devise a more potent, more addictive formulation. One that will be spoken about in hushed whispers across the city, the mountains, and every last battlefront in the realm with an air of exclusivity and scarcity that will have the armies of our enemies clamoring for a taste—a taste we will gladly provide. While the demon and the vampire-fae devise and test the new formulation and my own soldiers begin feeding the rumor mills, the gargoyle will serve as my appointee in overseeing the harvest and transport of the corpsevine flowers from all known fields as well as any new territories we discover."

"You're trying to take them down from the inside?" I asked. "By getting them hooked on your dark fae crack?"

"A general must use every tactic at his disposal."

"Why not just poison them?" I asked. "Make them believe they're getting the good stuff, then… *wham*. Little black bottle of death."

"Darkwinter have powerful fae witches among them. Witches able to sniff out poisons."

"And you don't think this shit is poison?" I set the bottle back on the table. Elian shifted in his chair. If not for the chains, I was pretty sure his knee would be bouncing.

"Not in the same way," Keradoc said. "Dream is a recreational drug like any other. By the time the enemy soldiers realize the effects of its enhanced potency, they will be too weak to counteract it. Too addicted. It happens quickly, Miss Barnes." He gestured at Elian as if he were the newly appointed poster boy.

*Just say no, kids. Be cool, stay in school.*

"Dastardly," I said, unable to keep the disgust from my tone. "Another trick you picked up at the Academy? Bet you were the star pupil, weren't you?"

"Would you rather I—what's the term you use back home? *Nuke* them?"

"It *would* be faster," I said.

"Yes, and I suppose I have the magickal backing to devise a weapon of that sort. One that could take out the entire realm at the press of a button. The problem, Miss Barnes, is that whatever you think of Midnight fae, we do not—to borrow another quaint phrase from your homeland—shit where we eat. This is my *home*, for all that my enemies are attempting to claim it from me, and I do not wish to destroy it."

A glimmer of fierce pride shone in his dark eyes, and for a moment, I couldn't look away.

A strange understanding passed between us.

I knew what it felt like when your home was being threatened. What it felt like to want to defend it with your very last breath, by any means necessary.

The really fucked-up thing was… I could almost understand why he felt that way about Midnight. I'd only been here a couple of weeks, yet the place had already gotten under my skin. The thought of it falling under

Darkwinter reign—under the reign of *any* enemy who sought to trample and destroy it...

Bile rose in my throat at the realization, but I couldn't deny it. Some part of me—a very dim, deeply buried part—actually wanted to help him.

And maybe, if he'd come to us with a proposal instead of demands—instead of soldiers and spelled chains—we'd be having a very different conversation right now.

"So your entire strategy for winning the war and saving the homeland you claim to love rests on the ability of four prisoners—prisoners you've already beaten and tortured, mind you—to remain loyal to your cause and carry out your orders without issue?" I laughed. "Really?"

"And here she thought you were the star pupil," Jax said to him. "Perhaps you need a refresher on your coursework."

"There is no such thing as loyalty, Miss Barnes," Keradoc said coolly, ignoring Jax. "Not in Midnight. But for the right price, certain insurances can be bought, and trust me when I tell you I've invested *heavily* in the ensuring of your cooperation as well as my own safety throughout our *entire* arrangement."

"What do you mean?" I asked.

"Let me keep this simple—for all of you—so there's no confusion later." He leaned even closer, his cold-roses scent slipping past my defenses, trying desperately to remind me of that stupid kiss. In a dark, dangerous voice, he said, "Should anything befall me or my personal guards, my generals, my staff, or anyone even *remotely* connected to me or this castle, your friends will be tortured while you watch. Should you attempt another escape, you'll get as far as the Sanctuary before you're captured and forced to torture one another for me and my guests, whom I assure you will pay quite handsomely for the entertainment. Do you sense a theme here?"

Yeah, I sensed a theme. Douchebag, with heavy accents of narcissistic personality disorder and toxic masculinity, framed in a neat little package of *complete* flaming asshole.

But I was pretty sure it was a rhetorical question.

I lowered my gaze and sighed. I didn't doubt Keradoc would hurt us. Badly. But he hadn't threatened us with *execution*, which further cemented my belief in what he'd admitted earlier: no matter what, he needed us alive.

His pathway to victory rested entirely on us—my spells, the guys' drugs.

Which meant we still had a bargaining chip.

No idea how much it was worth, but there was only one way to find out…

"Suppose we tell you to take your grand plans and fuck off?" I asked. "Suppose we throw ourselves over the wall the first chance we get, sparing your guards the trouble?"

At that, his eyes widened a fraction, as if it hadn't occurred to him that we'd be anything less than compliant in the face of his threats.

*Cards shown, asshole. Cards fucking shown.*

"You've got demands," I pressed on. "You've stated them. You need me to do a ritual summoning. You need the guys to make a better, stronger pill to dose your enemies."

"Was something about that unclear?" he asked.

I folded my arms across my chest and shrugged. "Only the part where I tell you what we want in return."

"I do not take orders from captives."

A low rumble vibrated through Hudson's chest, but I smiled to let him know I was just fine.

"It's not an order," I said to Keradoc. "It's a bargain."

He laughed. That purple-eyed fae fucker actually laughed at me. "You and your pets are hardly in a position to trade."

I got to my feet and leaned forward, hands on the table, just like him. We were so close, our noses were almost touching. A ripple of unease moved through the soldiers on the perimeter, but Keradoc raised a hand, silencing them.

"Look around, Keradoc," I said, my voice just as low and dangerous as his. "Take a good fucking look at who you're dealing with here. You think the threat of pain scares any of us? You think we haven't endured our share of torture?" I laughed at the ridiculous notion of it. "Do you honestly believe you're the first asshole in my life who threatened to put his hands or weapons on me just to get what he wanted? Now, you may think I've got pull with Darkwinter fae, but let me tell you something, *sir*. Before I stepped foot in your realm, Darkwinter assholes and their human hunter minions kidnapped me, imprisoned me, tortured me, and killed people I cared about. I've been stabbed, electrocuted, poked and prodded, starved, whipped, beaten, burned, cut, waterboarded, and those were the more pleasant abuses. Jax is a demon, for fuck's sake. You think you've got something on hell's torture chambers? Hudson doesn't even speak, so you can use your imagination on what happened there, but I'm guessing he didn't stop talking just because he lost a bet. And Elian? He's his own best torturer-in-chief, and the only way he can survive another day with his ghosts is to pop those little pills you're so ready to feed to your enemy. Now, tell me again how we're supposed to cower under the threat of *your* whips and brands."

Tension crackled in the air between us, my heart jackhammering against my ribs, Keradoc's eyes sharp with anger and mistrust and—though he was trying *damn* hard not to show it—raw, uncut lust.

As much as I hated to admit it, I was pretty sure he saw the same thing reflected in my gaze.

No matter. I refused to look away. Refused to back down. Refused to give a fucking inch on this—it was too important.

Through a jaw clenched so tight it damn near trembled, the warlord finally spoke.

"State. Your. Requirements."

"First, I need assurances my sisters will be kept safe. So whatever you need to tell Melantha to make that happen? Do it."

"Your sisters have nothing to do with—"

"The only reason I came here at all was to protect them. If they're not okay, *I'm* not okay, and if I'm not okay? I've got nothing to offer you."

"You seem to think I hold sway over the dark goddess."

"Don't you?"

"Melantha sent you to me in the hopes that I'd reverse her banishment and allow her to return to Midnight, which I cannot do. Very soon, word will likely reach her that I've captured her Darkwinter blood witch, yet I've made no move to commute her sentence. She will grant me no additional favors."

"Then send a *new* word to her that the witch you captured at the Feast wasn't me, but an imposter. Convince her I haven't yet arrived—you're still waiting for your so-called gift."

"Miss Barnes. *Haley…*" His eyes softened a fraction, the tiniest flicker of guilt shining through. "Eventually, she'll learn the truth. If Melantha is set on destroying your sisters, there's nothing I or anyone else can do to prevent that."

"Prevent it, no. But you can at least buy me some time to figure something else out."

"But that's—"

"Lasagna, Keradoc. It's lasagna, and it's what I need from you right now, whether you understand it or not."

He clamped his mouth shut. Closed his eyes. Muttered a whole string of curses under his breath, some in a language I'd never even heard before. The sound of it, even at a whisper, cast my whole body in goosebumps.

*Goosebumps? Really? Since when am I the type of girl who falls apart over a sexy foreign accent?*

"We're also going to need food, water, and clothing," I continued, straightening my spine and forcing myself to break free of whatever dark fae magick-mojo he'd obviously used on me. "And not the cheap stuff, either. I can't be expected to work magick if I'm not comfortable, protected, and stylish."

"*Stylish?*" He scowled and shook his head, but when he finally opened his eyes again, there was no more fury there. The tiniest smile twitched at the corners of his mouth, there and gone again, but his eyes held the ghost of it, glittering mischievously beneath those dark lashes. "Very well. Will there be anything else, little thief?"

Beside me, all three of my guys stiffened at the sudden informality in his tone.

"One last thing," I said firmly, refusing to show him how that nickname, that tiny bit of teasing was already worming its way into my chest, trying to spark up a little fire that needed to stay cold. "I'm spending the night with my friends. *Every* night, actually, for as long as we're here."

With a laugh, he said, "Your friends will be sleeping in the dungeons, and trust me—the dungeons are no place for a woman. Especially not a woman whose spellcraft requires her to remain in top form."

"Top form?" I fisted his fancy metal-tipped lapels and grinned. "Then I guess you'd better upgrade the boys to the executive suite, Keradoc, because along with fresh bedding, hot bubble baths, and green smoothies spiked with gin, your new favorite drug dealers are an integral part of my self-care regimen. So I suggest you unchain them, hand over the fresh towels, and escort us to those luxury accommodations, or you're going to find out why everyone says Scorpios are the craziest bitches in the zodiac."

# 17

## JAX

*J*'d just settled into a steaming-hot bath in one of the suite's massive onyx tubs when she appeared in the doorway—my angel of darkness, freshly scrubbed and polished, damp hair piled into a messy bun on top of her head, some kind of short, black lacy little number clinging to her curves.

My heart almost liquified, though I couldn't say the same for my cock, now standing at full attention beneath the water.

"I should probably apologize for barging in on you," she said with a dreamy smile, "but I'm not actually sorry to find you naked and wet. Not. At. All."

"Nor should you be. Damn, angel. Aren't you a sight for sore—" I grunted as I sat up straight, taking in the sight of her smooth, unmarred skin. "—everything. I take it Saint healed you?"

"Yep. Vampire blood," she said, shrugging. "Hell—"

"—of a drug."

"Exactly. So why do *you* still look you fell into a wood chipper?" Her smile faded as she perched on the edge of the tub, her eyes scanning the mess of cuts and gouges on my arms and chest. "He promised me he'd heal you, too."

"Yeah, well. Give him points for trying."

"Trying isn't doing."

I shrugged a shoulder, skimming my palms along the surface of the water. "He annoyed me, so I staked him."

"Jax!"

"What? It wasn't a lethal hit—just a jab in the thigh. Believe me, he had it coming."

"He *always* has it coming, but..." She swung her bare legs over the edge and dipped them into the water, toes gliding along my thigh. "You two can't keep going like this."

"Wanna bet?"

"You went back for him. You could've left the Sanctuary with me and Hudson, but you risked your life to go back for him."

"Don't read into it, angel. I told you I'd get him out, and I did."

"Did you see Oona again?" she asked, her voice softening to just above a whisper.

I nodded. "They were both still in the cell, but we split up after I let them out. We all agreed it was best—couldn't risk her getting caught helping us escape. She's still a soldier of Midnight—our history doesn't change that."

"Do you want to talk about it, or...?"

"No, angel. I really don't." No point. It was all in the past now. A past I'd just as soon bury than drag out into the light for Haley or anyone else to sift through. "What I felt for her back then? It's gone. Even if she hadn't lied to me, I just don't feel that way about her anymore." I glanced up at her. "I'm not making any assumptions about what you feel or don't feel for me, Haley. But Oona's not someone you need to worry about. Ever."

"That's not why I was asking." Haley sighed and shifted her legs between mine, sending tiny ripples across the surface of the water that lapped at my chest, right beneath my tattoo. "It's just... You and Elian have this crazy-intense bond—it's so obvious you care for each other. Deeply. But then there's this huge wall between you, and I know it's not just about what happened with Oona. I can feel it, Jax."

"That wall took lots of years and lots of fuckups to build." I reached between my thighs and grabbed her foot, sliding my thumb over her arch. "Fuckups on both sides, as much as I'd love to blame it all on him. And a wall like that won't come down overnight—not even at the request of an *impossibly* stubborn blood witch with superior negotiating skills."

She laughed, the sound of it erasing all the cobwebs from my past. "I don't know about all that."

"Don't sell yourself short," I said. "It's no accident I'm sharing my bed with you tonight instead of with the rats and corpses."

"With *me*? Aren't you a presumptuous little demon?"

"You wouldn't turn down the last wishes of a broken, bleeding man, would you?"

"No, I suppose not." She blew out a breath, her smile fading once again. "I hate that you're in so much pain, Jax. You should've let Elian heal you."

"Why don't you give it a try? I'd much rather your hands on me than his."

"I don't know how to do healing magick."

"But you *do* know blood magick, so maybe you're halfway there." I squeezed her foot. "You certainly can't make things worse, right?"

"That's a bold assumption, considering I'm operating at half-capacity." She rolled the iron cuff around her wrist.

"I think we both know I'm just looking for a reason for you to put your hands on me."

That got another laugh, and she shifted along the edge of the tub so she could reach me better. "Just tell me if it hurts, okay?"

I nodded, watching in fascination as she closed her eyes and ran her hands over my shoulders and chest, brow furrowed, lips muttering an incantation I couldn't hear.

Aside from the defensive maneuvers in Blackbone Forest and the throne room—both times when we'd been under threat—I'd never really seen her work her magick. Now, I took great pleasure in studying her face, the tiny wrinkle between her eyebrows, the way her chest rose and fell as her breath settled into a deep, steady rhythm.

After just a few moments, a soft, warm light emanated from her palms. Red, as her magick had always appeared to me, but fainter than before. Despite its lower wattage, it warmed me at once, and I felt my blood humming through my veins in response, following the call of her magick, encouraging the gashes in my skin to heal, the bruises to fade.

My pain receded, though whether it was more because of her magick or her touch, I couldn't say.

Eventually, the magick faded, and she opened her eyes and inspected her work.

"Holy shit!" A new smile broke across her face as she touched the now-smooth skin beneath my collarbone. "Does it still hurt?"

I shook my head. "Good as new, angel."

"I can't believe I just did that. I actually did that. I healed you!"

"Oh, I can *totally* believe it."

"You're just saying that."

"Angel, not an hour ago, I watched you stare down the warlord of

Midnight. You put the fear of hell in that man's eyes, and that's no easy feat. Something tells me there's a *lot* you can do that you haven't quite tested yet."

"Maybe." She trailed her fingers through the water, the ripples lapping at my skin. "Jax, listen. I wanted to apologize about before. In the Sanctuary? I'm sorry I snapped at you after the chokeweed thing. It just happened so fast, and I wasn't ready for it."

Guilt bubbled up inside, and I took her hand, pressing a gentle kiss to her palm. "You have nothing to apologize for, angel. I can't even imagine how frightening that must've been for you."

"You saved my life, and I pushed you away."

"I forced you to relive your worst memory—one your subconscious wanted to keep buried. You were terrified, and you had every right to be."

She didn't deny it. "Honestly, I'm still feeling a little… unsettled about it all. I only just learned about what my birthmother did recently. She found us again in the Bay. Wanted us to reconnect and join her fucked-up cause. My sisters and I… we banished her to hell."

She met my gaze, and I nodded silently. No one knew better than I did what banishment to hell was like. The fact that she'd had to do that to her own flesh and blood just to save herself…

It was an agony she never should've been forced to endure.

"Haley, I'm so sorry. You—"

She pressed her fingers to my lips and shook her head. "Don't say anything. I don't want to get into it now—not yet. I still haven't even fully processed what happened in the Bay. Right after that battle—after we sent my mother off—I had to leave my sisters to answer Melantha's call. The blood on my boots and daggers wasn't even dry yet." She ran her thumb over her wrist, tracing the words of her tattoo. *This too shall pass.* It seemed to steady her. "I'll tell you about it," she said. "All of it. I want to. Just… just not tonight. Tonight, I just need you to know that as scary as it was to relive my near-drowning, I'm not terrified of *you*, Jax. I never could be. Not now."

When I spoke again, my voice was dark and low. A warning. "Maybe you should be."

"Probably." She grinned, her eyes lighting up. "But I think we both know it's too late for that. I mean, it's kind of hard to be terrified of a demon when he's super sexy, naked in the bathtub, and you know the sound he makes when he comes."

Without warning, she slipped both hands beneath the water, trailing her fingers down my cock, which had been rock hard for her since she walked in. She fisted me and squeezed. Stroked, hot and slippery in the water.

"*Fuck*, angel," I growled, and she tightened her grip.

Every time the woman touched me, I lost my damn mind.

"Question about the drowning thing..." I ground out, barely able to keep my voice even. "Are you afraid of water now? Of being submerged? Anything like that?"

"No, that's the weird thing. I *love* being in the water. I'm—"

I grabbed her and hauled her into the tub, cutting off her squeal with a deep, hungry kiss as the water sloshed over the sides, puddling on the floor around us.

"Jax!" she gasped, breaking away to admonish me. "Your injuries!"

"The strangest thing, angel. Suddenly, I feel like a new man." I kissed her again. "Guess you really do have the healing touch."

She pulled back and kneeled between my legs, bracing herself with her hands on the edge of the tub. The position gave me a perfect view of her breasts, her nipples outlined by the dark silk chemise that clung to her. I brought my mouth to her breast and bit, teasing and sucking her through the wet silk.

A soft moan, the slide of her fingers into my hair, the warmth of her skin as I ran my hands along her arms... If demons believed in heaven, I'd swear I was already there.

And maybe I could've stayed. Maybe I should've stayed, kissing her soft and slow, teasing her, making her whisper my name like a prayer.

But the silk in my mouth... it wasn't hers. And once that realization slithered into my mind, I couldn't let it go.

"What are you wearing?" I asked, pulling back.

"This? Found it in my fancy-ass wardrobe closet." She laughed. "Apparently, Keradoc took my demands to heart. Elian said some servants came to deliver a bunch of stuff while I was in the other shower."

"And you thought you'd give it a go, did you?"

"It's real silk. I'm not turning *that* down."

"That's not silk, angel. It's made from the petals of the Black Slipper— an extremely rare flower that grows in the Razorback Mountains." I rubbed the edge between my finger and thumb. The material was so finely woven, I could barely feel it.

If I could put a price tag on this flimsy garment in American terms, it would be in the six-figure range.

Keradoc was toying with her. Trying to lull her into trusting him. Liking him.

I'd seen the way he'd looked at her in the war room. Seen the bulge in his pants as she'd given him a piece of her mind, and I'd held my tongue.

But now, the idea of the warlord dressing her up like his own personal paper doll sent me into a fit of frenzied anger so hot, I was surprised the bathwater didn't boil up around me.

"He's trying to impress you," I ground out.

"Give me *some* credit, Jax," she said, frowning. "If Keradoc wants to impress me, he's going to have to work a *little* harder than silky pajamas."

"If that's how you truly feel, then you won't mind if I tear them off."

"Have I ever?"

With a deep, satisfying growl, I gripped the hem of the chemise in both hands and said, "Now would be a good time to heed my warnings, angel. Because I'm going to utterly *ruin* you tonight."

# 18

## JAX

*I* ripped that chemise right the fuck in half, then made equally short work of the bottoms. They tore away like tissue paper, and I pitched the wet scraps over the edge, more than eager to welcome her naked flesh into my hands.

Her naked, Keradoc-free flesh.

Well, aside from the fucking cuff he'd clamped on her wrist.

Noticing where my gaze had landed, she sighed and said, "Don't even look at it. It doesn't matter."

"It *does* matter. It's like he's got a dog collar on you."

"Jax," she said, capturing my face between her hands, forcing me to look into her eyes. "Right now, in this bathtub, it's just us. *Nothing* else matters. Okay?"

She lowered her mouth to mine, and the taste of her kiss obliterated everything else—Keradoc's power games. This fucking place. The drug mission Saint and I may or may not be able to pull off.

The complete insanity of our lives.

Haley was right. Here, now, there was only us. And nothing else mattered.

I stretched out my foot and twisted the faucet, replenishing the water we'd splashed out, filling the bathroom with steam.

Haley deepened our kiss, her tongue sliding into my mouth, her thighs clamping around my hips, my cock hard between us.

Our first time together, I'd taken her hard and fast in the woods near the corpsevine fields, where we'd clawed and bit and howled like animals. After that, I'd taken her hard and fast in the apartment. I'd taken her hard and fast in front of Saint, bold and brash as I pleased, and then on her knees in the shower. After that night, I'd taken her in so many other ways it made my head spin. My wild angel matched me every time, always desperate for each crazy, searing-hot touch.

Slow and soft had never been our style. But tonight? It was all I wanted. Needed. No, not because of my wounds—she really had healed me. But because being here in this fucking castle at the whims of the warlord I'd barely survived during my last tour of Midnight only reminded me how fleeting everything really was.

Tonight, I just wanted to feel her. All of her. One sexy, devastating inch at a time. And I wanted to make it last.

I broke our kiss and grabbed her hands, stopping her from fisting me again.

"Relax," I whispered against her throat, buzzing a trail of kisses along her warm skin. She was already resisting my hold, aching to get closer, to take, to receive. "Don't fight me. Not tonight."

"But we're so *good* when we fight, sinner," she teased, nipping my lower lip—a move that had me claiming her in another ferocious kiss, my hands sliding down to cup her backside as she writhed against me.

*Fuck*, I was so ready to just slide inside her and take her in every dark, wicked way, slow and soft be damned…

*No.*

I fisted her hair and pulled her back once more.

"Sorry, angel," I whispered against her mouth. "Tonight, you're *mine*."

Her eyes blazed with heat, with desire, with the pleasure of submission. She relinquished control, her muscles softening, her eyes dancing with curiosity.

I drew her close once more and brushed her lips with a soft kiss, then turned her around in my arms, settling her between my legs, facing away from me. Her hair slipped loose from the bun, falling in strawberry-scented waves, and I pushed it gently forward, baring her back and shoulders.

With a firm grip, I squeezed her neck, then slowly worked my way down to her shoulders, to the muscles between them, loosening the knots. She drew her knees up, resting her cheek on them as I continued to massage away the tension.

"That feels… amazing," she breathed. "You're turning me into rubber, which is awesome, don't get me wrong. But it's not exactly *ruining* me."

"Hmm." I kissed her shoulder, trying to work a particularly stubborn knot from her neck. "I'm merely softening you up so I can bend you to my every whim."

"It's torture. You know that, right?"

"What's torture, angel?"

"The way you're touching me. Teasing me. It's… God, Jax. Your hands are fucking amazing."

"*These* hands? These hands right…" I slid them down her back, down to her hips, then around the front, gently parting her thighs. "…here?"

"Yes, that's…" Her words trailed off into a moan.

"Lie back, angel. Close your eyes."

She did as I asked, resting the back of her head on my shoulder, her body stretched out before me. Her breasts peeked out above the waterline, and I blew a cool breath down over her shoulder. Her nipples hardened in response.

I cupped a handful of water, then poured it over her shoulder, watching it slide down between her breasts. My other hand snaked around her hip, dipping between her thighs again, a slow and lingering brush of skin on skin as I teased her clit with the barest pressure.

"Why?" she breathed. "Why are you still single?"

I laughed. "Fairly certain the answer to that question would fill up several volumes, not to mention completely kill the mood." I stroked her again, applying a little more pressure but keeping my movements slow and controlled.

Torture, just like she'd said.

From the bright flush of her skin and the hard points of her nipples, I knew she was enjoying every second of it. I slid a middle finger inside her, then drew back, circling her clit before dipping back inside, deeper this time, then out once more, every touch bringing her closer.

"I'm going to make you come now, angel," I whispered, biting her earlobe. "But I want you to remain *absolutely* still for me. Don't arch your back, don't tighten your muscles, don't even curl your toes. Just let it wash over you."

She murmured my name, her breath turning shallow as I stroked, my touch still so soft, so slow, until I felt the barely perceptible quickening of her heartbeat and knew she was right there.

Plunging my fingers inside, I finally brought her to ecstasy, and my angel did just as I asked, holding herself completely still in the water, my name a sharp gasp on her breath as the pleasure rippled through her body.

After a few silent, blissful moments, she finally turned around again in my arms. Her cheeks were darker now, her damp hair curling around a soft smile.

I held her face in one hand and gazed into her eyes, black pupils swimming in a green sea.

"Every time I look into your eyes," I whispered, "I forget how to breathe."

Never before had I so desperately wished for the eye I'd lost. Wished for my full vision, so I could see every contour, every shadow as it was meant to be seen.

As if she could read my thoughts, Haley traced her fingertips along the edges of my makeshift eye patch.

"Let me see you," she whispered. "All of you."

I grabbed her wrists and shook my head, ducking her intense gaze. "You don't need to see all of me, angel. Trust me on that."

"Jax."

I didn't respond, shame burning through me. It'd never bothered me so much before—the scars, the mottled, caved-in flesh where my eye used to be. I'd gotten used to it, and there was no point in dwelling on shit that couldn't be fixed anyway.

But now, the thought of her seeing me... Finding me lacking...

No. I couldn't bear it.

"Jax," she said again, and I finally looked up at her again, everything in me suddenly wound tight with new fury.

It wasn't Haley I was furious with. It was Saint. Keradoc. This fucking place, and everything we'd done to stay alive here the first time. Everything we'd done to get the fuck out and try to start over in New Orleans.

And now we were back here, doing the bidding of a warlord who took pleasure in threatening the woman we both so obviously loved.

But Haley was the one in front of me now, soft and beautiful next to my hard, ugly, jagged edges, so she was the one who took the brunt of my anger.

"You really need to see the monster behind the mask?" I snapped. "It's that important to you?"

"Actually, yes. I do."

"I'm not your personal freakshow, Haley. If that's what you're looking for, take a walk through the Hollow. Plenty of freaks to choose from, most of them more than happy to show you anything you'd like."

"Is that what you think? That I'm just looking to satisfy some morbid curiosity?"

"Aren't you?"

"Jax, I already saw you without the patch in the throne room."

"I see. So now you just want a closer look? Trying to decide whether you can bear to look at it for however long this thing between us lasts? Or maybe you're ready to cut and run now, and you just want to make yourself feel better about—"

"Stop." The word was firm, but her touch on my face was gentle. "I'm not going anywhere, Jax. And I'm not trying to make you feel like you're under a microscope. That's not it at *all*. So keep it covered if that's what you truly want, but don't let it be out of shame or embarrassment or some fucked-up story you're telling yourself about what I'll think if I see you. I want you, Jax. Every bit of you," she breathed, kissing my jaw even as I turned away from her, shame still burning through me as sharp and hot as her words.

"I want every sexy line," she whispered, another kiss brushing my lips. "Every dip and hollow. Every scar, no matter how terrible."

Silence descended, hanging as thick as the steam in the air.

I turned back to face her. Held her gaze. Searched her face and knew she'd meant every word.

"It was my price, angel," I admitted. "My ticket back home."

A soft gasp slipped from her lips, but she'd done it—popped the lock off the vault—and now that those words were out, I couldn't stop the rest.

"It was Melantha," I continued. "She was in Midnight at the time. She's the one who cast the portal spell to get us out of here. So while Gem and the other Midnighters who'd helped us had their own price—a cut of our operations, which we'd be forced to continue in New Orleans—Melantha had another. Money would never be enough for her, no. She demanded one thing from each of us—the most important thing, the thing that truly made us who we were."

"Your sight."

I nodded. "For a fear demon, our vision is what allows us to see into a person's mind and soul. To see their fears."

"So she just… carved out your eye?"

"She wanted me to do it, actually. But I… I couldn't. I held that dagger in my hands, the blade heated by fire, glowing red, and I just… I couldn't do it, Haley." I held my hands before her, both of them trembling at the memory. "I was damn near ready to shove it into my chest instead—just be done with it. But Saint grabbed the blade from my hands. Finished the job that I could not."

"Jax! Elian did this to you? He cut out your *eye*?"

"Not like that, angel. Saint did me a favor that night. There was no joy in it for him, believe me."

*You hurt her, demon, and I'll take the other eye…*

Saint's old threats echoed, but I knew how badly that night still haunted him. He put on a good show, but half the reason we couldn't stand to be in the same room together was that most days, Saint could barely look at me. The guilt of what he'd done chewed him up inside; I could read it almost as clearly as his fears.

"Just… just take it off," I finally whispered, all my anger draining away. "If you want to see all of me, take it off."

Her fingers slid into my hair and stilled when she reached the tie knotted at the back. "Are you sure?"

I nodded, and she brushed another kiss to my lips, so soft and sincere I damn near melted.

With a gentle touch, she slid the patch over my head and set it on the edge of the tub.

It took me a moment to gather the courage to tilt my face up again. To let her see everything up close, the old wounds in all their gruesome glory.

I closed my other eye before I did, not wanting to see the change come over her face. The inevitable horror, or worse—pity.

I held my breath. Waited for the telltale gasp. The awkward stuttering.

But all I got was the tickle of her warm breath on my brow bone, her soft lips as she traced a path of sweet kisses along the ridges of my eye socket.

I winced, and Haley drew back.

"Did I hurt you?" she gasped.

"No, it's… Some areas are still a little sensitive."

"Elian couldn't heal you?"

"He did his best, Haley. But vampire healing isn't always a sure thing with demons, and… Well, this was about all we could hope for."

She traced her fingertip across my eyebrow, then down the long scar that bisected it, all the way to my jaw. "And this one? Did Elian do this too?"

"That one… That was *my* doing," I said. "After we left Midnight, I started having these nightmares. Migraines too. Melantha, this place… I never quite shook free of it. And every night I'd wake up with my entire skull feeling like it was on fire, and in those moments, I felt like I'd do *anything* to make it stop. Anything. So one night, delirious from lack of sleep and wild with rage and completely fucking devoid of all hope, I grabbed a dagger and I just…" I made a slashing motion, then shook my head. "Terrible idea, obviously, but when you're desperate and you feel helpless and you just… Fuck. Sometimes I feel like I'll never really be free of Midnight, even if we do make it out, and I swear to the moon and the stars, Haley Barnes, if you fucking cry so much as *one* tear for me over this, I will leave you here without a second—"

"Jax." She cupped my face, tilting it up until I looked at her again. "You survived. You're *still* surviving. So no, I'm not crying for you. I'm fucking *proud* of you."

She kissed me then, fierce and fiery, and wrapped her thighs around my hips, my cock hard between us, the water making us both hot and slippery. She was a survivor too, my angel, and had her own scars and stories to prove it, her own darkness to carry. And in that moment, I knew she understood me. Right down to my tarnished fucking soul. She'd seen it, and she was still here. Still in my arms. Still looking at me like she couldn't imagine a life where I didn't exist.

Without another word, she smiled and slid down over my length, taking me inside with a shudder I felt right down to my balls.

*Fuck, this woman…*

The bathwater was slowly beginning to cool, but in my arms, Haley was on fire, my angel of darkness and flame, burning me from the inside out. When she pulled back from that intense kiss, the darkness swirled in her eyes again, matched in intensity only by the bright light of her heart, a juxtaposition that made my head spin and my entire body ache for her in ways a demon shouldn't be allowed to feel.

For us, love should only hurt, like it had with Oona—a fae woman who'd allegedly cared for me enough to fake her own death to get me to leave Midnight, but not enough to trust me with the truth.

It should hurt, like it had with the men I'd once called brothers in a place where bonds were more often than not cast aside for a better offer.

It should hurt, like it had with my first family—the parents who'd condemned me to hell as a human, so certain I was a sinner beyond saving that they hadn't even bothered to try.

But Haley…

She made me feel almost whole again. Made me believe that it was even *possible* to feel whole again. And even as every warning about love and fear blazed through my mind, as my skull burned with old memories, as my chest constricted with old regrets, I couldn't help but feel this. But fall. But bring her closer to me with every deep thrust, every soft breath on my lips, every kiss. And when her eyes locked on mine and her body tightened around me and she came for me once more, my heart expanded in my chest, filling me, filling in the holes and gaps, softening the old hurts, muting the fears I'd so fervently fought against for so long.

"Jax," she breathed, and I swallowed her soft moan with another kiss—her lips, then her chin, then her throat, the sweet taste of her skin a fucking gift I still wasn't sure I'd earned. And when I finally came for her, it shook me right down to my bones, and I bit down hard on her shoulder, marking her with a silent promise as deeply as I'd marked her with my teeth.

A promise to love her the right way—not with the kind of false, fleeting, conditional love that hurt and destroyed, but with the kind that was *real*.

Now that I'd gotten a glimpse of it, I'd never settle for anything less.

We lingered in the water a bit longer, just holding each other, Haley humming another of her blissfully off-key, post-orgasm melodies—a sexy-as-sin lullaby that soothed me like none other.

When our skin had sufficiently pruned and the water had turned cold, I got out of the tub, grabbing a towel and one of the guest robes hanging on a hook behind the door.

But I didn't grab the eye patch.

I was done with it. For good.

"You coming?" I asked her, watching her naked form rise out of the water like a damned goddess.

"Soon. I'm just going to take a few minutes alone to finish up."

"Fine. I'll be waiting for you in bed."

"Whose bed, demon?" she teased.

*"Mine.* Also known as yours, since that's the only bed you'll be sharing for the foreseeable future."

"We'll see about that." She laughed, stepping out of the tub and looping her arms around my neck. "You're not ready to call it a night? Get some sleep before your mission tomorrow?"

Ignoring thoughts of tomorrow's mission, as well as thoughts of any other beds she might want to share, I pressed my lips to her warm skin and growled against her neck, the vibration making her squirm.

"It seems you misunderstood my intentions, angel. When I said I was going to ruin you tonight? I meant it. So no, I'm not ready to call it a night. In fact, I'm just getting started."

# 19

## HALEY

*J*ax made my head spin as fast as he made my heart race.

Being with him was like climbing Everest and walking on hot coals and skydiving all in the same day—danger mixed with excitement mixed with raw adrenaline and an obsession that just kept growing inside me, every time we were together.

When I first met that sexy-ass bartender at Saints and Sinners, he'd intimidated the hell out of me. Now? Now he pushed me. Hard, then soft. Made me question my assumptions and challenge myself in ways I'd never bothered to before—ways I hadn't thought I was capable of. He made me want to stop running, to turn around and face my proverbial demons head-on.

And when things got to be too much, he brought me right back from the brink with a seductive growl or a heart-melting kiss or the simple pleasure of a back rub that made me feel cherished and cared for.

Jax was a fear demon, a monster forged in hell who fed on the terror of others and had the power to bring people to their knees… Yet somehow, I was stronger and braver because of him.

And the sex?

*Holy. Fuck.*

My whole body flushed all over again, the ghost of his hands and mouth lingering, my nerves still buzzing with pleasure in all the places he'd so expertly touched me. Teased me. Claimed me.

But more than that—more than *all* of that—the way he'd trusted me tonight, the things he'd shared, the moment he'd finally lowered his guard and let me behind his walls…

When he left the bathroom without his patch, I knew. Right then, I knew.

I was falling for him. Hard.

And I was pretty sure he was falling, too.

The thought set loose a thousand butterflies in my stomach, making me feel light and giddy despite our current predicament.

After I finished up in the bathroom, I slipped into one of the thick, luxurious guest robes and headed out with every intention of joining my demon in bed, more than ready for Operation Ruination to continue.

But on my first night as Midnight captive, locked away in a massive stone castle carved by trolls, curiosity was an invitation I couldn't ignore.

Rather than heading back into the suite, I found myself padding out into the gallery hallway on bare feet, my heart thudding like it used to when I was a kid sneaking into Nona's kitchen for a stolen, late-night piece of her homemade tiramisu.

Back then, even when I got caught, it'd always been worth it.

*Just a little exploring,* I told myself now. *Five minutes, ten tops.*

The first three sets of doors beyond the suite were locked, but the fourth opened easily, revealing an impressive library larger than our entire suite, with rows upon rows of bookshelves. The back wall was curved, its towering windows offering a stunning view of the city.

There were no magickal chandeliers. No torches lit along the wall. Only the light of the moons and the flicker of red lightning on the horizon, illuminating the jagged peaks beyond.

Incredible.

I headed inside, slowly taking it all in. It reminded me of the city itself, an entire room carved out of raw black obsidian, a mix of smooth, polished-glass surfaces and rough-hewn edges jagged enough to slice through flesh.

Like much of the castle, the library was spotless and pristine, but it held a coldness to it. A darkness that had nothing to do with the absence of light and everything to do with Midnight itself.

The sight of it stirred something inside me—something beyond mere curiosity. With every step that brought me deeper into the room, my heart galloped harder, the hairs on my arms standing at attention. It felt as if the red lightning had charged the air, electrifying everything it touched.

Silently, I crept along the rows of shelves, skimming spines etched with symbols and elegant script I couldn't decipher—probably an old fae language. I longed to touch them, to crack open their leather covers, but the last thing I needed was to open the wrong book and summon a demon —not the sexy kind—or unleash an ancient curse on the realm.

I continued on toward the curved back wall and found a reading alcove tucked off to the side, complete with a soft leather chair and a small table set with a flickering black candle. Beside it, a stack of old journals tipped precariously, the top one spread open.

A glass of amber liquid caught my eye too, and when I picked it up for a sniff, the ice inside shifted and popped.

Freshly poured, then. And—sadly—*not* the fae elixir I was hoping for.

Just bourbon.

I set it back down with a sigh, my senses picking up another familiar scent.

Roses.

Suddenly, Keradoc's scent was everywhere, charging me up like the lightning, the magick, the forbidden thrill of sneaking around in his library in my bare feet, naked beneath the robe, my hair still dripping water.

I took another deep breath of it, sickly sweet and ethereal, and tried to convince myself the sudden fizziness in my stomach was unpleasant.

I blew out a breath and shook my head, as if that alone could somehow shatter the invisible hold Keradoc had on me.

*As if you really* want *to shatter it, girl…*

Right. The voice in my head was obviously sleep-deprived, bordering on delusional, so I ignored it and focused instead on the stack of journals.

Careful not to disturb them, I crouched down and peered at the neat lettering inside. The entry was dated decades earlier, the page already starting to yellow:

*Another setback tonight after the Parvaillian fae took the Towers of Wrath and Vengeance.*

*They felled my useless, gutless soldiers with an army of undead, their necromancers stronger and more powerful than any I've ever encountered.*

*No matter. Soon those necromancers will bend the knee, and the surviving soldiers who failed me will know what it is to wish for a swift death.*

*In personal matters, Ashera has finally succumbed to her injuries, bringing an end to the experiment.*

*The child is inconsolable, clinging to me as viciously as the leeches of Hanging Lake. I know not what to do with her.*

*I fear she has inherited neither her mother's strength nor her intelligence, but perhaps that will turn out to be a blessing.*

*Those who lack spine and wits are much easier to break.*

*Tomorrow night, we send another company to the Towers to face the Parvail-*
*lians and reclaim what's mine. Should my soldiers fail me again, I will order them*
*to march to the beach as soon as the Fog arrives.*

*—Keradoc of Midnight*

"Holy shit," I whispered.

These were Keradoc's journals. Why was he re-reading them? Did he
get off on revisiting his old tortures? His greatest hits?

And who were the Parvaillians?

Where were these so-called Towers?

And Ashera… Was that Oona's mother?

And what did he mean, "bringing an end to the experiment?"

Before I could read another word, a whisper of dark magick tingled
across the back of my neck, the scent of roses thick and inescapable.

"Looking for a bedtime story, little thief?"

# 20

## KERADOC

The witch startled at my sudden intrusion but didn't scream or gasp. She simply drew in a deep breath, turned to face me, and stood her ground, just as she'd been doing from the very first moment I'd looked into her eyes and demanded a dance.

"If wars could be won by lurking and skulking," she said, "you'd have every last enemy cowering at your feet by now."

"It's my castle, Miss Barnes. My right to lurk and skulk is practically written in the stones. Well, chiseled in them, anyway. This place *is* rather ancient." I tried for a smile, but as usual, she wasn't impressed.

"Is it written in your diaries too?" she asked.

"I know not. I was interrupted from my reading."

"Reading your own diaries." She clucked her tongue and shook her head, as though I should be ashamed. "Wow, and I thought *my* Saturday nights were pathetic. Have you ever considered dating? Or maybe joining a club?"

"I wouldn't know the first thing about joining a club. I haven't participated in group activities since my Warlord Academy days."

She laughed. By the moons and stars, the witch laughed. But then, as if she'd been caught breaking some sacred oath, she schooled her features and cleared her throat, her gaze shifting back to the stack of journals on my table.

"Why *are* you re-reading them, anyway? Wait, don't tell me. Your therapist suggested it as a way to identify the lifelong patterns of self-loathing that led to your toxic, abusive behavior and complete inability to form intimate relationships?"

I had no idea how much she'd already read, but I didn't owe her an explanation or a justification. I reached forward and closed the open journal, my arm inadvertently brushing against her ribs.

She sucked in a sharp breath.

The unintentional contact sent a spark skittering across my skin, unleashing a barrage of memories I'd been desperately trying to ignore.

When our gazes collided once more, she shivered, then quickly turned away as though looking at me was a burden she simply couldn't bear.

My lips twitched into a grin. "The unexamined life is not worth living. Isn't that what they say on your realm?"

"Pretty sure pining over your emo-warlord high school diaries was *not* what Socrates had in mind." She headed for one of the towering bookshelves nearby, running her slender fingers along the spines of leather tomes that'd been shelved there long ago. Her hair fell in loose waves down her back, damp and curling at the ends, the wetness leaving a dark imprint on her bathrobe. My fingers ached to slide beneath the curtain of that hair, to discover whether the back of her neck would feel cool from the dampness or warm from her skin. Her magick.

The sight of that dark fall of hair, the wetness on her shoulders, the *very* recent memory of soft, shuddering moans echoing across the bathroom…

Her very presence tonight stirred an old longing inside me, like a bellows stoking a fire to life from ashen coals long presumed spent.

I could forbid it, of course. The cavorting. I could keep the prisoners separated, focused on their work, punished for any breach of whatever boundaries I chose to establish.

But eventually, I'd need to earn the witch's trust—enough to allow us to work together and see this mission through.

I'd met her demands thus far—provided food and clothing for her and her fugitives, set them up in accommodations fit for a family of noble fae. I'd even sent word to Melantha that I was still awaiting the witch's arrival, thereby securing the relative safety of her sisters for a bit longer.

Despite all of this, she still seemed unsatisfied.

She was more than demanding. More than obstinate. For all the fire she possessed inside, Haley Barnes was cautious, guarded, and—the trait most difficult to overcome—*discerning*.

It was a challenge from which I would not, however, back down.

I *would* earn her trust, whether it was warranted or misplaced, and I would do so sooner rather than later. Taking her away from the men she so obviously cared for—the touch she so obviously needed—would only hamper those efforts.

Besides, I'd be lying if I said I didn't take a good deal of my own pleasure from spying upon hers. Even now, the scent of her desire still lingered, her cheeks flushed from her very recent interlude.

"Where did you get all these books, anyway?" she asked, stretching up on her toes to reach a leather-bound book of so-called fairy tales. It remained, however, just out of reach. "I didn't think a warlord would have time for pleasure reading."

"Most of the works in my library were smuggled here from your realm. Some of them are quite rare." I reached above her head and retrieved the fairy-tale book. "This is a first edition. The Brothers Grimm, if the name means anything to you?"

Her eyes widened with interest, and she reached for it, our fingers brushing. But that brief touch had her drawing back once more.

It shouldn't have irritated me, yet it did.

For fuck's sake, the woman had kissed me so passionately in the throne room, so eagerly, yet now she recoiled as if my touch might possess the power to leech the strength from her bones.

"You're welcome to borrow it." I held it out once more, but she was as defiant as ever, already shaking her head. "In any case," I said, "the library is yours to roam, should you choose. You may find some interesting occult or fae history books to aid in your ritual. But no lurking or skulking—*that* is strictly my province."

She cast her gaze to the chandeliers and sighed at my attempted humor. When she finally saw fit to look at me again, she crossed her arms over her chest and scowled. "How very Beauty-and-the-Beast of you."

"I'm afraid I don't understand the reference."

"Let me break it down for you. You're the beast in the equation."

*Oh, you have no idea, little thief...*

I reached for a lock of her hair, aching to brush it from her shoulder, but stopped short of touching it. My hand simply hovered between us, tickled by the soft whoosh of her breath. She gazed at it intently, mesmerized, and for a moment I wondered if she could sense the magick coursing beneath my skin the same way I could sense hers.

"I suppose that makes you the beauty, then?" I asked, lowering my hand and stepping closer. Too close. The scent of her freshly washed hair and skin intoxicated me.

"It makes… It makes me…" She blinked rapidly, then shook her head, ice hardening her features once more. "It makes me the prisoner, Keradoc.

Nice clothes and soft sheets and a library full of first editions pilfered from the homeland doesn't change that."

I forced myself not to bristle at the rebuke. "Your stay here will be more pleasant if you stop thinking of yourself as a prisoner."

"I didn't come to Midnight for pleasantries, *warlord*. And even if I had, I wouldn't look for them here. I'm pretty sure you're not capable of anything even *remotely* pleasant."

"Your concept of what I'm capable of, *Darkwinter*, is severely limited."

"As is *your* concept of how good my imagination is."

"Oh, I've no doubt your imagination is rich and fathomless. So I want you to imagine this." I closed the very last of the gap between us and grabbed her arm, peering down into her glittering green eyes. "When you crawl into the bed of your precious demon tonight... When the others are fast asleep and he alone touches you... When he whispers against your pale neck... When he puts his warm, wet, demanding mouth on all the places that give you such wild and fevered dreams, I want you to imagine how it would feel to see him stripped bare, tied to the underside of the drawbridge, whipped until his very bones wept, and lowered into Beggar's Moat during the full triple moon when the light would grant the most *exquisite* view of the carnage. I wonder, *angel*, would he scream? Or would he hold fast, imploring you with that singular eye not to fear for him, not to mourn him as I sent his soul back to its eternal torment in hell?"

Tears filled her eyes, but she refused to let them fall. When she spoke, her voice was tight with emotion. With rage. "You're a *monster*."

"But not a fool." I released her arm. "Do *not* test me again, Miss Barnes. You'll not enjoy the outcome."

A flicker of fear danced through her eyes, mingling with a vile hatred that for some inexplicable reason made my cock stiffen.

Suddenly, I wanted nothing more than to bed that obstinate little witch. To fuck the hatred right out of her. To break her until she softened and moaned my name as she had the demon's, *begging* me not to stop...

We glared at each other in the flickering candlelight, another unspoken challenge rising between us.

I was tempted to use fae magick on her, if only to keep her in my company for the rest of the evening, to enjoy more of her sharp wit and my own dark, twisted fantasies.

But I wouldn't. Not now. Despite what she thought of me—despite the urgent ache in my cock—no, I wasn't the kind of man who drugged and manipulated women for my own entertainment.

I preferred to save *those* tactics for more important missions.

With a final warning glance, I replaced the book on the high shelf above her head and turned on my heel, leaving her alone in the library, trying not to chuckle at the sound of her soft grunts as she tried in vain to jump up and grab the book.

# 21

## ELIAN

Fifteen minutes into our new gig, Jax and I were already at each other's throats.

Thanks to Haley, neither of us had slept much.

Jax, on account of making my little sparrow sing for him all night long.

Me, on account of having to listen to that shit, even locked away in my own sleeping alcove with pillows jammed up around my head and my heart slamming against my ribs and the thunder of a fresh storm rattling the windows.

On top of all that, the meager meal Keradoc's staff had prepared for us left us hollow and irritable—cold, congealed oatmeal and a few overly ripe pieces of fruit, along with a watered-down bottle of blood for me. Haley had taken one look at that shit, pushed up her sleeve, and offered the vein.

I was too hungry to resist, even though the sight of her made me want to jump off the highest turret.

What the fuck did she see in that demon, anyway?

And why the hell did she keep looking at me like she no longer wished me dead? Like she was actually glad I was here? It was my fucking fault we were in this mess in the first place. My fault for trusting Gem. My fault for not protecting Haley.

I should've been there to stop that fucking monster before he'd ever demanded a single dance.

Now, we were all caught in the same web, and I couldn't even kill him.

Couldn't even try. One whiff of betrayal, and we'd all be on the torture racks.

*Fuck.*

When I'd had my fill—as much as I'd been willing to take, at least—I wiped my mouth with the back of my hand and said, "If you insist on sharing his bed, sparrow, at least stuff a sock in your mouth so the rest of us can get some sleep."

Yep. Championship asshole, going for the gold.

But every night that passed with Haley in my presence but not in my arms was another night some part of me shriveled up and blew away. Wasn't her fault, but still. It was better for both of us if she stopped trying to help me. Stopped acting like my personal blood bag and looking at me like she still cared—like I still deserved it.

When I looked into her eyes, there was still too much fucking hope there.

And hope, as she'd so eloquently told me that night in the apartment, was its own kind of poison.

Every night since, her words had echoed through my skull like a warning.

*Hope? It's a drug worse than your Devil's Dream. A drug that causes delusions so powerful, you re-route your whole life around them until all you have left are the bullshit stories you tell yourself just to get through another day...*

Now, trapped in Midnight, I didn't want any hope. Didn't need it. What I *needed* was another fix, but Jax's supply was limited, and until we could either make or steal more pills, I had to slow down—a task that would've been a hell of a lot easier if the bastard would actually tell me how much he was carrying, but he was keeping that card close to the vest.

It was all I could do not to trail him like a lost puppy sniffing after a bone, which sucked, because what I *really* wanted to do was beat the shit out of him for making Haley sing. Again and again. Fucking opera house, that suite last night. I wasn't surprised to learn Hudson had left early for the fields. Considering Haley was his fated mate, the poor bastard probably wanted to strangle Jax, too.

So, after the meager meal and a well-deserved scolding from Haley, Jax and I left the castle, marching through the cramped streets of Amaranth City in hostile silence as we searched for our new job site.

We'd just turned down another dank, festering alley when out of nowhere Jax pounced on me, shoving me to the ground.

Two circular blades whizzed over our heads. We got to our feet and bolted toward the direction where they'd come from, but our would-be attackers were already lost in the crowd.

"Fuck," Jax hissed.

"What did you see?"

"Nothing. It was more what I felt—a spike of adrenaline."

"You think it was Keradoc's men?"

"I think there are plenty of people in this city who want us dead, and plenty more who want *anyone* dead, and maybe we just happen to look like easy targets." Then, giving me a quick once over, "You good?"

I nodded and scratched my head, grateful it was still attached to my neck. "Thanks for—"

"Old habits, Saint. Don't thank me." He shoved past me and stalked back down the alley, and I followed just behind him, trying to pay better attention to my surroundings. I was part vampire, for fuck's sake. *I should've* been the one to sense that attack. And if I wasn't going out of my mind about Haley, about those fucking pills, about all of it…

Excuses didn't matter.

Right now, I just had to get through this night. Check out our new work situation, figure out what we'd need to do to get Keradoc whatever drugs he needed, then make it happen.

"This the place?" I asked when Jax stopped in front of a low, squat building built into the side of a rocky outcropping. A few dusty windows lined the front, and I tried to get a look inside, but they were tinted.

"It's the address Keradoc gave me, so I'm guessing it's either our new office or a setup."

"Let's find out then, shall we?" With a grin, I pushed open the front door and stepped inside.

A bright magickal floodlight kicked on, temporarily blinding us as the door closed behind us with a heavy thunk. I'd just lifted my arm to block the light when four projectiles slammed into the door around our heads.

Not blades this time. Stakes.

Shot from crossbows.

Wielded by none other than our favorite purple-haired traitor.

Flanked by six guards, Gem stepped out of the shadows with a grin.

"Hello, boys. Miss me?"

I was on her in a flash, my hands wrapped around her throat. But before I could properly crush her windpipe, a painful electrical current surged through my body, dropping my ass to the ground.

Gem only laughed. "What about you, demon?" she said to Jax. "Want to give it a go?"

Glaring at her, Jax crouched down to help me back to my feet. My muscles were still twitching with whatever dark magick shielding I'd hit.

Fucking Midnighters.

"What the *fuck* are you doing here, Gem?" Jax ground out.

"Apparently, Commander Keradoc doesn't trust Elian not to steal the product," she said, "or you not to flee. So I've been assigned to supervise."

Hurt, rage, betrayal… all of it collided inside me, sending my heart into overdrive.

"Why?" I asked, my voice a broken whisper, and she knew damn well I wasn't asking about why she'd been put on babysitter duty.

Something dark and sad flashed in her eyes, but before I could make sense of it, she turned away from me and dismissed her entourage.

When she looked at us again, I saw that same sadness in her eyes and for a second, I thought she might actually talk.

Instead, she shoved that crossbow into my chest and said, "No more questions, *Elian*. Now, considering you two already know your way around a drug processing facility, we're going to skip your orientation and get right down to business."

"That right?" I asked. "And what do you know about our business here, you fucking traitor?"

"I know I told you to stop asking questions. And I know if you two don't get to work, we're going to have a serious problem involving *my* boot up *your* ass. So move."

She shoved us ahead, steering us to a section at the back of the cavernous space where several tables had been set up for us, some of them holding trays of dried corpsevine flower, others covered with various pieces of lab equipment—beakers, test tubes, scales, burners, goggles.

There were other tables, too—manned by fae and demons and vampires alike, all of them working on various stages of the production line: crushing the dried flowers into powders, preparing it to be pressed into pills, counting out and bottling the final product.

My mouth watered at the sight of so much Dream, but my infatuation was short-lived. There, on the far side of the space, were the testers.

Dozens and dozens of people of every supernatural race, all crowded together on the floor, all in various stages of delirium. Some of them scratched at invisible bugs crawling beneath their skin, others moaned through the pain of withdrawal, others trembled and twitched, desperate for their next dose. A few were stretched out on cots with IVs hooked up to their arms, concentrated black liquid dripping into their veins, their eyes glassy, their mouths open in a perpetual, blissful grin.

Several testers had already become corpses. No one had bothered to remove the bodies.

"I'll leave you to it, boys," Gem said. "But remember—I'm watching you."

Jax and I exchanged a look, then bent our heads to the work, rearranging the equipment until we had it optimized.

"Just like old times," I said.

"Yeah, except in the old times, our closest ally wasn't a fucking sellout."

I nodded, ready to let loose a barrage of curses about the bitch I'd once considered a friend, but something held me back.

The events of that night still didn't add up for me. If Gem had truly wanted to betray us, why did she wait until the feast? Why did she go to the trouble of getting us the apartment, the tickets to the feast, the formalwear, all of it? She knew we were heading back to Midnight, so why didn't she just have an ambush waiting for us on arrival?

And what was that look in her eyes all about just now?

"Jax," I said softly. "She keeps calling me Elian. Even that night after they shot us. She said, and I quote, 'it's like I always say, *Elian*... Nothing in Midnight is ever what it should be.' And just now she did it again —Elian."

"That's your name, asshole. How much Dream have you *had*?"

"That's not my name in Midnight. Gem only ever called me Saint."

His eyes widened as he considered the implications. "You think she's trying to tell us something?"

Another stake slammed into the wall behind us.

"Shut the fuck up and get to work, boys," Gem shouted across the room, "or the next one's going in your fucking skull. And don't think you're getting off easy either, demon. We're taking bets on who gets to pluck out that eye the minute you give us any shit."

I blew out a breath, my heart sinking into my stomach. "Guess that answers that."

**22**

HALEY

*H*ow's things, babygirl?"

A deep, gravelly voice rumbled across the common room, and I couldn't help the ear-to-ear grin that stretched across my face.

Abandoning my latest failed magickal experiment at the dining table, I ran to my gargoyle, giggling like a schoolgirl as he swept me up in his powerful embrace, spinning me around.

"What are you doing here?" I asked when he finally set me back down. I handed over the notebook I'd started carrying in case he needed to scrawl out a message. "I thought you'd be out in the fields for another few hours."

He pushed away the notebook. "Starshowers closed us down early. Thought I'd come check on my girl."

I grinned again, loving the sound of that voice rumbling through his chest. He was in his human form now, fully clothed, his blond hair hanging in loose waves to his shoulders. I couldn't help but lean in for another hug, wrapping my arms around his waist and pressing my head to his chest. His heart beat strong and steady against my ear.

"So many words in one sentence?" I teased.

"For you? Hell yeah." He laughed, the rich sound of it reverberating through his chest, making my heart skip.

Hudson never spoke in front of the guys, and after everything that happened the night of the feast, he hadn't spoken out loud to me either. I

320

didn't push him—just assumed he'd retreated into his old strong, silent protector mode.

But now, the first time we'd been alone together since he'd rescued me from the Sanctuary last week, it seemed he was ready to talk again.

And I was more than ready to listen.

"Hudson," I said softly, pulling back to look up into his chocolate-brown eyes, "what happened the night of the feast? I was so worried about you."

A current of white-hot fury swirled in his eyes—a darkness I'd never before seen in my sweet, protective gargoyle. "Ambushed by some fuckers from my past who ain't got no business calling themselves gargoyles."

"Ambushed?" My heart slammed against my ribs. "But... who? Keradoc's guards?"

"Not exactly. See, I knew something was up that night. Saw Saint and Jax running off with Gem, felt like you were in trouble, too. I searched everywhere, finally spotted you tied up in that throne room. But that's when they nabbed me."

He told me the story of the attack, the spelled bullets, how they'd imprisoned him.

"Oh my God," I gasped. "But... How did you get out of that?"

"Like I said, I knew you were in trouble. I could feel it. And I wasn't about to stay locked up like a statue when my girl needed me. So I got out, made my way back to the city, and found you and Jax in the chokeweed. You know the rest."

I shook my head, still marveling at him. I still had so many questions, though. How did he break that spell? And who were his attackers?

"And these... these guys from your past," I said. "They're... dead, I'm assuming? Hoping?"

Hudson laughed, but it was dark and hollow, like something scraping along the basement floor. "Yeah, babygirl. They're dead. They don't know it yet, but they'll get that memo soon enough."

"But—"

"Hey." He tucked a finger under my chin, tipping my face up as he brought his close. In a soft voice, he said, "I don't want you worrying about all that, okay? It's being taken care of. You got your hands full here, and that's a good thing."

"How do you figure?"

"Ain't gotta like what Keradoc's doing, but as long as he needs this spell, I know the bastard's gonna do everything he can to keep you protected."

"Imprisoned, you mean."

"Safe and alive, for as long as it takes for us to find a way out."

I nodded, leaning into him once more. Hudson wrapped his arms around me, so solid, so warm, and I sighed with pleasure. I didn't care how many walls Keradoc had built or how many guards he had watching over me. *Nothing* made me feel as safe and protected as a single hug from this man.

"Show me what you're working on," he said. "I'm feeling a little short on words now. I could use some Haley-speak."

"All right, Gargs, but you asked for it." Laughing, I took his hand and led him to the dining table, narrating my progress on the ritual prep in excruciating detail.

Rather, my *lack* of progress.

After our run-in in the library last week, Keradoc had pretty much ghosted me, which was just fine by me. The following night, I'd raided the library again, scrounging up a few books about Darkwinter history, along with some general texts on summoning spells and blood rituals. I looked for his journals, but no luck. After he busted me looking at them that night, I was pretty sure he'd locked them away for good.

So, for the next few nights, I read. Took notes. Ran a few small experiments—nothing too intense, considering I was still limited by the dampener cuff, but enough to deepen my understanding of how my blood magick might work in a summoning ritual.

My setup was pretty bare-bones, though—I needed some herbs and other ingredients, and I hadn't been able to find them in the kitchen. After the encounter with the chokeweed, I wasn't about to go traipsing through the gardens for a few clippings, either.

"You'll get there, babygirl," Hudson said now. "I know you will. And if you need shit from the city, just let me know. I can try to find it for you on my next run."

"Yeah?"

"Make me a list. I'll help you out any way I can."

I smiled, but the idea of it made me sad. Hudson and the guys had it way harder than I did, and there wasn't a damn thing I could do to help any of them. I didn't know how to make drugs, and I certainly couldn't fly over corpsevine fields and guard them from the many vicious creatures of Midnight.

It'd been less than a week since Keradoc had put us to work, and already the guys were exhausted.

Their nightly return to the castle at the end of their shifts had quickly become the best part of my time here, because it meant they'd survived another day. That we'd be together under one roof for at least a few hours before we had to get up and start the grind all over again.

We always ate dinner together, no matter how late it was, and thankfully the food had gotten better—not quite as rich and resplendent as the Feast of Midnight spread, but an upgrade from that first day of cold, bland mush. I fed Elian my blood whenever I could—usually when he'd gotten too weak to resist.

But our conversations were short, all of us too wiped out for anything else. There was no way to avoid it—we all wanted to get the hell out of Midnight as quickly as possible, even if it meant working ourselves to the bone to make it happen.

*Later*, I'd tell myself each night as I crawled into bed with Jax, or sometimes with Hudson if he was having trouble sleeping. *Later* we'd have time for fun. For lively conversations over decadent meals. For stories told around a crackling fire about that crazy-ass time we all went to Midnight and helped the warlord secure another hollow victory.

Though they were all curious about my magick and the things I was learning each night, they never talked about their own work, and I never pushed the issue. What could they really say, anyway? They were making drugs. Testing them on people. Overseeing the harvesting and production of a substance that would ultimately—if Keradoc had his way—end the lives of hundreds of fae. Maybe thousands.

Fae whose same dark blood ran through my veins.

And yet, despite the cruelty of Keradoc's assignment, despite the regrets my guys carried about their involvement, there were times when I couldn't help but feel sorry for the warlord. All this subterfuge, all this violence, and to what end? Midnight had been at war for an eternity. Midnight *was* a war. What did he hope to accomplish?

And even if he achieved his goals and eradicated every last Darkwinter fae in the realm, even if he defeated every last rebel faction and claimed Midnight for himself once and for all, what then?

What did it mean to claim a place as your home if you had no one to share it with?

The thought sent a wave of goosebumps rippling over my skin, and I rubbed my arms to chase them away.

Even though I hadn't seen him, I could still feel the tingle of Keradoc's magick, still smell a whisper of roses around every corner. It always felt like he was watching me—even now—though I'd never caught him in the act.

"Hey," Hudson said now, bringing me back to the moment. "You got this. You know that, right?"

I returned his smile, bolstered by the vote of confidence. "You know it, Gargs." Then, blowing out a breath and glancing across the mess on the table, "I just have to keep experimenting until I get it right. I'm a powerful blood witch, for fuck's sake. Right?"

"Damn straight. And with all that Silversbane Darkwinter magickal woo-woo running through your veins? Hell, *I* wouldn't want to meet you in a dark alley."

I picked up a vial of blood I'd drawn earlier, swirling it in the glass, watching it cling to the edges.

"If my Silversbane Darkwinter woo-woo is so special," I said, "maybe the guys should be selling my blood instead of Devil's Dream. Probably get more money for it. Maybe we could just buy our way out of this mess instead."

"Your blood is not for sale, Miss Barnes." Keradoc's chilling voice echoed across the room as the warlord marched in uninvited. Then, plucking the vial from my fingers and replacing it in the rack on the table, "Your blood will turn our fortune in this war."

"My blood and your malice." I rolled my eyes. "Sounds like a winning combo to me."

"I've come for an update on your progress. In all this time, I do hope you've made some."

"Oh, and hello to you too, Keradoc! Hudson and I are doing just fine today, thanks for asking. And what about you?" I reached up and smoothed out the lapels on his impeccable military uniform, then tapped one of his many patches, which was probably completely disrespectful, but I didn't care. "Did you have a good night spilling the blood of your enemies and setting their puppies on fire?"

"Your *progress*, Miss Barnes." He reached up and fingered a lock of my hair. "Unless you'd like me to set you on fire as well?"

Hudson stepped between us and folded his arms over his chest, a warning growl rumbling through him.

"The skies have cleared, *gargoyle*," Keradoc said with a sneer. "You're needed back on the southwestern front."

"Hudson." I stepped out from behind him and glared at Keradoc. "His name is Hudson. And if you can't remember that, *fae*, you don't deserve to address him at all."

The three of us stood like that for a long moment, locked in a battle of wills.

Finally, Keradoc backed off.

"*Hudson*," he said—through gritted teeth, but still. "You're needed back at your post. And Miss Barnes, I really would like to understand what you've been working on. So, if we might continue?"

"We might, assuming you can behave in a civilized manner for at least fifteen minutes." I shot him a warning glare, then took Hudson's hand and walked him to the doors that led out to the balcony. Stretching up to kiss his cheek, I said, "I'll be fine, Gargs. Don't worry. Just be careful out there and come back to me in one piece, okay?"

He looked over at Keradoc once more, then back to me, his eyes full of worry.

"Go!" I teased, swatting him on the very firm, very nice ass. "The sooner you leave, the sooner you can come home."

With one more warning growl for Keradoc, Hudson finally took off, heading out the door and leaping into the sky, wings unfurling behind him.

Reluctantly, I dragged myself back to Keradoc. "So. This is my performance review? Because honestly, I'm doing a terrible job. You should totally fire me."

Keradoc's violet eyes darkened, and he turned to look out the glass doors, hands clasped behind his back, his spine ramrod straight. "What do you truly know of this realm, Miss Barnes? That it's a prison? A form of hell? Or—what's the term you and your kind are so fond of—a shithole? Not that I can disagree with *that* assessment."

Looking out across the dark expanse beyond the balcony, I felt oddly defensive of the place. "If you feel that way about Midnight, Keradoc, why are you so determined to slaughter everyone who tries to take it from you?"

"Ah, but if it were that simple." He opened one of the doors and gestured for me to follow him out onto the balcony.

The air was cool, fresher up here than down on the streets, the din and squalor of the city muted.

"There are places on your realm," he said, "where beauty and riches are found not in what the eye can see on the surface, but in what lies beneath."

"Do you mean literally? As in gemstones and metals? Oil?"

He turned to me and grinned, his eyes twinkling in the moonlight. "All things the men of your realm pay great sums to acquire."

"Or to have someone else acquire for them." I glanced at the bloodstone ring on my finger, then met his eyes again, not wanting to draw too much attention to it.

"Or to steal it for them."

"Or they just declare a war and take it."

"Precisely," he said with a nod. "And so it is in Midnight. Only in our case, it's not diamonds or oil we're fighting for. It's magick. A magick that runs through every rock, every tree, every lake of blood in this realm. The magick of Midnight is a precious thing, Miss Barnes. Far more valuable than our cities and walls."

"Why are you revealing state secrets to your prisoner?"

"It's no secret. Not for the ones fighting to take it, nor the ones fighting to keep it. And not, I suspect," he said, turning to face me full on, "for you."

The intensity of his gaze made my skin burn.

"You're... right," I finally admitted. "I can feel it. There's a hum in the air—in the ground as well. More than a vibration. There's a palpable magickal energy here—sometimes I feel like I can actually *see* it. Like a phantom glow."

"It's palpable to *you*," he said. "Because you're a witch with Darkwinter blood coursing through your veins. The magick of Midnight—dark magick—is your birthright. The longer you remain in my realm, the more connected to it you will feel."

Even as I blanched, his words sent a little thrill through my heart, making my pulse race.

But... no. Just because I had Darkwinter blood—severely diluted Darkwinter blood, considering how many generations ago my Darkwinter ancestors lived—that didn't make *me* dark. Didn't make me any more capable of harnessing and wielding dark magick than Hudson or Jax, for that matter.

"I'm not dark, Keradoc. Not in the way you're thinking."

"No?" He crowded me, backing me up against the rough barrier that surrounded the balcony. "What do you see when you close your eyes, Miss Barnes? What do you find when you search deep in your soul, past all the things you believe make someone a good person, past the things you believe keep you safe from the dark?" He was standing so close to me now, I could feel his breath misting on my lips. In a soft whisper, he said, "When you sleep, little thief, where do the nightmares take you?"

He drew a fingertip across my forehead, his touch soft and cold, his magick whispering through my mind. It was the barest caress, but like

Jax's fear demon mojo, this magick unleashed a flood of images so real I swore I could reach out and touch them.

*Flame and shadow bending at my command, breaking the laws of physics and magick both.*

*Power surging through my veins, crackling at my fingertips.*

*Death rising, a thousand raw-boned corpses clawing out of the black earth and bowing at my feet...*

I drew back with a gasp and shut my eyes, struggling to believe it. No, I didn't mean the visions themselves—those were as clear as the red-and-gold stars in the black sky, and I knew, somehow, they were real—as real as the fears Jax had brought to the surface to save me from the chokeweed.

Keradoc had just given me a glimpse of my future—that much was certain, even if I couldn't yet make sense of what I'd seen.

But the *feelings* those visions had unlocked inside me... How could I accept them?

How could I admit to the fact that rather than gasping in fear, I was gasping with excitement? With wonder? With hope that all of those things might one day be mine?

My whole body trembled with the possibility of it, and I clenched my fists at my sides, trying to calm myself. To bring myself out of whatever trance his magick had put me under.

"I... I should get back to my work," I said, glancing desperately toward the doors. Keradoc was still in my space, too close, too... everything.

"Yes, you should," he said smoothly. "But Miss Barnes?" He reached for my un-cuffed wrist, lifting it with a delicate touch, his thumb sliding across my tattoo. As I unfurled my clenched fingers, a black rose bloomed in my palm. Keradoc brought it to his nose and inhaled, unleashing a moan so lush I could've sworn he'd just come.

"Next time," he whispered, finally releasing me, "perhaps you'll think twice before passing judgment on my motives."

# 23

## KERADOC

*ands and teeth as sharp as knives, he chased me.*

*He always chased me. It was his favorite game. Refusing to play only made the punishment worse.*

*So I ran.*

*I ran in the dark. Ran through sharp-bladed grass that sliced my feet to ribbons, and I hid among barren trees that seemed to relish in giving away my position. They were nothing like the silver-leaved trees of home, the trees that cradled and nurtured and soothed.*

*These were the trees that burned and bled, that fed from the wounds of their victims.*

*Yet still, I hid behind them, just as he wanted me to.*

*And still, the wolf of Midnight found me.*

*He always found me, for it was his game, and it was as rigged as any could ever be.*

*Hands and teeth as sharp as knives.*

*"Don't struggle, pretty little fae," he said, his hand on my shoulder as he winked at me. "You'll only make me angry, and you know what happens then."*

*"My apologies, master." I dropped to my knees. Bowed. This too was part of the game, just like what came next.*

*A fist in my hair.*

*The sharp crack of a leather switch against bare skin.*

*Face pressed hard into the wet earth, his cruel hand as large as my head.*

*Gasping for every breath as he held me down in the rancid mud and took.*

*And took.*

*And took.*

*The pain, the blood, the darkness…*

*It crashed upon me in heavy waves, my screams muted only by his wicked laughter…*

---

"No, stop! Please! *No!*"

I awoke with a start, heart hammering against my chest like the beating of war drums. Sweat rolled down my back, and my every muscle quivered in fear.

Nightmare. Just a nightmare. I was safe in the library, nowhere near the old forest. As for the wolf… the monster in the shadows had since been de-fanged. Now he rotted away breath by breath, bone by bone, no longer the master. No longer the predator, but the prey.

*Don't struggle, pretty little fae…*

I picked up the half-full glass of bourbon from my table. Pitched it against the wall. The clear, unmistakable sound of something breaking calmed my nerves.

I had no idea how long I'd been carrying on in my half-sleep, but soft footsteps on the polished floor on the other side of the bookshelves told me it hadn't gone unnoticed.

*Haley.*

In the week or so she'd been living here, I saw to it that our paths had rarely crossed. I preferred to let the guards keep watch, reporting back to me on the comings and goings of all my new guests. Being close to her was too distracting for me. Too dangerous. Too confusing, for the inexplicable pull I felt toward her had only intensified since that night on her balcony.

Yet I'd be lying if I said I hadn't watched her on occasion. Hadn't lingered outside her door or peered through the windows of my own suite, hoping for a glimpse of her on the balcony, her long hair blowing in the breeze, her spine straight and determined as she looked out across the city lights, held out her palms, and tried to make her roses bloom.

"Kcradoc?" came her soft call in the darkness now, as I knew it would. I recognized the cadence of her steps as easily as I recognized the warm touch of her magick. The scent of her skin. All of it reaching me before she finally appeared before me.

She was dressed for bed, wrapped up in the bathrobe she'd seemed to so love, her hair woven in a loose braid that hung over her shoulder. In her hands, she held a steaming mug of peppermint tea.

"Are you all right?" she asked, her brow knitted with concern. "I thought I heard you shouting."

I felt as if I had one foot still in the land of dreams, the room blurring at the edges, her face as pale as an apparition.

"Something is… hunting me," I whispered. "A dark and vile thing."

The moment the words had left me, my thoughts cleared, the ridiculousness of my confession making the back of my neck burn with shame.

But Haley said nothing. No mockery, no sharp-tongued repartee about how I deserved to be hunted. Deserved to suffer.

Instead, with a look one could only describe as empathy, she handed over the mug of tea.

"Peppermint and lavender," she said softly. "I find it helps keep the nightmares at bay."

I thought to deny the offer, but the simple kindness was a balm on my still-fractured heart, and I took the mug with a silent nod of thanks.

Her gaze locked on mine, she leaned back against the windowsill, the shape of her illuminated by the moonlight.

I closed my eyes and sipped the tea, grateful for the warmth as much as the excuse to look away from her.

"Thank you for the tea," I finally managed, "but I've no need of your company. You may go."

She shrugged. "Needs and wants aren't always the same thing. Besides, I'm feeling a little restless tonight, too."

"Yes, well… As you can see, I've got plenty of work to…" I gestured at the book I'd left on the table—a collection of hand-drawn maps of the realm—but my weak excuse faded away in a sigh. "Why are you here, Miss Barnes?"

"I just came from the kitchen. I was on my way to my suite when I heard you."

"And?"

The compassion in her eyes deepened, the weight of it almost unbearable. "And… and maybe I know what it's like to be haunted by a past you can't even remember."

Her words struck a deep chord, and I couldn't help but wonder what was haunting her. Was it the mother who'd tried to drown her as a child? The sisters she'd never even gotten the opportunity to know?

Something knifed into my chest at the thought, but I dismissed it, chasing it away with another sip of tea.

"*Hunted*," I said softly. "I felt as if something were hunting me, not haunting."

"Is there a difference? Ghosts. Monsters. Memories. All of them can destroy us if we give them the power to."

"Power isn't always given away. More often than not, it is stolen from us. Stripped when we're at our most vulnerable."

"Then wielded like a weapon, keeping us cowed and fearful—yeah, I've seen this episode before." A heavy sadness touched her eyes, and in that moment, my own evaporated, replaced with a deep anger at the very thought of anyone wielding a weapon against her.

But then, as quickly as it had risen inside me, the anger vanished, hot guilt bubbling in its wake.

In my efforts to save Midnight, to pursue my own needs, I had done just that—taken her power. Wielded it like a weapon against her and her companions both.

Literally and figuratively.

Yet still, she'd come here tonight offering tea and a sympathetic ear.

Shaking my head at the wonder of it, I finally said, "It seems I've misjudged you, Miss Barnes."

"Hmm. You think?" A smile flickered at the edges of her mouth, and something deep inside me stirred, warm and hungry.

Longing.

The witch was getting under my skin in ways I should never have allowed, but it was happening, bit by bit, each night. Each moment, even this one.

When Melantha had first bargained with the Darkwinter witch, I'd been more than curious, more than eager to see how she might be of use. To see whether the summoning and resurrection of the Darkwinter ancestors really could turn our fortunes in this war.

In my mind, she was a means to an end. A weapon the enemy would never be able to defeat, just like I'd told her from the start.

But she wasn't just a weapon. She was a marvel. She was kind and generous. She was fierce and resourceful. She fought for herself, fought for the people she cared for. I wasn't certain of her combat skills, or whether she could even *hold* a sword, much less use it. But she was smart and quick on her feet. And she was powerful. In her presence, I could feel the threads of her magick even through the dampener cuff, the force of a thousand caged birds desperate to break free.

"Miss Barnes, I—"

"Haley," she said. "You need to call me Haley. Miss Barnes makes me feel like a naughty schoolgirl. Besides, I kind of like how it sounds when you say my name."

She shrugged like the admission meant little, but the dark stain on her cheeks said otherwise.

"Haley," I said softly. "There's something you should know. I never meant for you to… The situation in Midnight is complicated. I realize you and your companions feel like prisoners here, and in some ways, I suppose you are. But I do not wish you harm, Darkwinter. Only—"

"Darkwinter," she snapped, her eyes flashing, the momentary peace between us vanishing in a blink. "Your so-called enemy. The ultimate evil, right? Which is saying a lot in a place like Midnight."

"Haley, no. I didn't mean—"

"You *did* mean it, though. In your mind, that's what I am—an enemy. An enemy to be broken, bent, and reshaped to suit *your* needs. You've tortured those Darkwinter fae. Hunted them, just as they hunt you. So every time you say that name—every time you call *me* the name of your sworn enemy—you jam the knife a little deeper into my gut. So don't you *dare* tell me you don't wish me harm. The fact is, you *are* harming me. You can't just wish that away with some bullshit platitudes about how complicated your situation is. *Life* is complicated, Keradoc. Get over it."

"Midnight is at war—has been for a long time. I'm only doing what's best for my people."

"And who are your people, Keradoc? Your daughter? Your generals? The soldiers you leave to rot on the field? Or maybe the ones you parade through the streets until they finally succumb to their wounds? What about the people starving right outside this very castle, begging your servants for the scraps you've left on your plate? What about the people you feed to your ghouls?" She shook her head, a bitter laugh escaping. "If that's how you treat your so-called *people*, I'm happy to be your enemy."

My stomach churned and roiled. Every one of her accusations rang true.

But those daggers weren't meant for me. They were meant for the man whose mask I wore. Whose mantle I now bore, along with all the power— and the judgment—that had come with it.

I'd taken on those things willingly, gladly, all in service of my ultimate goal.

But when all was said and done, which of us would be called to atone for those sins?

Did it even matter?

I turned the ring on my finger, the skin burning and blistering beneath.

It was getting more painful by the night; the magick was faltering, the bond between us unraveling. His death was close.

And mine was probably not far behind.

"I don't know why I ever thought we could have one nice conversation," she said, standing up to leave. "You know what? I hope whatever's chasing you in your dreams finally catches you, and I hope it bites off your—"

"Your sisters," I blurted out, desperate to defuse her. To make her stay, even for a moment longer.

To prove to her I wasn't the monster she believed me to be.

Her face turned the color of the first moon. "What about them?"

I rose to my feet. "I wanted you to know that they're safe, Miss Barnes. Haley. I give you my word."

"And what, exactly, is that word worth? Can I trust you, Keradoc?"

"On this? Yes."

She held my gaze for a long moment, scrutinizing me through narrowed eyes, her breath stirring a strand of hair that had slipped from her braid.

*Moons and stars*, she was lovely. A dark flower blooming in an even darker world, and when I'd said I had no need of her company, it was a lie as bold and black as I'd ever told.

"I've got associates in Blackmoon Bay keeping a close eye," I said. "Your sisters are alive and well, as are the witches with whom they practice their craft and the men with whom they share their lives. A vampire and two demons, I believe? And a wolf shifter and a mortal man, or so I'm told? Honestly, the arrangement sounded rather tedious and confusing, but nevertheless, all are safe and well."

She pressed a hand to her heart with a gasp, and tears filled her eyes. "My sister Gray. Those are her mates. Asher and Ronan are the demons, Darius is the vampire, and Emilio is a wolf shifter. Liam used to be Death, but now he's mortal."

"Death?" I couldn't help the curious lifting of my eyebrow.

"Long story."

"Indeed." I offered a tentative smile. "Such a strange realm, your home."

"You have no idea." She returned my smile, and it felt like forgiveness. "Did you mean what you said? Really? My sisters... Everyone's okay?"

"As I last heard from my associate earlier this evening, yes. Everyone is okay."

"Thank you, Keradoc," she whispered, her eyes glittering with tears. This time, there was no hatred behind them. Only gratitude. Only warmth.

She took a step closer and offered another smile, and for the briefest, oddest moment, I thought she might embrace me...

*"Haley."*

The gruff voice shattered the moment.

Elian. Her vampire-fae companion. The fugitive, drug-addled doppelgänger whom I still couldn't bring myself to look at with more than a passing glance, for every time I saw the face that tugged at my memories, Melantha's treachery burned anew.

She would pay. Dearly.

At the sound of her name passing through his lips, Haley's eyes filled with longing. Regret. Heartache.

And there, flickering around the edges, hope.

I hated him for it, though I didn't understand why.

"Be right there, Elian," she replied. Then, turning to me one last time, she placed her palm against my cheek and said, "Sleep well, Keradoc. Tomorrow is a new night."

**24**

ELIAN

here's Jax?" she asked as we headed back into the common room.

Of course that would be the first question out of her mouth.

"Don't know, don't care. I'm more concerned about what you're doing having tea with our jailor like you're old chums."

Haley laughed. "Seriously, Elian? I think we've got *slightly* bigger issues to worry about than who's attending afternoon tea. I mean evening tea. Or… whatever the hell time it is. Either way, I'm beat, so I'm going to bed."

Pushing past me, she headed for her bedroom.

Jax's bedroom.

*Fuck.* Even when he wasn't home, she still wanted to be close to him.

Jealousy, that old friend, burned through my gut as I watched her remove her robe and strip down to nothing but a thin T-shirt and panties.

She crawled beneath the blankets, then glared at me. "Um, you here to tuck me in, or…?"

In response, I took a seat in the chair beside the bed. Folded my hands in my lap. Smiled. "Just keeping an eye on you, little sparrow. Since your boyfriend can't be bothered."

She rolled her pretty green eyes and punched down her pillow, then settled in with a sigh. "You can stay as long as you want, Elian, but only if you promise not to be a dick."

335

"Can't promise I won't *be* a dick, but I'll do my best to hide my true nature."

This got a smile. "Fair enough. So… what's on your mind?"

"Nothing, I… I just thought maybe we could… talk?"

"Talk? About what?"

I leaned forward, watching her in the light of the triple moons that shone through the window, searching through my fractured mind for a safe topic—one that wouldn't send me into a jealous rage or cause her to kick my ass out.

There was no real purpose for my visit. Only that Jax and Hudson weren't here, and it was the first time I'd been alone with her since that night in the apartment—the night Jax had made her come with my name on her lips—and I just… I needed to be with her.

And this was the only way.

Talking.

"You have sisters," I said finally.

Her eyes softened, a sweet smile touching her lips. "Gray, Georgie, and Adele."

"And you. The four Silversbane witches," I said, remembering what she'd told me in Keradoc's war room that night. "I still can't wrap my head around it. You're part of the prophecy—that's insane, Haley. I'd always assumed it was a legend."

"Nope. You're in the presence of greatness," she teased. "Practically witch-fae royalty right here. Maybe you should kiss my feet." She stuck a foot out from under the blanket and nudged my knee.

I grabbed it, gave it a squeeze. Held it, soft and warm in my hand, unable—unwilling—to let go.

The playfulness in her eyes shifted to something more serious, and in them I saw a deep longing I wanted nothing more than to dive right into.

"Haley," I whispered, and she bit her lip and lowered her gaze, pulling her foot out of my grasp.

"Elian, I… I'm…" She sighed, and I was already feeling the crushing weight of her rejection, knowing she was about to kick me out.

Probably for the best.

But then she scooted over to the side of the bed, looked up at me again, and patted the empty space next to her.

I didn't move.

"Just for a little while," she said softly. "Please? Yes, I know I'm needy and whiny and impossible, but—"

"You know I can't say no to you, little sparrow." I rose from the chair.

"You sure your boyfriend won't get mad if he comes home and finds me in bed with his woman?" I teased, but I was already sliding in next to her.

Like I gave a fuck what Jax would think. It was his fault for not being here.

*That's right, asshole,* the little voice inside my head said. *She was* your *girl first. Just because you can't fuck her doesn't mean you can't* think *about fucking her. Doesn't mean you can't lay next to her and remember what it was like…*

Ignoring the pulse of heat in my cock, I settled in next to her, rolling onto my hip to face her. The bed was warm from her body, the moonlight painting her face, and for a long moment I just… watched her. Drank her in. Tried to set aside my complicated feelings and the pain and the regrets and all the fucked-up shit between us and just appreciate the fact that for right now, whether it would be for an hour or fifteen seconds, I had her all to myself.

I didn't even care that we'd stopped talking. Just being here, just looking at her was enough.

But then she reached up to touch one of my silver braids, and sadness washed through her eyes, her mouth pulling into a frown.

"Elian," she whispered, and I held my breath, knowing—just fucking *knowing*—what would come next. "Who's Evander?"

A smile touched my lips, but then it vanished, swallowed up by the ache inside me that would never heal.

"You used to dream about him," she continued softly, as if I could ever forget. As if I didn't *still* dream about him, didn't still see him every time I closed my eyes. "Back in the Bay sometimes. I remember you'd—"

"I know, sparrow. It… it was a long time ago."

"That night in the throne room, though… What made you think of him?"

I didn't answer her. Couldn't. The truth still sounded too fucking crazy, even in my own drug-addled brain—a place that practically thrived on crazy.

"Is Evander the reason you…" She trailed off into a sigh, then lifted her other hand, the unmistakable black pill pinched between her thumb and forefinger.

"Haley!" I bolted upright and leaned over her, trying to take it. "Where did you get that?"

She closed her fist around it and shrugged. "I found it in the kitchen. One of the staff probably dropped it."

"Give it to me."

Still clutching it in her fist, she said, "What does it feel like? I used to turn my nose up at the idea of trying it, but I have to admit—I'm kind of curious now."

"Please, sparrow," I whispered, tracing a soft line down her cheek. "You don't want to get mixed up with the Devil—trust me on that."

She blinked up at me with those endlessly green eyes, and once again I wanted to fall into them. I was already leaning closer. So close I could almost kiss her...

"Wasn't that long ago you suggested I try it," she said. "Take the edge off, right? Escape reality. Be a little less uptight." She was teasing me, taunting me, but there was a sharpness to her words, too. A baited hook.

"I was being a dick. I didn't mean it."

"No, you never do." She let out a deep sigh, her breath ghosting across my mouth.

I cupped her face. "I wouldn't wish it on my worst enemy, sparrow."

"I'm not your enemy. And lucky for both of us, I'm not your responsibility, either." In a flash, she popped the pill and closed her mouth.

*Fuck.*

Images flashed behind my eyes—the poor souls in our facility, so strung out they could no longer tell whether they were dead or alive. All that mattered was the Black. The next hit. The comfortable numb.

Cold dread settled in my gut, and I squeezed her jaw. "Damn it, Haley. Spit it out."

She shook her head and pressed her lips into a tight line, the brat.

"Do *not* make me bite you," I warned. "And no, that's not the idle threat of a dick ex-boyfriend."

With a slow roll of her eyes, she finally did as I asked, and I plucked what was left of the pill from her tongue and set it on my own, for all the good it would do her. She'd never tried it before. It would take some time to kick in, but when it did, even that tiny little taste would fuck her up good.

Best I could hope for now was that she'd burn through the buzz quickly and pass out, then wake up tomorrow with a headache murderous enough to scare her away from the shit for good.

The headaches only happened your first time, but I wasn't about to tell her that. Better to let her believe the stuff was pure torture.

I closed my mouth and leaned back on the pillow, gazing up at the ceiling, but her soft touch on my cheek had me turning toward her again.

"I want to watch," she whispered. "Let me see it."

Powerless to refuse, I opened my mouth, frozen in place as her fingertips slid down along my jaw.

Haley was transfixed, mesmerized as the last of the pill dissolved, the magick swirling on my tongue and reflecting in her eyes.

"Do you feel it?" she asked.

I closed my mouth. Swallowed. "Not yet."

"Me neither. Maybe it's from an old batch."

"It's not an old batch, Haley. It's your first time—it might take a minute before you feel anything."

"What about you?"

I shook my head. "Half a pill? My body won't even register it."

"How many do you need before it registers?"

"Lately, three or four. I take what I can from the facility—whatever I think won't be missed."

The admission—both of them—burned on the way out, but if Haley was surprised or disappointed, she didn't say.

Instead, she closed her eyes and went quiet, and I did the same, and for a long time, neither of us moved.

She wasn't sleeping, though. Her heartbeat had quickened, her breathing jagged.

"What are you thinking about, little sparrow?" I finally asked, opening my eyes.

I found her already watching me.

Smiling, she said, "How did you know I wasn't sleeping?"

"I remember how you sound when you sleep, and this isn't it."

Her smile fell away and her eyes glazed with unshed tears.

"Tell me why you said his name," she whispered. "When the guards brought you to the throne room."

She was talking about Evander again, and this time, I couldn't keep it inside.

"Because when I looked into Keradoc's eyes, I thought I saw Evander's ghost." I sighed and shook my head. "I know how it sounds, Haley. The drugs talking, right? Or some trick of Keradoc's meant to confuse me. I *know* that now—so fucking obvious, right? But in that moment? I looked up into the face of the man who'd bested us, and I swore I saw… someone else."

"I… I saw someone else too, Elian. His face, his eyes… They kept changing. I thought… I thought he was you, and I—"

"*What?*" I sat up, my heart thudding in my chest.

"There's something I need to tell you. I don't know why I feel guilty… I mean, it's not like you and I are together, or… But I feel like you need to know, and it's…" She was babbling, talking a mile-a-minute, my heart jackhammering with every word, still hoping I hadn't heard her right, still hoping this story would end some other fucking way, and then…

"I kissed him, Elian," she said. "The night of the feast, when Keradoc first brought me to the throne room alone, I kissed him."

Fury burned through me. It was one thing to see her chatting him up in the library, offering him tea. It was one thing to see the way he looked at her.

But this?

Knowing she'd fucking *kissed* him?

"Why are you telling me this?" I ground out, practically throwing myself out of the bed.

"He was wearing your face!" she said, as if that explained it. She followed me out of bed, followed me right into the common room. "Your eyes!"

"You kissed a warlord because he glamoured himself to look like me? Is that supposed to—"

"Elian." She reached up and cupped my face, forcing me to look at her. "I kissed him because he *was* you. At least, that's what I believed. God, it was all so confusing. I hadn't seen you in days, and suddenly there you were. You—I mean, he—he'd taken me to the throne room. We were alone. I saw the glamour slip away, or—I don't know. Maybe he is Keradoc and your face was the glamour, but either way, in my mind, it was you."

I pulled out of her touch, turning my back on her. I couldn't look into those eyes right now, couldn't see the passion and longing in them, knowing that fae-fucking bastard had looked into those same eyes and seen those exact same things.

"Say something," she whispered. "Please."

"Fine. You want me to say something? Here it is, sparrow. I wish you'd never told me. I wish I didn't have to live the rest of my immortal life with that image stuck in my fucking brain. I wish…" I shoved my hands through my hair, ready to tear it all out. "Keradoc isn't just a warlord and a murderer, Haley. He's worse—so much worse."

"What are you talking about?" she asked. "What could be worse?"

"He's a trafficker, Haley. He steals fae kids from their home realms, enslaves them, and sells them off to his rich, noble friends. So yeah, you want to know what happened to Evander? Here's an idea—the next time you open your mouth for that fucking bastard Keradoc, why don't you ask *him* what happened instead of letting him stick his tongue down your throat."

I stormed out of that room, down the gallery hallway, down the stairs, and out into the dark streets of Amaranth City.

And there, in the loneliest fucking corner in the darkest, dankest alley I could find, I fell to my knees and screamed into the night until my throat bled and the ghosts in my heart fell still.

## 25

# HALEY

My head clanged as if the bells of every cathedral in Italy had been relocated to the inside of my skull.

I wondered if Nona had something to do with it—a scolding from the great beyond. I smiled at the thought.

Last night, the Dream made me feel floaty and warm, but tonight there was only pain. Regret.

Still. Despite the ache in my body, I couldn't deny the appeal. I'd only gotten the barest taste of the stuff, yet when it finally kicked in, it sent me to another fucking planet.

Which was precisely why I wouldn't touch it again. It was too tempting. Too fucking dangerous.

"Sorry, am I interrupting?"

I glanced up at the now-familiar voice of Keradoc as he waltzed into the common room.

"Yes, but that's never stopped you before."

"No, I suppose it hasn't." He smiled, but tonight I found it irritating rather than charming. I was still feeling a bit prickly from the Dream, and at the sight of our warlord captor, all of Elian's warnings from last night came rushing back.

*Keradoc isn't just a warlord and a murderer, Haley. He's worse—so much worse...*

"Is there something you need, Keradoc?" I asked, my tone clipped.

342

"Otherwise, I've got a lot of reading to do and a laundry list of missing ingredients to compensate for, so if you don't mind…"

"I need to go to the marketplace in East Amaranth," he said. "I thought—"

"Really? A whole castle full of servants, and suddenly you're doing your own shopping?" I narrowed my eyes. "Spill it. The truth, if you've got it. If not, kindly return later. I'm too tired right now to shovel bullshit."

He smiled again, and this time his cheeks flushed a bit. "Actually, my kitchen staff told me your gargoyle wasn't able to find all the ingredients you needed for your work. So I thought… I was wondering if you might… That is, if you're not too preoccupied with the spellwork… On second thought, forget I mentioned anything." He shook his head, flustered. "I'll… I'll leave you to it. Good evening, Haley."

I let out a deep sigh, still trying to reconcile everything in my mind.

The man Elian spoke of last night was a vicious criminal who deserved to be tortured, strung up by his balls, and dropped into his own moat for the most gruesome death possible. And everyone he'd ever wronged should be invited to piss on his corpse, and *then* he should be forced to come back as one of the ghouls, cursed for eternity.

But the man I looked at now? The man fumbling over his words to invite me for a stroll through the marketplace?

The man haunted by nightmares and ghosts?

The man who gave me visions of a dark, powerful future I hadn't stopped dreaming about?

The man who sometimes, when we first met, looked like Elian?

How could they be the same person?

*Because you're fooling yourself on account of his epic dark-fae hotness, and every time he looks at you like that, you can't help but remember how good that kiss tasted…*

No. That wasn't it. Not at all. I mean, sure. Obviously, I liked my men a little rough-around-the-edges, full of shadowy secrets and deep, dark wounds.

But I wasn't the fall-for-the-villain, blinded-by-Stockholm-Syndrome, he's-sexy-so-he-gets-a-pass-on-all-the-evil-doing type.

Still, something wasn't adding up. I had no idea who our captor truly was, or what—if anything—he'd known about Evander's disappearance or the alleged kidnapping and trafficking of the other fae children Elian mentioned.

I didn't know who Evander was, either—or anything about his true connection to Elian, who'd spoken about him as if he'd died long ago.

Maybe he had.

But deep down, my gut told me the man standing before me now wasn't behind any of it.

And the only way I was going to find out for sure was by spending more time with him.

Starting right now.

"Actually," I said, "I'd love to get out of the castle and pick up a few things. Just give me fifteen minutes to get changed."

A new smile broke across his face, making him look younger. Less troubled. "Great. Perfect. I mean, yes. Of course. I need to change as well. I'll meet you in the gallery."

I dressed quickly in some of the clothing he'd sent up for me, glad to finally have an excuse to wear it—black leather pants, a dark gray metallic shirt, platinum armlets, leather straps and belts for days. The whole thing was pretty badass.

Ready before Keradoc, I wandered down the gallery. The doors to his suite were ajar, and I couldn't help but sneak a quick peek inside.

The place was massive—probably three times the size of our entire suite, and that was just the part I could see. Everything was black—black walls, black furniture, black bedding.

And there, standing before a full-length mirror, was Keradoc. He'd just pulled on his shirt—but not before I saw the scars.

I held my breath to keep from gasping. His entire back and both arms were covered in scars—some thin and silver, others red and ropey. He'd been whipped, burned, shot, and the entire left side of his torso was mangled with some sort of vicious bite marks.

Heart in my throat, I stepped back from the doorway and scooted back to the stairwell, fighting to get my breathing under control.

When Jax and Elian had first told me about Keradoc, they'd said he wasn't even a real warlord. That he was a politician who played war games from behind a desk.

But if that were true, what the hell had happened to him?

And how the hell had he survived?

"Sorry to keep you," he said, and I glanced up, plastering on a smile. He looked over my outfit appreciatively, then pursed his lips. "Lovely, but I think it's missing something. Something to tie it all together."

Flashing one of his wicked grins, he handed over a bone-handled dagger.

*My* bone-handled dagger. The one Jax had given me that Keradoc had stolen the night of the feast.

"Seriously? You're trusting me with this?"

"It appears that I am. Don't make me regret it."

Before he could change his mind, I took it and fastened the sheath to one of my belts.

"Perfect," he said. "Besides, it's better to be safe than sorry in Amaranth City. My guards and I will be watching over you, of course, but... I'd just feel better knowing you had some way of defending yourself, should the need arise. Shall we?"

He held out his arm, and I linked mine through it, letting him escort me down the stairs.

Just before we headed outside, he said, "Oh, there's one more thing."

When I looked up, Keradoc was gone. The man who stood at my side now was blond, with striking amber eyes and a shorter, stockier build than the warlord's.

"Another glamour?" I asked.

"I can't risk being recognized in the marketplace. Not while I'm escorting you. I've got too many enemies, Haley. So as much as I despise wearing a glamour, I must remain incognito."

Two guards joined us outside—gargoyles in their human form—and together, we walked to the marketplace.

Before Keradoc had decided I was his secret weapon and locked me up in the castle, I hadn't actually seen much of Amaranth City. Other than that first night in the pub with Gem, I'd spent most of my time in the apartment practicing my spells and going over our plans for the Feast of the Beast.

Since then, I'd seen the city only from a distance.

Now, up close and in the thick of it, I was experiencing massive sensory overload... And loving every minute of it.

The marketplace was packed with vendors selling goods out of stalls and carts—everything from weapons to spices to exotic meats to glittering jewelry. Crowds rolled through the narrow passageways like water, jostling each other to find the best bargains, haggling with the shopkeepers, stealing whatever they could get away with.

In less than an hour, I'd managed to find everything I needed, all paid for by Keradoc without question. He also bought me a hot cider and a pastry that reminded me of a giant Pop-Tart.

"So," I said, licking the last of the sugary, flaky crust from my fingertips. "At what point do you tell me this was all a setup and I'm actually about to meet my untimely demise?"

Keradoc laughed, low and smooth. "You still don't trust me, little thief?"

"You've spent the evening being nice to me and buying me things. I'd be a damn *fool* to trust you."

He laughed again, deeper this time, the skin around his temporarily amber eyes crinkling. They were the wrong color, but somehow I felt like I could still see the real Keradoc behind them.

I just didn't know who that real Keradoc was.

Still studying him, I recalled Elian's earlier accusations again, letting them roll around in my mind, trying to see if any of them stuck.

*Murderer.*

*Kidnapper.*

*Fae child trafficker.*

I knew the first was true—I'd seen him execute two shifters the night of the Feast. It was a thing I couldn't excuse, but... What if I didn't have the whole story? What if the shifters were guilty of crimes even more heinous than Keradoc's crime of beheading them?

And that night, Elian had mistaken Keradoc for Evander. He'd called him by that name several times. If Keradoc had been involved in Evander's death, wouldn't he have shown a glimmer of recognition? Guilt? Something?

I closed my eyes and shook my head. None of this made any sense.

"Haley? Are you all right?"

We'd stopped walking, I realized. I opened my eyes and forced a smile, intending to tell him I was fine.

But then, ducking into a building across the street, another fae caught my attention.

A Midnight fae with purple hair.

Everything inside me burned with rage.

"Gem," I hissed.

Keradoc turned to follow my line of sight.

When he looked at me again, he nodded. "Gem is supervising the operations your companions are working on. That's the processing and testing facility."

I handed over all my shopping bags. "Wait here," I said. "I'm going in."

"Not alone, you're not."

"Incognito, remember? You can't waltz in there with me and your goon squad. We'll draw too much attention."

"But—"

"No buts," I said. "You can wait for me right across the street. I just need five minutes. Ten tops."

*Just enough time to bleed a bitch dry…*

# 26

## ELIAN

*I*'d been doing my level best to keep my shit together and do my job, but I'd also been high as *fuck* for the last two nights, so maybe I wasn't the best judge of my performance.

Gem had just returned from wherever the fuck she ran off to half the time, and as usual, she brought back a nasty glare for me. And a glower. And a roll of the eyes for good measure.

"How's it going?" she asked. I didn't know whether she was talking to me or Jax, but I decided to appoint myself spokesperson for that particular question.

"Excellent." I grinned, scooping up a handful of the little black beauties. "Truly excellent."

That, at least, was the truth.

This latest batch was our best yet—way more potent than the last, and it didn't wear off as quickly either. I had no doubts that any fae who tried it, Darkwinter or otherwise, would murder his own commander for a taste.

The high was fucking *exquisite.*

I thumbed at my chest and smiled again. "Exhibit A."

"Exhibit A, what?" she asked, and I realized I'd just said most of that shit inside my head.

Before I could repeat myself out loud, the front door banged open again, ushering in what I assumed was another desperate Amaranth City soul looking to volunteer as a test subject.

348

The woman was soft around the edges, a little smudgy. When I tried to focus on her, she doubled in my vision.

And both of them were marching toward us like they were on a *mission*.

"Haley?" I asked, finally recognizing her. She was just one person again, close enough to touch, so I reached out and fingered a lock of her hair. "Have you come to sing me to sleep, little sparrow?"

"Actually, I've come to stick a knife in *that* bitch's throat." She beelined right for Gem. Caught her off guard, too—enough to get that dagger pretty damn up-close-and-personal.

"Give me one reason not to slit your throat," she gritted out.

With another roll of her eyes, Gem arched a purple eyebrow, then touched Haley's shoulder.

That was it. One touch. One finger.

And Haley went down hard on her ass, her muscles spasming.

"Ouch," I said, remembering all too well the feeling of that zap.

Something deep inside me said I should probably be furious about what Gem had just done to Haley, but I couldn't seem to focus on that thought long enough to bring it to fruition.

Jax didn't seem to have any trouble with it, though. He was on Gem in a blink, grabbing a fistful of her shirt and hauling her close.

"Touch her again, *traitor*, and I don't care how many devil's trap bolts you threaten me with. I will *end* you."

"Yeah?" Gem laughed. "Let me know how that works out for you, cowboy."

And then she stalked off to harass someone else for a change, thank fuck.

"You'd think threatening the boss would get us canned," I said, finally realizing I should probably help Haley off the floor. She ignored my outstretched hand and got her own ass up, though.

Fine by me.

"Unfortunately for us," I continued, "we're too good at what we do. Job security, I guess." I popped another pill like it was fucking candy and grinned. "Boss says we're not supposed to steal from the stash, either. But I learned a little trick." I leaned in closed and fake-whispered in Haley's ear, "It's not stealing if you say it's for quality control purposes."

"Control?" Haley snapped. "Interesting word choice for a man who's clearly *out* of control. Look around you, Elian. Is this what you want? Really?"

Her eyes flashed with anger, but there was sadness there, too. Worry.

More shit I didn't need to see right now.

I shrugged as if I didn't give a fuck. Considering the amount of next-level Black I had coursing through my system, I shouldn't have been *capable* of giving a fuck, but still, there I was.

Giving fucks.

"No choice," I said, my words slurring. "You asked for my help getting to Midnight, and… Hell, sparrow. You were there every step of the way. You don't need me to give you the recap of how I landed *this* cushy job."

"I know you didn't have a choice with the job, Elian. I'm talking about…" She gestured behind me, a whole bunch of sympathy flooding her eyes now too. On top of everything else.

I didn't need to turn around to know she was talking about the Dreamers.

My fucking people, for all intents and purposes.

"So you've gone from dancing with the Devil to turning your nose up at it in a matter of…" I glanced at my wrist as if I were wearing a watch. "Ten hours? Might be a new flip-flop record for that not-so-shiny moral compass of yours, Haley."

Her eyes blazed, and she opened her mouth like she was about to spit venom. Or fire. Or venomous fire, all of which I'd welcome.

Because in that moment?

Yeah, I wanted the fight. Needed it. Needed her to hurl those insults my way, sharp daggers I could catch right in the heart.

Anything—*anything* to feel something other than this soul-sucking void chewing through me.

But my little sparrow wouldn't give me that. She was too good for it. Yeah, she was pissed, but that was only because she was so damn worried.

I knew her well enough to know she wasn't truly judging me. Wasn't judging those poor souls lined up behind me with their mouths open for the next pill, their eyes rolled back, their bodies quaking, some of them so far gone they didn't even realize they were sitting in their own waste.

"Why?" she whispered, her voice breaking. "Why do you do it?"

"Because sometimes there's a hole inside that's so fucking big, nothing can fill it. And sometimes there's a *lot* of holes—gaping fucking craters— and in case you haven't figured it out yet, sparrow, that's where I'm at. Gaping fucking craters."

"And this?" she asked softly, plucking a pill from the pile in my hand and rolling it across her palm. "This can fill them?"

"No." This time, she didn't fight me when I tried to take it from her. Just let me have it, watched as I tossed it into my mouth. "All it does is make me high enough to numb the edges a little. But I'll take being high and numb over the full-blown pain of my reality any day."

"Even if that reality includes people who care about you? People who… people who love you?"

"People who love me? Please. Even *I* couldn't conjure up a fantasy *that* good."

Hurt flooded her eyes, and I knew at once I'd said the wrong thing again.

Earlier tonight, Jax had told me I was poison to her, and that motherfucker was right. Every time I looked at her, every time I opened my mouth, all the wrong words fell out.

Because I wasn't allowed to say the right ones.

I wasn't trying to hurt her. But then, neither was a poison trying to kill its victim. That was just its nature.

Now, once again, I struggled to find the words to fix the mess I'd made, to explain how I didn't mean half the dumb shit I said, to string something together that made a fucking *lick* of sense amidst all the bullshit.

But Haley was already heading for the door, Jax following after her, two of the only three people I cared about leaving me to fall back into those dark craters alone.

So I did what I do best.

Popped another pill, sat down with the other dreamers, and waited to catch the next wave to fucking oblivion.

# 27

## HALEY

$\mathcal{I}$ hadn't realized I was running until I felt Jax's hands on my shoulders from behind, slowing me to a stop not far from the nameless tavern where we'd met up with Gem on my first night here.

The sight of it—the reminder of what she'd done to us, the reminder of her smug face inside that awful facility—only fueled my anger. If not for her, would we have been back in New Orleans by now? Would I have gotten Keradoc's blood and satisfied Melantha's demands? Would my sisters be free from her ever-present threat?

Would Elian have already turned his back on the drug that had so thoroughly imprisoned him?

"Let me go." I tried to shrug off Jax's touch, but it was a weak effort, and we both knew it.

Gently, he turned me around to face him.

"Tell me what's going on," he said softly. "Let me see what's behind those eyes."

I looked up, unable to stop the tears from spilling.

"I'm sorry we didn't tell you about Gem," he said. "Keradoc assigned her to supervise. Saint and I didn't want you to worry."

"It's not just Gem, as much as I want to stab her with something rusty." I shook my head. "I hate seeing him like that, Jax. It breaks my heart."

"I know, angel. I know." He drew me in close, his warm embrace and campfire-and-lemons scent grounding me. "You shouldn't have seen it. Any of it. Keradoc never should've brought you here."

I pulled back and smeared away the tears. "But even if I *hadn't* seen it, it's still happening to him. He's still going through it and I'm just... God, I feel so helpless."

"Saint's problems are not your burdens to bear. Believe me, I've tried, and that's the fastest way to an early grave."

"But he's my—"

"Your what, Haley?" He sighed and released me, suddenly defensive. "Your ex? Your first love? Your *only* love?"

I searched his face, trying to get a read on his emotions. He knew how I felt about Elian, and he'd never gotten worked up about it before. Not like this. So no, it wasn't jealousy tightening his voice, despite how badly he wanted me to believe it.

It was pain. Anguish.

I knew in my bones Jax cared deeply for Elian, despite everything they'd been through. Maybe even because of it. They were truly brothers, in all the ways that counted.

And I knew this was killing him as much as it was killing me.

"No, Jax," I said softly. "I was going to say family. Elian is my family. And no, it's not perfect. It's messy and complicated and crazy and *hard*. So much harder than it should be. All I know is I feel like we're watching him kill himself, one little pill at a time, and there's not a damn thing I can do about it."

Jax scoffed and shook his head. "Whatever."

His flippancy ignited my rage all over again. "Fine. You look at him, and all you see is a fuckup—I get it. I see his mistakes too, Jax. So many of them. Hell, that man is a walking reminder of the darkest nights of my life. But I still care about him. I don't want him to..." I trailed off, unable to say the words.

*Die.*

*Take his own life.*

*Overdose.*

*Succumb.*

*Fall.*

"You think I want Saint to kill himself, Haley?" he spat. "You think I want to stand by and watch him disappear, or worse—turn into one of those strung-out corpses back there? A hollowed-out shell of a person? They're barely breathing, for fuck's sake!"

"Yeah? And how much easier would your life be if Elian suffered the same fate?"

"*Way* easier—no question. But easier doesn't... Damn it, Haley. It doesn't mean better." Then, softer than the breeze down the rancid alley, he whispered, "My heart is broken too, angel. And every night I see him like this, every night I have to decide whether to watch him suffer through withdrawals or give him another pill to take away his pain, it breaks my heart a little more."

A tear slipped down his cheek, and he brushed it away.

"Then why do you do it?" I asked. "Why do you do it at all? In all the years you two have been stuck together, why the hell haven't you left him? And don't tell me it's because of some weird demonic principles about carrying debts and who owes who. It's more than that and you know it."

"I've told him a thousand times I'm going to leave. Hell, before we left New Orleans, I swore to him if we made it out of Midnight alive a second time, I was packing my shit and leaving for good. But that was all bullshit. I stay because he needs me. I stay because when I needed him, he was there. Maybe not in the way I wanted him to be, but still. He was there. So yeah, maybe it *would* be easier if he just fucked off and died, sparing us all the torture of watching this shit. Of cleaning up his messes. But when you call someone a brother—when you make that oath—it's not just for the perfect, squeaky clean stuff, Haley. It's just like you said—messy and complicated and hard. That's what you sign up for when you choose your family, and as much as it fucks me up inside, no, I *wouldn't* have it any other way. You ask me why I stay? I stay because I *choose* to. Every day, every moment, that choice presents itself again—stay or go. And I make it. I stay. I will *always* stay. With Saint. With Hudson. With you, because you're my fucking family. So if you can't trust that—if after all this time you actually think I'm the kind of guy who walks out when shit gets real— then maybe you're not the woman I thought you were."

"Jax, that's not—"

"Haley, there you are." Keradoc appeared around the corner, trailed by his two guards. "I was worried you'd finally run off."

Jax glared at me, as if he were waiting for me to tell Keradoc to go fuck himself.

When I didn't, he just shook his head and scoffed like he couldn't believe he'd wasted so many weeks of his life with me.

Then, without another word, he turned on his heel and stormed off toward the facility, knocking into Keradoc's shoulder as he passed.

Keradoc let it go, his eyes never leaving mine. "Are you all right?"

"I'm fine. Just… just take me—" I caught myself before I said the word balanced on the tip of my tongue. *Home.* "Take me back to the castle. Please, Keradoc. I just need to be alone right now."

# 28

## HUDSON

*J*'d never been big on cultural shit like the ballet or the opera or all them gallery tours. Back in New Orleans, that'd always been Saint's bag. My boy liked to take his rich vampire clients out for a show— all part of the fake-ass fantasy that scoring a bunch of Black from a fae dealer was a classy affair, not some shady back-alley drug trade.

Who the fuck had time to wade through that much bullshit? To sit through some boring-ass, artsy-fartsy show, oohing and ahhing and jerking off about metaphors and color palates and artistic integrity just to seal a deal both parties knew was a sure thing anyway?

I never understood it.

But now, watching Haley work her magick?

God *damn*, that felt like watching a fine artist carve a statue out of marble or paint the ceiling of some sacred place, her every move a study in elegance and grace, her eyes dancing with a passionate light that warmed every part of me.

*She* was a work of art. A gift from the gods the rest of us had no business even looking at, yet there I was, lurking in the shadows in a state of awe and wonder as she brought her blood magick to life.

I'd just flown back after wrapping up Keradoc's latest assignment helping his guards secure a newly discovered field of corpsevine just north of the Boiling Glass Sands—when I noticed the telltale red glow shining from our balcony. I knew I should've left her in peace, let her practice her spells alone, but I couldn't help myself.

Now, I stayed hidden behind a pillar of obsidian while she kneeled in a pentacle made of dirt and muttered her latest spell, two bowls of blood on the ground before her, both glowing red.

When she finished her spell, the bowls glowed brighter, but then fizzled out quickly.

"No," she hissed. "No no no… *Damn* it! Why? Why have you forsaken me? Have *thou* forsaken? Hast thou? Ugh." She tilted her face to the moons and shook her fist.

I couldn't help the laugh that slipped out. She was so fucking cute.

She heard me, though. Let out a little yelp and jumped back, hand pressed to her heart.

Busted, I stepped out of the shadows and shrugged, like, *what are ya gonna do?*

"Didn't see you there, Gargs." Her eyes widened as she took in the sight of me, then my girl cracked up. She swept a hand up and down, indicating my naked form. "Wow, so you're pretty much always free-balling it these days, huh?"

"What can I say? I like the feel of the wind on my—"

"Biceps. I get it."

I laughed again—couldn't be helped. Hell, the woman had made me smile more in a few weeks than anyone else had in my entire existence. "Gargoyles ain't got the same hangups about flesh that you humans do. Not that I don't appreciate and venerate certain forms of it, mind you. Just that I don't feel a sudden need to duck and cover after I shift back into human form."

"Nor should you." She crossed the balcony to meet me in the middle and grinned up at me, stretching up to loop her arms around my neck, seemingly undisturbed by my nudity.

"Careful," I teased. "Keep greeting me like this after a hard night's work, and I might start getting used to it."

"Like I'm getting used to seeing your naked, tattooed ass on full display?"

"No one said you had to look."

"As if I could tear my gaze away." She let out a dreamy sigh. "Maybe you're onto something, though. Maybe *I* should try it. Saunter around the castle in the nude. Give Keradoc's guards something to gossip about besides the size of their swords."

"Hate to rain on your parade, but that's *definitely* not happening. Long as those creeps are near, you're staying fully clothed. Matter fact, why aren't you wearing a coat? And a scarf? And maybe a cape, just to cover the bases?"

"Excuse me?" she teased. "That's hardly fair."

"Just saving lives, babygirl." I picked her right up, tucking her close against my chest as I carried her to the far edge of the balcony. "Anyone other than my boys so much as twitched an *eyelid* near your fine naked self, I'd snap their heads off, dump out the shit-for-brains inside, and use their empty skulls as beer mugs and no, I wouldn't feel bad about it. Not even a little."

Haley laughed. "That was… oddly specific. Very creepy. But also kind of sweet? In your own special gargoyle way, I suppose."

"As it was meant," I said with a wink that had her shaking her head and laughing. I set her on a flat part of the barrier and took a seat next to her. "Speaking of shit-for-brains… Where are the boys? They usually beat me back home."

Her eyes dimmed, the smile dropping from her face. With a deep sigh, she said, "As far as I know, they're still at the facility. I haven't seen them at all these last two nights. I'm pretty sure they're avoiding me."

"What? Why?"

"Keradoc took me to the market. I saw the facility. Things got… heated."

She told me the story—all the crazy shit she'd seen, the bullshit with Gem, her fears about Saint, her fight with Jax.

"I'm so worried about them, Gargs," she said softly. "And when I saw all that, it just hit me really hard, and I just opened my big, fat mouth and stepped *right* in it. I tried to wait up for them last night so I could smooth things over, but I passed out before they got back. I wouldn't be surprised if they decided to stop talking to me altogether."

"No. No fuckin' way."

I saw the way they looked at her—Jax like he was always ready to step in front of a flaming arrow to keep her safe, Saint like he wanted to turn himself inside out just to erase the sadness from her eyes.

Sadness I was pretty damn sure he'd put there in the first place.

So what, they'd argued. Didn't make a damn bit of difference. Nothing she could do or say would send either one of them packing, and I told her as much.

"I hope you're right." She curled up against my chest, and I tucked her in close, just holding her. Breathing her in.

We sat like that for a long time, me and Haley.

Silence had never been a problem for us. Lots of people thought silence was awkward—they couldn't deal with it. But with Haley, it'd always felt like a respite—a little place we could retreat to together and just… just breathe.

Just be.

After a while, she pulled back and smiled up at me again. "I'm glad you stopped by. I needed a break from all this summoning business."

"Yeah. I suppose I should leave you to it." I stood up, and she followed, already shaking her head.

"Confession? I don't want you to leave."

"Confession?" I blew out a relieved sigh. "I wasn't planning to leave. I was just gonna go sit in the dark where you couldn't see me and keep right on watching anyway."

"Seriously?"

"Couldn't leave you if I tried, babygirl. Not really."

"Can I tell you something crazy? I mean, you're used to that from me, right?"

I grinned and took her hand. Brought it to my mouth and kissed her palm. "Lay it on me."

"When I'm with you, I feel this… this intense connection. It started that first day in the garden at Elian's place, even before I'd met you. When I touched you? There was this weird spark and I *swore* you felt it, too. Even through the stone."

I squeezed her hand and nodded. "I thought I was going crazy, too. But that wasn't it. We do have a connection, Haley. Runs deep."

"I feel connected to all of you. Elian and I… well, we have history, obviously. Jax came out of nowhere, but my feelings for him came on fast and furious. And you… I can't even explain it. I just know that when I'm with you, I feel like nothing bad could ever touch me."

"None of that sounds crazy to me."

"There's more. It's… it's this whole place, Hudson." She looked out across the city and sighed. "I feel connected to Midnight too. The magick, the air, the stones, the stars and moons. God, even Keradoc is—well, I won't say I've got any love for the creep. But I'm starting to understand him a little. I don't think he's evil, Gargs. A complete douche, yes. But not an *evil* douche, which feels like an important distinction. Anyway, the longer I'm here, the more I feel like I was always supposed to end up here. Like maybe I just got lucky all these years—somehow, I stayed off the radar, and the Midnight fae never came looking for me."

When she looked up at me again, her eyes were glassy, and I swore I saw all the red-and-gold stars in the sky reflecting right back at me.

"Do you remember the roses?" she asked.

"Beauty in the darkness, babygirl."

She nodded and held out her hands, studying her palms like she was trying to memorize every line etched in them.

When she finally spoke again, I had to dip my head low just to catch her whisper.

"Do you think I'm evil, Hudson? Like the Darkwinter fae?"

My heart cracked in half at the pain in her eyes.

"Evil isn't a bloodline, Haley. It's a choice we make. Don't always feel that way for some, I suppose, but it's still a choice. Darkwinter fae… Hell, they're just trying to make their way in this world, protect what's theirs. Same as Keradoc. Same as you and me."

"Yeah, but the things they have to do to protect what's theirs? To save the people or places they love? Maybe that's where the evil comes in."

"Does it?" I ran a hand across my beard and shrugged. "Then sign me up for team evil, because I'm telling you *right* now. Anyone comes out here —soldier, gargoyle, Keradoc himself—and threatens your life? I'm taking that fucker down. I will *not* hesitate." I tucked a finger under her chin and tilted her face up, waiting for her to meet my eyes again. "No one with love in their heart is evil, babygirl. But all of us are capable of doing evil shit. Beyond that, I can't make a blanket call. None of us can."

"So you're saying there's a chance I'm evil?"

"I'm saying it's a word, a label. And it's not up to you to decide—it'll be written by your enemies, if it's written at all. But if you really wanna know? No, babygirl. I don't think you're evil. Far as I'm concerned, you're just… well, you're the right amount of bad."

She laughed and wiped away a tear. "I guess I can live with that."

A cool breeze skated on through, making her shiver. I flexed my shoulders and let my wings unfurl, curling one around her to block the wind.

"You can do that?" she gasped. "Wings, even when you're totally in human form?"

"It's a partial shift, yeah. Not that great for actual flying—the human body isn't made for it. Mostly, I just use it to impress the ladies."

"Well, it's working."

I laughed, but soon it faded away, the serious shit rising back up to the surface.

I had to tell her.

Now or never.

"Haley, there's something I need you to know. That connection you feel? You're right. I feel it too. From the first time I saw you walk into Saints and Sinners, and no, it wasn't just 'cause of that hot little dress you had on."

"It *was* a hot dress, though, wasn't it?"

I nodded, but I couldn't stop to joke. This was too important. I had to get it out before I ran out of words.

"Gargoyles... We have mate bonds. And for whatever reason, the universe—or fate, or the stars, or whatever you want to call it? Something saw fit to make you mine. Mine to protect and guard. Mine to cherish. Mine to love. That don't mean we have to... you know. Be *in* love. But there's the potential. Either way, the bond will tie us for life."

"Mate bonds?" She looked up at me, her eyes wide, a smile tugging at her lips. "I'm your mate? As in, fated mate?"

"That's one way to put it, yeah."

"Is that how you were able to sense I was in trouble the night of the feast?"

"Sure was. And I suspect that's how I got out of that cave, too. Your fear... I felt it through the bond. It just... it fucking *enraged* me, babygirl. So one minute I was locked in stone, and the next thing I knew, I felt you—felt that panic. Something just exploded inside me, and suddenly the spell they'd used on me shattered. I shifted into my warrior form, ready to murder some motherfucker just to find my way back to you. And that's just what I did."

She held my gaze for so long, not saying a word, I thought maybe she was about to laugh. Or worse—cry. Or, worse yet, run back into the suite and lock my ass out here.

But then she just smiled up at me with her sweet Haley-smile, and said the one thing I didn't even realize I needed to hear.

"Well, that's fucking cool."

Now, I laughed. "Cool? I tell you we have this mystical, fated connection that may or may not lead to love, and you go with 'cool?' No questions, no denials, nothing?"

She shook her head, her face turning serious. "No, Gargs. I can't explain it, but it just... I don't know. It just feels right. Like, as soon as you said it, something clicked in my mind, and I thought, of *course* we're fated mates."

"In that case, I need to ask you something, babygirl, and I need you to be real straight with me."

"Always," she whispered.

"The way I see it, you got a choice to make. And whatever you pick, I'm good with it—no questions asked, no pressure, no awkwardness between us. That night when I told you I got you? There's no expiration date on that. I'm here for you no matter what. *That* is a promise."

She nodded. "And it means more to me than you know."

"Here it is, then." I blew out a breath. Jumped in headfirst, no net, hoping like hell I wouldn't crash and burn. "You're either gonna ask me to kiss you right now, or you're gonna send me to bed with a broken heart. Pick one."

I smiled to let her know I was kidding—sort of. But she just… well god *damn*, her whole face lit up like I'd just told her I found a way to bust us all out of here.

"That's it?" she asked. "Just two choices? No third option, no clauses or sub-clauses, no contingencies?"

"Just the two. So what'll it be, beautiful?"

"Hmm." She smirked. "I may be bad, Gargs, but sending some poor, defenseless gargoyle home with a broken heart? *That* would make me downright terrible."

"Agreed."

"And I'm not terrible."

"Not in the slightest."

"I think I'm more—"

"Haley? I love hearing you ramble. I swear it. But right now, I *really* need to kiss you. So if you could make your decision and put me outta my misery, I'd appreciate it."

"I *really* need you to kiss me, so that works out well. And also—"

I didn't get to know what she was planning to say after that. Swallowed up her damn words with a kiss so deep, so devastating I thought maybe we created a whole new galaxy with the explosion.

The bond, fate, the stars, destiny, whatever the fuck you wanted to call it…

That shit had *nothing* on this.

Yeah, she was mine to protect. Mine to watch over. But what I felt right now as she slid her arms around me, as she parted her mouth, as I deepened that kiss and unleashed a sweet little moan from between her cherry red lips?

That was more than the bond.

That was love, or a good deal of the way to it.

When we finally broke for air, we were both a little bewildered. Took us a minute to realize we'd accidentally knocked over one of the bowls of blood. It mixed with the Midnight dirt, glowing brightly.

"Hudson, look," she gasped.

And there on the ground between us, a whole 'nother mess of them black roses of hers bloomed in the moonlight.

# 29

## HUDSON

*H*udson?" She glanced at the flowers, then back up at me, her eyes filled with a mix of wonder and fear. "I know you said there's beauty in darkness, but this whole black-roses thing is seriously starting to freak me out."

I stared down into her pretty face, her sparkling eyes. My lips still tingled from her kiss. Hell, she was honey and spun sugar and all the brightest stars in the blackest sky.

But she was my spooky little monster girl too, and right now, I needed her to know just how much I appreciated it—all of it.

"Haley," I growled, determined to make her listen. To make her believe it. "I've never seen anything so fucking remarkable as you and your black-magick roses. So whatever worries you got about that? Squash it, babygirl. You've got nothing to be ashamed of."

"Do you mean it?" she whispered, the sweetest little smile curving her mouth.

"Wouldn't say it if I didn't. Figured you knew that about me by now."

"Hmm. Maybe I just like hearing you talk."

"That so?" I pulled her close to me again, running my nose down along hers and dusting her lips with another kiss. Damn, one kiss and I was already addicted to her. "What else you like?"

My wings hovered over us, fluttering in the breeze, and she glanced up at them and smiled even bigger. "I like the wings, Gargs. A lot."

I stretched them out, giving her a show.

"Can I touch them?" she asked. "Or is that... not a thing you're supposed to ask? I'm sorry. You're my first gargoyle."

"And you're my first little monster girl," I said with a wink, "so I guess I'll allow it."

I kissed her forehead, tucked my wings in close, then turned and got down on my knees, giving her unrestricted access.

She ran her fingertips along the edges, then flattened her hands, stroking me with her palms.

I shuddered in the wake of her touch.

"What does it feel like when I touch you?" she asked.

"It feels..." My words trailed off into a groan of pleasure. "God *damn*. Do that again."

With a soft laugh that whispered across my skin, she stroked the edge of one wing, then the other, back and forth with the gentle touch of her fingertips, then the soft scrape of her nails, her every movement driving me wild.

I had no idea how long she stood there mapping my skin with her fingers, but it felt like hours. Hours and hours of sheer bliss as I lost myself to her sweet caress, every stroke sizzling with the magick of our bond.

By the time she came around and knelt down in front of me, I was so hard for her it hurt, no way to hide it. She continued her soft strokes, grazing my chest, my abs, lower, fucking *lower*, until my little monster girl finally wrapped those fingers around my cock.

I hissed through my teeth. Fucking hell, her touch was like living fire. It'd been so long since anyone had touched me—centuries. And Haley? She was in a league of her own. Just being near her made it hard to breathe. Now she had her hand on my cock, her wet mouth parted, her eyes blazing with a fire that seemed to be *daring* me to cross that final line with her...

How had I not dropped dead of a fucking heart attack yet?

How had Jax and Saint survived her?

"Hudson," she whispered, her voice turning shy, that fire in her eyes dimming a little, though she didn't let go of my cock—a thing I was *supremely* grateful for. "Is this really happening?"

Everything was so oversensitive, so hot for her, all my wires felt like they were short-circuiting. I could *think* the words, but couldn't seem to make my lips move.

Once again, I'd forgotten how to fucking talk. But this time, it wasn't because of some unspeakable trauma.

It was because she'd left me tongue-tied, my nerves buzzing, my muscles trembling for more.

*Damn it.* Much as I loved the feel of her touch on my wings, I needed to be a man for this. *All* man, or I wouldn't be able to concentrate long enough to find those words I so badly needed to find.

I flexed my shoulders and shifted the rest of the way into my human form, no trace of the warrior left, other than the heart jackhammering inside my chest. A warrior's heart that'd somehow never beat as hard in battle as it was beating right now, all for this woman. This witch. My mate.

"I'm… sorry," she whispered as my wings vanished, confusion smothering the last of the fire in her eyes. "Did I… did I hurt you? I thought… Maybe I was too rough? I wasn't sure if—"

I pressed my fingertips to her lips and shook my head. It was all I could manage in the moment, but I needed her to know it was okay. More than okay.

She smiled softly, and I knew she understood me, just like always.

"I'll give you a minute to find the words," she said. "But I've got some for you first, if you don't mind?"

I nodded. I loved her words. All of them. Always.

"I need you to know something, too," she said. "I believe you about the bond—I feel it too, and it means more to me than I could ever say, which sounds crazy since I never seem to run out of things to say. But I'm doing this because I want to, Hudson. I want *you*. Not just as a friend and protector and a fated mate, or whatever you call it. But something more."

She stood and stripped out of her clothes, revealing herself to me in the moonlight, naked and perfect and damn near stealing my breath away.

I held her at arm's length, searching her face, unable to hide my goofy grin.

I wanted something more, too. All of it.

"But if that's not where you intended things to go tonight," she continued, "then you can be honest with me about that. Words, notes, hand gestures—however you need to say it, just say it. No games, no sugar coating. Not with us."

The fire in her eyes, in her voice… It finally broke through the haze in my mind.

I fisted her hair and brought her close, running my nose along her jaw, inhaling her scent. Desire rumbled up through my chest, my throat tight with it. "Haley fucking Barnes. How can you not know?"

"I know it seems obvious, right? I mean, all the signals are there." She glanced down at my hard length and smiled. "But I can't make guesses and assumptions. Not with this—it's too important to me. *You're* too important. So please, Hudson. Tell me what you want."

"You need to hear me say it, then?"

She bit her plump lower lip. Nodded. That sweet blush darkened her cheeks, and I could tell from the tightness in her shoulders she was holding her breath.

Time to end this torture… for both of us.

"What I *want*," I growled, "is for you to ride my face until *you're* trembling and *I* can't remember the taste of any damn thing in the world but you. I don't need notes, don't need hand gestures, and I sure as shit don't intend to play games. I just need you in my mouth so I can make you come so hard you forget how to fucking *breathe*. That clear enough for you?"

She gasped, her cheeks blushing a few shades deeper, and for a second I wondered if I'd pushed it too far.

But then my girl just busted up laughing, a sound that made my heart kick up a few more gears.

"Oh, you think that's funny, do you?" I teased. "I'll give you funny." I grabbed her in a bear hug and dropped, taking her right down with me. I stretched out flat on my back in her bed of black roses and dirt, Haley straddling me, heat radiating from every inch of her.

"Seriously?" She was still laughing. "*Seriously?*"

"Depends on what you're seriously-ing me about."

"Before tonight, I could've counted the number of words you've said out loud on one hand. Maybe two. Now you're coming at me with words like *that*?"

"Yeah, well. Ain't no point in mincing them now, right?"

She leaned forward, hands sliding up over the tattoos covering my pecs, her hair falling against my face. Her mouth was kissably close when she whispered, "Say more, Hudson."

The taste of my name on her breath… *Fuck*.

I swept back her hair, gathering it in my fist at the base of her neck so I could see her eyes. They glittered like emeralds in the darkness, two bright jewels that felt like another gift from the gods.

"I loved kissing your sweet mouth," I said softly, "But now it ain't enough. I need to kiss you *everywhere*, Haley. I need to know just what my spooky little monster tastes like as I make her shatter."

"Holy shit," she breathed. "Where have *you* been hiding, filthy-mouthed gargoyle superhottie?"

"I'm not hiding, babygirl. I'm right here. And I need *you* to get your fine ass right up—" I grabbed her hips and hauled her close until she was finally straddling my face. "—*here*."

Another gasp slipped out from her cherry-red mouth, her thighs brushing against my ears as she hovered above me, still just out of reach.

I slid my hands up and cupped her ass, urging her closer, a groan of frustration rumbling through my chest. "Closer."

"So impatient," she teased. "Naughty gargoyle."

"You're killing me." *Fuck.* At that point, I was pretty sure I'd turn to stone and crumble into dust if she refused me for even one more minute. "No more talking. *Please*, babygirl. Let me taste you."

The desperation in my voice was pathetic, but that shit was real. I felt it all the way down to my bones, that deep ache for her, the feeling that she belonged to me in ways that went beyond the mate bond. Ways I wanted to show her right the hell *now*.

A soft breeze whispered across the balcony, making her shiver. Her nipples hardened, and she leaned her head back and let out a sigh of pleasure.

And finally—fucking *finally*—Haley lowered herself down, her hands fisting my hair, holding on for the ride.

My mouth was on her in a heartbeat, stealing the taste I'd wanted for so long, licking and teasing and kissing her and... fuck *me*. She started moving, rocking her hips—slow at first, then grinding down against me as she lost herself in the pleasure.

Pleasure I was more than happy to give her.

I was so turned on, all I wanted to do was grab my cock, stroke, and fall right over the edge with her. But that would mean taking my hands off her ass, and some motherfucker'd have to chop off my arms before *that* would happen.

So I ignored the ache in my stone-hard cock and focused entirely on her, on making her squirm, on making her gasp as I licked and sucked and devoured her until I finally got my wish.

There was no other taste in the world but her.

And when that sweet little tremble I so desperately wanted to feel finally rippled through her thighs... When she tossed her head back and gasped my name over and over as she came all over my face...

Hell, if I wasn't already halfway in love with her before?

That did it. That fucking did it.

# 30

## HALEY

*I*'d always wanted to be ravaged.

And as it turned out, my sweet teddy bear—my fated mate—was a ravager.

The sounds of his deep, gravelly moans vibrated through me, his beard tickling my thighs, his demanding mouth so fucking amazing…

God, I wanted it to last all night.

But Hudson was too good, his kisses too intense, and it wasn't long before the first ripples of pleasure were already rolling through me.

When I finally came, I gasped, calling out his name, tears flooding my eyes, my heart thundering until slowly, beat by beat, it settled back down.

I pulled back, lying down to curl up beside him.

When he met my gaze again, his eyes were dazed, his mouth curved in a sweet and sexy grin.

"You gave me what I want," he said softly. "Now tell me what *you* want, babygirl."

"As if that wasn't enough?"

"Apparently, it wasn't." He ran a thumb along my lower lip, shaking his head with a mock frown. "I don't hear you singing."

"Give a witch a minute, Gargs!" I laughed, everything in me buzzing and light. "I'm still trying to catch my breath!"

"Don't bother. I'm only going to steal it again." He captured my mouth in another kiss, his beard still damp with the evidence of what he'd done to me, and the thought of him wearing my scent like that…

It sent another jolt of pleasure right through my core.

I wanted him inside me.

*Now.*

I pulled back. Grinned up at him. "So, about those wings…"

"You want the wings?" He flipped us so he was on top, then flexed his shoulders, and his wings unfurled once more, curling around us and cocooning us in our own dark little world.

I reached up and ran my fingertips along the inside edges, making him shiver.

"You have *no* idea what that does to me," he growled.

"Is it like that with everything that touches you? The breeze? Another person?"

"Breeze feels nice, sure. But it ain't got shit on you, Haley. It's you. Your touch, your… your everything. I can't explain it."

"Does it—"

The sound of another pair of wings fluttering—not Hudson's—cut off my words.

I lifted my head with a start, shocked to find one of Keradoc's gargoyles standing on the balcony and glaring down at us, supremely annoyed.

And I was pretty sure he was one of the assholes who'd shot magickal arrows at us the night Hudson had pulled me out of the Sanctuary.

Before I could even grab my clothes and cover up, Hudson had already gotten to his feet and shifted into his warrior form. His wings blocked me from view, and I stood up and tugged on my clothes, more than ready to push this asshole off the balcony.

"Stay behind me, babygirl," Hudson whispered. His voice was soft, but the warning in his tone sent a chill skittering down my spine.

The other gargoyle lifted his hands, as if to show he meant no harm. "Relax. I'm here on official Midnight business."

"Tell Keradoc I'm busy," I snapped. *Shit.* Things were just getting good out here, too. Well, good *again.*

"Keradoc is in a meeting with his generals," he said. "I'm here at the behest of Gem."

"Gem?" I laughed, shifting to stand in front of Hudson. "You can tell *her* to fuck right off the edge of—"

"It's the vampire-fae, Miss Barnes. There's been an incident at the facility. He's… not well."

Alarm shot through my veins. "Elian? What happened?"

"I don't know the details. I was asked to find you and bring you back."

"Gem?" I asked. "Gem asked you to find me?"

"Gem and the one-eyed demon both. The demon told me I'd likely have trouble convincing you it was a legitimate request, so he sent a message. Something about the saint needing his little sparrow, and it's time to make the choice—stay or go. I assume you know what that means?"

I looked at Hudson, and my gargoyle mate nodded, no questions asked. No debate.

"It means," I said to the guard as Hudson scooped me into his arms, "we're going. Step aside—I've got my own ride."

# 31

## KERADOC

eeks ago, I demanded regular reports from the Road of Silence. And in all that time, my highest-ranking officers have provided little more than shrugs and guesswork." I tossed the papers across the table, shaking my head.

More reports. More bullshit. More empty words that would never help us win this war.

"It appears the Darkwinter fae are lying low, sir," the general said.

"It *appears*? Or it is *fact*? Only one of those things is even remotely useful to me. Care to guess which one?"

"Facts, sir."

"Yes. Facts. So if you do not have facts to provide, then *you* are not useful to me either. Dismissed."

"But sir, we must—"

"Dismissed!" I shouted.

The general rose from his chair as ordered, but his face looked stricken.

Once, they'd been used to my short temper, my gruff demeanor.

My cruelty.

I'd let it fade in recent months. Gone too easy on them.

Mistake.

One of them—the general overseeing the southern outpost—hadn't even shown up tonight.

They were losing respect for me. Growing complacent.

But as much as I'd love to blame the incompetence of my generals for my current mood, I couldn't. The foulness that had crept into my bones tonight was all on account of one infuriating, passionate, beautiful, untouchable blood witch.

I scarcely remembered having a life before Midnight, though I knew from my nightmares I hadn't always lived here. Still, I'd gotten so accustomed to this realm, I hardly noticed its charms anymore. Not just the magick humming through the rocks or the splendor of the triple moons, but the small things that made a city unique in *every* realm—the food, the people, the sights and the scents, the oddities.

Showing her around Amaranth City, I saw everything through new eyes. Through *her* eyes.

She'd moaned in pleasure at the taste of our food, our cider. She stared in wide-eyed wonder at the crowded marketplace, her eyes darting from one vendor to the next, excitement coloring her cheeks. She'd laughed for me, and her smile had felt like the sun upon my face—a sun I only ever saw in my dreams.

Yet that smile was fleeting. It had never been meant for me.

Only for them. Her demon. Her vampire-fae. The gargoyle I'd watched pleasuring her on the balcony tonight, making her smile in ways I could only dream of.

They were the monsters who held her heart.

Me? I was nothing more than a merchant. The bastard warlord she'd bargained with for a fair trade—the safety of her sisters and companions in exchange for the ritual that would bring me the so-called weapon to destroy my enemies.

Now, I looked upon the faces of my generals, my daughter, all of them awaiting orders on how to crush our enemies.

Never before had I so longed to drop this pretense. To tear off the ring and the glamour that came with it. To turn my back on my plans and let this place fall to ash.

But that was not an option. I would *not* let Amaranth City fall to ruin. I would *not* let the Darkwinter fae claim Midnight for themselves.

I would *not* become someone else's slave.

It was Oona who spoke next, when it was clear that I could not.

"We've received reports of additional Darkwinter advances through Dead Claw," she said, "though the gargoyles in and around Stone City are keeping some of them at bay. Skirmishes continue on the edges of Blackbone Forest as well. Darkwinter is certainly our main concern at this point, but the other factions are gaining ground. We're also hearing rumors—and yes, I realize rumors are not facts, but they *are* still worth an assessment.

There are rumors of increased magickal activity around the borders, suggesting there are other players at work. Other forces we're not yet aware of."

With a deep sigh, I said, "I'm not concerned with a witless army of imps or half-breeds breaking through our defenses at Amaranth, or with wizards playing games at our borders. Darkwinter is and shall remain our primary—"

"My apologies for being tardy, sir." My missing general barged in, finally ready to make an appearance. He was disheveled and out of breath, his eyes wide with fright. He didn't even salute. "If I may—"

"You *may* explain the reason for your lateness, your rudeness, or the despicable state of your appearance," I snapped, "but I will *not* sit here and listen to—"

"We've received a report from the southern outpost," he barreled on, clearly distressed. "A new threat is making its way across the Boiling Glass Sands."

"What new threat?" I scoffed. "None but dragons can cross that wretched landscape, and none of those beasts have been sighted in—"

"Not dragons, sir."

I stood up. Crossed the room. Grabbed a handful of his shirt and pulled him close, my whole body trembling, ready to erupt, eager to find an easy target for the rage the witch continued to inspire within.

In a deadly whisper I said, "If you've come to tell me that Darkwinter armies have not only built ships to sail the un-sailable Sea of Tranquility, but have devised some way to cross the Boiling Glass Sands without liquifying their very bones, I will tear the tongue out of your mouth and gut you where you stand."

"It's not Darkwinter, sir. Not fae at all." He didn't so much as blink at my threat. Simply glared at me, unflinching in his determination to deliver this dire message.

My mouth turned as dry as the obsidian sands beyond the wall.

"Speak," I commanded. "What new devil has set his sights on my realm?"

"*Her* sights, sir," he said grimly. "The intelligence has been corroborated. The Dark Goddess Melantha has found a way to reverse the banishment spell and return to Midnight. And this time, she's brought the Army of the Dead."

# BLOOD AND MADNESS

BOOK THREE

# 1

## HALEY

*T*error.

It vibrated from my demon's very soul as he paced the oily street in front of the facility, raking his hands through his hair.

Hudson landed and set me on my feet, and when Jax looked up and met my gaze, I saw it right there in his eye—that raw, unguarded fear that could only mean one thing.

Whatever had happened, Elian was in bad shape.

I swallowed hard, momentarily frozen in place as a dozen horrific scenarios played through my mind. *An overdose. An attack. Hawthorn stakes. Gem. Bleeding out. He's dead...*

I didn't have the courage to voice a single fear. When I finally opened my mouth, the only word I could manage was, "Jax?"

"Angel," he breathed, pulling me close and holding tight. A tremor rolled through him, and I caught it like a virus, my whole body quaking in his embrace. "You came."

I glanced up at the other gargoyle who'd followed us here—one of Keradoc's goons. "As soon as we heard. I—"

"Fuck, I'm so sorry, Haley." Jax pulled back and cupped my face, his eye searching me in the glow of a flickering streetlamp. "For all of it. What I said the other night... that you're not the woman I thought you were? Way out of line, and not even remotely true. You're so much more than that, angel. So fucking much more, and I can't even... You didn't deserve that shit from me. I'm sorry."

We hadn't seen each other since our argument about Elian the other night. I'd been so convinced he was upset with me—that he and Elian were both avoiding me. But now, staring into that bright blue eye, feeling the lingering tremble in his muscles, knowing Elian was in trouble, I could barely remember why we'd argued at all. All those harsh words and accusations suddenly felt so meaningless. So insignificant.

"I'm sorry too." I nestled in closer and stayed in his arms for another beat, stealing a final moment of warmth and comfort. I knew it would vanish as soon as I let go; whatever terrible news he had about Elian would fill up all the space between us like a dark shadow.

But it was Jax who broke away first, pulling back to cradle my face in his hands.

"It's bad this time," he whispered. "Real bad. None of us can get through to him."

I blew out a breath, relieved to know that Elian was still alive, at least. "Tell me what happened."

Jax searched my face again, then gripped my hand and gestured for me to follow him inside.

The knot in my throat tightened. My heart was beating so loudly I could feel it pounding in my ears.

*What could be so bad that he has to show me? That he can't even say the words?*

With Keradoc's guard and Hudson on our heels, we entered the facility. The darkness enveloped me completely, the iron scent of blood heavy in the air. It was too sweet, though. Cloying, like a vase of dead roses long forgotten.

It reminded me of Keradoc.

Step by precarious step, Jax pulled me deeper inside the room. The stench grew so heavy it made my eyes water, and when my gaze finally adjusted to the darkness and revealed the scene, I nearly gagged.

In that moment, had my heart remained whole, I probably would've choked on it.

But it *wasn't* whole. The moment I saw him, it shattered into a thousand pieces.

"Elian," I gasped.

He didn't acknowledge me. Didn't acknowledge any of us—not even Gem, who paced in silence behind him, her face sheet-white.

Elian was kneeling on the floor, staring blankly at his trembling, blood-slicked hands as if he didn't even recognize them. The same dark blood stained his clothes. Spilled from his mouth. Covered the lifeless bodies strewn around him.

Corpses.

"They're all dead," I whispered, shock stealing my breath. "How… how did this happen?"

Jax put his hands on my shoulders, his voice low against my ear as we continued to watch Elian. "We were finishing up the last batch of the night, and out of nowhere, he just… He lost it, Haley. Started grabbing pills, downing them by the fistful. Gem and I couldn't even get close to him—no one could. Eventually he headed for the Dreamers. I'd thought maybe he'd burned himself out and needed to sleep it off, but before we even realized it was happening, he… he just…"

Jax trailed off into a dark, broken sigh that made me shiver.

"He murdered them," Gem said suddenly, her voice too loud. Too shrill. Her hands trembled as badly as Elian's, but still, my vampire-fae didn't even blink. "He *mutilated* them."

"But why?" I asked. "The pills I understand, but the *people*? Elian isn't a killer. Not like this."

"Once the pills were gone," Jax said, "there was only one place to get the Black."

I choked back a sob, the horror of it almost too much to contemplate.

"Their blood," I whispered. "He drained them for the drugs in their bloodstream."

Tears brimmed in my eyes. I knew Elian was struggling—getting worse with each passing night. We *all* knew it. But to do something like *this*? To slaughter nearly two dozen people—supernatural and human alike—just to get another fix? Just to chase down one more second of that elusive high that never seemed to give him what he truly needed?

My entire body recoiled in disgust, and I wanted to welcome it. The revulsion. Hatred. Some vicious, vile rage that would allow me to turn my back on the man I loved and walk away from his mess for good.

But when I looked at the fae who still held my heart in his blood-soaked hands, all I felt was a devastating heartbreak. An anguish that penetrated my very bones and filled me with a desperate need to help him. To take care of him, because clearly, he couldn't do it himself.

I took a step toward him, but Jax placed a hand on my shoulder and leaned in close.

"Careful," he said, a soft warning. "He's not himself. Not even close. Honestly, I'm not sure he'll even recognize you at this point, but we have to try. If anyone can get through to him…"

I swallowed the knot in my throat and schooled my features, nodding once. Jax was right. Whatever Elian and I were to each other now didn't matter. We had history—a deep, intense bond that hadn't faded no matter how messed up things had gotten. And that history had bled into our present—twisted, but nevertheless real. Nevertheless important.

I just needed to bring him back to it—to whatever bond still connected us.

Ignoring the stench of death and blood, I knelt down alone beside him, brushing his shoulder with tentative fingers. Blood soaked into the knees of my pants, chilling my skin.

Elian didn't even acknowledge my presence. My touch.

"Elian," I said softly, forcing a smile. "It's me. Sparrow. Can you hear me?"

No response.

I lifted a hand to cup his face, my thumb tracing his cheekbone. The gesture felt so intimate, so familiar, it threatened to yank me straight back into the past. My heart slammed against my ribs, aching with every beat as I fought to stay in the present.

"Elian, please look at me," I whispered. "Please come back to us."

Haunted, silver eyes finally slid my way, locking on my gaze, then narrowing. In that moment, I felt his rage, his confusion, his shame, all of it mingling into a dangerous brew that had his muscles twitching. A warning growl vibrated in his chest, but before I could think of something to say that might calm him, he lunged for me, knocking me flat on my back and pinning me to the blood-soaked floor.

"Elian, stop!" I shouted, but it was no use. Fangs burst through his gums as he lowered his mouth to my throat and—

Vanished.

# 2

## HALEY

The weight of him, the heat, the rage… all of it was gone in a blink.

I bolted upright to find Hudson—still in his winged warrior form—pinning Elian to the wall behind us, one hand around his throat. Whatever urge had sparked the attack on me, it was gone. Elian's body was suddenly limp and pale, as if someone had turned on the spigot and drained away his life force.

His head slumped forward, and Hudson finally released the deadly grip, scooping him into his arms and carrying him back to me.

"He needs clean blood," I said, getting to my feet. Elian's eyes were closed, his breathing so shallow his chest barely moved.

Hudson met my gaze briefly, his own full of anguish. With a brief nod, he looked down at the broken man fading away in his arms.

"Haley," Jax said, "he fed more tonight than he's fed in weeks."

"He hasn't though—not really. The dreamers he drank from…" I closed my eyes, swallowing back the bile in my throat as the smell of all those fresh corpses rose anew, mingling with the sickly-sweet smell of the drugs. "Their blood is full of Dream. It's not enough to nourish him, Jax. It's only going to keep amplifying the effect of the pills. We need to flush it out of his system with fresh blood. It's the only way I can think of to reset him."

"I can get him another donor," Gem said, chewing her thumbnail in an uncharacteristic show of nervousness. She was still pacing, but when Elian had lunged for me, she hadn't moved to stop him.

Needless to say, I wasn't exactly team Gem at the moment.

"What are you saying?" I asked.

"There's a place a few blocks over where humans like to hang out, and—"

"No." I glared at her, barely keeping my simmering rage in check. "Why are you even still here, Gem? Waiting for another chance to betray your so-called friends? Or are you just following orders like a good little soldier, keeping watch over the lowly prisoners?"

Her eyes hardened. She spat out a jagged bit of thumbnail and gritted her teeth. "Better a soldier than a prisoner, witch."

"In Midnight?" I laughed. "It's cute that you believe there's a difference." I took a step toward her, refusing to fall victim to her latest little power trip. If she'd wanted to shoot me full of magic or steel bolts from her damn crossbow, she would've done it by now.

"Back off, Barnes." She lifted a hand, as if that would stop me, but I ignored the gesture and took a step closer, getting so far up in her business I could count her fucking eyelashes.

"You know, Gem," I said, my voice low and menacing. She tried to take a step back, but I followed her, backing her up to the wall where moments earlier, Hudson had throttled Elian. "Where I come from, friendship is something to be cherished. Honored. Whatever fucked-up shit you went through in this realm? Elian—Saint—he was your friend. And he believed you were his—enough to trust you with our lives."

"You don't know what you're talking about, witch."

"The fact that you so carelessly pitched that friendship into the trash for a shot at your own glory tells me *everything* I need to know."

"Haley," Jax warned from behind me, his hand curling over my shoulder.

But I wasn't done yet. Not even close.

"You take a good look at him, Gem. A good look at the man who trusted you, because *that's* what your so-called friendship got him. And if you think we need your help saving him now, then you must be hopped up on the Black too, because bitch? You are fucking *hallucinating*. So do us all a favor and stop pretending like you give a shit whether he lives or dies, because whatever happens to him tonight? *That's* on you. All of it."

Gem lifted her crossbow. Shoved it right into my sternum. "Keep pushing me, witch."

Tough talk, but she wasn't going to shoot me. Not tonight, anyway. The thing wasn't even loaded.

"Leave," I demanded. "Run back to your master and give him the full report. Unless *you're* volunteering to donate blood tonight, in which case…" I thumbed over my shoulder toward Elian, still lying limp in Hudson's arms. "By all means, Gem. Offer up the vein. Prove my ass wrong. Show us what a good friend you really are."

Something dark and broken flashed behind her eyes, but before I could even guess at her thoughts, she lowered the crossbow, turned, and stalked right out of the warehouse.

She hadn't even looked at Elian once.

*Fucking coward.*

"Angel," Jax said softly, and I turned to face him, blowing out a pent-up breath as he tucked a lock of blood-matted hair behind my ears. "I understand why you don't want Gem to drag in some poor human to feed him. But why does it have to be you? Why does it always have to be you?"

I glanced back at Elian. He was still breathing—barely—but his eyes had fallen closed, his mouth hanging slack. He was trembling again, his body twitching even as Hudson tried to hold him steady.

I had no idea whether he was reacting to the drugs in his system, the tainted blood, the trauma of what he'd done, or something else entirely. I just knew that we were his only chance right now.

That *I* was his chance.

"Because he's drowning, Jax. He's fucking drowning. And no matter what he's done, no matter what he deserves, no matter what it might cost me in the end, I can't just stand by and watch him suffer. Not when I'm holding a possible lifeline." Cupping his face, I said softly, "You wouldn't have called me here if you wanted me to sit on the sidelines."

"You're right. I wouldn't have." Jax touched his forehead to mine and gripped my arms. "But now that you're actually standing here covered in all this blood, I just…" His warm sigh ghosted across my mouth, fingers tightening possessively. "If he hurts you, Haley, I'll—"

"He won't." I pulled back so I could look into his face again. He wasn't wearing the eye patch—I hadn't seen it since that night in the bathtub— and looking at him now, I finally felt like I was seeing the real Jax. The man behind the demon, the person he was at his very core.

And that person wanted to end Elian's suffering as much as I did.

"You and Hudson will make sure I'm safe," I continued. "We just… we have to try, Jax. I don't care how badly he's fucked up or how many second chances he's already burned through. It's like you said the other night—when you call someone your family, when you *choose* them? It's not just for the easy stuff. So yeah, this is me, choosing to stay. Choosing Elian even when he's at his absolute rock-bottom worst."

He held my gaze for another long beat, then finally drew me close once more, pressing a lingering kiss to my forehead.

"Okay, angel," he whispered. "Do what you need to do. I've got your back."

With Jax's blessing, I finally turned my attention back to Elian.

A quick slice of my dagger across my fingertip, a few drops of blood squeezed into his mouth, and I held my breath, pulse quickening as I waited for a response.

*Any* response.

After what felt like an eternity, those silver eyes slowly blinked open, and Elian licked his lips, getting his first taste of fresh, untainted blood.

He stiffened in Hudson's arms as another growl tore through his chest, his fangs descending violently. He thrashed against the hold, but my gargoyle kept him steady, Jax standing close with a hawthorn stake at the ready, just in case.

Lacing my fingers through Elian's tangled hair, I pressed my other wrist to his mouth.

And then, stroking his hair, I began to sing. Soft, completely off-key, but clear and true. A song to remind him that he wasn't alone, no matter how deeply he'd fallen into that gaping hole. A song to bring him back to us. A song to let him know I still loved him as my family, even if I couldn't love him as my mate.

His growl turned into a desperate moan, his eyes filling with anguish as he gave in to the temptation of my blood. Unlike all the other times I'd offered the vein, he didn't fight me tonight. Those razor-sharp fangs sank deep into my flesh, his mouth latching on and sucking, sucking, *sucking* until the room spun before my eyes and my muscles quaked, until heat spread from the bite throughout my entire body, until my song gave way to gasping breaths. The pain was sharp and acute, chased by waves of pleasure that rolled over me again and again like I'd fallen into the ocean, tossed up on the shore only to be sucked back out to sea, exhilarated and begging for more.

Elian was absolutely *starved* for it, his gaze locked fiercely onto mine as if I truly was his only lifeline, a tether back to the world of the living.

"Come back to me," I whispered. "Please come back."

Another moan and the bite deepened, the pressure of his clamped jaw nearly crushing my wrist.

"Angel," Jax whispered, raising the stake, but I shook my head.

"Just another minute. A little more. He just needs a little... *damn it...*" I swayed on my feet, the dizziness finally overtaking me. I tried to pull away from the bite, but Elian only clamped down harder, sucking deeper, relentless in his need to feed.

"That's enough, Elian," I said. "Please stop. Stop!"

I begged him to release me, but he was beyond hearing. Beyond caring.

"Fuck this," Jax said. He gripped his stake and stabbed Elian in the thigh.

The unexpected jab of the hawthorn made Elian gasp, and I yanked my arm back and dropped to my knees, fighting to catch my breath. Blood gushed from my wound; Elian had been too far out of his mind to do things the neat and tidy way tonight, which meant I'd be healing this mess on my own.

With a little assist from my bloodstone ring, I whispered a quick spell, just like I'd done for Jax in the bathtub. The magick was weak, but it answered my call immediately, tingling down my arm and warming the skin around the puncture wounds. Slowly, the blood began to congeal, the skin knitting itself back together until all that remained were two angry pink welts.

When it was clear Elian was back to himself again—as back as he could be anyway, given his physical state—Hudson yanked the stake out of his thigh and knelt down beside me, keeping one arm around Elian's midsection, holding him upright against his chest.

Elian was still as pale as a ghost, but his eyes had finally cleared. Blood stained his mouth and shirt—mine, the victims', his own—and when he looked at me, the depth of his misery nearly swallowed me whole.

"Sparrow." He didn't even say the word—not really—just moved his lips, the faintest breath passing through them. But even in the stone-cold silence, I knew the shape of my name in his mouth, knew the look in his eyes he'd always reserved just for me. The one he couldn't hide, no matter how desperately he'd been trying to keep me locked out.

My entire arm still throbbed with white-hot pain, my head swimming from the loss of blood and pleasure both, but I refused to let an ounce of discomfort show on my face.

"It's me, Elian." I smiled and cupped his face. "I'm here. Jax and Hudson too. All of us are right here with you."

"What... what have I..." His voice finally broke through, but the words evaporated as he took in the full sight of the carnage that surrounded him, the stink of the dead, the black glaze of rot and ruin that was already beginning to set in. Tears slipped down his cheeks, his face reddening with shame. "I killed them. All of them. I fucking *killed* them."

Locked in Hudson's embrace, he trembled and heaved as if he might puke.

"Breathe, Elian," I said. "You need to breathe. Let my blood work its way through your system." I gestured for Hudson to release him, then I took my gargoyle's place, kneeling behind Elian and rubbing his back as I whispered the words over and over like a mantra.

*Breathe, Elian. Just breathe.*

He grabbed my arm and wrapped it around his chest, clinging to it as if he'd slip away again without it, and I let him. I let him hold me close, let him tremble and sob in my embrace, let him take and take and take.

Jax and Hudson said nothing, but when I finally looked up into their eyes, I saw the same silent tears I felt running down *my* cheeks, the same silent understanding passing between us.

Elian was a mess in every possible way. A dangerous, reckless, self-destructive, selfish fucking mess who'd bring us all down with him if we let him.

But...

I closed my eyes and took a deep, steadying breath.

He was *our* fucking mess. And right now, we needed to get him the hell out of here.

"Let's go," I said softly. "Gem can deal with the bodies. We need to go home."

Wordlessly, Hudson lifted Elian back into his arms, and I rose and leaned into Jax's waiting embrace, and together the four of us headed out into Amaranth City, leaving the dead behind.

# 3

## KERADOC

athered in a grim circle around the table, my most trusted war generals and elite guards stared up at me, their collective breath drawn and held tight, no doubt awaiting my inevitable eruption.

I felt it simmering inside, churning from the depths of my soul and aching for an outlet.

But as deeply as my muscles trembled with the effort of holding back, I couldn't erupt. The news was too shocking. Too deadly.

The general in charge of the southern outpost held my gaze, his warnings echoing through the cold room like one more illusion cast by the vile goddess herself.

*The Dark Goddess Melantha has found a way to reverse the banishment spell and return to Midnight… She's brought the Army of the Dead…*

My hands clenched into fists at my sides, aching to wrap around his throat and choke him for his vicious lies. Perhaps watching the life drain out of those mud-brown eyes would mute the other images seared into my brain—my blood witch on her knees, bared to the night air, thighs spread over her gargoyle's bearded face. Her head tossed back with careless abandon, the breeze caressing her long hair as her mouth parted on a sweet, decadent moan…

For him. All for him.

My jaw cracked from the pressure of clenching my teeth, the audible pop snapping me back to the present.

War council. Melantha. My general.

I swallowed the rage. I could no more kill him than I could convince myself he'd lied to me. The look in his eyes was too grave, too terror-stricken for his words to be anything other than the truth.

With a wave of my hand I dismissed him, allowing him to take his seat among the others. His relief was palpable.

*My* relief, however, was non-fucking-existent.

"How long?" I asked, my voice stone-cold, hands still fisted at my sides. "How long until she reaches our borders and unleashes her wicked ghouls on my city?"

Squaring his shoulders, the general whose life I'd spared cleared his throat and said, "We're working with very limited intelligence at this time, given the difficulties of entering the Boiling Glass Sands. Our men at the southern outpost have been working with our dark witch allies to track her movements through spellcraft, but it hasn't been easy. Melantha is moving quickly, never lingering in one place too long."

"Is she in her true form? Or has she taken the shape of another?"

"Neither, sir. Our scouts don't believe Melantha has physically manifested—not fully, anyway. At this point she's merely an entity—a magickal field, so to speak. But it's only a matter of time. Every moment she spends on Midnight soil is another moment she's leeching its magick, channeling it to her own dark ends."

Bitterness churned in my gut. Stealing magick—that had always been her modus operandi. For a long time, the leaders of the past had let her get away with it too. All part of the deal.

But I wasn't them. Wasn't *him*. And I would be a dead man in the moat before I let her use the magick of *my* city—my fucking *realm* against us.

I leaned forward, my fingertips pressed so hard against the table they turned white. "How. Long."

Clearing his throat again, the general said, "Assuming she's able to draw enough magick to both manifest and continue working whatever protective spell is allowing her to travel through the Sands, she'll likely clear the desert in a few weeks—that's *if* luck is on our side. Otherwise we're talking about two weeks, maybe ten days at most."

"If luck were on our side," I said, "we wouldn't be having this conversation. What of her army?"

"They'll follow her in any form, sir. As long as Melantha is present—fully manifested or no more than a whisper in the air—the dead will march on the orders of their queen."

*The dead.* I practically scoffed. Such a common, everyday name for her mystical, otherworldly beasts.

Melantha's soldiers weren't like the ghouls of Beggar's Moat—weak and festering, strong only for short bursts when riled by their prey. The Army of the Dead was relentless—the vicious dead, resurrected and animated by the darkest, most ancient magick imaginable, driven by a singular purpose:

To consume everything in their wake.

And she wielded this power not only through her own army, but through *any* corpses she happened upon, in any realm, no matter how long ago those poor souls had passed on. Melantha had the power to call upon them all—including my own ghouls—bending them to her will and turning them against us.

"Darkwinter invades from the north," I said, pacing the dark chamber. "Melantha and her gruesome army from the south. Rebels eat a million tiny holes in the realm like a fucking cancer. One by one, the dead of Midnight—*our* dead—will answer the call of the dark goddess, and we will become nothing but fodder for the…" I closed my eyes and pinched the bridge of my nose, willing myself to pull it together. As hopeless as our situation appeared, it would do no good for the generals and guards to witness a breakdown. Now more than ever, I needed to be strong. A leader. A tyrant, if that's what the situation called for.

I was close—so *fucking* close to achieving all that I'd set out to achieve. The realm was within my grasp, and I would not let these vile enemies waltz into my home and unravel *decades* of planning. Of sacrifice. Of pain.

"Who beyond Vanderham's Wall still has the courage to fight?" I asked, my voice cold and impassive once more. "To stand with the armies of Midnight? To stand with their commander?"

After a brief commotion of comparing notes and ruling out the factions we absolutely couldn't trust, the generals came to a consensus.

We were, in a word, fucked.

Oona named a handful of factions whose loyalties hadn't yet turned, but they amounted to little more than an army of renegade demons and weak humans who'd do anything to commute their sentences in Midnight. We also had the ghouls of Beggar's Moat, bound to serve their commander for eternity, but what good would they do against Melantha's forces? Even with constant feeding, my ghouls wouldn't last more than a handful of minutes against the true Army of the Dead. And though we hadn't yet been tested, there was a good chance that if the dark goddess called upon them, they'd answer, turning on me in an instant.

"What of the gargoyles in Stone City?" one of the other generals asked.

A fair question, as most of them had remained somewhat politically neutral, making themselves available to the highest bidders as needed.

"Mercenaries," Oona confirmed. "Most of them can be bought, but they won't come cheaply. Not for such a dangerous task. And if Darkwinter decided to make a better offer, they'd easily turn."

"We need more allies," I said. "Fighters. Not riffraff and mercenaries."

A shuffling of feet. A clearing of throats. A general murmur of agreement, yet none of my generals offered any viable solutions.

How could they? They hadn't risen to their ranks by spoon-feeding me lies and wishful idealism.

"We will reconvene tomorrow evening to review any new intelligence we can gather," I announced, a sudden bone-deep weariness gripping me from head to toe. "Tonight, I want all of you to return to your posts at once. Apprise your troops of the news about Melantha, as well as the ongoing threat from Darkwinter. All of us must work together to recruit as many others as we can to this cause, by conscription, coercion, or any means necessary. Our realm—our very home—is at risk. If we fail to defend her now, then…"

I glowered at each of them, every single soldier and hired guard positioned around my table, ensuring they understood exactly what was at stake.

They didn't need me to speak the words.

A shudder rippled through the room as all of them undoubtedly contemplated life under the reign of Melantha—an unhinged dark goddess with an army of ghouls at her command. In the face of such a gruesome alternative, the vile acts perpetrated by the legendary Keradoc of Midnight looked like mere party games.

Certain they understood, I dismissed the room, gesturing for just one of my advisors to remain—Oona, my Lieutenant General. My most trusted.

The warlord's daughter, always eager to serve her father and homeland both.

The old guilt churned anew.

Ignoring it, I said, "Give me your honest assessment. Are there *any* in Midnight still willing to risk their lives for the realm? Soldiers, mercenaries… hell, at this point I'd enlist mothers and children if I thought they could help."

Oona's eyes flickered with something that looked a lot like frustration. Like anger. I'd never seen it in her before, and the sight of it sent fresh worry blazing through my chest.

"You know this realm better than anyone," she said, her jaw ticking, her eyes fixed on me. "Do you honestly think there are others? People willing to fight and die for us? For *you*? After—" She bit off her words, shaking her head as if she couldn't believe the gods had damned her to this fate. To this bloodline.

To me.

"Speak plainly, Oona," I commanded. "You weren't raised to shrink in the face of conflict."

She met my eyes again, her own steely and unflinching. A sight to make any father proud.

"Our armies—your very generals and personal guards—are no more loyal than the factions sniffing around the wall willing to trade a lifetime of servitude for safe harbor in Amaranth City. All of them are forced to do your bidding under threat of torture and death—by the wilds of Midnight or by their commander himself. You cannot *possibly* rely on soldiers like that to defend us. To *truly* defend us. If you don't see that by now, then neither I nor your other generals can help you. *Sir*," she added with a belated salute.

I glared at her, shocked at her newfound audacity.

But glad of it nevertheless.

We watched each other in tense silence for another beat before I finally allowed myself a thin smile. "No, daughter of Midnight. We cannot rely on soldiers whose only loyalty has been forced or bought."

The woman didn't breathe a sigh of relief. Didn't show an ounce of softness.

She was strong. Stronger than I'd given her credit for.

I didn't know whether to be glad of it or... or defeated by it.

Oona deserved better. But better was not her lot in life.

"Then my path is clear," I said finally. "There is but one final option. One final faction upon whose quest for blood and vengeance I might be able to rely."

Her eyes widened, her jaw going slack as the realization set in. "Sir, you... *Father*. You can't be serious."

"I fear I have no choice."

Some of the steel melted from her eyes, her shoulders sagging under this new weight. "But they're... they're nearly feral. All traces of humanity eradicated. Fighting for us? Risking their lives when... No. They wouldn't. They simply wouldn't. It's an impossible request with nothing but disappointment and death as the answer. How can you even *consider* it?"

"Because, *daughter*." I stepped close, so close she had to tilt her face up to hold my gaze. Her violet eyes held a lifetime of suffering, a sight that threatened to bring me to my knees with rage and regret in equal measure. Tucking a finger beneath her chin, I said softly, "In a war with no *possible* path to victory, we must seek out the *impossible* and hope—against the most devastating odds—it shines its light on another path."

I withdrew my touch and headed for the exit, hoping she would do the same.

Hoping, against more impossible, devastating odds, she might find some peace tonight.

"What new orders, then, sir?" she asked, still so eager to obey. To serve. "What would you have me do before your journey?"

"Send word to Gem and my fugitives that the production schedule has been moved up. I want that product packaged and ready to distribute in two days' time."

"I'm not sure they've completed the testing. We don't know how potent or effective the new formulation—"

"I care not, Oona. We must move soon if we've got any hope of weakening Darkwinter and the other factions working against us."

She nodded once. "Very well, sir. And the blood witch? Any orders for her?"

*The blood witch…*

A fresh barrage of images assaulted my mind, each one more torturous than the last.

Haley Barnes kneeling in the moonlight. Haley Barnes crying out as the pleasure took hold. Haley Barnes, her entrancing beauty haunting my dreams and nightmares both, making my blood boil, my heart race, and my cock stiffen painfully.

I closed my eyes, allowing myself the briefest, darkest indulgence…

*The things I would do to that soft, sweet little mouth…*

"Sir?" Oona pressed, breaking the fantasy's hold.

Just as well. I couldn't afford to be sidetracked by foolish notions of pleasure. Notions of *her* on her knees for *me*.

"Inform Gem about the schedule change, Oona. I will deal with the witch myself."

# 4

## HUDSON

$\mathcal{T}$he sight of her standing alone on the balcony, shivering in the moonlight like all the hope had been sucked right outta that great big heart of hers…

It was enough to squeeze the breath from my lungs.

But when she turned toward me and I saw them big, fat tears on her cheeks?

*Fuck.* My heart damn near liquified.

If Saint wasn't in such bad shape from the Black, I'd march right back inside and put him in bad shape with my fists.

*Damn it, Saint. You* asshole. *What the fuck were you thinking?*

I shoved a hand through my hair, squashing those shitty thoughts. Wouldn't help matters. Besides, he was seriously messed up right now in ways I couldn't even begin to imagine. Deep down, I fucking bled for the guy, just like the rest of our motley little crew.

But none of us hurt as much as Haley. She truly loved the sonofabitch. Whatever drove them apart all those years back—whatever kept them apart now—it wasn't her choice. That was pretty damn obvious.

"Feel like some company, babygirl?" I asked.

She nodded, but then turned away to stare out over the balcony again. Wordlessly I draped a blanket over her shoulders, and my girl sighed and leaned back against my chest, letting me wrap my arms around her. Resting my cheek on top of her head, I held her close, the two of us gazing out across the Amaranth City hellscape.

"He's going to be okay, right Gargs?" she finally whispered.

I didn't have an answer on that one, so I just squeezed her a little tighter and said the one thing I knew to be true about Saint just then. "If anyone can pull him outta this fucked-up nightmare, Haley Barnes, it's you."

A sad sigh rushed out, making her crumple in my arms. "I'm the one who dragged him into this nightmare in the first place."

"Not true. Saint's addiction isn't your—"

"He's only in Midnight again because of me, Hudson." She turned around in my arms, blinking up at me with a wide, sad gaze that stabbed something deep inside me. Hard. "Keradoc's got him working with an even higher-potency version of a drug he's already completely addicted to, with unrestricted access, and Elian's only going along with it because he's trying to help me. To make sure we give Keradoc whatever the hell he wants so my sisters are kept safe and I'm..." She shook her head and closed her eyes, fresh tears slipping down her cheeks. "How is this not my fault?"

"Just ain't. Not unless you're some kind of mad goddess pulling all the strings." I hooked a finger under her chin and tilted her face up. When she finally opened her eyes again, I grinned. "Something you forget to tell me?"

This got a smile. A faint one, barely there, but hell—anything was better than her tears.

"Oh, right." She rolled her eyes. "I'm a goddess, of course! Must've slipped my mind, what with me being a fae-blooded Silversbane witch and all. Hard to keep track of so much badassery in one little package. Forgive me?"

"So long as you keep me in your good graces, goddess, we're just fine." I lowered my mouth to hers, stealing a soft kiss in the moonlight. The touch of her lips sent a zap of electricity straight to my heart.

Haley felt it too. She pulled back with a yelp, brushing her fingers across her mouth. "Damn."

"Shocking, ain't it?"

"Yeah, it's... *Wait*. Did you just..." Her eyes narrowed playfully. "Did our resident stone-cold gargoyle just make a pun?"

"You're smiling now, so yeah. I'm gonna go ahead and take credit for that." I slid my hands down to her perfect ass and lifted her up, tucking her against my chest. She wrapped her legs around my hips and settled in *just* right, the feel of her warm little body stirring my cock to life. Girl was lucky I'd pulled on a T-shirt and sweats before I came out here, but now I kinda wished I hadn't. All that fabric between us was just getting in my way.

I ran my lips across her brow bone and down to the tip of her nose, then lowered my mouth to brush another soft kiss to her lips, bracing for the inevitable sparks. I groaned at the feeling, and she sighed and deepened our kiss, threading her fingers into my hair.

Goddamn, I'd never get tired of her kiss, her touch, her everything.

When she finally pulled back again, she granted me another smile, the tears finally starting to evaporate.

"I'm glad you're here, Hudson. Not just tonight, but…" She drew a hand down along my face, caressing my beard with her palm. "I'm grateful the gods or destiny or whatever the hell's in charge out there saw fit to put us on the same path, no matter how fucked up that path may be."

"Hmm. Even if I shock you every time we touch?"

"Is it every time, though? Like, *literally* every time?" She pursed her lips and glanced up at the moon, pretending to be deep in thought. "I think we need to do some more research here, Gargs. Bigger sample size, you know? Otherwise it's not statistically significant."

"If it's something big and significant you want, I've got you covered." With a dark chuckle, I shifted her ever so slightly lower on my hips, letting her feel *exactly* what was going on below the belt.

Haley let out a sigh, sweet as sin and twice as inviting.

"Damn. I'm in so much trouble with *you*, babygirl." My words were soft and low in the darkness, but she heard me just fine, a flare of desire brightening her eyes.

"Hudson?" she breathed. "Maybe this makes me selfish and insensitive, but after everything we just went through, I… Okay, fuck it." She cradled my face and laid a searing-hot kiss right on my mouth. Then, pulling back with a desperate gasp, she fisted my hair and made her demands. "Take me to my room. *Now*."

I didn't respond. Didn't give her a chance to ask twice. Just held her close and marched right back through the suite and straight into her bedroom, where I unceremoniously kicked the door shut behind us.

Jax was keeping watch over Saint, and I didn't want to hear shit from any-fucking-body tonight.

Only my girl begging me to make her come for me.

Again and again and again.

*Fuck*. I'd meant to be gentle with her, especially for our first time, sweet little thing that she was. But the way she was looking up at me now, that unchecked hunger burning in her eyes, her mouth parted as her chest rose and fell with every shallow breath... Nope. I just couldn't hold back.

I threw her down on that bed and climbed right the fuck on top, groaning at the perfect feel of her body squirming beneath me. I was all over her in a fucking heartbeat, hands tangled in her hair, mouth on her skin, my stone-hard cock digging into her thigh.

"I've never wanted anything so damn bad as I want you right now," I whispered, kissing a trail from her throat to her ear. "We were interrupted before I could give you everything you wanted tonight, but I promise you... We start this again? I ain't stopping. Not for the boys. Not for Keradoc's guards. Not for the entire fucking army of Midnight. Once I'm inside you, babygirl, I ain't stopping until I break the goddamn bed."

She moaned in response, nipping my lower lip and sucking it between her teeth, tracing it with her tongue. The gesture kicked my heart into overdrive and sent a red-hot pulse straight to my balls.

I broke away from her just long enough to tear off my clothes, and she did the same, wriggling out of her top and bottoms until she was completely bared for me. I took a moment to appreciate the view of her silky curves in the moonlight, her damp thighs parted, dark pink nipples rising in anticipation of my mouth.

One more second to take it all in, and then I was right back where I needed to be, kissing the woman breathless as my cock inched closer and closer to her soft, inviting pussy.

I teased her with the tip, stroking her, nearly losing my damn mind at how slippery she was. "*Fuck*, Haley. You're already so wet for me."

"Um, you kind of have that effect on me, Gargs."

"Since when?"

"Pretty much since the first time I saw you standing in Elian's kitchen wearing your tight T-shirt and too-cool-for-school sunglasses."

"You're kidding me. You've been crushing on me the *whole* time?" I was damn near giddy at the thought, but I needed her to admit it out loud.

"Yes. Okay? *Yes.*" An adorable giggle bubbled up, the blush in her cheeks darkening. Her breathing quickened, misting across my mouth in hot, shallow puffs.

"You all right?" I swept her hair back, searching her gaze.

She smiled up at me, my fucking sunshine in the darkness. "Why wouldn't I be?"

"Dunno. You seem a little nervous is all."

"No, it's just... You're very... um..." She blew out another breath and shifted beneath me, her skin flushing hot from head to toe. "*Gifted*. Physically, I mean."

My chest rumbled with a laugh. "You sound surprised."

"Maybe a little? I mean, now that you're here, up close and personal. *Really* up close and personal. And like I said. Gifted."

"Pretty sure my so-called *gift* is the same size it was earlier when you shamelessly groped it." I nuzzled her neck, making her squeal. "Not that I'm complaining about *that*, mind you."

"You were naked!" She laughed. "And it was just… out there. Practically *begging* to be touched. Was I supposed to ignore it?"

"Either way, I'm glad you didn't." I rolled back onto my hip to give her a little breathing room, then trailed a hand down between her thighs, fingers gliding lazily between them. She was so wet, so warm, but like she'd said to me earlier—I couldn't make assumptions. Not with something so damn important. "Haley. You sure this is what you want? We don't have to—"

"No! I mean yes, I want it. Yes. Absolutely. Just…" She bit her lower lip, her eyes dancing with a mix of pleasure and trepidation as I ghosted my thumb across her clit. With a soft shiver, she whispered, "I'm all for breaking the bed, Gargs. Sign me up for that—my bed, your bed, all the beds, pretty please and thank you kindly. But maybe… maybe we should go slow at first? Just to make sure you… you know. Fit?"

"We can go as slow as you want, but…" I leaned close to her ear, my voice a deep rumble against her skin as I slid two fingers inside her, gently stroking. Deeper. Deeper still, curling to hit the perfect spot, just to give her a little taste of what I had in store for her tonight. "I know you can take it, babygirl. *All* of it."

A sigh of intense pleasure drifted from her lips, and she opened herself wider to me, hips tilting up, her every sound and movement sending shockwaves of desire down my spine as I slowly worked in a third finger, then a fourth.

"God, Hudson. Whatever you're doing to me? Don't ever stop. *Please*," she begged, and fuck if I didn't want to replace my fingers with my cock right then and there and make good on that promise to break the damn bed.

Hers. Mine. All of 'em.

But I couldn't—not yet. Not until she was truly ready for me.

"You're close," I whispered, brushing my thumb over her clit again, rubbing slow circles as I continued my deep thrusts. "I can feel it."

Her mouth fell open on another moan, green eyes rolling back as her body arched to get closer.

"Please don't stop," she said again, her thighs just beginning to tremble. Having enjoyed the pleasure of those thighs wrapped around my head as I kissed her sweet pussy into oblivion earlier, I knew she was seconds from going over the edge.

"Already told you I ain't stopping," I said. "Thing is, I can't let you fall just yet. Not like this." I drew my fingers out and rolled back on top of her, repositioning myself between her thighs. Slipping a hand beneath her ass, I angled her body just right. Then, in a low growl, "When you come for me tonight, babygirl, it's gonna be on my cock, not on my hand. You ready for me?"

A dark blush stained her bare chest. She lowered her lashes and gave me the sweetest, softest smile I'd ever seen. "More than ready."

Once more, she had me stopping to appreciate the view.

"Haley Barnes. Your smile is..." I swept a thumb across her lips, searching for the right word. Beautiful? Heartbreaking? A goddamn showstopper? All true. But the word I finally settled on was... "*Mine*. It's mine, Haley. *You* are mine. Understand?"

"I'm yours."

"That's my good girl."

I couldn't wait another minute.

Claiming her mouth in a possessive kiss, I finally sank inside her, one slow, torturous inch at a time, doing my damndest not to completely lose it right there. The feel of her was... fuck *me*, it was everything.

If soft touches and stolen kisses caused sparks, then being inside her set off a fireworks show the likes of which I'd never seen, not even during all them drunk-ass festivals in NOLA.

My girl responded immediately, her thighs tightening around my hips, her body pulsing around my cock, so tight and perfect and...

"Jesus *fuck*, Haley," I ground out. She was already moving beneath me again, arching to get closer, to take more of what she needed. "You gotta slow... slow down."

"I thought you wanted it... hard and fast," she breathed, knotting her fingers in my hair. "Break the bed, yes?"

"That's the idea, but... Damn it, woman. If you don't slow down, I'm gonna come before you, and I'll tell you something *right* now, babygirl. That's *never* happening. Not on my watch."

"You're a prince, Gargs. Truly." She cracked up. It made her clench around me even harder, her body vibrating with her laughter.

Definitely not helping the situation.

"Then lie back and let me give you the rest of this royal dick, princess, before you make me *completely* lose control. I'm barely hanging on by a thread." I slid in a bit more, my muscles rippling with the effort of holding back when all I wanted to do was fucking *pound* into her, show her just how badly I wanted her. "*Goddamn*, you feel good. So fucking good."

"Hudson." The breath left her lungs in a rush. "That dirty mouth of yours is just... My god. Pure perfection."

"Only for you."

She grinned up at me, a thin sheen of sweat shining on her upper lip. I wanted to lick it off. To taste every bit of her.

So I fucking did. Dragged the tip of my tongue across that smooth, salty skin, then bit her lower lip with a possessive growl that had her moaning and writhing all over again.

Going slow was pure torture, and I just couldn't fucking deal. I plunged the rest of the way inside, making her stretch to accommodate me. Making her gasp.

Making her fucking *beg*.

"Say more, Hudson," she whispered, just like she'd done earlier. "*Please* say more."

"Well, since you asked so nicely." I winked, then brought my mouth to her ear, taking my time kissing the sensitive skin behind it before I finally whispered, "Still can't decide if I wanna be soft and sweet with you tonight, babygirl, or fuck you so damn hard you can't take a single step tomorrow without remembering the feel of this cock buried inside you. But I'll tell you this—I'm leaning *heavily* toward the latter."

"Hudson, I want..." She trailed off and fisted my hair so tight my eyes watered, then gazed up at me with a fire that scorched the air between us.

"Tell me," I said. "Tell me what you want, and it's yours."

"*More.*"

"More dirty words? Or more of this cock you were so worried you couldn't take?"

"*Yes.*"

*Well, hell.* Who the fuck was I to deny my girl's wishes?

I gripped her hips and gave her a few more deep, delicious strokes, working her into a white-hot frenzy that had her panting, but it wasn't enough. Not for her, and sure as hell not for me. Haley was so hot and wet, so needy, so beyond ready for the rest of what I had in store. For that bed-breaking, soul-destroying, mind-altering *fuck* I'd been dreaming about since the night she'd first marched into Saint's and Sinners in them hot little black boots.

So, with a growl I couldn't fucking contain, I pulled out. And before she even had time to protest, I flipped her onto her belly, gripped her hips and hauled her ass up, then slammed right back inside that hot, wet haven, absolutely *claiming* her.

"*Fuck*, babygirl," I gritted out, barely able to speak. "You're taking it so fucking good for me."

She bit back a curse I couldn't understand, gripping the headboard and pushing back to meet my every thrust. All that nervousness was long gone, leaving only a fierce, hungry little monster-girl in its wake.

One I was more than happy to feed.

Haley's entire body was on fire, that long dark hair spilling down her back, skin glistening with sweat... I'd never seen anything so damn perfect in my life.

And right now, she was *my* perfect. No one watching us. No one banging on the door. No one else kissing her and touching her and making her scream.

Only me.

"Hudson," she breathed, arching her back. "I'm *right* there. I can't... I can't hold on much longer."

"Then let go, babygirl." I slid my hand around to stroke her clit. "I got you. I always fuckin' got you."

"I know you... you... oh, shit. Yes. Hudson, yes! Right there... I'm... *Fuck*!"

She went absolutely supernova for me, her whole body shaking with the force of it—the force of her, of me, of our bond, all those fireworks exploding between us in an epic finale that had me chasing the same damn pleasure I felt shuddering through her. Still facing the headboard, she rose up onto her knees, grinding that sweet little ass against me as she rode out the intense waves.

"Haley, that's... Goddamn, you're making me... I'm... *Fuck*."

I fucking *shattered* for her, coming so hot and furious it made me dizzy, made me see the stars, made my damn wings burst free. Them fuckers shot out across the room, took down a statue from the dresser, and smashed right through the goddamn window, but all we could do was laugh about it, lost in a sea of bliss, drifting away together into pure oblivion.

Losing myself in this... In Haley... Hell, it was pure fucking magick. A thing so rare and special, in nearly a thousand years with a beating heart, I'd never even come *close* to experiencing anything else like it.

And in that moment, I knew I never wanted to experience it with anyone but her.

---

When the laughter and aftershocks finally faded, Haley sighed and leaned back against me, and I dropped a kiss on her shoulder and breathed in the strawberries-and-cream scent of her, memorizing the feel of her skin as I wrapped my arms around her and held on tight.

"Mine," I said again, squeezing even tighter, wishing I never had to let her go.

"Always, Hudson," she whispered. "Always."

I tucked my wings back in, ignoring the shit I'd broken, and together we stretched out on the bed, facing each other in the darkness.

Skimming my palm along her thigh and up to the sexy curve of her hip, I said softly, "Feeling okay?"

"Oh, I feel amazing. But I'd like to file a complaint with the management."

"That a fact?" I laughed, sliding my palm around to cup her ass. My big hand spanned the entire width of it—a thing that had me wanting to claim her all over again. "Was something not to your liking?"

"Only the part where you broke your promise. I mean, sure. You destroyed the window and whatever poor statue was on the dresser, but this bed?" She reached back and knocked on the headboard. "Still intact."

"True, but you're forgetting one important point." I rolled on top of her and lowered my mouth to her nipples, sucking and biting one, then the other, teasing her until my cock was rock hard again and she was wet and willing, all wound up for another round.

Then, pulling back just long enough to see the light in her eyes as I slid right back inside her, I said, "*That* was just the appetizer, babygirl. We ain't even *close* to the main course yet."

# 5

## JAX

Tremors wracked Saint's body as I tried in vain to get him to lie still. I'd cleaned him up as best I could and put him in my bed; I was pretty sure he'd stashed a supply of Black in his room and there was no fucking way I'd risk him ingesting more of the shit.

He'd suffer hard the next couple of nights, but it was the only way through it. We needed to dry him out.

"Jax," he said, his eyes frantic in the dark. "Jax. I just need… a little. Two or three to help with the…" He clenched his gut, doubling over in pain. "Please, Jax. I know you've got some on you. Just a couple. Then I won't ask again."

"No."

"Fine. One. One lousy fucking p-p-pill. That's it."

The request fell on deaf ears.

I pulled a chair up next to the bed and pressed a cold cloth to his forehead. His temperature was spiking, and if I didn't get it under control, he might start hallucinating, which would make all this a hundred times worse.

"Please, brother." He grabbed my wrist, desperation flooding his eyes. "I need it to feel better. Help… help me f-f-feel… better."

"I don't want you to *feel* better, Saint. I want you to *get* better. And unfortunately for you, getting better is going to feel like shit for a good, long while. Now stop fighting me and try to relax."

"F-fuck you," he gritted out, jaw clenching against some new wave of pain.

"Pretty sure I'm already fucked, brother."

"You're so... so smug. I hate myself, Jax. I... I... I hate the man I've... I'm not... Is that what you want to hear? Does it... does it make *you* f-f-feel better? Better than me? You... you fucking *are* b-b-better and you know it, so... fuck you. Fuck... *Fuck!*" He kicked off all the blankets, his whole body contorting against another bolt of pain.

Every movement, every groan of misery sent a burst of agony through my chest. I didn't even have the strength to argue with him. To yell back. To tell him just how badly he'd fucked up this time.

Maybe because deep down, I knew I'd fucked up too.

I should have seen this coming. I should've been able to stop him tonight before he got so out of control. I could've made up some bullshit story to get him out of the facility earlier, or... hell, I don't know. Knocked him out with a few hawthorn stakes to the chest. *Something.*

"It hurts," he moaned, tears filling his eyes.

*Fuck.*

"Deep breaths, Saint," I said softly, repositioning the cloth. "In and out."

He tried to do as I asked, but the trembling was so violent, he couldn't maintain steady breathing. Fear clung to him like the blood still blackening his teeth, still streaking his silver hair.

He really was drowning, just like Haley had said.

Her blood had done its job, neutralizing a good deal of the Black he'd ingested from the Dreamers. But now his system was starving for the drugs again, and there was nothing we could do but try to keep him comfortable as he went through his withdrawal.

I'd never seen him in such rough shape. In so much abject pain.

Another spasm gripped him, this one so vicious I had to lay across his body to keep him from flinging himself off the bed.

After an eternity, it finally passed, taking most of his remaining energy with it.

I sat back down and blew out a breath. Maybe now he could just pass out. Sleep. Give his body a chance to start healing.

I dipped the cloth into a bowl of cool water, then used it to wipe the rest of the blood from around his mouth. He was still a mess. Still reeking of death.

His gaze locked on mine, his eyes half-lidded, consciousness fading fast.

"Haley," he whispered.

"Sorry, Saint." I tried to smile. "I'm your nurse tonight. I'm not as cute as she is, perhaps, but I've been working on my bedside manner."

This got a response—something that almost sounded like a laugh. But of course it didn't last.

"Where… where is she?" he pressed.

"She's with Hudson. I promised her I'd take care of you. She needed the break."

"G-good. I don't want her to s-s-see me like… like…" He trailed off and turned away from me, but not before I saw the tears leaking from his eyes.

*Then you shouldn't—*

I stopped the thought from even forming. What the hell was I going to say, anyway? *You shouldn't put yourself in this situation? You shouldn't be addicted to a drug I helped you invent? You shouldn't have been stricken with an illness you can't fucking control and sure as hell didn't ask for?*

"She won't," I said instead. "Hudson won't let her out of his sight."

He nodded.

"Jax?" he whispered.

"Yeah. I'm here." I watched him, waiting for his question, but no more words came.

He was, blissfully, out.

I sat at his bedside for another hour as he fully succumbed to sleep or unconsciousness or some combination of both. Made no difference to me. I was just glad the pain had subsided enough to let him rest.

I needed to stretch. Get a drink. Clear my fucking mind.

I'd just headed out to the kitchen to get some water when an intruder barged into our suite, her mouth pressed into grim line, her traitorous eyes blazing.

Three quick steps and I had the bitch pinned to the wall, my forearm pressed to her throat. "You'd better have a *damn* good reason for showing up here, Gem."

She raised her hands in surrender, but didn't flinch. Didn't look away. "I do."

"Convince me. Five seconds."

"Orders from Keradoc," she choked out. "New intel from the war front."

With my free hand, I hastily patted her down, surprised she wasn't packing. No signature crossbow. No daggers that I could find. I released the pressure on her throat just enough to let her speak, but I wasn't about to turn my back on her.

"New enemies inbound," she wheezed. Then, attempting to clear her throat, "According to Oona, the generals are estimating a couple of weeks at most before the enemy forces reach the wall."

"*What* enemy forces?"

"Sorry. Specifics are above my pay grade. All I know is they're all freaking out, everything's completely fucked, and Keradoc needs us to move up the release date on the new Black. *That's* why I'm here."

The dread in my gut turned to cement. "How soon does he want it?"

"Two days."

"Not happening. We have to start over with the testing—that's *if* we can even find anyone willing to risk volunteering after what happened tonight. Gem, there's no fucking way."

"Keradoc isn't interested in scientific integrity, Jax. He doesn't even care if the shit's pure. He just wants it out on the streets and quickly making its way onto the battlefields."

"Well that's just fucking great." I finally released her. "I've got one man down for the count, and Hudson and I need to do everything we can to get him back on his feet again. Not to mention Haley—she's not going to be able to work until she knows Saint's out of the woods. We need more time, Gem. At least a week, maybe longer."

She reached up to massage her throat, shooting me a dark glare.

*Good. I hope it leaves a fucking bruise, traitor.*

"Figure it out, demon," she hissed. "Keradoc said two days. Nothing more I can do for you."

"Nothing more." I let out a bitter laugh. "Right. Nothing more than stabbing us in the back. Oh, unless you can find another place to stick a dagger, perhaps?" I gestured toward my bedroom across the way, where Saint muttered and twitched in his drug-induced stupor. "Pretty sure he doesn't have an inch of unmarred flesh left on his entire body at this point, inside or out. But hey, don't let that stop you. Clever woman like yourself, I'm sure you can find a way to finish the job, right?"

She glared at me, hands clenching into fists, her body vibrating with a dark rage. But then her gaze shifted over my shoulder, undoubtedly catching a glimpse of Saint, and all the fight leaked from her limbs.

When she met my gaze again, there was only sadness in hers... And fear. I felt it wash over me like a hot desert wind, fierce and all-encompassing.

"Is he… is he going to survive the night?" she asked, her voice suddenly timid.

When I didn't immediately respond, her fear kicked up a few notches.

It made no fucking sense. What the hell was she afraid of? Saint's death? It was her fault he'd been forced into Keradoc's drug dens in the first place. Now she felt bad about it?

Correction. Now she was *pretending* to feel bad about it. Saint may have believed there was more to the story of Gem's betrayal, but I sure as hell didn't.

She'd fucked us. Simple as that. And if she thought I had so much as a *shred* of sympathy for her, she was barking up the wrong fucking demon-tree.

"What's wrong, Gem?" I taunted. "You worried Saint might actually live long enough to finally take his revenge on the woman who set us up for death?"

"Jax, I… It wasn't like that. I didn't…" She closed her eyes and shook her head, cursing under her breath.

"You didn't what? Sell us out?"

In a flash, she lunged for me, swiping the dagger that was strapped to my hip.

She brandished it between us, pointing it right at my chest, but I was beyond fearing her. Beyond caring.

"You didn't lay a trap you knew we'd walk right into?" I continued. "You didn't convince us you were on our side—a friend—then pull the rug out from under us right when we needed you the *most*?"

"It's complicated," she said. "Keradoc—"

"*Keradoc.*" I practically spat out the name. "You can stand behind your warlord protector all you want. But after what you did to us?" I took a step closer. "To Saint?" Another step. "To *Haley*?" I took the final step, ignoring the press of that dagger against my chest as I backed her all the way up against the wall again. "I don't care who you were before all this went down. I don't care why you're doing what you're doing. I don't care that you're a pureblood Midnighter who's got Keradoc and a whole army of fae witches backing you up. You hear me, Gem? I. Don't. Care. So if you feel like you need to shove that blade into my heart? Fine. Do it. But know this. Whether Saint survives the night is irrelevant to you. Because as long as *I* survive? You don't have much time left." Then, in a cold whisper that made her shiver, "I'm coming for you, Gem. *That* is my fucking promise to *you*. And unlike you? I *keep* my word."

Gem shoved me away, but the gesture was just that. A gesture. Empty and useless, just as her friendship had been. With one last glare, she dropped the dagger and said, "Keradoc wants the first shipment packed up and ready to move in two nights. Make it happen."

"Keradoc can go fuck himself, and you're welcome to join him."

Gem's eyes narrowed. "Don't forget who owns you, *demon*."

Unlike her weak excuse for knife play, *that* weapon actually hit the mark.

She was right. Keradoc did own me. For now, anyway. Because if I didn't obey him, Haley would be paying the price.

And that wasn't something I'd *ever* allow to happen.

I blew out a breath. I'd have to get back to the facility first thing tomorrow. Maybe even in a few hours, assuming I could get Saint stabilized enough to leave him. In his absence—and after all the Dream he'd taken tonight—I'd have to work my ass off to pick up the slack. I had to make more. A lot more. Make sure it was packaged up and ready to move, no more incidents. No more fuckups.

The task felt fucking impossible. But if that's what it took to keep Haley safe?

That's what I'd have to do.

"Leave," I ground out, hauling open the door. "Just fucking leave."

Gem opened her mouth—no doubt for one last jab—but then thought better of it, walking away with nothing more than a warning glare.

I slammed the door hard behind her, then returned to my vigil at Saint's bedside.

I pressed a hand to his forehead. His fever was breaking, sweat beading on his skin. His body shook and shivered, his face the color of old milk, limp locks of hair plastered to his pillow.

But he was still breathing.

I squeezed my eye shut as the images from earlier tonight slammed into me, one painful frame at a time. Saint, swallowing all those pills. Going after the Dreamers. Tearing out throats just to get at more blood, more Black, all of it...

And the stench of all that fear. All that gore. All that sudden death.

I shuddered at the memories, once again wishing I could've stopped him. Wondering why I didn't. Hating myself for it all over again.

He slaughtered so many people. Fae. Demons. Humans.

And he'd nearly killed himself in the process.

My insides churned and roiled. Suddenly I felt like I'd swallowed a handful of broken glass and chased it down with boiling oil. But it wasn't fear that held me in its cruel grip now—no way. Fear I could deal with—

squash it before it ever took root. That's how I was made. Forged in hell into a ruthless monster who could outrun the terrors that would bring lesser men to their knees.

This? This was fucking *helplessness.* And as much as I hated myself for not being able to prevent this tragedy, I hated him for making me feel this way at all.

For making me face the truth of how much I truly cared for the bastard.

I opened my eye and glowered at him, ready to give him the same old litany.

"When this is over, I *swear* to you, Saint. I'm—"

"Jax." Saint stirred, muttering something under his breath. I leaned in closer, and suddenly his arm shot out. He gripped my hand in a fierce lock, the tremble in his muscles vibrating straight into my fucking heart, and all my harsh words died away.

The old refrain I'd been threatening him with—*I'm leaving, we're done, fuck off*—it was bullshit. All of it.

I returned his tight grip. Held onto him for dear life.

And said the only words that mattered. The only words I truly meant.

"Fucking survive the night, asshole," I whispered. "You hear me? Fucking *survive.*"

# 6

## HALEY

*H*udson was… a lot.

*So* much.

And tonight? Holy hell, I was *here* for it, so grateful he'd kept his word about not stopping. Not until I told him I was done, and I was *far* from the finish line with this man.

Our connection was undeniable, the magick of our bond sizzling through my veins, lighting me up inside and out. Being with him just felt so natural, so right. So inevitable. With every punishing thrust, he filled me and stretched me and pushed me to the edge in every possible way— with his words, with his kiss, with his body…

*God*, that body.

And I was loving every second of it.

He'd left me exhausted and panting after just one round, yet I still wanted nothing more than to take him deep inside me again. And again. And yeah—spoiler alert!—*again*, until all I could feel, all I could breathe, all I could even *remember* was the way this man made me feel.

Safe. Protected. Cherished.

And absolutely on fire.

"You're amazing," I whispered, my eyes rolling back as he hit me with another deep, punishing thrust. "You feel… God, Hudson. I can't get enough of you."

"Same page, babygirl. Same page." He brought his mouth back to my breast, kissing and licking, sucking my nipple until I cried out from the overwhelming sensations. Then, his beard tickling my chest, he slid his mouth to the other one, teasing me until I was trembling beneath him, begging him for more.

My words spurred him on, driving him to a frenzied pace as he gave me *exactly* what I craved. What I needed. A chance to lose myself in this intense pleasure, safe in a perfect little bubble where nothing could hurt us.

Hudson's lips brushed my ear, his breath ragged as he whispered all the sweet and naughty things that left me gasping and wet, my muscles coiling tight, my body begging for the blissful release I knew was coming.

His wings burst free again, and this time I begged him not to hide them away. I loved his wings, loved how he shivered when I touched them. And with every stroke of his perfect cock, with every kiss of those soft lips, with every commanding touch of his hands on my skin, I lost track of which parts of him were the man and which were the monster. It didn't matter, though. I'd already fallen for him—man, gargoyle, warrior, the whole impossibly strong, incredibly sweet, and absolutely *filthy* package.

He'd said I was his, and that was true. But he was mine, too. And I needed him to understand that.

"You're mine," I whispered, pressing a hand to his cheek. "*Mine.*"

"Haley," he moaned, but whatever he'd meant to say next faded into soft murmurs until eventually the words stopped making sense altogether, both of us swept up in the moment as we brought each other closer and closer to that sweet oblivion.

Hudson shifted on top of me, rearranging my legs until they draped over his shoulders, his cock hitting me even deeper. I gasped at the feel of him, the heat, the intensity as both of us began to unravel. Pinning my wrists to the bed, he bit my shoulder, my neck, stealing the last of my breath with another kiss as he fucked me harder, owning me, absolutely *wrecking* me until…

"Hudson!" Heat exploded between my thighs, the orgasm ravaging my body, consuming me in an inferno so intense it made the room spin. Hudson's grip tightened on my wrists, and he slammed into me one last time. A loud crack was all the warning we had before the bed buckled beneath us and my fearsome gargoyle came inside me, letting loose a wild, feral growl that echoed off the walls and made me shiver.

With a final shudder, Hudson sighed and collapsed on top of me, smothering me with his hot, hard body, his hair falling into my mouth as our chests rose and fell together and our heartbeats answered each other's thundering calls.

A chill swept through the now-broken window, ushering in the sounds of an approaching thunderstorm.

Hudson finally pulled back, and I sucked in a deep breath of cool night air.

He swept the hair from my eyes and kissed the tip of my nose, a wide grin stretching across his face.

"Okay, okay," I teased. "Mission accomplished. Complaints to management officially rescinded."

A quick wink. A soft, slow kiss. And then he put those wings away and rolled onto his hip, just watching me in the moonlight, no more words necessary.

Outside, the storm drew closer, the rain beginning to plink down on the castle rooftop, the air heavy with the electric charge of the not-so-distant lightning. But here in our suite, safe in Hudson's arms, knowing Jax was taking care of Elian, I felt a sense of peace wash through me. A deep knowing that bolstered me despite everything we'd been through tonight. Everything still to come.

This was my family. And this was our home. No, not because I felt drawn to the place. Not because I felt its magick calling to me, the pull growing stronger with each passing day. Both of those things were true, but that's not what made Midnight feel like home.

It was home because I was with *them*. My men. My monsters. My heart. And as long as we were here together, that alone made Midnight a place worth fighting for.

After a quick break to clean up, we returned to our bed, now little more than a mattress on the floor, and snuggled in close. We continued to gaze into each other's eyes, and I trailed my fingertips up and down his arm, tracing the lines and swirls of his tattoos. Every one of them told a story, and even though I wanted to know them, I sensed that he was out of words for now.

So I just settled in and enjoyed the silence. The perfection of a moment that seemed to last forever. Looking into those deep brown eyes, I felt like I was falling into him, like I could lose myself. But I knew without question Hudson would never let that happen. He was there to catch me. To anchor me. To protect me, just like he'd promised.

As the thunder rumbled closer, Hudson's lids began to grow heavy, and so did mine. Certain we couldn't fight off sleep much longer, I finally turned over, and he pulled me in close, his chest warm and solid against my back, his breath hot on my neck as I drifted into serenity.

<hr>

I didn't know how much time had passed from the time I fell asleep in my gargoyle's warm embrace until a shuffling noise pulled me back to consciousness, but it must've been a few hours at least, judging from the stiffness in my muscles. The storm had come and gone, and when I cocked my head to listen, I heard it again—footsteps passing just beyond our room. Seconds later, the door to the bathroom clicked shut.

*Elian.* He was moving slowly, still weakened from his ordeal, but I knew the cadence of his steps like I knew my own.

I held my breath, waiting for the telltale sound of running water—a toilet flushing, a sink running, even a shower—but it never came.

There was only one sound now. Soft and muffled, barely discernible at first.

And when I finally figured out what it was, it tore a hole in my chest big enough for my heart to fall right through.

*Weeping.* Elian was weeping.

*No...*

I pictured him curled up on the floor in a shivering mess, feeling lost and alone and broken as his body rebelled against the loss of the Devil's Dream. In that moment, I didn't care that he'd done it to himself. Didn't care that he'd hurt people—killed them. Didn't care that he'd hurt us too.

Whatever he'd done, whatever had set him on this path of self-destruction, it wasn't all Elian's fault. People succumbed to addiction for all sorts of reasons—some I understood, others I didn't—but that kind of sickness didn't come from a place of peace and contentment. No way.

You don't climb into bed with the devil unless the darkness is already chasing you.

I didn't know what darkness had chased Elian into that bed. I just knew I didn't want him to suffer anymore.

Silent tears spilled down my cheeks, soaking the pillow beneath my head, soaking Hudson's arm. I tried my best not to move, not to wake him, but of course my protector was already awake. Already listening, just like I was.

"He'll be all right, babygirl," he whispered into my hair. "And so will you."

I turned around in his arms, facing him. "I hate that he's so alone. I hate that he's completely falling apart right now, and we're here talking about him, and I've never felt so helpless and—"

"Hey. Hey, listen to me. Shh." He pressed a kiss to my forehead, sweet and soft. Calming. "There are some parts of this we can help him through, and it's gonna take all of us standing by his side to get him through it. But the rest?" Hudson sighed, reaching up to cup my face and wipe my tears with his thumb. "Hell, it breaks my heart to say it, but it's the truth. Some of this stuff Saint's just gonna have to ride out on his own. All we can do is pick him up off the floor when it's over and help him put the pieces back together."

"Will you, though?" I whispered. "Given everything he's done, given the risks he's taking, the risks he's putting us through? Will you still help him put the pieces back together? Even if he breaks again?"

"Again and again and again." He took my hand and pressed it against his heart, right over the tattoo of the skull weeping blood, its mouth full of roses. It was the same tattoo Elian and Jax had, the mark of their oath. "Blood before roses, babygirl," he said adamantly. "You're damn straight I will."

# 7

## KERADOC

*A*n overdose. A fucking overdose on *my* product—the weapon I'd hoped would sufficiently weaken our enemies. The drugs he'd sucked down represented weeks of work, weeks of careful harvesting and preparation, all of it gone in a flash.

According to Gem, he'd also managed to slaughter our test subjects and scare off several other employees who now wanted nothing more to do with the facility if we couldn't keep our hand-picked fugitives in line.

*Fuck.*

I should've seen that particular writing on the wall, but I hadn't. I'd assumed Haley was too important to the man for him to risk disappointing me in such a grave manner. But that was not the case, and now— not only was I down the vampire-fae whose services I still required—but my witch was undoubtedly distracted as well. The demon and gargoyle too, all of them caught up in the swirling vortex of their associate's demise like fragile soap bubbles sucked down the drain.

The only good news to come out of it was proof of the new formula's potency. It'd been enough to drive the vampire-fae to the brink of insanity. Enough to make him turn on the innocent.

I could only hope that even in smaller doses, it would still have a similar effect on the enemy soldiers. And if not? Well. We'd simply have to make more. To utterly flood the market with it until not a single Dark- winter or rebel soldier remained untainted by its deadly allure.

After I'd learned about the accident at the facility and the ensuing recovery efforts, I'd given Haley and her band of infuriating fugitives two nights without interference from me—two nights before I confessed the worst of the news from the war front—and that was merely because I needed time to prepare for my upcoming departure, and I didn't want the witch worrying about what Melantha's rumored arrival might mean for her sisters in Blackmoon Bay.

But as much as I wished I could spare her any further distress, I simply couldn't wait any longer. Melantha and her army wouldn't rest, nor would the Darkwinter fae. I needed to make my move, and I needed the witch's aid.

Without her magick as leverage, it would all be for naught.

Strapping one last dagger to my chest, I headed out of my chambers and down to the suite housing my fugitives. I didn't bother knocking; the demon was working overtime at the facility and the gargoyle was on security detail out in the corpsevine fields. Haley was alone with the vampire-fae, and according to my guards, he'd barely left his sleeping quarters these past two nights.

I found Haley on the balcony, kneeling in a pile of dirt that looked as if it'd been intentionally spilled there. Unlike the night of passion she'd shared with her gargoyle, tonight was dedicated to her craft. On closer inspection, I noticed that the dirt was poured into the shape of a pentagram. Several spellbooks lay open before her, and thirteen flickering black candles encircled her.

The scents of dirt and melted wax drifted to my senses, and I took a moment to watch her from the shadows as she worked her magick, making the candle flames jump and dance at her command. She muttered an incantation, lifted her hands, and every candle extinguished at once. A heartbeat later, the lost flames flickered to life in her outstretched palms, then turned a bright, blazing red.

"It worked!" she exclaimed, her smile as bright as the magick itself. Then, hopping up to her feet, she began dancing in the dirt, laughing and spinning, the magick arcing over her head in a dazzling display.

"Who's the witch?" she sang. "Who's the motherfucking witch?"

A strange warmth buzzed through my chest at the sight, a smile tugging the corners of my mouth. I couldn't help myself; I needed to speak with her. To see the light in her eyes.

I stepped from the shadows, straight into her path.

# 8

## KERADOC

*I*'m going to take a wild guess here and say it's you, Haley Barnes," I announced. "*You're* the—*ahem*—motherfucking witch. Yes?"

She gasped at my sudden intrusion, but that smile refused to dim, even as the magick finally fizzled out.

"Tell me you saw that," she demanded, grabbing my hands and pulling me into a childlike spin. Her eyes shone with pride. With happiness. "Tell me you saw that epicness, Keradoc!"

*Damn it*, her excitement was contagious. Despite everything, I felt myself drawn to it, the proverbial moth to the flame.

Grinning, I ran my thumbs over her knuckles and said, "Yes, I did indeed witness something… quite magickal. It would seem congratulations are in order, though I must admit—I've no idea what feat you've just accomplished."

"No idea? No *idea*? Keradoc, after weeks of failed attempts, I just summoned freaking *fire* spirits with my own blood. Fire sprits! Something that allegedly hasn't been done in Midnight since ancient times!"

"Fire spirits? Well that's… something. I… suppose?"

Stopping our makeshift dance, she rolled her eyes playfully, a soft laugh slipping free. It sounded like the tinkling of bells. Like birds taking flight. Like I imagined flower petals unfurling after a storm would sound, were we able to hear such a thing.

"Right," she teased. "The next time I unlock a new witchy achievement, remind me not to look for praise from a stuffy old fae warlord. You couldn't possibly appreciate the nuances of… Oh." Her eyes widened, and she glanced down at our still-entwined hands, gasping as if she only just realized she'd touched me at all.

She drew back at once, shoving her hands into her pockets and taking a step backward. Her eyes dimmed, that beautiful smile slipping.

*Fuck.*

I'd done that, I realized. My words. My touch. My very presence.

Never before had I so badly wanted to throw myself off some great height.

"Was there something you needed?" she asked, her tone suddenly forced. Awkward. "I mean, is everything okay? How are… things? Haven't seen you since our shopping trip. I figured you were off doing… I don't know. Warlord stuff."

"Yes. Warlord stuff. Keeps me quite busy these days." I didn't tell her that while she hadn't seen me, I'd seen her. I'd seen her kneeling on this very balcony, thighs clamped tight around another man's face as she came on his tongue and cried out for him…

I cleared my throat and turned to look out over the balcony, hoping she hadn't noticed the sudden bulge in my pants. Being so close to her now made my cock fucking *ache.*

An obsession that would only lead to madness, no doubt.

"My associates informed me about what happened at the facility," I said firmly, forcing myself back to the matter at hand. "I wanted to discuss—"

"I know."

"You… know?"

"I know what you're going to say." She blew out a breath, coming to stand beside me at the low stone wall, all that kept us from toppling over. Running her hands along the rock, she said, "I'm sure it sounds bad to you. I mean, it *was* bad. Those people died, and Elian… He isn't… He isn't well. But Jax is covering for him and Hudson's helping out where he can and I'm doing everything in my power to figure out the ritual and—"

"Haley, stop." I glanced down at her, so fierce and fiery in the moonlight, always ready to defend her friends. To fight for them, even if it meant confronting her captor. Despite my best efforts *not* to feel such things, it endeared me to her for reasons I couldn't explain.

"I'm well aware that the demon is picking up the slack where the vampire-fae has failed me," I continued. "That's not why I've come here. I need to speak with you about some new developments with—"

*"Failed* you?" Her eyes turned to cold steel, the last of the warmth evaporating in an instant. "Elian is risking his life for you. All of us are. Yet you've offered no protection, no assistance, not even the most basic information about your so-called strategy. We're soldiers in this war now—all of us. Fighting for *your* home. For you. Yet you treat us like minions, like chess pieces you can just move around the board at your whim. This isn't a game, Keradoc. This is real life. *Our* real life."

"You act as though these men hung the very moons in the sky. But your so-called friends are fugitives of this realm. Fugitives of *mine*. They're fortunate I didn't execute them on sight the moment they were dragged into my throne room. Not only did I spare their lives, I entrusted them with positions of great responsibility. Positions anyone else would've been honored to—"

"Trust and honor? Are you serious right now?" She laughed again, only it was nothing like the sweet music I'd heard earlier. This laugh held nothing but venom and ice, and it took everything in me not to shudder in its wake. "You didn't put Elian in that position to spare his life, or because you trusted or wanted to honor him. You did it because it benefitted you, and if you believe otherwise, then you are truly delusional."

"I'm disappointed in you, Haley Barnes. You call me delusional. You attack *my* character, yet you're ready to go to blows over an addict. A scheming, conniving criminal who would just as soon sell you on the streets for his next fix than—"

"I'm defending my *family*, Keradoc. And I'm not saying Elian is innocent—far from it. But what the hell did you expect? You knew he struggled with the Black—it was obvious the second you flashed that pill bottle the night you gave us these assignments. Yet that's exactly where you put him —ground zero in the drug den. You can't throw a man to the wolves and then blame him when he gets bitten."

"Open your eyes, Haley!" I said, my voice rising. "We're *surrounded* by wolves. And every moment we lose to bickering and petty indulgences is another moment those wolves close in. Another moment we grant them an opportunity to snap their jaws around our throats."

"Wolves. Right. Do you mean literal wolves? See, I have no idea who the enemies really are. Wolves? Raven gryphons? Dark fae? Ghouls? All this talk of war, yet all you do is dress up in your flashy weapons and finery and walk around your castle brooding."

"That is hardly—"

"Right, my bad! You're also fond of drinking alone in your library and waxing poetic over your old diaries. Oh! And let's not forget torturing prisoners and parading your own wounded soldiers through the streets until they drop dead or get trampled or murdered by their comrades." She folded her arms across her chest and narrowed her eyes. "Quite a list of accomplishments, Keradoc. I'm surprised they haven't erected a statue of you in the town square!"

"And I suppose you think you deserve a statue as well?" I shouted, no longer caring whether the guards heard us, whether we awoke the sleeping vampire-fae, whether the whole of Amaranth City gathered around the castle to hear this battle. "Oh, yes. Haley Barnes, ladies and gentlemen. Ever the diligent little witch, playing in the dirt like a child with her charms and potions, no closer to crafting my ritual than she was the night she flounced through my ballroom dressed like a delicate rose freshly plucked from the vine. Why is that? Ah, yes. Because she's been too busy cavorting with criminals and entrancing them into her bed to pleasure her for—"

The crack echoed across the night sky, the sound of it so shockingly unexpected it took me a moment to feel the ensuing sting on my face. To even realize what had happened.

Haley stood before me, her cheeks dark with rage, her hand still outstretched between us, her lips parted in the same shock coursing through *me*.

She'd slapped me. The witch had slapped me.

I was too stunned to do anything but gape at her, the blood simmering in my veins, my heart galloping with the need to grab her, bend her over this wall, and teach her a much-needed lesson about insubordination...

"First of all," she snapped, refusing to back down even in the face of my mounting anger. "I did *not* flounce. I was undercover on a mission for the Dark Goddess, having no idea that she had already betrayed me— obviously. And furthermore, I just summoned the fire spirits—the first step in figuring out how to summon ancestors—and you have the gall to accuse me of playing in the dirt?"

The fire in her tone snapped me out of my momentary stupor.

"Haley, you have been in this castle for weeks, and you're no closer to—"

"I'm not finished. You criticize my methods without knowing jack *shit* about witchcraft, when all I've been doing—all I *keep* doing—is working my ass off for you, never mind the fact that you've got me leashed and neutered like a dog." She curled her fingers into a fist and shoved it in my face, not to assault me this time, but to remind me of the dampener cuff I'd locked around her wrist.

*Moons and stars*, her every word, her every feisty action set my cock ablaze with a deep, clawing need I was ashamed to admit even to myself, the pulse of reckless desire thrumming through me, making me crazy, making me burn, making me utterly *desperate* to put her on her knees, slide my cock between those plump lips, and fuck her mouth until she was *begging* me for more...

"And why am I doing it, Keradoc?" she continued. "Why? Because you demanded it, yes. But there's more to it now. More to all of this. Because some stupid, hopeless, ridiculous part of me actually *wants* to help you. How crazy is that? And now you stand here and judge my choices in *men*?"

"I merely pointed out—"

"You say you're disappointed in us? In me? Fine," she barreled on as if my protests meant nothing. "I'm disappointed in you, too. I'm your so-called secret weapon, yet you've kept me in the dark the entire time. You think taking me shopping for ingredients for *your* damn ritual and giving me a pastry makes us square? No way. You haven't had my back once. Not once."

"If you'll just let me—"

"You avoid me for days, then you show up here—once again dressed in your silks and leathers and blades—just to berate me and my men because we're not meeting your ridiculously impossible standards. Well you know what, warlord? Fuck off." She shoved me with both hands, hard enough to make me stumble a step backward. "Yeah, that's right, I'm telling you to fuck yourself right off the balcony, because you *completely* suck. And if I didn't think we'd all be executed for it, I'd give you a good shove—"

I crashed into her with a savagery so intense, it nearly knocked us both over the wall.

I couldn't hold back another moment. Not when she was so warm and alive, so bright, so damned infuriating, so... *everything*.

One hand gripping her jaw, I sealed my mouth against hers, taking, taking, *taking* the kiss I'd been fantasizing about since our very first kiss in the throne room, ignoring the pummeling of her fists against my chest.

Like so much about my little thief, her resistance was nothing more than a temporary show. The moment I shoved my tongue between her lips, she relaxed into my hold, parting wider for me, her soft moan vibrating into my mouth. I fisted her hair and backed her up against the low stone wall, my cock as hard as my sword as it dug relentlessly into her abdomen.

And oh, how she *burned* for me, grinding her lithe body against me, her tongue fighting mine for dominance, fingers clawing at my buttons and buckles as if to tear them loose and release the monster behind them…

But just as quickly as it had consumed me—consumed us both—the inferno died. Our kiss suddenly broke, and Haley shoved against my chest until I finally relented and set her free.

Panting and disheveled, we glared at each other in the moonlight, dark magick crackling between us, the electric hum of it buzzing in my ears. She felt it too—I was certain. It was written in her eyes, her gaze as furious as it was intrigued.

"Are you quite finished?" I asked, the fresh-berry taste of her lingering, making me dizzy. Drugged.

"Are *you*?" she shot back. "What the hell was *that*?"

"*That* was a mistake." I dragged the back of my hand across my mouth, disgusted with myself for allowing her to so thoroughly distract me. To bewitch me. "One that will *not* happen again."

"You're damn right it won't, asshole. Touch me again without my consent, and I'll steal one of your sparkly, fancy-ass daggers and use it to carve out your fucking tongue." She grinned without warmth, a mouth full of ice and venom once more, then turned to stalk away.

The little thief thought she could escape me, but I wasn't finished with her yet. Not by a long shot.

"I don't think so, witch." I grabbed her arm, spinning her around to face me, my voice rumbling with a deadly warning. "You accuse me of masterminding this war as if it's no more consequential than chess, yet *you're* the one treating this like a game. I've tried to impress upon you the seriousness of our situation time and again. I've spent every night since your arrival planning and strategizing, doing everything in my power to keep my enemies at bay. Enemies that would *take* you in ways so vile I cannot even bring myself to speak the words, then roast you over an open fire and eat you for dinner if I let them get anywhere *near* you. So yes, Haley Barnes, I *have* had your back, and I *respectfully* request that the next time you feel the need to physically assault someone, you channel that rage into your spellcraft where it might actually be useful to me."

My throat burned at my own hypocrisy, but the warning had the desired effect. The first sign of real concern flickered in her eyes, and the smart little mouth I so badly wanted to fuck finally snapped shut.

With a deep sigh, I released her arm.

"Despite what you believe—despite what my actions would indicate," I grudgingly admitted, "I did not come here tonight to berate or judge you."

"No, you came here to shove your tongue down my—"

"I *came* here with news from the southern front. News that requires me to travel to… I need your help with… Something dire has happened in the south, Haley, and I…" I rubbed my jaw, frustration and worry boiling over, melting away my words.

Melantha was invading Midnight. All of us were in grave danger. And Haley was absolutely right—for all my demands and talk of war, I'd done little to prepare her for its actualities.

Now those actualities were rapidly advancing toward my doorstep, and my little thief had no idea what was coming for her.

*Who* was coming for her.

"I need to show you something," I finally said.

Her eyes narrowed. "Another close-up of your dental work? Hard pass, K-Doc."

"Come with me." Ignoring the buzz of magick still sizzling between us —as well as the endless ache throbbing in my balls—I turned and headed for the balcony doors, leaving no room for argument. "It's time I gave you the crash course."

# 9

## HALEY

*Something dire has happened… Time I gave you the crash course…*

He'd just hit me with the mother of all cliffhangers. And that kiss? What in the seriously fucked-up seven hells was that?

*A mistake, girl. Just like he'd said. Snap the fuck out of it.*

I closed my eyes, cursing myself from here to eternity. I never should've allowed him to claim me like that—like some piece of property he could use and bend to his will. I never should've kissed him back, either. And I *definitely* shouldn't be following him now, ensnared by his cryptic words like some sad, clueless little fish on a hook.

But how could I refuse? If Keradoc had something to show me—something that would help me understand what the guys and I were risking our lives for—then yes, I wanted to see it. *Needed* to see it, dignity be damned.

Resigned, I followed him back inside, just as the bastard knew I would.

"I can't go anywhere with you until Hudson's back from the fields," I said. "He should be back in an hour. Elian can't be left alone."

I expected an argument, but Keradoc only nodded. "One of my gargoyles will meet us outside. Dress warmly—there's a chill in the air tonight."

———

My gargoyle wasn't thrilled about the idea of sending me on an unsupervised field trip with our captor, but after promising him I'd keep it short—and make up for my absence in bed later tonight—he reluctantly let me go.

"You've got two hours," I told Keradoc when I finally made my way downstairs. "If I'm not back by then, Hudson will come looking for us, and trust me—you do *not* want a pissed-off gargoyle up your ass."

"I'll have to take your word on that particular warning, having no experience with such things myself." He winked at me, a thin smile twitching his lips as he opened the front door.

Okay, *fine*—I laughed. But only for like, a second. Then I reminded myself he was a complete narcissist *and* a dickhead I wanted nothing more to do with aside from finishing the damn ritual and securing our freedom.

Even if that stupid kiss *had* unleashed a flock of butterflies still twirling around inside me. Clearly, those assholes were drunk. Because there was nothing even *remotely* okay about what Keradoc had done tonight.

Didn't matter that the air still crackled between us as we walked out onto the castle grounds, everything charged up like an impending storm. Didn't matter that he'd made me hotter and wetter with every stroke of his tongue, my thighs still trembling at the memory. Didn't matter that I kept replaying everything about that stupid kiss in my mind—the firm command of his touch, his unrelenting grip in my hair, the way his control had completely unraveled in a blink, the heady rush of his cold-roses scent washing over me, the feel of his lips melting against mine like the darkest chocolate…

I shook my head and dug my fingernails into my palms, dragging myself back to the harsh reality.

*Warlord, girl. Fucking dark fae warlord who may or may not decide to murder you after he gets what he wants…*

The cool Midnight air was a relief on my hot skin, and I sucked it down in big gulps, clearing my head. One of the gargoyle guards was already waiting for us, just like Keradoc had promised.

"Where are we going, exactly?" I asked Keradoc when the guard wrapped his arms around us both. It was the same gargoyle, I realized, who'd tracked me down the night of Elian's disaster at the facility.

The same one who'd shot at us the first night we'd tried to escape.

"To the wall," Keradoc said.

And with that, we were off, the breeze whipping through my hair as we sailed out across the city.

# 10

## HALEY

S oldiers," I gasped, my eyes watering with awe and wonder at the sheer magnitude of Keradoc's forces. "So many of them."

The drawbridge was lowered across the moat, and Keradoc and I looked down from the top of the wall as thousands of troops began their long, slow march into the city.

Fae. Demons. Vampires. Witches, even. Most of them were on foot, but there were several supply wagons pulled by the fae-tamed Mares of Night, their eyes glowing red in the darkness. Standing all the way up here, a cold breeze buffeting me, I couldn't hear the din below, but I could imagine it. The thunk of heavy boots. The creak of the wagon wheels. The soft nickers of the mares.

The moans of the wounded as they limped across, desperately trying not to fall into the moat.

My wonder suddenly turned to disgust as I remembered again what Jax had told me about Keradoc's infamous parades.

"Are you going march *them* through the streets of Amaranth City tonight, too?" I asked, dragging my gaze away from the soldiers to glare at their cruel commander. "Let your vicious Midnight nobles tear them apart until the streets run red with blood and the mourners throw roses at their feet? Or better yet, command your guards to pick them off with flaming arrows as they cross the bridge, taking bets on how fast the ghouls will rise up and devour them?"

Something that looked like regret flickered in his eyes, but then it was gone, his cold demeanor sliding back into place like a shutter slammed over a window.

"The ghouls will not feast tonight, Haley. And these soldiers will not be harmed. Not unless they fall upon the swords of our enemies." He sighed as if he carried the weight of the world on his shoulders. "I've called them back to the city to defend the wall. Some of them will be transferred to the northern border as well, once the Fog of a Thousand Knives recedes."

"To fight the Darkwinter fae," I confirmed. Of course that's why he wouldn't harm them. He needed them alive so they could defend his castle. His home. *Him.*

"They're crossing the Sea of Tranquility in droves," Keradoc said. "An attack is imminent."

"From the north though, right? Why are you also fortifying the wall down here?"

He watched me a beat longer, another sigh slipping from his lips. Then he said, "Come with me."

I followed him to a curve in the wall a bit further down, far enough from the torchlights at the moat crossing that I could see more clearly across the dark obsidian below. The guards in the tower behind us moved away the moment they spotted Keradoc, giving us some privacy.

"Do you see that?" he asked, pointing far out into the distance.

A series of strange starbursts illuminated the night sky, dancing and flickering before quickly fizzling out. It wasn't like the deep red lightning I'd gotten used to seeing here in Midnight, but a pale indigo that reminded me of cheap fireworks—the kind that never quite burst large enough or bright enough, dying in a puff of smoke before they even reached their zenith.

"What is it?" I asked. "Another storm? Starshowers?"

"The southernmost reaches of the realm are home to the Boiling Glass Sands," he said, coming to stand close behind me. "Far, far in the distance. What we're looking at is happening over those lands. A magickal reaction to something dark and unnatural. Something that shouldn't be, but is."

With a gentle hold, he took my hand, lifting it to point to the next burst of light, then the next, as if he could predict where each would appear.

Here on this dark, lonely stretch of the wall, his touch was reassuring. Comforting, even, despite our earlier arguments. And when he leaned in over my shoulder and spoke again, mouth close to my ear, I couldn't help but shiver at the touch of his warm breath on my skin.

*Damn.* Even his scent made my heart flutter now.

Images of our earlier kiss flooded my mind again, but I blinked them away. Fast.

"The guys told me about the desert before we came here," I said, my hand still wrapped in his as another starburst glittered to life. "Too hot to handle, right? No one can cross it."

"That was our belief, yes."

"So what's the issue? What's causing the lights?" I turned around to meet his gaze, and he finally released my hand, searching my face like he was trying to decide how much to tell me.

"We'd always assumed no one—nothing—could survive such an inhospitable landscape," he said. "Only dragons, and we're not even sure they exist anymore."

"There's a but coming," I whispered, the unspoken weight of it squeezing my lungs, making it hard to breathe.

"I'm afraid so." With a sad smile that softened his eyes, he reached up and tucked a lock of hair behind my ear, holding it there against the chilly breeze. His touch was warm and protective, and for a moment I wondered who he saw when he looked at me like that.

His secret weapon? The witch who'd stolen into his castle and tried to steal his blood for an adversary? A prisoner he could bend to his will?

Or did he see me as a woman? One he'd wanted to kiss earlier? One he might want to kiss again?

And, million-dollar-question-of-the-century…

Why the *fuck* was I even thinking about this again?

*Therapy, girl. If you ever get back home again, the first thing you're doing is making that appointment.*

The breeze died down, and Keradoc lowered his hand, weariness seeping back into his gaze.

"Haley, I…, I don't know how to tell you this, other than to just say it. We've received intelligence—confirmed it—that Melantha has broken the banishment spell and returned to Midnight. She hasn't yet manifested in her physical form, but her essence is here, making its way across the desert with the Army of the Dead, a force of nearly indestructible ghouls against which we don't stand a chance. Not with our current numbers."

It took a few seconds for his words to sink in. To rearrange themselves in my mind into something that made sense.

*Melantha.*

*Broken spell.*

*Desert.*

*Army of the Dead.*

*Indestructible ghouls.*

*Don't stand a chance.*

And when those words finally clicked into place, the horror of the images they unleashed stole the last of the breath from my too-tight lungs.

"Melantha!" I gasped. Her vile name echoed through my skull, sending shockwaves of fear reverberating through my body. "But that's… No. How could she break the… And if she's…" I closed my eyes, forcing myself to take a deep breath. Then, glancing up into those enigmatic violet eyes, "Keradoc, if Melantha is here, what does that mean for my sisters?"

That was the most important thing. The thing I still cared about above all else, despite everything that'd happened here. With him. With the magick and wonder of this dark, beautiful, mysterious place.

My sisters.

"I don't know, Haley. I've lost contact with the associates I'd sent to keep tabs on things in Blackmoon Bay. Melantha's arrival is interfering with our travel spells and portals—with *all* of Midnight's magick—in ways we can't even predict, let alone counteract. I've sent two of my best witches to the Bay in hopes they have better luck than their predecessors, but I have no way of knowing whether they've even reached—"

"Luck? *Luck?*" I shoved my hands into my hair, damn near ripping it out of my head. Fear pounded through my veins, making me jittery and wild. "That's not good enough! She knows by now I failed to complete her quest. And you promised me—"

"Melantha's fight isn't with you," he said firmly, as if that would make everything better. "It's with me. She used you because she saw you as a means to her next end against the enemy she *truly* despises. My hope is that she's not interested in your family. That her focus will remain on me and—"

"We're talking about the lives of the three sisters who've only just come back into my life. Sisters I fought and nearly died to protect just to give them a chance at a normal life. Your *hope* isn't good enough for me, and neither are the promises you can't even keep."

"I didn't mean to imply—Haley, wait. Where are you going?"

I tossed up my hands, stalking past him and back toward the drawbridge, wishing I could find a gargoyle to take me out of there. Wishing I could find some way to get back to Blackmoon Bay and leave all this behind me.

But of course Keradoc wouldn't let me leave. He was on me in a flash, his grip tightening around my arm as if I was his pet. His property.

"Let. Me. *Go!*" I raged, already reaching for my dagger. He didn't release his hold, but he didn't stop me from fisting the hilt, from drawing my weapon and pressing the tip to the soft flesh beneath his chin. A tiny drop of blood beaded on the end, but if he felt the sting, he didn't show it.

His grip finally loosened. Then, in a voice so tender and sad it almost unraveled me, he said, "You cannot leave Midnight. Your sisters are beyond your help. Either they're safe, and we've nothing to worry about. Or they're already in danger and you'd merely be walking into the same trap."

"Or worse—I'd be walking into a graveyard, because they're already—"

"Shh." He pressed a fingertip to my lips, his eyes blazing with a sudden fiery resolve. "Don't speak it. Don't even *think* it."

With a resigned sigh, I finally lowered my blade. Killing him wouldn't do any good.

Besides, I didn't want to hurt him. Not really. Maybe that was crazy, but…

No. Scratch that. It was *definitely* crazy.

Still. Crazy didn't mean false. Keradoc had gotten to me. The mystery, the darkness, the magick… I was drawn to him, and I suspected he felt the same way, our strange connection growing stronger every time we crossed paths.

Every time we touched.

"I will do everything in my power to look after your sisters," he said. "But I cannot allow you to return to your realm. Not until your task is done and this war is—"

"No." I sheathed my dagger. "You *won't* allow it. There's a difference."

"Oh, is that so?" He let out a dark chuckle, that fire crackling back to life inside him. "If not for my forbidding it, you'd leave this place without so much as a backward glance? Right this instant? I very much doubt it."

"What part of the word *prisoner* don't you get? You threatened to torture and kill us if we tried to escape. I have no other reason to stay otherwise."

"No?" He stepped closer—impossibly close—and hooked a finger under my chin, forcing me to meet his mesmerizing gaze. "Tell me something, Daughter of Darkwinter. If I were to grant your freedom, no strings attached, would you accept it? Would you truly leave Midnight?"

I opened my mouth. Hesitated.

And in that tiny space of nothingness, Keradoc saw the truth.

One I hadn't even accepted for myself—not until that very moment.

No, I wouldn't leave Midnight. Not when the realm was under threat and I might be able to defend it.

To protect it, this place I was all too quickly—all too strangely—coming to think of as home.

Wordlessly Keradoc released me, turning back to look out across the wall. To look out at the hazy light still flickering in the distance, a warning of what was coming our way.

A warning of what I'd somehow—despite the dangerous impossibility of it all—decided to stand by his side and fight.

# 11

## HALEY

"Melantha and her army will be here in a matter of weeks," Keradoc said. "Perhaps even sooner than that."

"Do you still think we have a chance? Against Darkwinter and Melantha and her army?"

His eyebrow arched at the mention of "we," but he still didn't call me out. Didn't need to. He'd baited the trap, and I'd leaped right into it.

We both knew I was in this for the long haul now, come what may.

Oddly, as much as I'd hated the fact that he'd seen through my facade, it was almost a relief that he knew. That *I* knew.

Yes, I was a prisoner. An unwilling hostage.

But I was also a fighter. A defender. A witch who wouldn't turn her back on the people she cared for, even if one of them *was* a vicious warlord.

Yeah… That therapist? I would *definitely* be putting her kids through college. Probably her grandkids, too.

"Tell me about your experience with the Darkwinter fae," he said.

I joined him at the edge of the wall, crossing my arms over my chest to keep the chill at bay.

"There was a faction of human hunters making waves again, trying to mobilize their forces across the globe to mount a coordinated attack against witches. We couldn't understand how they'd grown so powerful in such a short time, but it turns out they hadn't. Their backers, though… They were the real force behind the madness."

"Darkwinter," he ground out.

"Yep. They got in bed together on a plan to eradicate witches and enslave the rest of the supernatural and human populations. We're talking some epic-level conspiracy shit, too—turning humans against each other, outing supernaturals in communities just to stir up fear and instability, crossbreeding supers to create powerful hybrids with ten times the strength and none of the weaknesses. But it was real—all of it. My sisters and I lived though it."

"And survived."

I nodded, that old word settling around me like a familiar security blanket. "Thanks to countless allies and a whole lot of magick, not the least of which involved my calling on the Dark Goddess, yes. We survived. Took their asses down, burned them to the ground, and fucking lived to tell the tale." I shook my head, a bitter laugh bubbling up. "Kind of hoped I'd seen the last of them."

"You defeated them once before, Haley. I have every confidence you'll do it again."

"That was in my home realm, though. Not in Midnight."

"If it was possible there, it's possible here."

"I'm not so sure about that, Keradoc. You said Darkwinter shouldn't be able to sail the unsailable sea, yet they have. They've outsmarted your soldiers and rebel factions both, slowly tearing their way across your lands. If they were cross-breeding supernaturals in the Bay, imagine what they can do in Midnight? In a place where they can feed off the same dark energy that runs through their veins?"

At my words, my own blood began to stir, buzzing suddenly through my veins as if my latent Darkwinter magick had heard me talking about it and decided to join the party. The faint scent of sulfur tinged the air, a hint of sweetness following.

Keradoc watched me a long moment, his eyes narrowed in silent assessment, and I wondered if he could feel it, too. The darkness. The strange mix of my magick—Darkwinter, Silversbane—mingling with the strange magick of Midnight.

But when he finally spoke again, he said only, "We need more fighters, Haley. That is another reason I brought you here tonight." He nodded back toward the gatehouse, where the bridge was now lifting, sealing us inside the city once more. "These were all the troops the outposts south of the wall could spare, and they're still not enough."

"What about the people?" I asked. "The regular people? Maybe if you leveled with them, they'd—"

"The people of Amaranth City are not soldiers. They're street fighters, Haley. Scoundrels and renegades one and all."

"Doesn't mean they can't fight." I thought of everyone who helped us in the Bay. How we'd all come together—witches, law enforcement, supernaturals—all of us ready to defend our home and the lives of everyone we cared about. "Doesn't mean they *won't* fight, especially if they know what's at stake."

"This isn't Blackmoon Bay. It's not even Earth. It's Midnight. A brutal, terrible realm built from the blood and bones of all who've been cursed with the pleasure of calling it home." He dropped his gaze and shook his head, dark hair falling into his eyes, shielding them from my view. "They won't fight for us, Haley. Not against a faceless goddess commanding legions of skeletons and ghouls who rise just as soon as they're slain. Not even against Darkwinter."

"So what's your plan, then? Wander the realm and see if you can round up a few monsters, recruit them to the cause?"

"Something like that, yes."

"Something like that," I echoed, air-quoting the words, "is not a strategy. And if there's anything I've learned about you in my weeks of captivity, it's that you always have a strategy. Some plan you're cooking up, ten steps ahead of everyone else."

He arched a delicate eyebrow, a hint of laughter shining in his eyes. "Is that what you've learned?"

"Well, that and how to summon fire spirits, an accomplishment we've already established can't impress you."

"Everything about you impresses me, little thief."

His words sent another jolt skittering through my veins—one that had nothing to do with my Darkwinter magick. But before the moment turned any more awkward, he glanced back out across the wall and said, "Many years ago—centuries, actually—several members of a prominent family of noble fae were slaughtered in Amaranth City. It was a coordinated attack, a betrayal by the very gargoyles hired to protect them."

I swallowed hard, picturing the gargoyles that had attacked us the night Hudson and I had tried to escape. They were formidable fighters, just like Hudson himself was. That night, they'd only been trying to stop us, but it wasn't hard to imagine what it would be like to be on the receiving end of a gargoyle murder spree.

Goosebumps rose along my arms, and I rubbed them to no avail.

Keradoc shook off his cloak, the movement shifting his shirt and revealing a stretch of bare torso, the skin puckered with scars. I'd gotten a glimpse of them before—a stolen glance into his room as he was dressing for our trip to the marketplace—yet the sight of them still stole my breath, making my chest tight.

Those scars told me he'd been bitten. Mangled. And the ones I couldn't see now, the ones that'd left their vicious marks across his entire back and both arms, told other stories. The stories of a fae who'd been burned and whipped. Shot by arrows or bullets or both. Tortured.

Another chill rattled my spine, and Keradoc draped his cloak over my shoulders, immediately chasing away the shivers. I wanted to refuse it, but it was so warm and soft, his body heat still clinging to the fur lining, the scent of sweet roses lingering.

"The remaining family members retreated into the Razorback Mountains," he continued. "And there, they carved out a new home, a new life, a brutally bleak existence in an inhospitable land that would drive lesser men to their graves. And all the while, they sharpened their grief like swords, using it to drive them to become stronger, more vicious, more bloodthirsty than those who'd murdered their kin."

"So they could avenge them?" I asked, completely captivated by the gruesome tale.

"That was the assumption, yes. But the retaliation never came. Now, all this time later, we know very little about them. We know they're still there —generation after generation—still living their bleak existence. Through their own fae magicks, they learned how to domesticate some of the raven gryphons, among other deadly creatures. And while it's said they rarely venture outside the boundaries of their mountainous home and the Hanging Lake where the gryphons dwell, it is *also* said the most feral, most fearsome among them can be bought."

His words were nearly a whisper now, an appropriately ghoulish end to a tale that bordered on urban legend. But I knew from the dark look in his eyes, from the severe line of his mouth that this story was one hundred percent true.

And all at once, Keradoc's plan became clear.

"I see," I said, a new chill seeping into my bones despite the warmth of his cloak. "And what's the current market value on a merc army of pissed-off, vengeful fae?"

"They have a price, just as we do."

"How much? A million? Ten? A billion?"

"They're not interested in money, Haley. Only in something that's eluded them for all these years—the one thing that for all their strength and cunning they've never been able to control or possess." He placed his hands on my shoulders, his violet eyes boring into mine so deeply, I just *knew* what the price would be.

And I knew, with that same cold certainty, who was expected to pay it.

"Magick," I whispered. "Not fae, but darker. *My* magick."

Keradoc nodded solemnly.

"But… What for? You said it yourself—they're feral. They can control those monstrous raven gryphons, for fuck's sake. Why would my magick possibly interest them?"

"Four children were slaughtered that day in Amaranth City," he said grimly. "The purest heirs of their bloodline. Their bodies were repaired by witch healers, and to this day they are kept in a state of suspended animation with intricate spells and rituals. They are physically alive, yet they do not age. Do not speak or move. And worse, they are soulless."

Nausea spun through my gut as the realization dawned.

"Necromancy," I whispered, the very word sending an icy tendril of dread down my spine. "You're talking about necromancy."

# 12

## HALEY

*B*ut you have necromancers in your employ!" I said, desperate to find a way out of this. "You said as much the night of the feast. You don't need me for that."

"None of my necromancers are skilled enough to resurrect fae children felled by their own protectors."

"But… why does the cause of death make a difference?"

"Gargoyle mythology is steeped in its own magick, Haley. When a protector breaks his bond and commits such a heinous act, it leaves behind a darkness that not even the strongest fae witches can overcome."

"And you think *I* can overcome it?"

"You haven't even *begun* to taste your true power. To imagine your full potential." Heat blazed in his eyes, and an answering ember sparked to life inside me. "So yes, I do think you can overcome it. But I—"

"Keradoc. Necromancy is…" I blew out a breath, turning away from his intense gaze. "Look, I've… I've dabbled, okay? But I've never actually brought a soul back from the Shadowlands. And I don't even know how that would work with a fae, let alone a noble Midnight fae *child* cursed by some bad-gargoyle mojo. This is just… It's beyond. It's… No. It can't be done."

"*But,*" he repeated firmly, "if you'll kindly let me finish, I would tell you that it doesn't *have* to be done. Even the possibility that it *could* be accomplished would be enough to win their favor. If they merely *believed* you could bring their loved ones back, we could use that as a bargaining chip to—"

"Great. Now you're talking about manipulating them. People whose ancestors—whose ancestors' children—were slaughtered in *your* city."

"Before my time, I assure you."

"That doesn't matter! It's wrong! God, this is so many completely fucked-up shades of wrong there isn't even a word for it."

"You have the audacity to judge?" He laughed, as cold and bitter as the wind kicking up behind us. "Look me in the eyes and tell me that everything you did in Blackmoon Bay to defeat the hunters and the Darkwinter fae, to save your home, to protect your sisters... Look me in the eyes and tell me it was morally just. That you took the high road *every* time, even when your enemies had sunk so low you could scarcely contemplate the depths of their depravity. And if you can do that, if you can truly convince me, then and only then will I allow you to condemn me for suggesting something so many completely fucked-up shades of wrong there isn't even a word for it."

I blew out a ragged breath, wishing so badly I could tell him off. Tell him he didn't know me, didn't know what I'd done. That I could *never* do what he was suggesting, not even to save the people I loved.

But I couldn't tell him those things, because they simply weren't true.

And once again, my silence was my answer.

Keradoc shook his head, scoffing. "Morals. Nothing but pretty jewels afforded by the privileged few whose safe, perfect lives are kept that way because there are still those of us willing to bathe in blood. And we do it for them again and again. Gladly. Because deep down, *we* know the truth —a truth discovered from living a life that was forced upon us rather than a life we bought." He took a step closer and backed me up against the wall, caging me against it with his arms, his gaze sweeping down to my mouth, then back up to my eyes. In a deep, deadly-calm voice that rolled across my skin like water, he said, "When Death knocks upon the door, Haley Barnes, morals are the first thing we offer to trade for just one more precious heartbeat, one more precious breath. And you of all people cannot tell me otherwise, for I *know* you've stood at the threshold and made that very bargain yourself."

My heart slammed against my ribs like a fist trying to punch free. His words stripped me bare, left me exposed, turned me inside out until every last one of my nerves burned with an unquenchable fire that can only come when someone truly sees you—the darkness, the blackness, the worst of the worst—and doesn't turn away.

I lifted my hand to his face, wanting so badly—so inexplicably—to touch him. To feel his skin against mine, to feel our connection and know without any more words or arguments that it was real. That it was unbreakable, even in a place as twisted and corrupt as Midnight.

Even if *we* were twisted and corrupt ourselves.

But the moment my palm skimmed along his jaw, he hissed, jerking his head away from my touch.

My heart faltered. "Keradoc, I... I'm sorry. I didn't mean to—"

He grabbed my wrist, yanking me close once more. The wind screamed against me from behind, blowing my hair into his face, into his mouth, but still he didn't release me. Didn't drop his penetrating violet gaze, a new rage burning in his eyes, his grip almost painfully tight.

For a minute I worried he might try to steal another kiss.

Or worse... that he wouldn't.

But before I could talk myself out of those dangerous thoughts, he brought my wrist to his chest and shoved a tiny silver key into the lock on the dampener cuff. The metal burned hot for an instant, shining the same bright gold as his magick, then fell away, the heavy iron hitting the ground with a clink.

"What... what are you doing?" I breathed, my voice swallowed by the wind, by the intensity of the moment, by his very presence.

"It was never my intention to dim your fire, little thief." Keradoc offered a sad smile, all that fire and fury receding in a blink. "Only to save myself from being hurt by it. But it seems I've failed in both endeavors."

*Failed? What is he talking about?*

"How could I possibly be a threat to you?" I asked. "How could I hurt you?"

He shook his head, a soft laugh slipping free, and suddenly I felt like the dumbest woman in the realm.

"Keradoc, it isn't—"

He pressed his thumb to my lips, sending another spark of awareness straight to my core, where it inconveniently smoldered for him all over again.

"You have a choice to make," he said softly. "And all I ask is that you give it due consideration before making it."

"What choice?"

"Accompany me on the journey to the Razorback Mountains to bargain with the feral fae who dwell there. Or remain behind the wall, continuing to practice your summoning spells. Regardless of what happens with the nobles, I'm still counting on you to devise that ritual against the Dark-winter forces."

"You… You're really giving me a choice in this?"

"For what it's worth, yes. I am. But I think we both know the truth." He brushed his fingertips along my cheekbone, the soft touch making me gasp. When he drew his hand back, his fingers curled around the stem of a single black rose, the bud closed tight. "You've already made your choice."

I took the flower and brought it to my nose, closing my eyes and inhaling its scent. It was sweeter than the red roses of home, with a lingering spiciness that reminded me of the magick here. The darkness.

And it called to that thing inside me, that wild, unnamed buzzing, the potent mix of my blood and magick—the blood and magick of all who came before me—and I knew he was right. I wouldn't turn my back on him. Wouldn't turn my back on Midnight. On its people.

*My people,* a distant voice echoed.

And in my grasp, the black rose unfurled to a lush, full bloom.

Then the wind tore it from my grasp, scattering the petals across the dark sky.

"Thank you for hearing me out, Haley," Keradoc said. Leaning in close, he brushed a chaste kiss to my cheek that left me aching for more of him— for more of the dark, delicious things I had no business wanting.

Not from our captor. Our warlord. Our mystery that deepened with every passing hour I spent in his unnerving presence.

He glanced away and lifted his hand, signaling to the gargoyle who'd flown us here.

It was time to return. To tell the guys about what I'd learned. About what I knew in my heart must be done.

"Take her back to the castle," he commanded, and the gargoyle saluted in response.

"What about you?" I asked. "You're not coming?"

"I need to meet with the tower guards and prepare them for the new arrivals. I'll see you back home later though to continue our conversation."

*Back home.*

I nodded, a faint smile touching my lips, and then Keradoc was gone, heading off in search of the tower guards.

I watched until he reached the top of the gatehouse, then descended what I assumed were stairs that led to the bottom. Taking a deep breath, I took a few more minutes to gather my thoughts, gazing out across the black lands of Midnight. The flickering lights over the desert had finally dissipated, and I wondered whether that meant Melantha's forces had stopped for the night.

Whatever it was, though, I knew it was just a temporary pause. Keradoc was right—Melantha was coming. I could *feel* it.

And I would be right here waiting for her arrival, more than ready to roll out the red carpet for that traitorous bitch.

With a surge of determination and a newfound sense of purpose, I turned to the guard and let him know I was ready to go back to the castle. To my guys and the undoubtedly long night of conversations ahead.

The gargoyle nodded and reached for me, but in his dark eyes I saw the glint of something malicious.

My instincts prickled, and I took a step backward, trying to shake off his hold. "On second thought, maybe I'll just wait for Ker—"

"No take-backs, witch." Tightening the already uncomfortable embrace, he jerked me against his chest and leaped over the wall, sailing away from Amaranth City.

Out of the darkness, two more gargoyles appeared at our sides, the trio zooming me out across the moat. On the far edge, I caught sight of a shepherd's wagon drawn by two mares, the whole rig facing away from the crossing, as if waiting to return to the wilds of Midnight.

Waiting for cargo.

*Witch* cargo, to be precise.

Even before the two fae riders came into view atop the mares, I knew what was happening. These psycho gargoyles and their fae accomplices were planning to kidnap me.

I struggled in midair, my arms mostly pinned to my sides, my fingers reaching for the hilt of my dagger, stretching… just a little farther, and…

*Got it.*

Hudson had once told me a gargoyle's only weak spot was the throat—a soft bit of flesh just begging for a well-aimed arrow. I didn't have that, and his throat was too far away to reach with my dagger.

But I did have magick—unconstrained, now that Keradoc had uncuffed me—and just enough wiggle room to draw blood.

I nicked my thumb with the blade and whispered a quick attack spell, hoping like hell my aim was true.

A blast of red light exploded from my palms, slamming into his throat and sending him reeling.

A howl of pain pierced the night sky, the gargoyle spinning through the air as he tried in vain to hold on to me. His grip loosened, and I kicked and fought as hard as I could, jabbing my blade up into his belly.

It wasn't enough to slice through the thick hide—just enough to make him recoil.

To make him drop me.

There was no time to brace for impact. I slammed into the ground with a thud, my right side taking the brunt of the hit, the force of it knocking the wind right out of me and sending my dagger skittering out of reach. Stars danced before my eyes, my mouth filling with the hot tang of blood from whatever I'd bitten inside. Tongue? Lips? Cheek? No fucking idea. Everything was throbbing and spinning, my head clanging like a bell, a thousand times worse than a Devil's Dream hangover.

It took me a minute to scramble to my feet and catch my breath. To find my dagger. To blink the stars and dirt from my eyes. To finally get my bearings and figure out where the hell I'd landed.

And holy fuck-me-in-the-ass-with-a-broomstick, I should've just taken my chances with the kidnappers.

Because now, instead of being hauled off in a wagon, tortured, and held for ransom—a predicament I *might've* actually survived—I was bleeding at the bottom of Beggar's fucking Moat.

# 13

## HALEY

There was no time to make an escape plan before the low rumble vibrated up through my legs, the sound so unnatural it made the hairs on the back of my neck stand on end. I whipped my head around in search of a way out—a ladder, a handhold—but the dirt walls of the trench were too soft and too steep.

"Damn it!" I shouted, frustration and pain colliding in my chest. My ribs were definitely cracked, my shoulder dislocated, and my knee was completely jacked up, too. "Fucking gargoyle *assholes*!"

But I could scream all I wanted. They weren't swooping down to rescue me—just turning tail and zooming back over the wall, back to the relative safety of the city. The fae riders with the wagon had taken off too, everyone fleeing the scene the minute their well-laid plans imploded.

Dead witches commanded no ransom.

Another deep rumble echoed from the bowels of Midnight, and suddenly the ground cracked open, a deep, black fissure that tore straight down the center of the trench, as far as the eye could see.

I leaped out of the way of the gaping maw, slamming my back against the trench's outer wall.

Dirt rained down into my eyes and mouth. I hacked out a painful cough.

Adrenaline flooded my system, my pain momentarily forgotten as every one of my senses sharpened.

I knew what these ghouls did to their prey, and I was *not* going out like that.

Keeping my back pressed against the dirt wall, I brandished my dagger, peering into the dark fissure as my heart slammed against my wounded ribs.

The air was thick and heavy, and all around me, the world just… stopped.

Soundless.

Breathless.

Not even a breeze.

Tears streamed down my cheeks, my heart nearly bursting from the agony of waiting. I was standing on the very edge of death, and suddenly I thought of Keradoc and his stupid violet eyes and his smug certainty… and I knew he was right. Knew I'd trade away every last moral, every good little bone in my body for one more chance. One more day. One more hour.

One more *minute* to see my men, to say goodbye, to set things right…

To look into the silver eyes of the fae I still loved so deeply…

*Elian*, I breathed. *God, I'm so sorry…*

But there *was* no fucking chance. No one here to offer me a trade.

In this, I was alone. I would fight alone, and I would probably die alone, and in the end there'd be nothing left of my body to bury or mourn or even remember.

"What are you waiting for?" I screamed, smearing away my tears with the back of my wrist. "Rise up, you fuckers! *Rise!*"

As if answering my command, a deep, terrifying howl exploded out of the trench, chilling my blood and paralyzing me where I stood.

And then, no more than sixty feet away, they began to emerge.

I watched in horror as mottled gray bones bloomed from the gash like weeds—fingers. Skulls. Spines and ribs. As bare skeletons they rose, a hint of translucent flesh filling in the dark hollows as they shambled out of their eternal tombs.

I thought I was prepared. I thought I would at least put up a good fight, maybe knock off a few heads, even if I was ultimately destined to end up as dinner.

But this…

*Oh my god.*

The sight. The stench. The ancient rot and ruin clinging to creatures that should've died and disintegrated long ago—creatures that shouldn't even exist…

No. It was too cruel a fate, too monstrous for my mind to even process.

Time slowed to a crawl.

My body began to shut down, as if it had already decided we didn't stand a chance against this abomination and noped the hell out. Adrenaline faded from my limbs, the pain of my injuries rushing back to me in a hot, sickly wave that left my legs shaking and my stomach roiling. My chin dropped to my chest, my head suddenly too heavy to hold upright. Blood spilled from my mouth, splashing onto the broken earth as the ghouls continued to rise, rise, rise in the distance, skulls swiveling on bent necks, their ghastly nose holes sniffing the air, finally catching the scent of their new prey.

All at once they turned to me.

And the sound…

A thousand undead monsters squealed into the night—my final warning before they charged.

That terrible, ear-splitting, gut-wrenching sound skittered up my spine and grabbed me by the throat, shaking me out of my stupor.

Fuck. *Fuck*!

I gripped my dagger, but what the fuck would that do against the undead?

I needed something… magick. A spell.

My mind raced as the ghouls closed in, their feet not even touching the ground.

*Fifty feet. Forty. Thirty.*

They'd swarm me, just like the hybrids in that prison compound beneath the Olympic National Forest back home—the place where I'd first petitioned the Dark Goddess to help me fight.

That was it. That's what I needed.

*Twenty feet.*

The spell came back to me in a rush. I wouldn't dare call on Melantha again, but a quick change of the last verse should do the trick…

*Ten feet, and…*

I sliced my palm, clenched my bloody fist, and with a feral cry that ripped through my lungs, I cast my magick out into the darkness.

> *Blood of hell, blood of night*
> *I call on the darkness to show us the light*
> *May evil and malice and violence intended*
> *Return to its hosts uprooted, upended*
> *Magick of Midnight, hear now my plea*

*Grant me this power, and so mote it be*

The ghouls surrounded me, leaped on me, *smothered* me as they dragged me to the ground. I flipped onto my stomach and tried to cover my head, but they were relentless. Jagged finger bones tore at my scalp, yanking chunks of hair from my head. I felt the first piercing sting of skin tearing along the back of my neck, then down between my shoulder blades as sharp claws shredded Keradoc's cloak and my shirt, scoring the tender flesh beneath. Teeth snapped hard around my shoulder, more around my thigh, and I cried out as the pain exploded through my arms and legs.

They dragged me on my belly toward that great maw in the ground, the abyss, the end.

Kicking and flailing, I struggled against the onslaught, shaking one loose, then another, but there were too many of them, too demanding, too hungry, and now they were all around me, flipping me onto my back once more, teeth snapping at my neck, claws spilling my blood into the earth, and then...

A surge of blinding red light exploded from my palms, blasting them away and shattering the skeletons into piles of loose bones.

But just as quickly as they'd come apart, the bones were reassembling, ghouls rising once again.

Choking down a few deep breaths, I scrambled back up to my feet and commanded the magick to form a shield around me, sealing me off from their next attack.

Only... the attack never came. The ghouls went as still as statues, staring at me with vacant black holes for eyes, as if someone had flipped a master switch and put them all in sleep mode.

But they weren't sleeping. I knew it in my gut.

They were merely waiting.

*Shit. Shit, shit, shit!*

My spell wouldn't hold much longer. I could already feel it weakening, my body too banged up to handle the strain as the magick sucked away my energy.

The shield flickered. Flickered again.

My muscles quaked, blood running from a dozen gaping wounds. I was beaten and broken. Wasted. And I couldn't hold out for another second.

With a desperate cry, I dropped to my knees. The magick shield vanished. Blood ran down my face, my chest, my fingers. It soaked the dirt, so much of it I wondered how the hell I was still alive.

The ground trembled once more, making my vision blur.

There, before my weary eyes, a riot of black roses burst from the fissure, filling the air with their sweet, spicy scent.

My head spun.

And without a sound, the skeletons dropped to their knees, bowed their terrifying gray heads, and vanished.

# 14

## HUDSON

*I* ain't never flown so fast in my entire fucking life.

One minute I was hanging out with Saint in the common room, cracking two beers open to celebrate his return to consciousness.

And then I felt it. The bond, jackhammering a dire warning at the base of my skull that my girl was in deep shit.

I sucked in a breath, and then it came again. The call. The urgency.

Her fear lanced my heart like a blade.

I didn't even bother telling Saint what I'd felt. Where the fuck I was going. Just dropped that beer and took off at a run, crashing through the balcony doors and soaring out into the night.

Now, I was picking up the signature of her magick right alongside the unmistakable burn of that fear, but it was coming from outside the wall.

*Sonofabitch*, I knew I never should've let her leave with Keradoc tonight.

Fucking hell.

I tucked my wings in close and dove right over that fucking wall, following the insistent tug of our bond as it grew stronger, so strong my skull felt like it was about to burst.

Right over Beggar's Moat.

No. No fuckin' way was she in there. It just wasn't possible…

The sight unfolding below was so fucked up I almost didn't believe it was real. Like maybe it was some dark fae mojo making me hallucinate. I

447

blinked rapidly, my eyes adjusting to the dark shapes… ghouls converging on their latest victim… a flash of dark hair splayed in the dirt… the bright burst of red magick.

Magick that could only belong to Haley.

Tucking my wings close, I torpedoed down toward that moat so fast, everything else became a smudge in my peripheral vision, the wind a dull roar in my ears as I pushed harder and faster, desperate to reach her before—

The magick. It vanished. It fucking vanished and my girl dropped to her knees.

*Fuck, Haley. Don't you give up now! Don't you fucking dare…*

I was so close… so fucking close, and then…

Her beautiful black roses exploded across the ground, and every last ghoul in the moat dropped to its knees and bowed.

And then they were gone.

A heartbeat later, she was finally within reach. I didn't think, didn't even draw a breath. Just snatched her right out of that pit like I was snatching her from the jaws of hell, because that's exactly what it was.

Hell.

And she'd survived it. My girl had fucking survived.

As gently as I could, I laid her on the ground just beyond the trench, skimming my hands over her arms and legs, searching for wounds. She was conscious, but she was in bad shape. Broken bones for sure, probably a concussion, but the blood loss was my immediate concern. I did my best with the shredded clothing still clinging to her body, tearing off a few strips for makeshift bandages.

"Tell me what happened," I said as I worked. There was no way I'd be able to follow the story—my mind was singularly focused on patching her up, stabilizing her enough to get her back to the castle, where hopefully Saint would have the strength to heal her with his vampire blood. But I needed to keep her talking. Conscious. Needed to know she was still fucking with me.

"Keradoc… Keradoc's guard," she managed, her voice cracking. "The gargoyle and… two fae. From the…" She gasped in pain as I wrapped her ankle, the sound of it fucking gutting me. "From the castle. I recognized… trying to…. take me…" She was panting now, her pupils dilated, her face covered in sweat and grime and blood.

*Fuck*, I needed to get her home. Now.

"Keep talking, babygirl," I said, sliding my arms beneath her. "I need to pick you up, and it might hurt a little, so be brave for me and—"

"Hudson!" she gasped, her eyes going wide with some new fear. "Incoming!"

I whipped my head around just in time to see them—three gargoyles swooping in for the kill.

One I recognized as Keradoc's man.

The other two were my dear old friends, Mad Marco and Draven. No Garrison tonight, but that was fine by me. I'd hunt him down eventually. Obliterate him just like I was about to obliterate these three fuckstains.

I didn't care *who* they worked for now. Keradoc, some other fae nobles, some secret Stone City faction, the fucking all-powerful devil himself... Didn't matter.

They were *all* going down.

I made sure Haley had a strong grip on that dagger—strong as she could manage, anyway.

"Sorry, babygirl." I cupped her face. "I'll do my best to keep 'em away, but you might have to defend yourself. You good?"

"Magick, or... aim for the... the throat," she managed, a weak smile lighting up her grim face.

"That's my girl." One more second to look at her, and then I was gone, shooting up into the air and crashing into Draven like a damn missile.

We rolled and spun and smashed back down to the ground with a crash that tore up the black earth. I gave him no time to react—just pounded him, smashing my elbow into his nose, slashing at his throat with my talons, but it wasn't enough.

The other two gargoyles touched down, Keradoc's man wobbling on his feet, clutching his throat. His hide was charred with the remnants of magick, and I knew right then my girl must've nailed him good. He was still suffering from the aftereffects, which was a relief.

No wonder he brought backup.

A faint red glow flickered to life behind me. Good—Haley still had some juice left. Wouldn't last long, given her condition, but I'd make it work. Had to, or she'd be easy fucking prey.

A swift punch to the face snapped my head back. I'd been distracted, and fucking Draven finally got in a shot. Now, the motherfucker grinned up at me, blood staining his teeth and spilling down his chest.

Through the telepathic bond that connected us, he taunted, *Your little witch is even hotter when she's bleeding.*

*Wonder what she sounds like when she screams,* Marco chimed in. I turned to see him and the other bastard circling Haley's shield, waiting for a break.

Waiting for *her* to break.

"Guess we'll know soon enough, eh?" Draven again, this time speaking the words out loud, his eyes filling with lust. "I can't wait to stuff that tight little ass full of my—"

I don't know if he ever finished that thought. Don't know if he said the final word and I just didn't hear it.

All I knew was now I had him pinned to the ground, groaning and writhing under my weight like a little bitch, one of my hands wrapped around his throat, the other tearing out the wet, bloody meat that used to be his tongue.

The sound he made... God *damn*.

I leaned in close, grinning ear to ear as I inhaled the scent of his blood. "Guess we know what it sounds like when *you* scream, Draven. And fucking hell, it's enough to drive a man insane."

I shoved the loose tongue right back into his mouth, choking him with it.

Haley's magick was fading behind me, Marco and Keradoc's other gargoyle looming closer, their filthy, vile thoughts invading my mind. They didn't seem to care that I was slice-and-dicing their pal.

They only cared that—in a matter of minutes—they'd have their hands on my girl.

Channeling a strength I didn't know I possessed, I slashed open Draven's face, tearing the thick hide right off the bone. I rose to my full height, dragging his mutilated body up with me, then slamming him right down onto his knees. With a swift kick to the back, I sent him sprawling face-first into the dirt.

Haley gasped, her magick finally sputtering out, Marco's evil taunts echoing through my skull.

*She's going to choke on my cock...*

Pure, white-hot fury boiled up from deep inside me, a violent nuclear explosion that could only be quenched with one final, desperate move.

It was a thing unheard of among the gargoyles—an act so foul, so profane, we didn't even commit it against our worst enemies.

Doing it would mean turning my back on the last of my kin, on all the ancestors that had lived and died before me. It meant tarnishing my name in this life and the next. It meant severing all ties with everything I'd ever known.

It meant I could no longer claim the status of protector. Of guardian.

It meant I couldn't even call myself a gargoyle anymore.

But what the fuck kind of protector and guardian would I be—what kind of gargoyle—if I let my bonded mate come to harm?

No. I was beyond honoring some ancient bullshit creed.

I was here. Now. And I would protect the woman I loved with everything I had—with everything I was.

Draven lay twitching before me, face down in the dirt.

Without another thought, I pounced on him.

And with trembling hands, I gripped his wings—the one thing more than any other that made him who he was—and ripped them from his back.

Blood sprayed from the wounds, and Draven cried out once more in agony, knowing that whether he lived or died in this moment, his life was over either way.

But he wasn't going to live. No fucking way.

The other two gargoyles finally fell silent, their shock reverberating through me like an electrical current. It was one thing for them to stand by and let their man get his ass whooped. Killed, even, if they were in the mood for a little bloodshed. It's not like mercs had any true loyalty to one another.

But this?

I'd just committed the *ultimate* sin.

And I wasn't even done yet.

My hands slid through the bloody mess of his back, and I grabbed his head and bashed it against the ground, again and again and again, until I heard the crack of bone and felt his brains slipping out between my fingers.

Slowly, I got to my feet and gathered up his body parts—headless torso, pieces of broken skull, and those precious wings—and tossed them into the fucking moat.

The ghouls rose again. And this time, they didn't bow. Didn't vanish.

They fucking *consumed*.

Turning on my heel, I took a deep breath and locked eyes with Mad Marco, his mouth hanging open in utter disbelief, that gap-toothed fucking maw just begging for my fist.

*You're next*, I warned. *Any last words?*

But before I'd even taken another step, Marco was in flight, Keradoc's bitch-ass gargoyle right behind him.

I watched them vanish into the night sky. Cursed them for it, making a silent vow to end this, one way or another.

"Gargs?" Haley's soft voice filtered through the mess of my thoughts, and I turned my attention away from the skies and back to the ground. To her. "I think I… I think I need…"

She was on the ground, clutching a gaping wound in her side.

Blood spilled out from between her fingers. Her face was the color of the first moon.

Only my fear for her life could quiet the rage inside me. As I knelt down beside her, that shit went stone-cold silent.

"It's bad, right?" she muttered, barely forcing a smile. "You look like you just saw a ghost. I really… I really hope I'm not dead. I didn't get to tell you—"

"Don't talk, Haley." With bloodstained hands, I lifted her up, cradling her against my chest, hoping like hell she couldn't hear the terror thundering through my heart. "I got you."

She met my eyes for a second—just a second—and smiled, real and true. And that smile was like the sun rising in a place that had never even seen such light. *This* fucking place. And then it was gone. Her eyes rolled back into her head, and she went as limp as a rag doll in my arms, blood spilling out of so many wounds I was afraid she was more holes than solid parts.

*Fuck.*

"Hold on, babygirl. You fucking hold on, hear me?"

---

"Hudson, there you are. Where the…" Saint's words fucking died as I marched in through the broken doors and he took in the sight of us.

Me.

Haley.

All that fucking blood.

He met my gaze, his own wide.

The look in his silver eyes just then… Hell. I didn't know if it made me want to break something or just break, period. I was pretty damn close to doing both, and if she wasn't in my arms in that moment, I was pretty damn sure I woulda smashed everything in my path as readily as I'd smashed Draven's skull into the dirt.

I carried her into my bedroom—the one we'd been sleeping in since we took her bed out of commission. I set her down as if she were made of glass, because right then, that's what it felt like. Like she was fragile. Like she'd been shattered.

"What... what the fuck?" Saint gasped, trailing on my heels. "What the fuck happened?"

I turned around and wrapped a hand around his throat—put him right up against the wall. And finally—after more years than there were ghouls in the damn moat—I gave him some of my real words.

Only two of 'em—all I needed to make the fucking point.

*"Fix. Her."*

# 15

## ELIAN

$\mathcal{E}$lian?"

My name was a faint whisper on her lips, the sound full of anguish even as my little sparrow tried to smile through the pain. Blood leaked from her mouth, matted her hair, stained her tattered clothing.

Most of it was *her* blood. I could smell it.

*Fuck.*

Normally, the scent of Haley's blood drove me wild. Now, it just made me want to go on a murderous fucking rampage.

But there was no time for that.

"The... guards," she sputtered. "Keradoc's men. They... betrayed... Tried to kidnap and... I fought."

"I know you did, sparrow. I know." I glanced up at Hudson, who was staring at her as if he still couldn't believe what the fuck he was looking at. "Go get Jax," I said. "He's probably still at the facility. Bring him back here. *Now.*"

No response.

"Hudson!" I snapped.

He finally met my eyes again.

"Jax is still at work. You need to find him and bring him back."

He glared at me, mouth pressed in a grim line, his bloodied face tight with fear.

"I can heal her," I assured him, a promise I wouldn't dare break. "I've got this. Go."

Another beat. Two. And then, as silent as he ever was, he took off.

"All right, sparrow." I blew out a trembling breath and took her hand, forcing a smile. "I think you've caused enough trouble for one night, yeah?"

She smiled back, but before it even touched her eyes, a wave of pain gripped her tight, making her grit her teeth and arch off the bed.

"Elian!" she cried, crushing my hand in a death grip.

The sight of her in so much pain broke me inside, but I wouldn't let her see that.

"You're going to be fine, Haley," I said, needing to hear it out loud myself as badly as I suspected *she* needed to hear it. "I can heal this—piece of cake. You're not gonna like it, but you don't have a choice in the matter because I'm a fucking vampire, I'm sober tonight, and I'll *definitely* kick your ass if you try to step to me. Deal?"

Another smile, faint. Soft. Familiar. Fucking *heartbreaking*.

"D-deal," she whispered.

I squeezed her hand. My fangs descended. I bit my wrist and pressed it to her mouth.

"Drink, sparrow. Don't think about it. Just drink."

I knew it the moment the first drops hit her tongue. Her nose wrinkled in disgust, her body convulsing as she fought off the instinct to gag, but she had no choice. Haley was a powerful witch, but she was still human, and she'd suffered a lot of injuries tonight. Not even her own magick could heal her as quickly as vampire blood.

And if her body didn't start knitting itself back together in the next few minutes, she'd...

*No*. I wouldn't even allow the thought.

She swallowed past the initial discomfort and continued to drink, and soon her body relaxed, the blood working its potent healing powers.

"That's it," I murmured, squeezing her hand as I held my other wrist to her mouth. Her lips were soft and warm, her breath ragged against my skin, tears streaking her stained cheeks as she swallowed, but the lacerations on her face and neck were already closing, her bones mending, her pain receding.

Her gaze stayed locked on mine, her grip fierce.

"I'm right here, sparrow. Right here with you. Just a little more you've got this."

Finally, certain she'd ingested enough to do the job, I pulled away from her mouth, my wounds healing instantly.

"Better?" I asked, wiping a trickle of blood from her chin.

Haley nodded, her eyes flooding with relief. In a hoarse voice, she said, "Thank you, Elian. For a minute there, I thought I might... Well, anyway. Yeah. Thank you."

"Are you kidding me?" I teased. "After all the times you've served as my personal juice box, this was the least I could do."

Another smile touched her lips, but it faded just as quickly, exhaustion finally settling over her. Part of me wanted to keep her talking, but she needed to rest. Her body would heal more quickly in sleep. Still, I wasn't leaving her side tonight. I'd keep watch over her, just as she'd done for me more times than I could count.

In Midnight and Blackmoon Bay both.

When her muscles finally relaxed and her breathing became deep and even, I pulled the blankets up to her chin and leaned in close, pressing a kiss to her forehead.

"Sleep, little sparrow. I'm right here. I promise you—"

"Where the hell is she?" A dark voice bellowed, edged in panic. "What happened?"

*Jax.*

The moment he found us in the bedroom, he fell to his knees at the bedside, his hands fisting her blankets, the anguish on his face twisting like a hot knife through my gut. It was so intense, so acute, it amplified my own pain a hundred times over until it filled every hollow part of me like cement, rooting me to where I stood.

"Angel," he whispered.

"She's going to be okay," I said softly, risking a hand on his shoulder. He flinched, but didn't pull away. "Where's Hudson?"

"Don't know," he said. "He's still not talking. Dropped me off and bounced again. But if I had to guess? He's out looking for whoever did that to Haley. Now tell me what the fuck happened."

With a heavy sigh, I did my best to get him up to speed, but I didn't have the whole story either. "From what little I could gather from Haley, Keradoc's guards ambushed her on the wall. She fought back—ended up in Beggar's Moat. That's where Hudson found her. She was in bad shape when he brought her back."

"And now? Is she... Hell, Saint. Is this all her blood? I can't even... I'm..."

"She's unconscious, but yeah, she's okay. Just processing the vampire blood. I think she's through the worst of it, but it may be a few hours before she's fully healed."

"Healed? Wait, you *healed* her?" he demanded, his voice suddenly tight. He got to his feet and fisted my shirt, his eye narrowed. "What were you thinking? You damn well could've turned her!"

"She needed my blood. We had no other options—she was too fucked up." I shook loose of his grip and turned my attention back to Haley. "Besides, you're freaking the fuck out over nothing. The only way I could turn Haley into a vampire is—"

The words died abruptly on my lips.

*Oh. Fuck.*

# 16

## ELIAN

$\mathcal{A}$ human could only be turned into a vampire through a blood swap. She'd have to drink my blood, but before that, I'd have to drink hers within a relatively short span of time. Hours, maybe.

Which I was pretty sure I'd done.

And the worst part?

While humans were turned all the time, as well as the occasional fae, witches were not. Other than her sister Gray, who was allegedly some kind of crazy powerful witch from the prophecy, no witch had ever survived the change.

Jax must've sensed the fear spiking inside me. He grabbed my shirt again, his grip trembling, his voice deadly cold. "When was the last time you fed from her?"

My mind reeled. "I don't… I don't know. A few hours ago, maybe?"

"Maybe? Think, asshole. Fucking *think*."

I closed my eyes, trying to remember. She'd been feeding me regularly ever since the slaughter at the facility, trying to keep my blood clean. Sometimes I was awake for it, other times barely present. But… I'd fed from her earlier tonight, hadn't I? Before she'd left with Keradoc? Wait, was that tonight, or was it last night?

Fuck, all the time was blurring together, no sunlight to differentiate one night from the next, my brain still addled from all the drugs and the sickness that followed…

*Damn it.*

"I don't know, Jax," I said honestly, my voice barely a whisper. I opened my eyes and looked at her, still breathing, still with us, but that could change in a heartbeat. "I think it was a few hours ago?"

"Great." He shoved me away, glaring at me with so much disgust and hatred, I didn't know how he could fit it all in one eye. "So she'll either wake up a *bloodsucker,* or she won't wake up at all because she'll fucking *die*. Not liking the odds here, asshole."

"She's not going to die."

"You don't know that. You *can't* know that." He turned away from me, shoving a hand through his hair, his cold composure unraveling. "For fuck's sake, Saint. You put her life at risk."

"I know. I fucking know! Hudson just showed up here and there was so much blood and she was in pain and I... I didn't think. I just—"

"That's the point! You didn't think. You *don't* think. All you do is react. And most of the time you're too fucking stoned to even do that. I can't *believe* you gave her your blood. How could you even... How did... Fuck, Saint. Fuck! I'm telling you *right* now, and hear me good. If Haley dies tonight—"

"She *won't*," I seethed, glaring right back at him. "You would've done the same thing in my position, and you fucking know it. So you can hate me all you want, Jax, but if you say another word about my girl dying, it'll be *your* ass in the moat. We clear?"

"Clear? Are you serious right now? I'm... Wait, what am I saying?" Laughter burst from his lips, high and hysterical. "Of *course* you're not serious. You're probably fucking high again, aren't you?" He stepped to me once more, his face looming close, that eye boring right through my damn soul. In a voice so calm it scared the hell out of me, he said, "Tell me you're fucking high right now, Saint. Tell me. Because if you are, and you just fed her a batch of blood tainted with Devil's Dream, I swear to every demon and devil in hell I will decapitate you and set your ass on fire where you stand."

"I'm. Not. High," I said, my jaw clenched so tight my teeth ached. "I haven't touched a single pill since the night at the facility."

"You sure about that?"

I shoved him away. "As sure as I'm about to tear out your throat and leave you bleeding to death on this floor."

"Oh, you'd love that, wouldn't you. Selfish fucking asshole. I bet you're just counting down the days, waiting for the right moment to take me out. Well, why keep me in suspense? I'll make it real easy on you. Take your fucking shot." He tore open the top of his shirt, baring his jugular. "Yours for the taking, asshole. Do it. Fucking do it! Oh, what's that? You can't kill me yet, because you need me to keep cleaning up your messes? Right. Of course. That's what I'm good for, after all. That's why you dragged me out of Midnight in the first place, right? You couldn't stand the idea I might actually be happy with Oona. That you wouldn't have your demon bitch-boy to keep following you around, wiping your ass, dealing your drugs, picking up the pieces of all the lives you fucking shatter every time you pop another pill. And for what, Saint? All those pills, all that fucking ruin, and for what?"

His voice broke on the last word, his whole body shaking with rage, and that eye—that fucking eye drilling through my skull like he believed if he just went far enough, deep enough, he might find all the answers.

For a long, intense moment, neither of us spoke. Haley was still passed out, her soft breathing the only sound in the room as Jax and I continued to stare each other down. Tension crackled in the air between us, the room so thick with it I was certain if anyone struck a match, we'd all blow up.

Then, I took another step closer. One more, until we were nose to nose again, and I was staring into the gaping maw of his eye socket—yet another injury I'd caused.

"You know why I took those pills?" I said softly, my trembling breath stirring the hair flopping over his forehead. "You know why I keep dancing with the very devil that's *literally* killing me, no matter how badly I want to give it up? Because that devil is the only thing keeping my fucking heart from *exploding* every time I'm in the same room as Haley. Every time I see the way she looks at you and Hudson. I loved her, Jax. I fucking *loved* her—the kind of love you don't even get to read about in the fairy tale books because it doesn't fucking exist. *That's* how rare and special it was. I loved her like that, and I never stopped. Not for one night. I *still* love..." I shook my head, the words turning to dust in my mouth. "You think I dragged you out of Midnight last time because I was jealous of what you had with Oona? Because I needed a warm body to push my drugs and work behind my bar? To clean up my messes? Fuck you, Jax."

I shoved him again, so hard this time he stumbled back and hit the wall, but I wasn't done yet. Not even when the tears fell hot on my cheeks, not even when my heart ached to say all the words out loud, not even when I thought admitting it all might be the thing that finally killed me.

"Fuck. *You*," I continued. "I took you with me because I couldn't fucking *stand* the thought of losing another brother. And you *are* my brother, you asshole, in every way that counts, yet somehow I've lost you anyway, and here we are in this shithole realm, right back where we started, and I keep on making the same damn mistakes I always do, and everything around me is falling apart and there's not a damn thing I can do about it. So you wanna judge me? You wanna look at me like I'm the monster who ruined your life and the fuckup who destroys everything and everyone he touches? Like I'm some junkie who doesn't give a fuck about anything but his next fix? Like you wish Keradoc would fucking execute me already? Do me a favor and spare me the one-eyed glower, Jax. Just pick up a sword and chop off my head. Set me on fire and throw my burning corpse to the ghouls, if that's truly what you want. Put me out of my fucking misery *right* now, once and for all, because I can *not* take another minute of existing in this pathetic, wasted life in a place where the woman I would *die* for a hundred times over shares her bed with a demon who would rather see me in a pile of ashes than admit he still gives a single fuck about me or tell me he's got my back, come what may. And no, I don't deserve your loyalty or your brotherhood or your pity. I don't even deserve a quick death. But this is how I feel, Jax. Every word is true—maybe one of the few times you'll ever hear it from me—so take it as you will or end it. Fucking end it."

For once, Jax said nothing. Didn't move away from the wall. Didn't even breathe.

But I'd ignited something fierce inside him, some new rage that surged through him in silence. I could smell it in his blood, and his whole body hummed with it, like a bowstring just plucked, its arrow mere seconds from shredding a soft heart.

He finally opened his mouth to speak.

And I opened mine to accept whatever sentence he'd hand down.

But one word, one soft voice doused the rage in us both, blowing all the tension and ire from the room like the gentlest spring breeze.

"Guys?" Haley's voice was thin, but when she opened her eyes and looked at me, I knew she was okay. Alive.

"Sparrow." I couldn't hide my relief. Somehow I forced my legs to carry me to her bedside when all they wanted to do was collapse under me. Brushing the matted hair from her forehead, I said, "How do you feel?"

Jax was at her other side in a flash, his hands clasping one of hers, pressing it to his mouth. "Angel, you gave us quite a scare."

She smiled, weak and watery, but her eyes were full of light. "And here I thought you were fearless, sinner."

When he spoke again, it was so quiet I knew she couldn't hear him—only a vampire could. "That was before I met you."

He leaned in and brushed his lips to hers, as soft as a whisper.

"Jax," I said, a little harsher than intended, but fuck it. "I need a moment with Haley, if you don't mind."

"Actually, I do mind, Saint. Think I'll stay put for now."

"Jax," I said again. "*Leave.*"

I glared at him until he saw whatever he needed to see in my eyes. Then, without another protest, he got to his feet.

"I'll be back to check on you soon, angel." He traced his thumb along her brow bone and smiled. Then, sparing me one last scowl, he stalked out of the room and shut the door.

With a shaky sigh, I knelt beside the bed. Took her hand in mine.

And asked her the only question that mattered.

"How do you feel about human blood?"

# 17

## ELIAN

*H*uman blood?" Haley's nose crinkled in a way that made me want to press a kiss between her eyebrows. "Is this a metaphor for something, or have you finally scrambled your brains completely?"

"Warm and salty," I continued, "the faint taste of iron hitting the back of your throat as it slides down and—"

"Are you trying to make me puke, or just punch you in the face? Because I'm pretty close to doing both right now." She smacked her lips a few times, scrunching up her face again. "And *your* blood isn't much better. God, this is *gross*. Can I get some water? And can we please not talk about your meal preferences again until I've had a sandwich or something? Actually, that reminds me, I could use a sandwich, too." She snapped her fingers and pointed in the direction of the kitchen. "Near-death experiences really make a bitch hungry."

"But not for human blood, right? You're sure?"

"Elian! What is *wrong* with you?"

I laughed, my chest still so tight with worry it hurt on the way out, but I didn't care. Sparrow was okay. Perky, demanding, hungry—definitely back to normal.

"Be right back." I headed out to the kitchen to get her some water and a snack. Jax was pacing before the fireplace. "She's fine," I told him. "Mostly healed. All human."

A grunt was all the response he could muster.

Then he stalked right out the door, probably to go help Hudson track down the traitors.

Best thing he could do right now. For all of us.

Back in the bedroom, I said, "Confession? I kinda thought I'd accidentally turned you into a vampire. Well, Jax thought so, anyway. I was in complete control the entire time. Mostly. Partly."

"A vampire?" Her eyes widened, and I felt the strain of her muscles as she tried to bolt upright.

"Don't," I said softly. "You're *not* a vampire, which means you're not strong enough to murder me, as tempting as the idea may be."

She narrowed her green eyes. "Well, you healed me, so clearly I'm no longer incapacitated."

"Clearly."

"Then why won't you let me sit up?"

"Maybe I just like having you horizontal in a bed."

She laughed, but all too soon, it triggered a coughing spasm.

"Breathe, sparrow. Just breathe. You've probably still got fluid in your lungs, maybe even blood." I pressed my hand flat against her sternum and continued stroking her hair, trying to calm her. When she finally caught her breath again, I cradled the back of her head and lifted the glass of water to her lips. "Just a few sips. Go slow."

She managed to get some of it down, then gestured for the sandwich.

I helped her take a few bites, her color looking better and better with each one.

"Better?" I asked, setting the empty plate on the side table.

"Yeah, except…" Her face scrunched up again. "I need a shower. This is… *ugh.*"

"Just rest up for now, Haley. Worry about being clean later."

"My skin feels like it's crawling. Half of this is gargoyle blood. I want it off. So you can either help me or stand aside, because—wait. Why are you laughing?"

"No reason. Just… it's good to have you back, sparrow. That's all."

---

I walked her to the bathroom and turned on the shower for her. "I'll be right outside the door if you need anything."

"Actually, I was hoping… Will you stay?"

"In here?"

"I don't want to be alone. Not yet." She let out a soft exhale. "Every time I close my eyes, I see the bones. I can still feel them on my skin, just… just clawing at me and tearing and…" A shudder wracked her body, head to toe.

The bones. The ghouls. The fucking moat. My heart broke just to think of her in that awful pit, and once again I wanted to murder someone. *Multiple* someones.

"Are you sure you want *me* in here, though?" I asked, tempering my fury and meeting her eyes once more. "We could wait for Jax to get back, or Hudson—"

"No, Elian. Just you." She held my gaze for a beat, then stripped out of the tattered clothing still clinging to her body. Blood, bruises, and welts decorated every inch of skin, but the blood was dried, her wounds healed. Eventually, the bruises and welts would fade and vanish, too.

Instinctively, I reached for her, but then pulled back just before my fingers brushed her shoulder. "Sorry," I muttered. "I didn't mean to—"

"Don't be weird, okay? It's nothing you haven't seen before. I just… I really need the company. Please?"

"I… right. No, it's… it's fine. I'm staying. I'm here, so… yeah. Carry on."

Relief flooded her eyes, her smile making it all worth it.

I turned away as she stepped into the shower, my whole body a fucking inferno. The shower door was made of some kind of frosted glass that obscured all but a blurry shape, but I didn't need to see her to clearly imagine those soft curves, the water sluicing over her shoulders and breasts, the blood and grime swirling down the drain and revealing fresh, pink skin.

I was already fucking hard for her, which was completely inappropriate given the circumstances, but hell. Nothing I could do about that. It's not like I could actually touch her, anyway. Not like I could strip off my clothes, step into that shower, take her into my arms, and slowly reacquaint my hands and mouth with every sinfully hot, wet curve until she was singing for me again and I—

"Still with me?" she asked.

"Still with you, sparrow." *Fuck*, my cock throbbed as if someone had kicked me. I shifted on my feet, trying to relieve the pressure, but that was a useless endeavor. Fucking woman was going to kill me even faster than the demon.

Still. Hers was a torture I'd happily endure. Especially knowing she was alive. Whole.

*Not* a fucking bloodsucker.

"You're too quiet," she said with a laugh. The air filled with the clean, fruity scent of shampoo. "Makes me think you're up to no good out there."

*Just trying not to imagine lathering you up with soap and running my hands over your slippery—*

"Just wondering when you're going to start singing, little sparrow," I teased. "I know how the shower *inspires* you."

"What? Oh, you wish!" An arc of water leaped out over the shower door, dousing me right in the face.

I cracked up. And for a few minutes, it actually felt good to laugh with her again. Like maybe things were... Well, I wouldn't say normal, but...

What the hell was I talking about?

Nothing was ever normal in Midnight, and nothing between me and Haley could even come *close* to normal.

Not like what we'd had in the Bay.

The thought sucked all the lightness from my heart, leaving a heavy weight in its place.

No, things wouldn't be normal between us. I'd made sure of that the night I left her, vanishing without a goodbye.

Guilt churned through me, eating everything in its path.

"Hand me a towel and bathrobe?"

"Hmm?"

She turned off the water and stuck her bare arm out. "Towel. Robe. Preferably sometime before I freeze my ass off, if it's not too much trouble?"

I hadn't realized how much time had passed. How long I'd spent dwelling on the past.

Dragging myself back to the present, I did as she asked.

When she stepped out, she was shiny and pink, her hair wrapped in a towel, her body wrapped up in the bathrobe, her eyes a few shades brighter.

*Damn*, it hurt to look at her.

"What?" She grinned at me, cheeks darkening with a new blush, but all I could do was shake my head.

Kept right on staring at her though. Couldn't tear my gaze away.

"Elian," she whispered, her voice faltering, that megawatt smile fading. Her eyes, though—they only grew brighter.

I said nothing. Didn't move. Didn't breathe. And for the span of a hundred heartbeats, we just watched each other, lost in thoughts and memories, all the what-ifs and could've-beens that would torment me until I took my last immortal breath.

There was a time when I'd sworn I could read her thoughts like this—just by looking at her, just by letting the silence linger.

But she was a mystery to me now. One whose innermost thoughts I no longer had a right to know.

"Where are you, little sparrow?" I whispered anyway—the old question we used to ask each other whenever one of us drifted into our own darkness. It was a way to bring each other back.

"I can't believe you still remember that," she said softly, her eyes misting.

"How could I forget?"

Hurt flooded her gaze, and I wanted to stake myself.

How could I *forget*?

I'd fucking walked out on her. In her mind, I *had* forgotten—everything we'd shared, everything we'd promised, everything we'd ever meant to each other.

And now I was standing here in the bathroom of a fucking warlord after I'd nearly lost her all over again, and it seemed all I could do was keep on saying the wrong shit, no matter how many chances I'd been given.

"Years," I whispered, knowing I should shut the fuck up, stop the inevitable train wreck of a confession that would only hurt us both, but I couldn't. "So many years when I couldn't look into those green eyes. Yet not a single night has passed when I haven't thought of you. Haven't remembered those eyes, your smile, your laugh, the smell of your skin. Haven't tried like a damn fool to hold onto something I never even deserved in the first place. And now you're here and I'm here and I'm looking at you like this—looking at you after you nearly died tonight, and you're still a million miles away, and I just... *Fuck*, sparrow." I took her still-bruised face in my hands, my thumbs ghosting across her lips. "You're so damn beautiful it's a wonder someone like me is even *allowed* to look at you. To want you the way I still do."

She gasped, our gazes colliding with all the unspoken things—the heartache, the loss, the love, the friendship, the fuckups and regrets—*my* fuckups and regrets—and she parted those soft lips and drew closer and I lowered my mouth to hers and...

"Sparrow, I... I can't. We can't." My whispers fell across her lips, my hands trembling with the urge to do it—just fucking do it—but I couldn't.

Beneath the desperate touch of my palms, I felt her jaw clench, the air cooling between us, all the old aches marching right back into my heart and planting their fucking flag.

"I'm… sorry," I said stupidly, turning away from her. "Sorry."

*Sorry.* That fucking word again. Pretty soon there'd be nothing left to say to her— just that word on an endless loop, echoing for eternity.

But even then, it wouldn't be enough. Not for all the pain I'd put her through.

"For what?" she asked, grabbing my shoulder and spinning me around to face her. Her eyes blazed with emerald-green fire. "You… you mess with my head. You say these things to me like… And then you just… God, Elian! You ask me where *I* am? Where are you? Where the fuck are *you*?"

"In a place I hope you never, ever see."

"Why? Why don't you want me to see it?"

"Because I…" I squeezed my eyes shut, wishing I could make this all go away. That I could rewind five minutes. Five weeks. Five fucking *years*.

But I couldn't. All I could do was look her in the eyes once more and try to be honest.

"Because I can't stand the thought of you ever getting to such a dark, hopeless place," I said. "I know I keep screwing up, I know I've hurt you. But I only want good things for you. You have to believe that."

"Excuse me, but no. I don't have to believe *shit*." She folded her arms across her chest, the hair towel dropping to the floor, wet locks cascading over her shoulders. "You confuse me so much, Elian. One second you're about to kiss me. The next your pushing me away, or ignoring me, or acting like a jealous asshole."

"I'm not acting. I *am* a jealous asshole. You haven't figured that out yet?"

"But… but *why*?" She fisted her wet hair, her voice rising in frustration. "I told you how I feel. How I *still* feel. If you wanted to be with me, all you'd have to do is—"

"I *can't* be with you." I shook my head and turned away from her, leaning against the sink, steeling myself to put a little more force into my voice. "It *can't* happen. What we had… it's over, Haley. Forget my mixed signals and bullshit attempts at flirting. I'm an asshole, and I can't deal with my own shit, let alone yours. You have to accept it and move on. I know it sucks, but it's just the way it is. Period."

"Accept it and move on? Like I've been trying to do for five fucking *years*?" She stood behind me, meeting my gaze in the mirror. "Trust me, Elian, I would love nothing more than to move on. But you know what? I can't. It's like… like I'm stuck in the past. I feel like I *literally* can't get over you, and you know why? Because I don't even know what it is I'm supposed to get over! You never told me. One night I'm in your arms, singing for you—fucking singing for you—and then I wake up and your just… poof! Gone. No trace. No note. No goodbye. No closure. I told you I wished you dead, that I pretended it, but even that didn't work. Because all it left me with was a dead man without a body to bury. You're just…" She pressed her fingertips to her lips—lips I'd come so close to kissing tonight—and shook her head, tears spilling down her cheeks, each one carving a fresh path through my heart.

And in the silence that followed, the weight of her pain surrounded me, so heavy and sharp I could almost taste it.

"I know I said I wouldn't ask," she finally said, turning away from me to pick up the fallen towel. "I *keep* saying it. Keep trying to convince myself it's all in the past and I don't need to know and I should just let it go, but… Tonight, when I landed in that moat, when I saw those bones rise up and I felt their hands on me, I almost didn't see a way out. I truly thought I would die there. And all I could think about was how we never set things right. How I just wanted one more chance to talk to you. One more chance to ask—"

"There's nothing to—"

"I can't *breathe*, Elian!" she shouted, turning back to meet my eyes in the mirror once more. "Every time you touch me, all I can think about is all the ways you're *not* touching me. And your eyes? God. I used to get so lost in them. Remember? My whole life could be going to shit, and five minutes of staring into your eyes would set the whole world right again. But now, every time I look into your eyes, I remember what it felt like when you took that away from me too. My fucking *lifeline*. And it's like it just happened last night. Like it's happening all over again right now, and I can't…" She pressed her hand to her chest and took in a ragged breath. "I can't let you go."

Her voice broke, and she crumpled to her knees on the cold stone floor, and it was all I could do not to fall apart right along with her.

I was on my knees before her in a flash, clutching at the robe, tongue-tied and stupid and dying inside. Just fucking *dying*. "I know, sparrow. I know."

"*End* it, Elian. Tell me your reasons for leaving and just… just end it for good, because I can't survive this again. The wondering. The questions. *You*. I just can't. So you look me in the eyes right now and tell me there was another woman, a man, *someone*. Tell me you never loved me. Tell me it was all a lie—that I was nothing more than a warm body in your bed to keep the nightmares at bay."

Everything inside me burned and shriveled. I reached up and cupped her face again, uselessly swiping her tears with my thumbs, wishing I could cry them all for her. "You *know* it wasn't a lie," I said. "Fuck, Haley. You were the *only* real thing in my life. The *only* real thing I ever—"

"No." She wrapped her hands around my wrists, clenching me tight. "I don't care. I don't care what you tell yourself, Elian, I just need you to tell *me* it was a lie. Convince me. I need a reason to hate you and walk away one last time. So fucking give it to me, asshole. You fucking give that to me if it's the only thing you can get right for the rest of your damned immortal life."

My eyes fell closed, as if that could ever block out the image of her wounded gaze, her broken heart, the endless pain my very presence caused her.

In a dark whisper, I said, "If I haven't given you enough reasons to hate me by now, then nothing I can say tonight will change that."

"Answers," she whispered. Pleaded. "I need answers. I need them like I needed your blood tonight. Like I need fucking *air*."

"You think you want them, sparrow, but the answers—the *real* answers —they're going to cut even deeper than you know."

"Not as deep as the questions. The what-ifs and whys and what happeneds I could never, ever explain to myself."

"There are so many, I don't even know where to start unraveling this story."

"Pick a thread. *Any* thread. Just…" She rested her head on my shoulder, her breath warm against my neck as her tears soaked into my shirt. "Say *something*."

Seconds stretched into minutes that stretched on into a thousand little eternities, time slowing down until it started moving backward. Suddenly I was back in Blackmoon Bay, tracing the outline of her lips, her cheekbones, her eyebrows, memorizing the feel of her with my fingertips as she slept, knowing I would be leaving her that night.

*Damn it, Haley.*

I placed my hand on her back, stroking softly, a dark acceptance settling deep in my chest. I owed her this. As much of the truth as I could bear to tell.

"The other night, you asked me about Evander?" I whispered, the very name sending a shudder down my spine, a fresh ache blooming in my gut. "That's where this starts. Where it *all* starts."

She pulled back and met my gaze once more, her brow furrowing. "Evander? The one you used to dream about?"

"He was my brother, Haley. Not in a blood-before-roses way, in a literal way. *Quite* literal—he was my twin. My fucking twin. My best friend. My hero. And the boy whose absence left a hole in my heart so massive, it's still eating its way through my life." I swallowed the tightness in my throat and got to my feet, holding out a hand to help her up. "And it's nowhere *near* done with me."

**18**

ELIAN

our brother. Evander is your twin brother?" She shook her head, shock and disbelief still clinging to her eyes, even though I'd answered the same question a dozen times now. "I'd always thought you were an only child."

She was back in bed now—mine, since she'd left Hudson's covered in blood—and I sat in the chair next to her, still trying to figure out where to start this story. Trying to find the words to get it all out without completely falling apart.

"I was," I said. "For a long time, anyway. But before that, I had Evander. We were inseparable. Two peas in a pod, as the saying goes." I smiled, some of the old memories coming back. "He was older by about ten minutes, and he never let me forget it. That boy took his big brother role very seriously."

Haley mirrored my smile, a bit of the light returning to her eyes. "Yeah? You let him boss your stubborn ass around?"

"*Save* my stubborn ass, more like it. Remember this?" I pushed up my sleeve and leaned across the bed, revealing an old scar on my forearm— one she'd seen hundreds of times before. One she'd kissed and caressed as I'd embraced her in the bed we'd shared in Blackmoon Bay and told her the story of how that scar had come to be.

Part of it, anyway.

"You were bitten by a silver wolf in Autumnshire," she said softly, tracing her fingers over the craggy crescent-shaped mark. "Brutal."

"Would've been a lot worse if not for Evander."

"He was with you?"

"He saw me go down, then jumped right into it, taking the brunt of the attack. Fucking wolf was relentless, too—cracked a few of Evander's ribs, punctured a lung, chewed him up good before my brother finally smashed a rock over his head and killed him."

"Oh my god, Elian. Is that… is that how he died? From the injuries?"

"No. Came damn close to it that day, though. Our healers got to him quickly—their magick and my mother's prayers saved him. Well, that and the fact that he was certain if he died, I'd change up the story so that I was the one who killed the wolf, and poor Evander was the one who got eaten." I laughed. "Crazy fae fuck, that kid. But he survived."

Haley let out a soft sigh, her eyes dimming. "Then what happened to him, Elian? What happened to your brother?"

I lowered my gaze, grief blurring my vision, as raw and sharp as it ever was. "The forest where the wolf had died—that was our favorite place. He and I spent more time there than we spent in our own house, always off on our make-believe adventures. Even the wolf attack couldn't scare us off. Soon as Evander was well again, we were right back to our old tricks—digging tunnels, climbing trees, making weapons. All the trouble you'd expect from two eight-year-old boys.

"But one day, during one game or another, he hid from me. Hid so well, for so long, that he…" I shook my head, as if my brain still didn't want to believe it. "He never came out again. Not even when I gave up the game and begged him to reveal himself. Not even when I offered up all my favorite toys in exchange for him to just stop screwing around. Not even hours later, when I brought my parents back to help me search. All of us—my family, the neighbors, the other kids we knew—we scoured those woods for weeks. Searched under every rock, every leaf. But in the end, he was just… gone." I leaned back in the chair, gazing up at the black ceiling, a strip of moonlight reflecting off the dark obsidian. "The only evidence we found was the footprints of an adult male fae and… and drag marks. They never caught… never…"

I trailed off, my eyes blurring with tears. I could hear Haley's heart thundering through her chest, her breathing tight, and I knew if I looked at her I'd find the same tears streaming down her cheeks.

So I didn't look. Didn't even move. Just stared at that little patch of moonlight and forced myself to get the rest of the words out.

"People kept telling us that we'd move on, that eventually it would stop hurting, that maybe my parents should have another child. It was all bullshit, Haley. You don't move on from something like that. You don't stop hurting. I was a fucking ghost, and my parents?" I let out a shuddering breath. "They were never the same after that. My father practically went insane—caused a lot of trouble for the royals of Autumnshire, who refused to help search for my brother and eventually banished our family to the earthly realm. For years, my mother would call me by Evander's name, and I didn't know if it was because she'd simply confused us, or because she believed if she said it enough times, the fates would see fit to return him. Sometimes I wondered if she wished… if she wished I'd been taken instead." My throat closed around ancient pain, the edges of it as sharp as they were the first night I realized Evander was truly gone—was truly never coming back to us. "I didn't blame her. I used to wish for it, too, because then at least my mother's suffering would end and Evander would be okay."

"Elian, no," she said softly, her voice full of sympathy, but she could no more talk me out of those old beliefs than I could talk myself out of them.

"As I got older," I continued, because if I stopped now I'd fucking shatter, and I needed to hold on long enough to tell her the rest, to get us back to that night in Blackmoon Bay so I could make her understand, so I could ease her suffering even just a *fraction*—a thing I was never able to do for my family. "I just… I assumed he was dead. How else could we go so many long, long years without hearing a word about his whereabouts? If he were still alive, I'd reasoned, he would've been an adult at some point, and he would've found a way to get in touch. To get back to us. So I tried, Haley. I tried to do what everyone said and move on with my life as best I could."

"But you couldn't," she said softly. "That's not how it works."

"No. It isn't. I was ready to give up, sparrow, I really was. But then…" A smile touched my lips at the memory, and I finally found the courage to look at her again.

She was sitting upright in bed, cheeks pink, her eyes bright despite the tears. "Then what?"

"Then I spilled coffee on some crazy, green-eyed witch on a pier in Blackmoon Bay, and she made me feel like life might just be worth living after all."

She smiled at the memory, too. It would always be a good one, our first meeting. Me spilling that coffee. Her pushing me into the Bay. Everything that had come after.

"You were my light, sparrow. My reason. And no, it's not fucking fair to put that on a person. But it's true. As true now as it ever was, and I shouldn't even tell you that, because even that confession feels like another burden I'm laying on you, but I don't want to lie anymore. Not to you. Not about us. See, the pain of losing my brother never went away. Never even faded. But being with you... I felt happy in ways I didn't think I ever would, and it just... You helped me learn to live with that loss. To believe that it was okay to keep both things in my heart—joy *and* anguish. Love *and* loss."

Haley nodded. Of course she understood.

When you lose someone you love, you're never the same again. No matter how many years pass, no matter how many different ways you might find love with someone else—even in friendship—your heart never quite beats the same way after a loss like that.

Yet Haley was still alive, still shining like a bright beacon even after I'd put her through the worst kind of loss. No, she hadn't gotten through it unscathed—if she had, we wouldn't be having this conversation.

But somehow, she'd learned to live with both, just as I had.

"We *were* happy, weren't we?" she whispered, fresh tears slipping free. "I didn't imagine it?"

"Sparrow, I was never happier than I was all those nights I spent in your arms. Our life together was... It was everything. If you take one thing from this story, one truth, please let it be that." I moved over to the bed, sitting beside her so I could take her hand. "But one night, I got word from some of the fae in Blackmoon Bay—there'd been rumors from a pureblood Midnighter they knew, a smuggler who claimed that a guy fitting the description of my brother was spotted in Midnight. That he was taken from his home and enslaved as a child, passed around among the noble dark fae of Midnight. Then, somehow, he'd ended up in the dungeons after assassinating half the royal guard and making a play for Keradoc. They were going to execute him, but he escaped."

Her eyes widened, a soft gasp slipping from her lips—not just from the news about Evander, but from the timing. I could practically see the wheels spinning behind her eyes. "When... when did you hear this?"

I tightened my hold on her hand. "Five years ago, sparrow. The last night I saw you in the Bay."

# 19

## ELIAN

*I* felt the change wash over her as the realization took hold, rooting in her heart like a poisonous seed that bloomed with a hundred new impossible questions, a hundred new impossible answers.

"I *knew* the story about Evander was true," I said, sparing her the pain of having to ask me to go on. "I felt it in my heart, like our connection had just reignited after all those years. I could practically feel him calling out to me, calling for my help. Calling for me to come and find him. I didn't think. I didn't plan. I just... I spent one last night with you, then I left Blackmoon Bay and traveled to the royal fae court in Summer's Vale—my one-way ticket to Midnight."

"How? How was that your ticket?"

"The royal family of Summer's Vale used to be close with ours, but they turned their backs on us after Evander's kidnapping. Eventually, my parents discovered that they played a role in getting us booted out of Autumnshire. So yeah, I already had reason enough to want them dead. But this? This was the final nail in that particular coffin."

"What... what did you do?"

I took a deep breath. Held her gaze so she knew I was speaking the truth, because the story would only get darker and harder to bear from here on out.

"I assassinated the two crown princes in cold blood, right in the middle of a festival. Hundreds of witnesses. A crime so heinous, there could only be one sentence."

"Banishment to Midnight." She closed her eyes and shook her head, but she didn't release my hand. "You left me. You murdered two innocent fae. All so you could save your brother."

"Save him? No. I knew if Evander was really here—if he'd been here for that many years, decades, a child slave forged into a bitter killer—there would be no saving him. I just wanted to see him one more time. To let him know that I'd never forgotten him." I turned away from her, wiping an errant tear from my cheek. "That I never *could* forget him."

"Oh, Elian," she breathed, her voice as broken as mine, lost to this story, to this past. "God, I don't even know what to say. This is… I'm sorry. I'm really angry with you, and I hate that you left me, and I hate that you killed those fae. And I hate that your brother was stolen from you, and that you had to grow up without him, and know that kind of pain… I can't… Fuck, Elian. Just… fuck."

I shifted closer to her, wrapping an arm around her shoulders and pulling her against my chest. "You know, as crazy as it sounds? After all that… I still believed I could find a way back to you. I left you that night because I had some blind, foolish hope that if I only tried hard enough, fought hard enough, I could make it back to you. And then I could tell you about Evander, and I knew you'd understand why I'd had to try, because family was everything to you—your Nona, and—"

"And *you*, Elian. *You* were my family." She glanced up at me through dark, tear-stained lashes. "Didn't you know that?"

"I *did* know it, sparrow. Logically. But at the time, I still blamed myself for his disappearance, as if I should've been able to see who'd taken him. As if I could've stopped it from happening. Eventually I'd convinced myself that he'd died, and I thought that was my fault, too. I didn't… I didn't believe I deserved a love like what you were offering, any more than I deserve your forgiveness now."

"It wasn't your call to make then, and it's still not your call to make now."

"It doesn't matter," I said. "Obviously. I never found him. I spent two years searching, and I never even found him, and I lost you in the process. So ultimately, it was all for nothing."

"Do you think he's still here?"

"No."

"But Keradoc's glamour! Maybe he knew Evander, and that's how he—"

"Melantha, Haley. It's all her doing—maybe it always was. She knows how to manipulate us. At this point, I don't even know if I believe Evander was ever in Midnight to begin with. And if he was? You can bet your ass Keradoc was likely behind it."

"But he—"

"Haley, don't. Please don't. I know you see something else when you look at that man, but all I see—all I will *ever* see—is a brutal warlord who makes my crimes look like minor skirmishes."

Haley bristled, but she still didn't pull away. "So what happened then? You found a way to escape Midnight, just like you'd hoped."

"I did. But it cost me, sparrow. Dearly." I tightened my hold on her. "So no, in all the ways that count, I didn't *really* escape Midnight. And now I know I never will."

"Jax... He told me about his eye—his vision. He said that in exchange for helping you guys leave, Melantha demanded the most important thing from each of you."

I nodded. "The thing that truly made us who we were. Her exact words."

"Tell me what it cost you," she whispered, and I knew she wasn't asking me about the drug-dealing empire I'd been forced to set up in New Orleans. "Tell me the price you paid to get out."

I took a shuddering breath, the weight of my confessions pressing on my heart from all sides. "There's a saying, you know, about a man who's got nothing left to lose. How it makes him the most dangerous bastard in the room. And Midnight? Hell, you'd think we were all there already—the rock-bottom basement of our terrible lives. How else could someone end up here, of all places? But you know it now, sparrow. The truth is, some of us come here by choice. And for me, the real rock-bottom came after. When I gave up the only thing that had ever truly mattered to me."

"Tell me, Elian," she demanded. "Tell me what you gave up."

It took every last bit of strength I possessed to slide my fingers under her chin and tilt her bruised face up toward mine. To look at her—truly look at her. To hold on to that beautiful green gaze as I dredged the words up from the basement of my heart. And even when I finally did it, even when I could taste them on the tip of my tongue, I still couldn't bring myself to give them a voice.

Not the actual words of Melantha's curse. Not the gruesome, vile, despicable things she vowed would happen to Haley if I ever really touched her again. If I ever came close to sharing with her all the intimate, beautiful things I so desperately, desperately wanted to share.

"You, little sparrow," I finally admitted, the words catching like barbed wire in my throat. "I gave up *you*. It's why I never reached out to you after

I got to New Orleans, despite how badly I'd wanted to. It's why I can't touch you now, even when all I want to do is take you into my arms and kiss you breathless. It's the price I promised to pay, and if I go back on that promise, if I so much as touch you any more closely than this... You won't survive, Haley. And if you don't survive, neither will I."

Her heartbeat raged against my chest, a fathomless ache swimming in the depths of her eyes. She stared at me for an eternity, searching my face. For what, I had no idea. The truth? She had to see it there, written plain as fucking day, etched in every deep line, every broken shard of glass in my silver eyes.

After an eternity, she pressed her palms to my cheeks and smiled. My sparrow heard the worst of all my confessions, and she fucking *smiled* at me.

God, that smile. It had the power to break me and glue me back together again. Always had.

But her next words punched a hole through my chest and ripped out my beating heart.

"I love you, Elian," she said plainly. So clear and matter-of-fact it was if it'd been written in the stars at the dawn of time, utterly unchangeable. "I will *always* love you."

"You love a ghost. The man you knew—I'm not that man anymore. I'm—"

"No. You're *not* that man." She pressed a hand to my chest, right over the heart I'd sworn she'd just carved out. "You're *this* man. The one who brought me back from the dead. The one who followed me to Midnight— to the worst hell he's ever experienced—just because I asked for his help. The one who made mistakes but never turned his back on me—not really. And for all those past fuckups, for all your present faults, for all the future things you don't even know you should be sorry for yet, you're still *mine*. Do you hear me? I'm *claiming* you as mine, even if I can't be yours because of some dark goddess bullshit price. You're my heart, Elian. You've always been my heart. I love you. *You*. This man, right here." She patted my chest, harder this time. "I never stopped, and I never will, and no mistakes or dark goddesses or death sentences in a terrible realm will ever change it. Not for me. So I don't know what that means to you—if it means anything at all—but I'm saying it anyway because I need you to know it."

*If it means anything at all?*

Fucking hell, her love and loyalty meant everything. Absolutely *everything*.

I just couldn't do a damn thing about it. Couldn't even say the words back to her, because they were true. And that particular truth, if given a real voice outside my head, would put her in the fucking ground and damn her soul to an eternity of... Fuck, I didn't even know what.

Melantha's cruel hiss echoed through my skull, splitting it with a blinding pain.

*And she shall perish in flames for an eternity... And you shall know the true depths of a grief you have not yet begun to fathom...*

I shook my head, clearing away the words before the rest of the curse bubbled up through my memories. It burned inside me like a hot blade, and it made Haley's forgiveness and her love all the more bittersweet. All the more torturous. The world's most precious gifts I could never, ever reciprocate.

She waited for me to speak, to say *something* even if it wasn't what she truly deserved to hear. But I was a fucking coward, and if I heard the sound of my own voice just then, I knew it would fucking break me, and before I could untangle the knot of my feelings and put them into words that wouldn't get her killed, the guys were back, barreling into the room at the sight of her sitting up in bed, whole and healthy.

Sitting up in my arms.

"Did you find them?" I asked, untangling myself from her and getting to my feet.

Hudson gave a quick shake of his head, his jaw clenched tight with frustration.

"Angel, you look perfect," Jax said, and I watched with a fire blazing in my chest as he kissed her. Hudson moved in next, pressing his mouth to hers with a lingering tenderness that made me ache. When Hudson finally broke away, she turned back to Jax for another of his kisses.

It was the happy reunion they all needed. Deserved.

But it wasn't long before those sighs of relief and happiness turned into soft gasps of pleasure, each one crashing into the next until the soundtrack of her miraculous recovery became the soundtrack of my most abject pain.

I closed my eyes as her scent washed over me—her strawberries-and-cream skin, the scent as familiar to me as my own. Her warm blood, heated even more by their insistent touch. Her desire, that intoxicating perfume that had hypnotized me every time we touched, back when we still could, and every time they touched her now.

I burned for her. Ached for her. Longed in a way that left me gasping for a breath I couldn't take.

I couldn't watch this. Listen to it. Smell it, for fuck's sake.

I was going out of my damn mind.

Again.

I took a step toward the door. But my girl, she saw me leaving, and she wasn't having it. She reached for me, her eyes full of forgiveness and hope and desperation and yes, desire too. Desire for me, in whatever way she thought she could have me.

*Damn it, Haley.*

"Stay," she whispered. Begged. "Stay with us, Elian. Please."

My heart galloped like the wild mares of night, and I took her hand once more. I wanted to tell her no. To remind her she had to let me go. Let me fucking *go*, but I couldn't.

Because no matter what I'd told her earlier about moving on, about accepting our inevitable end, deep down, I *didn't* want her to let me go.

"You're still mine," she whispered again, her soft smile another balm on my cracked heart. "Always."

I squeezed her hand. And in that moment, something passed between us, some new understanding that this was it—this was how it had to be. The only way we could have anything at all. Friendship and loyalty up close, but love only from a distance. Words unspoken. Desires unfulfilled but for the fantasies we could both conjure, and the pleasure I could watch my brothers give to her.

And in that moment, I knew what she needed. The only gift I could give her that would ever mean a damn thing.

Not permission, no—she certainly didn't need my permission to love who she loved. But I sensed she wanted a blessing of sorts. A smile that said it was okay for her to want this, to desire it. To feel the things she was feeling for men that *weren't* me. Men I still called my brothers, even if they didn't feel the same way about me.

And that it was okay for her to want me to bear witness to it, however crazy it might've seemed.

Earlier, I'd told her I was a jealous asshole, and that was the fucking truth. But I'd also told her I wanted only the best for her, and that was the truth too. I wanted her to be happy. To find love, even if it couldn't be with me. Even if it tore me apart to see it happening.

So maybe, after all the secrets and lies and the darkness, this was the middle where we met. The soft, safe place where the jagged edges of our darknesses and brutal pasts overlapped, creating something new and undefined. Something magick.

Hudson and Jax glanced up at me as if they, too, needed me to be okay with this.

I appreciated it more than they realized.

"Take care of her," I said, swallowing back the last of my tears. "Make her sing for us."

# 20

## HALEY

My skin was still crawling with the cold, dry scrape of bony fingers, the wailing of the ghouls an endless echo in my skull. I'd tasted death tonight, felt it tearing at my skin, witnessed it bend and bow before my magick, watched it claim a ruthless enemy that my gargoyle protector destroyed before my eyes.

I hadn't even gotten the chance to tell them the whole story yet, or to share Keradoc's news about Melantha. About the choice he'd asked me to make.

Between everything I'd been through tonight and everything Elian and I had just shared, I felt hollowed out inside, like a jack-o-lantern left to rot long after Halloween had passed.

Right now, I just needed my monsters, the solid weight of their warm bodies and fevered touches. I needed to feel the pounding of my human heart, the hot rush of blood in my veins, the spark of desire between my thighs that could only come from within a body still *very* much alive. Very much healed and whole.

And, for the first time since fate had set us all on the same twisted path, I wanted them all together.

At the same time.

"Tell us what you need, angel," Jax said. "We're not going anywhere. No matter what."

I nodded, but I still bit my lower lip, nervous despite his reassurances.

Jax and Hudson knew I cared for them both, knew I'd been spending time with each of them. But we'd never really talked about what that meant for all of us. If there could even *be* an "all of us."

My heart fluttered, my stomach turning fizzy at the thought. This was what I wanted, and there was no reason to feel shame or embarrassment about it. No reason to feel nervous.

I just had to tell them how I felt, and let them decide for themselves whether they wanted to be part of it. Part of the "us" that set my soul on fire. That made a family. That made a future together, even if that future was here in Midnight.

"I need… I need to be reminded that I'm alive," I finally admitted. "I need to *feel* alive. And being with you—all three of you…" I shook my head, a shaky laugh bubbling up from inside. "So many things about this life are so fucking complicated. Messy. Disastrous. But not this—not us. The way I feel about you guys is like… God, it's the simplest thing there is. Your mine, and I'm yours, and whatever shades of gray fall in between all that, whatever labels we need to give it or not give it, I don't care. I just know that I want you—all of you. Elian included, in whatever way he can be here. So if that's not what you guys want, if you're not a hundred percent okay with me sharing my bed and my heart with all of you, then tell me. No judgments. I promise I won't—"

"Stop." Jax cupped my face, his eye blazing. "Just stop. There's *nothing* I wouldn't do for you, angel. Not one fucking thing. So if this is what you want, then this is what I want, too. I'm *in*, a hundred percent."

Hudson growled in agreement against my neck, kissing a path up to my ear and nipping my earlobe, no words needed.

And when I looked up at Ellian, my first love, my tortured, silver-eyed fae, he simply nodded, the promise in his eyes all I needed to see.

He was okay with this, too. With *us*.

And he was staying. Watching. Bearing witness to this crazy thing unfolding between me and my monsters—this precious, nameless thing that Elian was as much a part of as the rest.

Jax looked to Elian, his eye narrowed. "Are you… joining us?"

"No," I said, saving Elian from having to answer. The others didn't know about the price he'd paid—Melantha's curse—and whether he decided to share it or not, now wasn't the time.

Elian smiled, a mix of gratitude and sadness. "Haley and I have… an agreement."

"You sure?" Jax asked, and Elian nodded.

"I'm just here to watch, brother. And to hear my little sparrow sing."

"It's okay." I reached up and touched Jax's face, tracing my fingers over his brow bone, down along his scar. "This is what I want. I promise."

"Then let us take care of you," Jax whispered, already undoing my bathrobe, unwrapping me like a present. "Let us give you what you need."

A deep sigh of satisfaction and happiness floated from my lips as I leaned back and closed my eyes, focusing on the feel of the robe slipping away, his palm skimming across my bare stomach, the brush of Hudson's beard against my shoulder as he kissed me, the familiar weight of his massive hand caressing my breast. Even with my eyes closed, I felt Elian's gaze on my body, a smoldering heat that melted me straight down to my core.

Jax's fingers worked lower, gently gliding between my thighs and circling my clit before finally dipping inside me, his expert touch making me gasp.

"So wet for us, angel," he murmured, slowly drawing back to tease my clit. I arched my hips, begging him to drive in deeper once more, but apparently my demon had other plans.

He and Hudson rose from the bed, my body screaming at the sudden loss of their touch, and I opened my eyes to watch them strip out of their clothes, both of them rock-hard and ready, a sight that made my pussy throb with need. Hudson moved to the end of the bed, and without warning, grabbed my ankles and dragged me down until my legs were hanging off the end. Hands gliding up to my hips, he gripped me tight, his eyes sparkling with mischief. His lips quirked into a devious grin—my only warning before he thrust inside, impaling me on his massive cock.

"Fuck, yes... Yes!" I gasped, the exquisite burn quickly turning into intense pleasure as he found his rhythm and gave me what I'd asked for, every one of those punishing thrusts obliterating the cold touch of those ghouls.

But, just like with Jax's fingers, all too soon, Hudson was pulling back

"More," I begged, shamelessly reaching for his cock. "*More.*"

A low chuckle rumbled up through Hudson's chest, and he leaned in close to my ear and whispered, "Not yet, babygirl. I'm just getting you warmed up." He glanced behind me at Jax and winked, keeping his voice low so only I could hear him. "We've got other plans for you."

He stood up, pulling me up with him and repositioning me so I was kneeling at the edge of the bed. Across the room, Elian watched all of this in silence, utterly transfixed, his mouth parted as his chest rose and fell with short, rapid breaths, his cock straining hard against his pants, knuckles white as he clutched the arms of his chair. I held his gaze, a thousand unsaid words passing between us, my body blazing for him as much as it was blazing for the men who were actually touching me.

My heart broke again and again to know what he'd suffered in childhood, to finally understand after all this time why he'd left me, why he'd let me go. I still hadn't even processed it all yet, and when I did, I knew I'd have a hundred more questions—undoubtedly leading to more answers that would break my heart all over again.

But for now, it was enough that he'd stayed here with me. With us.

It was enough to know that he loved me, even if he couldn't say it. That I loved him, and I'd stand by his side through whatever darkness he still had to face.

"Sparrow," he mouthed, and I nodded, giving him the softest smile.

The bed dipped, and Jax knelt behind me, sliding his hands into my hair and lifting it off my back, leaving a trail of hot kisses up my spine. Hudson bent down and claimed my mouth in a fierce kiss, stirring me into another frenzy.

"Sit back, angel," Jax whispered against my neck, his cock dipping between my thighs from behind. "I want you to ride me until we make you come for us."

I was powerless to do anything but obey. With a soft moan into Hudson's mouth, I arched my hips and lowered myself onto Jax, shuddering with white-hot pleasure as I took him all the way in, Hudson's tongue gliding across mine to mimic the stroke of Jax's perfect cock.

"Fuck," Jax whispered, burying his face in my hair and bringing his hands around to cup my breasts. His thumbs scraped over my nipples, unleashing another moan from my mouth.

Hudson broke away, and then my sweet, possessive gargoyle dropped to his knees, his massive hands gripping my thighs and wrenching them as far apart as they would go in my current position. He blew a soft breath between them, then lowered his filthy, beautiful mouth to my clit, tonguing me as Jax thrust into me from behind.

*Holy. Fucking. Hell.*

The dual sensations sent me into sensory overload, my nerves humming, tendrils of pleasure snaking down my spine and coiling low in my belly, making me ache and moan.

"That's it, angel," Jax murmured, biting my shoulder, my neck. "Take it. Take what you need."

"Oh god," I breathed, the sting of his bites making my pussy clench. "That's... yes. Just like that."

With a growl of satisfaction, he bit down harder, marking me, claiming me, my breasts heavy and aching against his palms, my body a raging inferno.

I pushed up on my knees, then slid back down, rolling my hips and driving Jax deeper inside me, riding him, fucking him as I slid my hands into Hudson's hair and brought him closer, his tongue swirling over my sensitive flesh, beard scratching my thighs.

Across the room, a deep rumble echoed, and I looked up once again to find Elian watching me, his silver eyes wide, his body trembling. Everything in me was spinning and hot, Elian's fiery gaze and the wicked touch of my monsters driving me closer and closer to that blissful edge, further and further from the brutal death that had nearly claimed me earlier.

I was alive. Fucking *alive*.

My vampire-fae smiled at me.

And I responded with a smile all for him, because he was here. Because for all he'd endured, he'd survived.

*We'd* survived.

And we'd keep *on* surviving. That, more than anything, was our promise to each other now—one I intended to honor for the rest of my life.

To fucking survive.

**21**

ELIAN

A groan born of frustration and pleasure both tore through my chest, my cock straining hard against my pants, but I didn't dare look away. Didn't move. Not with my little sparrow's hungry gaze locked on mine, her mouth parted in ecstasy as Hudson devoured her sweet pussy, Jax fucking her hard and deep, the scent of her wild desire making me drunk.

Jax palmed her breast and bit her shoulder, and with a cry of pure ecstasy she slid her fingers into Hudson's hair and rode them both harder, taking what she wanted, what she needed, unleashing a deep growl from Hudson's throat, the whole scene making my heart pound as fiercely as a Midnight storm.

Just like that night in the apartment with Jax, I almost felt guilty watching her like this—seeing that blush creep up her thighs and over her breasts, knowing it was the mouths and hands of other men that'd put it there. But there was something *so* fucking right about it too. About being here with them, being part of this, all the blame and our bullshit fights and the last few weeks of anguish and torment on hold for just a little while— just long enough to offer a night of pure pleasure to the woman we all loved.

And I knew it then, truly and deeply, that we *did* all love her. That something beyond logic or obligation or even the loyalty born of our blood-before-roses oath connected us to her and—if I was being honest, which wasn't the easiest fucking thing for me these days—to one another. She was the center of it, though. The beating heart of us all.

Haley met my gaze again, the pulse of her immense desire echoing through my balls, my cock throbbing for her, my blood simmering. The scent of her in that moment was overpowering, making my head swim.

I must've smiled at her, because suddenly my girl was smiling back again, the sight of it warming me head to toe.

I'd nearly lost her tonight. Nearly lost all of them tonight, and so many fucking nights before, but they were still here. Yeah, Jax and I had fought —we probably always would. But we were still fucking brothers, just like I'd told him. And for all my fuckups, for all that I'd put them at risk, I wanted to be better. So much better, because they deserved a friend and brother who could take care of them. Who wouldn't fall apart or fall prey to some vicious addiction.

And I wanted to be better for me, too. To find a way to live with the pain of the clawing emptiness inside me, the losses, the unanswered questions, the fucking tragedies, because living with them was the only way I would ever truly appreciate the beauty as well. The love. The brotherhood that was all around me.

I closed my eyes, shame coursing through my veins, my gut churning. Fuck, I'd been dancing with the devil for so long, those little black pills felt like my oldest friends. Even now, two nights clean, feeling better than I'd felt in years, I still hungered for them. Still felt the whisper of their dark promises on the back of my neck, the sweet oblivion that was never more than a swallow away.

They were killing me. Ruining me. Destroying everything and everyone I cared for.

But as badly as I wanted to turn my back on the Black for good—as badly as I *needed* to—I just didn't fucking know how.

And that, more than anything, fucking terrified me.

# 22

## JAX

*A*fter all the time I'd spent chained up in the fiery pits of hell, I thought I knew fear. Thought I'd experienced it so often, in so many different forms, I'd never succumb to its dark powers again—that I wasn't even *capable* of it.

But earlier tonight, seeing her broken body on the bed, blood spilling onto the floor from her wounds…

There was a moment—a single heartbeat—where I thought she might actually be dead.

And in that moment, fear—the truest and sharpest blade I'd ever felt—sliced right through my heart, putting every last one of hell's brutal tortures to shame.

Now, having her with us again—warm, alive, moaning my name as I slid deep inside her—felt like a second chance. One I hadn't even realized I'd been begging for.

Since our very first kiss in the corpsevine fields—and the chase that ensued—I've *loved* fucking my sweet angel, teasing and biting her in all the sinfully delicious ways I knew drove her absolutely wild. I never thought I'd even consider sharing her—not at the same time, anyway—but tonight? When she'd looked at each of us in turn and put her whole heart on the line just to tell us what she wanted? To tell us how to make her feel whole again?

*Fuck.* It was just like I'd told her—there was *nothing* I wouldn't give her, nothing I wouldn't do for her, nothing I wouldn't accept if only to bring one more smile to her beautiful face. It didn't matter that I was still pissed at Saint for risking her life with his blood earlier, or for all the things he'd done to put his own life in danger. Yeah, he and I had some bad blood between us. But that shit was nothing compared to the bond that connected us as brothers. Not just because of our oath, but because of Haley. Through her. Our heart.

"You feel amazing, angel," I growled against her soft neck, sliding my hands down to grip her hips as she took me in deeper.

Across from us, Saint sat in the chair, his eyes smoldering like hot coals. I wondered what their agreement entailed, why he was keeping his distance. I wondered what he was thinking—whether he was imagining himself in my position, fucking her hot and deep, or in Hudson's, sucking her sweet little pussy while she raked her hands through his hair, begging for that hot mouth. Or maybe he was thinking about where he might fit into this tangle of arms and legs, of sweat and seduction. Would he take her mouth, fucking her until he lost himself to the velvet slide of her tongue? Or would he wait his turn, claiming her in all the dark and devious ways she'd never even imagined before her monsters crossed her path?

Just knowing how much pleasure that would bring her made my cock stiffen even more, and Haley rocked back against me, her every movement sending waves of red-hot euphoria straight to my balls.

*Fuck*, I wanted to come inside her so badly.

To know and believe—just as she needed to know and believe—that I was still fucking alive, despite the universe doing its damndest to take our asses down.

I wanted to fucking *feel* it.

I bit her shoulder again, and she gasped, her thighs already starting to tremble, Hudson's relentless mouth claiming her flesh as I rolled my hips and fucked her harder, deeper, the strawberries-and-cream scent of her skin making my heart stutter, the smoldering coals of Saint's eyes igniting into a blazing fire as she whispered his name and reached for him, riding me harder and faster, her soft whispers cascading into a moan of heady pleasure that threatened to shatter us all.

Her body tightened hard around me like a fist as the orgasm slammed into her, and with one hand reaching back and sliding into my hair, she reached again for Saint with the other, crying out all of our names as we made our sexy, beautiful witch come.

Burying my face in her dark hair, I tightened my hold on her hips and railed into her once, twice, three more times, carrying her through the aftershocks of her release as the same heat spiraled through my chest, my abs, right down into my balls and finally—fucking *finally*—I exploded inside her, the intensity of it ripping a deep and primal growl from some ancient, dark place inside me, a place as old as Midnight itself, a place that no one else had ever reached.

And no one else ever would. Only Haley. Only my angel.

Hudson and I gave her a minute to catch her breath, but apparently the gargoyle couldn't wait much longer than that. Suddenly he was lifting her up off my cock and tossing her back onto the bed, climbing on top to claim her mouth in a suffocating kiss.

"Let her breathe, asshole." I laughed, shaking my head. "Poor girl needs to recuperate."

Haley pulled back and shot me a dark glare. "Speak for yourself, sinner. As for me, I'll recuperate when I'm dead."

With a grunt, Hudson rolled onto his side, keeping Haley close and hooking her leg over his hip as I stretched out behind her. He grumbled something into her ear that I couldn't hear, but Haley nodded enthusiastically.

"Now," she breathed, touching his face. "I want you inside me right fucking *now*, Hudson. *Please.*"

"Don't mind me," I teased, gathering her hair into my fist. "I'll just be back here, enjoying the show."

I dragged my tongue along the back of her neck, making her shiver as Hudson gripped his massive cock and speared her. A deep, gravelly rumble vibrated through his chest as she took him in, more animal than human, but I didn't care *what* kind of crazy-ass sounds he unleashed tonight. All I cared about was Haley—that we were giving her what she wanted. Taking care of her. Keeping her protected.

The fact that she was begging for more? That was just an added bonus.

I was already hard for her again, my cock pressing insistently against her back. She reached behind and fisted it, stroking me so fucking tight, so perfect…

*Oh, fuck…*

"You're going to *destroy* me, angel." I rocked into her hand, kissing her shoulder, skimming my fingers across her hip and down her belly, brushing her clit with soft, teasing strokes as Hudson filled her again and again, his massive hand spanning her thigh, his other wrapped around her throat, our combined efforts making her writhe and moan.

He met my gaze across her bare shoulder, his eyes crazed and unfocused, dark with desire. One look told me he was as close to losing it as I was, and we both knew Haley wouldn't be far behind, either.

"Are you ready to come for us again?" I whispered, biting her delicate earlobe as I increased the pressure on her clit. "Because your monsters are more than ready to come for *you*."

"Yes," she panted, still stroking me, damn near stealing my ability to speak. "God, yes."

Hudson thrust into her, hitting her deeper, sending her legs into a spasm as she arched her back for more, more, *more* of his cock, more of my fevered touch, more of Saint's fierce gaze, all of us crazed and frantic and lost.

And then, in a singularly perfect moment of bliss…

Found once again.

She came for us like a wild thing, reckless and bold, her back arching as the pleasure exploded inside her, setting off a chain reaction. Her fist tightened around my cock, and I came in a blinding rush that spilled hot and slippery between us as Hudson slammed into her one last time, his whole body shuddering against her soft, sweet curves.

"*Fuck*," Saint ground out, the first word he'd uttered since ordering us to make her sing. The strangled grunt of his voice told me he'd just come too, right along with us, clearly by his own stroke. But when I chanced another look at him, I saw his hands still fisted around the arms of the chair, his pants still fastened. He hadn't even touched himself. Just fell apart as he'd watched the three of us bring each other to ecstasy once again.

In that moment, it didn't matter that I resented him. That we still had unfinished arguments about the past, the present, the fucking future.

Deep down, I still fucking loved him like a brother, and seeing that fathomless longing in his eyes—longing for a thing that for some reason he couldn't have—damn near broke my heart.

*Fucking Saint.*

He watched us for a few more heartbeats, but then he closed his eyes and shook his head, as if he were trying to clear something away. Images of us touching the woman he loved? Of her bleeding out after the ghoul attack? Remnants of the Devil's Dream still lingering in his mind?

Some other dark horror I couldn't even imagine?

Whatever it was, something finally snapped inside him, and without a word he rose from the chair, his cock still half-hard, his release damp and obvious on his pants, his shattered heart shining like a torch in his silver eyes.

With one more soft, broken smile for Haley, he slipped out of the room and shut the door.

None of us spoke, but as the three of us stretched out on our backs, breath slowly returning to our lungs, I felt Haley's heartache for Saint like another person in the bed, the weight of it pressing down on all of us.

But no one dared bring it up. Maybe we wanted to respect his privacy. Maybe we were too scared to hear the truth. Maybe it was a little bit of both.

Eventually, Hudson let out a deep exhale, then rolled over to steal another kiss from our girl. Rising from the bed, he collected his discarded clothing and got dressed. He and Haley exchanged another one of their long and silent glances, and then she nodded.

"Be careful," she said.

A nod. A grin. One more passionate kiss, and then Hudson was off, presumably to head back out in search of the fuckers who'd eluded us tonight. I still didn't know the whole story, but I'd gotten enough from his earlier grunts and gestures to put some of it together. Keradoc's men were behind the attack, along with a couple of Stone City gargoyles Hudson was more than looking forward to murdering.

"I should *probably* go with him," I said, turning to face her. I traced a long, lazy path up and down her arm. "But I rather like being naked next to you, so… yeah. Decision made. I'm staying."

"Good. I missed you." She cracked up. "You work too much. Maybe I should have a talk with that boss of yours."

"I'd rather you didn't. And also, don't mention his name while we're naked. Not if you want me to stay hard for you."

"As if you have a problem staying hard for me."

"Fair point." I kissed her, lingering just a little longer before I pulled back and said, "How do you feel, anyway? No side effects from your little blood transfusion?"

She rolled her eyes and laughed again. "Yeah, I heard you thought he'd turned me into a vampire."

"It was definitely a concern."

"Unfounded, obviously. If I were a vampire, I'd be the one biting *you*." She rolled on top of me and nipped at my neck, a gesture I happily returned, again and again until she was squealing and flailing against me.

*Fuck*, everything about her felt so damn good. So damn right.

I smoothed my palms down her back and cupped her ass, and she propped her elbows on my chest and cradled her chin, staring down at me in the moonlight.

Damn, those eyes. Those lips. I was lost.

"Jax?" she said softly, a frown tugging the corners of her mouth. "If I *had* been turned, would you still look at me the way you're looking at me now?"

"How am I looking at you, angel?"

"Like… I don't know. Like you'd die if I pushed you away."

"The day I stop looking at you like that is the day you're planning a funeral," I whispered, "because angel? It would mean I was already dead." I captured her face between my hands and kissed her fiercely, emotion rising like a tidal wave in my chest, sweeping me under and sucking me out to sea.

She was everything to me—my woman, my witch, my angel, and though I never thought it was possible to feel this way, I knew, deep down, why I'd been so terrified of losing her earlier—what the bite of that hot, deadly fear inside me actually meant.

The words gathered behind my teeth, the taste of them foreign and sharp, once again terrifying me, as if I needed the reminder of how dangerous those words could be. Everything inside me trembled at the prospect of speaking them aloud—of accepting the promise and responsibility that came with them.

But I had to set them free. I couldn't deny it for another moment, and I couldn't keep them locked inside.

I clung to her, holding her tight, breathing in the scent of her.

And then, in a dark whisper, I finally made my confession.

"The first time I saw you in Saints and Sinners, when you staked that asshole vampire at the bar, I started falling for you. And every moment since—every argument, every chase, every kiss, every breathless shudder —has taken another piece of my armor, baring my heart until I finally felt that fear I'd spent so many centuries outrunning. Now I'm naked and exposed and you… You have the power to absolutely fucking *wreck* me, and there's not a damn thing I can do to change that because I don't want to. Because I'm in love with you, Haley Barnes. And that fucking *terrifies* me—more than every monster in Midnight, more than every nightmare I ever faced in hell. But it's the truth. I love you. And I will spend the rest of my immortal life making sure you damn well know it."

Tears glittered in her eyes, and she took my face in her hands and opened her mouth, and I felt it the moment she was going to say the words right back to me—the three that would forever alter the course of my immortal existence. Hell, I could see it in her gaze, that raw emotion, the truth that cut us both to the bone.

My heart damn near exploded with happiness.

But I couldn't—I just *couldn't*—hear those words from her—not yet. Not in Midnight, when we still had so many battles to fight, so many risks to take. So much fear to face.

I wanted to savor it. To wait for it, even though I couldn't wait to say it to her.

"Not yet." I brushed my fingertip to her lips, then followed with a soft kiss. "Tell me when we're back in New Orleans."

"But what if... What if we don't—"

I silenced her with another kiss, another promise. Then, whispering against her lips, "We will, angel. Because I *swear* to you, I will burn this realm to the fucking *ground* just for a chance to see you back in Saint's kitchen in NOLA, moaning over Cajun Jeb's jambalaya and yes, Jeb's the only other man besides Hudson and Saint that's allowed to make you moan."

This got another laugh, a smile through her happy tears.

"For now," she teased, those green eyes flashing with a wicked gleam.

"Excuse me!" I rolled on top of her, pinning her wrists over her head, stealing another kiss that left her breathless. "If you've got any other monsters on your list, I'm gonna need names. Right now. Addresses too."

"Why, so you can hunt them down and kick their asses? So chivalrous, sinner."

"No, angel. So I can hunt them down, kick their asses, light them on fire, and watch them burn, if you want to get technical about it, which—"

"Jax!" she gasped, her face suddenly falling, eyes wide with shock. "Oh my god! I just realized... Keradoc!"

I groaned. "*Please* tell me the warlord presently holding us hostage is not on your fuck list. I thought we agreed not to talk about him while naked."

"The scars!" she exclaimed, as if this made any fucking sense at all.

"What scars? Haley, what are you talking about?"

"Keradoc's scars. I can't believe I didn't... Fuck." She wriggled out from under me and stumbled out of bed, hunting down her bathrobe. She was still wobbly on her feet—either from her ordeal in the moat, or from what we'd done to bring her back. Either way, I didn't want her storming off into the castle in search of the fucking warlord on her own. Or at *all*, for that matter, but if there was one thing I'd learned about Haley Barnes— well, other than how to make her come—it was that when she set her mind to something, nothing would stop her from seeing it through.

"Mind telling me where we're going?" I asked, following her out of bed and hastily pulling my pants on. "You haven't even started singing again yet, and now you're—"

"Where's Elian?"

"If I had to guess? Probably giving Keradoc a few *more* scars, considering what he did to you tonight."

"*He* didn't do anything."

"His hired lackeys tried to..." I pinched the bridge of my nose and sighed. "Seriously, angel. Why are you so worked up about fucking Keradoc all of a sudden?"

She knotted her bathrobe tight, her face suddenly pale. "Because fucking Keradoc *isn't* fucking Keradoc at all. And I need to find Elian before he does something that'll fuck him up worse than all the Devil's Dream in the realm."

<h1 style="text-align:center">23</h1>

<h2 style="text-align:center">ELIAN</h2>

*I* stayed, just like she'd asked me to.

Watched with a desperate agony bleeding through my soul as Jax and Hudson gave her everything I no longer could. It was a torture worse than any withdrawals, worse than any hawthorn stakes I'd ever taken to the gut.

Yet I wasn't able to look away. Not once. Because my *god*, seeing her like that? Watching my brothers take care of her, put that blush in her cheeks, make her sing her sweet little off-key songs?

Haley had never been so happy. So alive. And witnessing that was like witnessing a goddamn miracle. It was incredible. Breathtaking. And yeah, so fucking hot I'm surprised we all didn't burst into flames.

But it broke my heart nevertheless. Because as much as I wanted them to make her happy, *I* wanted to make her happy, too. And I fucking couldn't.

Ever again.

*Fuck.* I had to get out of there. Right fucking now.

Not because my heart was smashed—that was a small price to pay for all the things I'd put her through, and I was willing to endure it for as long and as often as she granted me the privilege of watching her.

No, I had to get out of there right fucking now because I had business to attend to.

Haley had been hurt tonight.

Someone had put her life at risk.

498

Which meant someone needed to *die.*

Didn't matter that I still wore the evidence of her effect on me, a cold dampness spreading across my pants. Didn't matter that I was hard for her all over again, a sharp ache in my balls to match the one in my heart, twin pains that would never ease. *None* of that mattered. Lust mingled with pain mingled with rage into a fierce determination that propelled me out of that room and down the dark hallway in search of the only man who—in the absence of the guards Hudson and Jax hadn't been able to locate—could pay tonight's hefty price.

I slipped three pills from my pocket—last of my emergency stash— then downed them in quick succession, ignoring the shame in my chest. Ignoring the self-hatred.

I needed them, just this last time. Needed the devil to steady me as only he could. To keep me from succumbing to my fear or sadness or worry or anything—*any* fucking thing—that might interfere with me completing this singularly important task.

I followed the scent of him—dead roses, a hint of bourbon and ice from a freshly poured drink.

I hoped he enjoyed that drink.

It would be his last.

Two fae guards trailed him, hovering like flies on a steaming shit pile. Their heads swiveled toward me as I waltzed into the library, hands shifting at once to their crossbows.

Keradoc was standing at one of his bookshelves, the bourbon in one hand, a book spread open in the other, his brow knit tight with consternation.

He knew I was there the moment I'd taken a step across the threshold, but he waited until the guards had drawn their weapons before finally glancing up to meet my gaze.

Whatever he saw in my eyes, he knew I was *not* fucking around.

His eyes widened a fraction, the scent of his blood tinged with the barest whisper of adrenaline.

*You should be afraid, you sonofabitch. Death is calling for you, and he won't be satisfied until he claims your tarnished soul...*

Quickly schooling his features into an expression of boredom, he said evenly, "Elian of Autumnshire, finally crawled out from the bottom of the barrel, have you? Looking for something to read, perhaps?"

"Not exactly."

He snapped his book shut and slid it back into place on the shelf, then swirled the ice in his glass.

Bored. Unaffected. Ever-so-slightly annoyed.

It was a good act. Pretty convincing, really, but for the adrenaline still coursing through him, mingling with his rich fae blood like an invitation to a gourmet fucking meal.

"I wasn't aware you'd recovered from your... incident," he said, his words clipped.

I *hadn't* recovered. Not really. I'd slaughtered two dozen people whose only crime had been falling prey to the same addiction that still gripped me in a chokehold. I'd damn near turned Haley into a vampire tonight because I couldn't think straight anymore. I'd put everyone I loved at risk, and I kept doing it, again and again and again, because I was a worthless junkie and a selfish fae fuck, and unless and until I could pull myself out of this pit, I didn't deserve to call myself anything else.

But that wasn't why I'd come here tonight, seeking our warlord.

"I'm not here to discuss my fuckups with you, Keradoc. As much as I'd *love* to regale you with the tales of my utter ineptitude—and trust me, there are many, as I'm sure you can imagine—I've got other business here tonight."

He glowered at me a long beat, then slid his gaze to his guards. "Go check on the other prisoners. This parasite is nothing I can't handle alone."

The guards bowed, then did as he asked, closing the doors behind them and leaving us in the library alone.

*Fatal mistake, fuckers. Fatal mistake.*

"So tell me, *slave*," he sneered, enunciating the word as if I might've forgotten my place here and needed the reminder. "What is it you think I can do for you?"

Despite his attempt at belittling me, his bravado had slipped away with the departure of his guards, leaving behind a tired, worn-out ghost of a man. I stepped closer, taking in the sight of the fine lines around his eyes, the tension in his jaw, the bone-deep weariness that clung to him like a second skin.

Putting him out of his misery would be a kindness.

"Oh, it's a small thing, really," I said. "Quick little favor."

"Get on with it then. I'm a busy man, as you might imagine."

I flashed a grin. "*Die.*"

I blurred into him, slamming him into a towering shelf clear on the other side of the room. Books and statues fell to the floor, but I didn't give a fuck. My fist was a piston, smashing into his face and breaking his nose, the sweet scent of his blood making my mouth water for more.

My fangs descended, the imagined taste of his rich fae blood already warming on my tongue, but I wouldn't give him the satisfaction of feeding on him. He'd expect that. A vampire out of control, driven by rage and bloodlust.

*Couldn't be helped,* he'd convince himself as his soul slipped away. *The poor savage.*

Fuck that. I wanted him to know I was in *complete* control. That killing him was my choice—one made in a singular moment of clarity. That it was my fucking *pleasure.*

With a firm grip on his hair, I jerked his head back and pressed the tip of my dagger to the soft underside of his chin. One quick thrust, and I could skewer his brains.

"What you did to her tonight?" I seethed, barely able to grind out the rest of the words. "I will *end* you."

"Ah." He rolled his eyes. "So the little thief told you about our kiss, then? Yes, I know I was wrong to steal it, but it couldn't be helped. The way she was looking at me, the scent of her..." He closed his eyes and inhaled, his lips twisting into a cruel smirk. "She was practically *begging* for it."

*Kiss? Begging for it?*

A fresh wave of fury descended over me, sucking me down deep, threatening to drown me. My hand trembled, yet Keradoc didn't fight back.

No matter. Whether he'd truly kissed her or this was just another manipulation, it mattered not. My mission didn't change.

"You'll *die* for her." My blade pierced his skin, blood welling at the tip. Keradoc didn't even wince, yet my hand still trembled inexplicably, my resolve weakening. "Give me a reason to let you walk, filth."

*Fuck.* What the hell was wrong with me? Keradoc *deserved* to die. Slow, fast, I didn't care, as long as he stopped existing.

So why the hell was I hesitating? *Bargaining* with the cocksucker?

"You've come here to assassinate Keradoc of Midnight," he said, still refusing to fight me, his tone heavy with exhaustion. "And you're asking me to talk you out of it? Well, I'm sorry to disappoint you, slave, but that is a request I cannot grant. You see, I've made similar attempts against the warlord's life—seventeen, to be exact. All failed."

I blinked rapidly, trying to stay focused. Was I fucking high? Or had the dream not worked its way through my system yet?

He'd made seventeen attempts against the warlord's life? What was he even talking about? Suicide?

"Stop taking me in circles," I snapped. "You've got fifteen seconds to come up with your last words. I suggest you make them count."

I dug the blade in deeper, blood sliding down the cold metal.

Keradoc closed his eyes and sighed.

"Do it," he whispered, and fuck *me*, how I wanted to. More than anything. I felt it all the way in my bones, the desire as powerful as any drug craving, *sucking* at me, begging me. The old devil whispered on my shoulder, pushing me to shove that blade in just a little harder. Deeper. To end him. To spill his warm blood until he was nothing but an empty husk.

*Do it,* the devil echoed. *End his life. You've earned this. Remember everything he took from you. It's why you came to Midnight. It's what you've always wanted...*

And it was, too. The desire wound tight inside me, threatening to explode.

But something more powerful steadied my hand, even as I tried to obey the devil and Keradoc both.

Something—some wild, inexplicable force—was physically preventing me from shoving in that blade.

"*Do it!*" Keradoc roared, the force of it rattling my teeth, spraying my face with his blood. "What are you waiting for, slave? *End this!*"

Instinctively, my tongue darted out to lick his blood from my lips.

Salty, warm, coppery. A hint of sweetness lingering on the end like the rarest, finest wine.

*That's it, boy,* the devil goaded. *Taste it. Drink it in. Take it. Take what's yours...*

The decadence of dark-fae blood was legendary, and the taste of it sent me into a spin, finally breaking the strange hold that'd so far steadied my hand.

But now, I didn't need the dagger. Didn't care whether Keradoc thought I was a savage.

I only wanted one thing.

Blood.

The dagger clattered to the floor. I wrenched his head back again, and sank my fangs deep into his throat.

Keradoc cried out in pain, but he didn't resist. Didn't struggle as I began to drain the life from his body.

And oh, that sweet, perfect taste.

I was drunk on him, quickly falling under the heady influence, the taste of that blood even more seductive than the Black coursing through my system. Keradoc's muscles relaxed, his body sagging against me, no longer able to hold itself upright.

If I didn't stop soon, I'd kill him.

I didn't care. Two birds, one bloody stone, far as I was concerned.

A moan of pure pleasure vibrated through my chest, and I took another deep drink, savoring the salty tang as it slid down my throat, and then...

A flash tore through my mind, splitting my skull in two, a rush of memories spilling forth.

The flicker of silver eyes, the flutter of silver hair in the breeze.

A laugh like the tinkling of bells, two boys stealing golden nectar from the yellow-and-white sun blossoms growing in their mother's garden.

A laugh like the tinkling of bells, two boys giggling behind the hedges.

A laugh like the tinkling of bells, and a whisper like a ghost in the graveyard, calling out across the realms...

*Look what I found, Evander...*

*Come play with me, Evander...*

*Come back, Evander! Where are you? Why have you left us?*

*Evander, no! Evander...*

"Elian," the whisper called, the name changing. "Elian."

The voice was louder now, but still soft. A voice I remembered. I voice I *knew*—the only one with the power to reach through the all-consuming haze of my bloodlust, my fury, my fantasies, my memories, my regrets...

And blow them all away like dust.

*Sparrow.*

My fangs receded. I squeezed my eyes shut. Counted to ten.

And when I opened them again, the haze of the past had cleared, and the man leaning against me was Keradoc once more.

Not the silver-eyed fae who haunted my past. Who lived as a ghost in my heart.

"Elian," she whispered again, reaching up to cup my face, her gentle touch as soft as her voice. "Please don't do this. You have to let him go."

Blood still coated my fangs, sliding down in fat, delicious drops on my tongue. I wanted to obey her, to give her what she wanted. But...

"Keradoc deserves to die," I protested.

"Keradoc deserves *worse* than death," Haley said, her voice turning icy cold. But the look in her eyes was warm and devastated, fresh tears shining on her cheeks. "But the man in your arms isn't Keradoc."

That man and I both stared at her in silence, awaiting the drop of the guillotine.

"Elian," Haley whispered, scattering the last of the haze from my mind like a child blowing away the dandelion seeds. "He's your brother. He's Evander of Autumnshire."

# 24

## KERADOC

*B*rother…
     *Evander of Autumshire…*
*He's your brother…*
*Brother…*
*Brother…*
*Elian, he's your brother. He's Evander of Autumnshire…*

Her gentle words were a dim echo in the recesses of my mind, but I couldn't make sense of them. Couldn't acknowledge the dawning realization that'd been dancing on a razor-thin wire in my mind ever since my guards had dropped the vampire-fae on his knees in the throne room the night of the Feast, staked and bleeding, and through his agony he'd gazed upon me as if I were a benevolent god come to deliver him from death.

Because now, in this moment, there *was* no vampire-fae. No brother. No murky, forgotten childhood I couldn't recall even if I forced myself to try.

No. Right now, there wasn't even a weakened, broken body drained of blood and very near collapse after a vampire bite, a warlord who hadn't even tried to defend his own life.

There was only Haley Barnes, my witch. My weapon. My feisty, fiery little thief with her wild eyes and soft, expressive mouth and tossed hair and—an unbearable sight that gripped me in a rage so sudden and violent, everything else vanished in its stark presence—a series of dark, angry bruises blackening her beautiful face and neck.

I reached for her, my hand shaking as I brushed a gentle thumb across her cheekbone.

She winced at my touch, then lowered her eyes, cheeks darkening as if she were ashamed to be seen in such a state.

A fury like the end of the world ripped through my chest, making me tremble.

"You're… wounded," I gritted out.

"I'll survive," she said softly. "Elian healed the worst of it already—no permanent damage."

Emotion swelled inside, but I slammed the gates down on it. There was no room for emotion now. Only action. Swift, resolute action.

I lowered my hand, fisting it to stem the uncontrollable quake. Turning away from her, I looked at the man she claimed was my brother, then at the one-eyed demon who'd followed her into my library.

When I finally found the will to speak, I couldn't keep the tremor from my voice. *"Who. Did. This?"*

The demon scoffed. *"Now* you care what happens to her?"

*"Answer me!"* I roared, the words scraping my throat raw, making the puncture wounds in my neck throb—wounds my so-called brother had made. Blood trickled down my throat and soaked into my shirt, but I was beyond caring. Beyond all reasonable thought. Beyond anything but the sudden need to vanquish the vile creatures who'd *dared* to bruise her.

Again, the silver-eyed fae drew close to me, nose-to-nose, the ghost of Devil's Dream sweet on his breath. "You left her alone on that wall with a fucking *mercenary* after warning her for weeks that your enemies could hurt her. And she *did* get hurt, *Keradoc,*" he sneered, enunciating the name as if he didn't want to believe Haley's proclamation any more than I did. "Barely made it out alive. But you were wrong about one thing—the attack didn't come from your enemies. It came from your hired thugs, bought and paid for with Midnight currency. *Your* currency."

I opened my mouth to deny this blasphemy, but the intensity in his eyes told me he spoke the truth.

The fury in my gut simmered. My arm shot forward and I fisted his shirt, yanking him closer. *"Which* hired thugs?"

He and the demon remained silent.

"They die tonight," I vowed. "All of them."

*"Haley* nearly died tonight," the demon snapped. "Because of you."

*"Name them!"*

"It was the gargoyle," Haley finally said, wedging herself between me and the vampire-fae until I was forced to release him. Her voice was clear and commanding, her eyes blazing with righteous indignation as she glared up at me. "I asked him to bring me back to the castle, but he grabbed me and flew over the wall instead. A few other gargoyles showed up too, and I saw a wagon with two fae guards I recognized from the team that normally watches my room. The whole thing was a setup."

She told me the story, my vision blackening around the edges with every word as I imagined the fear she must've felt. The pain. Her insane bravery in the face of the ghouls.

I was certain she was the only living being to *ever* survive a fall into Beggar's Moat, let alone an attack by the very ghouls for which it's named.

But there would be time for admiration and wonder later. Right now, I had another mission.

I held her gaze for only a moment longer. Just long enough to make my silent vow.

*I will find them, my little thief. And for every bruise, for every welt, for every smudge of dirt they left upon your perfect skin, I will make them suffer a* thousand *unimaginable tortures...*

"Rest tonight, Haley. I will return to check on you later." I reached for her face once more, nothing but a soft brush of my fingertips along her jaw.

She shivered at my touch, but there was a smile there too. Soft. Sweet.

And with that smile held firmly in my mind, I turned on my heel and stalked out of that room.

I marched down the stairs. Searched every level, floor by floor. When the sprawling rooms of the castle turned up empty, when the hallways and basements and dungeons revealed no sign of the men I sought, I moved out to the grounds.

And there, in the Sanctuary, I finally found them.

The two dark fae soldiers and the gargoyle who'd been on my payroll for years, huddled together with a handful of other guards and kitchen staff in the shadowed back corner, cavorting and sharing bottles of bourbon no doubt pilfered from my stash.

Women and booze—popular pastimes among the guards. Pastimes I'd always overlooked, preferring to lure them into the false sense of security one often develops when he believes he's more clever than his master.

When he believes his master isn't watching.

I was *always* watching. Except for tonight at the wall—a momentary lapse when my attention was needed elsewhere. A lapse they'd taken full advantage of, conspiring to kidnap and torture my beautiful witch.

My vision turned red, but I kept the monster inside me at bay.

For the moment.

"And what are we drinking to this evening, gentlemen?" I stepped out into the courtyard, beaming at them. "I do hope it's a worthy cause."

"Sir! We, um… That is to say… Did you need something?" The only guard brave or stupid enough to make eye contact with me squared his shoulders, trying desperately to hide a bottle behind his back.

"No salute tonight?" I taunted. "Well, no matter. This will only take a moment—I won't keep you." *Alive*, I resisted adding. Then, glaring at my head cook, "I'm sure you and the other kitchen staff have work to finish, yes?"

"Of course, sir." She bowed her head, then gathered up the others, shooing them back inside like a mother hen saving her chicks from the fox.

"Is everything all right, sir?" another guard asked. "Thought you'd still be at the wall, or I would've checked in sooner."

I turned my gaze to him.

*Him.*

He was in his human form now, drunk and stinking of booze, but there was no mistaking the gargoyle. The bastard who'd taken Haley over the wall and dropped her into Beggar's Moat.

Clearly, he didn't know she'd survived her ordeal. Didn't know I'd learned of his treachery. His final, fatal mistake.

"Actually, no, it isn't all right. I'd like to talk to you about a few changes we'll be making to the guard. Staffing… *cuts*, if you will." With that, I removed my sword.

He opened his mouth to question me, or perhaps to utter his final words, or voice an objection about the unfairness of it all. His fetid breath curdled my stomach.

So I took his head.

Clean cut, which was better than he deserved, but no less gratifying when the spray of blood gushed from his neck and his wasted body dropped to the ground.

Shocked and confused, a few of the guards dropped their drinks and reached for their weapons, clumsy in their drunkenness. The others stood mutely by, likely trying to decide which side would offer them better odds of survival.

Neither.

I lifted my sword again and advanced on another guard—one Haley had identified as one of the riders. He clutched a dagger in his hand, but the booze had left him unsteady. He stumbled backward against the court-yard wall, and I shoved my blade into his belly, eviscerating him.

The remaining guards roared in fear, scrambling to mount an attack. But they were drunk, and I was…

Not alone.

Suddenly I felt a presence at my back, and turned around just long enough to confirm my suspicions.

Haley's men.

The demon, the blood-drenched gargoyle who'd apparently just returned from some other fight, and the vampire-fae—my brother, if Haley's presumptions were correct.

I didn't know whether to be repulsed by the idea or glad of it, but right now, there was no time to contemplate the family tree. No time to ask why they'd followed me out here.

Only time for vengeance.

We were bound by it, this blood and madness that had brought us together. And that, more than anything, made them *all* my brothers, even if it was just for tonight.

Without another word, we charged, our individual strengths merging into an unstoppable force—the vampire-fae's speed and lust for blood, the demon's fear manipulations, the gargoyle's raw power, and my unwavering determination to end the lives of anyone who dared harm Haley Barnes.

It felt like only minutes before the gardens were awash with the blood of our enemies, the chokeweed twisting out of the soil to claim the bodies —all but the heads we'd so dutifully severed, clutched in our blood-stained fists like an offering, all for her.

# 25

## HALEY

*J*'d paced the suite for so long I was sure I'd worn a groove in the stone floors. But then, after a damn lifetime, Keradoc and my monsters finally returned.

Covered in blood and gore, reeking of death, but I'd never been so relieved and happy for such a homecoming.

"I take it you found them?" I asked.

"We did," Elian said. Blood dripped from his hands onto the floor.

*Pat-pat-pat-pat-pat.*

"And?" I pressed.

"They won't touch you again," Keradoc said. There was a massive canvas bag slung over his shoulder, and he dropped it at my feet, spilling its contents.

Heads. A bag full of severed heads. At least a dozen of them.

"I am sorry for the mess." He sketched an apologetic bow, but his eyes held a joyful malice that sent a spark right through my core. "I wanted you to be assured that the situation had been... dealt with."

"No it's... it's great. I... thank you."

"We all helped," Elian said, puffing up his chest a bit.

"I bet you did." I covered my smile with my hand, trying not to laugh. Gratitude bloomed inside me, as if the monsters had brought me a chocolate peanut butter milkshake and a burger and fries smothered in cheese rather than the heads of the mercenaries who'd hurt me.

I tried not to think about what that said about my ever-darkening moral compass, but still, I *was* appreciative. I'd always said I was a chocolates-and-weapons kind of girl. Guess I needed to add the severed heads of my enemies to the Haley Barnes gift list, too.

After a quick recap of the fight, my guys went to wash up, leaving me alone in the suite with Keradoc.

He watched me in silence, his eyes still holding a glint of that malice, a hint of the dark well of depravity I suspected ran bone-deep inside him.

Suddenly, completely uninvited, Jax's earlier words echoed.

*Please tell me the warlord presently holding us hostage is not on your fuck list...*

I sucked in a breath and closed my eyes.

Keradoc? On my so-called fuck list?

No. No way. Impossible. I didn't even *like* him, let alone...

Memories rushed through me in a hot torrent, his fist in my hair, his strong, lean body pinning me against the wall, his cock grinding against me, his tongue sweeping into my mouth as my all-too-eager fingers tugged at his shirt buttons like I wanted to strip him bare and—

"Haley, are you all right? You look a bit peaked, all of a sudden."

"Yes!" I blinked away the memories and met his gaze, his face pinched with concern. "No!" I rushed to add, fucking awkward as hell. "I mean, yes I'm all right, no I'm not peaked, and... So, are you... going to shower, or... tea? Tea! Excellent. I could make us some, I mean. If you want. That lavender mint blend—I remember you liked that one. It's calming, so..."

I clamped my mouth shut and turned toward the cupboards, my hands shaking.

Why the hell was I so nervous around him?

*As if you don't know, girl...*

"Haley." I felt his presence in the kitchen behind me, his breath stirring my hair, his voice soft and warm, a direct contrast to the vicious, blood-soaked beast I knew him to be. "There's something I need to show you. Something I should've shown you sooner."

"If it's another bag of heads, I appreciate the sentiment, but I'm good. Really."

"It's not—I assure you."

I turned to face him, my stomach bubbling with nerves that had nothing to do with his status on my fuck list. "The last time you wanted to show me something, I ended up fighting for my life in a moat full of—"

"Leaving you unguarded on the wall with a gargoyle mercenary was a grievous error I will *never* make again, and not just because I've decapitated most of my private guard." He took my hands in his and brought them to his mouth, the touch gentle despite the rage in his voice. Despite the blood caked under his nails. Then, with the softest brush of his lips against my fingertips, he whispered, "I vow to *never* leave you in the care of anyone but myself or the men who fought by my side to bring your attackers to justice. On that, you have my word, Haley Barnes."

"I... I'm... Okay. I appreciate it. I believe you." I pulled out of his grasp, unable to take the warring sensations battling in my chest. Desire, where there should only be revulsion. Trust, where there should only be wariness.

And sympathy, for a man who'd been stolen from his family, his entire life rerouted, molding him into something he was never meant to be.

"Evander," I whispered, my heart nearly shattering for all that he and Elian had lost. "I—"

"It can't wait," he said urgently, ignoring the name. "You must come with me now. It... it may change everything for you."

"Change everything, how?"

"The choice you've yet to make. The decision that will determine your role in this war. In this... in this everything. I need to—"

"Seriously?" I let out a sigh, my shoulders sagging. "Would it be too much to ask for *one* night where we don't have to talk about this freaking endless war? Like, I totally appreciate that you and the guys teamed up and went all psycho on the guards for me, and no one has ever brought me heads before, so that was kind of... special. But what if we just, like, stayed in tonight? We could bake brownies and make hot chocolate with little marshmallows on top, and stretch out before the fireplace with a game of Scrabble, or maybe do a little Netflix-and-chill? Or whatever the Midnight equivalent of all that is?"

I smiled at him, knowing it was futile, but losing myself in the fantasy nevertheless.

"I... only understood about half of those words, but..." He blinked at me, shaking his head. "There is so much to explain, yet so little time to do so. Please, Haley. Come with me. Trust me once more and come with me."

The malice in his violet eyes vanished, replaced with a desperation that told me he was telling the truth.

He held out his hand.

And I took it, ready to follow him into whatever new Midnight insanity awaited.

———

It wasn't until we reached the dark, dank corridor that led to the dungeons that he finally spoke again, his voice so soft and tentative, I almost couldn't be sure it was even him.

"Do you truly believe he's my brother?" he asked. "That I'm..." He stopped and turned to face me, his eyes dancing in the golden torchlight that illuminated our path.

"Evander of Autumnshire," I said.

"How... Why do you even know that name?"

"At this point, the better question is... Why do you *not* know it?"

His eyes clouded, his gaze shifting to some faraway place I couldn't even begin to imagine.

"I feel as though I should," he whispered, "and yet... I can't explain it, Haley. Evander... The name exists on the very edges of my memory, but it won't solidify into anything real, anything I can grasp. It's... it's like a ghost that haunted me as a child. An imaginary friend, perhaps. A monster hiding beneath the bed, only to vanish with the first flicker of torchlight shone into the shadows. Yet you... you seem so certain. Why?"

"Let me see your face," I said softly, reaching up to press a palm to his cheek. "Your real face."

He leaned into my touch, a soft sigh catching in his throat. "This *is* my face, Haley. At least, it is the one I..." He blinked, then cleared his throat, turning away from me to continue along the corridor, stopping when we reached the door to the cells. "Just in here."

"Just so you know?" I folded my arms across my chest and leaned against the dank wall while he fumbled with his keyring. "If this is a trap, my guys will carve off your limbs and leave the rest of you to rot in here, so—"

"There's no trap, Haley. Not for you, anyway." He unlocked the door, then turned to me, handed over the keys, and stripped off his weapons, leaving all of them outside the door except for one—the biggest, scariest looking dagger of the bunch. The blade was gleaming obsidian, so sharp it looked as if it could split the dust motes floating between us. Violet jewels the same shade as his eyes studded the hilt.

Thing must've been worth a small fortune, yet he handed it to me with nothing more than a wicked grin slashed across his face. "If at any time you sense a trap, you have my permission to finish the job my brother Elian could not, and leave whichever parts of mine you choose for the dungeon rats."

I peered over his shoulder into the darkness on the other side of the door—a small chamber that held several ancient-looking cells.

Curiosity sunk its hooks in deep.

Shooting him a final warning glare, I reached out and grabbed the hilt, keeping the dagger close as I followed him into the room, the stench of rot and waste making me gag.

"Prisoner 6712," he called out across the dark space. "How are we feeling this evening?"

Out of the shadows of one of the cells came a grumble and a cough, the sound of iron chains clanking. The sound of struggle. Of quiet rage.

"What the hell?" I whispered, narrowing my eyes as the shapes emerged from the darkness.

The man on the cot was old and sickly, his dark hair hanging in limp locks around a gaunt face.

A wheeze rattled through his lungs, and when Evander brought his torch close to the bars, the prisoner recoiled from the light.

"Who is he?" I asked, my heart already pounding its way up to my throat, my skin prickling with unease.

After a long, impossibly tense pause, Keradoc finally said, "*He* is a man who tortured me for decades. Brutalized me as a child in ways I dare not speak of, for naming them would mean releasing them from the depths of my soul where I've kept them chained for all these long years." Then, with a dark sigh, "The man whose life I've been living—wearing—for the past eighteen months."

"I… what?" I pressed a hand to my chest, struggling to keep my heart from bursting as his words filtered through my mind. "Evander… Keradoc… I… I don't understand."

He slid his torch into an empty sconce on the wall, then turned to face me, his eyes holding an apology for something I was only just beginning to grasp.

"This *filth* is Lord Commander Keradoc of Midnight." With more than a little difficulty, Keradoc—*my* Keradoc—removed the ring from his finger—a ring I'd seen him twisting and toying with many times. Blood ran down his finger, but he either didn't notice or didn't care.

"Who or what that makes *me*," he continued, "I know not. I was kidnapped and brought to Midnight as a child, my identity and past lost to its darkness."

Suddenly, the man before me transformed, his hair streaked with more silver than black, his face shifting, his eyes flickering from deep violet to silver. To the eyes I'd seen that first night in the throne room and mistaken for Elian's.

They were *never* Elian's. They were Evander's, his twin brother. The man who Keradoc—the *real* Keradoc—had stolen as a child, just as Elian thought.

All of the pieces clicked into place.

"But… but how is this possible?" I touched his face again, mesmerized by the change. But just before I lost myself in those silver eyes, Evander slid the ring back on, his eyes turning violet once more.

"Dark magick," he said. "A glamour spell that allows me to maintain his appearance at all times. To become him, for all intents and purposes."

"But… why?"

Through gritted teeth, he said, "So that I may take *everything* from him, just as he has taken everything from me. His soldiers have become mine. His daughter has become mine. His entire kingdom, and all the magick and power it possesses, will become mine, and all the while he will molder and fester, dying a slow, agonizing death, knowing that the boy he once called a slave has finally exacted his revenge."

Evander was trembling now, the force of his convictions thrumming through him like an electrical charge.

"And what about Elian?" I whispered, reaching out to touch his arm. "What about your brother?"

He turned away from me, shaking his head. "You're so certain, Haley, but as I've told you, I have no memory of him."

"But he's your—"

"Brother, yes, so you've said. But tell me, Haley Barnes." He turned and stepped close to me once again, the rotting, wheezing Keradoc temporarily forgotten. "What is he to you?"

"Elian? Well, he's my… It's kind of hard to explain, but we sort of…"

"Love each other?" he offered. A cold laugh followed. "Your connection to him runs deep. Deep enough that on our first night together, you were able to see through my glamour to the silver-eyed fae beneath." He took a step closer. "And when you kissed me, you believed you were kissing him."

"Yes, but only… Only at first."

He arched an eyebrow, a challenge flashing in his now-violet eyes, a new intensity that stripped me bare.

I couldn't lie to him. Not about this.

"I knew it the moment our lips touched," I admitted. "I knew I wasn't kissing Elian."

"Yet you didn't stop. Why?"

"I… I don't know. I guess I felt… something."

He took another step closer, chasing the last of the air from the room. *"Something."*

"A connection. A spark. Just like earlier on the wall, when you kissed me again, I…" I pressed my lips together, forcing myself to stop. I'd already said too much, and this was as close to the truth as I was willing to go.

Evander held my gaze for a long beat, his own fiery. But then he closed his eyes and exhaled, his head bowing low to his chest, a heaviness settling over his shoulders once more.

"For your sake, little thief, I wish I *could* remember my past. A happier time. Some hope to cling to on the darkest nights." He lifted his chin and looked into my eyes again, his own clearing. "No matter. That was a long time ago. I must move forward, as we all must."

"Why did you bring me here?" I asked. "Why did you tell me about Keradoc?"

"I left you vulnerable on the wall tonight, and the consequences of that were a wake-up call. I've kept you in the dark for too long, yet I'm asking you—once again—to risk your life for my war. My cause."

"Your revenge," I said, tightening my grip on his dagger, still not entirely sure where this was heading.

"My revenge," he whispered, taking my other hand in his. The cool metal ring that held his glamour in place clinked against my bloodstone ring, making me shiver. "Whatever you choose, I want you to do so with open eyes. To know who—and what—you're choosing."

"Who else knows about this?" I asked, glancing into the cell. Keradoc was silent, his desperate breaths the only indication that he was even still alive. "Oona, I assume?"

He shook his head and released my hand. "It's a ruse I've kept even from her, though she remains the only advisor I trust. This prisoner is unrecognizable even to her, and as for me, well…" He let out a soft laugh. "She must think her father has gone soft, but that is a small price to pay for her continued loyalty and counsel. Besides, that woman has suffered enough at the hands of a loveless father. I've read his diaries—I know this."

The diaries. Of course. "You read them so you can understand him better. To play the part."

"I was taken by him as a child, Haley. Kept as his personal slave—one he loved to share among his noble friends." A shudder wracked his body, his jaw tight, but he squared his shoulders, continuing. "I knew his inner circle quite intimately. Knew how to speak like them, act like them, *destroy* and *take* like them. I didn't need his diaries to study my part, only to glean some useful intelligence that might help me win this endless war and claim the realm once and for all."

"Who, then?" I asked. "If not Oona, who else have you told?"

"There are only four alive who know about this, Haley. And three of them are in this very room."

Evander. Keradoc. And now me.

"And the fourth?" I asked.

"The Dark Goddess, Melantha."

Dread gripped me in an icy fist. "That's why you banished her from Midnight. She discovered your secret."

"Discovered? Who do you think crafted this spell?" He twisted the ring around his finger, then clenched his fist. "After the deed was done, I knew I had to be rid of her. So I called upon the darkest magick from the darkest Midnight fae witches at my disposal—Keradoc's witches, who were more than happy to perform such services for the man they believed to be their master—and banished her. Despite her promises to the contrary, she's too vindictive to ever trust with something so important. I couldn't risk her exposing me."

"Yet you're telling *me*? What makes you think *I* won't expose you? Use this as leverage to get me and my guys out of Midnight?"

He crossed the space between us again and grasped my chin between his thumb and forefinger, tilting my face up toward his.

In a soft whisper laced with warning, he said, "Let us not pretend we don't *both* know the answer to that."

I blinked up at him, my body heating at his touch, at the softness of his breath against my lips, at the firelight dancing in his violet eyes.

"So tell me," he continued. "Now that you know my deepest, darkest secrets, where does the little thief I've captured, imprisoned, and forced to do my bidding stand?"

"You're... you're seriously still giving me a choice?"

"I am."

"Then I stand with Midnight," I said, more resolute than ever. "With Evander of Midnight."

The dank air felt charged and heavy, Evander's gaze blazing right through me, his grip firm on my chin, his mouth so invitingly close...

And then he released me, yanking the torch from the wall sconce and marching toward the door. "We leave in six hours. I'll collect you from your suite at that time. Be packed and ready—we do *not* have time to dally."

"You'll *collect* me?" I laughed, pushing past him and stalking out the door. Just past the threshold, I crouched down and scooped up the rest of his weapons, strapping them onto my chest with practiced ease. "Let's get two things straight about our upcoming adventure."

Evander glared at me, his jaw rigid, but he couldn't hide the new spark of light in his eyes. "What things, witch?"

"One? You don't collect me. I collect *myself*. And two? I'm not going on this crazy-ass mission with you alone. My guys and I are a package deal, just like I've been telling you from the start. So you'd best talk to Oona or whoever else is on your payroll and tell them they're going to have to run your drugs themselves, because from here on out, we're a team. You, me, Elian, Hudson, and Jax."

He opened his mouth to protest, but I cut him off, pressing the blade of his fancy-ass dagger to his throat.

"Oh, did I say two things? I meant three." I beamed up at him, and in my most saccharine-sweet voice, I said, "Don't piss off a Scorpio blood witch when she's the one holding all the weapons."

# 26

## HUDSON

*A*nother night in Midnight, another bullshit mission for its self-appointed commander.

*Usurper*, more like.

I believed Haley about Keradoc being Elian's brother. About the *real* Keradoc rotting away in a cell, and all the fancy fae mojo that went along with that particular setup. Now that we knew the whole fucking story, a lot of the missing pieces had clicked into place.

Didn't mean I trusted the guy, though. Which was precisely why none of us were about to let him take off with Haley into the Razorbacks in some fucked-up ploy to win over the hearts and minds of the crazy-ass fae that lived there.

That point was non-fucking-negotiable, but thanks to our demanding little witch, Keradoc didn't fight us on it. For better or worse, she seemed to have the fake warlord wrapped around her pretty little finger.

Now, I shouldered my pack, keeping my eyes peeled for any signs of danger. Specifically, the asshole gargoyle kind of danger—I'd worry about the feral fae later.

"You doing okay, Gargs?" Haley asked, gazing up at me as we walked along the trail. Keradoc—sorry, *Evander*—had taken point, with Jax and Elian bringing up the rear, all of us on foot. Mares in the mountains would've drawn too much attention, and that was one thing we did *not* need on this journey.

I was in my human form for now, but that was just so I could be closer to my girl. The moment I got a whiff of trouble, I'd shift.

I ran a hand over her head and smiled. "Just keeping a lookout, babygirl."

"You're nervous. I can feel it."

"Yeah, I am. Aren't you?"

She shrugged, tugging the straps on her pack. She looked real at home in the mountains, so fucking cute I wanted to grab her and haul her off the trail, have my way with her in the woods.

But, that would be frowned upon by the rest of the team. So, onward we marched.

"No more than I was on our way up to Amaranth City when we first portaled in," she said. "Besides, now we've got Evander with us, and—"

"And the rest of the realm believes he's a fucking warlord, so he's more of a target than all of *our* asses combined." I shook my head, trying to clear the bad mojo. "Sorry. He ain't even what I'm worried about, to tell you the truth."

"Then what's wrong?" She glanced up at me again, her face so earnest. So sweet.

*Fuck*, my heart kicked up a few gears every time I looked at her.

"Hudson?" she pressed. A tiny wrinkle appeared between her brows. "What is it?"

"Haley, I…" Hell, I didn't wanna lay this on her—not now. But Marco posed a real threat, and she needed to know it. "The gargoyles who attacked us outside the moat? That wasn't just some random attack. It was personal—highly personal."

"Well, yeah. They were working with the guards to kidnap me."

"Even more personal than that, babygirl." I stopped her on the path, tugging her behind a rocky outcropping for a moment of privacy. "The one who took off that night before I could nail him—his name's Marco. Mad Marco, to be exact. And me and him?" I blew out a breath, my cheeks puffing up with the force of it. "We got some dark shit between us. Real bad shit."

"You know him?"

"From way back when."

That wrinkle turned into a deep crease. "And what about the other one? The one you… took care of."

"Draven. And that's just it. After what I did to him? Marco—"

"Let me guess." Haley lowered her gaze, kicking a stone off the side of the mountain. "You killed Marco's wingman, so now he wants you even more dead than he did before?"

"Well, yeah. I mean, that fucking meathead's *never* gonna stop wanting me dead. Not until I'm a pile of dust."

She shuddered at my words, then looped her hand through my arm and tucked in close. "We're not going to let him touch you again. *I'm* not. I swear, Hudson, if that asshole comes within fifty yards of you, I'll… Well, I'm not sure what I'll do. But you can bet your firm, tattooed ass it'll be something suitably bloody."

"Aww. You are just *adorable* when you threaten another gargoyle's life for me." I cupped her face and brushed my thumb across her sweet smile. "And as much as I'd love to hire you as my bodyguard…"

My grin dropped. I couldn't keep up the pretense of jokes when so much was at stake. When her very *life* was at stake.

"Haley, this ain't just about retaliation for a dead wingman." I clenched my jaw so hard my entire face ached. "Marco was there the night I found you in the moat—obviously. He was working with Keradoc's mercs—part of that fucking crew waiting to take you away from me."

"Yeah, but he *didn't* take me. We stopped him."

"But not before he saw what I did to Draven. *Exactly* what I did to Draven. Now he knows."

"I don't… I don't understand. Now he knows what?"

"There's a code among gargoyles. Even the worst of 'em follow it. You don't mutilate the wings. I broke that code—and before you even say a word, hell yes, I'd do it again a hundred times over just to keep you safe. But that's the problem right there, babygirl. There's only one reason a gargoyle would do something so… so reprehensible to our kind." I took her hands. Pressed my mouth to her fingers. "A gargoyle would only do it to protect his mate."

Her eyes widened as the realization hit her.

"Now he knows you're the most important person in the world to me," I continued. "He knows I'd violate that one unspoken law—that I'd mutilate my own kind to get to you without a second thought. Which means—"

"Which means…" She sighed and dropped her head into her hands. "Shit, Hudson. It means I'm your weakness. You're a target now, and they know *exactly* how to get to you. Right through me. I— "

"Hey. *Hey.*" I gripped her chin, forcing her to look up at me. "Weakness? Don't even *think* it, babygirl. You've given me a reason to… Fuck, Haley. I'm… I just… You're the only… You're…"

The words were coming at me hard and fast, crashing together in my head like a car wreck. But I forced myself to take a deep breath. To steady my thoughts and start again, because she *needed* to know this, even more than she needed to know about Marco.

And she needed to know it now.

Tears slipped down her cheeks, but I cupped her face and swiped them away with my thumbs. "You listen to me, Haley Barnes, and listen good, 'cause I don't know if I'll be able to make sense for too much longer here, but… God *damn*. Falling for you has changed me in all the best ways. You're my girl. My fucking soul mate. Weakness? *Weakness*? Fuck that bull-shit right now. I ain't *never* been as strong, as powerful, or as brave as I am when I'm with you, and that's the truth of it."

She gazed at me, her eyes wide and shining, her breath as shallow as mine. She didn't say anything at first, but that was just fine by me—I wasn't going anywhere. Not unless she sent me packing, and if that happened? Hell, I was pretty sure I'd fucking die.

But when she finally opened her mouth to speak, the hope and happi-ness flooding her eyes told me she wasn't sending me *anywhere*. She was keeping me. Right fucking by her side, right where I belonged.

"You… you're falling for me?" she breathed.

I took her hands. Pressed them to my chest so she could feel that wild, warrior heartbeat.

"Yeah, babygirl," I said softly, a nervous laugh making my words shake. "I'm in love with you. Not sure what you think about that, but there it is."

"I think… I think I'm… No, wait." She shook her head, her exaspera-tion only making her more adorable. "This isn't thinking, Hudson. It's knowing. I *know* I'm in love with you, too. So I'm going to do us a both a favor and just… Yeah. Just *this*." She pressed her lips together and grinned, and for the first time in the history of the whirlwind that was Haley Barnes, she stopped talking. And then, she stretched up on her toes and planted those luscious pink lips right on mine, sealing the promises we'd just made on the side of a damn mountain under the triple moons.

I was so caught up in the moment, I didn't even realize what new dangers had dropped into our laps until the first icy flakes hit my face.

"Is it… snowing?" Haley asked, pulling back and holding out her hand. Her palm immediately filled up with dark, heavy snow. Red snow. "Holy shit! It's like… blood snow. This is insane!"

"Hudson!" came the call, and I whipped my head back toward the path just in time to see Evander sprinting down it. "Weather witches!"

My gut twisted, but one glance at the sky confirmed it. Five raven gryphons soared overhead, mounted by figures I couldn't quite make out, but didn't need to. The unique, bright-yellow glow of their weather magick arced through the air.

No idea how the fuck they'd managed to tame those gryphons, but that was a question for another night.

I grabbed Haley and shoved her toward Evander.

"Get her someplace safe," I ordered—first words I'd ever spoken to the fucker. Didn't love the idea of sending her off with him, but right now, I just needed her out of range before that snowfall turned deadly. "The boys and I will take care of the witches."

I expected an argument, but the dark fae didn't utter a word. Just nodded and grabbed her arm, already dragging her back up the path. "We need to move, Haley. Now."

"Hudson?" she turned and looked at me one last time over her shoulder, her eyes wide with fright and confusion, red snowflakes catching in her hair.

"Go," I said. Then, forcing a smile just to ease her worry, "I'll see you soon, babygirl."

One more second to look at her, to memorize the shape of her face, and then I was off, charging down the path toward Jax and Elian, shifting into my warrior form.

They'd already spotted the enemy, their weapons drawn as I leaped off the cliff and shot up toward our attackers.

Weather witches were a Darkwinter breed—magickal fae who could command and control all kinds of storms. And in a matter of minutes, they'd whipped their blood snow into a full-on blizzard, cutting off all visibility as I tried to navigate through the sky and reach the raven gryphons. My muscles were already seizing up on account of the plunging temperature, but if I could just take down a few of those fucking birds, the witches would have to fight us on the ground—a much more level playing field.

A dark shape swooped past up ahead, and I finally had one of them fuckers in range. I tucked my wings in and pushed myself harder, faster, my talons drawn, body bracing for impact—

A bright yellow blast of magick exploded beside me, cutting a path through the snow like a missile as it soared down toward the mountain.

But this was no missile.

This was fog.

The kind that could slice-and-dice you to shreds the moment it grazed your skin.

*Fuck.*

I banked hard and changed course, arrowing back down toward the boys, a race against the witch-spelled Fog of a Thousand Knives as I desperately tried to reach them. The snow was so impossibly thick, there was no way they'd see the danger coming their way.

Not until it was too late.

With a roar that echoed across the bleak night, I zoomed down, down, down, pushing myself harder than I've ever pushed, hoping like hell I could snatch my boys out of the Fog's destructive path...

The mountain finally came into view. There was a flash of silver, Elian's hair whipping in the wind. The dark shape of Jax's coat, and a blue backpack discarded on the ground in haste. I blinked the snow from my eyes, wishing I could shout for them, wishing they could hear me, but I was still too fucking far away and the Fog was outpacing me and the red snow was so fucking heavy and cold and...

Another blur, a flash of silver and black, the breathtaking speed of a vampire-fae as he shot from one side of the path to the other, slamming into the demon and knocking him out of the way just as the Fog finally descended upon the path.

And, in a gruesome and devastating explosion of gore that not even the heavy snowfall could mask from my eyes, claimed its victim.

# 27

## HALEY

Tucked inside a cave in some craggy, unknown peak in the Razorback Range, I peered out into the storm, searching for any signs of the others.

A useless attempt.

Blinding snow the color of blood poured down from the skies, swirling into vicious eddies that scoured the mountainside like hundreds of mini tornados.

I was pretty sure no living thing could survive out there—a thought that threatened to unravel me.

*They're not stupid*, I reminded myself. *They've survived Midnight before, and they probably found shelter tonight, just like you did. Not to mention the fact that they're fucking immortals.*

Immortals. Right.

Comforting myself with the word, I peered out into the darkness once more, scanning the peeks until my vision went blurry.

"Come back to the fire, Haley," Evander called from deeper inside the cave. "You didn't come all this way just to freeze to death."

"But what if the others pass us by? What if—"

"They won't," he said, his warmth radiating behind me as he drew close. He wrapped his cloak over my shoulders, the feel of it heavenly against the frigid bite of the storm. "They're smart men, Haley. They'll wait out the storm just like we're doing, and then they'll come. You'll see."

Blowing out a breath, I turned to him and smiled, feeling marginally better. "You really think so?"

"If there's one thing I know about those men, it's that they'd *literally* move mountains to get to you." He smiled and touched my shoulder. Then, with a nod of his head toward the inner chamber, "Come on. I'm making dinner."

I laughed, a much-needed moment of levity. "*You*, man of a thousand servants, actually know how to cook?"

Kneeling before his pack, he glared up at me and shook his dark head, his violet eyes glittering. "I suppose we're about to find out, aren't we?"

Joining him by the fire, I sat on a fur bedroll he'd laid out for me, letting the heat of the flames wash over me in blissful waves. If not for the fact that we'd just escaped some weird witch attack and were still awaiting word from the guys, the whole thing might've felt cozy. Nice.

As Evander set up a small cooking pot and dropped in some basic ingredients—water, a few hunks of dried beef, herbs—I watched him in silent appreciation, mesmerized by such simple gestures. Building a fire. Setting up the bedroll. Cooking a meal for us to share.

These weren't the gestures of a warlord bent on vengeance, a cruel murderer willing to destroy anything—and anyone—that stood in his way.

But then, he *wasn't* a warlord. Not really. Just a man who'd had his entire life stolen from him, remapped and remade by the most brutal kind of monster imaginable. Every torment Evander had endured at the hands of Keradoc—the hands of the man he'd pretended to be for so long—had led him right here. To *this* cave, in *this* moment, with *this* witch.

The fact that he still had the capacity for any kindness at all felt like a bit of magick in itself, and I didn't want to squander it. Only to understand it. To understand how the man that had been our captor was now becoming something else.

Something that, if I wasn't careful, might just sneak up on me and steal my heart.

"The key to enjoying this meal," Evander said suddenly, scattering my thoughts, "is to keep your expectations low. That way, you're less likely to be disappointed."

He handed me a mug of steaming liquid, his smile turning a bit shy.

"Considering what you had to work with," I said, smiling right back, "I'm calling it a gourmet meal. Thank you."

"I will hold you to it." He kept his amused gaze locked on mine as I brought the mug to my lips, blew a breath across the top to cool it, and took a sip. It was far too thin to be of much nutritional value, and way too over-salted, but it was hot, and it was edible, and I was beyond grateful.

"Well?" he asked.

"Like I said. Gourmet."

Evander laughed, the sound of it warming me even more than the fire and the soup. "You're no better a liar tonight than you were the night I caught you crashing my party, little thief."

The reminder of our first meeting sent a shiver skittering down my spine and snaking into my belly. Suddenly his gaze felt too hot, his attention too smothering, his presence too… too everything.

I finished the rest of the soup quickly, then got up to stretch my legs and check the situation outside.

It wasn't long before the chill chased me back to the fire, my whole body shivering as I pulled the bedroll closer to its crackling warmth.

"See anything?" Evander asked.

I shook my head.

"You need to sleep tonight, Haley. I'll keep watch for you."

I nodded, but I was pretty sure I wouldn't be able to sleep. Not until I knew my men were safe.

A long moment passed, nothing but the hiss and pop of the fire keeping us company.

Then, out of nowhere, Evander said, "You truly love them, don't you?"

The note of wonder in his voice surprised me, and when I glanced up at him across the fire, I saw that same wonder reflected in his eyes, as if he couldn't possibly imagine what it would feel like to love someone enough to worry about them.

To *be* loved by someone like that.

"I do," I said. "It's funny—I haven't even known Jax and Hudson all that long, but sometimes you just… I don't know. Click with people."

"And… Elian?" he asked, his voice thick, as if he still had trouble saying his brother's name.

"I've… I've loved Elian for a long, long time. It's… I don't know. I'm not sure you'd understand."

"No? I wouldn't understand love? Or I wouldn't understand that what you feel for him is strong enough to override the fact that he's an addict and a criminal?"

I bristled at the turn in the conversation. At the sudden hint of irritation in his voice.

"Elian is in *pain*. Can't you see that? Isn't that enough of a reason for you to have a modicum of compassion?"

"I supposed it *would* be, if he actually allowed himself to feel that pain. He avoids it by escaping into drugs, no matter what the collateral damage is to those around him, and you shrug and continue to stand by his side as if the man can do no wrong."

I rubbed a thumb along the scar on my wrist, the old ache blooming in my gut. "Show me a person who *hasn't* longed for escape, no matter who they might hurt in the process. No, he's not perfect, and I've got a lot of bitter history with him to back that up—a lot of reasons to be angry with him even now. But his addiction—no matter how much it affects me—isn't one of them."

"Many people would turn their backs for lesser faults."

"I know. Many people have turned their backs on *me* for lesser faults. But Elian never did. Not even when I was at my worst. Not until he..." I blew out a shaky breath, the rest of those words evaporating.

*Not until he left me to come to Midnight in search of* you. *His brother. His twin.*

It wasn't Evander's fault that he'd been taken, and it wasn't his fault that Elian had tried to find him.

Glancing down at my wrist again, I focused instead on the tattoo etched above the scar.

*This too shall pass.*

"I've got Elian's back," I said simply. "And that's that. Whether you understand it or approve of it is irrelevant."

Again, that strange sense of wonder appeared in his eyes. "He's lucky to have such a loyal friend."

"That's an oxymoron. A friend *is* loyal. Not perfect, not without cracks and flaws, but yeah. When life tries to steamroll you, a friend—a real *friend* —either has your back, or they don't deserve the honor of the title."

Evander finally allowed a smile. "I can only hope to achieve such an honor as to be your friend one day, Haley Barnes."

The sincerity in his tone, in his eyes, melted some of the ice that'd crept in between us.

"You're on the right track," I said. "I mean, you *did* decapitate your own guards for me, which is saying something."

"I did. I also sacrificed not one, but two cloaks to protect you from the elements."

I cracked up. "In that case, friendship achievement unlocked."

In the wake of Evander's soft laughter, I yawned and stretched out on the bedroll, surprised at how comfortable it was. The fire crackled before me, the rock walls trapping and radiating the heat, making this the perfect place to wait out the storm.

My eyelids grew heavy, my body finally giving in to the siren call of sleep.

I'd just drifted off when I felt it—a strange new iciness filling my chest and gripping my heart, cold claws scraping my insides, tendrils snaking through my mind, unleashing images so terrifying, they paralyzed me.

Thousands upon thousands of ghouls marching across the desert sands, devouring everything they touched, the land turning black and ashen in their wake.

And there, leading the charge on a bloodied, bedraggled raven gryphon ten times larger than any I'd ever seen, was the woman who'd haunted my nightmares ever since I'd promised her my service. Pale white serpents slithered around her sleek ebony limbs, her hands and feet curled into deadly talons, the feathers of her wings razor-sharp and dripping with blood.

And at last, the Dark Goddess Melantha swiveled her vicious head toward me, her eyes two red embers waiting to ignite, her voice hissing through my skull like an omen.

*I have come for you, Daughter of Darkwinter.*

## 28

### EVANDER

 t's all right, Haley." I was kneeling at her side in a flash, desperate to pull her from the nightmare's claws. "Wake up, my witch. Wake up."

"No!" she cried out, bolting upright as her body finally jerked free. Her eyes fluttered open, and she looked up at me in the firelight, fear still keeping her in a tight grip.

"Just a bad dream," I said softly, stroking her hair. "You're all right now."

"It wasn't…" She closed her eyes and shook her head, a shiver rolling through her. When she met my gaze again, she looked even more terrified than she had when she'd first awoken. "It wasn't a bad dream. It was a message."

"From whom?"

"Melantha. I felt her—her presence, her scent… I saw the Army of the Dead—they burned the very desert with their touch. She was leading them, riding this massive raven gryphon, and then…" She swallowed hard, a shiver taking her once more. "She looked right at me and spoke to me. Her voice was just… It was in my head."

"What did she say?"

"I have come for you, Daughter of Darkwinter."

I sat down next to her and drew her close, holding her as the tremors worked through her limbs. "She's not here, Haley. Not yet. But if she's

530

reaching out to you through your dreams, she's obviously found a way to connect with you. To tap into your magick."

"That… can't be good."

"No, but it's not necessarily bad. I don't know that she can harm you that way—only scare you. But I'm going to let you in on a little secret about Melantha."

She turned her face up toward me, her eyes shining with fresh hope. "What's that?"

"She's extremely powerful, as you know. She doesn't need a show of force, doesn't need to announce herself before an attack. The fact that she's actively reaching out through your magick and trying to frighten you tells me that she's as terrified of *you* as she wants you to be of *her*."

"Well, she definitely understood the assignment on that one, because newsflash? I *am* terrified!"

"It's your power she's after, Haley. Your magick."

"If I thought it would make her go way, I'd give it to her."

"No, you wouldn't."

Haley blew out a breath, rubbing the last of the sleep from her eyes. "No, I wouldn't. You're right."

"I have a theory. See, all this time, we were operating under the assumption that she sent you to Midnight for *me*, so she could either barter her way back into the realm or steal my blood for her spell."

"So what's your theory?"

I tucked a lock of hair behind her ear. "I don't think she sent you here for me at all, Haley. I think Melantha sent you here for *her*. She must've known you'd be able to tap into Midnight's dark magick—that you'd not only be able to feel it, but to channel it somehow. To grow stronger through it. And you *have* grown stronger—I've seen it. And you're still just *beginning* to touch that potential."

"But why would Melantha care about that? What good would it do her?"

"She must've thought she could trick you into fighting for her. If it's Midnight's magick she's after, what better champion than a dark witch she could install from a distance, biding her time until she was finally able to break the banishment and join her newly-appointed ally?"

"But I would *never* fight for her. Not anymore."

"And that, my little thief, is why she's so damn terrified of you." I took her hands in mine, rubbing some warmth back into her fingers. "She knows you're already powerful. Knows that the longer you remain in

Midnight, the more powerful you'll become, until eventually you'll surpass even her."

"But… but my sisters. We still don't know whether they're safe. She'll use them against me."

"Let her try."

"*Try*? She's a crazy-powerful goddess with the backing of an army of ghouls."

I smiled, if only to ease the worry clouding her eyes. "And *you're* a crazy-powerful blood witch. And a Scorpio, if I recall correctly. One who's no slouch when it comes to fending off ghouls. Or dark fae warlords, for that matter."

A laugh finally broke through the darkness, lighting up her entire face.

"That smile," I whispered, brushing my thumb across her cheek. "Stars and moons, little thief. That smile could light up the darkest places of the realm."

I hadn't meant to say it out loud, yet I had, and the admission left something hot and uncomfortable in its path. I couldn't acknowledge it, couldn't name the thing that spun and fluttered inside me like a trapped bird. I was accustomed to the feelings Haley inspired below the belt—the constant ache, the raging, stone-hard steel that longed to sink into her wet heat. But this? This spiraling warmth, this explosion of tenderness and possessiveness left me completely unmoored, my mind grasping to make sense of something utterly beyond comprehension.

I couldn't take the words back. Couldn't explain them away.

So the moment she parted her lips to respond, I lowered my mouth to hers and kissed her.

It was just for a moment—barely a brush of soft lips and a warm sigh before I realized what I'd done and jerked back, turning away from her so she couldn't see the shame heating my face.

"Evander," she breathed.

"My… apologies." Clearing my throat, I forced myself to look at her again. To meet her eyes and ensure she knew I spoke the truth. "That was out of line."

"It's… it's okay. I—"

"No, it isn't. You asked me not to kiss you again without your consent, and I meant to honor that. I was… overcome. Again. I'm sorry, Haley. Truly."

She nodded, fingers pressed delicately to her lips, her eyes glazing over as if she'd just awoken again from another dream. "It wasn't just you. I wanted…"

I waited for her to finish, my heart raging inside me, hope spinning wildly…

*You wanted what, little thief? Tell me what it is, and I shall make it yours…*

The light in her eyes changed, and for a moment that hope expanded inside me, nearly bursting, and then—

"Wait, I heard something," she said suddenly, glancing out toward the cave entrance. "Do you think it's them?"

She scrambled to her feet and bolted, and in that moment, I knew that the light in her eyes hadn't been for me.

It would *never* be for me.

She returned a few minutes later, her light dimmed.

"Just the wind," she said.

I frowned, hating the sadness in her voice. The disappointment.

"I guess I should get back to sleep," she said. "I mean, if you're still okay to keep watch a bit longer?"

"Of course."

"Wake me if the storm breaks, okay? If you see them?"

"You have my word."

*And my heart*, I thought, but that was impossible.

My heart had been ripped from my chest and burned to ash long ago.

# 29

## HALEY

The roar and crackle of a freshly made fire stirred me from sleep, and I sat up on the bedroll and stretched my arms over my head, feeling better than I had in days.

"I didn't mean to wake you." Evander offered a quick smile, but then ducked my gaze, turning his attention back to the fire. He'd just set another log on the flames, sparks cascading up to the cave ceiling. "You can keep sleeping if you'd like."

"How long was I out?"

"Not long. Three, four hours at most."

I got to my feet and stepped closer to the fire, rubbing my hands over the flames. Outside, the wind continued to howl, red snow blotting out the view.

My heart sank. "Still no break in the storm?"

"I'm afraid not." He stood up and went to his pack, rearranging and repacking, setting a few supplies aside. I watched him for a few minutes in awkward silence, wondering if he still felt bad about the kiss last night. The near-kiss. The sweet, tender brush of lips that lingered in my dreams, making my stomach swoop even now.

"About last night," I began, but he was already shaking his dark head.

"You don't need to say anything, Haley. I meant what I said—I'm truly sorry for my actions."

I nodded, but he wasn't even looking at me, still so focused on his task.

It hit me then, what he was doing. Why he was divvying up his cooking supplies, his weapons, and transferring only a few essentials to a smaller pack.

"Are you... leaving?" I asked, unable to keep the alarm from my voice.

Evander let out a sigh, finally looking up to meet my eyes. "If the storm continues and your men don't arrive in the next couple of hours, I'll need to travel on ahead. We're running out of time."

I folded my arms across my chest, my panic turning into irritation. "I'm *not* leaving this cave without them."

"No, you're not."

"I'm serious. You'll have to knock my ass out or drug me or... I don't know. Do something *really* bad, which means I'll have no choice but to take back your friendship achievement." I glared at him like a smug, petulant child, but the look in his eyes sent a new wave of panic crashing over me.

Evander got to his feet, coming to join me before the fire. In a soft voice full of regret, he said, "You're not coming with me, Haley. I need to locate the fae who dwell in the mountains and begin the negotiations. You can meet me there when your men rejoin you."

"How will you convince the fae to help without me? You said it yourself—it's my magick they'll want. My magick they'll think can bring their ancestors back."

"I must try, Haley. Melantha's army encroaches. Every hour we wait is another hour she gains on us."

"That doesn't mean you should waltz out of here on your own, trying to be a fucking hero."

He cupped my face, his gaze fierce. "I won't risk taking you out in this storm. You're too important. End of discussion."

My heart fluttered at his words, at his touch, but I shut that nonsense down *real* quick.

I wasn't important to *him*. I was important to his mission. The war. The magick.

He'd said Melantha wanted to use me, but so did he.

After all, he'd told me that from the very start.

*Haley Barnes. A weapon the enemy could never defeat.*

I turned away from him and stared into the fire, frustration simmering inside me. I felt him shifting on his feet, opening and closing his mouth as if he had more to say. But then, after a few tense moments, he returned to his packing, stripping out of his shirt and digging through the bag for a clean one. When he stood up again, the map of scars across his torso shone in the firelight, the sight softening my heart.

"I know how you got those scars," I said quietly. "The bite marks, anyway."

"Then you know more than I."

I crossed the small space until we were standing close once more, so close I could smell the scent of him, the sweet roses, the spice. But Evander kept his back to me, still fumbling with his shirt.

"Elian told me that when you were boys, you saved him from a silver wolf attack." I ran my palm over the bite marks alongside his ribs, and he hissed, but didn't flinch or pull away. His skin was rough there, but red-hot, his muscles taut beneath it.

"Is that what he said?" he asked, turning to face me.

I nodded. "He was bitten too, but you nearly died fighting off the beast, protecting your twin."

"Such a *brave* boy," he snapped, but the softness in his eyes belied the venom in his voice.

"Do you really not remember?"

He put his arms through the sleeves of his shirt, but didn't button it, the scars harsh and terrifying in the firelight. But they were beautiful, too. His stories, just like I had *my* stories.

When I lowered my gaze to take in the rest, he didn't shy away. Didn't tell me to stop.

The smooth, hard planes of his abs gave way to a trail of soft, dark hair that dipped down below his beltline, and in that moment, all I wanted to do was run my hands down his chest, trace the story of his life with my fingertips, with my tongue. My heart pounded behind my ribs, my breath catching, the fire making everything impossibly hot. Impossibly close.

Evander took a step closer, and I dragged my gaze up to his face. To the deep violet of his borrowed eyes.

He reached for my hand and placed it against the bite marks, holding it there, his heart thudding just as wildly as mine.

"It's said that when one suffers a traumatic event," he said, his voice barely a whisper, "the mind will sometimes block out the memory as a way to keep us from reliving the trauma, from experiencing that pain over and over." He touched the scar on my wrist with a delicate stroke of his thumb, making me shiver. "I suspect you might know something about that."

I nodded. There was no point in denying it. In hiding it. My scars were part of me, the history that had shaped me into the woman I was now, just as his history had shaped him.

Pain and understanding flickered in his violet irises.

"In my case," he continued, "my mind did the opposite, magnifying the traumatic experience until it was *all* I knew. All I'd *ever* known. Until those incomprehensible brutalities became so large in my memory, they choked out anything that had ever existed before."

"But you survived," I said. "You fucking survived. The worst possible things, you survived."

"I survived, Haley, because I took all of that fear, that pain, that helplessness, and I channeled it into a weapon. Almost as soon as I arrived in Midnight, I began plotting, and I continued to do so, year after torturous year, enduring all manner of sadistic abuse and suffering that had me begging for death more often than not, all in the hopes that when Keradoc finally made a mistake, I would have my opportunity. Every time he laid a hand on me, every time he..." Evander closed his eyes and clenched his teeth, struggling with the memories of his oldest, darkest pain, his anger radiating from him in waves. "Every time he did those unspeakable, unconscionable things to me and the others, it was as if he'd tossed another log onto that fire raging inside me. Eventually, he'd built an inferno. And then, when he finally slipped up, when I finally saw my opportunity, I took it, unleashing the fire that he himself had stoked to terrible life."

I pressed my cheek against his bare chest, sliding my arms around his waist, holding him tight. He was stiff at first, but then I felt him relax, his arms coming around to embrace me, his head resting on top of my head.

And for a long moment, we just stood there, holding each other, keeping each other company, having each other's backs.

Like friends were supposed to.

What Evander had endured... I couldn't even *begin* to imagine that much pain. That much torment. My birth mother had been cruel and brutal, but I'd still had people in my life looking out for me. People who'd made sure that I was safe, that I was adopted into a loving home, that I was cared for and cherished as a child ought to be. And even though it meant being separated from my sisters, in the end, I still got them back. I still had my family.

Evander was ripped from *his* family, from his childhood. From Elian. He was stolen. A vulnerable child with no one there to keep him safe.

"I can't pretend to know what you went through," I said, pulling back to look into his eyes. "But I understand why you feel the way you do about Keradoc. Why you want to take everything from him. Why this war is so important to you."

"Then you understand why I must leave."

"I understand why you *believe* you must leave, but..." I sighed and shook my head. "Your need for revenge drove you to survive, and I get that. In that situation, yes, you absolutely do whatever you can. But the problem with vengeance as a survival strategy is that it's not good for the long haul."

"What do you mean?"

"What happens when it's done? Let's say you win this war, squash Melantha and Darkwinter and all the rebel factions, claim the realm for yourself, and wipe Keradoc from the records so no one ever speaks his name again."

"That's the plan."

"And what will keep you going after all that?"

"Keep me *going*?" A dark laugh echoed through the cave, so cold and lifeless it made me shiver despite the roaring fire. "That's the thing about revenge, Haley. Those who live by the sword, die by the sword."

"That's not an answer."

"I don't expect to live long enough to need one." He turned from me again, buttoning up his shirt and crouching down to sift through his pack.

"You are fighting a war for a home you've got no plans to live long enough to enjoy? You're about to leave me here alone, hike out through a storm you probably won't survive, all because you think you need to just... keep fighting? Keep carrying out your revenge? For who, yourself? The soldiers you're hoping will write battle hymns about you?"

"It's not for them. Don't be ridiculous."

"Then for who, Evander? *Who*?" I demanded, my voice rising, my blood simmering as the reality crashed over me. He *wouldn't* survive the storm—no amount of fae magick could keep him safe. If it could, then my own fae would've found a way to get here by now, and we wouldn't even be having this conversation.

"Oona isn't your daughter," I continued. "She's Keradoc's. And if you truly cared for her, you'd tell her that her real father is rotting away in your dungeon, so don't tell me you're doing this for her. Your guards are gone—slaughtered by your hand or fleeing out of fear that they'll be next. Your generals remain loyal, but for how long? The minute they sense they're fighting a losing battle, they'll choose new sides. That's just how this works."

"I don't need you to tell me about the challenges of war, Haley. I'm well aware."

"Your entire life in Midnight is a ploy. A scheme that you plotted for a single purpose—to ruin the man who tortured you. Well, you've already won in that regard. Keradoc is a relic, barely clinging to life. And you say you want his realm, his magick, but you know damn well that if you walk out of this cave tonight, you'll very likely die before you even make it a full mile, and the kingdom will be lost anyway. So you look me in the eyes and tell me, Evander of Midnight, what are you *really* fighting for?"

He stilled at his pack, every muscle in his body drawn tight, his breath held, the tension so thick I thought I might choke on it.

And then, finally, an answer. Low and dark, a whisper I could barely hear above the hissing of the flames.

"For a long time, I thought I knew," he said. "I *did* know, Haley. With utter certainty. For decades, I planned this. And if you'd asked me the night of the Feast, I'd have told you my answer—I was fighting for the realm. The magick. And no, I would never have risked my life on a fool's errand such as this. I would've sent my men to do my dirty work, while I stayed safely behind the wall, moving my chess pieces around the board as I'd always done."

"Then what the hell changed?"

He exhaled and got to his feet. Turned to me. Closed the gap with a single, powerful step.

He raised his hands before me, and in one swift move, jerked the ring free.

Blood ran down his finger, black and viscous.

And before me, a silver-eyed fae stood in the firelight, magnificent and beautiful. Real.

"Evander," I whispered, my throat tight with emotion, tears brimming in my eyes. He and Elian may have been identical twins, but their lives had diverged long ago, and the tragedies shaping them had altered them in small but perceptible ways. Looking at him now, it was a wonder to me that I'd ever mistaken him for Elian, even for a little while. The angles of their faces were different, and Evander's hair retained some of its black sheen, whereas Elian's was completely silver. Their eyes were the same shade, but in them shone such different pain, such different history.

I reached up and touched his face, my thumb sliding across his mouth.

"You asked me what changed, Haley Barnes?" He smiled beneath my touch. "A fierce, devious, beautiful little thief kissed me on the dais and turned my entire world upside-down. And every moment since that night, she's held me captive. Every moment I've spent in her presence has made me question all the things I thought I believed, all the things I thought I was. And the times when she wasn't near, she still haunted my dreams. My thoughts. My very breath. So when you ask me why I fight? Why I risk my life for a home I've no intention of living long enough to claim as mine?" He shook his head, a tear slipping down his cheek. "Maybe you've finally given me something truly worth fighting for, little thief."

The breath rushed from my lungs, and I closed my eyes, lost in his words, his touch, his heat.

Before I could even respond, Evander swept me into an embrace so fierce, it knocked me off my feet.

I didn't fall, though. I couldn't. He'd caught me and held me close, the lean muscles of his body rigid against mine.

A deep ache throbbed between my thighs, an inexplicable need for him that had sparked to life the very first time he held me in his arms and waltzed me across his ballroom at the feast. And every time he touched me, every time he stole another kiss, every time he looked at me, that spark burned a little brighter. Hotter.

And now, tonight, it finally caught, the fire raging to life inside me.

I couldn't explain it any more than I could explain my feelings for Hudson and Jax, despite not knowing them all that long. I only knew that it felt right.

I opened my eyes, gazing into his, the heat between us cresting.

Evander had been an outsider for so long, and now he stared at me fiercely, an unanswered question in his eyes.

Another challenge.

Would I push him away?

Or would I fall headlong into this madness with him?

# 30

## EVANDER

$\mathcal{T}$he witch trembled in my hold, but it wasn't fear that had set her body to shivering.

My own muscles quivered with restraint, a monumental effort to temper a raging storm when all I wanted to do was break upon her shores and fucking *devour* her.

"Tell me you look into *my* eyes and still see the man you loved before," I demanded, our mouths so close I could already taste her lips. Her hair was like warm silk in my fist, her taut stomach trembling as I lifted the hem of her shirt and pressed my palm to her skin, then slid down lower, desperately seeking more of her. *All* of her. "Tell me my touch makes you burn for *him*. Tell me there's no room in your heart but for the men who've already claimed it, and I will bury this blaze in my chest so deeply I will never again feel its warmth."

She arched into my touch, an instinctive gesture born of a need unmet, a desire unfulfilled.

My fingers slid inside her pants, gliding down past her clit to tease her hot, wet center.

"I... I can't." She clutched my arms, her grip fierce even as her voice trembled. "It would be a lie. I... I feel you, Evander. I see *you*."

"You call me by my so-called given name, but I'm still your captor, am I not? Your..." I pushed past her entrance, her heat enveloping my fingers, the smooth, silky feel of her unraveling my thoughts faster than I could hold onto them. "Your *enemy*."

I was losing the ability to speak, all logic and reason consumed by the unchecked desire raging through me. Touching her wasn't enough. I needed to claim her, to drive my aching cock inside her and fuck her until I absolutely *owned* her. Until I could look into her glittering, jewel-bright eyes and see the same blinding need reflected right back at me.

"We're all our own worst captors, Evander," she breathed. "Even you."

Her eyes flamed, and then she was reaching for the buttons on my shirt, swiftly unfastening them.

I pulled out of her and moved to slide the ring back on, already feeling the effects of removing it. The slowing of my heart, the slight weakening of my muscles.

But Haley stopped me, closing her fingers around the ring before I could put it on.

I stilled, my heart stuttering. "Even after everything you've claimed, you still need to see *him* when I touch you? My brother?"

"No. I need to see *you*, Evander. The *real* you, not the glamour of another man."

New heat blazed inside me, but as much as I wanted to her grant her request, I couldn't.

I sighed and slid the ring on, my strength returning at once. "It's not just a glamour, Haley. My soul is bound to Keradoc's—that's how it works. You might prefer my original face, but the ring... I must not remove it for any length of time."

"Why not?"

"I'll die without it."

"What?" she gasped. "But... but Keradoc... the *real* Keradoc... He's *already* dying, isn't he? What happens when he—"

Her words cut off abruptly, the answer obvious.

"You can't be serious," she said. "If he dies, you die? That's how the magick works?"

"If that's the price I must pay, then so be it."

"Your life?"

"And his."

She opened her mouth to speak again, no doubt with another protest, another argument. But I had no more words for her tonight.

Only the promise of a pleasure so rich, so exquisite it bordered on pain.

I gripped her jaw, pressing the pad of my thumb to her lips to silence her. "If it's conversation and debate you desire tonight, seek it elsewhere."

She glared at me, incredulous, but her skin was still pink with heat, her eyes dark with desire, and after the span of several heartbeats, her lips finally parted, her tongue darting out to skim the tip of my thumb.

I very nearly came right there.

"Kiss me, Evander," she whispered. "Just kiss me."

With a feral growl, I slid my hands into her hair and claimed that hot, smart little mouth with the kiss I'd been dying for since our very first embrace in that ballroom.

The *real* kiss—no teasing and taunting, no holding back, no apologies.

And my little thief kissed me right back, her soft moan of pleasure sliding into my mouth like melted caramel as she parted wider for me, taking me in deeper, my fists tightening in her hair, my cock hard and throbbing.

We broke to take a breath, and in a mad frenzy I tore the clothing from her body, ripping her shirt down the center, yanking her pants to her ankles as I dropped to my knees and pressed my mouth to her divine cunt, savoring the taste of her as I licked and sucked, her fingernails raking over my scalp as I fucked her with my tongue.

"Yes," she breathed. "That's… right there. So… fucking good."

I drove my tongue inside her, kissing and devouring her, harder and faster, losing myself in the intensity of the moment, of her, and then—

"Oh my god! Evander!" she cried, the sound of my name—my real name—echoing through the cave as she trembled and shook and came, hard and beautiful, all for me.

Her captor. Her enemy.

The brother of a man she once loved. A man she still loved.

I got to my feet, drunk and dizzy with lust, and claimed her in another possessive kiss, my mouth salty with the taste of her.

She stepped out of her pants and pushed the shirt off my shoulders, and with quick fingers I unfastened my pants, not bothering to remove them. I was too desperate for her, too needy.

I couldn't wait another minute.

I fisted my cock, and Haley hooked her leg around my hip, guiding me to her entrance, her heat radiating across my aching flesh.

"Okay?" I whispered.

Another kiss. A smile. A nod. "Okay."

That was all I needed to hear.

I lifted her up, her legs wrapping around me as I backed her up against the wall and slammed inside her, burying myself in that hot, silky haven. A jolt of pleasure skittered down my spine, and when I claimed her mouth in another bruising kiss, the air around us began to crackle and hum, sizzling with dark magick—mine, hers, the ancient magick of Midnight, all of it colliding and conspiring to push us closer, deeper, harder.

*More.*

I dragged my cock out slowly, only to pound into her once more, fucking her harder, our tongues and breath mingling, the magick gathering in strength and intensity as it twined around us, an invisible force that swirled and roiled, connecting us, binding us, revealing to me with every deep thrust the truths I'd suspected since that night on the balcony —the night I'd told her about the magick of Midnight, and a perfect black rose had bloomed in her palm.

Haley *belonged* to Midnight. Belonged to me, as surely as she belonged to the others. I didn't pretend to understand our connection, but I could no longer deny the pull of her, the fire I would willingly allow to consume me if only she wished it so.

"Evander!" she cried out once more, and her body tightened around me, everything inside her pulsing with heat, with pleasure, with a fury of magick and flame neither of us could contain.

I reached up and grabbed her throat, pinning her to the wall as I fucked her harder, faster, my fingers sliding down between us to graze her clit, and this time, when my fierce little thief shattered for me, I fell right over the edge of that dark, jagged peak with her.

Right into the deep abyss.

---

"You don't have to leave, you know," Haley said, gazing up at me.

We were stretched out on the bedrolls beside the fire, warm and content and naked, my fingers trailing along her bare curves.

If not for the fact that I *did* have to leave—and soon—I would've called it a perfect moment.

No, that wasn't exactly fair. It *was* a perfect moment. The fact that it would soon come to its end only made it all the sweeter.

"If there is a way to win this war," I said, "I must find it, Haley. And I must do it soon."

"Not alone, though. You've got allies. "

"No, little thief. *You've* got allies. Friends. Lovers. Me? I've got prisoners. People forced to do my bidding merely because they fear the consequences of refusing my command." I sat up and gazed into the fire, my thoughts drifting to my men. To Oona. To the generals I was relying on to hold the northern front. "Loyalty inspired through fear and coercion can only last so long."

"I don't want you to go," she whispered. "Elian wouldn't want—"

"Do *not* speak for him."

She sat up beside me, drawing her knees to her chest. "I'm not. I just… I *know* him, Evander. I know what he would say if he were here. Can't you at least consider that? Consider the possibility that he might want the chance to get to know you again? Not as the children you once were, but as the men you are now?"

"He may be my brother, as you say. I can't deny it—we share the same face. But I have no memory of him. No memory of my past. No memory of our bond."

"Memory is not the only thing that binds brothers, Evander. Elian spent most of his life searching for you. He never gave up on you. He *still* hasn't, even while you push him away."

"*Elian*," I gritted out, the name still tasting like bitter blood on my tongue. "He and I are strangers tethered by a single thread—you." I cupped her face, gazing into her eyes for so long I feared I might fall into them. "You aren't just the thread that binds us, either. You're a formidable witch and strategist. A woman I've come to know as a trusted advisor. Whatever comes of this war, I *need* you by my side. Tell me you'll fight with me, Haley. Tell me you'll continue this fight, even if I perish. And not just because we…" I trailed off, unable to find a word perfect enough to describe what we'd shared tonight.

For me, that word simply didn't exist.

Haley nudged me in the ribs. "If you think my loyalty can be bought with a few little orgasms, you are an egotistical—"

"Little? *Little*?" I shook my head, a wicked grin breaking across my face. "You nearly brought down the very walls of this chamber with your screaming, woman. Not to mention the terrible singing that followed."

She laughed, a sound even more beautiful than the singing, which—however terrible—had filled me with endless pleasure.

"Yeah, that's kind of my… thing," she said. "When I… you know. Finish."

I was still holding her face, and now I drew her closer, my lips brushing hers ever so gently. "When you *come*, you mean?"

She shrugged, her cheeks darkening with a new blush.

Sliding my hand down to cup her breast, I whispered, "If you'll let me make you come again right now, woman, I will gladly endure another round of your terrible singing."

She rolled her pretty eyes. "So romantic."

"I'm not trying to romance you." I leaned back on the bedroll, pulling her down on top of me. "I'm trying to make you—"

"*Haley.*" A dark, broken voice shattered the moment, and Haley scrambled to her feet, grabbing my shirt and wrapping it around her body.

I myself had no use for modesty in that moment. I rose from the ground, my cock still hard from the thought of making my little thief sing for me again, and followed her toward the cave entrance.

"Jax! You made it!" she cried out, but the moment the demon's face came into view, she faltered. "I… What's wrong? What happened?"

He spared a glance for me, his singular eye barely meeting mine before it returned to her.

Something prickled along my spine. I'd expected a reaction from him. Jealousy, perhaps. Anger about what he'd so clearly just interrupted.

But this was… not right. His face and chest were splattered with blood, and when I looked more closely, I noticed he was trembling.

A chill crept into the cave that had nothing to do with the waning snowstorm.

The gargoyle lumbered in behind him, still in his warrior form. His wings were torn, and blood coated his hands and arms, as if he'd been digging through a river of it.

"Hudson?" Haley gasped. "What… what happened? Where's Elian?"

The alarm in her voice sent an unexpected jolt of fear through my chest.

Time slowed to a crawl, and I watched in horror as the battered demon fell to his knees, the gargoyle standing mute behind him, the walls closing in on us all.

After an agonizingly long beat, the demon finally glanced up at Haley again, tears leaking from his eye.

"I'm so sorry, angel," he began, his voice hoarse. Broken.

And in that brief instant, before the rest of the words fell like shattered glass from his lips, I knew.

Deep in my ashen heart, I knew.

The vampire-fae called Elian, the fugitive of Midnight, Haley's lover and friend, my prisoner, my brother, my twin… was dead.

# BLOOD AND MAGICK

## BOOK FOUR

# 1

## JAX

*I* was an immortal fucking demon. I'd lost my humanity centuries ago.

But I wasn't so old I didn't remember what pain felt like. Human pain —the crushing immensity of it. The helplessness. The way it could steal the breath from your lungs and make you feel as if you'd never be able to breathe again.

I'd been human when my kid sister died in my arms. When my original family sold me to hell. When the cruelest, most vicious monsters in the pit tortured me until everything mortal about me had finally fled, leaving only a broken, brutal demon behind.

And as that demon, I'd endured brutalities that made hell look like Disney World, especially here. Even when we'd escaped to New Orleans, I couldn't shake free of Midnight's nightmares. Of that feeling of loss and emptiness more vast than the Boiling Glass Sands, so dark and bleak I was certain one night it would swallow me whole, spit me out right back into the bowels of hell.

But tonight, when that stupid, infernal, *reckless* fae fuck shoved me out of the way and I watched from the ground, powerless to do anything but gape as the fog just... just fucking *pureed* him.

I'd sworn my insides disintegrated right along with his.

Saint—my enemy, my bane, my brother and best fucking friend, was dead.

And I finally understood—as the wet, wine-dark spray of him slid down my face—that I'd never really known pain at all. For all that I'd suffered, I'd never even come close.

I was still blinking the blood from my eye when Hudson came into view, his face a mask of death. He knew at once what'd happened—witnessed the whole thing from above and just couldn't fucking get to us in time.

I saw the rage come over him then, his eyes smoldering with it, his muscles spring loaded as he leaped back into the air and went after the closest raven gryphon. They attacked him ferociously, but in the end, the gargoyle proved victorious. He took down two of those fucking hellspawn beasts—a shower of blood and bone and black feathers—before the witches called off their storm and retreated.

Hudson and I scoured that mountainside for hours, desperate for any sign that Saint had escaped—that somehow, the scheming bastard had found a way to pull off the ultimate trick. To beat death. To come back to us, but... nothing but blood and mist and memory.

It wasn't a fucking trick. Saint had sacrificed his life for me. For all of us. Even after all the horrible things I'd said and done. The cruelty of it all, and he was just...

Gone.

Fucking *gone*.

The storm had long since passed, no sign that the witches planned to return with reinforcements, but Hudson refused to fly. We trudged up the path in silence. Shock. I kept telling myself it was the cold, even though the snows had eased. I kept telling myself it was the cold because the alternative—that grief had rendered him flightless—was too much to bear when my own heart was already shattered.

With every step, the silence of Midnight grew more deafening. My chest tighter. Breathing more impossible because my lungs just couldn't fucking expand under the weight of the ugly truth filling up my heart.

Yet still, my mind refused to budge.

Saint would be waiting for us with Evander and Haley, it kept insisting. We'd get to the cave, and he'd stand up from behind the fire, a bowl of stew in hand, that cocky, crooked smirk shining out across the dim. *Took you long enough, brothers,* he'd say. And sure, maybe he'd be high again, maybe—ever the schemer—he'd be laughing his stoned ass off that Hudson and I had so thoroughly fallen for his ruse. I'd beat the shit out of him, but I wouldn't be mad. Wouldn't judge or condemn him for his antics or his little black pills. No fucking way. Never again would I so much as glower at him in distaste, if only... if *only* he'd just fucking *be* there.

But now, as we finally neared the cave at the top of the rise, the entrance glowing with firelight from inside, the soft and all-too-intimate sounds of Haley and Evander drifting out on the chilled breeze, that stupid hope inside me guttered out.

She was in there with our warlord. Our captor. Saint's brother.

She was… for now… happy.

And I was about to fucking destroy it.

No, not out of a jealous rage.

But because someone she loved had died for me, and I couldn't bring him back.

I turned to look at Hudson. He held my gaze a long moment, defeat casting his eyes in shadow. His wings had been torn in the fight. His spirit broken.

I nodded once. I would do this alone. I would fucking do this, because Saint died for me. For my pathetic life, and I owed him this much. I owed *her* this much.

Giving Hudson a moment of privacy, I stepped inside. Saw the whole scene spread out before me, just as I'd feared.

Haley and Evander, naked before the fire. Embracing. Laughing.

I didn't know what was worse—the fact that he'd made her laugh, or the fact that it might be the very last time I ever heard it.

*"Haley,"* I said, my voice hoarse. Broken. I dropped two packs on the ground—mine and Saint's.

She gasped and jumped to her feet, grabbing a shirt to cover up.

*His* shirt.

Evander rose behind her. Nude. Erect. Proud and smug, glaring at us as if we'd better have a good reason for the interruption.

"Jax!" she cried out, her smile breaking my heart a little more. "You made it!"

I tried to memorize it. That smile. The light in her eyes, no matter who'd put it there. The warmth. Tried to hold on to it, knowing I was about to blow it all away.

I drew in a shuddering breath, trying to find the words. But before I did, she saw it in my face. My eye, that fathomless window to the dark soul inside.

"I… what's wrong?" she whispered. "What happened?"

I glanced at Evander. Still nude. Still smug. His shoulders tightened under my gaze, though. And there, behind all that self-righteousness, I sensed it.

His fear.

Sharp and acute.

Hudson finally entered the cave, silently looming behind me. Blood dripped from his hands—his blood. The raven gryphon's. Saint's. The blood snow that'd finally vanished from the skies but still stained his skin.

Haley's eyes widened as she took in the sight of his torn wings.

Her fear spiked, the scent of it mingling with Evander's.

"Hudson?" Haley gasped. "What... what happened? Where's Elian?"

Evander's fear morphed into pure terror. He met my gaze again, his face etched in shock, the first glimpse of real pain flickering beneath.

My legs could no longer hold me up.

I dropped to my knees. Stared down at my useless, blood-stained hands. Tears blurred my vision.

Blood dripped onto the floor behind me—the last of the snow melting from clothes and shoes and packs. The fire crackled and hissed, and I finally lifted my head to look into Haley's eyes.

"I'm so sorry, angel," I said, every word scraping my throat raw. "Saint... Elian... he died."

And as I watched the look—*that* fucking look—bleed into the eyes of the woman I loved... the woman who loved Saint more than all the stars in the Midnight sky... I was reminded all over again just how little I'd known about true pain.

Endless. That look in her eyes was endless.

Haley fell to her knees before me. And Keradoc—Evander—whoever the fuck he was now finally had the decency to put on some pants.

"What happened?" He crossed the chamber, knelt down beside Haley. He wrapped a hand around the back of her neck, steadying her. "Where the fuck is my brother?"

"The—the witches," I stammered. Helpless. Dying inside. "They conjured the fog and he just... He saved my life. I didn't even see it coming, but he... One second he was across from me on the mountainside. He dropped his pack, the two of us bracing for incoming witches. And then... A flash in his eyes. A blur, and he just..."

The images rushed through my mind. Torture. Fucking *torture* as I'd watched my brother turn into red mist. A body made of muscle and bone, blood and hair. Silver eyes and a rare but wicked laugh. Memories and mistakes and loss and loyalty... An entire fucking immortal existence... All of it rendered utterly insubstantial by the fog. The cold, cruel breath of the realm blew across the mountain pass, and Elian was gone.

The Saint of the Hollow, the Saint of New Orleans. Just... gone.

The cave walls wavered, and Haley touched my face, her own pinched. Tears glazed her eyes, but they didn't fall.

"It's fine," she whispered. "*He's* fine."

"No," was all I could manage.

She glanced up at Hudson. Frantically shook her head. When she spoke again, her voice had risen in volume and pitch, echoing throughout the cave. "You guys are being ridiculous. We just need to… We need to go out there and find him, is all."

"Angel," I breathed, reaching for her, but she was already getting to her feet, flitting away like water, like smoke, and I stayed on my knees and kept right on reaching for her as if I could grab her and hold on long enough to make this okay. To fix it.

To bring him back.

My fingers clutched at nothing but the chilly air, and I watched with my heart stuck in my throat as she quickly dressed and then knelt before Saint's pack, her hands trembling.

"He needs… something," she murmured, yanking open the ties. "Warm clothes. Maybe different boots… Is it still snowing? He'll definitely need good boots if it's still snowing. These mountain paths are no joke."

Evander got to his feet. Offered a hand to help me up, and I took it, both of us exchanging a pained glance as Haley carried on, babbling as if Saint had merely lost the trail. As if he actually needed boots. As if he still had feet to carry him back home.

Releasing Evander's grip, I forced myself to go to her. I had to make her understand. To accept this, no matter how devastating.

Hudson still hadn't moved. Hadn't made a sound but for that blood still drip-drip-dripping from his body.

I slid my hands over Haley's shoulders, my touch unbearably gentle when all I wanted to do was crush her against my chest and never let her go. Never let her take a step outside of this cave, because inside it maybe there was a chance… A chance I could keep her safe. Keep all the cold, brutal things from ever laying a hand on her. Keep her whole and warm and fucking *alive*.

Hear that laugh again, even if it was Evander who brought it out.

"Haley, listen to me," I said, struggling to keep my voice from breaking. My fucking heart. "I know this is hard, but you need to hear this. Saint is gone. He's dead, Haley. He's not lost. He died. We have to—"

"*Find him!*" she shouted, rocketing to her feet and whirling to face me. Her green eyes flashed—not with grief, but frustration. Fury. "We have to find him, Jax!"

I wrapped my arms around her. Held her tight, even as she beat her fists against my chest. Even as her whole body shook. Even as she just kept saying it, over and over.

*Find him. Find him. Find him…*

The agony in her voice ripped me to shreds all over again, and I knew —I fucking *knew*—it didn't matter if I chained her up in this cave for the rest of her life.

This pain, right here, was worse than any brutal thing that existed outside these walls.

And I—an immortal fear demon forged in the bowels of hell—didn't have the strength to protect her from either.

# 2

## HALEY

For the first time in my life, I had absolutely *zero* tears for Elian. Seriously—not a single drop—not even when the hopelessness in Jax's voice threatened to break me. Not even when the dark clouds in Hudson's eyes were so all-encompassing, I worried they might swallow us all.

Nope. Not going there.

Because if I let even one stupid tear fall, it would mean I actually had something to cry about. And I didn't. All I had was something to be *annoyed* about—that Elian had gotten himself hurt and separated from the others, and now everyone was staring at me like I'd lost my damned mind just because I wanted to go back out there and get him.

Well, they'd obviously been through hell fighting off those weather witches. Hudson was in rough shape. Jax was completely out of sorts. Both of them were bloody and filthy. They could stay here by the fire—clean up and recuperate, if that's what they needed—no judgments.

But me? I needed to get back out there and find my man.

"Gloves," I said firmly, freeing myself from Jax's crushing embrace and returning to Elian's pack. "*That's* what he needs. Maybe some hiking socks, too. You have to protect the extremities in cold weather, right?" I fished a pair of soft leather gloves from the pack, and something else fell out with them, hitting the cave floor with a quiet tick.

A piece of paper folded into a square the size of a cracker.

I picked it up, gently unfolding it. Smoothing out the creases.

Even as my hands trembled, blurring the image before me, I knew at once what it was.

*Holy shit, he must've been carrying it with him all this time…*

I felt Jax hovering behind me, his breath catching.

"There was a street fair in Blackmoon Bay," I said softly. "This guy was doing caricatures and portraits—I dragged Elian over to him. Elian laughed and rolled his eyes the entire time, but he indulged me." I traced my fingertips along the lines—me, sitting in Elian's lap, my smile wide. Elian whispering in my ear, a glint of mischief in his eyes.

I still remembered what he'd said that night. That moment.

*When we get home, you're going to pose for me, naked and blindfolded. And I'm going to lick every part of you until you're singing all my favorite songs…*

The lines of my face were smudged and faded, as if he'd unfolded this paper and ran his fingers across it ten thousand times.

How many nights had he spent looking at us? Touching my face the way I now touched his? Remembering me, missing me, when all along I'd thought he'd forgotten?

Grief wrapped my heart in a vise, but I refused to let it break me.

I folded up the paper and tucked it back into the pack, resuming my hunt for warm socks.

"Snacks," I said. "He might need snacks. Is there any cheese left?"

The light flickered as someone moved closer, footsteps like whispers in the darkness. I hoped it wasn't Evander. I couldn't look at him now. Couldn't risk seeing even a *glimmer* of his twin's face…

But it was Hudson who came to stand behind me now. I felt his love for me through the bond, sweet and all-encompassing. His sadness, too, as heavy and immovable as the mountains themselves. All of it slipped beneath my ribs, and the defenses I'd built up around my heart began to crumble. A crack. A fissure.

I sucked in a sharp breath and closed my eyes, willing away those fucking tears that stung the backs of my eyes…

*No. Do not cry. Do not fucking cry for him…*

The air shifted, and my gargoyle knelt behind me. He was in his human form now, the blood vanishing along with his wings. He rested one strong hand on my shoulder. Warm. Solid. Reassuring.

His breath stirred my hair, and then his voice was in my ear, the soft rumble making me shiver. "Babygirl, I can't pretend to know how you're feeling, but—"

"*Worried*, Hudson. That's how I'm feeling. I'm worried about Elian because he's out there somewhere, alone, scared, injured… and we need to find him. We just need to *find* him, okay?" I nodded as if to affirm it for myself, cementing all those words in my mind. What choice did I have? I certainly wasn't going to sit around wringing my hands over it. Searching for him was a thing I could actually *do*. My one fucking piece of lasagna, which was about all I could manage in that moment.

Hudson squeezed my shoulder, but didn't say anything else. Didn't even move.

"You're injured," I finally managed.

"I'll heal."

"But… there was so much blood. I saw it."

"Gargoyles have a lot of extra blood vessels. It's what helps us shift so quickly. But I'm okay, babygirl. I promise."

I turned to meet his eyes, and he watched me for a long beat, his face tight with the effort of holding back his pain. No, not the pain of his torn wings, his surface wounds. But something I refused to truly see. Refused to acknowledge, because for him to be in pain like that could only mean…

*Nope. Not possible.*

So I turned away from him and dug around for the damn socks and told myself, again and again and again, that he and Jax were being over-dramatic. That they'd misinterpreted what they'd seen out there. That the stress of fighting off the weather witches and the raven gryphons, of making their way up the mountain through the blood snow, of finding their way back to me had simply confused them.

I took another deep breath. Focused on the scents of the cave—the wood smoke. The stew Evander had made for me, remnants congealing in the pot. The lingering warmth of our desire, the bedrolls not yet cool.

A spark of magick skittered down my spine, settling low in my stomach. Across the chamber, someone else inhaled sharply.

I knew without looking up it was him. My warlord. My dark lover. He'd sensed that spark—felt it—because the magick of Midnight belonged to him as well. It bound us to each other. To this land and all its beautiful darkness.

The thought should've brought me comfort, but it only cracked another chunk off that wall around my heart. The edges of it flickered with pain. Raw. Exposed.

"Haley," Evander whispered, but I still couldn't bring myself to look at him. To acknowledge the loss looming over us like a dark, inescapable cloud.

The magick inside me finally fizzled, and a tremor rumbled up through my legs. For the briefest instant I worried the ghouls of Beggar's Moat had come for me, tracked me through the mountains to finally claim what I'd denied them the night the guards left me for dead. I stared at the ground between my knees, waiting for the crack in the earth. Waiting for the bones to rise. To drag me to the deep places of a world without light. Without hope.

But it wasn't the ground that shook, I realized. It was me. A great wave rippled up from my feet, through my legs, into my chest and arms. My teeth chattered, every cell in my body vibrating with the effort of keeping my heart from exploding.

"Hey," Hudson murmured into my hair. He gripped my elbows, his massive hands warm and steadying as he gently urged me to my feet. "Mind if we step out and get some air? Something I need to tell you."

Still shaking, I nodded, grateful when he scooped me into his arms and tucked me in close, relieving me of the burden of having to walk even a single step.

I think we both knew that if I so much as tried, I would've collapsed.

I had just enough strength to reach up and touch his face, and when he met my eyes, I said the only word I could manage just then.

"Fly."

# 3

## EVANDER

$\mathcal{I}$ watched, stunned into silent paralysis, as the gargoyle carried Haley out of the cave.

How was it possible that only minutes had passed? Minutes since I'd held her in my arms? Since I'd kissed her breathless and she'd filled up the emptiness of this dark cave—of my heart—with her terrible singing?

Since her men had returned without their third—without my brother?

I blinked slowly, as if my mind simply couldn't keep up with the turn of events.

Across the dim space, Haley finally spared me a glance, her dark head lifting over the gargoyle's shoulder to meet my gaze. I don't know what she saw in my eyes, but her own suddenly filled with a terror so plain, so sharp, it tore through me as readily as a blade.

With that single look, I understood why the demon had fallen to his knees.

The helplessness I felt in that moment threatened to rise up and sweep me clear off the mountain.

The magick that had bound me to her faded, and it was only the demon's hand firm against my chest that made me realize I'd moved at all. That I'd reached for her as she vanished into the starry dark void beyond the cave entrance.

I blinked away the haze and looked at him, that blue eye glaring at me, glassy and raw, mirroring Haley's pain.

"She needs time," he said.

"We don't have the luxury of—"

"*Evander*," he snapped, and I finally relented, backing off.

"And you?" I asked, if for no other reason than to provoke him into conversation—*any* conversation. Anything other than the deafening silence of the dead. "What does her demon need?"

He groaned and scrubbed a hand over his face, massaging the skin above his ruined eye. Phantom pain, perhaps.

I suppressed a shudder.

"I don't know what the fuck I need," he said. "But even if I did, I sure as hell wouldn't be getting it from you."

I let it go without a response, and he turned his back and stalked toward the entrance. He didn't leave, though. Just leaned against the stone, arms crossed over his chest, eye undoubtedly roving along whichever route Haley and her gargoyle had taken.

Never before had I felt so torn between opposing worlds—opposing lives—as I felt in that moment, standing immobile between the darkness beyond the cave and the fire burning within it. My brother—their friend and ally—was dead. That alone should have given us some common ground, yet I was no closer to the demon than I'd been the night I'd put him on his knees in the throne room and watched as my guards riddled him with bolts.

I searched my heart for an ache, but found none. Only a deep, endless longing for the woman who no longer needed me—if she'd ever needed me at all. And why would she? Haley had her gargoyle and her demon now. Men who loved her. Men who loved my brother, when all I could feel was… empty.

And I'd meant what I'd told her earlier—time was not on our side. Regardless of the ill fortune that had befallen Elian of Autumnshire, I still needed to reach the fae who dwelled beneath this mountain range. Still needed to convince them to fight by our side, even if I had to do it alone.

I finished dressing in silence, then checked my pack, picking up where I'd left off just before she'd told me the story of my scars and the silver wolf who'd given them to me. Before she'd wrapped her arms around me and upended my entire world.

"Going somewhere?" the demon finally asked. He didn't turn from his watch beyond the cave, but still, I felt his gaze on me. His judgment.

"Melantha's army continues its advance through the desert. I don't believe she's manifested yet, but her presence grows stronger—I can feel it in the magick. It's… changing." As if it were listening in, the magick rippled through the surrounding stones. Barely perceptible, but there. Making itself known. Present.

I wondered if Haley could feel it now, too. If this magick would always tether us. Change us.

"I need to move forward with my plan," I continued, closing up the pack. I kept it light—either I'd find the fae and convince them to aid me, or I wouldn't be making a return trip. "We need allies, and—"

"Your brother is dead, Evander."

"So you've said."

"Your brother is *dead*," he repeated. "Your brother."

Again, I mined the depths of my heart, searching for something beyond that yawning dark emptiness.

But there was only the dim echo of memories I could no longer reach. Memories that belonged to another man in another time in another realm, as lost to me now as the brother I would never know.

# 4

## HUDSON

*P*lease tell me you've got the words to make this better, Hudson. *Please…"* Haley's voice broke, and whatever was left of my heart fucking cracked in half.

The one time I needed words more than anything, I couldn't find them —not even for her. Because the words to explain this fucked-up mess didn't even exist.

Ignoring the pain in my tattered wings, I'd shifted back into warrior form and flown us out about a mile down from the cave, desperate to escape the crushing sadness inside those suffocating stone walls. Now, Haley and I sat side by side on a nameless rocky ledge, legs dangling out over nothing but black air, the sprawl of Midnight's darkness stretching on for an eternity below.

All I could think about was the fall.

Would death claim us as swiftly as it'd taken Saint? A blink, a breath, and then… nothing? Would we find peace? Had *he* found peace?

*Fucking Saint.* All those pills. His pain. Was it possible he'd finally escaped it?

I tried to hold on to that thought. To the blind hope that no matter how badly the rest of us fucking hurt to lose him, maybe Saint was… maybe he was finally okay.

But I couldn't know that for sure, and hope and pretty wishes would never be enough to calm the storm raging inside me. To dry the tears from Haley's eyes and bring that smile back to her face.

Saint. Elian. Our brother. Our family. He was... gone.

"Tell me this isn't happening," she whispered, and I shuddered, desperate to keep the full extent of my pain inside. In that moment, it felt so fucking sharp I was pretty damn sure it would slice her up if she got too close to it.

I closed my eyes and squeezed her hand tight. Blew out a long, broken breath. Didn't matter how many times I'd witnessed death up close and personal, how many fucking times I'd seen the most violent, gruesome shit imaginable. It *never* got any easier, and it never made any sense. How could someone be standing there one second, and then—in a single heartbeat, in a *literal* blur—just stop fucking existing?

Still wordless, still spinning, I pulled her onto my lap and held her against my chest, tucking my torn wings around her as if that alone could keep her safe.

"He's not dead," she whispered, her whole body trembling in my hold, voice softer than the breeze. "Elian... what we had... what we *have*... If he were truly gone, I would know it. Deep in my heart, I would know it."

I stroked her hair, wishing like hell I could just leap off this fucking mountain and fly her somewhere else—to some other realm where the light still shone, where darkness and pain could never touch her again.

"Do you know what I told him?" she asked. "One night when we were still back at the apartment in Amaranth City? I told him that after he left me—after I was sure he was never coming back—I would fantasize that he'd died. He stood right in front of me, and I looked him in the eyes and told him I wished he *had* died, because it would've been easier than watching him disappear a little piece at a time... God. How could I say something like that, Hudson? How could I be so cruel?"

Tears blurred my vision, the breeze cold on my warrior skin. I could feel her pain through the bond. Her desperate ache. The dim flicker of hope that somehow this had all been a mistake.

"I just got him back," she said. "I spent five years hating him. Five years wasted to anger and bitterness, and all along, he was here. He was here with his brothers, fighting for you all, fighting for what he thought was right, and I finally... I finally *understand* him, Hudson. I understand why he made the choices he made. Turns out all those things I cursed him for are all the things I most admire about him, and if he's gone—truly gone —then I'll never get to..."

She sucked in a sharp, shuddering breath and pressed both hands to her chest, as if she could keep her heart from leaping right out and splattering on the rocks. When she opened her mouth again, no more words came out. Only gasps. Sobs.

Agony.

"Breathe, Haley. Please, babygirl. Just breathe." I could no longer keep the pain from my voice, from spilling right out of me like blood from a wound. I felt it wrap around us both, heavy and endless, as dark as the Midnight sky. I ran a trembling hand down her back. "I need you to breathe for me, because if you don't, I can't... I can't get through this without you..."

"I'm falling apart, Hudson. I'm falling apart and you have to tell me it's okay. Tell me this is just a nightmare. One of Elian's schemes. A trick of the realm. *Something...*"

*Fuck*, I wished I could lie to her, just this once. She wanted it so badly. Needed it—all that sugar coating.

But that's not how it worked with us. Never would be.

I slid my hand around the back of her head and held her against my chest, my tears soaking into her hair as hers spilled all over my skin, and I whispered the only words I could find.

"I got you, babygirl. I fuckin' got you."

She went boneless in my arms, and a howl so vast, so desperate, so full of anguish exploded out of her, the sound of it carving me out inside, my wings trembling as she clung to me and sobbed, and in that brutal moment, it was only my love for her—my fated promise to take care of her —that kept me from shifting into my human form, closing my eyes, and jumping right over that black fucking edge.

The cold wind scraped across my skin, and in the light of the triple moons, there we sat, the warrior and his witch, his mate, both of us succumbing to that gaping, gnawing hurt.

And then, finally... breathing. Just fucking breathing.

---

I didn't know how much time passed before the trembling stopped—hers, mine. The mountain itself. But eventually she pulled back to gaze up at me, and through them tear-soaked lashes, the change came over her swiftly.

Grief faded from her eyes, and in a blink, that fierce, steely, Haley Barnes determination lit a new fire behind them. A bright fucking blaze in the darkness.

"I know Death," she said. Then, in a whisper that sent a chill slithering down my spine, "I can bring him back."

My arms tightened around her instinctively, as if she might bolt right out of my hold and throw herself off the mountain just to find her way back to him.

"Haley…" It was a warning as much as a plea. "*No.* Necromancy is… No. Saint doesn't even have a—" I clamped my mouth shut over the word. *Body.* He'd been liquified by the fog. *Liquified.* All that remained of my brother had soaked into the Midnight soil. Into my skin. Jax's.

I could still taste his blood in my mouth. Smell it. Feel it.

But Haley was already shaking her head and wriggling out of my embrace, this new mission giving her strength. Purpose. "You don't understand, Hudson. I know Death. Literally. From everything in Blackmoon Bay… Death is one of my sister's mates, only he became mortal and the death mantel passed on to…" She swallowed hard, then said, "Reva. She was one of our witches. A kid—teenager. She helped save us from Darkwinter but she… she didn't survive the final battle. Not as a mortal girl, anyway. But Liam— Death—he found a way to… I'm not sure exactly how it all happened, but I know her, Hudson. So if I can find a way to get to her before Elian's soul crosses into the Shadowlands, maybe she can send him back to us."

The Shadowlands. The place where the dead found their eternal rest.

Assuming they made it that far. Assuming they weren't bound for hell.

But Saint… no. He wasn't going to hell. Not after all he'd sacrificed for us. If that's how the universe worked, then Death and everyone else involved could go fuck themselves, far as I was concerned.

"The Shadowlands weren't meant for the living, Haley," I said, as gently as I could. "You're talking about risking the loss of your own soul and facing down Death—that's assuming you can find her. Friend or not —*teenager* or not—it won't be an easy battle."

"If that's what it takes to save him? If there's a *chance*?" She wiped away the last of her tears, the color returning to her cheeks. "I don't care how hard it is. I'm doing it. And I'd do it for you and Jax, too. For… for anyone I care about."

"Evander." The name was out before I could stop myself. Stop the flames of jealousy that had flickered to life the moment we'd returned to that cave and still hadn't yet dimmed, despite the weight of everything else.

"Evander," she said firmly. It wasn't a question, but I could tell from the look in her eyes she wanted my thoughts on the matter.

I took her hands in mine. Pressed a kiss to every one of her knuckles, then released her hands so I could cup her face. "Evander… Saint's brother…" I shook my head, still not quite believing how much had happened in the last couple nights. "If you're telling me you care for him, and you're telling me he's worthy of it… Then hell. Doesn't matter what I think of him. You know I support you, Haley. Always."

A nod. A faint, relieved smile. "But it *does* matter, Hudson. It matters to me. For better or worse, there's something that connects him to me beyond the fact that he's Elian's brother. And that means he's connected to you and Jax as well. To all of us. I don't know how it happened, or why, or what it all means… And maybe I could make sense of it if I had more time. If we weren't facing this war and Melantha and everything with…" She sighed again, her lashes lowering. "With Elian. But that only makes me realize how important all of you are to me. Logical or not, we were meant to find each other. All of us. Which is exactly why I need to bring Elian back. To bring our family back."

Fresh tears slipped down her cheeks, wet and warm on my hands, but they weren't tears of grief. They were the tears of a fighter preparing for battle. Tears of a warrior who was ready to face down death for the man she loved.

I stared at her, awed and humbled. Still so fucking gobsmacked that the fates had seen fit to bring her to me. To make her mine. Ours.

I thought I'd understood loyalty. Bonds. Saint and Jax and me—we were brothers. Even without the blood oath and the tattoos, we were fuckin' *brothers*. But Haley? Her loyalty was unparalleled. She was talking about fighting Death. Literal death just for a slim chance to bring him back to us.

Now, looking into her infinite eyes under the triple moons of Midnight, I smiled. "I said it before and I'll say it again. If anyone can save him, babygirl, it's you."

"But you… you don't think it's possible." Her shoulders slumped.

"I don't think it's *likely*," I answered honestly. "But… That ain't a reason not to try."

She nodded and let loose a heavy sigh. "So you didn't bring me out here to convince me to just… accept that he's gone? To let him go, once and for all?"

Another shudder rippled through her body, and I drew her close and pressed a long kiss between her brows, wishing I could make sense of the feeling burning in my heart. Wishing I could turn it all into words so she would know—truly—what I felt.

My whole life in this body, in this universe… a thousand fucking years… and I could count on *one* hand the people who'd fight for me like that. Saint. Jax. And now…

"Haley, I'd no more try to talk you out of fighting for the man you love than I'd try to talk you out of casting spells or growing them gorgeous black roses. It's all part of who you are, part of the woman I fucking love more than all the stars in the sky, in this realm or any other, and I don't want to change that about you. Never. *Never.*"

She climbed into my lap again and I ran my hand down her back and buried my face in her hair. *Mine.* My fierce little monster girl, my mate.

"I brought you out here," I whispered, "because I need you to know you're not the only one who loves him." I closed my eyes as my throat tightened around the words. "I need you to know how much Saint means to *me.*"

# 5

## HUDSON

ou never asked me about the not-talking thing," I said softly. "Why it took me so long to open up to you, even though we clearly had a connection from the start. Why I still find it hard to talk to everyone else."

"I figured you'd share if and when you were ready. And if you didn't, well…" Haley's breath misted against my chest, her fingers tracing idle patterns along my forearm as I held her tight. "It's the same thing you said about me, Gargs. It's all part of who you are. Part of the man I love. Words or no words—that doesn't change how I feel about you. Doesn't change our bond."

"No, but knowing this… It might help you understand things better. Me. Saint. Why he… why he sacrificed so much to get us out of Midnight."

She stiffened, the weight of my old ghosts pressing in close. I knew she could sense it through the bond—my shame. My private darkness. The rage that would continue to simmer inside me until Mad Marco and the last of his traitorous fucking crew were dust in the wind.

But I had to tell her this story. Had to get it all out, once and for all, because I needed her to know it. To know all those things that'd made me the man she loved.

And to know how much Saint truly fucking meant to me, just like I'd said. Not just because I wanted her to know, but because I wanted him to know, too. And I never got the chance to tell him.

A fresh bolt of pain shot right through me, but I welcomed it. Pain like

568

that… it meant I'd lost something fucking important. The fact that I'd even had it at all was a blessing.

Keeping my wings tucked close around us, I shifted partially back into my human form and turned my right arm so she could see the tattoo—a field of wildflowers hacked by a bloody scythe, bright blooms scattered along the ground.

"I call it the reaping," I whispered, the word sending a cold shiver down the back of my neck. "Not a day goes by I don't look at this tattoo and remember it. Feel it."

She traced the outline of the scythe with her fingertips, down the handle and across the blade. When she spoke again, her voice was reverent. Awed. "What does it mean?"

"It means I'll spend the rest of my immortal life atoning for something I can't change." I turned to lay my cheek on the top of her head and breathed in the scent of her. Sweet. Home. I'd meant what I told her before the weather witches attacked—she *did* make me strong. Brave. And I needed every ounce of that courage to get this story out.

"Like all of Midnight's gargoyles," I continued, "I was born in captivity, bred at the behest of the dark fae nobles who saw us as little more than cattle. Most of us were used for grunt work—transporting goods, fighting on the front lines of their bullshit territorial skirmishes. Others, they…" I swallowed the knot in my throat. "…experimented on."

Haley gasped. "Do they still do stuff like that?"

"Experiments? Yeah, I'm sure they do. I mean, all this was even before Keradoc's time—the *real* Keradoc—but one look around will tell you… Ain't much changed. Same shit, new warlord, you know? Anyway, they had me working in the Stone City mines at first, digging up gems or metals or whatever the hell else they thought they could turn into currency. I was good—strong, fast. Did the job of guys twice my size in half the time. Eventually, the owner of one of the mines—an original Midnight royal, this guy—he took notice. Saw what I could do and decided he wanted me in his elite guard. Given the alternatives, it was a fucking honor to be selected for work like that, so off I went."

"But you had to leave Stone City?"

"Had to leave everyone and everything I'd ever known, yeah. But still —it was a better shot than what most of us ever got. So I said my good-byes and went willingly. Did the job with pride. Wasn't a bad gig, honestly. For the most part, he and his family treated me fairly."

"For the most part?"

A hollow laugh rang out, the old resentments twisting through my gut.

"A slave is still a slave, Haley. Not like they set a place for me at the dinner table, or even called me by my name, for that matter. I was just 'gargoyle' to them. Sometimes 'guard,' but never more than that. The kids, though? They were the good ones. Still young enough that the whole fucked-up system hadn't yet crushed their spirits." I laughed, remembering how they used to climb all over me whenever I walked into the room. Beg me to take them out flying, even though their parents had strictly forbidden it.

I told Haley a bit about my life at the royal estate in northern Amaranth City, not far from the sea. How I'd spent my nights guarding the noble lord and his family, telling the kids stories about life in the mines. Occasionally accompanying the lord on so-called diplomatic missions to territories beyond the wall, where I'd slaughter his enemies and let him bask in the glory, claiming another plot of Midnight wasteland just because he could.

"The royals never visited their claimed territories," I said. "Only time they ever left the safety of the wall was to wipe out some faction or another—expand their pointless empires. Whole thing was fucked. Always has been, always will be." I closed my eyes and shook my head, those old resentments turning into a quiet rage that rippled through my muscles.

Haley tucked in closer, her touch once again easing the ache inside me.

"One night," I said, "the lord of the manor decided to head out beyond the wall with some of the other high fae fucks on a hunting expedition. Looking for dragon's eggs, supposedly—way too precious a treasure to risk bringing a lowly gargoyle on the trip. I was left behind to look after his wife and their four children. The lady had heard whispers of a growing threat against the royals—the usual unrest. She'd begged him to cancel his trip, but he chalked off her concern to hysteria and left me to deal with her.

"She'd just put the kids to bed when we both heard it—a commotion on the roof. We grabbed the kids from their rooms, and I secured them with their mom in the master suite, then headed up to check it out." I sucked in a shuddering breath, no longer able to keep the quake from my limbs, the frantic pounding from the warrior heart that'd never forgotten its most brutal betrayal. "They were waiting for me up there, babygirl. Fuckin' ambush."

"Gargoyles?" she whispered.

"A half dozen of 'em, yeah. Three I'd never seen before. Three I'd once considered friends." I opened my eyes. Met her green gaze in the moonlight. "Garrison, Draven, and Mad Marco."

# 6

## EVANDER

*I* am… saddened by the news of Elian's passing," I finally managed, the lie leaving a bitter taste on my lips. "But I didn't know him as you did. I didn't know him as my brother."

"Because you threw away the chance. Even after learning who he was. Even after he fought by your side against your own guards in the Sanctuary. Even after he agreed to accompany you on this… this doomed mission."

"He was your friend," I said evenly. "That I *do* know, and for what it's worth, I'm sorry for your loss. But—"

"But you're leaving us, anyway. Leaving *her* when she needs all the support we can offer."

Something about the "we" in his statement sent an unfamiliar warmth unfurling in my chest, making me itch.

"War rarely gives us the luxury of doing what's right. Only of doing what must be done."

"Spoken like a true warlord." A dark laugh slithered across the chamber. "Tell yourself whatever you need to, Evander. Whatever gets you through the night, right?"

"And what would you have me do, demon?" I stood and crossed the dim space, joining him at the entrance. Outside, the darkness of Midnight shone like a black jewel, haunting and fathomless. "Shall I fall to pieces and weep for a brother I likely mourned centuries ago? Ask the kind, compassionate soldiers of Darkwinter for some bereavement time for a man who, until last night, was nothing but a fugitive of my realm? Perhaps I can inform Melantha and her Army of the Dead that we'll need to reschedule their sacking of the kingdom on account of the death of a vampire-fae who sacrificed his life for *you*." I fisted his shirt, hauled him close. So close I could see every scar and divot in his ruined face, harsh and cruel in the firelight. "Do *not* presume to understand my feelings on this or any other matter, *demon*."

A deadly smile slid across his mouth, and his eye blazed bright. Brighter still, until it was nearly glowing. A chill crept into my skull, scraping across my mind like a bitter wind.

I didn't resist the invasion of his power. His manipulations. I merely returned that smile—the grin of a corpse who didn't have the good sense to know he was already dead. In a dark whisper, I said, "If you honestly believe you can conjure a fear more terrifying than the nightmares haunting my head, be my guest."

Behind us, a log shifted on the fire, the flames hissing and popping, shattering the tense moment.

His smile faltered. The gleam in his eye finally dimmed.

That cold, invasive power retreated at once, leaving only shame in its wake.

"I'm... sorry," he said, and when he finally lowered that unnervingly intense blue eye, I knew he'd meant it.

I just didn't know what he was sorry for, exactly. That he'd invaded my mind? That I'd lost a brother I didn't even know? That Haley was in pain? That we'd nearly drawn daggers over all of it?

He let out a dark sigh and said softly, "I should've... I should've been able to protect him. He was my brother and friend, and I was supposed to have his back."

And there was my answer, right along with the common ground I so desperately sought.

No, it wasn't loss and grief that bound us now.

It was guilt.

All the anger inside me crumbled into dust, unleashing the dam on my own dark confessions. The first bite of pain lanced my heart, and I whispered, "I... I let him stay and fight while I retreated to the safety of this cave."

"You were merely protecting Haley."

"Still, I... I sent my brother to his death believing I wanted nothing from him but his unwavering allegiance. Nothing but what he could offer me as a soldier and spy. And now I'll never…" My voice splintered, and I closed my mouth, admonishing myself. It was more than I'd meant to say, more than I'd meant to reveal to the demon I'd treated as poorly as I'd treated my twin. My blood. My worst enemies.

"It was Elian's choice to join this mission," he said, plainly and without judgment. "All of us made the choice to back you, Evander. Same as Haley. And we'd do it again in a heartbeat, even knowing the risks."

"For her."

"For her," he confirmed, leaving no doubts about the limits of their loyalties.

And how could I blame them? Until last night when I'd finally revealed my true identity, I'd been their captor. The cruel warlord who'd threatened them, forced them to do his bidding, put their lives at risk again and again, all in service to this war.

*My* war.

And tonight, they'd walked into this cave carrying the weight of Elian's death—their brother's death—only to discover I'd bedded the woman they all loved. The woman he'd loved, too.

A surge of guilt burned away the last icy vestiges of his powers lingering in my mind.

Hastily, I stepped into my boots and grabbed my cloak.

Shouldering my pack, I said, "Keep her here. Keep her safe."

"What about you?"

"Watch for me by the second moonrise tomorrow. If I haven't returned, I want the three of you to gather what supplies you can and retreat to—"

"*Retreat?*" The hissing voice that broke across the night was not the demon's, but something unfamiliar, terrifying in its utter lack of warmth. Of humanity. "Such is the way of cowards and thieves."

The demon and I reached for our daggers and turned toward the cave entrance just as the pale faces came into view. On silent footsteps, they marched inside uninvited—a dozen feral fae soldiers, skin and hair as colorless as the first moon, all of them armed with swords carved of bone and obsidian. Three ancient dark fae witches accompanied them, magick curling from their very skin like glittering smoke.

Just beyond the cave, the shadows of two raven gryphons darkened the path.

Before I could even speak, a dark spell wrapped an invisible fist around my throat, squeezing. Crushing. The demon choked and gasped beside me.

"So tell us, *warlord*. Which one are you?" The general stepped forward and narrowed his ancient gaze, his black eyes like twin pieces of coal sinking into that eery, milk-white face as his witches surrounded us, the ancient magick crackling as it feasted upon the very breath in our lungs. "A coward or a thief?"

# 7

## HUDSON

*I*t was the fight of my life, Haley," I said. "For *hours* the six of 'em taunted me. Tag-teamed me like a rat in a maze, no escape. I left more blood on that rooftop than I've spilled in the nine-hundred-some years since, but no matter how hard I fought, there was never a chance for victory."

"*Assholes*," she seethed. "You were outnumbered six to one. By your own fucking kind."

"Wasn't just the numbers. Whole thing was rigged from the start. The fight was just a way for Marco to... I don't know. Feel like a man, I guess. Toy with me before the real attack came down."

"*Real* attack?"

"He and his boys had gotten tight with some dark witches. They were packing a sunlight spell that could immobilize any gargoyle on contact."

"Like the bullets from the night of the feast?" she asked.

I nodded. "Same shit, only this one was like a goddamn nuke compared to those bullets. One minute I'm on the ground bleeding, trying to think through some kind of plan. Then there's a flash and a fire across my skin like nothing I've ever felt. Next thing I know, I'm stone."

I shuddered again, the rest of the gruesome story boiling up like hot poison from the darkest, most ancient parts of me.

"I could see, hear, and feel everything around me," I said. "And they knew it, too—that's exactly how they planned it. I was trapped, Haley. Trapped and paralyzed as they broke through the wards in the house, dragged the woman and her servants and children out onto the grounds and... and did the most unspeakable... The way they... they violated them, and I just..."

My words tangled into knots and fell away on the Midnight breeze, tears leaking from my eyes. My girl didn't say anything, though. Just wrapped her arms around me and held me tight, giving me the space to catch my breath. Letting me find my way through the darkness, back to the tangle of my words. Back to her.

Long moments passed before I could speak again, and when I did, my throat ached with the effort. But I couldn't stop now. I had to get it out. All of it.

"I found out later that Marco... His family had paid off the nobles to get him out of the mines, but they'd chosen me as their guardian instead, keeping the money and denying they'd ever had any dealings with Marco's family. So Marco took it upon himself to exact his revenge—on me and the family both. In the end, he and his boys slaughtered everyone who lived on the estate. The lord and lady's siblings, random cousins. All the staff. Hell, even the mares weren't spared the wrath of the Stone City gargoyles. And the whole time—the whole fucking time they tortured those people, spilled all that blood—there wasn't a damn thing I could do but scream inside my prison of stone. Scream and fucking *scream* until it felt like my throat was shredded, but no one heard a sound.

"When they were sure all the fae and their servants were dead, they dropped me in the middle of all that carnage, still in my stone form. They painted me with the blood of the dead and left the bodies strewn around me like it was all some kind of... ritualistic sacrifice. I... I ain't never seen anything like it. Not before, not since. And I pray I never have to. Not with kids. Not like that."

Haley was crying now, too, the two of us clinging to each other in the darkness as the gruesome memories scored my heart all over again.

"When the spell wore off and I could finally move again, I was... I was beside myself, Haley. A total fucking wreck." I ran my thumb along the tattoo. "I kept thinking about wildflowers cut down by a blade—that's what I saw when I looked at those poor fucking kids. And all I wanted to do was find a way to put them back together again. But there was so much blood and... and it was too fucking late. They were just... gone. Exhausted, wasted, I fell to my knees and wept, but when I tried to scream again, no sound came out. So I stopped. Stopped screaming. Stopped fucking talking altogether. Words wouldn't bring them back, so what the fuck was the point?"

She laced her fingers through mine and squeezed.

"When the lord returned from his hunt the next night and saw what'd happened," I said, "I still couldn't speak. Couldn't bring myself to give voice to what I'd witnessed. He knew I wasn't the murderer—knew I loved his fucking kids like they were my own. But it didn't even matter, because my true crime was much worse than the murders. I was a gargoyle—*their* gargoyle. Slave or not, I was still honor- and duty-bound to protect that family at all costs, even if it meant sacrificing my own life. And in that single, most important mission, I'd failed.

"I remained in my human form, naked and vulnerable before him. I knelt. Bowed my head, hands clasped behind my back. I wanted him to execute me. Waited and wished for the bite of his sword. It was his right— I was their guardian, and I'd failed them. Completely and utterly failed them. But of course, an outright execution would've been too kind a punishment."

I rubbed the back of my neck, the dull ache where I sometimes still felt the blade that had never come. Still felt like I deserved it.

"He cast me out beyond the wall," I went on, "forbidding me from having any contact with other gargoyles. I wasn't allowed to return to Stone City. Wasn't allowed to meet my... my mate." I blew out a heavy sigh. "Yeah. Nine hundred years ago, I had a mate—only other time in my life. She was another gargoyle—one I didn't know. Felt the first tug of our bond just a couple months after the slaughter, knew it was my fated duty to protect her as well. But I couldn't—couldn't risk even acknowledging that pull. If I disobeyed the lord's command and returned to Stone City, I knew he'd find my mate and slaughter her as readily as Marco had slaughtered his family. The irony of it, though... Fuck *me*, Haley. She died anyway. A few years later, Marco took her out. I don't know how he found out she was my charge, but he did."

Another audible gasp. Haley tensed in my arms, but I pushed on. Hell, I'd kept the story locked up inside me for so long, I never thought I'd ever give it room to breathe again. Now that I had, I couldn't stop. Not until I got back to the fucking start of all this.

To Saint.

"Cutting a gargoyle off from his wards, from his pack... it does something to us," I said. "Not just emotionally, but physically as well. We *need* to protect. We're driven by that need, fed by it. Out beyond the wall, no charges to mind, no friends... I was dying, babygirl. Night by night, breath by breath, I was literally fuckin' dying."

At this, she cupped my face and looked up into my eyes, her gaze turning fierce as she caught my tears with her thumbs. "But you *survived*, Hudson. You were a gargoyle on your own, and somehow, you made it through."

"But that's the thing, Haley. I wasn't on my own. I felt something out there. Some kind of... spark." I lowered my mouth to hers, stealing the ghost of a kiss—the barest brush across her sweet lips. Then, in a voice as soft as the breeze, "I think it was you, babygirl. The promise of you. It'd be several hundred years before you were even born, but fate already knew you'd be mine. Not just a mate to protect, but a woman I might actually fall in love with. A woman who might fall right back. And even the idea of it... of you... It just... just gave me that little nudge. A reminder that life was worth fighting for, even if it would take me centuries to realize why."

She smiled and pressed a hand to my chest. To my heart. I covered her hand with mine and held her there, once again borrowing her warmth. Her courage.

"I decided to trust that little spark," I said. "Somehow, I made my way back to the wall. Snuck inside with a trading caravan. Changed my identity, started picking up odd jobs—mercenary work, private security detail for some of the most unsavory motherfuckers you can imagine."

"Unsavory..." Haley narrowed her eyes, the tiniest smile turning up the corners of her lips. "Let me guess. That's how you met Elian and Jax?"

"Hundreds of years and thousands of unsavory assholes later, yeah. That's *exactly* how I met them. Keradoc—the real one—was Midnight's ruler by then, making life hell for everyone—more hell than usual. The boys needed my help keeping their asses safe during their various... business dealings."

"Smuggling drugs, weapons, and secrets," she clarified. "Jax told me about it the first time I saw the corpsevine fields."

"Hey. Ain't none of us ever pretended to be the good guys." I sighed. "Despite all Midnight's bullshit, though, I was content. For the first time since I'd left Stone City to serve the nobles, I had a family to protect again. A purpose. Fucking *brothers* I could take care of, who took care of me just by being there. Letting me in. I wasn't naive enough to think it'd last forever—that's the first lesson you learn growing up in a place like Midnight. Don't get too fucking comfortable, right? But I *did* get comfortable. So much so that I almost forgot about my old ghosts. Forgot that they never really die, even if they lay low for a time."

She reached for my forearm again, fingers gliding across the wildflowers, making me shiver. "What happened?"

"One night, I was coming out of the tavern after a few drinks, and there he was."

She knew at once who I meant. Could probably hear my damn blood singing the fucker's name.

"Mad Marco," she whispered, and I felt the answering fury rise inside me all over again.

"He attacked me again, but this time, he was alone. Without his boys or his precious dark fae witches backing him, I beat his ass in a heartbeat. Would've killed him too, right there in the streets of the Hollow for all to see. But he reached out to Draven through their gargoyle bond, and the fucker showed up and saved him. They could've double-teamed me, but they didn't—just took off. I knew right then I was in deep shit—no way would they leave a loose end like me hanging around. Sure enough, the fuckers reported me to Keradoc as a fugitive. Said they had irrefutable evidence that I'd slaughtered the fae nobles all those centuries ago—an unsolved crime so heinous, it'd sent the noble lord and the remaining members of their bloodline fleeing to the mountains, never to be heard from again."

"Hudson... wait. The mountains? The... oh my *god*." She shot to her feet, the last pieces clicking into place. "The fae nobles... You're talking about the feral fae. The ones Keradoc wants us to meet."

**8**

HUDSON

*H*aley's face paled as I confirmed her suspicions about the fae.

"Those children are still… they kept them," she said. "Not alive, but…"

"Yeah. I know." Sickness roiled inside me, and I reached for her hands and tugged her back down into my lap again, needing to touch her, the softness and warmth of her skin the only thing keeping me from absolutely losing my shit at the thought of facing those fae again. I had no idea whether the noble lord himself was still alive, but it didn't matter. His bloodline lived on—all those who hadn't dwelled at the estate, anyway. And those poor fucking kids, kept in some kind of twisted magickal stasis, never allowed to find peace…

That alone was enough to make me rage.

"I… I didn't know," she said softly, tucking herself inside my hold once more. "When Evander told me about them, he mentioned the attack in passing. I didn't know you were involved."

"Pretty sure he didn't know it either. It was before Evander's time as Keradoc, and I've never spoken of this to anyone. Not even the boys know the whole story."

"You shouldn't be here. You shouldn't have to face them. To live through that again."

"There's a whole lot of shit none of us *should* have to face, but we do it, Haley. We fucking do it for the ones we love. So yeah, I absolutely *should* be here, because here is where *you* are, and if you think for a second there's anywhere else I'm gonna be, you need your head examined, woman." I ruffled her hair and leaned in close, stealing another kiss before she could say anything else on the matter.

When I finally drew back, she said, "How did you find out Marco reported you?"

"Keradoc gave his lieutenant general the order to hunt me down."

"Wait..." Her brow furrowed. "Oona?"

I nodded. "Saint never really trusted her, but apparently the two of them had worked out some kinda truce for Jax's sake. Soon as she got the order, she told Saint about it. Said she didn't want to do it—had no reason to hunt me, to deliver me to the dungeons for an eternity of torture. But hers wasn't the only crew out looking for me. It was a death sentence either way—I could either let Oona turn me over to Keradoc, or bide my time until Marco and his fucking lackeys found me again. And that was fine—I was ready for death. Thousand years was a good run, I figured, especially for a gargoyle of Midnight. But—"

"But Elian wouldn't let you die," she whispered, barely holding back a shudder as the reality slammed into us both. The reminder of why we were out here having this conversation.

My chest tightened, images of Saint getting swallowed up by that fog slicing through my mind once more.

"Saint gave me the lowdown from Oona," I said. "Told me not to worry—he was already working on a plan to get us the fuck out of there for good—all three of us. I didn't want him and Jax risking their asses for the likes of me, but Saint... You know how stubborn that bastard is. He dug his heels in. Refused to leave this place unless all three of us walked out together—those were his terms."

I shook my head, a sad laugh escaping as I remembered the look in the sonofabitch's eyes that night. The warning he gave me. *You bail on us now, brother, you're condemning us to this nightmare world for an eternity. So unless you want me to beat your ass until you're talking again, you're walking through that portal with us.*

"I didn't understand the hows and the whys at that moment, but I wasn't about to hold them back—not when he was flat out refusing to leave without me. I only knew that it would cost us—that we'd have to keep the business running in New Orleans, that Gem and everyone else would get a cut of the profits in exchange for keeping our escape secret. But there was dark magick involved, too."

"Fucking Melantha," Haley gritted out. The very mention of her name seemed to shift something around us, turning the air foul. Far in the distance, a strange indigo light flickered along the horizon.

The Dark Goddess and her army were getting closer. Stronger.

"For me, leaving my homeland *was* the price," I said. "Midnight was my last connection to my people, to the gargoyle I'd been for damn near a thousand years. The goddess knew I'd never really fit in down in New Orleans, even as I kept watch over Jax and Saint. And a place like that—all the sunshine? I spent more time as a statue in Saint's garden than I did anywhere else. Felt like my damn wings had been clipped, but still. Small price to pay to avoid the dungeons, and to keep Saint and Jax safe, too.

"The three of us never talked about what she demanded from us that night. No reason to—we got out, started over in New Orleans, and that was that. I always assumed that's why Jax had lost his eye—figured it had something to do with his powers. But with Saint, I had no idea. Until now." I slid my hand into her hair and fisted it tight, tipping her head back until she met my gaze. "It was you. You were the price Saint paid to get me out of Midnight."

It wasn't a question, and she didn't respond with anything more than a dark sigh.

"That's why he doesn't touch you," I said. "Even though you're both still so in love with each other, even a blind man could see it. You and me? We got a mate bond, Haley. But you've got a bond with them as well. Different, but just as real. Just as true. And when I see you and Saint... Fuck. Every time one of you walks into the room, the other one lights up like a damn star shower. Didn't make any sense to me—how even after you told us you wanted us all to be together, he still sat on the sidelines, watching us like it was tearing him apart inside not to touch you."

"He told me Melantha cursed us," she whispered darkly. "That if we ever touched intimately again, if he ever tells me how he truly feels... I mean, how he *felt*..." She trailed off into a silent sob.

*Fuck.* I hated everything about this.

"It destroyed him, babygirl," I said. "He never said it out loud, but that man was haunted. Utterly haunted. And I get it now. Holding you in my arms, breathing you in, falling in love with you... I finally fucking get it. What it cost him. What it did to him to lose you." My voice broke, every word a struggle to get out, but I had to. I fucking *had* to make this vow—to her, to Saint, to myself. "God *damn*, For *me*. He did that for me. And I swear to you, Haley, here and now, by all the stars and moons in the sky, I will spend the rest of my immortal life trying to be worthy of it."

Another sob rattled through her body, but she didn't flee. Didn't rage.

Didn't tell me I could never possibly earn that sacrifice. She merely wrapped her arms around my neck, brought her soft lips to my ear, and whispered, "You already are."

Her words, the warmth of her breath, the promise in her touch... I closed my eyes and fell into her, wrapping my wings around us again and just holding her. Protecting her. Loving her in the only way I knew how.

With every fucking thing I had left.

"Thank you for telling me," she whispered, settling back into my lap.

"I never wanted to," I admitted. "Never wanted you to know about all the terrible things that stole my words all them years ago. That brought me to Amaranth City. To Saint and Jax. How we all got out of Midnight. But tonight... Fuck, Haley. You need to know you're not alone in this. You need to know how important he was to me. To Jax."

"Not *was*, Hudson. *Is*. How important he is." She closed her eyes and pressed her lips together, and I knew my woman well enough now to understand she was gearing up for something, that smoldering fire inside her sparking to life once more. And sure enough, when she opened her eyes and met my gaze again, I saw it. That familiar blaze. That determination, undimmed by even *this* tragic fucking nightmare. "Elian is *ours*, Hudson, and it's on us to help him. You said you felt the spark of me all those centuries ago—the promise of your future mate? Well, I feel a promise like that with Elian, too. A promise that he's still out there—in some form. That he hasn't crossed into the Shadowlands yet. I know it sounds crazy—I'm sitting here listening to myself and I'm like, girl, you're out of your damn *mind*. But you know what? Nothing in Midnight is as it should be. Nothing—not even death. So I'm not leaving Elian behind just because *this* realm says he's dead. I can still feel him, Hudson." She pressed a hand to her heart, her voice trembling with conviction. With love. "I can *feel* him."

"Haley." I fisted her hair with both hands. Touched my forehead to hers and breathed her in deep. "I'd *never* leave him behind—you have my fucking word on that, and you know better than anyone I don't give out them words lightly. So if you're telling me there's a chance... even one fucking *sliver* of a chance that he's still out there somewhere... that we can bring him back before he crosses over... I don't give a fuck how crazy it sounds, babygirl. Say the word, and I got your back on this. Hundred percent."

Her face lit up like the brightest star in the sky. "You mean it?"

"You know I damn well do, babygirl."

"Will you take me to him, then?" She wiped away the last of her tears, brow furrowed with renewed intensity as her mind undoubtedly cobbled together a plan. "To where the fog came down and he… If there's anything left of his physical form there, maybe I can sense him. It's the best chance I've got at doing a spell and making the connection."

I'd watched the Fog chew Saint up and spit him right out again, and I knew—without a doubt—there was nothing left of him there but blood and memory.

But Haley was right. Nothing in Midnight was ever as it should've been. It was a place where all things were possible—the most terrible as well as the most miraculous.

So yeah, maybe it was fucking crazy. Stupid, even. But maybe—with a little faith and one fierce, beautiful, badass blood witch—we really *could* find a way.

With a grin that mirrored hers—a grin that matched the hope rising inside me for the first time since we'd set foot on these treacherous mountain paths—I stood up, shifted fully into my warrior form, and tucked her in tight, ready for the jump.

"Oh, one more thing," she said, and I braced myself for whatever law she was about to lay down next.

"Out with it, babygirl."

"If I *ever* see that fucking dickless gargoyle stain again, I *will* kill him. With a dagger, with magick, with my bare hands if I have to. Marco is a *dead* man if it's the last thing I ever do in this fucking realm. You have my word on that."

A low chuckle rumbled through my chest. "I ever tell you how sexy you are when you threaten my enemies?"

"If you think I'm sexy when I threaten them," she said with an adorable shrug, "wait until you see what happens when I mutilate them."

"Looking forward to it, my spooky little monster girl." I kissed her temple, then said, "Now, let's go get our boy before he fucks himself off to the Shadowlands for good."

# 9

## HALEY

*T*he blood snow had mostly melted, leaving a swamp of dark red mud along the path. Aside from a few sharp stones, there was very little to differentiate one wet patch of earth from another, but Hudson was absolutely sure about the location.

I felt it, too. The void left behind by a life unfairly taken. The absence of something that should've been there. That should've fucking *lived*.

I hadn't wanted to believe it before. Not when Jax had told us the story in the cave. Not when Hudson held me as I cried. Not even now.

But standing here, the chill creeping into my limbs, the smell of recently spilled blood a rich tang on the air, I could no longer deny it.

Elian was well and truly… dead.

The heaviness of it pressed on my heart anew, merging with everything Hudson had just shared about his past. About Marco and the fae nobles.

The dead children.

The sheer immensity of all that darkness and despair threatened to overwhelm me. My vision blurred, my heartbeat kicking into overdrive, my breath coming in short, staccato bursts…

*No.* If Hudson could survive that brutal massacre and everything that'd come after, I could certainly survive the telling of his story. And if Elian could survive death, then…

Then I would do whatever it took to bring him back.

"Okay, babygirl?" Hudson's voice rumbled against my neck, warm and comforting. And one touch, one gentle stroke of my gargoyle's hand over my head, and everything inside me settled. I felt his love for me through the bond. His belief in me—belief that I could actually do this.

"Okay," I said, sure of it now. I *was* okay. I *had* to be.

Then, steeling my spine, I sucked in a breath and knelt down in the mud.

Hudson moved around me like a silent sentry, keeping watch along the paths and in the skies in case the Darkwinter witches and their raven gryphons decided to return and finish the job.

I closed my eyes. Pressed my palms against the dirt.

Magick tingled at once across my skin, and the chilly breeze shifted, carrying his scent right to me—bergamot and rain.

"Elian," I whispered. "I... I need you." They were the first words that came to mind—the absolute truth—so I spoke them into the night, fingers sinking deeper into the muck. Into the Midnight earth soaked with his blood.

"I need you," I whispered again. "I *need* you."

Warmth filled my chest, and in my mind I saw the glint of his silver eyes, felt the touch of his silver-white braids falling on my cheeks as he lowered his mouth to mine and...

I gasped as the memory took root and bloomed. Our first night together, warming up in bed after I'd pushed him into the bay and then jumped in after him.

Our first kiss. Our first... everything.

Now, kneeling in the cold mud, I felt the gentle pressure of his lips on mine, tasted the sweetness of that long-ago kiss. Felt the hot slide of his fingers between my thighs, the scrape of teeth as he closed his mouth over my nipple and sucked.

The memory speared my heart and split me in two, every part of me throbbing with pain. Images continued to unfurl in my mind, each one revealing some deeply remembered facet—the sound of his roguish laugh, the way his cocky grin pulled up higher on the left side than the right. The warmth of his breath as he dragged his mouth across my skin, kissing me from one hip bone to the other. The firm press of a hand splayed across my stomach, holding me in place as he teased and taunted. The mischievous light in his eyes when he caught me touching myself in the shower, fanta-sizing about him. Singing after that sweet release.

The swirl of butterflies inside me the first time he brought his hot mouth to my ear and whispered, *Sing for me, little sparrow...* The nickname that would always remain. The name that'd made me his.

Every last one of those memories collided and shrunk into a single pinpoint of light, a bright spark I wanted to claim and swallow and keep inside me forever. In my mind, I tried to reach for it, but the moment my fingers brushed that tiny spark, it exploded, unleashing a hundred more. A thousand. A million.

My body trembled with the force of it, the force of *him*, the force of the love I'd never been able to bury—not even when I thought he'd turned his back on me. Not even when I thought he'd forgotten it.

Now, it thrummed inside me like a second heartbeat, and I knew he could no more forget than I could. Knew that not even death was powerful enough to smother this flame.

The dark, ancient magick of Midnight snaked up through my arms and into my chest, twining with my own and coiling around my heart, and I bent all my energy, my will toward finding Elian. Toward reaching out across the realms, across the void and shining a light so bright it would illuminate the way back to—

"Haley!" Hudson snapped. "We got company. Move!"

I barely had time to shake myself out of the near-trance before the gargoyle grabbed me, hauled me to my feet, and shoved me against the rocks, his body and wings instantly turning to stone around me. Protecting me, as only he could.

"Shit," I hissed. I'd gotten only the barest glimpse of the approaching figures before he'd encased me in his stone shield. I had no idea who or what was gathering behind him.

Darkwinter? The gargoyle traitors I'd vowed to eviscerate?

Through the gap between the bottom of his stone wings and the ground, I watched dark shadows ripple across the earth.

I pressed a hand to his stone chest, trying to get a read on the situation through our bond. I sensed his fear for me. His fierce protective instinct.

"Assume your human form, guardian," came the command, no more than a whisper on the wind, the scrape of metal against raw bone. I couldn't even tell whether it'd been spoken aloud or was just some spell rasping through my mind, but the order sent a chill down my spine.

"Release the woman and change form," the whispers continued. "Or you both die."

*Not gargoyles. Fae.*

I sensed the intrusive touch of their magick like an echo in the wake of their threat—a tingling on the back of my neck and a slight pressure around my chest, like zipping up a dress that didn't quite fit.

It didn't feel like Darkwinter magick. None that I'd come across, anyway. But they were definitely dark fae. As in… not friends.

My blood turned to ice as the realization dawned.

These were the fae Evander sought. The whole reason for our journey.

No one else lived in these caves. And any Midnight foes who would've risked their lives to follow us up this forsaken mountain would've killed us already.

The shadows shifted on the ground. They were closing ranks around us.

"We don't have a choice," I whispered, my hand still on Hudson's stone chest. "We can either fight them or try to talk our way out. But right now, you have to do as they say."

I felt his frustration, his fear for my life. The fact that he'd trapped me here rather than flying us out told me just how quickly—and silently—the fae had come upon us. By the time he'd noticed them, it was too late to do anything but put up the shields and hope for the best.

"Please, Hudson," I said. "We both know there's no other way out of this. You can't shield me here forever."

A flicker of agony through the bond. An apology. Shame, like a dark serpent slithering through his heart.

I didn't have time to tell him it wasn't his fault before he transformed, the stone protector turning into the man I loved, his chocolate-brown gaze catching mine for the briefest instant.

I smiled, if only to let him know I was okay. To give him some shred of hope to cling to.

Slowly, he turned to face our foes, keeping me tucked behind him. The well-defined lines of his massive, fully inked body glimmered in the moonlight, raw power locked away in every muscle. Even as a man, he was damned formidable.

"You are trespassing on sacred lands." Another hiss, another chill slithering down my spine. I peeked around Hudson's arm and spied the speaker—a tall, reed-thin fae male with hair the color of old parchment and skin so bloodless it was nearly translucent. He leaned on a gnarled wooden staff that looked even older than he did, but I wasn't foolish enough to think it was just a walking stick.

With his bulging muscles and imposing stature, Hudson may have looked every bit the deadly warrior he was. But this fae was just as treacherous. I saw it in his eyes—that gleam of violence. The hunger for it.

It reminded me of another kind of hunger. One that twisted up my insides.

Elian got that same look in his eyes whenever he'd gone too long without the Black.

"State your business," the old fae demanded. His voice had progressed from the raspy hiss to a watery calm, and he leaned on that staff like a frail creature, as if the night breeze might blow him clear off the mountainside.

A ruse. One that ignited a fierce rage inside me.

I stepped out from behind Hudson's shadow and opened my mouth to suggest the *perfect* orifice into which he could firmly shove that staff, but before I could get a word out, Hudson grabbed my hand. Squeezed. And did something that nearly stopped my heart.

Spoke to a stranger.

"We've come on behalf of Keradoc of Midnight," he said firmly, no hint of fear or uncertainty in his tone.

The hunger in the fae's eyes burned bright. "What does the warlord of the realm seek from the fae who dwell here?"

"An alliance."

A cruel grin split the old one's face, revealing a row of small gray teeth filed into razor-sharp points. Too many teeth, I realized. Far more than any fae I'd ever seen.

Darkness claimed us before I could even finish counting them.

# 10

## ELIAN

*I need you…*

The river churned and roiled, pushing me toward some unknown end as the current sucked and clawed at my limbs. Every surge of icy, dark water felt like another fist. Grabbing and pulling. Tearing. Dragging me under and drowning out the sounds of her voice.

*I need you…*

A voice I knew, but couldn't… *Fuck.* I just couldn't place it.

My thoughts scattered as the water yanked me in deeper, submerging me in its endless depths. Thick and red like wine. Like blood.

No… Not *like* blood. It *was* fucking blood—blood full of Devil's Dream. And I was drowning in it.

I kicked hard, bursting through the surface and sucking in air. Tainted blood ran into my eyes, into my mouth, the sickly sweet taste of the Black making me equally hungry and repulsed.

Fangs burst through my gums, everything in me burning with desperate need, but some deep, ancient part of me knew not to drink the blood. Knew if I swallowed even one drop, it wouldn't just trigger a relapse.

It would end me.

Swimming hard against the current, I glanced around as best I could, frantically trying to get a sense for where the fuck I was. What'd happened. Why I was so alone.

Didn't I have… friends? A family? Love?

An ache blossomed in my chest, crushing my lungs. Somewhere in the dark recesses of memory, that voice echoed... *I need you...* But the harder I concentrated, the quicker it faded away. When I looked around again, there was only the red river and a barren wasteland that stretched on for an eternity in every direction, the earth so black I couldn't tell where the horizon rose and the night sky began. Overhead, not a single star fractured the endless dark. But there, high above...

A quick flash of a white wing. Then another.

A glowing white raven gliding on the current. Following the pull of the river. Following me.

I fought to keep my head above the surface, my eyes fixed on the raven as the dark river carried me down, down, down, straight into the heart of the dead lands until it finally spit me up onto some rocky, unfamiliar shore.

Coughing up the strange blood, I dragged myself onto dry land, jagged rocks slicing through my palms. Behind me, the river vanished, but I could still taste it. Blood and Devil's Dream coated my mouth, ran down my chin. Slicked my skin, shining like black rubies under the moonless sky.

It was only my vampire sight that allowed me to see any shapes and colors at all.

In this wasted place, there was no light. Only death.

Spitting out a mouthful of blood, I rose, took a deep, trembling breath, and glanced up into the night sky. The raven circled, riding the currents lower and lower, its massive wingspan cutting through the inky darkness.

I stared at her for so long, the world began to spin beneath my feet. The tremble in my lungs spread to my arms. My legs. But at least I was on solid ground again.

For all the good it did me.

Every step was agony.

Blood continued to fill my mouth. To squelch up from the cold black mud between the rocks. My feet were bare, and for some inexplicable reason I was dressed in white robes as thin as sheets, every inch of fabric stained red. Clinging to my skin. Dripping.

*So much fucking blood...*

My fangs throbbed. Nausea twisted my stomach into knots, and an old companion flickered to life on my shoulder.

The devil I'd never quite left behind.

*Swallow it, asshole,* he whispered into my ear as my mouth continued to fill with that tainted blood. *Just fucking swallow it. Give the Devil one more dance. Let him take away your pain...*

I closed my eyes. Tried to sort through the feelings flooding my heart as swiftly as the blood filled my mouth.

Temptation. Shame. Hunger. Resignation.

I sank to my knees on the razor-sharp rocks. More blood spilled from fresh wounds. My muscles quaked. Heart pounded. Fucking *burned* for it, the promise of sweet fucking oblivion already humming through my veins…

*That's it*, the devil whispered. *Taste it. Just one taste. Remember how good we made you feel…*

I opened my mouth. Let the Dream-soaked blood spill out, but it just kept coming, filling me. More. So much more. Tears slid down my cheeks, tremors wracking my body, every part of me pushing me closer to that edge. The final one. All I had to do was close my mouth and swallow. Let it wash away the last of my sins on a wave of fantasy.

Let it wash away the last of my very existence.

A crack split my head in two, the pain like lightning. Like fire. My veins felt as if they were boiling inside me, then drying up. Blowing away.

*I need you…*

My heartbeat began to slow from a thunder to a trot. A throb.

*I need you…*

And fuck, how I wanted to give in.

*I need you…*

No more than a faint pulse now, the heart that'd once beat so wildly.

*Elian, I need you…*

Elian… the name as familiar as the voice. Lingering just at the edges of memory. If I could just… just fucking *remember* it. Just reach it, somehow…

"Elian," it came again—closer this time. Louder. The musical echo of a thousand voices, ancient and all-knowing. Not locked in a memory, but here. Now.

My name. I was Elian. Elian of… of Autumnshire.

And then…

The faintest breeze rippled across my face.

"I can end this for you," the voice promised. "Truly end it. Your struggle. Your pain. You've only to take my hand."

I spit out another mouthful of blood. Opened my eyes. And watched as the white raven landed on the earth before me, transforming into a figure enshrouded in a hooded cloak as colorless as her feathers, her pale hand outstretched in offering.

In her other hand, she held a scythe almost twice as tall as she was.

Her face was hidden in shadow, but I knew at once who she was.

"Death," I whispered. The word sent a bolt of ice to my gut, but I clung to it anyway. "Death," I said again, grateful for the shape of it in my mouth, for something other than the blood, which had finally stopped flowing.

The fog cleared from my mind, the pain in my head receding. I rose to my feet, standing once more on limbs that didn't tremble. The blood vanished from my wrappings, leaving them as bright as the moon.

No, not moon, but *moons*, I remembered suddenly. There were three of them. But... where?

Something shook loose inside me, and the memories rushed back, almost too fast to process.

I clutched my forehead, trying to slow the images. The feelings.

*Midnight. Blood Before Roses—my brothers. Keradoc. Evander, my twin. Melantha and the Army of the Dead and Darkwinter and—*

"Haley," I said out loud. Gasped as a new pain gripped my heart. "Sparrow..."

Loss. Regret. Longing. Love.

*I need you, Elian...*

"There was a fight on the mountain," I said. "Weather witches. Hudson tried to... But then Jax, and the Fog, and... oh, fuck." When I lowered the hand from my head and tried to search the face of Death, I found nothing but those shadows. "I'm dead. I died on the mountain. The Fog took me."

At this, she finally inclined her head, still not revealing herself.

"But I... no. Not possible. I'm immortal! I..." I paced the black earth before her, trying to sort through it all. How much time had passed? How long was I stuck in that river?

Was I in hell? Some kind of purgatory?

"Not purgatory," Death said, though I wasn't sure if it was because I'd spoken the thoughts out loud or she'd simply plucked them from my mind. "You're in the borderlands between realms. Take my hand, and together we'll cross into the Shadowlands where you shall find your eternal rest. Or..."

"Or *what*?"

She sighed and finally lowered her outstretched hand, and behind me, the blood river appeared once more. Wilder this time. Darker. Carving through the black earth like a wound.

In that same spectral voice, she said, "Or you return to the river."

"Return to *that*?" I asked as I watched the rapids whip the blood river into a frothy, red-black soup. Shadows moved beneath the surface now— some unnamed beasts ready to devour.

The old devil laughed in my ear once more. *Should've taken my offer, asshole…*

"What happens then?" I asked.

"Then," Death said, her otherworldly voice turning dark, "you will struggle mightily, but you will ultimately succumb, only to be delivered straight to hell. And there, your eternal hosts will make your worst nightmares feel like the *best* of friends."

# 11

## EVANDER

Fire flickered behind my eyelids, the scent of wood smoke and magick slowly drawing me back to consciousness.

Blinking away the haze, I waited for the blurred shapes around me to solidify.

A cave. They'd brought us to another cave. Moonlight filtered in through the cracks and crevices, and judging from the position of the shadows cast upon the rock walls, we weren't too far from where they'd found us.

I wasn't sure how much time had passed, though. How long we'd been under their dark enchantments.

The demon and I were chained to the wall by our ankles and wrists, shackled by iron and magick both. The metal bit into my skin, burning my flesh and draining my powers. Beside me, the demon groaned, fresh blood spilling from the side of his mouth. Iron couldn't hurt him, but magick... I had no idea what kind of spells they'd hit us with.

But for now, we were alive. Awake.

The fire burned before us, illuminating a large chamber bustling with activity. At least two dozen fae and several dark witches moved about, some carrying food and jugs of water, others consulting the general who'd taken us. Three fae males were busy carving symbols around the cave's wide entrance and down along the front wall—a fae language I didn't recognize from any of the hundreds I'd come across in Keradoc's library.

I wondered if they were wards. Or perhaps some sort of reckoning.

Despite the current frenzy of activity, it didn't feel like the cave was any sort of residence or permanent gathering place.

I glanced over at the demon, wincing as the iron cut deeper into my wrists. "Are you hurt?"

"Nothing I can't handle," he said. "You?"

"The iron is… most unpleasant."

The demon turned his head and spit out a mouthful of blood. "Fucking fae pricks."

"On that, we can agree. Unfortunately, we still need to convince them to—"

"You were not given permission to speak, warlord." From the opposite side of the chamber, the general reprimanded me, his tone ice cold as it cut through the din. Two other advisors had gathered with him around a stone altar, and they stopped whatever they were doing to turn and glare at us. I could just make out the feathered hide of some poor, small creature bound to the altar with ropes, its blood long since drained.

I wondered if that's how they kept control over the much larger raven gryphons. Some dark sacrificial magick.

It certainly didn't bode well for us.

"Still want to make friends?" the demon whispered, his eye fixed on that dead, bloodless thing.

"Can you access your abilities?" I asked, lips barely moving as the fae general stalked toward us.

"No. Whatever their spells, I'm effectively neutered. I can't get a read on any of these assholes."

So manipulating their fears was out. I tested the iron again, wrists straining against the binds. My skin blistered at the effort.

No chance of breaking free by force, either.

"Making friends it is," I grumbled.

As the general reached us, I forced a note of politeness into my voice and asked him, "Do you speak for the fae who dwell beneath this mountain?"

The question earned me a snarl and a backhand across the mouth. Before I even tasted the first trickle of blood, something flashed outside the cave entrance, and the murmuring around us fell silent.

More magick. I could taste it on my lips, in my lungs. The sharp, tell-tale bite of it.

I watched as several new fae stepped into the cave, dragging two more prisoners in behind them.

Haley and the gargoyle.

"Fuck," the demon hissed.

I yanked hard on my chains. For the effort, I was rewarded with a wave of nausea that made the room spin before my eyes. A gift from the iron that had no intentions of letting me go unscathed.

Haley and her mate were unchained and appeared unharmed, but a dark haze clouded their eyes, their movements sluggish. Their captors led them to the fire and ordered them to kneel.

Neither obeyed. Neither seemed to even understand the command.

"Kneel!" he bellowed again, kicking the gargoyle's legs out from under him.

At that, both of them dropped to the ground, palms splayed out on the rock to break their fall. Two heads dipped low, hair sweeping the ground, eyes downcast.

Defeated.

A new fire blazed inside me, burning away the lingering nausea.

"What do you *want*?" I demanded, no longer attempting politeness. "You've captured four innocents without cause, and you have the nerve to call *me* a coward? State your demands or release us."

Next to me, the demon whispered, "Apparently you missed the class on how to win friends and influence people."

A grin of ice and shadow slid across the fae general's mouth, his pale skin gleaming. "Those who trespass on our front door are hardly innocents. You of all fae should know that, warlord. Or is that wall around your city merely a decoration?"

"What do you want?" I asked again.

"As *you* are the ones seeking *us*, I'd hoped you might answer that question for me." He snapped his fingers, and in response, the shadows along the cave walls shifted, peeling away like phantoms, materializing before our eyes.

Three fae witches as pale as the others, but glowing with an ethereal light. Not the clear white light of the stars, but the deep violet light of Midnight herself. Its truest, most ancient magick.

Original magick.

It washed through the cave, through me, so raw and powerful it brought tears to my eyes. My own magick tingled with awareness, seeking the connection to its dark counterpart. Finding it.

The iron chains melted away, freeing me. Freeing the demon.

The general gasped, and in that instant, I felt Haley's gaze lift. Search for mine in the darkness. I met her eyes, saw the flames of the fire dancing in them. Gone was the dark haze of the fae spells. Gone was her fear and grief. Gone was the sense of defeat.

All that remained was my powerful, determined witch.

A witch ready to detonate.

Haley rose to her feet, the gargoyle following suit. Naked and forced into his human form, ink painting the entirety of his body, he looked as wild and unkempt as our captors. Feral. Beneath the tangle of long hair, those dark brown eyes held the promise of violence.

I was grateful he was on our side. On *her* side.

The three witches turned to face them and said, in a single voice that felt older than the mountains themselves, "The stones whispered to us of your arrival. A powerful dark witch and her consorts. But your intentions... they remain unclear."

"Our intentions are to rid the realm of the poison leaking through our borders," I said firmly, crossing the space to stand at Haley's side. The demon joined me as well, and I continued, "Darkwinter fae invade from the north. The Dark Goddess Melantha is already moving across our southern territories, drawing closer by the hour. We have not come here as enemies with veiled intentions, but as soldiers who seek an alliance."

The general sneered. "And why should the fae who dwell beneath the mountain fight alongside a warlord who's allowed war to rot this realm for millennia? Alongside a witch who is not even of our world?"

I stepped forward, my hands itching to close around his throat, but Haley was already speaking.

"Why should you fight with us?" she asked, her voice controlled despite the fire in her eyes. "Well, let's see. While you've been hiding out under the mountain pulling feathers off birds and drawing on cave walls for the past several hundred years, the entire realm has turned into a fucking powder keg that's about to go full-on nuclear thanks to the Darkwinter fae and a demented Goddess who—along with her legions of undead soldiers—have Midnight in their crosshairs. So unless they've been teaching you undead mortal combat along with those cave art lessons you're getting, you *might* want to shut your smug little fae-holes, stop with the hocus-pocus intimidation tactics, and give us a chance to strategize like grownups."

Her spark was a bright light in the dim hopelessness of the cave, and despite our circumstances, I couldn't help but grin.

If death was coming for us on this night, what better end than watching my witch burn us all to the fucking ground?

The witches remained silent. Unmoving. The other fae in the cave had gone equally still, all of them awaiting some final declaration. The determination of our fate.

The general narrowed his gaze, glaring at Haley with shrewd eyes. In a low whisper, he said, "Who are you, witch?"

The gargoyle let out a warning growl, but the general didn't flinch.

Meeting his gaze, refusing to be cowed by it, Haley said, "I am the Daughter of Darkwinter. A blood witch of the Silversbane prophecy. I was sent to Midnight under false pretenses by the Goddess Melantha in a bid to break her banishment, syphon the realm's magick, and enslave its people. Now that I'm aware of her true desires, I'm working to stop her and her army, along with my companions."

"And the Darkwinter enemy?" he asked. "Surely you don't mean to take up arms against your own kin."

"The Darkwinter invading these lands, brutalizing its people... They are *no* kin of mine."

The general held her gaze for another beat, then looked to the three witches.

At his nod, they moved to encircle us, assessing each of us in turn.

"We need to see your blood," they said. "The blood will reveal the truth."

Truth-seers, then. Witches who could scry with blood and detect lies... as well as a person's most closely guarded secrets.

Seeing no way around it, I nodded, pushing up my sleeve.

One of the witches produced an obsidian dagger. Another held a silver bowl.

"Do it," I said.

A quick slice across my palm, and I made a fist, dripping the blood into the bowl. They went down the line, taking some from Haley next, then the demon. The gargoyle went last, glaring at them the entire time, as if he might eat them.

When all of our blood had been spilled, the three witches added their own, then swirled the blood together, gazing into the dark pool.

"The Darkwinter witch speaks from a pure heart," the witches finally declared in that singular, eerie voice.

"And her companions?" the general asked.

"The warlord," they said, gazing up from the blood to meet my eyes, "wears many masks. His desire for an alliance is genuine, though his methods of persuasion are less than noble."

Before they could press me for details, they tore their unnerving gazes from mine and moved on to the demon. I tried not to sigh in relief.

"The demon is loyal and strong. He feeds on fear, yet has shackled his own fears deep within his heart, where they fester and weaken his resolve. Guilt will be his undoing."

The demon flinched as if the words themselves were daggers prying open his chest, but before he could respond, they shifted their attention to the gargoyle.

"A guardian tormented by his past," they said of him. "Haunted by the fae who screamed and bled and fell at his feet while he watched over them and did nothing." Their innate glow dimmed, the bowl suddenly trembling in their hands. Tiny waves rippled across the blood. "It is *he* who failed the Eternal Ones. He who spilled the blood of our noble ancestors."

**12**

EVANDER

*I* didn't think it possible for the general and his associates to turn any more pale, yet at the declaration of their witches, they did just that.

Every fae in that cave turned to look at the gargoyle then, a mix of sadness and rage filling their eyes. Creasing their faces. Rippling through the cave with a palpable tension.

My eyes widened as the realization hit me.

The Eternal Ones... the fae children who'd been slaughtered centuries ago. The ones they'd allegedly kept alive by magick, somewhere beneath these mountains.

It was him. Haley's gargoyle. Her mate. He'd been there the night they died at the hands of a gargoyle.

Was it possible he'd been the one to—

"Justice for the Eternal Ones," a fae male shouted from the back of the crowd.

"Justice and vengeance!" another echoed.

The anguish in the gargoyle's dark eyes just then...

Whatever doubts I'd had about him vanished as quickly as they'd appeared. Whatever his crimes, he did *not* kill those children. That family. I would stake my eternal life on it.

"Hey!" Haley shouted, breaking up the chants for justice that were now spreading like a sickness, the fae moving closer, their eyes locked on the gargoyle. "Hudson did *not* hurt those fae. He was attacked by ruthless cowards that night—gargoyles and witches. He would've *died* defending your ancestors, but he didn't get that opportunity, because those vile assholes stole it from him."

"*Haley*," the gargoyle warned, risking a rare moment of speech. But even I knew she wouldn't back down. Not when someone she loved was being threatened.

Ignoring his warning, she went on. "They trapped him in stone with a sunlight spell while they slaughtered his charges. His own kind—along with yours—betrayed him. By all accounts, he should've died that night too, or soon after. But he didn't. He fought to rebuild his life. To protect his friends. And he's here now, willing to fight all over again—fight to the death for a realm that has done *nothing* but brutalize him. Meanwhile, where the hell have you all been?" She turned on her heel, glowering at the fae, at their rage, her own vibrating in her every word. "*You*, who claim you want justice and vengeance for your dead. *You*, ready to attack a man who would sooner let you take his life than spill another drop of innocent fae blood. *You*, the great noble dark fae of old, hiding under the Razorbacks with your heads up your asses while the ones who slaughtered your people go free and the realm shatters to pieces around you."

The fae had fallen silent. All of us had. Only the fire dared break the silence, hissing and popping, flames dancing across the reflection in the blood. *Our* blood.

I chanced another look at the gargoyle, his face impassive now, the pain buried down deep. Most of the information about that ancient attack had been lost to time, lost to the very fae standing before us after they'd retreated beneath the Razorbacks. I'd heard the stories, but I'd never known which gargoyle had been in charge that night.

Which gargoyle had failed.

That he hadn't actually failed at all, but had been betrayed.

Something inside me twisted. Ached for him.

"Wait," said the witches, their attention once again reclaimed by the blood. "The stones spoke to us of five. Only four remain. Where is the fifth?"

"He… died," Haley said, her voice breaking. "The Fog of a Thousand Knives took him during an unprovoked attack by Darkwinter's weather witches."

A fresh slice across my heart, though whether it was for Haley or my brother, I no longer knew for certain.

"He died saving my life," the demon spoke up, reaching out to clasp

Haley's hand. "Died in the most gruesome way… And it's just a taste of what awaits us if we don't strike back and strike hard."

The general remained motionless, but something in his eyes had softened.

With a deep sigh, he turned to Haley and said, "I am sorry for your loss. But pure as your heart may be, Daughter of Darkwinter, my people have lived far too long to be so easily swayed by whispers of a fading relic of a goddess and an invasion of dark fae soldiers."

"Seems that fading relic didn't get the memo," Haley replied, "because she's *not* fading. She's making her way across the Boiling Glass Sands as we speak. She'll be here in a few days—maybe sooner. And she'll make the Darkwinter witches look like a few stray cats batting at mice."

"Have you any proof of this?" he asked.

Haley said nothing.

"Even if she *did* break her banishment," he said, "we can't know her true intentions yet. Midnight was her home for a time. Perhaps she's merely—"

"Oh, for fuck's sake," Haley snapped. Then, pointing at the witches, "Give me that bowl. I'll take that shiny dagger too, thanks."

They obeyed at once, stricken by her sharp tone or the determination in her eyes.

I had no idea what game she was playing.

Until she knelt on the ground before the fire, set down the bowl, and slid the dagger across her other palm, spilling more of her own blood.

"*Haley.*" *That* warning was mine, low and menacing, but it was too late.

The witch had already made up her mind—I could see it in those beautiful green eyes. Feel it in the surge of her magick, a soft caress against my own.

She was going to give them that elusive proof—a last-ditch effort to sway our hosts.

She was going to call the Dark Goddess here.

# 13

## HALEY

*E*ven the fire seemed to be holding its breath as I bent my head and gazed into the bowl of blood.

Nervousness made my stomach roll, but I forced those jitters down deep, refusing to show a single crack in my facade. It felt as if all my studies and practice sessions on the castle balcony had led to this—not to calling on my ancestors and binding them to fight for us, as Evander had first demanded. But to this bullshit task of proving myself to a bunch of crusty fae fucks who didn't think I had any real juice. Fae fucks who would die just like the rest of us if we didn't find a way to defeat Melantha and Darkwinter.

We needed them. Needed this alliance… Or we were already doomed.

*"Haley."* Across the fire-lit space, Evander met my gaze, his violet eyes bright with a desperate warning. I held it, waiting until I saw the warning give way to acceptance.

Then, finally—unexpectedly—encouragement. A soft smile. Warmth he'd never dare show anyone else.

The scent of his cold roses filled my nose, and I knew he sensed it too— the connection between us. The deepening of it, made all the more special by our shared loss.

*Elian…*

Grief slipped into my heart, but I kept it at bay. I *knew* Elian heard me. I felt him. I would try to reach out again as soon as I could. As soon as I got this over with.

Now, holding Evander's gaze, I returned his smile, feeling his magick curl around my heart. Keep it safe.

Hudson had mentioned the mate bond earlier—said I had a similar bond with all the guys, though each one manifested in different ways. With Evander, it was the magick. *Our* magick. I didn't pretend to know how it worked any more than I knew how the gargoyle mate bond worked, but I knew it was real. Knew it gave me strength. Hope.

*You can do this, little thief,* he seemed to be saying now. *I know you can.*

I shifted my gaze back to the fae—the general. The survival of the realm may very well rest with my ability to convince him we were worthy of their audience. That I hadn't been lying about the goddess and the threat she posed to Midnight.

It was all I could do not to snarl at him. His home was under direct attack, yet this fae required *proof* before he'd even deign to *consider* offering his aid.

And who was to say he'd accept my version of proof, anyway?

*Fucking fae-splaining asshole…*

Rage incinerated the last of my unsteadiness.

I clung to it, that fire. That heat. It fused with the love and support I felt from my men—all of them—and strengthened my purpose.

Without further delay, I dipped both hands into the bowl before me, sliding my fingers through the warm, viscous liquid until my bloodstone ring was submerged. My magick responded immediately, warming the blood and giving it a faint glow.

All around me, the assembled fae gasped and tittered.

*Oh, how I love when they underestimate me…*

I wanted to smirk at them. To roll my eyes. But the resting witch face was in full effect as I concentrated all my efforts on channeling this power.

On finding *her.*

I removed my bloodied hands and lifted the bowl before the fire, then spilled some of the blood across the ancient stone floor, painting a tight circle around me. Over me. Letting it infuse me with the power and magick of my men and the fae witches who'd spilled their ancient blood inside it, too.

With a dark pool of blood still gleaming inside it, I set the bowl back on the ground and placed my palms flat on the stone. Then, with a deep, clarifying breath, I closed my eyes and gave life to the spell that would decide our fate.

*Goddess of darkness, goddess of death*

*I offer this blood, I offer this breath*
*Across the Sands, I summon thee*
*Bound by the circle, so mote it be…*

Barely more than a whisper at first, then a soft chant that grew louder and louder with each repetition. The words wound through me and back out, tendrils of power that snaked along the walls of the cave and out into the cool night, up into the sky and past the moons and the stars, past the very darkness itself, and still I kept chanting. Again and again and again until my voice echoed cold and clear off the ancient stone, the fae awe-stricken, and the magick of Midnight finally heard my plea.

*Goddess of darkness, goddess of death*
*I offer this blood, I offer this breath*
*Across the Sands, I summon thee*
*Bound by the circle, so mote it be…*

Even with my eyes closed tight, I could see the glow of my magick, feel it rising up from the circle of spilled blood like a shield even as it drew the darkness near. Warmth washed over me in subtle waves, magick tingling across my skin, and then… a pause.

The glow held steady. The warmth undimmed. But for an all-too-uncomfortable beat, nothing else happened.

A sigh fell on the air, likely from the general. But before he could follow it with a dismissal, the fire extinguished, throwing the chamber into darkness, lit only by the red glow of my magick.

And then, as if I'd been grabbed and yanked out of the cave and straight up into the sky, I watched the mountains shrink beneath me. I watched as the whole of the realm whipped past in a blur—the Hanging Lake, the leafless black forests. Rivers of blood. Towering cliffs made of ice. Fields of jagged, gleaming obsidian.

And then, at long last—the Boiling Glass Sands, and the terrible sight laid bare across it.

Melantha's army, just as I'd seen it in my previous nightmare vision.

As one, they marched. Thousands. Tens of thousands, a sea of bone that undulated in an single, unrelenting wave that covered the desert as far as the eye could see, moonlight illuminating bare skulls, flames burning in the wake of their gruesome march.

There were more now—the force had nearly doubled in size since I'd seen it last.

A gasp born of both awe and terror escaped my lungs.

The skeletons halted. Looked up toward the moons. Toward me, their mouths open in a unified, silent threat.

Bile burned my throat, but I closed my eyes. Thought of Jax, my fearless demon. Everything he'd ever taught me about the nature of fear. About facing it, even when it damn near paralyzed us.

All fear was rooted in love, he'd said.

So it was love I clung to now—love for him. For Hudson. For Elian. For Evander, too—as new and surprising as it was.

Love for my sisters in Blackmoon Bay. My coven. The friends that had fought by my side back then—another lifetime, it seemed.

Love for the parents who'd adopted me. The grandmother who'd raised me after they died.

Love for myself.

All of it beat inside me like the familiar drumbeat of a favorite song, steadying me. Wrapping me in warmth and gratitude. Reminding me that it was only because I'd been blessed with so much of that love that I was even *capable* of feeling so much fear.

The thought calmed me. Gave me courage.

And when I finally found enough of it to open my eyes again and face what lay before me, she was there, hovering in the dark sky atop her gruesome winged beast.

**14**

ELIAN

The red river surged, unleashing the cloying scent of Dream-drenched blood once more, churning up that same mix of hunger and revulsion inside me. Blood filled my mouth again, warm and coppery, the drugs whispering promises so enticing, I nearly dove head-first into that river just to finally claim them.

To succumb to my demons and the eternity of torture they offered, once and for all.

An eternity of torture at the behest of bloodthirsty fiends who would make my nightmares look like old pals.

It was no less than I deserved.

Again, Death extended that pale hand. "You must choose, Elian of Autumnshire."

"Oh, it's *my* choice, is it?" A dark laugh hissed from my lips. "You think I've earned eternal peace?"

"It isn't my job to think or judge—that is for you to decide. I am merely here to acknowledge your final decision, then escort you on your path, one way or the other."

I glared at that hand, wondering if I could truly accept it. If I could truly rest in peace.

How could it possibly be so easy? For all the terrible, brutal things I'd done—all the pain I'd caused—how could *anyone* believe I'd earned that choice?

It hit me then. The fucking *tsunami* of it—all my worst, most despicable acts.

Murdering those royal fae to earn my first ticket to Midnight. All the monsters I'd killed across the realm on my first tour as I convinced myself again and again I *had* to do it—had to survive, had to find my brother, had to find a way back to Haley no matter what the cost. All the monsters I'd killed this time just to cross that moat into Amaranth City, to ensure safe passage for the ones I cared about—never mind the victims I left in my wake.

So much blood and death...

The lies I'd told. The secrets I'd kept. The hearts and bonds and oaths I'd broken.

Every little black pill I'd popped—little black pills of death that *I* invented. That *I* pushed, far and wide. That *I'd* consumed until they'd begun to consume *me*. Until my need for them obliterated my humanity. Drove me to slaughter a warehouse full of addicts just because I thought their blood would give me one more hit, one more hour of mind-numbing bliss.

All those people, dead. Fae and demons. Vampires. Humans. Mutilated. And the look in Haley's eyes when she'd realized what I'd done... what a monster I'd become...

Yet she knelt beside me anyway, offering up the vein to save my life. Singing me back from the darkness.

*Oh, little sparrow...*

My god, the things I'd put her through.

Never before had guilt felt so sharp and unwieldy, like a newly forged sword I just kept tripping over and falling on. Everything inside me ached with it. Bled for it.

By the time I opened my eyes, I was shaking so violently my teeth chattered, fangs slicing my lips. It wasn't the fear of death that held me in its grip—even as a so-called immortal vampire-fae, I knew my death had been a long time coming.

This was shame. Regret. Sorrow. All the hurt and pain I'd unleashed, finally boomeranging back to me, carving a wound so deep I was sure it would never heal.

Hell. Hell was where I belonged.

I took a deep breath. Glanced up into the shadows beneath that hood.

But the moment I opened my mouth to hand down my own sentence, something inside me shifted.

I pressed a hand to my chest. And there, fluttering beneath the razor-tipped barbs of my own guilt, beneath the desperate cravings the blood river ignited, beneath the rot of a wasted life, something good and beautiful and whole blossomed in the dirt.

As if in response to my touch, my heart slammed against my ribs, wild and untamed, lighter and stronger than it'd been in years. It was as if it'd been bound with chains and encased in cement, and now—for some inexplicable reason—they'd been obliterated. My heart could finally fucking beat again. And with every one of those wild beats, I heard the name of the woman I loved.

*Haley. Haley. Haley…*

"It's… gone," I whispered, almost afraid to believe it. "I can feel it. I can fucking *feel* it."

The curse. Melantha's curse. The dark spell that had kept me from truly loving Haley. From truly accepting her love in return.

"You died," Death said plainly. "The curse was placed for your immortal eternity, which has come to its end. The curse holds no more power over you."

And just as quickly as that good, beautiful thing inside me had bloomed, it withered and died.

Never mind Melantha's spell—the price I'd paid to escape Midnight. *This* was the true curse. To be free to love her again… only to have my life ripped from me.

I stumbled backward and crashed to the ground, my chest feeling like it was going to fucking cave in on me. All at once, Haley's words rushed back, echoes that felt as ancient as the stars.

*No. You're not that man. You're* this *man. The one who brought me back from the dead. The one who followed me to Midnight—to the worst hell he's ever experienced—just because I asked for his help. The one who made mistakes but never turned his back on me—not really. And for all those past fuckups, for all your present faults, for all the future things you don't even know you should be sorry for yet, you're still mine. Do you hear me? I'm claiming you as mine, even if I can't be yours because of some dark goddess bullshit price. You're my heart, Elian. You've always been my heart. I love you. You. This man, right here. I never stopped, and I never will, and no mistakes or dark goddesses or death sentences in a terrible realm will ever change it. Not for me. So I don't know what that means to you—if it means anything at all—but I'm saying it anyway because I need you to know it…*

A rage like nothing I'd ever felt boiled up inside me, erupting in a savage roar. *"No! No fucking way!"*

I'd left her too many times before. Disappointed her. Fucking *failed* her.

I would *not* let my demise be another one of those times.

Fury propelled me to my feet, and I crashed into Death and snatched the scythe from her pale hand, splintering it with a crack that echoed across the black wasteland.

A blinding white light exploded between us, knocking me back onto my ass.

When I finally looked up at her again, the cloak fell away, revealing…

Not a monster. Not a corpse or a skeleton or any of the images I'd always imagined when I thought of Death.

She was a girl. A teenager. Dressed in black leather pants and a bright pink crop top, with dark curly hair and freckles and big blue eyes that held the wisdom of the ages.

Now, fully revealed, she rolled those eyes and sighed.

"You're… Death?" I whispered.

"Um… yeah? Sorry to rain on your whole…" She bared her teeth and formed her hands into claws. "*Grrrrr, I'm a big bad vampire* routine, but the scythe and cloak are just props. I find most people are more likely to take me seriously if I look the part." She lowered her hands and shrugged. "But apparently you're not most people. *Apparently*," she huffed, "you're a *huge* pain in the ass."

I scrambled to my feet, not sure what to make of the turn of events.

The girl stared me down. Narrowed her eyes, sizing me up as if we were about to brawl.

Hell, maybe we were. When it came to dying, clearly I had some knowledge gaps. Or maybe…

"Am I stoned right now?" I asked. "I tried not to swallow it, but maybe… Or did I hit my head?"

"Did I say pain in the ass? I forgot to add *idiot* to the mix." She rolled her eyes again. "Haley's certainly got her hands full with you, doesn't she?"

I gasped. "You know *Haley*?"

"Oh, your girl and I go way back."

"But you're only… How long have you been here, exactly?"

"An eternity. But by your timeline, it's only been a few months." Then, seeing my obvious confusion, she sighed and said, "TL;DR version? As a human, I was part of Bay Coven. I fought with Haley and everyone in the Battle for Blackmoon Bay. Didn't exactly make it out unscathed, but… the last Death had just become mortal, so there was an opening for a Shadowborn witch, and *voila*! Here I am. But technically, I've only been on the job for a hot minute, so I'd appreciate it if you could cooperate and not make me look bad? I'm still trying to get the lay of the land, so to speak."

I blinked at her. A lot. "Um. TL;DR?"

"Too long, didn't read? Damn. Maybe you *did* hit your head. Anyway…" She held out her hand again. "Despite your theatrics, you still need to make that choice. You—"

Something rippled between us then. Some kind of rift, or…

"Haley," I whispered, her strawberries-and-cream scent wrapping around me, her voice whispering through my mind once more. Only now, she wasn't calling out to me, wasn't claiming she needed me.

It was a spell.

*Goddess of darkness, goddess of death*
*I offer this blood, I offer this breath*
*Across the Sands, I summon thee*
*Bound by the circle, so mote it be…*

Death's eyes widened, and I knew she could hear it too. Three times. Six. More.

"It's Haley," I said, and she nodded. "How come I can hear her?"

"She doesn't want to let you go. She called to you earlier."

"She said she needed me."

Death nodded. "She was trying to forge a connection. A bridge so you could find your way back."

"Find my way back?" Hope bloomed in my heart. "There's another choice, then?"

"It's… not that simple. You—oh, *fuck*," the girl whispered, her face going pale, those blue eyes dimming. She gripped my arm, and all at once, a great power swept across the land, dark and heavy. Ancient.

And so fucking evil it had me bending over and retching in the black dirt.

"Melantha," Death whispered, confirming my fears. "She's answering Haley's call. She's… connecting with her. Invading her."

"What? What do you mean, *invading* her?"

"For whatever reason, Haley's trying to communicate with her, but the goddess doesn't like to be summoned. She's… she's taking over Haley's mind, rent free."

"As in… possession?"

Silence.

Alarm shot through me like fucking hawthorn poisoning. "Send me back to her. Now."

"Elian, I—"

"I don't care what you have to do to make it happen. What *I* have to do. *That's* my choice. Not eternal peace, not eternal torment. I'll take door number three."

She released me and crossed her arms over her chest. "You do realize I can't just snap my fingers and abracadabra you back to your old existence. Your body's basically gone."

"Surely there must be *something* left of it. I was an immortal vampire-fae, for fuck's sake. I can't just—"

"Dude. That fog turned you into an immortal vampire-fae *smoothie*. An extra-smooth smoothie." She shook her head and blew out a breath, cheeks puffing with the force of it. "Brutal."

Rage boiled up once more. It was an effort to keep the tremble from my voice. "I. Don't. *Care*."

"You. Don't. *Understand*." Despite the bite in her tone, her eyes shone with sympathy, all traces of humor and snark gone from her face. "The pain you'll have to endure just to take another *breath* as a living being, let alone speak or walk or even hold her again... I know you want to be there for her, but... Elian, listen to me. *Trust* me. Going back to a body that's nothing but mush? Zero stars, do not recommend."

"Let me give *you* the TL;DR version, Curly Sue." I stepped close and glared down at her, towering over her by a foot. "I *love* that woman. Love. And I have fucked up so many times, made so many bullshit choices and wrong turns... You wanna talk about smoothies? I put Haley's fucking heart through the *blender*, and she *still* loves me. Still fights for me even now, even after I fucking died. And you're telling me Melantha's curse— the one thing that kept me from loving Haley the way she deserved—the way she was ready to accept again, even after everything I'd put her through—no longer applies?"

"Yes, but that's not the issue. You're—"

"So all that stands in the way of me finding my way back to Haley is the fact that I'm dead and boneless, and that dark goddess bitch is trying to possess her." I laughed at the insanity of it all. "Look, I'm not trying to make your job harder, but if you think I'm going to take your hand and frolic off into the Shadowlands or dive into that river and fuck off to hell just because those options are easier... Sorry, not happening. So whatever pain you say I'm in for, whatever unknown horrors await me in Midnight, you bet your freckles

I'm willing to endure it. Whatever it takes to get back to her and my brothers, I'm fucking in, because no, I will *not* leave my woman to face Melantha and the Darkwinter fae without me. I won't leave her to face so much as a damn paper cut ever again if there's anything—even a *single fucking thing* I can do to protect her from that pain. To take it for her. Understand?"

She glared up at me, nostrils flaring, defiance in her gaze.

Then, a sigh. Another roll of the eyes. "Seriously? I'm not sure you really get what TL;DR means, but… ugh. Fine. Compelling points."

"Send me back," I demanded again. "Now."

"You've got quite a fight ahead of you, vampire-fae. And I'm not talking about the war."

"I've been fighting my whole life." I spit out the last of the blood from my mouth and clenched my fists, ready for whatever awaited. "Dying didn't change that, and neither will going back."

Whatever the girl saw in my eyes, she believed me. I saw the change wash over her—from defiance to acceptance. Maybe even a little spark of something else.

Relief? Happiness?

"Just… do me a favor and try not to vamp out on me this time, okay?" she said. "The props aren't exactly unlimited around here."

The robes appeared and shrouded her once more, the hood casting her face back in shadow. In her hand, a new scythe materialized.

With a wave of of that gleaming weapon, the river of blood vanished. I watched in awe as a wooden footbridge appeared in its place, lined on either side with flowering dogwood trees and pink azaleas.

I recognized it at once. The bridge across my pond in New Orleans, the house and gardens Haley and I had dreamed up together over many sleepless nights in Blackmoon Bay, holding each other as we whispered and laughed and made plans for the future. I'd long since left her by the time I found that house, but I bought it anyway; it was the only way I could keep her close to me.

Now, that bridge called me home to her. I could already feel her pull, a tug on my very soul as all the old memories rushed through me, starting with the very first. The night she'd pushed me into the bay, then dove in after me.

"Why does it look like that?" I asked.

"Haley created it," she said. "From something that binds you."

Our dream, I realized. Our future. She still held that dream in her heart, just as I had.

"Why… why are you just revealing this to me now?" I asked.

"You weren't able to see it before. You weren't ready."

"I'm ready now," I said firmly.

"Follow it," Death said, her voice serene and otherworldly once more. "Follow it back to her. Just know that the moment you set foot on that bridge, you'll be beyond my aid."

"I understand. I… Thank you. Thank you for giving me a chance to…" I trailed off, the words lost to the wave of emotion that followed.

"Elian?" she said softly.

I turned to look at her once more, her robes already shifting back to feathers as her raven form began to take shape.

*Hurry,* she said, no more than a whispered warning in my mind.

I bowed my head in goodbye, sad that I didn't get the chance to say it properly. To wish her well, though I figured I'd see her again—hopefully not soon, but eventually. The thought gave me a small measure of peace.

When I glanced up again, she was gone, a white feather floating down in her wake.

I caught it mid-air. Held it tight.

Then, I turned back toward that bridge. Took that first step onto it. And fucking *blurred*.

# 15

## HALEY

The raven gryphon was massive, its feathers and flesh rotting even as it continued to hover in the night sky, bones protruding from its body. Melantha sat atop it, her own wings tucked behind her. Her sleek ebony skin flickered, revealing the blackened bones beneath—a sign that she still hadn't full manifested.

Despite her lack of substance, untold power emanated from her and the raven gryphon both, wrapping around me like a fist made of invisible iron. Just as it had during my last vision, an icy dread filled my chest, so cold I could hardly breathe.

Melantha glared at me with smoldering-coal eyes—bright red embers in that flickering dark face. A white serpent coiled around her throat, two more around her upper arms, all of them poised and ready to strike.

*How* dare *you summon me, Daughter of Darkwinter,* she hissed in my mind, her voice like a sharp talon dragging through the softest parts of me.

I heard myself say the words out loud—her voice on my lips, echoing through that cave—just as I heard the fae in that cave gasp. I was in both places at once—a liminal space that allowed me to communicate with Melantha while my body remained firmly inside the mountain, tethered by the blood of my men and the ancient witches.

Witches as old, perhaps, as the goddess herself.

"Tell us why you're here," I hissed right back, keeping my voice steady despite the suffocating force of her magick. "You were banished from this realm for a reason."

*Midnight is mine, foolish girl. Mine.*

A shiver rattled my spine at her words, at the unwavering conviction behind them. At the vile sight of her hideous form. Even tucked behind her, those wings promised a painful death, every razor-sharp feather glistening with blood, as though she'd already cut down an entire army. Mutilated them.

*Shit.* All I wanted to do was flee. Sever the magickal connection and return to my body. But I knew I had to keep her talking—long enough to scare some sense into those fae pricks. Long enough to make them understand that joining us was the only way they'd survive.

That *any* of us would survive.

"You think you can take the realm so easily?" I scoffed. "Like the people of Midnight will simply hand over their home like you tried to hand me over to Keradoc?"

*Keradoc?* She seethed, a surge of pure hatred rippling through her at the mention of the warlord's name. *I've no need for such traitors. I will destroy him. I will destroy you. I will destroy anyone who stands in my way as surely as I will destroy the lands you now claim as your home. The men you now claim as your family. All of you will writhe and bow before me.*

Again, I spoke her words aloud in the cave. Felt the answering fear rising among the fae—a fear that mirrored my own. As before, it wasn't the words themselves that sent terror pulsing through my veins—hell, her little speech was straight out of the evil villain mastermind playbook. But that rage inside her—dark and ancient, endless… I had no doubt she held the power to destroy worlds.

"We will fight you, Dark One," I said, aware that the undead army had started up its death march again. Aware that my hold on the spell was beginning to slip, my magick fading. But I needed her to say more. Something, anything… The fae remained unconvinced. As terrified as they were, I still felt their hesitation. Their desperate desire to retreat from a battle they didn't believe belonged to them.

"We will fight until the very last soldier bleeds out on the field," I said. "We will fight until… We… The…" I choked on the words, unable to form another thought. Unable to even draw breath as she tightened that fist of power around my chest and flooded my mind with images so horrifying, I was certain they'd melt my brain.

Black fire consuming thousands of fae soldiers on the stretch of obsidian sand between Vanderham's Wall and the White Cliffs of Oshen, so hot it boiled their blood. The Fog of a Thousand Knives enveloping block after block in the Hollow, turning its people into red mist. That unholy skeletal army flooding over the wall, tearing the flesh from anyone in their path, only to see their victims rise up in death and join them. Wounded guards on the wall and servants in the castle, limbs mangled, eyes burning, all of them begging for someone to kill them, *please* kill them. The screams of fae and vampires and demons and humans alike, a symphony of pain that echoed down every blood-soaked alley, off every obsidian wall.

"No!" I shouted, frantic to find that thread that would lead me back to my body, to follow the blood, to shatter the deadly spell that bound her to me. But all I saw—all I felt—was fire and torture and death. Melantha had fully invaded my mind, her dark talons tearing me apart from the inside...

"Haley!" someone in the cave shouted. Authoritative. Demanding. Fucking terrified...

*Evander.*

I opened my mouth to call out to him, but no sound came. No words of my own. Only hers.

*The Daughter of Darkwinter belongs to me. I have claimed her mind just as I will claim her power.*

"End the spell, Haley!" This, from Jax. His voice tight with a fear he'd never before shown. "Damn it! Do it *now!*"

I wanted to tell him I was trying. *Help me...* I tried to reach for him, to follow the sound of his voice, but it was no use.

*When I am finished sucking her dry of magick,* the goddess whispered through me, *I shall allow my serpents to dine on her blood. My ravens will feast on her brittle bones.*

"Fight her, babygirl. You fucking fight her!" Hudson. His strong hands on my shoulders.

*There will be nothing left of your precious witch but the memories I allow you to keep and the knowledge that none of you could save her...*

"Release her, you *bitch,*" came another command. Sharp and unwavering, filled with a dark terror that rivaled Melantha's.

I couldn't place the voice, couldn't focus long enough to... Everything was spinning, my body wracked with tremors, bile rising in my throat as I gasped for air and—

"Release her or I will drag you to hell myself. *Now.*"

That deep, unbreakable voice again. God... I *knew* that voice...

My heart thudded against my chest as if it'd just gotten a jump-start, and the invisible fist around my body loosened. A cold wind howled inside me, and Melantha's grip on my mind finally slipped.

I sucked in a deep breath and called to my magick, warmth tingling across my palms. But before I could close out the spell and free myself, the goddess returned, sharp talons scraping through my mind once more, digging in hard.

"I said *release her!*" His voice boomed across the Boiling Glass Sands, rattling the skeletons, rattling the very stars in the sky.

Her grip loosened once more, and in the dark, shuddering space she left behind, another presence flickered to life.

I felt him—his soul, his very essence. Scented him in the air—bergamot and rain. Felt his arms around me and tasted his kiss as memory after memory flashed through my mind…

Then he was inside me, filling me, our hearts and souls merging. The darkness faded from my vision, and…

"Elian," I breathed. And there, standing before my eyes on the bridge in his backyard in NOLA, was my silver-eyed vampire-fae. Live oaks and dogwood trees surrounded him, Spanish moss dripping from the boughs, mist rising from the pond.

"Elian," I whispered again, tears hot on my cheeks. My heart nearly burst with the force of missing him, of longing for him. Of needing him to come back to us more than I needed to breathe.

But just as soon as that unbearable pain carved my heart, it vanished, filling me instead with warmth.

With love.

"I see you, sparrow," he said softly, his silver gaze meeting mine across the mist, that sensual mouth curving into the cocky grin I knew so well. "I won't let her hurt you."

At his words, a shield of silver-white light rose between us, enveloping me. Protecting me.

All too quickly, Elian vanished, and again the vile goddess appeared, her coal-eyes blazing bright. The second Elian's shield touched her, she recoiled, yanking her talons free from my mind as if he'd burned her—as if *we'd* burned her. The fusion of our souls, our love. A bond not even death could splinter.

She glowered at me with such hatred, such determination…

Another image flashed in my mind—Melantha's parting gift.

A woman, bent and broken on a polished obsidian floor. A pool of blood spreading beneath her. Snakes slithering through the dark ruby spill, drinking… drinking… And that high, hollow laughter ringing out from atop the dais as black wings spread across a throne made of rock and bone…

Black roses bloomed around the woman, and I knew at once I'd witnessed my death.

And with that same bleak certainty, I realized it didn't matter whether the feral fae agreed to help us. Didn't matter whether we could pull a miracle out of our collective asses and defeat Darkwinter's forces and all the rebel factions fighting against us.

Because despite this temporary setback, Melantha would not retreat. Not until she'd gotten what she'd come for.

Me.

*I will see you soon, Daughter of Darkwinter,* the cruel voice echoed as she vanished into the night, the cave finally coming back into view. *Sooner than you think.*

# 16

## EVANDER

The transformation came over her without warning.

Pain twisted Haley's face into something sharp and wicked, her eyes rolling back into her head as the Dark Goddess slithered through her mind. We tried to reach her—to call out to her, to bring her back, to break the spell—but we were powerless to help.

The fae didn't move. Didn't speak. Simply watched her suffering, glazed eyes caught between confused horror and abject wonder.

In that moment, the raging helplessness inside me twined with my magick, no longer leashed by the fae spells and iron chains, and in its wake rose a thirst for violence so complete, so destructive, I knew only one desire.

Blood.

Leaving Haley with her gargoyle and her demon, I took a step toward the fae general. Reached for him, that smug, emotionless face, the pale skin suddenly so fragile and thin, my hands trembling with the need to rip out his throat and drain him as my half-vampire brother surely would...

A soft sigh in the darkness. A name whispered into the night. And I turned once more to my witch, the bloodlust relenting the moment I saw her face.

"Elian," she gasped. And as quickly as it had overtaken her, the pain vanished.

In its place, the face of my twin shone bright, his silver eyes flickering over her green ones. I heard his voice in my mind, clear as if he were standing beside me.

*I see you, sparrow. I won't let her hurt you…*

"Elian." I echoed Haley's gasp, reaching out through the darkness for him. For the face that looked so much like my own. Leaving the fae behind me, I knelt down beside Haley and touched her face. My brother's face.

But Elian vanished in a flash, and with him, the very last vestiges of the Dark Goddess.

"Haley?" I asked softly, unable to hide the relief in my voice. In my heart. "Are you—"

"Who was that fae male?" The general's shadow fell upon us, skepticism weighting his every word.

"Elian of Autumnshire," the three witches whispered. I'd nearly forgotten they were still among us. "The missing companion."

Haley flinched at the words, but her eyes were clear, her jaw set. I was still kneeling beside her, and now she reached for my hand. Held it tight.

*I'm okay,* she mouthed.

It took everything in me not to gather her into my arms.

"Our companion isn't *missing,*" the demon said, his blue eye narrowed on the general. "He died fighting the Darkwinter weather witches, as we've already explained."

His tone was murderous, but the general appeared unmoved.

Glancing down at Haley, those ancient black eyes shimmering like polished obsidian, he said only, "The witch can conjure the dead?"

A murmur of unease rippled through the fae, and I sighed.

In calling upon the Goddess, Haley had inadvertently revealed her other gifts. Gifts she wasn't even fully comfortable with— conjuring the dead. Or at the very least, communicating with them. And now it hung between us—the question in her eyes when I met her gaze.

Would we still attempt our original plan? To offer the trade? Their help in the war in exchange for our promise to revive their dead children?

Haley nodded once. Resolute.

*Whatever you think is best,* she seemed to be saying. *I'll stand with you.*

The murmuring around us turned to bickering as the fae began to question our motives. To question what it meant for a witch to reach across the veil.

"*Deathbringer,*" someone grunted out, the disgust in their voice clear even through the din.

My mind was set.

I squeezed Haley's hand again. Shook my head. No, we would not be offering a trade after all.

We got to our feet, the demon and gargoyle close at our sides. We all exchanged a glance—all seemed to be thinking the same thoughts.

These fae were dangerous. Seeking their aid had been a mistake. If what they'd seen through Haley's spell wasn't enough to convince them of the urgency, I wasn't about to put her through further scrutiny by floating the idea of necromancy.

Their arguing escalated, tension thick in the claustrophobic space. Cursing beneath my breath, I looked around the cave, quickly assessing our options. There was only the one exit. Dozens of angry fae stood between us and our escape.

We could mount an attack, but... no. I dismissed the idea before the thought even finished forming. We had no way of knowing the extent of their power or the size of their forces. Others could be hiding in the shadows, awaiting an opportunity to pounce.

I was still weighing the options when a gruff male voice barked across the crowd. "Fools! You're all fools! Can't you see? This was nothing but a performance! A trick masterminded by the conjurer of Midnight and the empty-headed *whore* who warms his bed."

I didn't recall leaving her side. Didn't recall charging through the crowd like a wolf on the hunt, sniffing out the bastard who'd uttered those words. Yet suddenly there I was, standing before another cowardly fae, his hair hanging in limp locks to his waist, his eyes black and beady.

My hand was so tightly wrapped around his throat, his parchment-pale skin had turned a shade of lavender I'd never before seen on living flesh.

In a dark, deadly-calm whisper, I said, "I'm certain I misunderstood you, so I'm going to do you the courtesy of asking you to repeat yourself. Think *very* carefully about your response."

Those black eyes filled with contempt. "You and your *whore* have tainted the very air we—"

I didn't grant him the courtesy of finishing before I jerked the obsidian dagger from the sheath on his hip and sliced off the lower half of his face. His jaw and tongue hit the floor, blood pouring from the wound.

"*Choke* on it," I taunted, then took a half-step back as his body dropped.

It took a moment for the rest of the fae to realize what'd happened. I had just enough time to turn and look at the gargoyle, his head towering above all the others, and give him a silent warning before the room exploded in utter mayhem.

He grabbed Haley and the demon both, shifting out of his human form in a blur I barely caught, his wings wrapping around them and turning to stone as the fae mounted their attack—magick and weapons, claws and teeth.

I still held the fae blade, and with it I made quick work of a fae male who lunged for me with his sword held too high, clearly untested in battle. One clean slice, and I opened him up from his throat to his balls. His guts spilled out onto the stone floor, and I braced myself for the onslaught, knowing the fae would converge on me. Knowing I didn't stand a chance against so many foes.

But the attack never came.

# 17

## EVANDER

*H*alt!"

The single command doused the uprising like a bucket of water poured over a candle.

The general stood among his people, all of them suddenly motionless but for their feral eyes, the three witches standing mute behind him.

"Rennick insulted the witch," the general said. "Gravely. By our own laws, the warlord was within his right to remove his tongue." Then, turning to his witches, "Heal him before he bleeds out, but don't re-attach the…" He made a vague gesture over his face. "Rennick will live with the consequences of his foul words for the rest of his immortal existence."

"And what of Jessian?" someone asked. "He didn't utter a word against the witch, yet the warlord—"

"Jessian's attack was unprovoked and unwise," the general said. "He knew as well as Rennick that the warlord, however violent, hadn't acted improperly. Jessian is beyond our aid."

Both fae—Rennick, Jessian—lay bleeding at my feet. I stepped aside to let the witches deal with them, adrenaline still surging through my limbs. The blade still clutched in my hand, obsidian gleaming with blood.

Across the crowded room, Hudson shifted from stone to his warrior form, releasing Haley and the demon but keeping them close, his wings out just in case he needed to shield them again.

The general approached me, one silent step at a time.

I made no move to relinquish my weapon.

Stepping over the bodies, his gaze locked on mine, the general arched a pale brow and said quietly, "So *this* is how you treat potential allies?"

"*She* is my ally," I spat, pointing across the room at Haley, unable to keep my simmering rage from boiling over. "Her companions are my allies. *You* are an unknown quantity, having taken us against our will by swords and dark magick both, refusing to even *consider* a partnership despite all that we shared with you about the coming threat. Haley risked her life—her fucking *life*—to secure your so-called proof, yet still, you remain unmoved. So pardon me, *general*, but if the best your people can offer is a childish insult toward the woman and witch who possesses the power to not only contact the Dark Goddess, but to reach across the veil and commune with the dead, perhaps I misjudged your desire to defend yourselves and the legacy of the children your ancestors so brutally lost."

Anger flared in those obsidian eyes, but the fae didn't move to strike. Didn't move to reclaim the weapon I'd stolen from his fallen companion.

With a deep sigh, he said, "You claim the witch has made contact with the realm beyond the veil. And I won't deny what our very eyes have shown us—a dark goddess making terrifying threats and a dead fae."

"Then what else could you *possibly* need?"

"Proof. Proof that this wasn't all some elaborate spell to—"

"Nope." Haley crossed the room to stand by my side, the others close on her heels. "Sorry, but I'm capital-D Done with this shit."

The general blinked, taking in the sight before him. Blood stained her hands, streaked her face. Clung to her hair from where she must've dragged her fingers through it. But that fire in her eyes refused to so much as flicker.

Behind her, the demon glared, unflinching. The gargoyle's shadow nearly eclipsed us all.

"The talent portion of tonight's competition is officially *over*," Haley said. "We didn't leave the safety of the wall and hike through these inhospitable bullshit mountains just so I could do a little song-and-dance routine. You saw what you saw, heard what you heard. After all that, if you honestly believe we're trying to trick you, fine. Cut our throats where we stand and be done with it. But I'm telling you, *sir*, that's the fastest way to ensure you'll *never* reconnect with those you've lost—in this life or the next. Because if you refuse to help us, if you refuse to fight, Midnight *will* fall. The Goddess Melantha and her army will consume this land from the Boiling Glass Sands to the Sea of Tranquility, from the Razorbacks to Dead Claw. Any scraps she leaves behind, Darkwinter will surely claim for their own. And you'd better pray to whatever old gods you still believe in that the two camps don't decide to join forces, or I can pretty much guarantee the caves you call home will be reduced to rubble, and the bones of your precious dead will linger in torment for the rest of their miserable eternity while the rest of you spend *your* eternities kissing the feet of your new dark rulers. Oh, and did I mention Melantha has a fondness for snakes? Poisonous ones who thirst for the blood of their master's enemies? Real cute, those guys. You'll see."

The general scowled at her, but Haley scowled right back.

My heart thundered with awe, with pride.

My little thief had fought for Midnight. For me. Not just in giving the general a piece of her mind, but in agreeing to this doomed trip in the first place. In everything she'd done from the moment I'd taken her captive.

And the moment I'd set her free.

She fought for me. Bravely. Recklessly. But through that fight, she'd… *Fuck.* She'd hollowed me out inside. I hadn't been exaggerating when I'd argued with the general; Haley *had* risked her life to channel Melantha, just to show these fae that she could. Just to give them a glimpse of the enemy's plans.

Her fucking life, just to put on a show. As if it was worth it. As if my powerful, beautiful witch had *anything* to prove to these fucking scum.

That rage bubbled to the surface once more. I stepped between Haley and the general, my eyes narrowing on his.

"We seek an alliance," I said plainly. "As Haley said, we're done belaboring the point. What is your answer?"

There was no conference. No weighing of the pros and cons among his people. The general didn't so much as glance at them as he said, "You needn't have made the journey. My people and I left the politics of this realm behind centuries ago. We've no need to entangle ourselves in yet another territorial skirmish."

"*That's* your response?" Haley stepped out from behind me. "We told you—we *showed* you—that your entire realm is about to be obliterated by a psychotic dark goddess who's convinced Midnight's magick belongs to her. We told you about Darkwinter fae who can wield weather like the deadliest of weapons. We laid all this out for you as plain as can be, and you're just… you're just gonna fuck off under the mountain and bury your heads again?"

"We will allow you and your companions to leave our lands unimpeded, Daughter of Darkwinter," the general said. "Be grateful for—"

"Don't you get it? *No one* will leave these lands unimpeded if we don't win this war," she said, seething. "All of you will *burn.*"

"My decision is made."

I felt the shift in her energy, the rise of ire inside her, crackling through the magick that bound us. Her eyes blazed, and before I could draw my next breath, she lifted a hand—to strike him? To clutch his shoulder and beg for the alliance? I knew not. She hadn't even touched him, yet the general recoiled as quickly as an oft-stricken child.

The look on his face wasn't fear, though. It was revulsion.

"You are touched by Death, *witch*," he snarled, all the feigned propriety gone from his tone. "We would no more lift our swords to defend you than we would choose to fall upon them."

Haley got right in his face again. "Death will touch you *all*."

He reached for the dagger at his side, but before he could even draw it, the gargoyle had his arms pinned behind him, and the tip of my stolen blade pressed against his throat. A trickle of blood leaked from a nick above his Adam's apple.

"Be gone," I warned softly, "or I assure you, you won't need ancient witches and bowls of blood to know just how impure our hearts can *truly* become."

He held my gaze, the promise of death simmering in his. But whether he decided we weren't worth the expense of their magick or their blades, or he simply calculated the odds and decided he'd be happy to let us fight the war for him, he nodded.

"Fight your battles, warlord," he said, and the gargoyle released his arms. "Leave us to our lives beneath the mountain."

"Deal accepted," I ground out, still not lowering the blade.

"Return to these mountains again," he said, "and you will *not* find such a hospitable welcome." A final warning glare. A wave of his hand. And magick flooded the cave once more, that same starlight-flecked dark smoke that had brought them to us initially.

When the smoke receded, the fae and their witches were gone.

Little remained in the cave. The fire, blazing once more. The bowl of half-spilled blood before it. A few scattered supplies, the altar and the dead bird, the fae runes carved into the stone, the stains left behind by the two fae I'd carved.

And the frantic heartbeat thrumming in my chest, the full weight of everything that had happened bearing down on me in earnest.

He could have killed her with that dagger. With his magick. He very nearly had.

As the demon and gargoyle checked her over for injuries, my gaze found hers in the darkness, magick sizzling between us. I had no idea if the others could see or sense it, but in that moment, I didn't care.

Eyes locked on hers, I said to the others in a tone that left no room for interpretation, "*Leave.*"

Silence. Nothing but heartbeats and breaths. The quiet violence of a gathering storm as my gaze burned through her, daring her to defy me. To push back.

Haley said nothing.

"An hour," I said to the men, taking a step closer to her, not once tearing my gaze away from those twin emeralds blazing right back at me. "Do a perimeter check—make sure the fae are truly gone. Haley and I have things to… *discuss.*"

<h1 style="text-align:center">18</h1>

<h2 style="text-align:center">EVANDER</h2>

Alone with my witch, I stared into those fathomless eyes, my heartbeat so deafening I was certain she could hear it.

*Thump-thump.*

"What?" Haley crossed her arms over her chest, suddenly defensive. She knew she was in trouble. Knew I was damn near *beside* myself with rage. "Why are you looking at me like that?"

I crossed the short distance between us and beheld her up close, firelight casting her blood-smeared face in harsh, terrifying shadows.

*Thump-thump.*

I couldn't find words. Couldn't form thoughts. Couldn't remember how to do anything but *touch* her. My skin burned with the need to slide against hers, to feel the warm solidity of her body, to know without question she'd survived this fucking encounter.

*Thump-thump.*

Gripping her arms, I slowly backed her up to the cave wall. Her shoulders hit the rock, and she gasped.

One hand slid into the back of her hair, the other snaking around her delicate throat. My thigh pushed hard between her legs, spreading her. Stealing the heat that radiated from her core. Fucking *delighting* in it.

*Thump-thump.*

"Evander," she breathed. "What… what are you—"

"*You,*" I finally ground out, my voice trembling with fury, "are the wildest, most reckless, most inconsiderate, most... *incredible* fucking witch I've ever known."

Her eyes widened, then narrowed, as if she were trying to decide whether to take my words as praise or scorn.

Behind us, the fire surged. Snapped.

*Thump-thump.*

After a torturously long pause, a mischievous smile graced her lips. In a soothing, seductive tone clearly meant to distract me from the fact that I was *blindingly* angry with her, the witch said, "And *you're* a schemer, a murderer, and a spy. The devil dressed in high-fae finery who grins as he cuts out the tongues of his adversaries and delivers death with a single thrust."

"Delivering death," I said, "is not all my *thrusts* are good for. Perhaps you need a reminder."

I ground my thigh against her center, giving her just that.

Her eyes shone bright, flashing with some new challenge. "Are you threatening me, warlord?"

A dark pleasure roiled inside me. Oh, how the little thief liked to taunt me. To play such dangerous games. Even before we'd finally given in to our desires last night, she'd always enjoyed walking along the knife's edge with me.

Enemies, lovers. Villains, monsters. A *very* fine edge indeed.

I tightened my grip on her throat, ever so slightly.

And ever so slightly in return, her eyes darkened with a need that stirred my cock to full attention. She felt it immediately, the way it pressed against her lithe body. Knew damn well how deeply she affected me.

How reckless the wild little witch made *me* feel.

A different sort of smile flickered across her lips now—knowing, mischievous—and I wondered if she, too, was recalling that first night in the throne room. Our passionate, all-consuming kiss on the dais.

Or perhaps she was recalling all the things I'd done to her last night. The way my tongue had painted her body with pleasure and unleashed her beautiful, terrible songs...

Before her men had returned with the bitter wind and the news that—

*Fuck.*

If I were a kind man, a compassionate man, perhaps I would've given her space. Time to grieve the death of my brother. To process the loss and prepare for the danger still lurking on our near horizon.

But the capacity for kindness had been ripped from me long ago, and I had *zero* interest in resurrecting it now.

All I wanted was Haley. To feel the hot press of her mouth against mine, to breathe in the raw scent of her sweat and desire as I fucked her into an oblivion so black it would chase away the pain that haunted us both.

She palmed my rock-hard cock, stroking me through my pants, and a growl unfurled inside me—her only warning before I pinned her against that wall, gripped her jaw, and fucking *claimed* that fiery little mouth with a kiss so rough it drew blood.

Unlike my twin, I wasn't Haley's vampire. But the taste of her blood in my mouth, warm and salty and bursting with life, tinged with the magick we shared...

"*Haley.*" I drew back, barely able to breathe. Barely able to speak the witch's name as my heart thundered into a fierce gallop.

I felt like I was dying. Like this feral heart of mine might very well burst from my chest, shattering the bones around it, leaving me to bleed out as I'd left that fae.

But I couldn't stop. Wanting her this way might end my life, but there was *no* putting this wildness back in its cage—a wildness that sparked and burned between us like the fire, eager to consume anything in its path.

Another feral growl, and I tore the shirt from her body, ripping it off her arms as I dropped to my knees before her. The pants were next, falling away in tatters as I shredded them in my haste to find that sweet, seductive heat.

"Evander..." She whispered my name like a spell, her fingers knotting in my hair, and I pressed my mouth to the apex of her bare thighs and breathed her in...

And then I licked her. A slow, torturous drag of my tongue across that hot flesh, unleashing a shudder that rolled through her body from her dark head to her toes.

"Please," she rasped. "More. Don't... don't stop."

Unable to refuse her for a single moment longer, I dipped two fingers inside, thrusting slow and deep, then drawing back, again and again, her hips undulating with the motion as her fists tightened in my hair. I licked her again, then slid my tongue inside, alternating with those deep thrusts of my fingers, not wanting to deny any part of me the sweet pleasure of fucking her.

She was so wet for me, so eager, my every touch echoed by her soft moans, by the tiny ripples of ecstasy I felt coursing through her magick. Whatever spell she'd cast tonight, it'd changed something between us, our magickal bond strengthening, intensifying. Driving me to that knife's edge she so loved to dance upon, leaving me aching and desperate to give her this pleasure and make her understand that *no*, we would not be risking her precious life again. Not for this war. Not for anything.

Raw, undiluted fury flooded my veins once more, and I slid my fingers out and gripped her thighs, spreading her wide for me, shoving my tongue deep inside her, fucking her with my lips, my teeth, the hot swirl of my breath, my very fucking soul as I feasted upon her and finally, when I could bear it no longer, growled her name against that hot, silky flesh and made her come, all for me.

Her captor. Her warlord. A dark fae with a withered heart who'd somehow fallen in love with her despite it.

I'd known it the moment I'd seen that fae general's hand twitch toward his blade and I saw her life flash before my eyes, and everything in me turned to ice with the thought of what I'd do to him if he so much as spilled a single drop of her blood.

I fucking loved her. And I would die before I let some fae beneath the mountain cause her pain.

Haley was still panting when I rose to my feet and met her half-lidded gaze.

I was covered in her scent, drugged by her very presence. She was trembling before me as the aftershocks rocked her body. Both of us were exhausted from the trek, from the night we'd endured... But we were nowhere *near* finished.

Shoving both hands into her hair, I claimed another kiss, just as fierce as the last one. She reached for my buttons and buckles, slow and fumbling, and I cursed the fucking gods who'd invented this clothing with all its many deterrents.

I tore away from the kiss only long enough to disrobe, and then I was on her again, hands tangled in that wild hair, mouth kissing and biting and teasing, stealing her very breath as she stole mine. Thoroughly entwined, we stumbled backward from the wall and crashed onto the hard stone ground beside the fire, my body breaking her fall, but I barely felt the crack of rock against my shoulders. Every thought, every breath, every feeling inside me was wholly attuned to her.

The need to dominate her, to protect her, to fucking *own* her was over-powering.

With a possessive growl, I rolled us, knocking over the witches' abandoned silver bowl as I pinned her beneath me. The remaining blood spilled—my blood, hers, the demon's, the gargoyle's, the blood of the truth witches who'd spied upon our dark hearts. It coated our skin and bound us to the ancient rock of the Razorbacks, mingling with the darkness and magick between us, the magick of Midnight, the magick of life and death and every fucking star in the sky, and as I thrust between her thighs and buried myself deep inside her, I felt it rise around us—a great, terrible power. A promise.

Haley arched her back and drew me in deeper, nails raking across my skin, the fire roaring, that dark magick so palpable it felt as if another lover had joined us. And for those long, hot, stolen moments in the cave, we shared no words, no tender touches, no sighs of languid pleasure.

No—my witch and I turned utterly *savage*, bound only by blood and magick, by its dark and ancient promise as I drove into her again and again, our skin slick with blood and sweat, breath mingling, mouths granting frenzied, feverish kisses until she finally cried out to the moons above and I shuddered inside her and came with a thunderous roar, clinging to her, crushing her against me as if I could somehow keep her alive and unbroken if only I held her tight enough.

# 19

## EVANDER

The magick slowly ebbed, leaving a sweet-and-smoky tang on the air. And when that wild, emerald-eyed witch finally opened her eyes and looked at me again, her hair tangled, lips swollen from my kiss, my heart surrendered itself fully. Irrevocably.

As if I'd ever stood a chance at all.

With a soft sigh, Haley rose to her knees, blood streaking her bare skin, the last vestiges of the primal delirium that'd so swiftly taken us both. I turned onto my hip and leaned on my elbow, head propped in my hand as I watched her intently. Waited.

"You're still upset with me," she said, reaching out to trace the crease between my eyebrows. "For speaking out against those fae."

"Not for speaking out, no." I closed my eyes and let out a long, slow breath, gathering my thoughts. "What you did was... I could never fault you for speaking your mind. For standing up for something you believe in." I opened my eyes, met her gaze in the firelight. Finally managed a smile, though it did nothing to ease the pain in my heart. The fear. "I'm sorry I was so... abrupt before. I was more angry with myself for dragging you into this. Putting you at risk was a mistake I—"

"You gave me a choice, Evander. I wanted to be here tonight. No, things didn't go as we'd planned, but still. I'd do it again, even knowing that asshole fae could've actually hurt me and—"

"Don't." I pressed my fingertips to her lips. "I can't think about what might've happened if your gargoyle hadn't been there. If I hadn't seen the

635

fae go for his dagger…" A chill slithered down my spine, and I had to hold my breath to still my nerves, to finally chase it away. "You… you were brave, Haley. Reckless, but brave. You showed more courage tonight than I've seen from all Keradoc's generals combined."

A smile touched her lips, but it quickly dimmed. Lowering her eyes, she said, "None of it mattered, though. In the end, they still turned their backs on us. On Midnight."

"Haley." I sat up beside her, hooking a finger under her chin and tilting her face up toward mine. "It mattered more than I can even… More than I can put into words. You fought for us tonight. You fought for—"

"I don't know *what* I fought for." She turned away from my touch, then got to her feet. Pacing before the fire, she said, "I thought… I thought I could make a home here. I saw it—a future in Midnight. As crazy as it sounds, *that's* what I wanted. What I was fighting for. But now…" A heavy sigh. "I don't see how it's even possible."

I stood up beside her, drew her into my arms. "That path is not closed to you yet. We don't know what awaits us after this war."

"I'll tell you what awaits us." She pressed her forehead to my chest, her whole body trembling in my embrace as some new fear took root. "You are going to *die*, Evander. Either because Keradoc wastes away in his cell or because someone else finds him and does the job. Hudson and Jax are barely holding on after what happened with the weather witches, and Elian… God. I *felt* him tonight. I literally felt his soul, and I know he felt mine, too. He saved me from turning into Melantha's puppet, but… But it wasn't enough. *I* wasn't enough." Her voice finally shattered, and she tipped her head back to look at me, the tears I suspected she'd been holding in all night finally breaking free. "I couldn't bring him back. So yes, we *do* know what awaits us —death. Always. And no, I don't know what I'm fighting for. Not anymore."

"You—*we*—are fighting for a chance," I whispered, tucking a lock of hair behind her ear. "Just a chance."

"It's not *enough*," she repeated, pulling out of my embrace. She turned away from me, heading off to hunt for her ruined clothes, as if they'd be of any use now.

But I wouldn't let her walk away. Not like that.

"A chance," I said, grabbing her wrist and drawing her in close once more, "is more than most people *ever* get in this life—even as immortals. So yes, little thief. It *is* enough." I cupped her face, brushed a soft kiss to the corner of her mouth. "We will make it so."

Her tears continued to spill, soft and warm on my fingertips, but my witch finally nodded, the tiniest smile curving her lips as she whispered, "We will make it so."

***

Rummaging through the supplies the fae left behind, I found a few jugs of clean water and a large soup pot. After setting it to boil on a grate over the fire, I headed outside to check on the others, leaving Haley to search through an abandoned trunk of clothing, hoping she might find something that fit and hadn't been torn to shreds by an overeager lover.

True to their word, the demon and gargoyle had granted us our privacy. After confirming they'd spotted no signs of the feral fae or any other trouble, I sent them back to our original cave—I'd been right in thinking it wasn't too far off—to collect our packs. Haley and I needed to be left alone for the remainder of the night, I insisted.

It took some convincing, but ultimately, they agreed. By the time I returned to the cave, Haley was kneeling on a blanket beside the fire, two large mounds of clothing stacked beside her.

"Keeper pile, discard pile," she said, pointing to each stack. "We can divide it up later. I'm too tired to do it now."

I nodded, joining her on the blanket. Steam was just beginning to curl from the pot.

"Your men have… enquired after you," I said, tearing a scrap of fabric from an item in the discard pile and dunking it into the water. "And by enquired, I mean the demon has nearly worn a groove in the mountainside with his incessant pacing and the gargoyle practically tore my arms off when I asked them to grant us a bit more privacy."

"They're… protective." She smiled again, but it was all too brief, not nearly bright enough to chase the lingering sadness from her eyes. "Especially now that—"

"Close your eyes, little thief," I said gently, unable to bear the weight of the words I knew she'd meant to say.

*Especially now that Elian is dead…*

I still couldn't quite accept those words. Still didn't know how I felt about what'd happened. But even as I thought about it now, I wasn't sure if those words were even true anymore. Elian was *physically* gone, yes. But Haley had made contact with him tonight. He'd saved her from Melantha. Protected her. So how could he be truly lost to us?

I wrung out the makeshift cloth and brought it to her face, gently clearing away the blood. Her blood. My blood. The same blood that ran through the veins of my brother.

*Especially now that Elian is dead...*

*Elian.* I took another breath, delved once more into the tangle of my emotions in search of... I wasn't even sure. Regret? Anguish? A deep sense of loss?

Haley and the others wore their pain so plainly, like a second skin they'd never be able to shed. My own pain came in flashes and flickers, if at all. Elian was my brother. My twin. Whether I remembered him or not... If he were truly gone, truly beyond our reach, shouldn't I be able to *feel* it?

*I see you, sparrow. I won't let her hurt you...*

My brother's words echoed, but a soft sigh brought me back to the moment, to Haley. Blinking away my confusion, I dipped the cloth back into the water, watching the blood leach away before smoothing it over her skin once more.

Upon every inch of clean, bare skin I revealed, I pressed another kiss— softer now. A promise rather than a warning.

*I see you, too, little thief. I won't let her hurt you, either.*

"Will you stay with me tonight?" she asked, when I'd finally finished bathing her and moved on to take care of my own blood-caked skin. "I... I really don't want to be alone, and I don't know when the guys are coming back. Unless... unless *you* want to be alone?"

*Alone.* Her voice was low and sweet before the crackling fire, and the word slipped into my heart, poking at old wounds.

"Alone," I whispered, shaking my head as I dropped the cloth into the pot, the liquid inside more blood than water now. "For so long, Haley, all I ever wanted was a night alone. An *hour* alone. One simple hour of peace, sealed away from the blood-curdling screams of the others and all the things I... But then I took on Keradoc's life, slipped into it like it'd always been mine to claim. And from that moment forth, I was surrounded by people. Guards. Generals. Sycophants. Day and night, surrounded." I laughed, dark and bitter. "Yet I never felt so lonely in all my life."

Haley smoothed her hand down my face, her thumb brushing across my lips.

"It doesn't have to be that way anymore. Stay with me," she whispered. Then, lowering her hand, "I... I know you're planning to leave. Things didn't work out with the fae, and now you're cooking up a plan B, and I can feel it, Evander. I can feel you pulling away from us. I don't want you to go."

Something thick and heavy rose up inside me at her words, at the sincerity in her eyes. It made my throat tight, my eyes water, my heart pound as ferociously as it had when I'd watched her deal with the fae. Not with the beat of pride, as it had then. Not with the thrum of fear, as it had soon after.

No. This was the beat of a death march.

For Haley was right. I *was* going to die. Whether on the battlefield, at the hands of the Dark Goddess, or by the very magick that bound me to Keradoc.

I thought I was ready for it. Thought I'd accepted it.

But it was all just another lie I'd been telling myself, night by night, secretly hoping I could somehow outrun it.

"Don't you *dare* leave me, Evander," she said. Demanded. And when I met her gaze again, I watched as a flurry of anger washed away the sadness.

"I'm not leaving *you*, Haley." I cupped her face, her skin so warm and smooth against my palm I wanted to spend the rest of my days caressing it. Kissing it. But I couldn't, because this war was far from over, and every hour I lingered here was another lost to Melantha and Darkwinter's advances. My failure to secure the alliance with the fae only made my mission more urgent.

"I must get word to Oona and the other generals before Melantha completes the desert crossing," I explained. "I want our troops moved from the northern border back to the wall, ready to defend against the Army of the Dead. They are the bigger threat right now. I also need to find Gem and ensure our drug supplies have reached the rebel battlefields. I can move faster on my own, and despite our differences, I trust your men to safely escort you back to Amaranth City before—"

"So that's how it is?" she snapped. "After everything we've been through, everything we've done and witnessed and lost, you're still clinging to those tired old plans? To the hope that your generals—*Keradoc's* generals—can be trusted?"

"There is no one else, Haley. These fae were our last—"

"Keradoc's guards tried to kidnap me, Evander. I only ended up in the moat because I fought back. Trust me—they had something *much* more sinister than death planned for me."

My whole body shuddered at the reminder, rage threatening to turn my vision red.

Through clenched teeth, I said, "Those guards are no longer a threat."

"My point is—we don't know who else was involved, or what they even wanted. So no, your generals can't be trusted. Maybe Oona—*maybe*.

But that's it. Meanwhile, you're wasting time and energy trying to take down a bunch of rebel factions with Devil's Dream… This isn't a gang fight, Evander. This is a war."

"Those rebels are my enemies. Which—assuming you mean to survive —makes them *our* enemies."

"Compared to what's coming across the desert, those rebels are nothing more than playground bullies and you know it."

I pinched the bridge of my nose, a headache building behind my eyes. "If you have a point, I'd appreciate it if you'd make it."

"Stop trying to sabotage them with drugs and trickery!" she shouted. "They may be bullies, but they're still fighters. And fighters can be turned into soldiers."

"Soldiers that would just as soon shoot a flaming arrow through my back? Through *yours*?"

"Not if you unite them under a single banner and—"

"Which banner? Mine?" I laughed, rising to my feet and grabbing some clothes from the pile. Yanking a stiff cotton shirt over my head, I said, "Do you honestly think they'd fall in line for the warlord who's been torturing and executing their people for centuries? For the warlord who paraded his own wounded soldiers through the city until they finally succumbed to their injuries, or worse—fell by the swords and arrows of their own men ordered to execute them?"

Haley stood up beside me and took my hands, refusing to release me even as I attempted to pull back.

"No," she said softly, her ire fizzling. "I know they wouldn't fall in line for Keradoc. But for you? For *you*, they might."

I closed my eyes, the realization settling into my gut like lead. "You want me to reveal myself to them. To remove the ring and show them the man behind the mask."

"Not… permanently," she said, touching the ring. The shackle. "I know you can't remove it for very long. Just… just long enough to show them who you are. To explain."

"To what end, Haley?" I opened my eyes to look at her once more, my own ire fading along with hers, leaving nothing but despair in its wake.

"Everyone in the realm will have to choose a side eventually. Even you."

"I choose Midnight. I've *always* chosen Midnight, even when my reasons weren't… weren't noble."

Vengeance. That had been my reason. My *only* reason.

Until I met her.

Haley watched me for a long moment. Then she rested her palm over my heart, a soft gesture in the heat of a brutal conversation.

"You're fighting *for* Midnight, Evander," she said gently. "But who are you fighting *as*? Are you the vicious warlord who executes his own soldiers and brings the people to their knees in fear? Or are you the fae who was stolen from his own life, forced to make a new one in a dark realm, fighting for that chance you whispered about earlier?"

Again, something thick and heavy gripped my heart. Knotted in my throat.

"*You* see the stolen fae," I said softly, not trusting my voice to remain steady. "Evander, the long-lost twin of Autumnshire. But I have no memory of that life, Haley. If there was ever anything good or noble inside me, I've long ago lost it. No, perhaps I'm not the *true* warlord of Midnight, but I'm no savior, either. I'm just one man, one fae trying to… to…" I trailed off, lost to the bleak emptiness that now hung over me like a Darkwinter storm cloud.

"Trying to what, Evander?" Haley's eyes softened, and I felt the touch of her magick curling around my heart. Strengthening me. Bringing me back.

In that moment, I felt more connected to her than I'd ever felt to another person, to a cause, even to the vengeance that had given me reason to keep existing for so many long, brutal years.

"When I look into your eyes," I whispered, "it enrages me to know that darkness and despair are even allowed to *exist* in the same universe as you."

She stretched up on her toes and kissed me, soft and sweet and deep. Another promise. Another tether, bringing me back.

I lifted her up, her legs wrapping around my hips, the weight and warmth of her stirring me to life all over again.

"Reveal yourself to the rebels of Midnight," she whispered against my lips. "The *people* of Midnight. Show them who you really are. Rally them to fight for you. For us."

I ran my hand up her bare back, beneath the dark curtain of hair that had always fascinated me. It reminded me of that first night she'd wandered into the library, fresh from a shower, damp hair curling at the ends. She'd caught me reading Keradoc's diaries over a glass of bourbon. Called me pathetic for it. And through all her taunts and teasing, all I could think about was touching that long, gorgeous hair, grazing my fingers along the back of her neck. I'd wondered if her skin would be warm or cool. If I'd feel the heat of her magick.

Now, her naked body wrapped around me, I had the answers to all of those questions and so many more.

I couldn't keep the tenderness from my voice when I said, "What do you see when you utter such things to me, little thief? A lover? A leader? Or perhaps a monster, no better than the ones hunting us?"

Haley smiled, equal parts sweet and wicked. Tempting and terrifying.

Magick crackled between us once more, her eyes bright with it.

"I see all of them," she whispered. "All of them."

# 20

## ELIAN

e're losing him. Damn it, Saint. Come on, breathe. *Breathe!*"

The harsh commands came to me in bursts, each one punctuated by the unmistakable blow of a fist to the chest.

"Fucking *breathe*, you asshole!"

Another shot to the sternum, and a cough spasmed through my body. Wet, rattling, fucking awful. But when the spasms receded, I finally —*finally*—took that breath. A real fucking breath, cool and deep.

Because I was… alive. Somehow, I'd made it across that bridge. Made it back to some kind of cave, a fire crackling behind me—

As soon as I had the thought, the pain rushed in. Fucking ambush waiting to strike.

Blinding. Soul-shredding. Fucking *devastating*.

I had no idea where I was, who'd been trying to get me to breathe, but in that moment, I couldn't even open my eyes. I wasn't even sure I *had* eyes—wasn't sure I had anything more than a collection of exposed nerves, every last one of them on fire.

A fierce roar exploded into the night, shaking the very ground I lay on.

It took me a beat to realize that sound had come out of *me*—a sound that tore through my chest and throat, ripping me apart on the way out.

Another cough. The coppery taste of blood in my mouth. Sharp claws and fangs slicing me to ribbons, over and over again as I fought to remain conscious.

"He's not going to make it," the voice said. "He's in too much pain."

"Give him something!" a second voice. Female. Both female.

"We can't risk—"

"Just a little bit. Something to ease his suffering. We can't leave him like this or—"

"We don't have a choice. That shit will *destroy* him. It's too—"

The roar—louder than the first, full of fury and anguish—drowned out their debate. But through the haze of pain, one line rang out loud and clear as a bell that clanged through the searing ache in my skull.

*Give him something… Give him something…*

Something. The Black. They had the Black. It was the only thing strong enough to take the edge off this wicked pain, but…

*Just ask them for it,* the devil on my shoulder said. *You know they'll hook you up. Come on—you need it. It's not even recreational this time. You fucking need it…*

Another ripple of pain rolled through me like a tsunami, taking down everything in its path, no fucking survivors...

"Fuck," I ground out. "*Fuck!*"

The devil was right. I *did* need it—another dance to get me through the night. Another hit to numb the pain.

I. Fucking. *Needed* it.

And that realization woke me up even faster than that fist to the chest.

Because if I couldn't survive this without the fucking Black, I didn't deserve to be here at all.

Death had warned me it would be like this.

*The pain you'll have to endure just to take another* breath *as a living being, let alone speak or walk or even hold her again…*

I'd sworn I could handle it. That I could face whatever awaited me if only I could go back to my life. Back to Haley.

Now, I was here. Suffering in ways so excruciating, I wouldn't inflict them on my worst enemies—but I was alive. And I had absolutely no doubts that if I gave in now—if I took even one more pill—I'd waste away and end up in that red river bound for hell. *Hell,* where the torment of losing Haley all over again—eternally—would be worse than *anything* my mutilated body could serve up now.

Gritting my teeth, I sucked in another breath and slowly opened my eyes. Glanced down at the naked wreckage of myself stretched out on the stone ground, blood pooling beneath me, the whole sight so fucking gruesome it made my stomach churn. A stomach I could fucking *see* through the mutilated skin. Bare torso full of holes, most of them leaking blood.

Bones protruding. The stump of an arm on one side, nothing past the shoulder on the other.

Both legs ended just below the knees.

It was a miracle I still had my dick, but given the state of things, I was pretty damn sure I wouldn't be using it again anytime soon.

I squeezed my eyes shut again as another red-hot fist of pain gripped my chest, so fierce I could've sworn my bones melted. Bile churned through my gut...

I turned my head to the side just in time to puke.

"Easy," came the soft voice. Soothing. Hands in my hair, gently scraping it back from my face as I continued to retch. Someone *else's* hands... because I no longer had my own.

Tears leaked from my eyes at the realization of what I'd become. At the unending fire tearing through me.

*Ask her for the pills, you stupid fuck. You're so fucked up right now, Haley won't be able to stand the sight of you anyway, so you might as well just swallow a handful of those little beauties and sail off into sweet oblivion...*

"No!" I shouted. "Fuck... *off!*"

"Saint, you need to breathe," the woman whispered, pressing a cool hand to my forehead. "You're body is trying to knit itself back together. You need to relax and let it do its job."

I opened my eyes again and slid my gaze up, following the sound of that voice. A voice I recognized...

A woman knelt beside me. Stoked my forehead, my hair. Her touch settled me—the touch of a friend.

Slowly, her face came into view. Sky-blue hair pulled back into a bun. Violet eyes so much like the ones my brother had borrowed...

Keradoc's eyes.

"Oona?" I whispered.

Tears filled those violet eyes, and she offered a warm smile. "You remember. That's a good sign."

"Where am I? What—"

"Welcome back, Saint." This, from the second female. Sharper. Clipped. "You fucking prick. Thought you were a goner for sure."

She came to kneel beside Oona, her purple hair shining in the firelight.

"Gem?" I blinked rapidly, not trusting my vision, but sure enough, it was her—another old friend.

The old friend who'd betrayed us.

"What the *fuck* is she doing here?" I asked Oona, my heart slamming against broken ribs, the effort of getting angry sending me into another coughing fit.

Gem only laughed. "I believe the phrase you're looking for is, 'thanks for saving my half-wasted ass, Gem. You're a real pal.' But if it's too painful for you to speak right now, you can just thank me later with… oh, I don't know. A fruit-and-cheese basket? Maybe a gift card for a massage?"

I glared at her. "Did you save me just so you could—" *Fuck*. More coughing. Another wave of nausea.

"Kill you?" The flash of her teeth, followed by the flash of a dagger. Gem pushed up her sleeve and drew the blade across her skin, drawing blood. Then, pressing her wrist to my mouth, she sighed and said, "Drink up, Saint. It's story time."

# 21

## ELIAN

*I* may have needed the Black, but I fucking *needed* the blood. I didn't resist as it slid into my mouth, clear and untainted, an inexplicable richness only a pure dark fae Midnighter could offer.

I lapped it up like a greedy bastard, literally starving for it. And as her decadent blood worked its way through what was left of my body and sped up my lagging vampire healing, Oona kept watch from the entrance of whatever cave they'd dragged me into, and Gem… Damn. That woman wove quite a tale.

She told me about how she'd begun to suspect something was up with Keradoc soon after the boys and I left Midnight the first time around. How the warlord was constantly on edge, but no longer demeaning his people. No longer executing them just for speaking out of turn or failing to deliver victories on Midnight's many battlefields. Oona, she'd observed, hadn't had so much as a black eye or split lip in months, despite the fact that she was constantly at his side.

"So one night," Gem said, "I was in the castle on business from the Hollow and caught the bastard sneaking away from his war council alone. So, being the intrepid little spy that I am, I followed him—straight down to the dungeons. I knew he'd been keeping a prisoner in seclusion—some fucker known only as prisoner 6712. I figured maybe Keradoc had grown tired of the nice-guy act and needed to spill a little blood. Hear the screams of some nameless victim to help take the edge off."

She shifted her position to give me better access to her blood—every precious drop easing a bit of the pain—then continued.

"But when he got there, he didn't torture the guy. Didn't even open the cell door. Just stood before it and said, 'I want you to remember who put you here.' Then he took off his ring, and he just..." She blinked and shook her head like she still couldn't believe whatever she'd seen. "He transformed. Keradoc literally transformed before my eyes into... Well, I thought it was *you*, Saint. I almost called out to you. But I knew it was impossible. I knew you'd left Midnight—I was still getting your reports from the operations in New Orleans. So I stood there, hidden in the shadows, watching this guy just... just gaze into that cell wearing your face. My mind went over every angle. Maybe he'd seen you in a crowd somewhere in the city, and he'd chosen your face—some random glamor he could slip into. Maybe you'd crossed paths in the castle on some shady deal or another with the guards or the staff. Maybe Melantha had fed him the image."

Sated and exhausted, I pulled away from her outstretched hand and shook my head.

By the time she tugged her sleeve down again, the wound had already healed, and I could finally draw a deep breath without feeling like someone had dipped me in a vat of acid.

Still fucking hurt, but not enough to have me wishing for the Black.

"I kept running through all the possibilities," she continued, "but then the guy wearing your face said to the prisoner, 'I will take *everything* from you, Keradoc, just as you took everything from me. And when it is done, when I've wiped the foul stain of your existence from history, not even your daughter will remember you.' I'm paraphrasing, but you get the idea. He slipped the ring back on, and once again, he became—for all intents and purposes—Keradoc. An ally, I realized. Whoever the guy was, whoever's face he was wearing, he'd found a way to imprison Keradoc, steal his identity, and destroy him. Happy dance, right? Still... I wasn't about to out myself by jumping out of the shadows and suggesting we get matching T-shirts. I had no idea what the fuck was going on—just knew I had to play it cool."

"I found out soon after," Oona said, coming to join us by the fire. "My father had summoned me to his chambers for some briefing or another, but I'd shown up earlier than expected. He didn't hear me approach. I saw him standing before a mirror, the ring held in his palm, the look on his face just... determined. That's the only way I can describe it. Like Gem, I thought it was *you* standing there, Saint—that maybe you'd returned to

Midnight to assassinate him. But before I could say a word, he put the ring on and became my father once more. We had our meeting, and I never asked him about what I'd seen. I was too damn terrified."

"Oona was completely freaked," Gem said. "We met up that night for drinks in the Hollow, and I knew something was wrong. Several drinks later, I sort of… let it fly. 'Keradoc isn't Keradoc,' I said. And her eyes got huge, and then we just… It all spilled out. We started comparing notes. Going over all the little things that no longer added up. Things we should've noticed a lot sooner than we did."

"From that night on," Oona said, glancing at Gem, "we decided we'd do whatever it took to help this mystery man bring my father down, even if we couldn't reveal ourselves to him. Even if we couldn't admit we knew his secret. It was all too fragile—too risky. So we just kept playing our parts, gathering intel, trying to suss out his angle."

"Ultimately," Gem said, "we realized he'd spoken the truth that night in the dungeon. He'd told Keradoc he wanted to wipe out his existence—and that was it. Revenge, pure and simple. Which, yeah. Lots of people want to kill Keradoc, but this guy… It always seemed so personal." She shrugged. "I mean, why is he going to such great lengths instead of just shoving a sword through Keradoc's heart and ending it?"

"And why does he look like you?" Oona sighed and trailed a hand through my hair, her face unreadable. "It's… uncanny, Saint. Truly."

I nodded and closed my eyes, trying to process everything they'd told me. The pain had dimmed a bit, but it still hurt to breathe. To think. I tried to shift positions, see if I could lift my head and check whether my wounds had closed, but even the slightest movement sent another wave of agony crashing through me.

"Your body is trying to repair itself," Oona said softly. "Making decent progress, too—the blood will help. When we first found you, you were barely more than a head and a partial torso."

*Fuck.* How long had I been lying there before they'd found me? I didn't remember anything after I'd connected with Haley and chased off Melantha—whole thing had been over in a blink. But somehow I'd gotten back to my… my former self. Whatever was left of me, anyway.

How long had it taken that vampire-fae smoothie to start knitting itself into a solid form again?

"Where?" I managed, still not opening my eyes.

"We're in the Razorbacks," Gem said. "About a day's march from the city. Darkwinter… they've taken the northern outpost, Saint. Our troops have fallen back to the city center to mount a defense, but it's… not going well. Then we heard rumors about an attack by the weather witches—an attack that supposedly killed a vampire-fae traveling with Keradoc. An attack that Melantha ordered."

My eyes flew open at that. "Melantha? So she *is* working with Darkwinter."

*Fuck.* We'd known it was a strong possibility. Just didn't think the Dark Goddess had made contact yet.

Gem nodded. "We came as soon as we could. We couldn't risk being tracked."

"We found you on the eastern passage alone," Oona said. "You were exposed on the trail, bleeding out, moaning... At first we thought it was a wild animal left to die by some cruel hunting party, but when we got closer..."

"Darkwinter will come for you again, Saint," Gem said. "They can't risk leaving you alive—not when Melantha is so desperate to take you off the map."

*Great.* Must've really chapped the bitch's ass when I'd shown up to help Haley.

"Why does she give a fuck about a washed-up fugitive?" I asked. I tried to sit up, but the pain was too much, chewing through every nerve until I was breathless and trembling again.

Oona winced, gently pushing my shoulders back down. "Be still. You need to rest and heal."

Gem said, "You're not a washed-up fugitive, Saint. There's more to this story—so much more."

I glared at her, the old resentments rising. Yeah, she'd probably saved my life with that little blood offering. Seemed to be playing for Team Good Guy again—Oona obviously trusted her. But that didn't explain why she'd fucked us over in the first place instead of just telling us about what she'd discovered in that dungeon. Could've saved us all a lot of blood and tears.

"Is this the part where you tell me why you sold us out to the not-Keradoc guy wearing my face?" I asked, not ready to reveal his true identity. "Why you ordered your men to shoot us full of hawthorn and bolts? Why you—"

"I know what I did, Saint. Every last sin." Gem had the decency to look contrite. "I can't even *begin* to tell you how much I regret hurting you guys. Not just the night of the feast, but... after. With the... Devil's Dream."

She was talking about the warehouse. How she'd threatened us, berated us. How she'd pushed and pushed and *pushed*, then stood by while I lost my shit and massacred all those people…

Guilt burned through me again, a pain almost as vicious as the rest.

"But even knowing how much I hurt you," she continued, "even knowing there was a good chance I'd never get to tell you this story and you'd just go on hating me for the rest of your immortal life… I'd do it again. No question."

"Because you're a fucking sadist?" I asked, not sure whether I should be pissed or disgusted or relieved that maybe I'd been right to think she hadn't actually betrayed us. That I hadn't been such a shitty judge of character when I'd entrusted her with our secrets.

"Because I fucking love you, you stupid asshole," she snapped. "You're… you're my best friend, Saint. You might not want that friendship, but I will *always* cherish it. So yeah, I've made mistakes. I've made bad calls. I've hurt people I care about. But you bet your chewed-up vampire ass I'd do it all over again just to keep you guys safe, and if you don't like that answer, you can fuck off over the side of this mountain."

"*Fine,*" I snapped right back. Then, with a deep sigh of resignation, "But you'll have to throw me over the mountain, Gem. In case you haven't noticed, it's a long walk and I don't have legs."

She stared at me for so long, I worried I'd short-circuited something in her brain.

But then that crazy, purple-haired psycho exploded into a laugh that bounced off the cave walls.

"Sometimes I really hate you," she said, but she was still laughing, tears sliding down her cheeks.

"Then stop checking out my dick and tell me the rest of the story."

One more bout of laughter, then the mood turned serious again.

Oona checked over my wounds, finally deeming them healed enough to earn me a cloak to cover up. She tucked it around my torso and hips, leaving what passed for my arms and legs exposed so she could monitor their progress.

"Haley," Gem finally said, and I could've sworn the fire beside us flickered. "She's the rest of the story, Saint."

## 22

HALEY

"Harder," Jax demanded.

"I... I can't. I can't take another minute of this... this pounding," I panted, sweat burning my eyes. "It's too much. You're... too much."

"Your *excuses* are too much. And frankly, I'm tired of them. You think you can take on the Army of the Dead? Melantha? You can barely throw a punch."

"Jax, I—"

"Hit me," he said. "Fucking *harder*, Haley. Do it."

Frustration surged. My fist rocketed into his face, but he dodged at the last second and my punch glanced off his rock-hard jaw.

"Close, but not close enough, angel," Jax taunted. "You need to give me *more*."

Watching from the sidelines beneath a gnarled, leafless tree, Hudson growled in warning. But my gargoyle had learned his lesson about interfering an hour ago, when he'd swept into the clearing and stolen me away from my ruthless trainer and the two of them nearly came to blows over their differing opinions on what constituted training and what constituted torture.

At the moment, wincing over my bleeding knuckles and the arms that now felt like overcooked lasagna noodles, I wasn't sure where I stood on the matter.

652

It'd been three nights since the fae had refused our alliance. Three nights since Evander left us. Left me.

My thighs still burned from those wild hours we'd spent in the cave, and every time I took a step now, I felt him inside me again, stretching me, claiming me, grinding my body into the stones beneath us, the very act calling up that ancient, primal magick that still simmered in my veins.

At some point, I'd fallen asleep, curled up in his protective embrace before the fire. But by the time I'd awoken a few hours later, he was gone. No goodbyes. No promises about when I'd see him again, if at all.

Evander, our captor-turned-friend. The brother of my first love. A dark fae who'd somehow slipped into my heart deeply enough to kindle the same sort of feelings inside me as the others... And in the end, he'd left, just like he'd told me he would.

I didn't know whether he'd gone to rally Keradoc's old generals, or whether anything I'd said about uniting the rebels had gotten through to him. I just knew that he was gone, and I missed him in a way I hadn't seen coming—a new hollow in my heart, right next to the one that belonged to his twin brother.

The guys and I had hiked our way down the mountain after that, setting up camp in the forested area that bordered the base of the Razorbacks, slowly making our way back toward Amaranth City. Since our descent, I'd spent my nights alternating between sparring with Jax, keeping Hudson company on his perimeter checks, and spilling my blood in a vain attempt to conjure another spell for Elian. With each passing hour, my magick was getting stronger, my spells more responsive... but nothing seemed to work.

I hadn't felt Elian's presence since that night with Melantha. Not even a flicker of those silver eyes or the barest whiff of his bergamot-and-rain scent. Whatever connection I'd forged in the place where the fog had taken him... whatever connection had allowed him to come to my aid when Melantha had taken my mind hostage...

Nothing but dead air now.

*Dead...*

The word echoed through my mind, making my knees tremble.

"Haley?" Jax's hands were on my shoulders, his eye full of concern, all traces of the brutal sparring coach gone. "What is it?"

"I... I can't do this, Jax. You guys are counting on me and... and I feel like I'm screwing it up at every turn."

"Ain't one damn ounce of truth in that statement, babygirl," Hudson said, coming to join us. The fact that he'd spoken a full sentence in front of

Jax only proved how worried he must've been. I hated making him feel that way, but I just didn't know how to keep up the brave face.

"It *is* true," I said. "Even after conjuring Melantha, I couldn't convince the noble fae to help us. I lost the connection to Elian. I can't throw a decent punch." I glanced up into Hudson's soulful brown eyes. "You said you're stronger because of me, but that doesn't work if you—if *both* of you —are so worried about me it distracts you during a fight." I shook my head, a dark laugh escaping. "You guys are here because of me. *Elian* came here because of me. You three had a life in New Orleans. No, it wasn't perfect, but it was still a *life*. Then I showed up at the club with my whole dark-goddess sob story, and you just packed up and—"

"We *lived* in New Orleans," Hudson said, tucking a finger under my chin and tilting my face up. "Don't mean it was a life."

"Pretty sure none of us knew what the fuck living even felt like until we met you, angel." Jax tried to smile, but he couldn't hold it.

I knew exactly where his thoughts had gone.

*Elian* wasn't living. Not anymore.

It hit me then, all at once. The hollow inside me expanded until I was sure it'd swallowed my whole fucking heart. My steps faltered, grief rising once more, a dark wave threatening to drag me down, down, down—so deep I knew I'd never see the light again. It crushed me, this weight. Sliced open some vital part of me I'd never get back.

Overhead, the dark sky flashed with an eerie green light—a light the color of poison. The color of war and rot. Melantha was getting closer, the magick of Midnight responding in kind—fighting. Preparing. I felt it, that magick. The same magick that flowed through Evander. Through the land itself.

The same magick Melantha wanted to steal. To twist and pervert to her own deadly ends.

We'd never even had a chance. Even if the fae had agreed to join us... No. We were outnumbered. Melantha's forces and Darkwinter's hatred... it was all too much.

I'd once told Elian I thought hope was a drug more dangerous than his Devil's Dream, and maybe it was. But right now, as I fell to my knees in the leafless forest and felt the last of my own hope drain out of me, I finally understood why he'd taken all those little black pills. Why he'd never quite been able to walk away from his addiction. The Dream might've destroyed nearly every good thing in his life—might very well have killed him if he'd actually lived through that Darkwinter attack. But it'd given him peace—enough to get him through the night. The hour. It'd blunted the pain of loss and regret and fear and all the terrible things that made a person wish they'd never even taken their first breath, and right now, if someone had offered me a bottle of those pills, I was pretty sure I would've swallowed down every last one without a second thought.

The shadows shifted around me, and Jax knelt in the dirt at my side, taking one of my hands and pressing a kiss to my palm. Hudson was there too, his big hand stroking my back. And together, without words, without hope, the three of us closed our eyes and wept.

---

By the time anyone spoke again, the sickly green light had faded from the sky, a blanket of clouds sweeping in and blotting out the stars.

I hoped it wasn't the weather witches.

Sluggishly, I dragged myself back to my feet. Brushed the dirt from my ass. Twisted my messy hair into a knot on top of my head.

It didn't matter if grief had swallowed up my heart. I still had to learn how to fight. Still had to try, if only for the men who still lived. The men who loved me as much as I loved them.

I looked at Hudson, my fierce gargoyle warrior. At Jax, my unrelenting, unstoppable demon.

And I thought of Evander. My warlord. My dark fae.

For them, I could do this. I could fight.

"Again," I told Jax, shaking off the haze of my grief. "Let's go."

He and Hudson stood up and exchanged a glance—one I couldn't quite translate.

"You sure about this, babygirl?" Hudson asked, his eyes glued to Jax.

I nodded. "I'm good. Definitely. Let's do this."

Uncertainty flickered through the mate bond, a low rumble of concern humming in his chest.

"I've got her," Jax said to Hudson as he made a show of rolling his neck and cracking every one of his knuckles like some kind of prize fighter. "We're gonna try a new tactic. See if the change-up can inspire a comeback for our feisty little witch."

"Go," I told my gargoyle, rolling my eyes at the demon's theatrics. "I'll be fine. I promise."

Hudson finally relented, and after a quick kiss on my forehead, he was gone, off to scout ahead for the location of our next camp.

When I turned my attention back to Jax, he was grinning at me—the old wolf's grin that had tied my stomach in knots from that very first night at Saints and Sinners. The one that'd sent chills skittering down my spine and set my heart thundering, just like it was right now.

*So my heart* hasn't *evaporated, then. Good to know...*

After another beat, the smile fell from his face. And in its place came a look so deadly, so primal, adrenaline flooded my limbs and every hair on my arms stood on end.

Jax folded his arms over his chest, narrowed his eye, and issued a single, bone-chilling command. *"Run."*

# 23

## ELIAN

’m sorry I couldn't tell you sooner," Gem said, her eyes glazing with raw emotion. "I had to be sure it was safe. Keradoc—the real Keradoc—has so many spies, so many people willing to sell out their own family members for a chance to win favor with him. I couldn't risk it. I had to keep playing my role. I'd already heard about Melantha's deal with Keradoc—well, the man posing as Keradoc. How she'd promised him a powerful Darkwinter blood witch in exchange for him breaking her banishment. Soon after, when I heard you were coming back to the Hollow with a blood witch in tow, I knew. I just knew it was all connected. I also knew the only way you guys would survive was if I kept up the ruse. I helped him take you prisoner the night of the feast because if I didn't, someone *worse* would take you. Fake Keradoc? At least he wanted you alive." She glanced at Oona, who nodded. "Only the two of us knew the truth. We trusted each other—no one else. And we kept up our little act, played the expected roles, at all costs. Even though it meant hurting you. Even though it meant betraying and losing my friends."

I nodded, still trying to make sense of everything they'd shared so far.

"I suppose you *tried* to tell me," I said with a sigh. "In your own shady-ass way. You were calling me *Elian* when you've only ever called me Saint. You kept telling me nothing in Midnight was as it should be. I thought maybe something was up, but at that point it was too much to hope for."

"I hated keeping this from you. There were so many times in that warehouse when I just wanted to drop the whole charade and throw myself at your mercy, but we couldn't risk it."

"What finally changed your mind?"

A shudder rippled through her body, and it took her a few beats to find the words.

"When I heard Melantha had sent Darkwinter weather witches after you, I made a promise. A prayer, if that's what you want to call it. If you survived and I ever saw you again, I'd come clean—that was the deal. Then we found you and…" She shuddered again, and scooted closer to the fire, eager to rub the sudden chill from her arms. "Took two nights for you to regain consciousness, but here we are." She reached over and pressed a hand to my chest. "And now you know."

The look in her eyes was so remorseful, so sincere, it shattered the last of my resentments.

She'd sacrificed my trust and friendship just to keep me and my friends alive.

I would've done the same damn thing in her place. Hell, I'd *been* doing the same damn thing… for years.

"I'm sorry I doubted you, Gem."

"After what I put you guys through, I would've been disappointed if you hadn't. But Saint? Let's *never* play that game again, shall we? I fucking missed you. I fucking missed my *friend*."

I put my hand over hers and squeezed, and… wait. My hand?

"I have a hand, Gem. I have a fucking hand!"

"Two of them, you dumb shit." Gem grinned like an idiot. "Look."

I checked it out. Sure enough, she was right. I was recuperating. Slowly, painfully, but damn. Hands! Two fucking hands!

"Tell me about Haley," I said, flexing my fingers, feeling like a badass. "You said she's the rest of the story."

Gem looked to Oona, who said, "Haley is a Silversbane Witch of prophecy, but she's also Darkwinter."

"I'm aware," I said.

"Yes, but just like Silversbane," she continued, "Darkwinter's got ancient prophecies, too. Haley's sister Gray was destined to unite the covens in the earthly realm and bring their oppressors to justice. But you know what the lore says about *your* witch?"

I shook my head, my heartbeat kicking up again, those shiny new hands tingling.

"Haley was never meant for the earthly realm," Gem said, getting up to go check the cave entrance while Oona sat with me. "They're calling her the Balance."

Again, the fire beside us flickered, and I wondered if it was a sign from Midnight itself. An acknowledgment of Haley's gifts. This so-called prophecy.

"The Balance?" I asked. "What does that even mean?"

"Exactly as it sounds," Oona said. "According to the translations, the Balance will bring light to the darkest realm, where the opposing magicks of each will come together in a true balance. Not in a blending, where each of them becomes watered down by the other, but in a way that allows for those unique powers to manifest in tandem. Creation *and* destruction, beginnings *and* endings, good *and* evil, order *and* chaos. An all-encompassing magick that sounds so simple, yet is vast and complex beyond our wildest imaginings. It's the very spark of life itself."

"I'm not sure I follow."

"Essentially, the Balance herself is neutral. She *brings* the light, but she does not seek to illuminate the darkness or stamp it out. She knows one cannot exist without the other, and has learned how to wield them both. To allow them to coexist. And through that union of light and dark, the Balance shall usher in a new world for all who understand and appreciate the duality of such magick."

"Beauty in darkness," I whispered.

Oona lifted her brows in question.

"It's something Haley says. Something she got from Hudson. Sometimes she makes these… these black roses. They bloom from her magick, her blood… I'm not exactly sure how it happens. Used to freak her out, but I think she's learned to appreciate them." A smile touched my lips as I thought of her—the fierce determination in her eyes whenever she was concentrating on a spell. The joy when she got it right. Those gorgeous roses…

"But… how?" I asked, still not sure what it all meant. "Even if the prophecy is real, how can you be so sure Haley is this… this Balance?"

A new light danced in Oona's violet eyes. "I believe you've already answered that for yourself, Saint. But…" She let out a breath, her eyes dimming. "There's another part to the prophecy, and it requires a bit of mental gymnastics to put it all together. It's probably best if I recite it for you."

I nodded for her to go on.

Oona touched my forehead once more, and a deep sense of calm washed over me, as if some part of me already knew what this prophecy would reveal. What it would mean—for all of us.

I closed my eyes, and Oona recited the verse.

> *Deep in the realm where the forests burn*
> *As one becomes two, the wheel shall turn*
> *A bond unbroken but by force*
> *United once more to right the course*
> *The Balance shall mend the tattered threads*
> *All that is false must now be shed*
> *With them she joins, through souls and hearts*
> *What is remade stronger shall never part*

As she spoke, the images appeared in my mind. Where the forests burn—the trees of Autumnshire, red and gold as the flames. As one becomes two—twins, like Evander and me, the one that became two inside our mother's womb. The turning of the wheel suggested the prophecy set in motion, perhaps by our very conception. The bond broken by force—Keradoc, stealing my brother from our family. Evander and I finding each other again in Midnight. And the Balance—Haley. She was the one who brought us back together. Not my searching, not my vow to find him, but Haley. And all that is false... Evander's mask. The lies we'd all told. The truths that had to come out in order for us to win this war. To survive.

And the joining...

"The joining," I said, opening my eyes. "It's literally—"

"Yes," Oona said. "The scholars believe that's a joining in the physical sense, but also through a deep emotional connection. You obviously have that with Haley, and some of the other pieces align as well."

"The burning forests of Autumnshire," I said, and she nodded.

But I wasn't the only one who had a deep connection with Haley. There was Jax and Hudson, obviously. But Evander... I'd seen it in both of their gazes the night she revealed his identity to me in the library. The night I went from trying to murder him to fighting by his side to take down the guards who'd hurt her.

I didn't know how it happened—only that it had.

Somehow, Haley and Evander had fallen in love with each other.

"We don't know what 'them' means in this context," Oona said. "Whether it's a translation error or a neutral pronoun or—"

"We *do* know what it means," I said. "I know." Then, looking up into those eyes that were so much like her father's, yet so different, I said,

"He's my brother, Oona. Evander of Autumnshire. That's why he looks like me. We're identical twins."

"As one becomes two," she breathed. "But you... you never mentioned—"

"Keradoc stole Evander from our home when we were children. Enslaved him in Midnight, where he's been ever since."

"What the *fuck*?" This, from Gem, who immediately abandoned her post by the entrance and joined us. Her eyes glazed with sympathy as she knelt beside me. "Saint, I'm... I don't even know what to say."

I told them the very briefest version of events—my time in Blackmoon Bay, the rumors of Evander's presence in Midnight, my first trip here to find him. The things Haley had figured out about him during our captivity. His memory loss, and finally, his admission that he was not, in fact, the warlord of Midnight.

"Outside you two and our group," I said, "there's only one other who knows about Evander." My gut soured at the thought of her. "Melantha helped him with the spell. The ring that allows him to wear Keradoc's face."

"She knows about the prophecy," Oona said, nodding. "It's why she wants Haley so badly. She knows Haley has the power to manifest all the magick of Midnight—magick she wants for herself."

"It's also why she ordered Darkwinter to kill you," Gem added.

"And why she cursed me. *Fuck*." I hissed out a breath as another bolt of pain shot through my gut, but the realization of what Melantha had done turned that pain into pure fire. "In order to get us out of Midnight last time, Melantha made us each give up something important. The *most* important thing we could offer."

"Haley," Gem said, and I nodded.

"I thought it was just part of her... her Dark Goddess bullshit, you know?" I said. "Nothing without a cost. But this... this was personal. She cursed me from ever truly loving Haley. I couldn't kiss her again, couldn't be with her. Couldn't even tell her that I still loved her." My voice broke as I remembered Haley weeping on the floor in the castle bathroom, desperate for an explanation. Desperate for a reason to hate me.

"Saint..." Gem's eyes softened. "Haley *is* the Balance. And you and your brother are part of this prophecy, too. Melantha only helped Evander become Keradoc because she believed it was in her best interest. She already had Haley in her sights—she was playing the long game here. She wants the magick of Midnight—its very lifeblood—and she'll stop at nothing to get it."

"Few can tap into it," Oona said. "But in the entire history of the realm, *no one* has been able to truly unlock it. Unleash it."

"And you're saying Haley… she has this power?" I asked. "To bring this Balance and unlock it?"

"It's why Melantha wants her," Oona said. "She believes that if she can prevent the joining, she can somehow control Haley and channel the Balancing power for herself." Oona blew out a breath. "Saint, Haley is more powerful than you realize. More than she herself realizes. Her coming to Midnight was no accident. Her arrival here was written in the stars before she was even born. Melantha knew as much, so she hastened things along by sending her to Keradoc."

"Rather, Evander posing as Keradoc," Gem said.

"But why would she do that?" I asked. "If the Dark Goddess wanted to use Haley to unlock Midnight's potential—to steal all that magick for herself—why would she send Haley here, knowing Evander only intended to use her as a weapon against Darkwinter?"

"Melantha was obviously counting on the fact that Evander didn't know about the prophecy," Oona said. "She assumed he would either honor their deal and accept Haley as a trade for breaking the banishment —thereby allowing Melantha to return to Midnight, where she could reconnect with Haley and set her plan in motion—or he'd break the deal and and betray her. That's why she needed a backup plan."

"She was already working on a spell to break her banishment," Gem said. "If Haley had succeeded in retrieving Evander's blood, or if he'd honored the deal, she would've gotten here a lot sooner. But Melantha was coming back either way, Saint."

"But she hasn't manifested in physical form, has she?" I asked.

"She doesn't need to," Gem said. "She just needs enough of a presence to lead her armies to the city. Now, she's got Darkwinter under her thrall… God, it's the perfect storm. She'll take the realm itself by force, then take Haley and all that magick."

"And what happens to Haley then?" I asked. It didn't sound like something she'd survive.

Their silence was all the confirmation I needed.

Fury tore through me all over again. "Yeah, well, there's one thing that bitch wasn't counting on. When she killed me, the curse died right along with me."

Gem and Oona both gasped.

"Haley and I are *finally* free to love each other," I said. "That's assuming she still wants me. And after everything I put her through—after everything I just went through to get my ass back here—I will *not* let some psychotic Dark Goddess with a lady boner for magick get in the way of me finding my woman and proving to her just how the fuck much she means to me, prophecy or not. So if that bitch wants to come at me again? She can fucking *bring* it."

A dark smile slid across my old friend's face, her eyes alighting with new mischief. "And *there's* that crazy, half-cocked, bastard Saint of Midnight we all know and love."

"*Full*-cocked now, thankyouverymuch," I said, gesturing at the situation below the blanket, which now included all four limbs, hands, feet, and a fully functioning... yeah. That.

Gem laughed. "Like I said, Saint. I'll accept your gratitude in the form of a gourmet gift basket or a spa day. Your pick."

I held her gaze. Her smile.

"A prophecy, on top of it all?" I rolled my eyes. It was all so fucking crazy.

Which—in a place as fucked up as Midnight—only made it all the more believable.

The fire hissed and popped, and I blew out a deep breath, steadying myself. Preparing to move.

"Excuse you?" Gem said, pushing me right back down again.

"I need to get to her," I said. "Tell her about all this. Make a plan to kick some dark-goddess ass clear across the realm."

"You can barely lift your head, Saint. You're lucky to be alive."

"Lucky. Sure." I laughed again. Yeah, I'd been lucky in life before. Lucky for the time I'd had with Haley before I fucked everything up. Lucky I didn't die of an overdose. Lucky my brothers hadn't turned their backs on me completely.

But this time? *This* second chance? No. I made a *choice*. Clear-eyed and clear headed, maybe for the first time in my entire pathetic life.

"Luck has nothing to do with it, Gem. I *fought* for this honor. And I'd die a thousand times over just to do it again for the chance to protect Haley. To hold her in my arms and keep her safe." Pushing through the agonizing burn in every part of me, I finally—fucking *finally* hauled myself up to a sitting position. Then, with what little strength I had left for the moment, I grinned at my old friend, grateful I could even call her that again. "So are you going to sit there pining away after me and my newly minted cock, or are you going to help me?"

# 24

## JAX

*I* can smell your *fear*, woman." I loped through the dark forest, every one of my senses trained on the hunt. "If I catch you, I *will* bite you."

A rustle ahead. A dark shadow skittering out from behind the trees.

Adrenaline surged inside me, and I shot toward that darkness—the black shadow, the fear, the raw scent of desire rippling from her in hot, intense waves that set my cock on fire.

She was scared. Not because she feared me, but because I'd intentionally triggered her primal instincts, hoping like hell it would be enough to jump-start that innate part of her that wanted to survive. The part that would fucking fight to the bitter end for one more breath—even when her heart was in pieces.

Haley darted out from behind a spindly tree—little more than a flash of dark hair and the gleam of a dagger strapped to her thigh. She ran deeper into the woods, leaping over roots, charging past trees, pushing herself harder and faster…

*Not fast enough, angel.*

I caught up to her far too easily, so close on her heels I could taste her. The strawberry scent of her. The sharp, unmistakable flood of terror coursing through her bloodstream.

*Good girl.*

Sensing me right behind her, she let out a groan of frustration and kicked it up a notch, putting a few more feet between us.

I closed the distance in a heartbeat.

"Haley," I taunted, and my witch made the fatal mistake of looking back at me over her shoulder.

She lost her footing. Tripped on a root. And down, down, down she went…

I caught her and twisted, breaking her fall as we crashed to the ground. Before she could even take another breath, I rolled us, trapping her beneath me.

"*Shit,*" she hissed.

"You're mine now, little mouse. *Mine.*" Straddling her body, I pinned her wrists to the damp earth and leaned in close, licking a path from her neck to her ear, savoring the salty taste of sweat as I growled, "I told you what would happen if I caught you."

I bit her neck, making her yelp, then swirled my tongue over the sting.

"Jax," she breathed, arching her hips. Grinding.

"No, little mouse." I sent another pulse of fear through her mind—the barest brush of my demonic power. "You need to fight me, not fuck me. Fight the big, bad wolf before he *devours* you."

Another bite, harder this time, and Haley's fear spiked again, reacting to the power.

"Get. *Off!*" She shoved against my hold, but I had her at a serious disadvantage, her wrists bound in my grip, my knees clamped tight around her outer thighs, my cock… *Fuck.* I was *throbbing* for her.

"You'll have to do better than that, angel. I'm stronger than you. Faster. I can get inside your head and make you—"

"Stop."

"Stop?" I tightened my grip. Nipped her earlobe with my teeth. "You think that's gonna save you from the *real* bad guys?"

"Jax, I… I'm serious." Defeat flooded her voice, her body going limp beneath me. "Like you said—you're stronger and faster. A fucking fear demon. I can't beat you, so… game over."

"That's your exhaustion talking. Your pain. Push through it, Haley."

She shook her head.

Frustration welled inside me. "Whatever you're feeling, I need you to fight it. Fight *me.*"

"No. I can't. I'm too—"

"Damn it, Haley. *Fight!*"

Tears glazed her eyes as she continued shaking her head, then finally just turned away from me completely. Closed her eyes. Sighed.

Gave up.

"No," I said. "You can't quit. Not like this."

No response. Nothing but a tear sliding down her cheek and disappearing in the Midnight earth.

Not because I was pushing her, no. That tear was all for Saint.

And seeing her like this—feeling her defeat, her grief...

I thought of Saint, pushing me out of the way on that mountainside. Exploding.

I thought of all the soldiers the old Keradoc had marched through the streets.

I thought of the oath, blood before roses.

I thought of hell and the demons who'd nearly ruined me.

I thought of my sister, dead at fifteen, bleeding in my arms after a brutal attack because *she* couldn't fight, and the look of terror in my parents' eyes when they found us...

Something inside me snapped. Just fucking snapped.

A roar tore through my chest, and I got to my feet and hauled her up. Got right in her face. "I will *not* stand by and let someone else I love be taken from me because they couldn't defend themselves. So you fight when I tell you to fight. You fucking fight! *Fight!*"

Her eyes blazed—fear, frustration, sadness, rage, all of it colliding into a storm that lit her up from the inside, unleashing a primal scream that echoed through the dark woods. In a flash, she unsheathed her dagger, sliced her palm, and—

*Magick.* A burst of the brightest red light, and my dark little angel finally fucking hit me.

The magick slammed into me hard, sending me skittering backward and crashing into a tree. She charged in right after it, shoving her bloodied hand against my chest, her eyes wild.

She didn't say a word. Didn't make another sound after that scream finally faded, but oh, that red-hot fury, the tempest in her eyes... it was a fucking sight to behold.

She let it all out, my angel of darkness, hitting me with everything in her arsenal until blood poured from my nose and I swayed on my feet, dizzy from the loss of it, her magick sizzling through my veins.

And then, as quickly as it'd exploded out of her, the magick vanished.

The forest was black once more, lit only by the moons, silent but for our ragged breaths.

I turned my head and spit out a mouthful of blood. When I met her gaze again, the world had stopped spinning, and the heart I was so certain had stopped beating kicked me hard in the ribs.

"Feel better?" I asked softly, reaching for her face.

"Do you?" With a bitter laugh, she took a step backward and scrubbed her hand over her mouth, leaving a smear of blood shining on her lips, rubies in the darkness. "Let's not pretend for a *second* you did this for me, Jax."

"Haley, you're holding it all inside. It's killing you. It's making you weak and sloppy and—"

"No. No fucking way. You wanted me to beat the shit of you tonight—to make you fucking *bleed* because you think I blame you for Elian's death. You think I wish your places had been reversed. That you'd sacrificed yourself and sent *him* back to the cave with the bad news. But that's not how it went down, and now you're trying to convince yourself that if I just hit you hard enough, just *hurt* you badly enough, you won't have to feel so fucking guilty anymore."

Every one of her words hit their mark, igniting a fresh blaze inside me. I pushed off the tree and closed the distance between us. "And what about your guilt, angel? You think I don't see it in your eyes? You think I don't hear you crying in your sleep?"

"You don't know what the hell you're talking about."

"No? So you don't blame yourself for his death? All of a sudden you're done telling yourself he only came to Midnight because of you? That every shitty, terrible, fucked-up thing that ever happened to him was somehow your—"

"It is!" she roared. "It is my fucking fault! It's all of our faults! Don't you get it? Every one of his so-called failures, all the things we've been so quick to judge and condemn… They weren't failures at all, Jax. They were consequences. *Brutal* consequences for the choices he made to save everyone else. He died protecting *us*. Again and again. He fucked up, he made mistakes, he gutted us more often than not, but at the end of the day… Elian put us first, we put him last, and *that* is a shame I'll carry with me forever. And I'll never get to tell him that. That I *saw* him, Jax. Saw the man he truly was. Saw what he did for the people he loved." Her voice broke on the last word, and she fell to her knees as a deafening howl erupted from some deep, dark place inside her.

I dropped down in front of her and pulled her close, wrapping myself around her, my own tears falling into her hair as she screamed and shook and fucking wept.

Wept for the man she'd loved and lost, only to love and lose again.

Wept for the sisters she hadn't spoken with, no idea if they were even still alive.

Wept for the birthmother who'd tried to murder her.

Wept for all the terrible, soul-crushing things that'd tried to take her down. It was as if I could feel her entire history wash through her, crushing her, suffocating her, and all I could do was wrap her up tight and try like hell to hold all the pieces together.

Silence. It settled over us like a shroud—sudden, all-encompassing. I had no idea how much time had passed since we'd knelt on the cold earth, but then Haley sucked in a sharp breath, drew back, and met my gaze.

Her eyes fierce.

I opened my mouth to ask what she needed, whether she was okay, to simply breathe her fucking name, but before I could even get a word out, she was on me. Her hands tangled into my hair, mouth smothering mine with a kiss that damn near sucked out my soul.

Maybe it made me selfish. Maybe it made me greedy. But in that moment, I needed her more than I'd ever needed anything—my lost family, my demonic sight, my missing eye, even my own fucking heartbeat.

I fisted her hair and pulled back just long enough to meet her eyes again. "Angel. You sure this is—"

"Yes. Just... I need to feel it, Jax. Make me fucking *feel* it." She crashed into me again, a violent clash of tongues and teeth and breath. I released her and stripped off my shirt, then hers, before shoving my hands back into her hair. I kissed her hard and deep, kissed her mouth, her jaw, her pale throat. She moaned and arched her body against me, and I bit her neck, her shoulder, my teeth scoring her flesh until I tasted the coppery tang of her blood.

"Jax," she cried out, and that sweet, delicious fear inside her spiked hard, but I knew this pain was exactly what she wanted. Needed. The hurt that would remind her what it felt like to be utterly fucking *claimed*. A reminder that she could still feel anything at all—that both of us could— when all we wanted to do was sink to the bottom of that dark well and never come back up.

"More," she begged. "Don't you *dare* fucking stop."

The intensity in her voice had me out of my fucking mind with desire, with the same need I felt shuddering through her.

I stripped out of my pants, then pushed her back onto the ground.

"You *belong* to me, angel," I said, kissing my way from her mouth to her ear. "To all of us. Saint may not be with us, but you're as much his now as you ever were."

"I know," she breathed. "I know."

"Haley." I wrapped my fingers around her jaw and met her eyes again, my grip unrelenting. "I don't want you to forget that. *Ever.* Tell me you understand."

"I… I understand."

I held her gaze for a long beat, memorizing every fleck of gold in the green, the arch of her delicate brows.

Then, when I felt like my heart might actually explode with all the things I felt for her, I ripped her out of her boots and pants, baring the rest of her naked body to me in the silver moonlight.

Even bloodied and covered in dirt and sweat, she was fucking *stunning.*

"*Good,*" I said firmly. Then, lips brushing her ear, I whispered, "Because I need you to know that what I'm about to do to you now has nothing to do with punishing myself for his death and everything to do with reminding you *we're* still fucking alive. That all of this is still worth fighting for. And I'm not going to stop, angel. I'm not going to stop until we're both fucking *empty.*"

"I told you I don't want you to stop," she whispered. Moaned.

A cool breeze whispered through the woods, and Haley's eyelids fluttered closed, her dark pink nipples rising.

I lowered my mouth to one of those inviting peaks, licking. Teasing. Scraping my teeth across it until I finally sucked it into my mouth. She moaned again at the contact, and I shifted my attention to the other one, flicking it with my tongue, driving her wild.

But it wasn't enough. Not for my dark angel, writhing and panting in the moonlight.

Not for me, aching to sink inside her.

I shifted and knelt between her thighs, my gaze raking over every curve, my cock hard and eager.

"Take it," she whispered, parting her thighs in the dirt for me like an offering to the old gods. "Fucking *take* it, Jax."

Another growl vibrated through my chest. I gripped her knees, spreading her wider and dipping my head.

She slid her hands into my hair and sighed for me, sweet and tender, but there was *nothing* sweet about what I had in store for her.

I bit the sensitive skin of her inner thigh hard enough to draw more blood, then licked, dragging my tongue up to her hipbone, then back down, kissing her everywhere but that *one* spot—that one soft, beautiful spot that would make her shatter.

"Sinner," she breathed. "I can't... I can't handle the teasing. I need... all of you. Inside me. Please, I just need... oh, *fuck...*" she gasped, suddenly breathless as I shoved my tongue between her thighs, no fucking warning, no more teasing, no more slow torture. Only the pressure of my thumb circling her clit, the sudden arch of her back, the roll of her hips as I licked and sucked and stroked... *Fucking hell,* the sounds she made, the sudden scrape of fingernails dragged across my shoulders, the warm trickle of blood running from the wounds, the fucking *taste* of her as I devoured that hot, needy pussy with every stroke until—

"Oh god. I'm... Fuck... *Jax!*" she cried out into the night, thighs quaking as the orgasm gripped her tight. I didn't stop, though. Just fucked her harder, faster, sucking her clit between my lips as I slid two fingers inside and stroked, sending her body spiraling into another orgasm that had her panting and thrashing beneath me, cursing my name from this realm to the next.

I didn't even wait for her to come down. Didn't wait for her to catch her breath, didn't wait for that wild heartbeat to settle. She was still trembling when I gripped her hips, flipped her over onto her stomach, and fisted my cock.

"Up," I commanded, teasing her backside with the tip. "I want my angel on her hands and knees for me."

She obeyed immediately, rising up on all fours, arching her back to give me another exquisite view.

"Fuck, angel," I whispered. "You're killing me."

"Take it," she said again. "It's yours, Jax. I'm yours."

"*Mine.*" I ran a hand up her back and grabbed her hair, my other hand curling around her hip.

"Yes," she breathed, so fucking wet for me. So hot.

"*Haley...*" A deep, dark sigh, and suddenly my own words echoed on the breeze, drifting though my mind.

*We're still fucking alive...*

*This is still worth fighting for...*

*Fucking alive...*

*Worth fighting for...*

"Angel," I said again—a whisper, a plea—and then I fucking *buried* myself. So fucking deep. So fucking hard. Again and again, fucking her beneath a canopy of black branches and Midnight stars until she tightened around me and another blinding-hot orgasm rippled through her body and I spoke those words out loud, those promises, over and over and over until I came hot and fierce inside the woman I loved and I finally—fucking *finally*—believed those promises, too.

# 25

## JAX

*S*aint died for me, Haley," I said softly, all the earlier anger gone, burned off by the frenzy of our fight and what had come after. "It wasn't an accident. He sacrificed his life to save mine, and I need to say it out loud because I don't want to forget it. Ever."

She offered a sad smile, curling into my embrace. "You won't. I know you won't."

We'd just finished washing up in a freshwater stream—damn near freezing to death in the process—and now we sat before a small fire, eating the meager meat from a few tiny rabbits Hudson had hunted down. He'd joined us for a few bites, but took off again soon after, wanting to do another sweep of the area. We were still trying to make our way back to the wall, and with every hour that passed, the skies grew more ominous.

The magick of Midnight knew what was coming for it. *Who* was coming for it.

We had no idea what horrors awaited us in Amaranth City—no idea whether Evander had even made it that far or whether he was even still alive. But the city was a destination—a mission. A piece of lasagna, as Haley was so fond of saying. And heading there felt like a better option than sitting out in the open, waiting to get picked off by a squadron of Darkwinter witches on raven gryphons or Melantha's ghouls or any of the other fucked-up monsters headed our way.

"I blamed him for trying to separate me from Oona," I continued. "For being jealous. When all he truly wanted was a chance to get me out of this hellhole. To give his brothers a better life. He was honoring our vow, Haley. Blood before roses. *I'm* the one who fucking…" I trailed off, not even sure what I'd meant to say. Only that it hurt inside. It hurt inside to say all these things, to think about them.

"I blamed him for a lot of things, too." She rubbed her thumb over the scar on her wrist, a spike of old fear hitting her bloodstream. "I haven't even… I haven't even fully forgiven him for leaving Blackmoon Bay without telling me about his brother—about his plans. I understand it, but it doesn't make it any easier to accept. He just… he thought it would be easier on me. Elian… he sacrifices for the ones he loves, Jax. That's what he does, no matter what the cost. What the collateral damage. And he's caused a *lot* of damage in his life—made a shit ton of mistakes. But no matter what the consequences, leaving me to try to find his stolen brother wasn't one of those mistakes. And saving you—sacrificing himself for you—wasn't a mistake, either. It was a choice he made. And even though I want him back—God, more than *anything* I want him back—I can't say I'm not glad he made that choice, Jax. Because losing you would *destroy* me. I—"

I cut her off with a kiss, still not ready to hear her say those words to me. I knew she loved me—it was written in her eyes when she looked at me, written in her touch, in her every kiss. But I just… I needed to get her back to New Orleans, just like I'd told her the other night.

Then, I would let her say it. Then, I would fucking *welcome* it.

"I'm sorry I pushed you so hard tonight," I said.

She tilted her face up to me and grinned, a bit of mischief shining in her eyes. "Right. Because the whole 'don't you dare stop, make me feel it, take it' thing gave you the impression that I wanted it soft and gentle tonight?"

I nudged her in the ribs and laughed. "No, smartass. I'm talking about the sparring. I want you to be strong, but… I could've been less of a dick about it."

"Jax. First of all? I don't ever want to hear anything about 'less dick' when it comes to you. But…" She blew out a breath, the mischief dimming from her eyes. "Being with you… I know you want me to be strong. And I *am* strong—you've helped me see that more than anyone."

"You're the strongest person I know, Haley. I just need you to believe it. To trust yourself."

"I get that. It's just…" A sad smile. A soft shake of her head, the fall of her still-damp hair shimmering in the firelight. When she spoke again, her voice was barely audible over the crackling fire. "Sometimes I wish I didn't have to be strong at all—even just for a little while."

Fuck, my heart broke for her. All I wanted was to take her into my arms and promise her she'd never have to be strong all the time. That she could sit out a few rounds. That Hudson and I would defeat the enemies of Midnight and take care of her forever.

Hell, I'd even make an allowance for Evander, too, if that's what she wanted.

But that wasn't the world we lived in. Wasn't this fucking place. Wasn't our reality.

"When I was a kid," I said, inching a little closer to the fire. "A *human* kid, I mean. I had a family. Parents. A sister."

Her eyes widened, but she didn't say anything.

"Long story short… I wasn't exactly every parent's dream. Fell in with the wrong crowds, made a lot of shitty choices. Cost my family a lot of money bailing me out of one fuckup or another. Eventually, my parents decided it wasn't safe for me to live there—not with my sister in the house. She was only twelve at the time."

"How old were you?" she asked.

"Seventeen, and they booted my ass out. Wasn't all that unusual for someone my age to be on his own—this was a few centuries ago. But I wasn't ready for it. No job, no prospects. I fell in with an even worse crowd. Gambling, drugs, illegal underground fight rings, all the bullshit you'd imagine. But I missed my sister. She missed me, too. We used to pass letters back and forth through a friend of hers at school—the girl was the sister of one of the guys I ran with. She kept begging me to take her to the fights. Wanted to learn how to throw a punch. Keep the boys on their toes, she used to tease."

I laughed as I remembered how she'd beg me to take her, swearing she wouldn't tell our parents.

"Anyway, this shit went on for a few years. I had *zero* contact with my parents—they were so-called decent, God-fearing folk, and I was a fucking degenerate, so it's not like our paths ever crossed. I got worse. Did things… things I'm not proud of. But my sister never stopped writing. Never stopped trying to make arrangements to see me. I always told her no—I didn't want my parents finding out and kicking her out, too. And I *damn* sure didn't want any of the assholes I associated with to know about her. The guy who exchanged our letters was decent enough, kept his mouth shut about her—probably because he had a sister, too. But I couldn't risk it."

"I'm... sorry. That's... Shit, Jax. A sister." She squeezed my hand, and I knew she understood. Haley had been separated from her own sisters as a child, only reunited recently in Blackmoon Bay. She hadn't even been able to see them or talk to them again since then—not since she'd come to Midnight on Melantha's orders.

"One night," I said, "my sister decided to come looking for me. I had no idea. Just got back to whatever shithole place I'd been crashing at—drunk, of course, booze being my drug of choice back then. I stumbled in through the front door, beelining for the couch I slept on, but even in my stupor, I knew something was..." I swallowed and shook my head, the old memories flashing through my mind, tying me up in knots. "I smelled the blood before I saw it. Then I heard the... gasping."

"Oh my god." Haley touched her fingers to her lips, her eyes glazing with tears.

"Room was pitch black. I lit a lantern, followed the sounds. The smell. My sister was... She was on the floor in the back room, curled up in a pool of her own blood. Still alive, but barely. She'd been... brutalized, and they..." I couldn't even bring myself to say the words. To describe it with any more than that single word—*brutalized*. "No one else was in the house. I ran to her, gathered her up in my arms, but there was so much blood and I just..."

A tear slid from my eye, my chest splitting open at the memory, at this darkness I hadn't ever brought into the light.

Haley said nothing. Just held me. Just fucking held me while I got it all out.

"I watched the light leave her eyes, Haley. Held my baby sister in my arms and watched the light leave—a fucking fifteen-year-old girl. And suddenly, out of fucking nowhere, I was surrounded by people. I hadn't even heard anyone come in. Didn't even realize the sun had risen on a new day. Didn't think it had a fucking *right* to rise after something like that, you know? But my parents were just... there. Looming. Gasping. My mother fainted. My father just fell to his knees and took my sister's hand and... He kept saying her name, over and over and over. And all I could think to say to him was, 'you're getting her blood on your knees.'"

I closed my eye and shook my head, the old shame burning through my gut. The memory of how my parents had looked at me after—when the shock had worn off and my mother had come back to consciousness.

A thousand years could pass and I'd never forget the hatred in their eyes. The blame.

"A cop was there, too, and a neighbor who'd claimed he'd heard screaming the night before. But then things got... I don't know. Strange. My parents said they didn't want word getting out about it. They wanted my sister buried privately. Didn't want an investigation—wanted it all swept under the rug. And the cop, for whatever reason, was fine to let it go. Sounded like a family matter, he'd said. To this day, I can't wrap my head around it."

"That's... insane," she whispered.

"Yeah. There's a lot about that night that doesn't add up. Never did."

"Did they ever find out who... who did it? Was it someone you knew?"

"No, I... I never found out. Considering the people I associated with, the shit we were into, the assholes who'd lost money betting on or against me in the fights, the fucking dealers and users flowing in and out of that house every night... There were so many possibilities, but in the end..." I shook my head as if I *still*—after all this time—couldn't fucking believe it. "Haley, my parents... They thought it was me. They took one look at the blood and the dead child in my arms and... that was that. Case closed. No, I wasn't an upstanding citizen by any stretch, but my own parents... My fucking *parents* actually believed I murdered my sister. A sister that I... I fucking *adored* that girl, Haley."

I didn't bother trying to keep my voice steady now. It felt like cheating. Like dishonoring her memory to pretend that speaking these words out loud didn't fucking *destroy* me.

"And here's part two of the short version of events... My parents, in all their infinite wisdom, did what any god-fearing humans with an unsolvable human problem would do. They tracked down a crossroads demon and made a fucking deal. Yeah, we knew about the supernatural back then. Wasn't talked about much, but it was around. I'd tangled with a few demons in my day. Vampires, too—the underground fight clubs were always popular among the bloodsuckers. Fucking buffets, far as they were concerned. Anyway, this asshole promised them he could bring my sister back from the dead—a sister they'd already buried, refusing to let me attend the funeral. And in exchange, all they had to do was sacrifice one little soul to hell."

"Jax. Holy shit. I... holy *shit*." Haley's face was as pale as the moon now, her cheeks shining with tears, her hand trembling as she tightened her grip on mine. "That's... that's how you became..."

"Yep. My own parents sold me out. I'm a demon because they sent me to hell in exchange for my sister's life. But you know the real fucked-up part of this story? I would've gone willingly. If there was actually a chance my sister could've come back, I would've done it in a fucking heartbeat. But I knew it was too good to be true."

"The demon was full of shit," she said.

"Yeah, there was no way to bring her back. She was already gone. Already at peace. So they signed me away for *nothing*, and they left me there to rot. And the demons? Fuck, Haley. They kept me human for years, torturing me at every turn. Then they made me immortal and kicked it up a few notches. And do you know the reason my tormentors in hell were able to do what they did to me? To literally *terrify* me for centuries until I was utterly incapable of fear? Because deep down, I actually *believed* all the terrible things I'd seen in my parents' eyes that night. All the things they'd said to me after. I knew I didn't hurt my sister, but I truly believed it was my fault. I couldn't protect her, therefore, I deserved what my parents had done. What the demons had done. I honestly believed I would never feel love again simply because I didn't deserve it, and—"

"Jax, I don't even know what to—"

"No. *No*, angel, I'm not telling you this because I want you to find some comforting words for me here. They don't exist—not for this. I'm telling..." I let out a deep sigh and cupped her face, some of the bitterness ebbing as I gazed into her eyes. Felt the love. Felt her. "I'm telling you all this because... Look, you were right. You shouldn't have to be strong all the time. You should be able to let your guard down, to laugh, to run through the woods without worrying about some psychotic monster slashing you to ribbons or a dark goddess stealing your mojo and feeding you to her snakes. And someday? I fucking swear to you, angel..." New emotion rose in my chest, my voice thick with it. "I *swear* I'll make that happen for you, but only if you—"

"If I make it out of here alive?" She lowered her eyes and let out a shuddering breath.

I tilted her face back up, forcing her to meet my gaze. "I was going to say, if you'll *let* me." A faint smile curved my mouth. "You're not exactly the sit-out-the-fights, let-the-men-protect you kind of woman."

"No, I suppose I'm not."

My smile faded, emotion rising inside once more. "But until that day comes, Haley, I *can't* let you give in—not even when it's just us sparring in the woods. I pushed you because I *didn't* push her. Didn't teach her how to fight, didn't push back when my parents kept me from her, didn't protect her when she needed it most."

"But that wasn't your—"

"I know it wasn't my fault. I *know* that, logically. But that doesn't change the fact that all of those things are true. I *didn't* protect her, *didn't* fight for her, and she died. I went to hell, but I paid a price more dear than losing my humanity. I lost my *sister*. She died in my arms. I was covered in her blood when I literally felt her soul leaving her body, knowing there wasn't a damn thing I could do about it because I was too fucking late. Because I didn't protect her, didn't get to her in time, didn't try harder to see her so she didn't have to come looking for me. And that image, that memory…" I slid my hand into Haley's hair, gripping her tight, needing her to truly hear these words. "It haunts me more than you'll ever know, angel, but never more than it did the night Hudson brought you back from Beggar's Moat. He's the strongest one of all of us, yet even *he* couldn't stop you from getting hurt. When I saw you in that bed, bloodied and broken and… Fuck, Haley. You were barely breathing. Seeing you like that… I can't get that image out of my fucking head. And the thought of you *ever* coming close to death again… It kills me. And don't think for one *minute* I don't know who saved you that night. Saint healed you. He brought you back to us, and now he's fucking gone. Just *gone*. So I need to do everything in my power to give you the best shot I can at defending yourself, with or without backup, with our without magick, with or without a vampire healer. Even if it means you hate me for what I put you through. Even if it means you walk away from everything we have. I'd risk that—*all* of it—just to give you a fighting chance."

Tears gathered in her eyes again, then spilled, each one leaving a glittering trail down her skin. Trembling, barely keeping it together, I drew her close, kissing one cheek, then the other. Kissing away her tears until there wasn't a single one to be found.

"I know there aren't any words to make this right," she whispered, pulling back to take my face between her palms. "But there's one thing I need to say. One thing I need you to trust me on, okay?"

I wrapped my hands around her wrists and nodded.

"You were wrong, Jax. You *did* deserve to be loved. Your parents failed you. They were supposed to love their son, but they utterly failed. And you don't have to carry their failure for them—that's on them. And you know what? You *are* loved. So just in case you need a reminder of what it feels like when someone loves you—truly, without reservation, without conditions? Well…" She smiled up at me in the firelight, and *fuck*, how I melted for that smile. "It feels a little something like this."

Haley leaned forward and brushed her lips across mine, soft and perfect, and even though I kept telling myself I didn't want her to say it until we got back to New Orleans, I let those words—*her* words—fill me up inside. I let them soothe the ache, let them heal the broken pieces inside me, let them put me back together again in a way *no* one—not in all my long centuries of existence—had ever bothered to even try.

*You* are *loved…*

It whispered through me like a mantra, again and again, until another word finally filtered in, past the echo inside me, past the sounds of Haley's soft sighs as she kissed me breathless, past the hissing fire and the Midnight breeze.

One simple word.

A word with the power to stop our hearts.

"Sparrow?"

**26**

ELIAN

Every step on solid ground should've been pure agony. Should've sent me crumpling to my knees, begging for death.

I'd only been on my feet for a few moments. Gem was able to create a portal, using the last of her reserves to transport us out of that cave and into the clearing at the base of the mountains. Every second in that portal had been torture, as if some great beast had reached inside me and tried to wring the last drops of blood from my newly formed veins.

But I'd endured it, following the tug of Haley's magick, the steady heartbeat that pulsed through the bond that now connected us. The bridge she'd built to bring me back.

And now, as I finally stepped out of the portal and spotted her there, sitting with Jax beside a low fire, my pain vanished. My weakness vanished. Everything vanished but her beautiful face and the taste of her name on my lips.

"Sparrow?"

Her eyes went wide, and she and Jax rose to their feet.

With a surge of renewed energy—renewed fucking hope—I blurred. Crashed right into both of them, taking them down to the ground in a hug so fierce it stole the air from their lungs.

"Fucking *Saint*?" Jax was the first to get back to his feet, his face splitting into a grin, tears glazing his eye as he hauled me and Haley back up. "You stupid fae fucking asshole!" He grabbed me again, hauling me against his chest. "You fucking shithead. You fucking fae… *fuck*!"

680

"I missed you, too, brother."

"But… how… how did…?"

I thumbed at the two women behind me, just coming into view as they walked across the clearing. "They'll fill you in."

"But… Oona?" he asked. Suspicion darkened his voice. "*Gem?*"

"She's with us, Jax. And she'll tell you everything. Just… just go."

I turned around to face Haley, who still hadn't spoken a word. Tears streaked her face, her mouth opening and closing, her eyes bright in the moonlight.

My heart melted. Fucking melted.

Everything I felt for her rose inside me, and I took a deep breath, then a step. One more, and she was there. Close enough for me to look into those eyes and see into her fucking soul.

"Saint," Jax said again, but I didn't spare him another glance.

"Leave," I ordered, not taking my eyes off Haley. Never wanting to take my eyes off her again. *Fuck*, she was beautiful. So fucking beautiful I could hardly breathe.

A soft sigh, a rustle in the grass, and the three of them were gone, finally—fucking finally leaving me alone with her.

"Sparrow," I whispered again, cupping her face.

And in the long, silent, heart-stopping moments that followed, neither of us spoke, and neither of us bothered to hide the tears that spilled.

Haley's eyes searched mine in the moonlight. After an eternity, she said, "You came back to me."

My hands trembled as I held her face, my gaze sweeping down to her mouth, then back up, slowly cataloging every inch. The precise angle of her jaw. The soft shape of each wave in her hair as it curled over her shoulders. The exact shade of pink coloring her cheeks. The dark, feathery lashes I used to kiss while she slept beside me—a memory that had gotten me through some of the darkest nights of my life.

By the time I met her gaze again, I was panting, my chest thundering with the beat of a heart that'd been bound for far too long, finally set free.

Death had warned me my return wouldn't be easy. That I would suffer and bleed with every step, with every breath. And I felt it churning below the surface—the burn as my skin and muscles worked to fully heal. The deep ache as my bones worked to grow strong again.

But the pain was a distant hum in the background of this moment. This fucking gift.

"I will *always* come back to you, sparrow," I said.

Another tear slipped down her cheek. "But... how? How is this possible?"

"Haley, you saved me in Blackmoon Bay. You saved me in New Orleans. You saved me here in Midnight so many times I've lost count." I swallowed through the tightness in my throat. "And then you built me a bridge and saved me again. I literally stared into the face of Death, but... One look into your eyes had the power to bring me back home. To life. To you."

"Death," she whispered. "You... you saw her face? Her actual face?"

I nodded, though I still couldn't believe it; the longer I'd been away from that place, the hazier the memory became. But I said, "She was a young witch—and a white raven, too. She said she knew you. That she fought with you in Blackmoon Bay."

"Reva," she breathed, wonder glazing her eyes. Sadness, too. Longing. Relief. "Is she... How is she?"

"She's... intense." I laughed, thinking of the girl's feisty spirit—*that* was something I was pretty sure I'd never forget. "But she helped me... figure out a few things. Well, first she called me a fucking *smoothie*, but then we worked it out."

Haley laughed, the sound of it a balm on my heart. "I can't... I can't believe this is happening. Tell me you're here. Tell me you're really here."

"I'm here. I'm right fucking *here*." I grabbed her hand. Pressed it to my chest. "Do you feel it?"

"Your heartbeat?" She laughed again, tears still falling. "It's racing like the wild mares of night."

"Because it's alive, sparrow. *I'm* alive. And I need to say something to you. I need you to hear it and know it and never, ever doubt it." I threaded my fingers into her hair and stared into those emerald eyes. *Fuck*, how I wanted to eat her whole. To taste every inch of her. To claim her so fiercely, not even death would ever dare part us again.

But first, I needed to get out the words. Words that'd been trapped inside my heart, bound by that fucking curse for far too long.

"I was *with* you," I said, my voice quaking with the force of it. Of her. Of *us*. "All those three-thirty-threes, those stone-cold lonely mornings when all you could do was stare out the window and wonder what the fuck went wrong. I was right there with you for every single one—missing you, aching for you, dying inside for how badly I hurt you. I know you felt alone, and I know my telling you this doesn't make up for the pain I caused. But you *weren't* alone. I was with you. Every time. Because I love you, Haley Barnes. With all that I am, I *love* you. I have *always* loved you.

You're my heart, my family, my fucking *soul*. Melantha's curse died with me. And I promise you—here and now and forever—I will *never* walk away from you again. From us. You are *mine*, little sparrow. And I'm yours, in any way you'll have me. And anyone—*anyone*—who tries to come between that again will fucking *burn*."

By the time all the words were out, I was panting again. Breathless. My heart thudding so loudly in my ears, I was pretty sure there *was* a wild mare in my chest.

But I waited. I waited and waited. I'd told Haley how I felt, let it all out, and she… she was still here. *We* were still here. Warm and solid and real and unbreakable.

"Tell me what you're thinking," I whispered, afraid that anything louder would pop this dream like a bubble.

Her eyes drifted closed, that heartbreaking smile gracing her face. In a soft whisper, she said, "I'm thinking I'll die if you don't kiss me, Elian of Autumnshire."

"A kiss?" I teased, my lips so close to hers I could already taste them. I bit down gently, my fangs descending, scraping across her lower lip and making her shudder. "Is that all my sweet little sparrow wants?"

"Is it true?" she whispered. "The curse is really gone?"

"Yes."

"Then no, Elian. I don't want a kiss." She opened her eyes, fire blazing inside them. "I want all of it. All of *you*."

I slid a trembling hand into her hair, the other down the front of her pants, her skin hot and smooth. I brushed past her clit and dipped two fingers inside her, and when she gripped my arms and gasped in pleasure, I captured her breath in my mouth and held it, memorizing the taste of it. Of her.

A tremor rolled down my spine, the last of my fear giving way to pure, red-hot desire.

I pressed my lips to hers, savoring the silky touch as she slowly parted for me. My tongue swept into her mouth, tasting every curve as I slid my fingers deeper into that soft, wet heat.

"It's been *far* too long since I've had the taste of you in my mouth, sparrow," I whispered, drawing back and bringing my fingertips to my lips. Still half-kissing her, I licked my fingers, savoring the twin sensations of her sweet mouth and the familiar, sweet-and-salty taste of her desire.

It unleashed something wild inside me, that kiss. That taste. Something that'd been chained up like an animal, finally cut loose.

With a growl, I unzipped my pants and freed my cock, then spun her around and fisted her hair. Lifted it up to reveal her bare neck. Kissed a blazing hot path from one side to the other, teasing and licking, biting, damn near weeping to even be *allowed* to worship her like this again.

"Elian," she breathed, trembling with every kiss. "You feel... you feel amazing. Everything you do to me is..."

"I know. I remember how you like it," I said softly, releasing her hair and wrapping a hand around her throat. With my other hand, I fisted my cock, teasing her from behind as she lowered her pants. "I remember *exactly* how you like it."

*Fuck*, how many times had I played this movie in my mind, so desperate to hold on to the memory, to find a bit of warmth and comfort during too many dark and endless nights to count. I would always be grateful for those memories, but now that I had her in my arms again, in my mouth... *Fuck.* Those memories felt like cheap imitations, and they would never be good enough. *Nothing* would ever be good enough—only this. Real. Fucking real.

"Tell me you want this," I whispered into her hair. Begged. "Tell me you still want this."

"I want this. I want you, Elian. More than you could even—"

I didn't give her a chance to finish before I slid inside her from behind, claiming her in one hot, slick thrust that had us both crying out into the night.

Buried inside her, my mouth on the back of her neck, hand still wrapped around her throat, I went completely still.

Being with her like this again felt like coming home. Home to all that I'd turned my back on. Home to all the things that'd kept me going, even when I'd wanted to give up. Home to the woman I'd never stopped loving.

And home to myself.

But as much as I'd fantasized about this moment, as much as I wanted to give it to her hard and fast from behind in all the ways I knew she loved... Tonight, I needed to see her face. To see the light glowing in those beautiful green eyes as I made her come, all for me.

I pulled out and slowly turned her to face me again.

She smiled, soft and sweet. And the love I saw there, the intensity...

My chest tightened, my eyes blurring with tears.

"Sparrow," I breathed.

She nodded, understanding without words, without explanation.

We stripped out of our clothes, then laid down on the soft earth, Haley on her back as I kissed her shoulder, her collarbone, her breast, her stom-

ach, slow and decadent, nothing between us but skin and heat and love—
so much love it filled me up, smoothing all the jagged edges inside me.
The black holes. The rage and the fear, the mistakes, the emptiness. Death.

She tugged on my hair, gently urging me back to her mouth, to another
perfect kiss, and she parted her thighs for me and arched her back, and I
slid inside her once more, whispering her name with every breath like a
prayer of thanks to all the gods of every fucking realm I knew.

There was no awkwardness, no re-learning. Our bodies remembered.
*We* remembered. She felt at once familiar and new, the years that'd passed
changing her in small ways, the men she now loved changing her even
more.

I nearly laughed at the thought. All those years ago, making love to her
in Blackmoon Bay, I would've murdered anyone for even *suggesting* I
might one day share her with another man. But now she had two other
men. Three, if my suspicions about her growing feelings for Evander were
true. And though it defied all logic and reason, I wasn't jealous, wasn't
spiteful. They made her happy. Fulfilled her in different ways—ways that
made her eyes light up. Ways that gave her happiness and hope, and
through her, gave me happiness and hope, too.

I loved them for it. All of them.

Now, my sparrow in my arms once more, I took my time, savoring
every stroke, every fevered touch, every sweet moan as I moved inside
her, our bodies drawing close, our souls knitting back together, the old rifts
repaired. Strengthened. In this moment, there was no war, no enemies, no
fear. Only love. Only this perfection between us, my every kiss another
promise—one I made to her. One I made to myself.

Death had given me a second chance, and I wasn't about to squander
it. I had no illusions that it would be easy, but I was ready to fight for it. To
fight to stay off the Black—that old demon I no longer feared, though I
knew it still had sharp claws. I would fight to stay present, releasing my
old resentments, the old wounds. I would fight for my brothers and the
woman I loved. I would fight for Midnight.

And every day, I would earn that second chance I'd been given. I
would fucking *earn* it.

I shifted and moved deeper inside her, and Haley gasped, her body
tightening around me.

I pulled back and gazed into her face.

"Open your eyes, little sparrow," I whispered. "Let me see you shatter
for me."

She did as I asked, dark lashes fluttering as she opened her eyes and looked at me again, her lips parted, her heartbeat wild, blood and magick singing through her veins as the pure pleasure swept her up and spun out inside her, making her quiver, making her cry out my name into the darkness, again and again.

Still trembling, she lifted her head and kissed me, and that was it. Everything inside me exploded, fucking supernova, and I came with a shudder and a roar in a blinding rush that made my whole world shatter, then come back together, piece by piece, breath by breath, until we were a single soul once more. A single heartbeat.

When I finally broke our kiss to look into her eyes again, tears streaked her face.

"Elian," she whispered, her palm warm against my cheek, and that was the last of it. No more words but the ones written in her eyes.

"I know, little sparrow." I turned and pressed a kiss to the center of her palm, my chest tight, my heart full. "I know."

I rolled onto my hip and shifted her so her back was against my chest, and I held her close and breathed in the scent of her skin. Her hair.

Moments later, with a deep, satisfied sigh, my little sparrow began to sing. Her chest vibrated with the sound of it, soft at first, then steadily growing until it echoed out across the clearing. Echoed through my heart.

And there, in those sweet, off-key notes, I found my salvation.

# 27

## EVANDER

*live*? What the fuck do you mean, he's alive? Move!"

Ignoring the halfhearted protests of Gem, the demon, my lieutenant commander, and the gargoyle—all of whom attempted to keep me away from the clearing where my dead brother had apparently manifested hours earlier—I barreled through the trees and headed straight for him.

Straight for them.

My witch… and my brother.

Elian.

Back from the dead, they said. Alive.

I'd been tracking Haley and the others for half the night, having only just secured the allegiance of a scant few of Midnight's most brutal, bloodthirsty rebels. Most of the others I'd found hadn't even granted me an audience. Many had already fallen prey to the enhanced Devil's Dream we'd pushed out through the ranks, the addiction spreading like wildfire, decimating entire camps in a matter of nights. Others had tried to kill me on sight, their hatred and bloodlust staunched only by my own cunning and quickness with a blade.

The few rebels who'd finally agreed to fight with us were a motley crew of barbaric demons and imps, dark fae mercenaries, and vampires from the human realm who didn't much care *where* their next meal came from so long as it screamed while they ate it. Their fealty had come at a cost—not just the revelation of some of my longest held secrets, as Haley had implored me to share, but the promise of full pardons for all past crimes, more money than I'd ever be able to produce, and precious real estate in the city... assuming we could save it.

Amaranth was already under Darkwinter attack, their forces moving in from the north, their weather witches controlling not just the Fog of a Thousand Knives but other phenomena as well—earthquakes. Floods. Just as Haley had predicted, most of Keradoc's generals had turned traitor the moment the enemies closed in, joining forces with the Darkwinter troops who promised to spare their lives.

Fools. Fucking fools.

Now, just about five miles south of the wall, I'd finally found her again. Them.

And learned that my brother was alive.

I stalked across that clearing, stopping only when I saw them lying in the grass, naked and entwined beside the fire.

My witch. My brother. Their bodies gleaming.

Whole. Alive.

Inside the darkest depths of my heart, twin flames burned bright.

One—relief and awe at the presence of my once-dead twin.

Two—a raging, unfathomable jealousy that he and Haley had already... reunited.

*Liar.* I closed my eyes, the word sliding through my mind. *Fucking liar.*

For when I searched my heart, I knew it wasn't their reunion that had set me ablaze. Haley was happy—I wanted that for her. Truly. I wasn't jealous of her love for Elian.

I was jealous, I finally realized, of her relationship with him. That she'd known him for so many years. That she had actual memories of him, a shared history that'd bound them, that'd allowed him to turn his back on death and follow her love home.

And I had... nothing. No memory of my twin brother, no matter how badly I wished for it now. No shared history, no matter how desperately I despised the yawning ache of that blank space in my mind. My old life.

"But... how?" I blurted out suddenly, startling them both.

They turned and gazed up at me in the moonlight. Haley smiled. And Elian... he smiled too.

Together, they rose, neither covering their naked bodies.

It was Haley, not my brother, who responded first.

"He heard me that night, Evander," she said softly, her smile as bright as the first moon. "He *felt* me. And when he sensed Melantha's hold on my mind, he..." She glanced over her shoulder, where my brother was standing at her side. "He broke it. And then, somehow, he fought his way through hell to come back to us."

"Not hell, exactly," Elian finally said, reaching for her hand. "I managed to avoid that particular destiny for now. But…" His silver eyes clouded, the usual smirk settling into a grim line. "It wasn't an easy journey. I'm still not entirely… healed."

I couldn't help my scoff, that irrational jealous ire flaring to life inside, looking for some target to hit—*any* target.

"Apparently you're healed enough," I said, raking my gaze down his naked form. Then, with no trace of emotion, "Get dressed and find some weapons. We march for the wall at—"

"He's still in pain, Evander," Haley said, her touch on my chest making my breath catch.

Glaring at his nude form once more, I said coolly, "If he's well enough to *fuck*, he's well enough to fight."

A growl. A shimmer in the air. A blur in my peripheral vision.

I was flat on my back and blinking up at the stars before I could even draw my next breath.

The vampire-fae had knocked me on my ass, and now he loomed over me, knee pressed to my chest.

"You're right, brother," he sneered. "I *am* well enough to fight. Are you?"

I shoved him off and tried to get to my feet, but another blur slammed me flat on my back once more—*this* blur accompanied by the bright red light and the smokey taste of magick I recognized as Haley's.

My only comfort was the fact that my brother had suffered the same fate.

"Really?" Haley stood over us, hands on her naked hips, green eyes rolling to the sky. "Look, I know you two are still coming to terms with this whole twin-brothers-reunited-after-one-was-kidnapped-and-the-other-one-*died* thing, but… guys. Seriously? You need to work it out."

"Because we're brothers?" I grumbled, getting to my feet and dusting the dirt from my backside. My brother did the same, finally locating his pants.

"Because you're family," she said. "*My* family. Look, I'm not forcing you into this just because you're blood relatives. I'm doing it because you're brothers in an even deeper sense. You care for each other—it's obvious. And we're all in this war together now. Fighting amongst ourselves is only going to make us easier targets for the real enemies."

"I *will* fight by his side for you, Haley," I said. "For this realm. That's not even a question."

"You know I'm with you on that, too, sparrow." Elian handed her some clothes.

With another roll of her eyes, she quickly dressed, then said, "What about fighting for each other? For our family?"

Neither of us responded to that.

Silence, for now, was better than coming to blows.

After a long, tense beat, Haley blew out a breath and said to me, "Tell me about the rebels. Were you able to scrounge up any additional fighters?"

I gave her the update—the rebels I'd secured, the ones I'd fought off. The ones the Devil's Dream had ruined beyond help.

At the mention of the drugs, Elian shook his head, his silver eyes bright with new anger.

I drew in a sharp breath at the sight. It was as if a veil had fallen away, and now I was seeing him for the very first time.

Guilt bubbled up inside.

My brother—my twin brother—was addicted to the very drug I'd forced him to work on, night after night. Forced him to deliver.

I couldn't hold his gaze. When I spoke again, my voice was tight. "Elian, I... I'm sorry."

"For what, exactly?" he snapped. "Shooting me full of hawthorn the night of the feast? Taking me prisoner and throwing me in the dungeon? Lying about your identity so the rest of us would continue to fear you and do your bidding?" He stepped closer, his eyes glowing even brighter, his entire body vibrating with rage.

I could nearly taste it.

Clearing my throat, I said, "I was... speaking of the Devil's Dream."

Elian scoffed. "Oh, don't give me that pitying tone, *brother*. I *invented* Dream. I earned every bit of torture those little pills put me through."

"No, I... I should've been more... understanding. About your situation. Haley tried to tell me and I..." I trailed off. This wasn't something I could fix with words, no matter how earnest.

"Did it work?" he asked. "Did you weaken any *actual* enemy forces, or just the ones who might've joined us?"

"Dream is a poison, like any other," I said. "Once it starts to spread, it's very difficult to contain."

"Quite an astute observation, Evander. Keradoc teach you that skill?"

Disgust rolled through my gut at the mention of the warlord's name, igniting a new fury inside me… But it faded quickly.

For all that I didn't remember him, Elian was still my brother. Not just by blood, but by the simple fact that Haley loved him. That he'd come back for her. That he was still willing to fight.

"I don't wish to battle with you, Elian," I said. "Haley's right. Our fight lies elsewhere."

"I suppose when you view the world through the eyes of a warlord," he said, "everything's a battle, isn't it?"

"Elian," Haley warned, her gaze darting between us. Then, with a sad sigh, "Guys, I don't… Look. I know you've got some things to… unpack. No one is saying you have to do that right now. I'm just asking you to drop the defensiveness and try to… I don't know. See each other the way I see you."

"And how do you see us, sparrow?" Elian asked.

She looked to me, her eyes brightening, her smile warm. It disarmed me, that smile. Always.

"Evander," she said, the sound of my name like the sweetest music, "is so much more than a warlord, Elian. He's decent and kind, he fights for what he believes in, and… and he's someone worth knowing as a man, despite the fact that you lost the chance to know him growing up."

I returned her smile, dim compared to the light gracing her face, but genuine nevertheless.

"And Evander, you need to know… Your brother *never* stopped looking for you. He walked away from our life in Blackmoon Bay—from love—just for a *chance* to find you. A chance—that thing you told me most people never get in this life. That thing we're supposedly fighting for."

I looked at my brother, waiting for him to deny it. To set the record straight. But his gaze was fierce. Unwavering.

"And as for the rest of this… situation," Haley continued, and I knew at once she was talking about our relationships. Our feelings for her. The tangled, thorny things I now found myself wanting. "Elian, I never stopped loving you. Not for a second. And I know you never stopped loving me, either. Now that I've finally got you back, I'm not letting you go again. And Evander?" She turned to me once more, lighting me up inside, obliterating the last of my earlier jealousy. "You… I'm not even sure what to say. You snuck up on me. My feelings for you are… complicated and surprising, but real. I can't deny them. I *won't* deny them. All I can do is give you the same choice I gave Jax and Hudson when I told them I wanted us all to be together. But that choice is about us—our relationship. It's not about the two of you working it out. That is *not* a choice."

Once again, I felt myself smiling at her. Completely undone by her. "That your heart has such a boundless capacity to love is a wonder and a gift, Haley Barnes. I would no more seek to dampen it than I would seek to dampen your magick."

"Well, other than the time you put an *actual* dampener cuff on her," Elian quipped, but there was no real anger there. The ghost of a grin twitched his lips, and Haley glared at him with the blazing heat of a thousand starshowers.

"What part of *working it out* don't you understand?" she asked him.

I tried but failed not to smirk.

Then, whirling on me, "And *you*? Wipe that look off your face before I blast your ass into the dirt again."

I raised my hands in surrender.

Elian sighed. "So you two," he said. "You're a thing, then."

"We've… gotten closer," I admitted.

He narrowed his silver eyes. "Define closer."

"Oh, for fuck's sake." Haley laughed. "Let's save the dick-measuring for *after* the war. We can make a game out of it. Family date night!"

Elian's eyes blazed, then dimmed, acceptance settling over him. "You know there's nothing I wouldn't do for you, sparrow. That *has* not and *will* not change. So if you have…" He swallowed hard and sighed again. "If you have romantic feelings for my brother, then I accept that."

"Accept, but not embrace?" she asked.

To his credit, he didn't scoff. Just met my gaze, assessing.

"We just… need time," he finally said. "To get used to your… feelings for us."

I nodded, grateful he was willing to leave it at that.

"And what about your feelings for each other?" she asked.

"Time," I echoed, and Elian—for once—agreed with me.

---

While the gargoyle and demon did another perimeter check, the rest of us sat around the fire, and I finished updating the group about the intel I'd gathered, the fighters I'd arranged to rendezvous with at the wall later. Oona and Gem shared what they'd learned, and we began to cobble together some sort of plan.

Get to the wall. Find the other fighters. Defend our city.

It was bare-bones at best. Hopeless at worst, but…

*A chance*, I reminded myself. *Just a chance. That's all we need.*

Haley smiled at me across the dark space, her eyes golden in the fire-light, filling me with a sliver of hope.

A hope that my brother shattered with a single word.

*"Fuck."*

We shot to our feet just as the demon came into view, running toward us across the clearing. By the time he reached us, he was panting and covered in filth. The gargoyle landed beside him, his face grim.

"A rift," the demon managed. "Melantha made some kind of rift. The Army… they're here."

He'd barely gotten the words out when I felt the telltale rumble in the ground. I met Haley's eyes again, the ripple of dark magick hitting us both.

I had just enough time to reach for her.

*"Fight,"* I commanded, gripping her jaw. "You fucking fight with every bit of magick you possess, every bit you can take from this realm, and don't you go down for *anything.*"

I kissed her. And then I was off, sword drawn, charging straight into the mayhem with the others.

Straight into our end.

<h1 style="text-align:center">28</h1>

<h2 style="text-align:center">HALEY</h2>

*A* wave of nightmares broke upon the hill, the skeleton army I'd seen so many times in my visions finally here. Black blood oozed from their mouths, clung to the white bone, glistened in the moonlight.

And the sounds—the endless droning of their empty moans, the clattering of bone against rock as they moved across the land…

Nausea churned in my gut. I wondered how many fae they'd already consumed. How many had risen again.

Overhead, a dark shadow blotted out the moons, and I glanced up to see it—that giant, rotting raven gryphon. And though I couldn't see its rider—still formless, still unable to physically manifest in the realm she so desperately wanted to claim—I felt her.

Her voice echoed through my skull.

*Here is where your friends perish, Daughter of Darkwinter. Here is where you bow to me.*

"Attack!" Evander roared. "Attack!"

And my men—along with Oona and Gem—followed the order. Swords flashed, striking bone. Shattering it. Some of the ghouls dropped. Others… others kept right on coming for us, seemingly unaware of their missing limbs, missing teeth, bashed-in skulls…

A bright flash of pale blue magick, and I turned to see Gem hitting the front lines with a blast that took out a few dozen at once. She couldn't hold on to her magick, though—it was as if it had grown unstable, just like the magick of Midnight. I could practically feel it—feel it thrashing around beneath the ground, upended by the chaos that had broken upon the realm.

Gem's magick finally fizzled out, and she followed up with her crossbow, shooting bolt after bolt through their skulls.

I lost sight of Elian. Of Evander. Of Jax. I had no idea if Jax's powers would even work in a fight like this—if the undead had fears he could manipulate.

Nearly impossible to kill in his warrior form, Hudson sailed out across that sea of death, grabbing skeletal soldiers and smashing them to bits. Dropping them, only to do it all over again. Again and again.

Chaos. There was only chaos. Chaos on the battlefield. Chaos in the magick as it shuddered beneath this dark invasion, this unnatural blight.

Chaos in my heart.

I dropped to my knees. Sliced my palm, letting the blood trickle over my ring. Magick whispered across my skin, tingled down my spine. Time slowed to a crawl, and I closed my eyes, trying to breathe. To focus.

My first love had just returned to me. Defied death, fought his way back to a body that hadn't even existed, fought through insurmountable pain... all for a chance—just one chance to tell me he loved me. To tell me our curse had been obliterated.

To stand by our side as we faced our enemies.

He'd also told me about the Darkwinter prophecy. The Balance. The seeds that'd taken root in my heart from my very first steps in Midnight and had since bloomed into something so vast, so all-encompassing it didn't even occur to me to question his story. The lore. The legacy. As soon as the words were out, I just knew. Knew they were true.

This was my destiny.

And the guys—Elian, Hudson, Jax, Evander—they were a part of that destiny, too. Part of my magick. My courage. My capacity for love and forgiveness.

We were a family in the truest sense of the word, and my heart had never been more full. More content.

Something else tingled down my spine then. Not magick. But fury. Cold, hard fury.

How *dare* the Dark Goddess try to take this from us. Try to shatter this bond. How *dare* her minions try to hurt the people I loved.

"Come see what happens when you piss off a Scorpio blood witch, you *assholes*." I slammed my bleeding palm into the dirt. A flash of red exploded around me as the magick of Midnight—the magick of my home

—surged up my arm, straight into my heart. It filled me. Fortified me. Set me on fire with a single purpose:

Take back what the goddess had so wrongly claimed as hers.

The ground trembled around me, and all at once, hundreds—thousands of black roses burst from the mud, blooming to brilliant life in the moonlight. The magick surged again, righting itself as if it was finally shaking free of the chaos, finally finding its purpose as I had found mine.

I closed my eyes, and images flashed unbidden through my mind—the vision Evander had shown me on the balcony during my first weeks here. Before I'd known he wasn't really Keradoc. Before I'd come to care for him —to love him.

*Flame and shadow bending at my command, breaking the laws of physics and magick both.*

*Power surging through my veins, crackling at my fingertips.*

*Death rising, a thousand raw-boned corpses clawing out of the black earth and bowing at my feet…*

As the vision played out in my mind, his words from that night echoed as well.

*It's not diamonds or oil we're fighting for. It's magick. A magick that runs through every rock, every tree, every lake of blood in this realm. The magick of Midnight is a precious thing, Miss Barnes. Far more valuable than our cities and walls…*

I'd admitted to him that I'd felt it, that magick. Like a hum in the air. A vibration in the ground. A subtle glow upon everything I looked at.

He'd insisted it was because that very magick was part of me—my Darkwinter legacy. The longer I remained in Midnight, he'd said, the more connected to it I would become. And even though I'd insisted—*insisted* I wasn't dark, he didn't back down.

*What do you find when you search deep in your soul, past all the things you believe make someone a good person, past the things you believe keep you safe from the dark? When you sleep, little thief, where do the nightmares take you?*

He'd said those words, soft and seductive, and then he'd touched me— traced a soft line across my forehead—and unleashed that vision. And rather than being terrified, I was excited. Filled with sheer wonder at the possibility. Hoping that one day, all of those things he'd shown me would indeed come to fruition.

I felt it then. The blood and magick of Midnight, of my ancestors— Darkwinter and Silversbane both. The blood and magick of the prophecy.

*My* blood and magick.

Now, when I opened my eyes and raised my arms, power crackling between my hands as if I'd reached into the skies and plucked the lightning from a storm, that same sense of wonder filled my heart.

And all of those things, those visions, came to life before my eyes.

"Fall back!" I shouted into the night. "Fall back!"

Hudson was the first to hear me—to sense the urgency through our bond. He swept down and grabbed Elian and Evander from the melee. A flash of blue hair, then purple, and Oona and Gem were clear as well. Jax came last, a final swing of his sword taking down another skeleton before he bolted out.

Power surged again, heat and starlight, building and building inside me until I could no longer contain it, and then—

A wall of blood-red fire exploded across the front line, rising into the dark night, consuming the bones as the bones had once consumed the living. The dead howled, an unholy wailing that made the very trees quake, but I didn't relent. Not for a fucking second. I lifted my hands higher, and the flames followed my command, surging ahead and chewing through Melantha's forces, destroying, devouring, turning everything in their path to ash.

Overhead, the raven gryphon shrieked, and an explosion of the darkest light burst through the sky, like a star going supernova, a black hole that swallowed the beast and the goddess both.

I lowered my arms. The flames vanished.

The men returned to my side, speechless, breathless. Awed.

For across that field of black, barren death, the Army of the Dead rose from the ashes, the bones reforming.

My friends gripped their swords and crossbows, ready to charge in once more.

But I merely stepped forward. Raised a single hand.

And tens of thousands of skeletons bowed before me.

"Are they… surrendering?" Jax whispered.

"Not surrendering," came the reply. Not mine. Not any of ours.

We turned toward the sound of that ancient voice, watching as hundreds of pale faces emerged from the trees behind us.

"The Army of the Dead is swearing fealty to its new commander," the fae general who dwelled beneath the Razorbacks said. "As are *we,* Daughter of Darkwinter. Deathbringer. She For Whom the Bones Bow."

Evander leaned in close, lips brushing my ear with a whisper meant only for me. "It appears I was right all along, little thief. You really *are* the secret weapon to turn our fortunes in this war."

Despite the insanity of the night, I laughed. "And to think you had me wasting all that time on ancestor spells."

"I should've known you'd only disregard my orders and do things your own way."

I brought my mouth to his ear, making him shiver. "*Always.*"

Turning back to the general, Evander cleared his throat and said, "Does this mean you'll fight with us?"

"We will fight the Darkwinter enemies for the deathbringer," he said. "It is written."

"*Written?*" Evander tensed beside me, clearly gearing up for a fight, but I put a hand on his arm and nodded. I didn't care what reason the old fae had for joining us. I only cared that they were here. That with them and the Army of the Dead, we actually had a fighting chance.

"Thank you," I said.

The general turned to his people. Raised his obsidian sword, the blade catching the moonlight.

"She For Whom the Bones Bow!" he shouted again, and the gathering fae echoed the call, a dark chant on the breeze as they all dropped to one knee. Then, as one, they raised their obsidian swords and let loose a fierce cry into the night. "To war!"

# 29

## HUDSON

*T*he sky over Amaranth City was as black as death, every last star blotted out by smoke and ash and the dozens of raven gryphons the Darkwinter witches now controlled.

Every few seconds, another flash of color exploded—magick, lightning —illuminating the burning city below.

Standing beside me at the top of the White Cliffs of Oshen, Haley said, "You'll need to bring me in close, Gargs. *Very* close."

"How close we talkin'?"

"I need to be *in* that moat."

"No."

She laughed. "Hudson. When I told you I'd have to spill my blood in the moat, I meant that literally. In the moat. There's no way around it."

I blew out a breath and tucked her in close, doing a partial shift from my human form so I could fold a wing around her body. "How the fuck did I already know you were gonna say that?"

"Because deep inside that strong, overprotective heart of yours, you know I'm always right, and you know I always get my way."

"Yeah." A low chuckle rumbled outta me, despite the fucked-up shit we were jumping into. "Pretty sure I heard that about you, babygirl."

She nuzzled in close, and together we continued to watch the wall, waiting for the signal.

Waiting for Evander to lead the others across the drawbridge and into Amaranth City.

My insides were all tied up like a damn pretzel. I hated that we'd split up, but they needed to get inside and start beating back the Darkwinter forces, and I needed to get Haley into that moat.

To round up the very last fighters Midnight could offer us.

The fucking ghouls.

After the feral fae had sworn their tenuous allegiance to our girl, Haley had ordered them to follow Evander's command. Saint, Jax, Oona, and Gem were under his command now, too.

And the Army of the Dead?

I shook my head, still not believing the damn sight.

They were already crossing the bridge over the moat. Tens of thousands of 'em, all marching on Haley's orders. Bound to her magick. Obeying her command through whatever dark Midnight mojo she'd harnessed.

Couldn't help but smile at that, my heart nearly bursting with pride.

*Spooky little monster girl.*

Now, we watched as the last of her skeletons finally cleared the wall. Watched as the city itself seem to ripple in the wake of their dark, all-encompassing wave.

Then came the screams.

They echoed out from the city, floating across the black sands between the wall and the cliffs, rising up to surround us both. If I closed my eyes, I could almost pretend it was an outdoor concert—cheering and whistling. Music. Life.

But this was no concert. No life. This was war. And those screams? They were merely the final, desperate, bloodcurdling cries of the enemy that had invaded our home.

So? Fuck 'em. Every last one.

"There," Haley said, pointing. "They're going in."

I peered out across the darkness, watching as Evander and his charges began crossing the drawbridge, following the Army of the Dead's path straight into the city. The feral fae went first, led by Oona and Jax. Gem was somewhere in the middle. Then came Evander's rebels.

Evander and Elian brought up the rear.

"Come on," Haley muttered, bouncing on her toes as she watched them disappear behind the wall, a few at a time. "Come on, come on, come on."

I tore my gaze away from our fighters and peered down at my girl, drinking in the sight of her. The dark hair, pulled back into a tight braid. The fighting leathers she'd pilfered from whatever the feral fae had left behind. The weapons—daggers and stakes, mostly. Her weapons of choice.

She was fierce, my little monster girl.

And she'd have to be. Tonight, more than ever.

My gut rolled again, and I bit back a dark curse.

We'd all seen Melantha vanish after her Army basically told her to get fucked. But according to Haley, Melantha wasn't actually gone. The Dark Goddess, she'd told us, would be waiting for her in Amaranth City. Waiting to exact her revenge and claim Haley's magick… and her life.

I had no idea how my girl knew all that, but I trusted her.

Just didn't like it. Not one fuckin' bit. And if she thought I'd let her march into that bitch's trap alone like some kind of sheep led to the slaughter—

"Now, Hudson," she said, scattering my dark thoughts. "They're in. We need to move."

I scanned the black obsidian sands once more. Sure enough, the bridge was empty. "You ready?"

She nodded, and I gathered her up in my arms. Then, just before I shifted into my full warrior form, I kissed her. Fucking breathless.

"For luck?" she asked, beaming up at me in a daze.

"Nah, babygirl. We don't need luck." I ran my nose down the length of hers, then kissed the tip. "We got *you*."

With that, I took off, leaping over the cliff and shifting into my warrior form, sailing us right down to that moat.

If I thought the sounds of Darkwinter's screams were loud before, this was… this was fucking deafening.

"Let's be quick," I said, then dropped us both down to the bottom, keeping a close watch as she knelt in the dirt.

She unsheathed a dagger and sliced her palm, the spell already on her lips as the blood welled, then spilled.

*Blood of hell, blood of night*
*I call on the darkness to show us the light*
*May evil and malice and violence intended*
*Return to its hosts uprooted, upended*
*Magick of Midnight, hear now my plea*
*Grant me this power, and so mote it be*

The ground trembled beneath us, and Haley got to her feet. "Up," she said. "Now."

I grabbed her and flew us back up to the ground level, landing on the south side of the moat just as those fucking ghouls exploded out of the ground like a goddamn oil strike.

Haley lifted her arms, magick red flames glowing in each hand, and I watched with my damn jaw on the ground as the ghouls—for the first time in their miserable eternal existence—climbed the north side of the moat.

They looked like them Army of the Dead skeletons at first, but then they started solidifying, rotten skin clinging to their bones, the stench of them making my eyes water as they kept coming and coming and coming, flowing out of the ground like cockroaches, like water, obeying the silent command of her magick.

She lifted her palms higher, and once more, the ghouls began to climb.

Not the moat.

Fucking Vanderham's Wall.

I took a breath to say something—anything—but before I could even get a word out, shadows eclipsed us and I felt the ground quake behind me and I knew... I fucking *knew* it wasn't from the ghouls.

I turned and shoved Haley behind me. Blinked as the full bullshit spectrum came into view.

My old fucking pal, Garrison. Two dozen Stone City meatheads I didn't know. And there, stepping out from behind the line of gargoyles who didn't deserve to call themselves warriors, Mad fuckin' Marco.

*So the whore* is *still alive,* he said through the gargoyle connection, that gap-toothed grin glinting in the moonlight. *Excellent. Now I'll get a chance to hear beg before I kill her.*

A fierce growl ripped through my chest, but before I'd even settled on whose wings I'd be tearing off first, a blast of red exploded into the night, illuminating every one of their stone-gray faces and sending them stumbling backward.

Haley stepped out from behind me and sighed. "I warned you, Gargs. Told you if I ever saw him again, I'd kill him."

I cocked my head smiled. Fucking woman would never stop surprising me.

"With a dagger, magick, or your bare hands," I said. "Ain't that right?"

"Aw, you remembered!"

"Sure as hell did. Thing is, babygirl, they ain't dead. Just stunned."

She shrugged. "Details."

Haley snapped her fingers, calling another red flame to life in each palm. Behind us, another wave of ghouls scurried out—this time, on our side of the moat.

Flowing around us like a river over rocks, they headed right for the shell-shocked gargoyles still bumbling around like dickless shitheads after Haley's blast.

I laughed. Couldn't be helped. This was gonna be fuckin' awesome.

One more smile for my woman. My mate. And then, together, we charged.

She headed for one of the nameless assholes in the middle. Me? I went right for Marco.

I grabbed him, slammed him into the ground. The impact must've jarred something loose in his head, because the bastard finally blinked up at me, awareness rushing back into his dead eyes.

He growled at me, then shoved me off, rolling on top of me in the black dirt. All around me, red magick surged and sizzled, Haley ordering her ghouls to feed. To feast.

And oh, how I welcomed *those* screams. A beautiful fucking symphony —the perfect accompaniment to the taste of their blood on the air as the ghouls devoured them. Wings, arms, torsos, heads.

But I wouldn't let them anywhere near Marco. He was mine.

"This ends *tonight*," I ground out, slamming a fist into his face, rolling us once more and pinning him beneath me.

He hit me with a jab to the throat, momentarily stealing my breath, but I managed to hold on. Got in another punch to the face, blood gushing from his nose. One more, and I finally knocked out those fucking teeth.

"Better," I said. "But you're still an ugly motherfucker."

He let out a roar, and before I could get in another hit, one of his asshole wingmen leaped on my back, an arm locking around my neck.

Fucking Garrison.

He wrestled me off Marco, forcing me onto my feet. Marco shot up in front of me, smashing my ribs with a battery of jabs to the chest, each blow more punishing than the last.

I twisted out of Garrison's death grip long enough to smash the back of my head into his mouth. He stumbled back a step, and I whirled on him, grabbed his head, and slammed my knee into his face.

T. K. motherfucking O.

He fell to the ground in a bloody heap, and Marco was on me once more, kicking out my legs and dropping me to my knees. He pounced on me, knocking me face-down, a knee jammed into my back, right between my wings. I thrashed, trying to throw him off, but before I could get any fucking leverage, another one of the bastards grabbed my legs, pinning them down.

I heard the sing of a sword drawn from a scabbard.

Saw the flash of that blade as Marco yanked my head back, exposing my throat.

Knew what he was planning.

But then—

"Oh, I don't fucking *think* so, asshole," Haley snapped.

Marco turned toward her. Toward the pulse of magick flickering around her. Toward the ghouls gathered at her sides, bloodied from their feast. Still hungry.

And with that single moment of distraction, she'd given me my opening.

I pushed up hard, finally throwing the fuckers off, then jumped to my feet and spun to face them head-on. Haley sent a blast of magick barreling straight into the nameless asshole. He wheeled back and fell into the moat.

The ghouls down there converged. Consumed.

And once again, my enemy was in my sights.

I didn't fucking hesitate. Just lunged for him. Tackled him to the ground. Pinned him on his belly like he'd pinned me, my knee digging into his back, his wrists locked in my grip, my other hand smashing down on the back of his head, grinding his face into the dirt.

I felt the rumble of that roar in his chest. Felt him squirming beneath me.

And suddenly, I thought of those kids. Those innocent fae kids he and his friends slaughtered, all because of some slight against his family. Some petty jealous bullshit.

The old rage rose up inside. Centuries upon centuries of it.

But then it faded away, and a sense of deep calm settled over me.

And without ire, without bloodlust, I released his head. Grabbed a wing.

And fucking ripped it out of his back.

He howled in pain, writhing, begging, but I was just getting started.

All around me, the remaining gargoyles went down, felled by my girl and her gang of ghouls.

And with that sense of calm still intact, I ripped off his other wing. Tossed them both into the moat for the lingering ghouls. I heard the crunch of muscle and bone as they bit and tore, fighting over the scraps of him.

After she'd finished decimating the other gargoyles, Haley came to join me. To bear witness. Her magick surged through the mate bond, lending me strength. Power. Without a second thought, I punched a hole in Marco's lower back. Gripped his spine.

Tore it halfway out before the fucker finally—thanks to some latent, ancient survival instinct—turned to stone.

But that wouldn't help him now.

That only made my mission easier.

I got to my feet. Pulled the half-mutilated statue upright and turned him around so I could see his face.

Twisted in agony. In terror. Frozen. His final act.

For so many centuries, I'd wanted him dead. Wondered if I'd been saving up all my words just for this moment, when I could finally let him have it—all the rage and disgust that'd been festering inside me all those years. The betrayal, the hurt, the fucking shame. I felt the words gather, churning inside me like a Louisiana hurricane.

But then, just like my fury, they fell away.

Marco didn't deserve my words. Not the ones in my mind, and sure as hell not the spoken ones. Haley was the one who'd helped me find my way back to those, and I had no interest in cheapening what we shared by wasting so much as another *breath* on this asshole.

So instead, I released the statue and took my woman's hand. Felt the strength of her magick once more. Her loyalty. Her love.

And with nothing more than a boot to the chest, I kicked that motherfucker into the moat.

He exploded into pieces so minuscule, not even the wind bothered to blow him away.

Haley leaned over that great gash in the earth and spat.

Me? I couldn't even work up the gumption for that.

A low, strangled moan drifted across the darkness, and together we turned to see Garrison—the only fucker still alive after the massacre—just getting to his feet.

"I got this one, babygirl."

"You sure?"

I ran a bloody hand over her head, ruffling her hair. "Yeah."

I didn't give Garrison the chance to fully regain his footing. Just slammed him to the ground and tore that fucking bastard apart, wing by wing. Bone by bone. He didn't bother turning into stone, and I didn't bother caring.

Just shredded him. Watched his blood spill into the earth. Then got to my feet and booted his carcass into the moat.

By the time I wiped the blood from my face and turned to take in the scene once more, the gargoyles who'd betrayed me were finally gone, nothing but dark wet stains on the earth to prove they'd even been here at all.

But Haley's ghouls were gone, too.

And so was my woman.

*"Fuck."*

I could still feel her, though. Her courage. Her determination. Her magick, more powerful now than ever before. Every part of her, every feeling came to me through the mate bond, giving me more strength. Giving me hope.

I looked up at the wall. Behind it, the battles raged, every army in the realm converging in a clash of steel and obsidian and magick.

I took another deep breath. Sighed. And then, I ran. Leaped over the moat. Flew up into the darkness and sailed right the fuck over that wall, straight into the jaws of death.

# 30

## JAX

ear. I tasted it with every breath I drew, let it linger in my mouth like a fine wine. Marveled at the subtle differences in flavor.

Maybe I should've felt guilty about this simple pleasure, but I didn't.

I absolutely *relished* in it, because I knew that every single one of these Darkwinter motherfuckers meant my woman harm. And *that* was a sin even a demon called sinner couldn't forgive.

So I made my way through the city, block by battle-ravaged block, following the enticing pull of that wild, delicious fear as it led me to our enemies.

Not as efficient as Haley's Army of the Dead or the Beggar's Moat ghouls that had arrived soon after us, sniffing out pockets of Darkwinter troops and consuming them in a frenzied feed. Not as elegant as the dance of a proper sword fight, the clanging of metal on metal that echoed through the night as Evander and the Razorback Mountain fae fought their way through the city. Not as brutal as the breaking of bones, the rending of flesh, and the spilling of blood Saint's vampire attacks offered. Nor was it the stunning visual beauty of black feathers and blood raining down from the sky every time Hudson took out one of those fucking raven gryphons.

But hell… It was a damned good time.

Now, ducking down the alley that ran behind our old pub in the

"

Hollow, I zeroed in on my next target. A Darkwinter grunt. Seemed to have lost his way, the poor fuck.

I cleared my throat. Welcomed the hit of fear that flowed through me as his adrenaline spiked. He drew his dagger, but didn't make a move as I stepped closer, rifling through his mind until I found his oldest, darkest fear.

*Fire.*

I grinned. A classic, to be sure.

With little more than a thought, I conjured an inferno in his mind. One that chewed through the buildings on either side of us, rising higher and higher, the heat nearly melting his skin.

He barreled past me and charged out onto the street, right into the path of another group of Darkwinter assholes parrying with some of Evander's rebels.

Safely hidden in the shadows of the alley, I watched as he stopped short behind his own men. Knew the moment he believed they'd all burst into flames.

At first, he tried to save some of them. Pushed them to the ground, one after the other, battering them, desperate to tamp down the flames even as they shouted at him to stop.

Another group merged in, Darkwinter about three dozen strong now, confusion spreading among them as quickly as that imaginary fire as my target continued to shove and batter. To scream. To turn their confusion into sheer fucking panic.

Some were trampled in the commotion. Others left themselves open to the thrust of a rebel dagger. The bolt of a crossbow.

Oona's, this time.

She stepped out from behind me and sighed.

"Let me guess," she said dryly. "Fire?"

"Wow," I said. "You're getting pretty good at this."

With a dark grin, I let the illusion drop away. The solider regained his mental faculties. Took one look at the surrounding carnage. Realized what he'd done. And then… the dumb bastard shoved his own dagger through his chest.

"Brutal," Oona said with a mock shiver.

We moved on to the next alley, locating two more enemies. I slipped into the mind of one—fear of the hybrid mutant shifters his own kind had created. He turned to his companion, his eyes narrowed in sudden suspicion.

Only a single heartbeat passed before he sliced the guy's throat.

Oona lifted her crossbow. Shot the fucker before I even had a chance to reveal the illusion to him.

"You are *no* fun," I said.

"I am *very* fun." She slung the crossbow over her shoulder and unclipped the water bottle hanging from her belt, downing half of it before passing it to me.

I nodded my thanks, then took a few sips. Smiled at her.

Somehow, bound together by this ruthless mission, the two of us had finally made our peace.

It'd begun after Saint's miraculous return, as she and Gem told me the story—his death, how they'd found him, the prophecy about Haley. How the two of them had been working together ever since the rest of us had left Midnight the first time. All the betrayals that weren't actually betrayals after all.

And then later, as Oona and I had peeled off from the group and begun our block-by-block sweep, that conversation continued, edging closer and closer to the real issue that had risen like a wall of ice between us. We worked in tandem, taking down hybrids, taking down dark fae soldiers, until she'd finally said, "I know the past is the past, and our lives have… diverged along very different paths. But for what it's worth… I'm glad you got out of Midnight, even for a little while. And though I regret hurting you, I can't say I wouldn't do it again if it meant giving you that same shot."

I'd stopped her then, right in the middle of crafting a mass hallucination about a cloud of poison gas, and looked into her violet eyes. Probably for the first time since I'd seen her in that fucking dungeon the night Saint and I had been captured. The night they'd admitted to faking her death just so I'd leave Midnight.

And when I saw the earnestness there, I knew. Knew I'd already forgiven her.

There was a saying about hatred. Something about drinking poison and expecting the other person to die. And in that moment, I realized I'd been doing just that.

Besides, deep down, I didn't really hate Oona. And despite Saint's miraculous return, we all knew life was too fucking short to hold petty grudges against people who might just turn out to be damn good friends.

"Admit it," she said now, bringing me back to the moment. "I'm *very* fun. Admit it or I'm not guessing any more of your fear tactics or shooting another Darkwinter."

I returned the water bottle and rolled my eye. "Fine. You're very fun.

The funnest. Now, can we please go scare the life out that fucking general over there?"

I pointed at another Darkwinter fae just before he slipped into an abandoned building across the street.

Checking to be sure we were in the clear, we crossed the street and ducked behind the building, knowing he'd be coming out on the other side eventually.

As we waited for him, Oona locked another bolt into place on her crossbow, then said, "You and I had some good times back in the day, Jax." Her voice turned serious, her violet gaze soft. "I cared for you, and I know you felt the same."

I nodded. No point in denying it.

"But," she said, "Haley makes you happy in a way I never did. It's obvious what you all have together is special. Real. I've always wanted that for you, Jax. That kind of family. That kind of love. I... I hope you know that."

I opened my mouth to tell her that I did, but before I could speak another word, a door banged open and our target emerged, two others in tow.

I reached out for him. Slipped into his mind.

The general had a fear of spiders.

I nearly laughed at my good fortune. Arachnophobia—another classic. *Very* easy to work with.

With a gentle pulse of my magick, I crafted the illusion, turning his companions into six-foot-tall spiders with hairy legs and iridescent bodies, crawling toward him, touching him, devouring him...

In his rush to escape, he lost his footing, crashing down flat on his back.

The other two tried to help him up, but our general saw only those spiders, ready to devour, ready to wrap him in their sticky web and suck him dry.

He stabbed them both through the belly with a sword, their hot guts spilling out all over him. And with another little nudge from me, those guts exploded into a million tiny spiders, all of them scurrying over him, covering every inch of exposed skin, slithering into his open mouth...

A bolt right between the eyes, and the general's misery ended.

Glaring at Oona, I said, "I take it back. You are so *not* the funnest."

She shuddered. "I don't like spiders either, asshole." Then, pressing the crossbow to my chest, "And if you *ever* use that fact against me—"

"I don't turn fear on my friends, Oona. Not like that."

She blinked at the sudden ferocity in my tone. "Is that... what we are? Friends again?"

I didn't hesitate. "Yeah, Oona. We're friends again." I put an arm around her. "Assuming you don't fake your own death to get rid of me again."

Oona laughed. "As if I could pull off a ruse like that more than once. I'll have to think of something *much* more sinister next time."

"Just remember, I know your deepest fear now." I wriggled my fingers in front of her in the approximation of a spider.

Oona shoved me away, but that smile still held. "You are *seriously* disturbed. You know that, yes?"

"*Some* women actually appreciate that quality in a man."

She sighed. "I can't decide whether I should congratulate Haley or warn her."

"Let's see how you feel at the end of the night." I jerked my head toward the street again, and together we crept back out, resuming our mission.

Block by block, enemy by enemy, each sweep bringing us closer to the castle. To the rally point Evander had established.

I wasn't sure how much time passed. Three hours. Eight. But eventually, we made it, ducking into the shadows behind the castle, heading for the servants' entrance off the kitchen.

We stepped inside, checking to make sure we were alone.

No enemies. No one.

Closing the door behind us, I leaned against it and let out a breath. Oona went to refill the water bottle, and I closed my eye, taking a moment to just breathe.

Outside, the battle raged on. Swords clashing. Magick exploding. Blood running red down every street, mingling with ash and fallen bodies and the feathers of dead raven gryphons.

But the fighting was starting to ebb. Battle by battle, we were gaining ground. Taking back our city.

Oona returned a moment later, nudging me with the water bottle.

I opened my eye. Took the offered drink.

Then, passing the bottle back, I said plainly, "Thank you."

She knew I wasn't just talking about the water, or even about having my back out there tonight.

Because of her, I'd gotten out of Midnight before. I'd survived. And that survival, as much as I couldn't see it at the time, was the only reason I was here now.

The only reason I'd found Haley. The woman I loved. The woman I wanted to build a life and family with—a future I never could've imagined when I was just a fucked-up, one-eyed fugitive.

As if she could read my thoughts, Oona smiled, emotion glazing her eyes. "You're welcome, Jax."

I held her gaze for another beat. Then said, "We should head up to the ballroom. See if the others made it yet. And if they haven't, we need to make sure we're not dealing with an ambush."

"Lead the way."

We'd just made our way through the kitchens and out into the main parlor when we spotted them—Saint and Gem, racing down the stairs from above.

Panic bleached the color from their faces.

"Melantha," Gem panted as we approached. "She's barricaded herself in the throne room. Spelled the doors and windows."

"If she wants that throne so badly," a dark voice seethed, "she can claim it."

We all turned to see Evander striding across the room, Hudson just behind him. It was clear they'd only just arrived.

He looked us over quickly, then turned to Gem and Saint. Relief shone in his eyes at the sight of his brother, but when he spoke again, that same dark rage echoed in his voice.

"I will burn this entire castle to the *ground* if it means ridding the realm of her foul presence once and for all."

Saint took a step toward his brother. Put a hand on his shoulder. A single tear glittered on his cheek—silver, like his eyes.

Then, in a voice so soft and broken it sounded like air leaking from a balloon, he whispered, "She's not in there alone, Evander."

And all at once, we knew.

*Haley.*

# 31

## HALEY

*J*'ve been expecting you, Daughter of Darkwinter."

Sneering at me from her perch on the throne of obsidian and bones, the Dark Goddess Melantha lifted a lazy hand, and the doors to the throne room slammed shut behind me. I had no doubt she'd spelled the windows, too.

A death trap, if the visions I'd seen when I'd conjured her were true.

*My* death trap.

She'd finally manifested in physical form. She was nude, her ebony skin gleaming, her eyes burning red. Long, dark hair fell in waves over her breasts. No wings.

For now, she looked… mostly human.

Didn't make her any less creepy, though.

With a hiss that slithered across the polished floor like the serpents coiled at her bare feet, she said, "So entitled, making me wait for your arrival as if *I* were the commoner and *you* the queen."

A shiver gripped my spine at the raw power in her voice, the promise of death whispering beneath every word, but I refused to shudder in her presence. Refused to show even a shred of fear.

Melantha had laid this trap for me, but I'd walked into it by choice. My own fucking free will.

I'd come too far, fought too hard to fall apart now.

I lowered my head and took a deep, calming breath. Steadying myself. Gathering my strength. My magick.

Beyond these dark obsidian walls, the battle for Amaranth City raged on. Through the thick velvet curtains, I could just make out the flickers and flashes of colored light—magick from the Midnight witches who fought on our side, magick from the Darkwinter weather witches who didn't. The violent tempests of Midnight herself, stirred to life by the utter *wrongness* of what was happening here.

I knew my armies were out there—the ghouls of Midnight, the dead Melantha had once commanded—all of them bound to me now, devouring Darkwinter's ground forces as they broke upon those enemy lines, wave after wave of destruction and ruin. Every grisly attack rippled through my magick like an electrical current.

And my men… my men were out there, too.

I closed my eyes and reached out through our bonds—magickal, fated, love—and tried to hear each of them. To draw strength and courage from them.

Evander, my dark fae warlord, shouting orders to the troops he'd rallied, to the feral fae who'd finally agreed to follow him in my stead. For all that he'd lived most of his life as Keradoc's prisoner, Evander had learned the role well, his fierce command inspiring courage despite the bleakest odds.

Jax, my demon, fearless in the face of our enemies, baiting the most terrifying Darkwinter soldiers with their own worst fears as he and Oona worked to secure the streets of our city, block by block, home by home.

Elian, my vampire-fae, tearing out the throats of every abominable creature Darkwinter had shoved through its portals and packed onto its ships. Creatures like those I'd fought in the Bay—hybrids, vampires who could turn into wolves, fae who could steal souls like demons. The magick in their blood would infuse him, every kill making him stronger and faster as Gem fought by his side with magick and weapons both.

Hudson, my warrior gargoyle, patrolling the dark skies and fighting off raven gryphons and traitorous gargoyles alike, breaking them, slaughtering them, finally freed from the shackles of his old enemies. His betrayers.

They all fought hard. For Midnight. For each other. For me. I desperately wanted to be with them, to fight with them, but in the battle for Amaranth City, I was hunting a different sort of beast.

I'd sensed the Dark Goddess's foul energy the moment Hudson and I had reached the wall. As soon as I knew for certain Marco and Garrison were dead, I'd followed that wave of Beggar's Moat ghouls straight into the city. Straight into the castle.

Straight into the place where Melantha had shown me a vision of my death.

Not on the battlefield. Not at the hands and teeth of her skeletal army or the poisoned swords of Darkwinter.

But here, from her self-appointed place of honor on the throne, where she planned to spill my blood, steal my power, and claim Midnight once and for all.

The worst part? She hadn't even risen to her feet. As if the task of ending my life would be nothing more than a minor inconvenience—something to pencil in between a manicure and drinks with a friend.

Magick simmered in my veins at the sheer *audacity* of this bitch.

I lifted my chin. Met her glowing red eyes. And said only, "You are *no* queen."

She shook her head, clucking her tongue. The serpents at her feet uncoiled, slithering down the dais, as lazy and unhurried as their master seemed to be.

"You've come alone, then?" she asked.

"The first time I faced you in the Temple of the Dark Moon, I was alone."

"And in all this time, you haven't managed to make any friends?"

"Oh, I've made plenty of friends." I grinned, taking a few steps closer to the dais, ignoring the warning hiss of the serpents now coiling at the base. "But sending you to hell doesn't require an audience."

Those red eyes blazed bright. Her anger rippled outward, thick and palpable. A crack shattered the obsidian floor behind me.

I raised my hands in mock surrender. "You're right, I misspoke. Sorry." Then, with a deeply put-upon sigh, I said, "I'm *not* actually sending you to hell. I'm just... eliminating you. Kind of like when you spill tomato sauce on your favorite white blouse, and you think it's totally ruined, but then you attack it with that stain remover stick and it just... vanishes? Poof! Gone! Where does it go? No one knows." I lowered my hands and bared my teeth, taking a step onto the dais. "It simply stops... *existing*."

"Do *not* disrespect me, child," she whispered. Then, with nothing more than another lazy flick of her wrist, both serpents sprang for me.

My magick shot up around me of its own accord, a shimmering red wall of light. Both snakes crashed into it and vanished.

The magick fell away.

Melantha finally had the decency to show a little surprise.

Still didn't move her ass from that throne, though.

"I swore an *oath* to you," I gritted out, taking another step up. "I vowed to do what you asked of me, and I would've gone to the ends of the earth to see it through, because I truly believed that however dark, however terrifying, *you* were a goddess worthy of my allegiance."

She gripped the arms of the throne, dark fingers morphing into talons that gouged the carved obsidian.

"Yet here you are," she shot back. "Simpering like a coward."

"Simpering. Right. Says the woman who slithered back into Midnight after she'd been banished? The woman who gave up her own army because she was too scared to face me?"

"You have no power over me, Daughter of Darkwinter."

I cocked my head, letting a little zing of magick sizzle up the dais. "You sure about that?"

She flashed a feral grin, teeth as sharp as swords. In a sickly sweet voice, she said, "Perhaps if you'd spent less time spreading your legs and more time practicing your spellwork, devoting yourself to your goddess, you would not find yourself in such—"

"Goddess?" I laughed. "You don't deserve the honor of such a title. You don't deserve the blood and magick of this land. You don't even deserve another breath." I lifted my hands, calling up my reserves, ready to eliminate this stain once and for all. But before I could unleash a single bolt of magick—

A wave of dark power slammed into me, knocking me on my ass as a thunderous crack echoed through the room. The throne and the dais crashed to the ground, and when I glanced up again, the Dark Goddess was standing on the rubble in all her nightmarish glory. Black wings dripping with blood, four more white serpents twining around her gnarled limbs, those deadly talons poised and ready to strike.

Blood spilled from my nose, my ears ringing, the room spinning, my vision turning gray at the edges…

"I warned you this night would come," she hissed. "Warned you that you and your men would writhe and bow before me."

She leaped from the rubble and landed beside me, eclipsing me in her dark shadow, her magick syphoning my power, my strength, my hope, all of it.

"Foolish girl," she sighed. "There was a time when you called upon me for help."

She was right. In my most desperate hour, I *had* called upon her. And she'd answered, granting me the power to fight enemies that were so much stronger than me. Than my sisters.

*My sisters…*

I thought of them now, my three beautiful sisters—Gray, Addie, Georgie. Sisters I would gladly die for, wishing I'd gotten just one more chance to hug them.

I thought of the other witches of Bay Coven. Witches who'd fought by our side. My friends. Reva, the shadowborn witch who'd become Death. Who'd help send Elian back to me.

I thought of Gray's men—how they'd protected and loved her through it all, just as my men protected and loved me.

I thought of them, of course. My men. My monsters. Fierce warriors who would fight until the bitter end for us. For Midnight.

I thought of the realm. A land of darkness and death. The place where I'd found light and love. Home. Belonging.

And then, I thought of myself. How far I'd come from that broken woman in the bathtub, desperate for an escape. I'd carried her with me all these years, and now, upon my death, I could finally set her free knowing I'd saved her. Knowing I'd made her proud.

The vision from the night with the feral fae flickered to life behind my eyes. Me, lying in a pool of blood. This blood, this room, this moment.

And I knew, without a doubt, I was going to die.

And that… that was just… fucking *unacceptable*.

Blood leaked into my mouth. Filled it. Filled *me*. Magick simmered in my veins once more, twining with my rage, and despite the pain in my body, I rose to my feet. Shaky but unbending. Determined.

Melantha only laughed. "Who will come to your aid now, little witch? Not the Dark Goddess. Never again will I heed your call. Never again will I help you fight your battles."

The magick inside me surged, chasing away the last of my weakness. The last of my tremors. The last of my fear.

I met her gaze, and I knew my own eyes glowed just as fiercely. And when I finally spoke to her again, my voice held the power of a thousand eternities, a thousand moonless nights, a thousand dark realms.

"I don't need to call upon the Dark Goddess to fight my battles." I lifted my hands, magick exploding from my palms, bathing the entire room in my red light. "I *am* the fucking Dark Goddess."

The floor rumbled and cracked, the polished obsidian splitting. Tendrils of dark mist curled up from the fissures, slowly taking form.

The restless spirits of all who'd died here. All who'd been executed before the throne, right or wrong.

Now, they would fight for me. Deathbringer. The Balance. She for

Whom the Bones Bow. The true goddess of Midnight. A goddess that had the power to imprison them for eternity… or set them free.

I lifted my hands higher, and the dead rose to their full height. Their gruesome glory.

And there, in the eyes of the once all-powerful goddess of darkness and death, true fear shone bright.

Ignoring the wings and talons, I grabbed her throat. Smiled. "Time for you to writhe and bow before *me*, bitch."

And with little more than a nod, I unleashed hell.

The dead swarmed her, devouring her as I held her in my grip, watching her glowing red eyes turn black, then burst. Black blood spilled from the sockets, eating through her face like acid. Skin melted from the bone, revealing an ashen skull and rows of those razor-sharp teeth.

And the power… so much power. It leaked out of her and poured into me, weaving with my own magick, filling me, healing me.

Remaking me.

And when it was done, the feathers and bones of Melantha turned to ash, and the dead of Amaranth City vanished, and I fell to my knees and wept.

---

"Come back to us, sparrow. Come back." A gentle voice, a soft whisper caressing my cheeks.

Warm hands in my hair, on my shoulder, rubbing my back, squeezing my hand.

I sucked in a sharp breath and opened my eyes. I was still on my knees in the broken throne room, but I was alive.

*They* were alive, I realized. Kneeling in a tight circle around me, covered in blood and filth, but unbroken.

Which meant… it was over. The war was over.

I looked at each of them in turn.

Hudson, my fierce winged warrior with a heart as big as Midnight.

Jax, the fiery, passionate demon who pushed me to my limits and refused to let me give up on myself.

Evander, our captor and warlord. Our commander. Our friend.

And Elian, my first love. The silver-eyed vampire-fae who'd refused his own death and found a way back to us. *For* us.

My monsters. My family.

*Mine.*

I felt it settle inside me then—all that wild, dark goddess magick. Felt it finding its home inside my heart just as I'd found my home in Midnight.

We'd done it. We'd defeated Darkwinter and Melantha both.

A smile burst across my face, and I rose to my feet, feeling lighter and happier than I had in years.

The guys rose, exchanging nervous glances.

"Does this mean you're well?" Evander asked.

"Take it easy, angel." Jax put a warm hand on the small of my back. "Just tell us what you need."

I laughed. "Totally appreciate the concern, guys, but seriously? What your girl *needs* is a hot bath, a hot meal, and some filthy, raunchy, *epically* hot sex… not necessarily in that order."

Evander's eyes widened.

Jax shook his head and laughed, his blue eye sparkling beneath a mask of blood and gore. "Good to know you're still *you*."

I shrugged and turned my palms up. Twin red-and-black flames danced to life across them, and my fingers curled into sharp talons.

"Mostly me," I said with a wink. "Just a few modifications."

"A *few*?" Evander said, at the same time Hudson said, "God *damn*, babygirl."

"*Fuck*," Elian said. "I think I just came."

Jax laughed again, giving Elian a playful shove. "Good to know *you* haven't made any modifications, asshole."

"So…" I doused the flames and talons and stretched my arms over my head, my back popping. "About those needs of mine…"

"Soon," Evander said, leaning in to brush a kiss to my forehead. Then, his eyes darkening, he clamped a hand over Elian's shoulder and said, "There's something I… Something I need to take care of first. And I'd appreciate it if my brother were at my side."

# 32

## ELIAN

*H*aley was right last night," I said as Evander led us into the cramped dungeon beneath the castle. For its lone prisoner, death was close at hand. The smell of rot nearly overwhelmed me. "When she said I never stopped."

A low chuckle. "No one in their right mind would stop loving that woman. I'm quite certain it's categorically impossible."

"True, but... I was talking about what she said about *you*, Evander. How I never stopped searching for you. Not when we were kids. Not when I turned my back on Haley and the closest I'd ever come to being happy. Not even after, when I was back in New Orleans and struggling to find a reason to get out of bed every day—stoned out of my fucking mind, totally lost, wishing death would finally claim me... Fuck. I still wanted to find you. Still hoped it was possible... Somehow."

He stopped in the center of the room and turned to face me, the torch he carried casting his face in a soft orange glow. "I'd like to think that deep down, maybe there was some part of me that never stopped hoping you'd find me." Genuine warmth glazed those strange violet eyes, but his smile turned sad. "I just don't remember it, Elian. I'm sorry."

Fuck, how my heart broke for him—for the childhood he lost. The innocence that Keradoc had stolen from him. All the good things in his life he'd forgotten, because it'd taken every bit of his focus and will just to survive Midnight. To survive all that Keradoc had done to him.

"No," I said, struggling to keep my voice even. "I'm the one who's sorry. *Truly* sorry for all you've endured. If we could trade places, I—"

"Don't even think it," he said, suddenly harsh. Then, with a sigh and a wry smile, "Besides, if it'd been you, I wouldn't have the pleasure of killing the bastard." He shoved the torch into the sconce on the wall and slid his blade from its scabbard—an obsidian dagger with a handle of carved bone, sharp and deadly. Perfect. "For as much pleasure as this filthy animal found in torturing me, I found *my* pleasure in imagining the night I could look into his eyes, look upon his wasted face, and decide the *exact* moment at which he'd draw his final breath."

In the cell before us, the lone prisoner rattled his chains and let out a watery groan, but he had no real fight left. He'd wasted away in here, his body kept alive—barely—just so my brother could exact his revenge.

"Haley told me your life is bound to his," I said. "That if you remove the ring or kill him—if *anyone* kills him—you'll…"

I trailed off, unable to finish the sentence. I'd only just gotten Evander back. And though I wasn't foolish enough to think we'd pick up where we'd left off as children, I'd started to allow myself the tiniest bit of hope that maybe… maybe we could start over. Not as brothers, but as friends. As men who'd fought for each other. Men who'd fought for the woman they both loved and the home they hoped to make with her.

"It's a distinct possibility, yes," Evander said, no hint of concern in his voice. "But with Melantha gone, I feel…" He pressed a fist to his heart and shrugged. "I can't explain it, Elian. It's almost as if she left a piece of her dark magick inside me—a splinter in the heart, festering. Poisoning. But now it's just… gone."

I nodded. I'd felt similarly when my death had broken Melantha's curse.

"For so long," he went on, "I assumed I'd die with him, and I made my peace with that. All that mattered to me was destroying his legacy, eradicating his name, and ending his life. If mine had to end as well? So be it. Collateral damage, a risk with any war. But now… honestly, brother. I believe with my whole heart I can be free of him. That I can go on living my life as I was truly meant to. I'm not sure I'd risk it otherwise."

"No? Even though you've been jerking off to visions of his dead corpse for centuries?"

Another low chuckle. "Yes, but you see… I have a lot more to live for now than I did when I first made this vow. This grand plan." He turned to me once more, his hand gripping my shoulder as his laughter faded. "I don't actually *want* to—you know. Cease to exist. But there are no guarantees with magick, and if the worst *does* happen, I thought… I would ask that you… I wanted…" He blew out a sigh of frustration and closed his eyes, gathering his thoughts. When he finally met my gaze again, his own was rock steady. "I wanted it to be you, Elian. The one to witness my final breath, as it was you who witnessed my very first."

My chest tightened, tears stinging my eyes. I was terrified—fucking terrified of losing him again. But my voice was resolute when I gripped his shoulder and said, "I'm honored, brother. But it won't be your last. I feel it, too. So let's end it. *End* it so we can return to our friends and our witch."

He held my gaze for another moment, then finally nodded and turned away, closing the short distance that remained between him and his prisoner.

I grabbed the torch from the wall and joined him at the bars, shining the light into the darkness. Keradoc recoiled and hissed, but I didn't draw back. He was a wraith—little more than a collection of bones sheathed in a translucent layer of skin marred with open sores and deep purple bruises. His mouth hung slack, gums bleeding, no teeth to speak of. Most of his hair had fallen out as well. The violet irises that had once been so vivid were little more than a pale wash of lavender.

He tried to rattle his chains again, but couldn't even lift his arms.

My brother unlocked the cell door. We stepped inside, the stench of waste and decay making my eyes water.

I shook my head, shocked at the sight. "Keradoc was truly a fearsome beast—I remember him, Evander. His cruelty. His utter lack of remorse."

I was pretty sure I'd never lose those memories. The blood running through the streets of Amaranth City as he paraded his wounded men before their families, some twisted punishment for their perceived failures. The roses, trampled underfoot by the mares of night and the soldiers who remained standing. The bodies he'd dumped over the wall for the ghouls of Beggar's Moat. The screams that echoed through the city streets whenever he came near.

"How did you manage to turn him into this… this *thing*?" I whispered, as though anything louder might reverse the spell and give the old beast his claws back.

"I didn't turn him into anything. I merely revealed him for the worthless coward he always was." Evander glanced at his sword, the black blade glittering in the torchlight. "That's the thing about power, Elian. He was so seduced by it, so convinced it was his by right, so secure in his belief that he himself *was* that power. He saw me as weak. As one more *thing* to be dominated and controlled, just like he controlled the others. It never once occurred to him that the fae he stole and ruined as a child would one day grow into a man who could ruin *him*."

We stood in silence for a moment, watching the ruined beast trembling on the straw-covered stone floor. He coughed again, and the scent of fresh piss filled the cell, a thin river of it trickling along the stone.

"I have to imagine there's a chance for all of us," my brother said softly. "A chance for a better life, even in a place as harsh as Midnight. And that chance starts right here—with trust. With me trusting the magick of Midnight. Trusting my own magick. My own power."

He wasn't talking about the power of a crooked warlord, the power that corrupted and destroyed. He was talking about the power inherent in all of us, if only we found the courage to claim it.

Haley had made me believe in it.

And now, as I stood beside my brother in the final moments of the darkest chapter of his life, I felt it swell inside me, too. Power. Courage. Love.

"It's strange," Evander said, testing the edge of that blade against his thumb. A bead of blood welled on his skin. "In all my fantasies of killing him, I never imagined he'd be so pathetic. So broken."

"You broke him, Evander. You truly shattered him."

"Do you judge me for it?"

"Wouldn't be here if I felt that way. Besides…" I smirked and thumbed at my face, a bit of levity to chase off the lingering darkness. "You're about to get your old face back. You think I'd pass up an opportunity to see which one of us wears it better?"

He arched an eyebrow. "Seems you've already made up your mind on that."

I laughed, and he returned it. Still restrained—still nowhere near the full and boisterous laughter I remembered from our childhood. But I welcomed the sound of it anyway. Just one of the many things I'd have to learn about my brother—his laugh.

Emotion rose inside me again, churning as swiftly as the river of blood that'd nearly swept me off to hell. I looked down at the vile beast on the floor. The beast who'd stolen my brother and hurt him in ways I couldn't even let myself contemplate for longer than a few seconds. The beast who'd destroyed my family and rerouted our entire lives.

"You mean to give him a painless death?" I asked. That blade was sharp enough to kill a man before the first trickle of blood showed on his skin.

"I have been giving him death for many, many months, brother. And it has been anything but painless. This is merely the end." He bent down and wrapped a hand around Keradoc's throat, hauling him to his feet as if he weighed no more than a child. The chains rattled with the movement, but the man himself remained utterly silent now, tears staining his sunken face.

Evander said, "In all my dreams of this moment—and there were many over the years—I always felt his blood on my hands."

"And now?"

"I won't let so much as a *drop* of it soil my skin," he said. Then, to Keradoc, "Your daughter has known for some time about my ruse. I offered her a chance to say goodbye, but she declined, sending no parting words to the father who brutalized her when he should have loved and cherished her. You were an abomination in life, and the stain of your foul deeds will linger in the scars of all those you've harmed. But eventually, you'll fade from our collective memory. With every home and business we rebuild, with every wounded soldier we heal, with every family we welcome into this realm, your deeds will be undone, your story rewritten. And the night will come when your memory is nothing more than a shadow, and then mist, and then… nothing. You will be nothing."

With a final exhale and a quick thrust, Evander shoved the obsidian dagger through Keradoc's chest, then dropped him and the dagger both. The Warlord of Midnight landed in the pile of his own waste, skull cracking against the wall, his final strangled breath sputtering out before the blood even rose to the wound.

Evander removed his ring. Dropped it into Keradoc's lap. And turned away.

Meeting my gaze again, he said only, "it's done."

His eyes were still violet, and something dark and sinister flickered behind them, but then it was gone. All at once, the light returned.

"I need to burn it," he said. "The body. The ring. All of it."

"Do you want the dagger?" I asked.

Evander shook his head.

"Then allow me." I was still holding the torch, and now I stepped forward to stand over the body. "I've never been one for big speeches or blathering on with pretty words, so—"

"Blathering on?" Evander said, feigning insult.

Turning to look at him over my shoulder, I said, "You did get a bit long-winded there, brother."

A smile. A little more light in those violet eyes. "I suppose you think you can do better?"

"Watch and learn, brother. Watch and learn." I grinned and turned back to the body. "Fuck yourself off to hell, asshole. I'm sure they've got a nice room waiting for you."

I tossed the torch into his lap, and together, Evander and I backed out of the cell and closed the bars.

The flames caught, the fire crackling to life.

I put a hand on my brother's shoulder. Not an embrace. Not the casual arm of an old friend. Just a touch. Just enough to let him know I was still here. Still with him. Always.

Side by side, we watched in silence as the flames chewed through the straw and cheap rags that clung to his body.

Watched as his skin blistered and split, ignoring the stench of burning flesh.

Watched until it peeled away and all the bones beneath it turned as black as his heart.

Watched as the metal ring glowed bright, then melted.

Watched until the fire retreated and the beast of Midnight was nothing but a pile of ash.

Evander turned to me and drew in a deep breath, then let it out slowly, as if he were blowing away the last of Keradoc's terrible hold.

And there in the darkness, revealed only by my vampire sight, my brother transformed.

His cheekbones sharpened, his mouth and jawline a mirror image of my own. His hair retained some of the black, but most of it had turned silver. Our build was the same, too.

The eyes, however, remained violet.

Still, the sight of him—the sight of my brother, my twin…

"Not bad." I coughed, loosening the knot lodged in my throat. "A little wrinkly around the eyes, and that hairline might be receding a bit, but… I suppose you're passable."

"You suppose I'm *passable*?"

I shrugged. "I've always been the good-looking one. *Everyone* knows that."

Evander laughed. Not the smooth, cultivated laugh of the warlord, or the bitter laugh of a man who'd clawed his way back from a life of torture and pain, but a *true* laugh, rich and warm, the promise of something better alive in every note.

Clapping a hand on my shoulder, he guided us out of that rancid pit and said, "Perhaps, *brother*, we should let the Dark Goddess be the judge."

# 33

## HALEY

$\mathcal{I}$ leaned back on the cool obsidian ledge, gazing up at the two fae warriors that towered over me. One was carved of moonstone, the other of onyx, their swords held high, clashing in their eternal battle. Spilling eternal blood.

That blood filled the fountain I now sat upon, the dark ruby liquid swirling in a dance as endless as their swordplay.

The first time I'd seen this fountain, Jax and I had been trying to escape the castle. He'd told me the fountain held the blood of the realm—that no one really knew where it came from, only that it never evaporated or froze. And all who attempted to touch or drink it perished, as evidenced by the collection of decaying vampire skulls around its base.

At the time, its sinister presence terrified me, but now I found it beautiful. Calming. This fountain, these warriors, they represented all of us. Strong, but flawed. Warriors who could just as easily destroy as we could create. Darkness and light. Death and life.

The Balance.

It was magick that'd kept the fountain flowing. Blood and magick. So many, many things in Midnight came down to that. So many things in my own *life* had come down to that.

Now, scrubbed clean of the blood I'd spilled in battle, I sipped from a fresh mug of lavender-mint tea and gazed up at the warriors once more, drawing a sense of safety and certainty from them. A reminder that Midnight would always be worth fighting for.

Blackmoon Bay would always be a part of me. And I couldn't wait to go back and visit my sisters. My friends. But Midnight?

Through all of this—the capture, the fear, the fighting, the blood and the magick...

Midnight had become my home. And I was staying.

While Evander and Elian had gone down to the dungeons to deal with the prisoner whose name I would no longer utter, Hudson and Jax had gone to the city center to check on Oona and Gem. They'd set up a triage at the former Devil's Dream warehouse with some of the realm's healers, all of them working diligently to treat the wounded. From what I'd seen and heard of the battle, I knew they'd have their hands full tonight. Tomorrow night. For many nights to come as we all worked to assess the damage, bury the dead, and slowly—ever so slowly—rebuild the realm.

I wasn't sure how many of Midnight's citizens had died tonight—on *either* side. How many would carry the scars and memories of all we'd done. But we *had* done it. Defeated Darkwinter, defeated those who'd sought to tear the realm apart, to destroy its magick, to claim it or bend it to their own ends. We'd united some of Midnight's warring factions—not all of them, of course. In a place as harsh as Midnight, there would likely always be strife. But every soldier who'd sacrificed his tribal allegiance for a chance to help the realm? He represented another bridge. And bridges could be built. Fortified.

And Melantha? She was gone. Not merely vanquished, not merely dead, but her very essence... well, that essence was mine now. Not to control and manipulate, but to nurture. In destroying her tonight, I'd become her. The Dark Goddess as she always should have been.

The creak of old metal hinges cut through my thoughts, and I glanced toward the gate, smiling at the welcome sight.

Two silver-haired brothers emerged from the darkness, freshly showered, exhaustion heavy in each step, but smiles gracing those mouths. *Twin* smiles, crooked and mischievous. Warm and familiar. Mine.

"Evander," I gasped as he knelt before me and placed his hands on my knees. The face that gazed up at me now was no longer the face of our warlord, but the face of the man I'd first glimpsed in the throne room the night of the feast. The man I'd kissed.

His eyes, though... They'd remained violet.

Sensing my confusion, Evander said softly, "I wore the mask of that man for so long, I suppose he's become part of me. A reminder of what happened here—all the things Midnight doesn't want us to forget, lest they happen again."

"I don't want to forget," I said. "Any of it."

"None of us do," Elian said, sitting on the fountain beside me and wrapping a hand around the back of my neck.

Still kneeling, Evander closed his eyes and let out a deep sigh, and together the three of us sat in the dark, peaceful shadows cast by the moonstone and onyx fae, listening to the gentle trickle of the blood fountain. Out beyond the walls of the courtyard, the sounds of recovery filled the night—shovels and pickaxes slamming against rock as the fae dug for survivors. Shouting—orders, questions, cries for help. The moaning of the injured, the weeping of all who'd lost someone they loved. Smoke and magick filled the air, barely perceptible over the smell of death.

"Thank you," I whispered to my men, tears slipping down my face. I didn't finish the thought, but the words flowed through my mind anyway. *Thank you for surviving. For finding your way back to each other. Back to me. Thank you for loving me...*

I didn't need to say them out loud. They understood.

When Evander finally met my gaze again, I cradled his face between my palms, still marveling at him.

Every facet in those violet eyes glittered. "Does it... displease you?" he asked.

"Is this your true face now?" I asked. "Your true self, fully embodied, because the warlord is finally gone?"

Evander hooked his hands around my wrists, squeezing gently. "He is *gone,* Haley. Nothing but ash. The man you see kneeling before you is me. Only me." Then, with a soft chuckle and a glance over at Elian, "Well, maybe a *little* of my brother as well."

"It's the hair," Elian said.

"As you can *clearly* see," Evander said, "it looks better on me."

Elian laughed. "We're supposed to let *her* be the judge, dickhead."

Violet eyes caught my gaze once more, his brows lifting in question.

"I'm not displeased, Evander," I said, tracing his cheeks with my thumbs. "You're beautiful. You're you, and you're beautiful."

The relief on his breath was palpable, then quickly turned into another laugh. "So this means we're in agreement about which of us is the handsome twin, yes?"

The three of us got to our feet, and I narrowed my eyes at Evander, then Elian, assessing. "I don't know, guys. It's not something I can just *declare.* I need more information."

"What sort of information?" Evander asked, brushing a soft kiss along one corner of my mouth, then the other.

Elian shifted to stand behind me, hands on my hips, breath warm on my ear as he said, "You know we're happy to provide some... additional evidence." He nipped my earlobe, and I leaned back into his warmth, that so-called evidence pressing urgently against my backside.

"If it's evidence the goddess demands," Evander whispered, biting my lower lip, then kissing a path from my mouth to my throat, "evidence we shall provide."

With slow, deliberate movements, he worked his way down my body, gingerly unbuttoning my shirt and unfastening my bra, sliding both off my shoulders, tracing swirls across the top of my breasts with light fingertips and teasing, languid strokes of his tongue. Behind me, Elian gathered my hair and lifted it off the back of my neck, replacing its warmth with the heat of his mouth, his breath, his increasingly passionate kisses.

"Beautiful, reckless little thief," Evander teased, then closed his mouth around my nipple, sucking hard as he palmed my other breast, stroking and teasing, all of my awareness zeroing in on the intense pleasure of his tongue, his teeth. I slid my hands into his hair—long and silver, just a hint of black remaining—and arched my back as he continued to lick and suck, flooding my core with hot, molten desire.

Elian's cock twitched against me, and a low moan of pleasure escaped my lips. Evander groaned, his kisses growing more urgent as he made his way down to my stomach, unzipping my pants and sliding them down my hips. I stepped out of them, and the panties quickly followed; eager fingers hooked inside the waistband, then ripped them away like tissue paper.

When I glanced down again at Evander, there was no hiding the bulge in his pants, his cock straining against the fabric as he brought his mouth to my flesh and inhaled.

"So fucking wet," Evander whispered, one finger gliding over my clit, teasing my entrance. "So fucking delicious."

I let out a whimper, everything in me winding tight, my entire body pulsing with an insatiable need for them.

"Do you like making my brother hard for you, sparrow?" Elian asked, a dark whisper against the shell of my ear as he snaked a hand around my throat, squeezing it just... God, just right. "Do you like bringing your captor to his knees?"

His other hand slid up to cup my breast, fingers tugging and teasing where seconds earlier, Evander's mouth had nearly unraveled me. Every part of me ached, throbbing and oversensitive and desperate for more.

"Yes," I breathed. "Fuck, yes."

With another groan of pleasure, Evander slid two fingers deep inside me, then pressed his hot, lush mouth between my thighs, unleashing that wicked tongue once more.

"Evander," I gasped, fisting his hair, tugging him closer.

Behind me, Elian stepped backward, releasing me. I was about to demand his immediate return when I heard it—the clink of a buckle, the whoosh of a zipper, the unmistakable whisper of fabric sliding off skin. Seconds later, he was back, one hand curling around my throat again, the other fisting his cock as he teased me from behind.

"I'm going to fuck you now, little sparrow," he warned. "While my brother sucks on your sweet pussy until you're singing your greatest hits."

"Please," I whispered.

Evander slid his fingers out but didn't tear his mouth away, his tongue drawing slow, deliberate circles over my clit.

And Elian—who knew my body so well, knew just how hard I liked it —tightened his grip on my throat, pushed his cock between my thighs, and fucking buried himself.

"Elian!" I cried out, my voice hoarse beneath the unrelenting hold on my throat as Evander sucked my clit between his lips and moaned, the vibrations humming across my flesh, my body pulsing as Elian dragged himself out slowly, then slammed right back into me. The orgasm was already building inside, glowing embers sparking to life, and then—

The creak of that gate. Shadows shifting across the courtyard.

Hudson and Jax both met my gaze, their own burning bright as they took in the scene.

"A demon and a gargoyle," Elian teased, slowing his thrusts but not stopping. Not releasing me from the chokehold that was driving me abso-lutely wild. "And what are you two reprobates doing in a nice place like this?"

Hudson let out a growl, but Jax laughed.

"Trying to decide if we should be offended that you started this party without us," my demon said.

"Less gawking, sinner," I panted. "More stripping. Both of you. I need… I need to feel you. *Taste* you."

Eyes widening, they both looked to Elian, who only laughed.

"You heard the goddess," he said, then slammed inside me once more, making me gasp. Evander licked another hot, delicious path along my clit, then sucked it hard between his lips, thrashing me with his tongue as Elian rocked against my backside, driving in deeper, harder, hitting that perfect spot inside me, his grip tight on my throat, the light dancing behind my eyes and then—

Elian released his hold, and the air rushed back to my lungs just as the fire inside me roared to life, heat sizzling across my nerves, the intensity of it spinning me out to the stars and moons and back again as wave after wave of pure, white-hot euphoria crashed over me.

A deep growl, a shudder from behind, and then Elian came inside me, thrusting against me as he tumbled headlong into those same euphoric waves.

Evander got to his feet, his mouth glistening, violet eyes dazed as he gathered me into his arms and kissed me. I tasted myself on his tongue, and I sighed into his mouth, reaching down to palm his cock as Elian slumped backward against the edge of the fountain.

I pulled back from Evander's kiss just long enough to glare at my demon and my gargoyle, who I just realized had been staring at us in utter silence for the past several minutes, mouths hanging open.

"Apparently, you two have difficulty following orders," I teased, raking my gaze down their fully clothed forms. "Do you really want to piss off the Dark Goddess on her first night?"

A burst of bright-red magick shimmered in the air between us, and I laughed as they gasped and finally obeyed, stripping out of their clothing.

"You, too, Evander," I teased. "This is not a clothing-optional event."

The magick faded as my men approached, naked and strong and beautiful in the moonlight.

Despite the teasing, a heaviness still hung on the air—the weight of all we'd lost, all we'd witnessed, all we'd survived. Maybe it was wrong to want this right now—to want this pleasure so soon after the chaos and destruction.

But the warrior fae towering above us reminded me once more that all things were a balance. Life and death. Order and chaos. War and love.

And tonight, right now, even for just a little while, I wanted love. Only love.

Silently, I beckoned all of them closer. Ran my hands over velvet-smooth skin and the hard muscles coiled beneath. Kissed the freshly healed wounds, the ancient scars, the trails of old hurts that could no longer be seen. Whispered away the pain, the loss, the fear, until all that remained was the bright beacon of love—a love we'd all fought so hard to protect.

Then, it was me falling to my knees, stroking my demon's cock in the moonlight, my tongue darting out to swirl around the tip, making him shudder.

"*Fuck,* angel," he growled, his fingers knotting in my hair. "You... you're..."

I moaned as I opened my mouth and took him in deeper, sucking him, worshipping, making him tremble and gasp. Behind me, Hudson knelt and ran his hands down my sides, my hips, gripping my thighs and urging them apart to make room for that perfect, stone-hard cock already sliding between them. I obeyed at once, and my gargoyle pulled me into his lap, impaling me as Jax slid all the way down my throat, making me choke. Making me gag. Making me so hot and wet, I feared I would literally melt.

Hudson growled in my ear, thrusting in deeper, circling his hips, spreading me, stretching me as Jax fucked my mouth.

Evander knelt beside me, kissing another blazing fiery trail from my jaw to my neck, and I reached for him and fisted his cock, teasing him with a soft, light stroke, my thumb brushing across the tip as I slowly increased the pressure.

Elian was in the dirt on my other side, mirroring his twin's movements, a trail of warm breath and soft lips that soon turned into the delicious graze of fangs. He scraped them across my nipple, then licked, making me moan. Jax hissed at the sound against his sensitive skin, and Hudson drove deeper inside me, my grip on Evander's cock tight as I stroked him harder. Faster.

"Open wider for me, sparrow," Elian whispered, that hot mouth sliding down my chest, my belly. "Now it's *my* turn to make you come on my tongue."

Evander captured my nipple between his lips, nibbling and teasing as Hudson gripped my thighs and spread them even wider, making room for Elian as he lowered his head between them and kissed. And sucked. And feasted until those embers inside me ignited once more.

It was wild. It was filthy. It was love. So much love, I felt it rise up around me like my own magick, radiating warmth and security and possibility and a promise that this was ours. That we *belonged* to each other. That every kiss, every touch, every deep stroke was another sacred vow to honor and cherish this. To fight for it, no matter what. To never give up.

In the long span of our collective lives, all of us had lost so much.

Evander was stolen from his family as a child, leaving Elian to wade through the wreckage, eventually losing the family he'd known and loved too. Jax lost his sister, only to have his parents abandon him to the most barbaric torments imaginable. Hudson was betrayed by his own people, scorned and exiled, never able to truly mourn the fae children whose gruesome murders he'd been forced to witness.

I was torn away from my sisters as a child, all of us hidden to protect us from a mother who'd wanted our magick so badly she'd tried to kill us for it. And though my adoptive family was loving and kind, they died young—to young—and I was left alone.

All of us were orphans. Outcasts. Yet somehow, we'd found each other.

We were part of each other's histories now, each other's hearts. And I was honored and humbled by it, this belonging. This love we all shared. I felt it glow and expand inside me with that fire—the knowledge and comfort that I was theirs. Their little sparrow and their little thief. Their babygirl. Their dark angel. And I was *me*, too. All me—the Dark Goddess, the Silversbane-Darkwinter Scorpio blood witch, wielder of magick and eater of lasagna, a woman who'd finally come to truly appreciate her life.

To appreciate all the beauty in that darkness, however painful, that had brought me here.

A deep throb pulsed through my core, and my body tightened around my gargoyle's cock as the fire inside me ignited again in earnest. I stroked Evander with a fevered touch, his body trembling beside me, Elian's silver head thrashing between my thighs, licking and sucking, Hudson sliding in deep as I moaned around Jax's cock in my mouth and then…

The orgasm detonated, bursting like a Midnight starshower inside me, hot and bright and endless as I shattered for them—all of them, my men, my heart.

Hudson was next, slamming inside me with a shudder and a growl that had me moaning all over again, and then Jax, fisting my hair as he spilled down my throat.

"Haley," Evander ground out, barely breathing, and then he was trembling again, his hot release spilling as he thrust into my hand.

Spent and sated, all five of us fell onto our backs on the dirt, panting. Dreaming. Breathing each other in. I curled my fingers into the dirt, and then, as if in response to some ancient call inside me, the ground rumbled, vines pushing up through the damp earth, reaching for life.

Jax sucked in a sharp breath, no doubt remembering our last encounter in this courtyard. The chokeweed that'd sprouted up in the darkness, nearly killing us both.

But even without looking at them, I *knew* these plants. Knew we had nothing to fear.

The blooms that caressed our bare skin tonight weren't chokeweed.

They were my roses. Black and lush and perfect. A gift from Midnight herself, welcoming us to the realm.

My men gasped as we leaned up on our elbows and took in the sight of this strange, wondrous new garden.

It was, most surprisingly, Hudson who spoke first.

"Beauty in darkness," came his deep, soothing rumble.

"Beauty in darkness," I echoed.

And when I leaned back again and glanced up into the Midnight sky, the triple moons all seemed to be smiling, and I let out a deep sigh and smiled right back at them, knowing in my heart that this view had *always* been meant for us.

Knowing we were finally, truly, irrevocably home.

# 34

## EVANDER

**One month later...**

$\mathcal{M}$emory was a strange thing. A curse or a gift, I still knew not, though lately I'd been more inclined to hope for the latter.

I used to tell myself I was better off without my past—that it could only ever be a burden that would weigh me down and distract me from my mission.

I no longer believed that. Our pasts were an integral part of us—part of who we became, who we were *always* becoming as one moment slid into the next. It was only in the present where we made that choice: would we allow our histories to be our burdens, or would we invite them to be our blessings?

Perhaps there was room enough for both. Perhaps, in the fine balancing of the two, we could find our peace.

I still didn't remember my childhood or my brother—not in a way that made sense. But things were coming to me more often now—a scene playing out in a dream. A flash triggered by my brother's laughter. A memory unlocked by the scent of fresh-baked bread cooling on the kitchen's obsidian countertop.

For so long, I couldn't see any of these things—not even the barest glimpse. But in saving our realm, in severing the chains that had once bound me to my vile captor, I'd finally shed the soul-crushing despair that'd hung over me like a death shroud for centuries. And in that place inside me where only darkness and nightmares lived, a light had finally begun to shine.

Not the light of memory, but the light of possibility. Of hope.

Haley had given me that.

"Is she ready, Evander?" one of my household employees asked as I paused before a decorative mirror outside the ballroom to check the fit of my clothing. Again. I'd lost count at how many times I'd changed, but everything had to be perfect tonight—my gift to her. Beauty in darkness.

And it was—I noted with no small amount of relief—perfect. The sleek, tailored jacket and pants, black as the Midnight sky but for their faint silver-and-violet whorls. I'd selected the pattern for Haley. The hint of color brought out my eyes—the violet irises I'd finally come to accept. To appreciate, if only for the way she looked at me each and every night.

"The people are eager to see her," he continued.

"As am I." I smiled and peeked inside the packed ballroom. For once, it wasn't just a crowd of sycophantic nobles who'd paid for the privilege of attendance, but the people of Midnight themselves. Those from the Hollow. Those who dwelled in the shadow of Dead Claw. The imps and the demons, vampires and fae, witches. Men and monsters all. Even the feral fae had re-emerged from their caves in the Razorbacks tonight—not to fight, but to celebrate with us. To rebuild. To remember those who'd come before us.

Their people. *Our* people.

Together, we'd buried the Eternal Ones—the children of their ancestors —in a place of honor on a high cliff overlooking the Sea of Tranquility, along with many others who died fighting for their homeland.

Hudson had spoken for them. Before a group of hundreds, he'd remembered them. Their light. Their boundless capacity for love.

In the month since our victory over Melantha and the Darkwinter fae, we'd made other changes as well.

Night by night, the people of Amaranth City were rebuilding. Homes, businesses, open spaces… More than ever, the city glittered like a jewel in the north, a beacon for all who wished to follow it home.

We'd signed treaties and trade agreements with many of the surrounding territories—Stone City, the Razorbacks, Dead Claw, Hanging Lake. Now that we'd gotten a taste of peace, very few wanted to return to the brutalities of the past.

Not everyone was so eager to make amends, however, and none of us were foolish enough to believe there would never be another skirmish, never be a territorial dispute or invasion, never be a battle for resources or weapons or drugs.

But we had to start somewhere. We'd fought and bled and died for the realm. For each other. Now, it was ours to protect.

We'd taken down most of Vanderham's wall so that no one would be denied passage into our city again. Part of it remained intact, however. A memorial to the fallen, as well as a reminder of our dark history—a history that could shape a better future, but only if we remembered it.

Beggar's Moat had been filled in, the magick that'd bound the fallen dead to the city eradicated, their trapped spirits finally set free—along with Haley's Army of the Dead.

From now on, the dead of Midnight would *always* rest in peace, no matter the manner of their deaths. No matter their deeds in life.

In the end, all of us deserved peace.

As for the living, Haley and I had worked with Oona, Gem, and some of the other purebred Midnight fae to reconfigure the portals so that anyone who wished to travel to and from our realm could do so freely—no spells or dark bargains required. Midnight would no longer be a realm of exiles, but a realm of free people. A realm of possibility.

And tonight, exactly one month after the attack on Amaranth City and the victory snatched from the claws of death, the castle reconstruction was finally complete, and our people were more than ready to celebrate.

Excusing myself, I headed into the throne room to await Haley's arrival. The others would be meeting us shortly, but I'd asked for a few moments alone with her first.

A few moments to just… be.

My back was turned on the dais, but I knew it the moment she stepped into the room. I felt her presence, the magick that connected us. The love.

I hadn't seen her all week—she'd been in Blackmoon Bay visiting her sisters. And now, I held my breath and turned to see her, my heart nearly bursting with anticipation.

I'd missed her. More than I could ever express.

Entering through the door behind the dais, she met my gaze and smiled, her green eyes glittering. She wore a delicate black-and-silver dress that clung to her curves like water, arms and shoulders bared, tiny blood-red jewels sewn into the hemline. With each step, the dress caught the light and shimmered.

Her hair was woven into a series of intricate braids that fell down her back. Behind her ear, a single black rose bloomed.

Resplendent. That was the word that came to mind.

The very sight of her brought tears to my eyes. I had never seen her so lovely. So fierce.

"Well," she mused, raking her gaze over me as I ascended the dais to join her. "You clean up well, warlord."

I didn't speak. Couldn't. Not until she said, "And how do *I* look? I wasn't totally sold on the dress at first, but Gem talked me into it. She said it would show off my—and I quote—hard-on inspiring shoulders."

"You," I finally whispered, daring to brush a single kiss to one of those shoulders, "look like the Dark Goddess and queen you were born to be. And allow me to be the first to concur with Gem's assessment."

I shifted on my feet, attempting to adjust the sudden bulge in my pants.

Mischief danced in Haley's eyes, the magick bond sizzling between us.

In that moment, I wanted nothing more than to drag her into that secret room behind us, shred her delicate dress, and—

I cleared my throat. Refocused on the matter at hand.

"I have something for you," I said, holding out my arm for her.

Her eyes raked down my body once more. "I bet you do."

"Something *else*, incorrigible little thief."

She finally took my arm, and I led her around to the front of the dais. To the new throne that sat atop it.

The room had been scrubbed clean of the stain of Melantha, the ancient throne of skulls replaced with something much more suitable.

A high-backed throne of polished obsidian, hand-carved with black roses and vines that twined around the arms and up along the top, where the triple moons—forged from the steel of melted swords—met in the center. Tiny flecks of amethyst and diamond sparkled down the back—the stars of the Midnight sky.

"It's... its beautiful," she breathed, running her hand along the rose motif.

"It's yours, Haley."

She stilled, and when she glanced into my eyes once more, I saw the hesitation there.

"Tell me," I whispered. "If you'd prefer a different design, we can—"

"No, it's not that. It's beautiful. It's perfect. But... I didn't get here alone, Evander. I haven't earned this."

I retrieved the wooden box I'd hidden beneath the throne earlier and held it out to her. "For millennia, Midnight was ruled by self-appointed kings and warlords."

"And now you think we need a war *lady*?"

"No, Haley." I unlatched the box and revealed the crown inside, finely-wrought silver vines blooming with flowers of onyx and moonstone. Delicate and fierce, just like she was. "Now, we need a queen."

Haley gasped, her eyes shining.

"Sit," I said softly. "Grant me the honor of being the first to bend the knee."

Her gaze snapped up to meet mine once more. A mischievous smile curved her lips. "The last time you ordered me to sit on the throne, it didn't end well."

I laughed at the memory. "As if I could forget. You blasted me with a blood spell and destroyed half the room. But I assure you, little thief. My commands can be quite… enjoyable. With the right intentions, of course."

She narrowed her eyes playfully. "Is that what you have? The right intentions?"

"Shall we find out?"

She lifted the crown from the box. "One condition."

"Name it, queen."

"You call me by all the names."

I arched an eyebrow. "*All* of them? But there are so, so many."

With another devious smile that sent a bolt of pleasure straight to my still-hard cock, she placed the crown atop her head, settled herself in the throne, and said, "Then I guess you'd better get started."

Resting my hands on the arms of the throne, I hovered over her, my mouth brushing across hers. In a dark whisper, I said, "Wicked little beast."

Then I dropped to my knees.

I pushed up her dress, revealing her bare thighs and the jewel-encrusted daggers strapped to each one.

I couldn't help but laugh. "I'm beginning to think you love your weapons more than the beautiful dresses that conceal them."

"Weapons are *always* the priority, Evander. Dresses are just the frosting on the cake."

"And oh, what a decadent cake it is." I gripped her thighs, spreading them apart as I brought my mouth to her hot, wet center. She wore a scrap of violet lace over smooth, bare skin, the thin fabric already damp with her desire.

After our victory, it didn't take long for word to spread about Melantha's defeat. About the Silversbane Darkwinter blood witch who'd fulfilled an ancient prophecy and brought peace and balance to the realm. They'd given Haley more names than we could count—names lauded in the taverns over wine and ale, names praised in the chapels, names exalted in every shop and home throughout the city and beyond as Haley had helped her people rebuild, wielding her magick as readily as she'd wielded a hammer and nails.

I'd memorized each and every name. Loved them, as much as I loved her. And now, I would show her just that.

"Haley Barnes, the first of her name," I murmured, then licked a hot path across the lace, making her shiver and writhe.

"She Who Claimed the Darkness," I said, unsheathing one of her daggers and slicing through the lace, baring her to me.

Another lick, this time directly across her hot, naked flesh. "Bane of the Enemies of Midnight."

"Oh, God," she breathed, her eyes fluttering closed, her body melting at my every kiss.

"The Great Balance." I gently bit her clit, flicking her with my tongue as I slid a finger inside her.

"Breaker of Walls, Builder of Bridges." Another finger to join the first, teasing her with long, slow strokes. I kissed the sensitive skin at the top of one thigh, then dragged my mouth across to the other. "Deathbringer. She for Whom the Bones Bow."

I curled my fingers inside her and slid in deeper, *deeper*, once more lowering my mouth to her flesh, tongue swirling over the sensitive apex.

"Dark Queen of the Realm," I whispered, my breath as shallow as hers, heart thundering in time with the red-hot pulse of magick emanating through our bond.

*Fuck.* I could no longer hold back. No longer tease and taunt.

With a final growl, I said, "*My* dark queen."

And then I was on her, my mouth devouring her as I fucked her with my hand, every part of me conspiring to give her this pleasure, to taste her, to feel her, to make my Midnight queen come for me.

I thrust inside her once more, hitting that perfect spot.

"Evander!" she cried out, and I moaned, licking her madly as she thrashed against my face and took every last bit of pleasure, every hot mist of breath, ever last silken kiss.

———

"What are you thinking about?" she whispered, fingers drawing lazy circles on the back of my hand.

I was seated on the throne now too, Haley curled into my lap, her lovely dress smoothed back into place.

The crown glimmered in her dark hair.

I could still taste her on my lips.

Pressing a kiss to her temple, I said, "Just recalling the time a devious little thief and her friends crashed my party in a vain attempt to steal my bodily fluids."

Haley laughed. "We've come full circle."

"And yet so much has changed."

"True." She shifted in my lap, her sweet berries-and-cream scent floating to my senses. "Last time, you didn't make me come on the throne."

"If you'd given me the opportunity, I assure you… I *would* have."

"Well, at least now we've got a fun game for later. And by later, I mean every time I'm sitting on this thing in a dress."

"Understood. I shall order you more dresses at once."

"Great." She ran a hand down the carved arm of her throne and grinned. "Now I'll *never* be able to walk into this room again without thinking of your *very* talented tongue."

"Indeed you won't. And don't believe for a second *that* was unintentional."

"My warlord," she teased with a roll of her pretty green eyes. "Ever the strategist."

She shifted again, drawing closer. I wrapped my arms tight around her and pressed my nose to the soft skin beneath her ear, breathing her in.

After several silent heartbeats, I said softly, "Do you remember when I told you my mind had blocked out all of the good things in my life, magnifying only the worst?"

She nodded, her body tensing.

"It's different now," I said.

She glanced up and met my gaze, her eyes sparkling. "You've remembered something?"

"Your dress," I said. "From the Feast of Midnight. You were a dark flower blooming in an even darker realm, and the sight of you stole the very breath from my lungs."

"You remember my dress?"

"You've beguiled me since our first encounter, Haley. I knew you were a spy—possibly even an assassin. Knew I should have ordered my guards to seize you at once. But one look, and I was just so desperate for a dance. A single dance, I promised myself. But then you were in my arms, and we were talking—all those little threats hidden behind teasing smiles—and somehow I'd fallen into those gorgeous emerald eyes, and I was already half enamored of you before the first waltz had even ended." I smiled, basking in the memory of that night. That dance. "I spent the next several weeks trying to convince myself it wasn't happening. Truly, I didn't believe my heart had the capacity to feel such things."

Her eyes misted. Through a soft grin, she said, "Only half enamored, huh?"

I laughed and closed my eyes, focusing on her warmth. The feel of her soft skin. The sound of her heartbeat. The magick simmering in her veins —the magick we shared.

"Maybe a bit more than half," I admitted.

The rest... it'd come to me slowly after that, sneaking in behind the cracks of my armor night by night, moment by moment. A mug of lavender-peppermint tea offered in my library after a nightmare. A stolen glimpse at a beautiful witch dancing on the balcony after accomplishing a spell. A gentle touch on scar-ravaged skin. The realization that this was a woman who would fight tooth and nail for the ones she called friends. The ones she loved.

"The truth is, I..." I swallowed hard and opened my eyes, meeting her intense gaze, losing myself in those eyes once again. "You saved me. You... you pushed me when all others cowered in fear. You believed in me when all others had turned their backs. And somewhere over all those nights, all those arguments, all the questioning and shouting and blood and tears and stolen kisses... *Moons and stars*, those kisses... I fell in love with you, Haley Barnes." I cupped her face, brushing away her tears with my thumb. "I *love* you. You have my *entire* heart, and even that doesn't feel like enough. It will never feel like enough because you deserve so much more. But if you'll grant me this chance, I vow to you I'll spend the rest of my immortal life trying to be worthy of all that you've already given me. Of all that you are to me."

"Evander," she whispered, her eyes fluttering closed, the tears falling freely even as she smiled.

When she finally looked up at me again, there was so much light in her eyes it made me gasp.

"Terrible things and terrible people have the power to make us feel unworthy," she said. "But only if we allow them to. Don't give them that power, Evander. You *are* worthy. I love you. And I'll spend the rest of my life taking care of your heart just as you've taken care of mine."

It was more than I could've asked for. Not just the words, but the promise behind them. The truth.

And yes, the hope.

---

The others were waiting for us as they'd promised, standing just outside the grand entrance in their Midnight finery.

As we approached, all three of them stared at her open-mouthed.

"Can we… skip the party, maybe?" Elian said, his gaze roving down her curves, then back up. "And just go back to the bedroom and—"

"No," I said.

"What if we just… show up a little late?" This, from Jax, who leaned in to brush a kiss to her cheek. In a low whisper not quite soft enough for me to miss, he said, "Our closet's still intact, angel. Maybe we should—"

"*Maybe* you should stop drooling before you stain your formalwear," I said. "Honestly, the three of you are so uncouth, it boggles the mind you even learned to walk without dragging your knuckles on the ground."

Hudson glared down at me. "Says the man who clearly enjoyed a little… ahem… *dessert* before the party." He swiped his thumb along my lower lip. "Speaking of staining the formalwear."

Haley laughed, stretching up on her toes to plant a kiss on his cheek. "Plenty more to go around later, Gargs."

"Enough salivating," I said to the men once more. Then, to Haley, "It's time to give the people what they so desperately need."

"Wine and chocolate?" she said, bouncing on her toes. "Oh! And those little pastries with the baked brie inside? I love those."

"I'm aware. And yes, all of those things await you. But I meant…" I took a breath, the mood turning serious once more. "A dark queen worthy of the title. Worthy of our loyalty."

At this, all four of us bowed our heads.

Haley allowed it… but only for a moment. Then she laughed and said, "I'll be *more* than happy to put all four of you on your knees for me later. But right now, your girl is hungry and those pastries are definitely calling my name."

She turned and opened the grand ballroom doors, revealing the vast sea of people behind them—dancing, laughing, some of them meeting and embracing one another for the first time after centuries of bloodshed.

All because a thieving little green-eyed witch crashed upon my castle and turned the whole realm upside down.

I watched as they noticed her entrance. Cheered for her. Offered her drinks and hugs and gratitude, and warmth filled me at every smile, at every teary-eyed kiss on her cheeks.

The magick of Midnight had chosen Haley as its keeper, as our goddess and queen. But unlike those who'd come before her, she wasn't interested in power and domination.

Only in peace and prosperity. In friendship. In family.

And now, as the many peoples of our realm celebrated the start of this new era, it wasn't the grandeur of the reconstructed ballroom I noticed, or the symphony of the realm's very best musicians, or even the crown glittering atop her dark head.

It was Elian. My brother, my twin. The fae Haley had fallen in love with years ago—lost and found again, brought back to me for a second chance just as he'd been brought back to her.

It was Hudson, the fiercely protective gargoyle who was just beginning to find his voice again. His place—the place of honor and friendship he deserved.

It was Jax, a brother to us all, the demon who'd taught Haley about love and fear and courage, more courageous himself than he even realized.

And it was Haley. It was her eyes and her laughter. Her heart. That boundless capacity for love. Her ferocity.

They were my family. Midnight was our home.

And together, we would continue to rebuild. To negotiate. To laugh. To honor. To love.

To fight for each other and for our realm.

And together, come what may, we would cherish the beauty that bloomed in all the darkest places, tonight and always.

---

**Thank you so much for coming along on this twisty, turny, happily-ever-after journey with Haley and her sexy monsters!**

It's always so hard to say goodbye to my characters, and these guys were among my favorites to write! I loved getting to know each of them, smashing all their hearts to bits, and then—of course—putting them all back together again (what kind of romance series would it be without that last step?).

I put them through the ringer in this story, but I know I've left them all in a good place—together, in love, and ready to build their new life in Midnight.

If you haven't read Haley's origin story in the Witch's Rebels series yet and want to jump in, now is the perfect time! Set in Blackmoon Bay, this spicy urban fantasy RH series is where it all began for Haley and her sisters. Start with book 1, Shadow Kissed!

**If you're all caught up with the Silversbane witches and you're ready for what's next... How do you feel about GARGOYLES?**

Claimed by Gargoyles is a *sizzling* hot reverse harem paranormal mafia romance series... with gargoyles.

That's right, friends. Our lucky witch teams up with not one but four fierce, brooding, *insanely* overprotective gargoyles to break an ancient curse and get revenge on the cruel dark mages bent on destroying her.

If you enjoy dark, supernatural thrills and *crazy hot* spicy romance featuring... *ahem*... special equipment, sensitive wings, and oh-so-dominant dirty-talkers, I've got you covered. **Start with book one, Wicked Conjuring,** and read on for a sneak peek!

Are you a member of our private Facebook group, <u>Sarah Piper's Sassy Witches?</u> Pop in for sneak peeks, cover reveals, exclusive giveaways, book chats, group therapy to deal with these killer cliffhangers, and plenty of complete randomness from your fellow fans! We'd love to see you there.

XOXO
Sarah

# WICKED CONJURING SNEAK PEEK

## CHAPTER ONE
### Jude

This many centuries into my cursed immortal existence, only three things have the power to remind me I'm not dead: fucking, fighting, and killing. Give me the full monty on the same night? Stuff of wet dreams, that. Bloody brilliant.

But thanks to the mortal feds crawling up our arses after a botched hit job on a crooked judge—not *my* botched hit job, mind you—Drae's got us on a real tight leash. Been a whole twenty-seven days since I broke a bone or spilled so much as a *drop* of someone else's blood, and he's still sore at me over the last bloke I put in the ground.

Human. Bastard abso-fuckin'-lutely deserved it too, but I digress.

As for my *favorite* way to pass the time?

Well.

I flick the lighter and hold the flame to the tip of the joint, sucking in a deep drag of witchweed. Across a pitch-black, dead-end street in Brooklyn's Park Slope neighborhood, a square of golden light spills from a third-story brownstone window. A dozen crows hang out on the eves just above it, flapping and tittering like old codgers fighting over dominoes.

Those fucking birds show up here every night, same as me.

Watching. Waiting.

I'm pretty sure the little scarecrow inside knows she has an audience, too. But she's a nice girl. Too polite to shoo us all away.

Lucky for us.

A shadow moves behind the sheer curtains, and I keep a close watch in anticipation of what's to come.

She's undressing for bed—my favorite part of the show.

Stripped down to her bra and panties, she saunters past the window, shaking out that gorgeous mane. Dark waves spill over her shoulders, covering her perfect, oh-so-suckable tits.

It's the color of crow feathers, that hair. Shot through with a few silver locks that set off the brightest blue-green eyes you ever saw.

Unfortunately, I only ever got to see them up close the one time. I was heading back to the office from a late-night coffee run when I caught her feeding her crows in Madison Square Park. Some pervert was harassing her, but I chased him off real quick. After that, I chatted her up a bit. Offered her the fancy-arse almond joy latte I'd bought for Auggie and made her laugh enough times to get the sound of it stuck in my head forever.

Before I knew it, I was half the fuck in love with her.

So a bit later, when she thanked me for the coffee and said she had to get home, I did what any self-respecting half-lovesick arsehole would do.

I followed her.

Never did get her name, but I've been showing up here like a stalker every night since, hiding out in the shadows across the way and hoping for a peek.

Yeah, I know. Who's the pervert now, right? Fuck it.

As for the shitbag who messed with her in the park… Would you believe it's been *exactly* twenty-seven days since anyone's heard from him? Poor chap. Although, there's a human skull on my desk presently serving as a paperweight that bears a striking resemblance. Coincidence?

The curtains flutter and her silhouette glides past once more. Every graceful movement makes my dick hard as stone, aching to sink inside her wet little cunt and make her beg for all the filthy things she never even knew she wanted. Needed.

And oh, I *will* make her beg.

In the end, they always do.

Her lights flick off. I hold my breath, heart slamming against my ribs.

*Please come back, darling. I've got so many naughty, delicious plans for us…*

Seconds later, the gauzy curtains part and I try not to squeal like a tween boy who's just discovered the dark side of the internet. I take another hit of the witchweed, then flick the butt into the gutter, my attention lasering in on that window. Her face fills the glass, blue-green eyes luminescent in the dark.

Searching. Always searching.

Perhaps she's looking for her white knight from the park, wondering if I've finally come to claim her.

*Fearing* it, as she damn well should.

The thought of making her tremble sends a dark thrill straight to my balls, and my human glamour ripples with the ancient magic holding it together. The real me is eager to come out and play.

Her neighborhood is quiet at this hour, all the happy little babies tucked into bed by their happy mums and dads, so fuck it. Keeping to the shadows, I give my surroundings a quick scan, then drop the glamour and let my true form stretch to fill the darkness.

If my little scarecrow saw me like this…

I nearly bust a gut at the idea. If the seven feet of muscle and massive leathery wings didn't scare her the fuck off, the horns and tail would certainly get the job done proper.

Gargoyles? We're not supposed to exist. Problem is, we do. What's left of us, anyway.

But my girl doesn't need to know that yet. All in due time.

These days, patience is a severely under-cultivated skill. Me? I'm old school. Reckless and impulsive most of the time, sure. But when something's worth the wait, my patience is damned legendary. Just ask any traitorous cunt who's had the pleasure of regaining consciousness after a beating, only to find himself chained up in my basement with his bodily fluids leaking onto my floor.

Death by a thousand cuts is the ultimate test of a killer's patience.

And this girl? Fuck. She's the reason patience is such a bloody virtue.

So as badly as I want to fly up there, smash through that window, and put her on her knees for me, I'll wait until she's ready. Until I'm *sure* she won't run off. Even if I have to show up here again and again, play our little game every night for another month. Six. Hell, I'd do it for a whole year if I had that much time left.

Drae doesn't think so. According to his calculations, unless we break the fucking curse, we've got about two months before it all goes to shit. And trust me when I say there are *plenty* of things worse than death for an immortal fucking monster.

Like being trapped in our statue forms for eternity—fully conscious—rather than just turning to stone while the sun's out.

Like being forced to watch the rest of our kind get pulverized into dust.

A rusty old ache stabs at my heart, but I don't have time for it.

Right now, there's only one rock-hard thing about me, and it's got *nothing* to do with some bullshit dark fae curse and *everything* to do with the girl upstairs.

Resting her forehead against the glass, my little scarecrow slides a hand down along her bare belly, hooking a thumb into the waistband of her panties. *Mmm.* White lace, this pair. Tiny pink bow at the top.

Back and forth her naughty thumb glides, driving me wild with every stroke. Her eyes drift closed as she tips her head back and sighs, one hand pressed flat against the glass, the other working its way lower, her back arching just so.

I'd give just about anything for a glimpse of her thoughts. Does she know I'm out here? Does she get off on the idea of being watched?

Does she have any idea what she's fucking doing to me?

I swear to the fucking devil I can almost *feel* her touch. Her small hand wrapped around my dick, eyes wide and scandalized as I command her to get on her knees, open her mouth, and…

*Just fucking take it…*

Pulling my wings close around me, I fist my dick with a tight grip, my gaze never leaving that window. That fucking girl.

Her eyes have haunted my dreams all month. Not even the feds or Drae's worries about the curse can break the spell this girl's got me under, and I don't want them to. From the moment I laid eyes on her in the city, I've wanted her.

And one way or another, I'll make her mine.

Her fingers continue their quest, finally dipping inside the panties as her mouth parts on a soft little moan only a supernatural beast could hear at this distance.

Grateful for my highly attuned senses, I stroke myself harder, faster, still imagining the feel of her soft pink lips, her velvet-smooth tongue, the scrape of her teeth as she takes me all the way in…

*That's it, darling. Just like that. God, you're so fucking good…*

I fight the urge to close my eyes, focusing entirely on her. On the fog of her breath against the glass. The smudge of her damp handprint. The pretty way her cheeks darken with lust.

And—most enticing of all—the desperate, wet sounds her greedy little cunt makes as she fucks herself for me, faster and more frenetic with every stroke, drawing back to circle her clit before diving inside once more…

*Fucking hell.*

A sheen of sweat glazes her upper lip. Suddenly, I want to lick her, and my mouth fills with the imagined taste of it—a mix of sweet and salty that has my balls tightening, heat racing through my veins, heart slamming in my chest as I fight to keep breathing, and then…

"Fuck!"

When I come for her, it's hard and fast and messy, and her answering gasp of pleasure echoes right through me, connecting us on a fucking *soul* level as she trembles behind the window and rides out the waves of her pleasure.

Then, just as quickly as it all began, it's over.

With a deep sigh, she presses her forehead to the glass and closes her eyes, sliding her hand out of the panties.

Again, I imagine the taste of her. The way she'll moan my name as I wrap a clawed hand around her throat and suck those fingers clean, one by delectable one.

*Such a good girl…*

Still gazing up at her beautifully flushed face, I grin.

For now, I'll let her rest. But tomorrow night?

Tomorrow night, I'll bring her a ring. Hand-carved, of course. Lovingly crafted from the bone of a man who once tormented a young girl in the park and was never heard from again.

My grin stretches wider. She won't be able to resist.

I'll make sure of it.

"Until tomorrow," I whisper. "Sleep well, scarecrow."

Overhead, the old crows finally take flight, and I stretch out my wings, leap into the air, and chase them all the way back to Manhattan.

---

What's in store for the little scarecrow and her fierce, obsessive gargoyles? **Find out in Wicked Conjuring, book one of the Claimed by Gargoyles series!**

# ABOUT SARAH PIPER

Sarah Piper is a witchy, Tarot-card-slinging paranormal romance and urban fantasy author. Through her signature brew of dark magic, heart-pounding suspense, and steamy romance, Sarah promises a sexy, supernatural escape into a world where the magic is real, the monsters are sinfully hot, and the witches always get their magically-ever-afters.

Readers have dubbed her work "super sexy," "imaginative and original," "off-the-walls good," and "delightfully wicked in the best ways," a quote Sarah hopes will appear on her tombstone.

Sarah lives in New York with her husband, where she spends her days sleeping like a vampire and her nights writing books, casting spells, gazing at the moon, playing with her ever-expanding collection of Tarot cards, and obsessing over the best way to brew a cup of tea.

You can find her online at SarahPiperBooks.com, on Patreon at patreon.com/sarahpiper, and in her Facebook readers group at Sarah Piper's Sassy Witches! If you're sassy, or if you need a little *more* sass in your life, or if you need more Dean Winchester gifs in your life (who doesn't?), come hang out!

Want to say hello or ask a question about… pretty much anything? Just email sarah@sarahpiperbooks.com!

www.ingramcontent.com/pod-product-compliance
Lightning Source LLC
Chambersburg PA
CBHW051421190726
48289CB00001B/3